MM +

Dee Williams was born and brought up in Rotherhithe in East London where her father worked as a stevedore in Surrey Docks. Dee left school at fourteen, met her husband at sixteen and was married at twenty. After living abroad for some years, Dee moved to Hampshire to be close to her family. She has written twelve other sagas including PRIDE AND JOY, HOPES AND DREAMS and A RARE RUBY.

Also by Dee Williams

Carrie of Culver Road
Polly of Penn's Place
Annie of Albert Mews
Hannah of Hope Street
Sally of Sefton Grove
Ellie of Elmleigh Square
Wishes and Tears
Sorrows and Smiles
Forgive and Forget
A Rare Ruby
Hopes and Dreams
Pride and Joy

Maggie's Market

and

Katie's Kitchen

Dee Williams

headline

Copyright © 1997, 1998 Dee Williams

The right of Dee Williams to be identified as the Author of
the Work has been asserted by her in accordance with
the Copyright, Designs and Patents Act 1988.

MAGGIE'S MARKET first published in Great Britain in 1997
by HEADLINE BOOK PUBLISHING

KATIE'S KITCHEN first published in Great Britain in 1998
by HEADLINE BOOK PUBLISHING

First published in this omnibus edition in 2004
by HEADLINE BOOK PUBLISHING

A HEADLINE paperback

10 9 8 7 6 5 4 3 2 1

All rights reserved. No part of this publication may be
reproduced, stored in a retrieval system, or transmitted,
in any form or by any means without the prior written
permission of the publisher, nor be otherwise circulated
in any form of binding or cover other than that in which
it is published and without a similar condition being
imposed on the subsequent purchaser.

All characters in this publication are fictitious
and any resemblance to real persons, living or dead,
is purely coincidental.

ISBN 0 7553 2264 9

Typeset in Times by Avon DataSet Ltd,
Bidford on Avon, Warwickshire

Printed and bound in Great Britain by
Clays Ltd, St Ives plc

Papers and cover board used by Headline are natural,
recyclable products made from wood grown in sustainable
forests. The manufacturing processes conform to the
environmental regulations of the country of origin.

HEADLINE BOOK PUBLISHING
A division of Hodder Headline
338 Euston Road
London NW1 3BH

www.headline.co.uk
www.hodderheadline.com

Maggie's Market

This is for my dear Les who is always in my thoughts, and whose idea it was to write about a girl on a market.

I would like to thank all the staff at Portsmouth, Waterlooville and Horndean libraries for their help with my enquiries, and their interest in my work. Thank you.

Chapter 1

Maggie Ross wandered over to her window and looked down on to Kelvin Market. It was a warm May afternoon, and below her people were lazily wandering about, chatting and taking their time over their purchases, the morning's hustle and bustle long over.

She sighed contentedly. At twenty-seven she had everything she could wish for – a loving husband, two wonderful children and another on the way. So far 1935 had been another good year for them, and with the new baby, the best was yet to come.

'Will Daddy take me to the park tomorrow?' asked Jamie suddenly. He pushed his straight fair hair to one side and looked up at her. With his twinkling blue eyes and fair colouring there was no mistaking he was Maggie's son.

'Shouldn't think so. Saturday's his busiest day. What made you ask that?'

'I'm drawing a lot of boys playing football.'

Maggie smiled. Her husband, Tony, had a stall in Kelvin Market, inherited from his father. Tony told people he sold antiques, but in fact most of it was junk – small stuff, chipped china, brass animals, tools and rusty door knockers.

Tony was very proud of his dad and had been helping run the stall for years, long before he left school.

The licences and stalls were very special and always handed down; many had been fought over in the past. Tony's was at the top end that opened out on to Rotherhithe New Road, considered to be a very favourable position. The Dog and Duck pub was at the other end. Kelvin Market had stalls lining each side of the cobbled stone road. It wasn't huge, but it did open every weekday come rain or shine. Everyday things were sold there, and had been for as long as most people could remember. Along with Tony's other deals the market provided the Ross family with a good living.

Maggie first moved here when they got married in 1928, seven years ago. The sounds and smells from the market below had become part of her life from then on. Their rented flat was above Mr Goldman's bespoke tailor's shop, where Tony always had his suits made. Mr Goldman was a kind widower, a real gentleman who loved the children despite their stomping and shouting above him all day.

Maggie glanced at the clock. Almost time to collect Laura from school. As she moved away from the window she caught sight of her reflection in the long ornate mirror leaning against the wall, one of Tony's finds, now waiting for a new home. She smiled; she didn't need reminding that her once-trim figure was expanding, the baby bouncing around inside did that.

She looked at the top of Jamie's bent head as he concentrated on his drawing. Up here he was a quiet, sensitive and very loving four-year-old, but when he got downstairs the traders seemed to bring out the devil in him, and at times

Maggie had to reprimand him for being cheeky.

'Come on, Jamie, we've got to go and collect Laura,' she told him.

'D'you like my picture?'

'Very nice,' she said, as the paper was pushed under her nose. 'You are a clever boy.'

'Mummy, when can I go to school?'

'I've told you, after the holidays.' Jamie was two years younger than Laura and couldn't wait to be grown up like his sister. Although Maggie knew it would be lovely to have the new baby, which was due in September, to herself, she would miss having Jamie's chatter and mess around.

'Can I stay with Daddy?' Jamie's voice interrupted her daydreams.

'I'll see. He might be too busy to have you touching everything.'

Maggie loved Tony very much. He was a warm, affectionate Londoner, loud when he needed to be, but very loving to her and the children. It was ten years ago, when she was seventeen and he was nineteen that she really took an interest in him. She knew he was always after the girls and Maggie and her best friend, Eve, would hang around his stall hoping he would take one of them out. Although he did go out with Eve for a while, it was Maggie he married three years later. He was everything Maggie had ever wanted in a man, tall with unruly dark curly hair, and very handsome. His lovely brown eyes could send shivers up her spine when he gave her a sly wink.

He always made a fuss of the old dears that visited his stall. He'd put his arm round them, telling jokes and teasing them. He said it helped business. Somehow, but Maggie didn't know how, he did make a good living from the stall and they enjoyed a comfortable lifestyle. If he did manage to find a real antique, it was either passed on very quickly, or found a home in their cosy flat till the right price was offered.

She stood in front of the mirror, brushing her fair hair and gently pushing the soft waves into place. There were times when she did wonder about some of Tony's shady associates, but if she mentioned them he would only laugh her off saying, 'You have to play up to all sorts in this business.' He would then put his arms round her and, pulling her close, whisper, 'Just as long as nobody touches me and mine life's a piece of cake.'

Maggie tingled at the thought of his arms round her.

'Right, my boy, let's go and get Laura, and then we can all have an ice cream.'

Jamie was down the stairs before she'd finished the sentence.

Maggie pushed open her front door, and was immediately in the middle of the market.

'All right then, gel?' yelled Fred, who owned the fruit and veg stall. He heaved a heavy sack of potatoes on to his shoulder. As usual a thin unlit hand-rolled cigarette dangled from his lips. Maggie had never seen him without one.

'Yes thanks. Busy?'

'Not too bad. All right if young Jamie 'ere has an apple?' he asked, banging the sack down and causing the dust to rise. Despite his pale watery eyes and the worried expression he always wore, Fred, a thin wiry man in his fifties, was as strong as an ox.

She nodded. 'Course.'

'Tell Laura I've saved her a nice shiny one.'

'Thanks, Fred,' Maggie smiled, and moved on. She had known these people for years; they too were part of her life.

She loved the whole atmosphere of the market: the sound of trains rattling above the arches; the smell of roasting chestnuts in the winter – even the rotting veg on a warm summer night helped give the market its certain smell. The organ-grinder with his monkey dancing on top always raised a laugh, but when it jumped down and rattled his collecting tin woe betide anyone who teased it or didn't pay up. It was known to bite.

Jamie ran on ahead. The clip-clop of a dray horse's hooves on the cobbles made him stop. Jamie turned and smiled at Maggie. He loved horses almost as much as he loved football. The smell of beer filled her nostrils. The dray was on its way to the Dog and Duck. The singsongs they had in the pub were always great occasions, and the new baby's christening would be the next excuse for a knees-up.

Tony liked telling everyone that he wanted to get a nice house and shop somewhere in the country for Maggie and the kids, but she couldn't imagine being away from Rother-hithe. Her parents had been born not far from here, and her father had worked in the tea factory. They were dead now, killed in a train crash seven years ago when they were going on holiday. The loss still upset her, especially the fact they had never seen their grandchildren, not even her brother's daughter, Doreen, who was a few months older than Laura.

Maggie sighed as she slowly moved past the stalls, giving a nod here and a wave there. She shouldn't be thinking about the past, the future was far more exciting.

For some unknown reason Maggie's thoughts were still clinging to her lost family. If only her brother, Alan, was a little more friendly. He was four years older than her, and had passed his exam and gone on to high school. He had a good job in the city in an office. When he married Helen they moved to a posh part of London, Hither Green. Since their parents died he and Maggie didn't see a lot of each other, but Alan always invited them over sometime during the Christmas holiday. Tony said it was only to show off their house and garden. He always came home discontented after visiting them, announcing that one day they'd have such a house. Helen and Maggie didn't always see eye to eye either. Helen and Alan's only child, Doreen, always stayed clean and immaculate while Jamie would end up looking a wreck. Maggie could always sense Helen's disapproval.

Arriving at Winnie's stall of new and second-hand footwear, Maggie picked up one of the shoes for sale. 'These are nice. I rather like these.'

Winnie grinned. 'You'll have ter wait till your feet go down. You can't go running up and down your stairs in those heels, not in your condition.'

'I do miss me high heels,' Maggie sighed.

'Yes, well, that baby's welfare is more important than you dolling yerself up. If you fell down those stairs and did you or that baby a mischief Tony would never forgive you.'

'Yes, marm,' laughed Maggie. 'And I shan't be sorry when it's here. I'm sick to death of these shapeless things.' She pulled at her navy-blue smock.

Maggie thought the world of Winnie, a warm round

woman. She had been a tower of strength when Maggie had lost her parents and had been heavily pregnant with Laura.

'How you gonner get that apple in your mouth?' Winnie asked Jamie.

'I'm gonner nibble it,' he said grinning.

Winnie bent down and, grabbing his face between her rough red, weatherbeaten hands, planted a very loud kiss on each of his cheeks. 'When yer looks up at me with those big blue eyes and flutters those lovely long lashes, I just gotter kiss yer.'

'Yuck. You better not do that when I go to school,' Jamie said indignantly, wiping his face and then running the back of his hand down the side of his trousers.

'Why's that?' asked Winnie, giving Maggie a wink.

'Don't want the other kids ter think I'm a sissy and keep getting kissed.'

'Come on,' said Maggie, laughing. 'See you on the way back,' she said over her shoulder to Winnie.

'And don't you kiss me again,' shouted Jamie, looking behind and grabbing hold of his mother's hand.

Winnie blew him a kiss.

Maggie ruffled Jamie's blond hair.

'Oh Mum, don't.'

'We only do these things 'cos we loves yer,' she said.

Jamie smoothed down his hair and ran on ahead. Maggie watched him. She was so proud of her family.

Suddenly she saw Jamie stop and look round, puzzled.

'What is it, Jamie?' she asked, getting nearer.

'Daddy ain't here.'

Maggie was close to the stall. ''Allo, Bill,' she said to the young lad that helped Tony. Bill had been with him for the past two years, ever since he left school at fourteen. 'Tony had to go off somewhere?'

'Dunno. 'E ain't been 'ere all day.' Bill was a tall, gangly boy who blushed easily while talking to women. When Tony wasn't teasing him he spoke very highly of the lad.

'But he got the stall out, didn't he?' asked Maggie.

'Yer, but he went off just after that, and I ain't seen him since. What shall I do about the takings if 'e ain't back be then?'

'Don't worry, he'll be back long before then.' Maggie frowned. Although Tony was often off buying and selling, it wasn't like him to leave Bill on his own all day, or not to tell her if he was going to be late home. 'He'll be here in time to pack away. Look, I must go and collect Laura.'

'Yer, yer of course.'

Maggie and Jamie were turning the corner just as the children came racing out of the school playground.

It was the same school Tony had gone to when he was little, and it hadn't changed. The old red-brick building with its small windows was cheerless, depressed and in need of a lick of paint. Everything round this area, including most of the children, had the same sad run-down look about them. Maggie made sure Laura was always well dressed and well fed but some of her little friends looked undernourished and sickly, and they were always glad of any of Laura's cast-off clothes.

Jamie ran up to his big sister, who was clutching a piece of paper. 'What you got there?'

'Look what I done at school. Don't you touch it,' she yelled at Jamie.

'I only want to look.'

8

'Well you ain't, 'cos you might tear it.'

'No I won't.'

'Stop it, the two of you. Let me see it,' said Maggie, taking the colourful sheet of paper from her daughter's chalk-covered hands. 'It's lovely.'

'What is it?' asked Jamie.

'It's a tree in a field. Can't you see that?' Laura rubbed her nose.

Maggie twisted the paper. 'Yes, yes I can see, it's very good.'

Laura smiled and a slight dimple appeared on her chalk-smudged face. She tucked a strand of hair behind her ear. Every morning Maggie painstakingly plaited Laura's long dark unruly hair, hoping to keep it under control, but the ribbon would always slip off and she'd end up tucking it behind her ears. Her large brown eyes lit up. She was like her father, and had inherited his good looks. Tony's mother had always been very proud of her Italian ancestors, as was her only child. 'It's where me good looks comes from,' was something he would often boast about. Tony's mother would talk about Italy as if she'd been there, but the truth was she'd never set foot out of London till the council started the slum clearance and demolished the row of terraced houses where she lived. Bella Ross was moved out to Downham. She was an opinionated woman who didn't take to change easily and they did wonder if she would go, but when she saw her lovely new house, with a bathroom and indoor lav, she couldn't wait. Although Bella had always had the last word with everyone, including her late husband, Jim, Maggie was very fond of her.

'You can put it on the wall if yer like, Mummy,' said Laura proudly.

'That'll be nice.'

'Oh, I nearly forgot,' Laura suddenly burst out. 'I'm gonner be a maypole dancer again on Empire Day.'

'That's lovely.' Maggie smiled. It was only last week on 6 May, the day they had all celebrated King George and Queen Mary's Silver Jubilee, that Laura had been chosen to dance round the maypole. That morning Maggie and Tony had sat on the tiny seats in the playground and laughed at the state some of the little ones had got themselves into as they twisted and weaved in and out of each other while holding on to the long coloured ribbons.

The week before Jubilee Day had seen the dull streets transformed, with red, white and blue bunting draped everywhere, and flags hung from every lamppost and window. The shopkeepers and stallholders had done their bit to join in the festivities and the many pictures of the royal couple showed how much they were loved. Everybody had been in a happy mood, laughing and singing patriotic songs, and wearing silly paper hats.

That afternoon a party had been held in the school playground for the local kids, some of whom had stood wide-eyed at tables that groaned with sandwiches, jellies and ice cream, before they set about devouring the lot. The food had been donated by the local tradespeople, all trying to out-do one another. The weather had been kind and all in all it had been a wonderful day.

That evening had been the grown-ups' turn to celebrate. The Dog and Duck was almost leaping in the air with all the racket that came from within. All kinds of musical instruments arrived to form an impromptu band and the customers spilled out into the street dancing and singing.

'What's Empire Day, Mummy?' asked Jamie, tugging at Maggie's hand and interrupting her thoughts.

'It's the twenty-fourth of May, the day when we remember our Empire,' said Laura confidently.

'What's our Empire?' came the next question.

'When you go to school you'll see all the pink bits in the atlas of the world, and all those pink bits belong to England.' Laura was obviously pleased to repeat all that her teacher had told her.

Maggie smiled. Her daughter must be taking an interest, and enjoying her geography lessons.

When they returned to Tony's stall he still wasn't there.

'If 'e ain't here in time I'll put the stall away for yer, Maggs,' said Bill. 'And I'll bring the takings up to you.'

'Thanks, Bill. There ain't a race meeting on somewhere, is there?'

''Spect so, but he would have said.'

'I'm sure he'll be back before long.'

'I hope so.'

Although Tony liked Bill and had a lot of faith in him he didn't like to leave him on his own for too long, and for Tony not to tell Maggie he was going out was unusual.

When Jamie saw Winnie was busy with a customer he quickly ran past her stall. Showing her drawing to Fred, Laura collected her promised apple. As they trooped past Mr Goldman's window Maggie gave him a wave. She opened her front door and the children clattered along the linoed passage and up the stairs. There was a back door along the passage that led out to the small yard and lavatory.

After the children had finished their tea, it was time for the market to close. Maggie didn't have to look out of the window, she was familiar with the scene. Men would be tying covers over the wares on their barrows and pushing them into the lockups under the railway arches where they stored them overnight. Mrs Groom would be taking down all her second-hand goods that she had draped round her stall, and old Mother Saunders, who sold haberdashery, would be packing away all her bits and bobs and stacking them neatly into boxes to be brought out again tomorrow. Mrs Russell would be filling her buckets with water, hoping the weather wouldn't turn too warm and wilt her flowers.

There were many women running stalls on this market, most of them inherited from their fathers or husbands who had been killed in the war.

Tony would be home soon.

Maggie sat up when she heard the front door slam, but was a little surprised when Bill came in alone with the day's takings.

'Where's Tony?'

'He ain't back yet. I've put the barra away.'

'Thanks, Bill.'

'Tell Tony a bloke was looking for him.'

'Did he say who he was?'

'Na. Shifty-looking sod. Ain't seen him round 'ere before.' He grinned. 'By the way, tell him I sold that old lamp he's been trying ter get rid of fer weeks.'

Maggie smiled. 'Nice work, Bill. Fancy a cuppa?'

'No, ta all the same but I'm off out tonight.' He twisted his cloth cap round and round in his hands.

'Meeting a girl?'

12

'Na.' Bill blushed.

Maggie was teasing. She knew Bill was embarrassed about his spots, but he was only sixteen and would grow out of them, and with Tony as a teacher he too would soon have the gift of the gab.

'I best be off. See you tomorrow. Bye, kids,' he yelled out before clattering down the stairs and slamming the front door behind him.

Funny about Tony going off like that, thought Maggie, but I expect he'll be back soon for his tea.

Chapter 2

Later, when Maggie went into the bedroom to tuck the blankets round the children, Laura asked, 'Why ain't Daddy here?'

'I expect he's had to go out on business.'

'Will he be back soon?' asked Jamie from his bed on the other side of the room.

'I should think so, but you may be asleep.'

'Tell him to come and kiss me good night.' Laura snuggled down under the bedclothes, clutching her teddy bear.

'I will.' Maggie kissed her daughter's forehead.

'And don't forget me,' said Jamie, popping his tousled fair head over the covers.

'As if we could.' She bent down and kissed him. 'Now go to sleep, the pair of you. Sleep tight.' She closed the bedroom door.

In the sitting room Maggie picked up her knitting. She was beginning to worry. This wasn't like Tony. He always told her if he was going out. Besides, he would dress up if he was meeting someone important or going to a special auction. She smiled to herself – at least if he had to go out with some of his cronies he would always bring her back flowers. When he went to play cards with Wally from the auction rooms, or to the dog track, he always brought her back a box of chocolates. He was so kind and thoughtful.

Maggie was restless and couldn't concentrate on the intricate pattern she was using for the new baby's matinée coat. She turned the wireless on and an orchestra's soft music drifted over her. She leant back in the armchair and closed her eyes.

As she drifted off she could see her mother and father smiling at her. She was dancing with Tony, the train of her long white frock draped over her arm. She looked into Tony's eyes, he bent his head and gently kissed her mouth. There were a lot of people shouting and laughing, but Maggie could only see Tony, her Tony – he was so handsome. She was so lucky that he loved her.

'Maggs, Maggs. Sorry, love, did I wake you?' A whispered voice brought her back from her dream.

Maggie quickly sat up. It was gloomy, the light hadn't been switched on, she was disorientated. 'Tony, is that you?'

'No, it's me.'

'Oh Eve,' said Maggie unable to keep the disappointment from her voice. Eve, like everybody else did, had used the front door key that hung behind the letter box to let herself into their flat.

'Well, don't sound so upset about it. You all right?'

'Yes. I was just dozing.'

'Kids in bed?' asked Eve, taking off her stylish beige straw hat.

Maggie nodded. 'Put the light on. What time is it?' She looked up at the wooden clock on the mantelpiece.

'It's nine o'clock.' Eve stood close to the mirror and ran her little finger over her bright red lips. She plumped up the back of her blonde hair.

'You on your own?' asked Maggie.

'Yer. Dan went in the Dog, so I thought I'd pop along to see if you was all right. Tony in the pub?'

'I don't know.'

'What d'you mean?'

Maggie sat forward. 'Eve, I'm getting a bit worried. Tony hasn't been seen all day.'

'What? Didn't he get the stall out?'

'Yes, but we haven't seen him since. Bill put the stall away. Eve, you don't think something could have happened to him, do you?'

'Don't talk daft, course not. He's probably met a mate and they finished up in a pub, and Tony's had a skinful and is sleeping it off somewhere. It ain't the first time, is it?'

'No, but he nearly always tells me if . . .' Maggie laughed. 'I'm beginning to sound like some nagging old wife.' Her laughter was false. Somehow, deep down, she knew something was wrong.

'I'll put the kettle on.' Eve stood in the doorway. 'You mark my words, he'll be back here with a big bunch of flowers and his tail between his legs.'

Maggie half smiled. 'I only hope you're right.'

Eve took the teapot from the kitchen cupboard. She knew this flat almost as well as her own, round the corner in Upper Road. As she clattered about with the cups and saucers her thoughts went to Tony. He was such a handsome devil. What was he up to? What if he was playing around? Maggie would go mad.

Eve smiled, remembering the time when they were silly young things and Maggie used to hang around his stall hoping he would take her out. It surprised them both when it was Eve he made the date with. Maggie got very upset over that and said she thought she'd lost him for ever. Eve managed to talk Tony into taking Maggie out. Eve's grin got wider; he hadn't got from Maggie what he'd got from her – well, not till he married her. He'd been a great lover. Not that she'd ever told Maggie. After all, it was Maggie he loved.

Eve stood watching the blue gas flame dance round the kettle. What had made her suddenly think about that? Was Tony starting to play around? He had never propositioned Eve since he'd married, but was that because she was too near to home? The whistle from the kettle brought her back to the present. She made the tea and walked into the sitting room with the tea tray. 'You feeling all right?' she asked Maggie.

'Bit tired. But no, I feel fine.'

'How many more you gonner have?' asked Eve, looking pointedly at Maggie's stomach.

'This will be the last. Only got room for one more bed in the kids' room.'

'What about in a few years' time? They won't wanner sleep together then, so will you move?'

'Dunno.'

'Tony still on about having that antique shop and the cosy cottage with roses round the door?'

Maggie grinned and nodded.

'Reckon he's been to too many films. I couldn't see either of you stuck somewhere down in the country.'

'Neither can I.'

When their conversation lapsed the usual sounds came drifting through the open window. Trains puffing and chugging above the arches, dogs barking and cats fighting, even the ticking of the clock seemed loud and invasive.

Although she knew the answer Maggie still asked, 'Will Dan come here for you?'

'I hope so. I ain't walking home on me own.'

'It ain't that far.'

'I know, but I still ain't walking home on me own.'

Later, when Dan came in, Maggie was again disappointed Tony wasn't with him.

Dan threw his trilby on to the chair and, bending slightly to peer in the mirror, smoothed down his dark hair. Dan was tall, broad and very good-looking, but then he had to be, Eve wouldn't settle for anything less. He had a steady job as a lorry driver, and with Eve working in the Council office, money wasn't a worry to them.

'Tony wasn't in the pub then?' asked Maggie.

'No. Didn't see him. Why?'

Maggie went through her story again.

'You sure he ain't been to the dog track?' Dan asked.

'He would have told me.'

'Yer, s'pose he would have. You ain't got a sandwich, have you? I'm starving.'

'What, after that bloody great dinner you had tonight?'

Dan grinned. 'Got to keep me strength up, gel, I'm a growing lad.' He put his arm round Eve and hugged her.

''Sides, you know I always perform better on a full stomach.'

'Not if you've had a skinful of beer you don't.'

'Ah yer, unfortunately that's when the mind's willing but the flesh is weak.'

Maggie laughed. She loved Eve and Dan like a sister and brother. Eve had met Dan at a dance and they'd got married very quickly, so quickly everyone had thought she was up the spout, but the truth was Eve didn't want children. Dan loved Eve, despite all the talk about her before they were married.

Dan sat down. 'Did he take his stall out this morning?'

'Yes, but Bill's been running it all day.'

Dan leant back. 'D'you know, I reckon he's met an old mate and they've gone out on a binge and he's sleeping it off somewhere.'

'That's exactly what I said,' said Eve.

'But it's not like Tony not to tell me.'

'Well, we all like to be let off the lead once in a while, gel.'

Maggie half smiled. Was she getting to be a nag? 'I suppose so,' she replied.

With no other suggestions, they all fell into a puzzled silence.

'Right, gel, on your feet,' Dan said briskly to his wife.

When Eve stood up Dan smacked her bottom. 'You ready then? Look, Maggs, sorry, but we've got to be off. I've got a long day tomorrow, got to take the lorry down to Dover to pick up a load.'

'What, on a Saturday?' asked Maggie.

Eve shrugged her shoulders. 'That's what 'e tells me. Reckon he's got a bit on the side.'

20

He looked at Eve. 'I told you, that's what the job's about. Go and see Tom if you don't believe me.' He winked at Maggie. 'Mind you, it's surprising what you can get up to in the cab, ain't it, gel?'

Eve looked away. 'I ain't saying.'

Dan laughed. 'Well, I wasn't the first to have your drawers off, now was I?'

'Yer. But in the end you was the lucky one that got me to the altar.' Eve put her hat on, and picked up her handbag. 'I'll call in tomorrow, Maggs.'

Dan bent down and kissed Maggie's cheek. 'And you give that old man of yours a right old ear-bashing when he gets home, making you worry like this. Bye, love.'

Eve checked her hat in the mirror, then kissed Maggie. 'I'll pop in tomorrow morning when I'm shopping, just to make sure you're all right.'

'You don't have to.'

Eve smiled. 'I'm so nosy. I've just got to find out where Tony's been and what he's been up to all day. After all, it might be somewhere exciting. Bye.'

Maggie stood at the window. The empty market looked eerie in the yellow glow from the gaslamps. She gave her friends' moving shadows a wave.

Although it was late she knew she wouldn't be able to sleep, so once more she picked up her knitting. The baby felt like it was doing a somersault. As Maggie gently touched her stomach, she smiled and let her thoughts drift to when Laura was born.

Tony had left early that morning, saying he had to meet someone, but would be home as soon as he could. Her pains had started almost as soon as he had closed the front door.

21

At first she didn't know what to do. If only her mother had still been alive. The doctor had told her labour could last for hours, plenty of time before Tony would be home. But what if the baby came before he got here? She'd been up in the flat alone. She'd had to get help.

Maggie had staggered down the stairs, and on opening the front door held on to it as a wave of pain made her legs buckle.

'You all right, gel?' Fred had yelled, coming over to her.

She'd shaken her head.

'Bloody hell. I'll get Tony.'

'He ain't here.'

'Where is he? Ain't he on his stall?'

'No. He left early, he had to go out.'

'What, 'e left yer like this?'

'I hadn't started then.'

Fred had begun flitting round her. 'Did he tell old Charlie where he was going?'

'I don't know.'

'Don't move,' he'd said in panic. 'I'll get Win.'

When Winnie had helped her back up the stairs she'd sat with her, holding her hand as the pains worsened.

'I gotter get you to the hospital,' Winnie had said, a worried look on her face.

'No, not yet. Not till Tony comes back.'

'Tony's old mate, Charlie, said he didn't know where he's gone.' Winnie had put a large warm comforting arm round Maggie. 'Come on now, love, think of the little 'en what's gonner pop out soon.' She'd looked concerned. 'I think the pains are coming a bit quick, don't you?'

'I'd rather wait for Tony to get home.'

Winnie had moved to the window and anxiously glanced out. 'Look, Mr Goldman will tell him you've gone.'

Maggie had gripped the arms of the chair as another pain took her breath away. 'P'raps you're right.'

'Good, I'll pop down and get Fred to get his van out, it'll be quicker in that.'

Winnie, red-faced and breathless, had been back almost at once. 'Right, got your bag packed?'

Maggie had nodded.

She had held on to Winnie's arm when they slowly made their way down the stairs. 'I must tell Mr Goldman,' she'd gasped.

'Don't worry, that's all taken care of.'

Everybody had shouted and wished her well as she'd staggered down the market. She'd even managed a smile as she climbed up into Fred's van. 'I suppose it's a bit different going to the hospital in a fruit and veg van.'

'Good job I ain't gotter call into Covent Garden first,' Fred had laughed anxiously. 'You might have ended up sitting on a sack of taters.'

'Or stinking of onions,' Winnie had said. 'Christ, that might make the little 'en go back in again.'

Laura had been born at six that evening. She had a mass of dark curly hair like her father.

When Tony had walked into the ward he'd been almost hidden behind the biggest bunch of flowers Maggie had ever seen. He'd thrown it on the bed and gently taken her in his arms. He'd kissed her mouth long and hard.

'Tony, don't,' Maggie had said, blushing and pushing him away. 'Everybody's looking.'

23

'I don't care. I want everybody to know what a clever girl my Maggie is. Is this ours?'

Maggie had nodded and smiled. She'd watched him lean over the cot at her side, and ease the blankets back.

'She's dark like me,' he'd beamed.

He had sat on the bed and held Maggie's hand. 'I love you so much.' He'd kissed her fingers. 'What we gonner call her?'

'I thought about Laura Margaret after me and me mum.'

'I like that. Welcome to the world, Laura Margaret Ross.'

Now tears began to run down Maggie's face at that happy memory. Tony had been with her when almost two years later, in September, her son had been born. James Anthony, a delicate-looking boy, took his father's and grandfather's names.

Maggie was told after that Tony had celebrated the first day of Jamie's life wandering round the stallholders with a bottle in his hand and they had all helped him wet the baby's head many times over. He was so proud to have a son and heir. Jamie worshipped his dad, who would take him to the park to teach him to play football. Some Sunday mornings he would take the children to Petticoat Lane while she prepared the dinner. Maggie was always terrified they would come home with a puppy or a cat, or even some baby chicks. Tony said he would like a stall there, but then he was always looking for new ways to make money, giving everyone the impression he was restless.

Maggie looked up at the clock. It was nearly midnight.

24

She suddenly felt alone and vulnerable, and very tired. Where was Tony? He should be home soon.

The ringing of the alarm clock woke her from a fitful sleep. It was early morning. The alarm continued its loud intrusive noise. Why didn't Tony turn it off? She put out her hand. His side of the bed was empty and smooth. It hadn't been slept in. Maggie sat up, cross. He had never stayed out all night before – well, not without telling her.

Maggie got out of bed and crept past the children's bedroom. It was Saturday so there was no need to wake them. She made herself a pot of tea and wondered about the stall. Today was the busiest day of the week. She was beginning to get very angry. If Tony had been out on the beer last night he should at least have thought about getting home.

She looked out of the window. Down below the market was beginning to come alive. She dressed herself. 'I'll be glad when you're born,' she said to the reflection of her bulge in the mirror.

She checked on the children, who were still fast asleep, then made her way downstairs and outside into the warm May sunshine. She knew if they woke up they would know where to find her.

''Allo Maggs,' said Fred. 'You're out and about early this morning. Keeping yer eye on yer old man?'

She gave Fred a smile. 'Something like that.' She didn't want to say too much at the moment.

''Allo, gel. Everyfink all right then?' asked Mrs Russell, standing back to admire the carefully arranged vases of colourful flowers she'd set out. The smell of the roses and carnations wafted on the early morning air. 'Hope it ain't gonner be too warm terday. This weather's a sod fer me blooms. Makes 'em all droopy in no time.'

'Could make yer bloomers all droopy an' all if yer ain't careful,' another stallholder called out.

'Don't want any of your old lip, Cooper.' She turned to Maggie. ''E can be a right saucy sod at times. Mind you, 'im and your old man always seem to hit it orf. Couple of saucy sods together, they are.'

Maggie liked Mrs Russell. She'd been on the market for as long as anybody could remember. Her trademark was the long black coat that she wore in all weathers. Tom Cooper reckoned she didn't wear anything under it in the summer. But come winter she sat with a piece of blanket wrapped tightly round her bent shoulders and secured with a large safety pin. Her hair was a nondescript colour and always hidden under a man's flat tweed cap.

Winnie was busy putting out the shoes. ''Allo, Maggs. What you doing out this time o' morning, and where's that old man of yours? Ain't seen him round here yet. He all right?'

'Yes.'

'You look a bit knackered. You OK?'

'Not too bad. I'll talk to you later.'

At the end of the market Maggie could see Tony's stall had been set up. 'Hallo, Bill,' she said to his back.

He turned quickly. 'Where's Tony? He got a bloody hangover?'

'Bill, I don't know where he is.'

'What? Didn't 'e come home last night?'

26

Maggie shook her head. 'Do you think you can manage on your own?'

'Looks like I'll have to. Where the bloody hell is he? 'E should be here.'

'I know.'

'Well, he'd better be back soon. I can't even have a Jimmy without asking someone to watch the stuff.'

'When I've given the kids their breakfast I'll be along and give you a hand.'

Bill looked guilty. 'You don't 'ave to, Maggs. Sorry if I got a bit, well, carried away. It's just it ain't my stall and I'm not always sure what to charge the punters.'

'Tony's got a lot of faith in you, Bill. 'Sides, he often leaves you. Just do your best for now.'

Bill blushed. 'Yer, of course.'

Maggie walked back to Win's stall and sat on the chair she kept round the back.

'So. Where's that bloke of yours this morning? Ain't he well?'

Maggie looked round.

'Come on, tell me. What's the trouble, gel, you two had a row?' Winnie tucked her short grey hair, held close to her head with hairgrips, back behind her ears. A fringe cut straight across her forehead made a frame for her weather-beaten face. She had been working on this market all her life, starting as a child helping her drunken father, who knocked her and her mother about. Her mother took over when he died; now it was Winnie who looked after her invalid mother. She had never married as her fiancé, another market trader, was killed in the war. She hadn't had much education, but could add up faster than anyone Maggie

27

knew, and she had a heart of gold.

'No. Win, I'm worried. Tony ain't been seen since yesterday morning.'

'You sure?'

'Yes. Why?'

'I thought I saw him yesterday, about lunchtime I s'pose. Yer, it was about then. I was just going into the Dog for a quick half. He was talking to a couple of blokes, shifty-looking sods, they was. One was an old man and the younger one looked a right bruiser.'

Maggie stood up. 'Where did they go?'

'Dunno. They went up Rovverhive New Road way.'

'Was Tony with them?'

'Yer, I think so. Didn't really take much notice.'

'Bill said he wasn't at the stall all day.'

'Well, he wouldn't be, would he? Not if he was at the pub. I thought it funny, him walking away from the stall, but I guessed he'd just been in for a quick one as well as it's a bit warm.'

'I don't know what to think.'

'He could have gorn on to look for Ding Dong. Tony likes a bet now and again, don't he?'

'Yes.'

'Don't worry about 'im, he's old enough and ugly enough to look after himself. Yes, missis, half a crown a pair.' Winnie moved to the front of her stall. 'No you can't try 'em on. Look at the colour of yer feet – dirty cow.'

Maggie left her arguing with her customer and went upstairs. The sound of her two running about told her they were up and would be wanting their breakfast. Dad or no dad, food was the most important thing in their lives at the moment. Then she would go along to the Dog and Duck and ask Gus, the landlord, if he knew where the bookie's runner Dougie Bell – known as Ding Dong – might be, and if Tony went to look for him yesterday. And, she thought grimly, she'd ask about the two blokes Winnie'd seen him with as well.

Chapter 3

''Allo, Maggie. Don't often see you in here.' Rene, the Dog and Duck's barmaid, gave her a beaming smile. 'How yer keeping then?'

'I'm all right, thanks.'

'If yer looking for yer old man he ain't been in yet.'

Maggie smiled. 'No, I'm not looking for him. You don't happen to know where I can find Ding Dong, do you?'

Rene laughed. 'Ain't seen him either this morning. Why, you gonner have a bet?'

'No, well . . . Is Gus in?'

'Now *there*'s someone I can help yer with. He's in the cellar. Mind you, he is a bit busy. Anythink I can do for yer?'

Maggie felt ill at ease. She didn't want to tell Rene as before long it would be all around the market that she was chasing after Tony. 'No thanks, just want a quick word, that's all.'

'I'll give him a shout.'

'No don't worry, not if he's busy.'

Rene's smile parted her bright red lips. 'He don't mind. Gives him a good excuse to come up for a bit of fresh air and a drink.'

31

Maggie watched as Rene walked through the door behind the bar, her hips swaying very provocatively in a tight black skirt. Rene did really look the part with her white low-cut frilly blouse and blonde hair. She was very popular with the traders and punters alike.

''Allo, Maggs,' said Gus, coming through the door wiping his hands on a grey piece of rag, which he ran over his florid face and bald head. 'It's warm work down there shifting and lugging all the crates and barrels about. Anyway, you didn't come here to listen to me going on, so what can I do fer yer?'

Maggie looked anxiously at Rene, who appeared to be busy at the other end of the bar polishing her bright red nails.

'I'd like to ask you something.'

'Well, ask away, gel.'

'Could we sit over there?' Maggie pointed to the corner of the bar.

'Don't see why not. Fancy a drink?'

'No thanks.'

'Rene, give us a pint of best, there's a love. Bring it over, we'll be at the far table.'

'Sure, Gus.' She gave Maggie a puzzled look.

Maggie waited till Rene put the beer on the table and was out of earshot. 'Gus, I'm worried about Tony.'

'Why? What's he bin up to?'

'I don't know. You see he ain't been seen since yesterday morning.'

After taking a great gulp of beer Gus wiped the froth from his grey moustache with the back of his hand. 'What, 'e ain't bin home?'

Maggie shook her head.

'That ain't like him not to tell you, is it?'

'No. Winnie said she saw him come out of here yesterday lunchtime. He was with a couple of blokes.'

'Yer, that's right. They sat here talking together. Very quiet, they was. Shifty-looking buggers.'

'That's what Winnie said. He didn't say where he was going, I suppose?'

'Na, in fact he didn't seem to be saying much at all.' Gus wiped his face again with his piece of rag. 'D'yer know, now I come to think of it Tony did look a bit worried.'

'Worried?' repeated Maggie in alarm.

Gus finished his beer. 'Shouldn't think it's anyfink for you to fret about. You know Tony, could always put on the right face for the right people, and if he thinks there's a good deal going he don't like to be left out.'

Maggie nodded. 'That's true. Win thought he might have been looking for Ding Dong.'

Gus shook his head. 'Na, don't think so. 'Sides, if he wanted to put a bet on he'd leave it here with me. Look, excuse me, Maggs, but I must get on.'

'Course, Gus. Sorry to waste your time.'

'No trouble, gel, and don't forget me and the missis is always here if you want us.'

Maggie thanked him. Gus and Beatie were a nice couple and the Dog and Duck was a good meeting place, old and tatty and in need of a lick of paint though it now was. Over the years everybody made full use of it for weddings, funerals and any excuse for a party. Once the doors were shut Gus always told the police it was a private do, and the drinking went on for many hours. Mindful of her own need to be getting on, Maggie left the peace and quiet of the pub and stepped out into the bright sunshine, and the noise.

The sounds of kids shouting and screaming and the loud cockney voices of the market traders trying to sell their wares were trying to compete with the small group of Blackshirts on the corner who were telling the world how good Germany was.

Maggie needed someone to talk to, but everybody seemed to be busy. Although it was Saturday and Mr Goldman's shop had the closed sign in the window, Maggie knew he was in his back room. She pushed open the door, causing the tiny silver bell above to ring melodiously. The smell of new cloth tickled her nose. Tony always got his suits here, and they were always of the best quality.

Mr Goldman, in his black striped trousers and black jacket, shuffled from the rear of the shop where he had lived since his wife died. His shoulders were hunched through years of sitting sewing. He always wore his tape measure round his neck like a garland, even today on his Sabbath when he wasn't working. Maggie often wondered if he went to bed with it draped around him. His white hair was permanently stuck up, looking as if he'd had a fright.

'Maggie, Maggie, my dear. Come in and take a seat.' His lined face lit up and he pushed a chair towards her. 'You are looking very well. I trust the little 'ens are also well?'

'Yes thank you. Mr Goldman . . . this might sound silly, but . . . could I talk to you?'

'Of course, my dear.'

Maggie waited till he got another chair and set it down beside her.

'Right, my dear, now tell me what's worrying you?'

'It's Tony. He hasn't been home since he left yesterday morning.'

Mr Goldman took her hand and gently patted it. 'Now you mustn't worry about that young man. I've known him all his life. I dare say he's gone off to look for that cottage he's always on about. You know how he likes to give you nice surprises?'

Maggie nodded. 'I know. But surely he would have said somethink.'

Mr Goldman smiled.

'Has he told you somethink?'

Mr Goldman touched his lips. 'Don't worry, he'll be home soon. Mind you, I'll have to tell him not to keep too many secrets from you.'

Maggie felt anger rising up in her again. If Tony had gone to look at a cottage why the hell hadn't he told her? What was the reason for all this secrecy? 'Thank you, Mr Goldman. What else did he say?'

'Nothing really, just that he was in a hurry. It was when I was on my way home from fitting a client. I'm surprised he didn't get home last night, though. He must have missed the last train.'

'Train? Did he say where he was going?'

'No, not really. We only walked together for a short while and he said he had to catch a train. I just assumed it was about the cottage he is always talking of.'

'Thank you.' Maggie stood up.

'Maggie, I will be sorry to lose you as tenants.'

'Don't worry, Mr Goldman. I can't see me living in the country.'

'But what if he's put a deposit down?'

35

'He'll just have to get it back.'

Maggie's steps were a lot lighter as she left, but she was also very annoyed. Why hadn't Tony told her about his crazy idea? And what about the stall? He should have told Bill. Just you wait till you walk yourself in, she thought. You'll get a real mouthful, making me worry like this.

For the rest of the morning Maggie was backwards and forwards helping Bill and seeing to the children. She was impressed at how efficient Bill was, but as yet he lacked the skill and easy banter Tony had with his customers.

Eve came along just as Maggie was leaving the stall to get the children's dinner. 'What you doing down here?' Eve asked Maggie as she picked up a brass door knocker from among the knick-knacks, a large black china elephant, rusty spanners and chipped china.

'Tony ain't back yet.'

'What? Where's he gone now?'

'I don't know.' Maggie looked at Bill, who was busy with a customer. 'I'll be back in a while,' she called to him. 'Just going to get a cuppa.' Maggie took hold of Eve's arm. 'Come upstairs, I've got somethink to tell you.'

'Is it exciting or dirty?' asked Eve.

'It's about Tony.'

'That's what I mean,' said Eve grinning.

The children were happy to play round the market stalls and everybody kept an eye on them just in case they got into mischief. Upstairs in the kitchen Maggie put the kettle on the gas stove, then moved into the living room.

'So, where's this errant husband of yours then?' asked Eve, settling herself on the sofa.

'I don't know.'

'But I thought you said—'

'I popped in to see Mr Goldman this morning and he said yesterday Tony told him he had to catch a train. Mr Goldman reckons it was to see about this bloody country cottage he's always on about.'

'What, he went without you?'

'Exactly.'

'But what if you don't like it?'

'I don't like it.'

'But you ain't seen it.'

'I know, and that's why I don't like it.' Maggie sat next to Eve.

'Surely he would have told you?'

'Mr Goldman reckons he wants to give me a surprise.'

'Well, it'll certainly be a surprise,' laughed Eve.

'In more ways than one.' Maggie stood up when the kettle began whistling. She went into the kitchen and Eve followed her.

'Maggs, how far away d'you think he's gone?'

'Dunno.'

'Surely he should be back be now? He couldn't have thought he'd be staying overnight else he would have taken his shaving things.'

Maggie leant against the sink. Worry filled her face. 'I hadn't thought about that. We all know how fussy he is about looking smart.' She glanced at the shelf. They didn't have a bathroom in their flat, so all washing had to be done in the kitchen sink, and once a week the tin bath was brought up from the back yard for their bath. 'His shaving stuff's still here, and without fail he shaves every day.' Maggie's voice had a slight catch in it.

'Go and sit down, I'll make the tea,' said Eve.

'I've got to get the kids' dinner.'

'Don't worry about cooking, I'll send 'em up to the pie and eel shop, they'll like that. Would you fancy a pie and a bit of mash?'

Maggie shook her head.

'Go and sit down. And I tell you somethink,' yelled Eve from the kitchen, 'when he does turn up he's gonner get a right old nagging from me. I don't like to see you upset like this.'

They finished their tea and Eve went looking for Laura and Jamie to take them out whilst Maggie went along to the stall so that Bill could have a bit of lunch in the Dog and Duck.

All afternoon Eve sat with Maggie, hoping and waiting.

'What time will Dan be home?' asked Maggie.

'Dunno.'

'Will he know where to find you?'

Eve smiled. 'I should think so, don't you?'

The quiet moments that followed were unnerving and it seemed unnatural when their conversation went dead, so unlike their normal time together – they always found something to laugh and chat about. In the silence Maggie went through so many emotions, from anger to gnawing worry. Finally: 'I must get the kids in for tea. You don't have to stay with me if you want to go and get Dan's ready.'

Eve stood up. 'I will pop home, just to let him know what's happening. I can see him punching Tony on the nose after all this.' Eve put on her hat. 'See you later.'

Maggie sat in the chair. A tear slipped down her cheek. 'Why are you doing this to me, Tony?' she said out loud.

The sound of the children clattering up the stairs made her wipe her eyes as she rose to open the door.

'Ain't Daddy home yet?' asked Laura, rushing in past her.

'Mrs Russell said you ought ter give him a right pasting when he gets back.' Jamie eased himself on the chair at the table.

So everyone on the market was discussing it.

'Auntie Eve bought us some pie and mash,' said Laura. 'And he,' she pointed to Jamie, 'made me stand and watch all those eels the man keeps outside. They was all wriggling about in the tins.'

Jamie laughed. 'It was good when the man chopped their heads off. D'yer know, they still wriggled even when they didn't have any heads. Would we wriggle if we had our heads chopped off?'

'Come here and let me see,' laughed Maggie, cheered by their irrepressible chatter.

'No!' shouted Jamie, jumping off his chair and hiding under the table.

'Well, I think it's horrid, doing that to those poor things,' said Laura. 'They can't run away and hide.'

'I'm sure it was so quick they didn't feel it.'

'I hope so. What's for tea, Mummy?'

Maggie smiled. Laura soon forgot things when food was around. 'Just a bit of cheese on toast.'

'When's Daddy coming home?' asked Jamie.

'I don't know,' said Maggie.

'He will come home, won't he?' asked Laura, anxiously.

'Course. Now go and wash your hands, then I'll get your tea, and as a special treat I'll pop along to Tucker's shop and get a bottle of cream soda and some ice cream.'

'Wow,' said Jamie, opening his big blue eyes wide. 'Can we have lots and lots?'

Chapter 4

Maggie couldn't settle, and once the children were in bed she sat and gazed out of the window. She was pleased when she caught sight of Dan and Eve hurrying down the road.

Dan was first in the room. 'Ain't he home yet?' he asked, kissing Maggie's cheek.

She shook her head.

'You can see he ain't,' said Eve. 'Damn silly question to ask.'

'Thought he might be down in the bog.'

'Dan, I'm really worried. D'you think we should go to the police?'

'What could they do?'

'Dunno.'

Eve sat next to Maggie. 'Maggs, I don't like to ask, and I know it ain't none of my business, but . . .' she shifted her position, 'he ain't playing around, is he?'

Maggie sat bolt upright. 'You think he's left me for someone else, don't you?'

Dan shot Eve a filthy look. 'Course she don't.'

'Eve, d'you know somethink?'

Eve looked uncomfortable. 'No.'

'D'you think there might be someone else?' Tears slowly ran down Maggie's face.

'No, course not.'

'Then something must have happened to him.' Maggie stood up. 'I'm gonner go to the police.'

'Maggie, sit down.'

She did as Dan told her.

He sat next to her and took hold of her hand. 'I don't think you ought ter start involving the police . . . well, not just yet anyway.'

'Why?'

Dan lit up a cigarette. 'Look, me and Tony being good mates often talked about all sorts of things, and well . . .' He rubbed his hand over his chin. 'Some of his dealings wasn't always . . . kosher, yer see, and yer know he liked a bet.'

'I know he was always doing deals, but surely none of it was that bad that someone would . . .? Why do you think . . .?' Maggie was beginning to get upset at these implications.

'Quite a while back he told me he was worried.'

Maggie sat on the edge of her chair. 'Worried, worried, what d'you mean, Dan?'

'It was years ago. He told me he was involved with some right villains,' said Dan very quickly. 'But as I said, that was years ago. They might even be doing time.'

'You don't think they're back on the scene now, do you?' Eve asked.

Maggie frowned. 'If they are, why should they be interested in Tony? He ain't ever said anythink to me about being worried. And I think I would be the first to know.'

'You don't always see what's going on, even if it's right

under yer nose, not if you're that close to someone,' said Eve softly.

'Maggs, has Tony got anything, you know, real valuable?' asked Dan.

'Don't think so. If he has it ain't up here.'

'Could it be in the lockup?'

Maggie shrugged her shoulders. 'Dunno. But surely if it was that valuable he'd hide it away till he sold it.' She looked at Dan, her eyes full of tears. 'Wouldn't he?'

'Give me the key. I'll go down and have a look.'

'I'm coming with you.'

'No, you stay up here, I'll go.'

'No, I'm coming with you. If there's anythink that ain't right, I want to know.'

'Please yerself. You coming as well, Eve?'

'Course. I ain't missing nothink.'

All three went along to the lockup. Although it was late evening and the market deserted, for some unknown reason Maggie looked around feeling guilty.

Dan pushed open the large door and turned on the light. The smell of Mrs Russell's flowers filled the air. Tony's stall was just as Bill had left it. He shared this lockup with Winnie, Mrs Russell, and Tom Cooper. Tony always said he was glad they didn't have the smell of fish and rotting veg in with them.

'Can't see anythink worth leaving home for,' said Dan, picking up some of the objects on Tony's barrow.

'Well, if he had something that was worth a bob or two he wouldn't leave it on show, now would he?' said Eve, walking round and lifting with the toe of her shoe some of the rubbish and old sacks that were lying around.

'No, I reckon you're right, old girl. Let's look in all the corners.'

'Don't know if I want to go poking around in here. What if a rat jumps out,' said Maggie, standing well back.

Eve jumped. 'Don't say things like that, you'll frighten the daylights out of me.'

A train rattling overhead made Maggie start, and the intrusive noise forced them into silence.

'You two stand over by the door while I have a look around,' said Dan, when the train passed.

'My brave hero,' said Eve.

'I'll tell you somethink for nothink. When he does walk his arse in I'll give him what for,' said Maggie, her tears turning to anger. 'Making me worry like this.'

Eve put her arm round her friend's shoulders. 'You won't be the only one. Me and Dan will give him a right old mouthful as well.'

Maggie smiled. 'If he hears us, he'll never come back, he'll be too terrified.'

'Can't find anything that's worth more than a few bob,' said Dan, walking towards them.

'Perhaps this gang of villains made off with the spoils as well as Tony,' said Eve, laughing and trying to look sinister. 'Come on, let's pop in the Dog for a quick one.'

'I reckon that's a good idea,' said Dan.

'I'd rather not,' said Maggie. 'If you don't mind I'd rather get back to the kids, just in case Tony comes back and starts looking for me. Don't let me stop you two, though.'

'You go on, I'll stay with Maggie,' said Eve.

'OK.'

'Dan,' Maggie gently touched his arm, 'you won't say

anythink in there about Tony just yet, not till we find out more?'

'Course not, love. I'll only have a quick one, then I'll be back.'

'I've heard all that before,' said Eve.

Dan ignored that remark. 'But what if someone asks about him?'

'Tell them he ain't well, got a cold or somethink.'

'OK. See yer later, girls.'

'Come on, Maggs, let's go and have a cuppa tea.'

Dan was true to his word and didn't stay in the pub very long. He told Maggie nobody bothered to ask about Tony. After Eve and Dan left for home Maggie was on her own once again. She knew deep down something had happened to Tony. 'Please, Tony, come home,' she whispered. She was sure he hadn't just gone off of his own accord. Maggie knew if there was any way he could get in touch with her, he would.

Sunday seemed a very long day. Maggie was short-tempered with her children and she wished she had taken them over to see Tony's mother at Downham, but what could she say to her? Could Tony be over there? No, his mother would soon send him back.

Although Dan had told Maggie not to go to the police, if she hadn't heard anything by tomorrow morning, that's where she would be going as soon as she had taken Laura to school.

On Monday morning, a letter plopping on the doormat sent Maggie hurrying down the stairs as fast as her bulk would allow. She desperately hoped it was news of Tony, but was filled with despair when after opening it found it was an invitation to her brother, Alan's birthday party.

'He only has parties to show off,' mumbled Maggie to herself as she mounted the stairs again. She looked at the date, it was going to be the Saturday after next, plenty of time to make sure everybody got him a present.

She tossed the letter on to the sideboard. 'Now come on, you two,' she said to Jamie and Laura, who were sitting at the table. They had been asking questions about their dad ever since they got up. What could she tell them? 'You should have finished your breakfast by now.'

She noted Bill had got Tony's stall out, but she didn't stop to speak and deliberately hurried past all the other stallholders. At the school gates she kissed Laura goodbye, and made her way to the police station.

When they reached the door Jamie held back. 'What we going in here for?' he asked, holding Maggie's hand tightly. He looked very apprehensive. 'Has Daddy done something wrong?'

Maggie quickly glanced down at him. 'No, why? What made you ask that?'

'Well, he ain't come home, and when Mr Ding Dong went away, Daddy told me he'd done somethink wrong and was put in prison.' He looked at his feet and shuffled about. 'Daddy ain't in prison, is he?'

Maggie bent down and held him close. 'Don't be silly, of course not. I'm just going to ask the policeman if he's been hurt, and find out if he's in a hospital, and can't tell anybody where he lives.'

'Why can't he tell 'em where he lives?'

'He may have been in an accident and been knocked unconscious.'

'Oh,' said Jamie. 'Come on then, let's go and ask.'

'Can I help you?' asked the young policeman at the desk.

'Please, could I see someone in charge?'

'What's it in connection with?'

'Well, I don't know really. I'm just trying to find out about my husband.'

'Done a runner then, 'as he?'

'No,' said Maggie indignantly.

The policeman took up a large writing pad and licked the tip of his pencil. 'Name?'

'Tony Ross.'

'Address?'

'Twenty-seven Kelvin Market.'

'How long's he been missing?'

'Since Friday.'

The policeman looked up. 'I know Tony Ross. He's got a stall at the market.'

'Yes. I'm Mrs Ross.'

'You say he's been missing since Friday?'

Maggie nodded.

The policeman's face changed to one of concern. 'Wait here.' He disappeared through a door behind the counter.

Maggie sat on the bench seat that lined the dismal brown painted wall. But almost at once the policeman was at the counter again, a man in plain clothes with him.

'Mrs Ross,' said the man, 'I'm Inspector Matthews. I think I may have some news for you.'

Maggie's face beamed. 'You have?'

The Inspector looked uneasy, and Maggie became agitated.

'Look, I think you'd better come round. Go through that door.' He pointed the way.

'What about Jamie?' The sound of her pounding heart was filling her ears. She was suddenly aware that this could be bad news and she didn't want Jamie to hear it till she knew for certain.

'Bring him round. PC Brown will look after him.'

Maggie's hand was shaking as she pushed open the door. The Inspector was at her side almost at once. 'Follow me.'

Maggie was in a daze. She was led into a small room that had the words 'Detective Inspector Matthews' painted in black on the brown wooden door. The shelves that lined the walls were overflowing with papers tied together in bundles, and stacked high with box files. The desk was strewn with papers and the ashtray full of dog-ends. The only furniture was just two chairs and a desk.

'Please, Mrs Ross, sit down.' He waved his hand at the chair opposite him.

'What news have you got about Tony?'

The Inspector took a packet of cigarettes out of his pocket and offered her one.

Maggie shook her head.

He lit up and blew the smoke in the air. He gently tapped the end of the cigarette into the ashtray.

Maggie wanted to scream at him to get on with it.

'Mrs Ross,' he said slowly, 'did your husband have any distinguishing marks on his body?'

Maggie felt sick. Tony was dead. He was trying to tell her Tony was dead. She felt numb. She could hear the Inspector talking but his words weren't registering.

'Mrs Ross, Mrs Ross, are you all right?'

Tears ran down her face. She shook her head. 'Is he dead?'

'We don't know. You see, we fished a body out of the docks last night, he didn't have any identification on him, and until we find out who he is, we have to eliminate any missing persons.'

'No, not my Tony. It can't be.'

'Now if I could have a few details about your husband, that will help.'

Maggie could hear herself describing Tony.

'Would he have been wearing any jewellery?'

She nodded. 'He had quite a large diamond ring on his little finger, and a wedding ring on . . .' She had to stop.

'I'm sorry, but we have to ask these questions. Would you like a cup of tea?'

She nodded again.

The Inspector jumped up and quickly left the room, almost as if he were glad to get away.

He returned almost at once. 'PC Thurly will bring one in. Now, back to these questions. The body we found wasn't wearing any rings, though it could be that robbery was the motive for an attack. Now what about any distinguishing marks, like birthmarks, tattoos or moles – did Mr Ross have anything like that?'

'No,' said Maggie softly. She thought about Tony's perfect body, so strong and lovely. She wanted him here now, to run her hands over him. Tell him how much she loved him. Tell him she needed him to be with her.

The door opened and a cup of tea was silently put in front of her.

'When is your baby due?' asked the Inspector, out of the blue.

'September.'

'Do you just have the young man outside?'

'No, I have a little girl at school.'

'That's nice. Mrs Ross,' he hesitated. 'I'm afraid I'll have to ask you to come to the hospital with me to identify the body.'

'Do you think it could be Tony?'

'We don't know.'

'Tony had dark curly hair, and was wearing a navy coat . . .'

'Mrs Ross,' interrupted the Inspector, 'the body was naked when we found him.'

Maggie sat very still.

'Look, if you like we could arrange for someone to go with you. Do you have a friend or relation?'

'My mother-in-law lives out at Downham, and my friend's at work. I could perhaps get Winnie from the market to come with me.'

'I'll send one of my officers to go and get her. Which stall is she on?'

'The shoe stall.'

'Oh yes, I know it.' Once again he left the room.

When he returned he had Jamie in tow.

'Mummy, that policeman showed me his handcuffs,' he said excitedly, 'and he let me see his truncheon. It ain't half heavy.'

Maggie struggled to smile. What would she do if the body was Tony? The children wouldn't have a father. How would she manage? Tears suddenly ran down her face.

'What yer crying for, Mummy?' Jamie's voice was full of fear and concern. 'They ain't gonner lock you up, are they?'

'No, course not.' She wiped her tears with the back of her hand and held out her arms. Jamie snuggled into her.

'Is Daddy in hospital like you said he might be?'

'I don't know yet. I've got to go and look at a man, just to see.'

'So he can't tell you if he's Daddy then?'

'No. I'm going with Auntie Win.' She looked up at the Inspector.

'It's all right, he can stay here. Would you like that, young fellow me lad?' He ruffled Jamie's hair.

Jamie gave him a dirty look. 'I don't like that, nor people kissing me.'

'I'm sorry, young man.' The Inspector bent down. 'And I promise not to kiss you.'

Maggie wanted to smile.

'Can I go back and wait with the policeman?'

'I should think so.' Inspector Matthews took hold of Jamie's hand and led him to the door. 'I'll be back. Did you want anything?'

'No thank you.' Maggie sat with her thoughts. What if it was Tony? She loved him so much, she couldn't bear life without him.

After a while the door burst open.

'What the bloody hell's going on round here? What you doing in a police station? I tell yer, girl, they'll be a riot down that market if they've got you in here and you ain't done nothink.'

The Inspector followed Winnie into the room.

'Win, I've got a favour to ask you.'

51

'Well ask away, girl. You know I'd do anythink for you, just as long as yer don't ask for money.' She laughed.

'Win, I think you'd better sit down.'

'Why? What's wrong?' Winnie looked puzzled as she glanced from Maggie to the Inspector.

Maggie began to tell her what had happened.

Winnie's eyes were growing larger and larger with every sentence. 'So what you're trying to say is that it could be your Tony what's laid out in the morgue?'

Maggie nodded and wiped her eyes.

'I'm afraid so,' said Inspector Matthews.

'Bloody hell, this is a bit of a shock.' Winnie fished around in her overall pocket for her handkerchief and blew her nose very loudly. 'What yer gonner do, gel?'

'I don't know,' whispered Maggie.

'Look, we mustn't jump to conclusions. Let's get down to the hospital and make sure first,' said the Inspector.

Winnie sprang up, 'Well, come on then, let's get it over and done with.'

'I'll take you in my car.'

'Thank you,' said Maggie.

'Come on, Maggs, hold on to me arm.'

Hanging on to Winnie Maggie walked out into the sunshine, but for her, everything had a black cloud hanging over it.

Chapter 5

The journey to the hospital had been made in silence. Now Maggie's mind was in turmoil as they hurried up the steps. What state would the body be in? She couldn't think of it as being Tony's body. Her stomach, like her mind, churned over. She didn't want to go in.

The Inspector noticed her distress and took her arm. 'Are you sure you're all right, Mrs Ross?'

'Yes thank you.'

Inside he said, 'Wait here,' and quickly made his way to the desk. He spoke intently to a young nurse, who nodded and glanced over at Maggie.

'This way,' said Inspector Matthews.

Maggie and Winnie followed him to the top of the stairs.

'It's down here.'

Maggie hesitated. Her legs felt like lead. She didn't want to go down.

'Come on, love,' said Winnie kindly. 'The sooner we get this over with, the better.' She took Maggie's arm and led her down.

They walked into the white tiled room. 'This is Mrs Ross,' said Inspector Matthews to a man in a white coat.

The cold clinical atmosphere with the smell of disinfectant and death made Maggie feel sick. She shivered. The man came towards them.

'Mrs Ross has come to look at the body we pulled out of the docks on Friday.' The Inspector hesitated before adding, 'It could be her husband.'

The man in the white coat nodded gravely. 'He's over here.' He moved across the tiled floor, his footsteps almost silent in contrast to the loud clomping sound the rest of them made as they followed him to a shape on a metal table. The shape was covered with a sheet.

'We were just going to start the post mortem on him.' He stood at the side and carefully lifted a corner of the cloth.

Maggie heaved, and the baby kicked. Her feet became rooted to the floor. They wouldn't move. She wanted to go and look, but couldn't.

Maggie swayed. Her head was spinning. Voices began to sound far away. Her legs buckled. In the distance she could hear Winnie shouting.

'Quick, get a chair.'

Then everything went black.

Slowly Maggie opened her eyes. The lights were bright and appeared to be moving round in circles. The man in the white coat was tapping her hand.

'It's all right, love. It ain't Tony,' said Winnie.

Maggie tried to stand up. 'Who . . .? What . . .?' she gasped.

'Just take your time,' said the man in the white coat, straightening up.

'It isn't your husband,' said the Inspector, 'and Mrs . . . here verified that. But I'm afraid you do have to tell me, just for the records, you understand.'

Maggie nodded.

'But only when you feel you are up to it.'

'I'm all right now.' She stood up and slowly moved towards the body.

Once again the corner of the sheet was lifted.

Maggie gazed down on a middle-aged man's face. It looked full of pain. 'No, this isn't my husband.'

'Have you any idea who it might be?'

Maggie shook her head and looked away. 'No, sorry.'

'Thank you. I'll take you back to the station. We'll have to ask you for a few more details about when you last saw your husband, and if you have any idea where he may have gone.'

In the car Maggie's feelings were confused. She was relieved the body wasn't Tony, but sad that she still didn't know where he was.

When at the station Maggie felt she had answered all the Inspector's questions, she asked, 'Is that it? Can we go?'

'Yes, thank you for now.'

She went to stand up.

'Mrs Ross.' He coughed, leant back in his chair and turned his pencil over and over in his clean, well-scrubbed hands. 'I'm sorry, but I do have to ask you this. Do you know if your husband was seeing another woman?'

'I can assure you he was not.' Maggie's answer was sharp.

'Thank you. But you do understand, we do have to ask.'

Maggie and Winnie, with Jamie between them, began to walk slowly back to the market.

'So how long's he been gone?' asked Winnie.

'I haven't seen him since Friday morning. Mr Goldman saw him at the station Friday afternoon.'

'What was he doing there?'

'If only I knew.'

Winnie stopped. ''Ere, you don't think he went to see his mum, do you?'

'No, he would have told me he was going. Besides, I normally do up a parcel for her. And it wouldn't take him all weekend to get there and back.'

'Yer, that's true. She lives out Downham way now, don't she?'

Maggie nodded. 'She was so upset when they pulled down all those old houses and moved the tenants away, but now she's got used to it she likes it. I think this is what Tony's got in mind for us.'

'Kent ain't that far away. Used to go down there hopping with me mum when I was a kid. She couldn't wait for August to get away from the old man.'

'Didn't he mind her going?'

'Na. Just as long as she was earning a few bob. 'Sides, with her out the way he didn't have ter bother to take the barra out, and he could get as drunk as he liked without her nagging.'

Maggie's thoughts went to her mother-in-law, who since tripping over in the garden and breaking her leg had been unable to get out as much as she used to. 'I'll have to go and tell her,' said Maggie out loud.

'Tell who?'

'Tony's mum.'

'Yer, but if I was you I'd wait till you've found out a bit

more. You know how she feels about him.'

Maggie smiled. 'Perhaps you're right. Tony's the apple of his mother's eye.'

They turned into the market and Jamie ran ahead. Winnie stopped for a moment and took hold of Maggie's arm. 'What yer gonner tell that lot?' She inclined her head towards the stalls.

'I don't know.'

'Well, you can guess we'll be having the coppers sniffing round here now, asking a lot of questions.'

'Yes.'

'And I don't reckon it'll go down that well with some of 'em. Most of 'em have got something to hide.'

'Even you?' Maggie gave her a faint smile.

Winnie laughed. 'Yer, I just see him asking, "And where did you get those boots from then, missis?" I could look up at him, flutter me eyelashes and say, "Off that bloke what you fished out the river." '

Maggie didn't laugh with her.

'Sorry, gel, that was a bit insensitive of me.'

When they reached Tony's stall Bill asked, 'Where's that old man of yours got to then, Maggs?'

'I don't know. Bill, he's not been around since Friday. I've just been to the police.'

'Bloody hell. The police? What for?'

'I want to find out where he is.' She lowered her head. 'And if he's still alive.'

Bill let out a long whistle. ''Ere, you don't think—'

'No, course not,' interrupted Winnie.

'Well look, you don't have to worry about the stall. I'll manage. I hope 'e don't stay away too long, though, otherwise we won't 'ave a lot of stock.'

'Don't worry about that for the time being, and Bill, if anybody, you know, who looks a bit suspicious, asks for him, send them up to me.'

'OK, Maggs. I hope this gets cleared up soon.'

'So do I.'

Winnie looked from one to the other. 'Bill, if anyone does ask for 'im, you'd better come and tell me first. Just in case.'

'OK, Win.'

Maggie and Winnie moved on.

'That's gonner be all round this 'ere market before you've had time to get the kettle on,' said Winnie.

'That might not be a bad thing. Someone might remember if he said anything to them. Then this mystery could be cleared up. Did you want to come up for a cuppa?'

'No thanks, I'd better get back to me stall. I never know if that Ada, what's supposed to keep an eye on it for me, helps herself to some of me profits.'

'She wouldn't dare.'

Winnie laughed. 'I've only gotter catch her once, then you wouldn't see her arse for dust.' She kissed Maggie's cheek. 'Now you go on in and put your feet up. I'll make sure Laura gets home all right.'

'Thanks, Win, I'll see you later. Come on, Jamie, up you go.'

For the rest of the day, Maggie's thoughts kept returning to that man laid out in the morgue. Somebody must be worrying about him. What if Tony was laid out in another place? Tears filled her eyes. How long must she wait for news?

At six o'clock Eve came hurrying up the stairs. 'Well, he back yet?'

Maggie shook her head and in a quiet voice told her about the trip to the morgue and the police station.

'Maggs, that must have been awful for you,' said Eve, putting her hand to her mouth and slumping down in the chair. 'What did the police say?'

'Not a lot really.'

'You don't think Tony's dead, do you?'

'I don't know what to think. Eve, what am I gonner do?'

Eve sat down and took a packet of cigarettes out of her handbag. She lit one and slowly blew the smoke into the air. 'You don't think he's gone off with another woman, do you?'

Maggie laughed. 'Course not. If there was any hanky-panky going on I'm sure I would have known.'

Eve nervously tapped the end of her cigarette into the ashtray. 'Yer, course you would have.'

'Eve, do you think Tony could be wandering around somewhere, you know, and lost his memory?'

'Dunno. I suppose that could happen, but then Mr Goldman saw him getting on a train.'

'I know.' Maggie sat on the end of her chair. 'But suppose after he'd been to see that cottage he hit his head. Those people wouldn't know who he was, would they?' Maggie was beginning to get excited about this theory.

'I don't know. But he must have something on him to tell them who he was, and an address for the cottage. They surely would know his name and where he came from.'

Maggie sat back deflated. 'I suppose so. It was just an idea.'

'I know.'

'Eve, I don't know where to turn.'

'I wish I could help. Now come on, let's try and be a bit practical. What about the stall?'

'Bill seems to be managing all right, but I don't know for how long . . .' Tears filled her eyes. 'Eve, what am I gonner do without him?'

Eve took her hand. 'We'll all rally round you.'

'Thanks.'

'What about your brother? You'll have to tell him.'

'That'll give Helen something to chew over. I'm not telling them just yet. By the way I've got an invitation to Alan's birthday party.'

'When's that?'

'Two weeks, I think – didn't really take a lot of notice.'

'You going?'

'Don't know. A lot can happen in two weeks.'

'You sure there's nothing around that might give you some idea where he is?'

'No. Mind you, I ain't been down his papers. They might give me a clue.'

Eve jumped up. 'Where are they? We can go through—'

'I'd rather not.'

'OK. Please yourself.' Eve looked a little put out. 'Did he keep a diary?'

'Shouldn't think so, never seen him with one.'

They sat talking and drinking tea for a while, then Eve said she had to go.

'I'll call in again tomorrow. You look after yourself.' She kissed Maggie's cheek and left.

After Eve left, Maggie thought about Tony's papers and

turned out his cupboard. Over the years she hadn't had a lot to do with his business, but hoped there might be a clue to his whereabouts amongst his documents.

For hours she sat poring over books and figures, surprised how detailed some of the transactions had been recorded. Most of the stuff came from the rag-and-bone man, Benny. Benny's name was in the book many times. Now and again the initial W was pencilled in, and some of the figures made her gasp. She didn't realise he had made that kind of money, but where was it? The book showed items he had bought at auctions. She remembered the times she went with him, and he'd mostly bought junk. But in this book were things she had never seen, or even knew about. Some had been bought and then sold on at great profit. So where was the money? The Post Office book didn't have a lot in, only thirty shillings, and she knew there wasn't any hidden in the flat. So how was he going to pay for this cottage? Was there money in a bank somewhere? If so, which bank? They didn't have a bank account. How could she find out? She straightened up, her back and head aching. She shoved the books into the cupboard. She would finish going through them tomorrow. She'd just about had all she could take for one day.

The following morning, as soon as Laura was at school, and Jamie went to play outside, Maggie opened Tony's wardrobe. At first she stood gently feeling his suits and holding them close to her cheek. Tears filled her eyes. They had his smell. 'Tony, where are you?' she whispered.

Quickly she went down all his pockets, fumbling, almost afraid he might come in and catch her. She found old train tickets, bus tickets, dog track tickets and cigarette packets. But there was nothing that gave her a clue or any hope.

Back in the living room she got down on her hands and knees and got his papers out again. Then she carefully ran her hand along the rear of the cupboard. She pulled out a child's exercise book that was wedged right at the back. She quickly ran her thumb over the pages. The book didn't have any figures in, but Maggie sensed it was very private. Guilt almost overtook her as she opened it. She had never poked her nose into his affairs before.

She sat at the table and began reading. There were names and addresses of most of the people they knew, also of some she didn't know. There was also a list of places with dates and times, with just an initial by the side. As she read on, the dates became more recent. They stopped before Friday, 17 May, the day he went missing.

If he was going to meet someone why didn't he write it down?

Jamie's yelling from the bottom of the stairs brought her back to reality.

'Mummy, Mummy, it's that policeman.'

Maggie stood up and quickly bundled all the books and papers back into the cupboard.

The door opened.

'Sorry, Mrs Ross. I hope it isn't inconvenient. Young Jamie here said it was all right to come up.'

'Yes, that's fine. Have you any news?' In her home he appeared tall, and he was quite nice-looking.

'I'm afraid not. But I thought I'd have a walk round the market and ask a few questions. You never know, someone may have heard something.'

'I bet that didn't go down too well.'

'You're right.' He smiled, and for the first time Maggie noticed he had a pleasant face and his smile crinkled his very blue eyes, quite unusual with such dark hair.

'I've been having a word with Mr Goldman, as he seems to be the last person who saw your husband, but he couldn't really throw any light on what we already know. What about Mr Ross's books?'

Maggie shrugged. 'Tony didn't really keep any.'

'You'll let me know if you find anything that could be useful, won't you?'

Maggie nodded. 'Would you like a cup of tea?'

'That would be very nice – if it's not too much trouble.'

'It's no trouble, in fact I was just going to make myself one.' Maggie suddenly felt very self-conscious at this man being in her home, and this silly bland conversation.

When she returned from the kitchen he was standing in front of the sideboard with her wedding photo in his hand. She noticed a small piece of paper with Tony's writing on poking out of the cupboard underneath. She quickly put the tea tray on the table, and wondered if the Inspector had seen the paper.

'You make a very handsome couple,' he said replacing the photo. 'Perhaps you have a photo of your husband we could have to place on file at the station?'

'Of course. There's one in this drawer. Do you take sugar?' It was the only thing she could think of to say. She felt desperate for him to leave so she might think about the list she had found in the book.

For the rest of the week Eve dropped in every evening, and

Inspector Matthews called in once again.

On Friday Maggie felt very low. Today was Empire Day.

Laura hadn't been sleeping well, and one night Maggie heard her shouting in her sleep. When she awoke she said she was worried about dancing round the maypole, but Maggie suspected it went deeper than that. Another night she was crying, and twice Jamie had wet the bed. A week had gone by since Tony left home, and it was having an effect on the children. Where was he? Was he still alive?

But today Laura looked very pretty in her pale blue frock that had frills from the waist down.

'This is Daddy's favourite,' she said, preening in front of the large ornate mirror. 'I wish Daddy was going to see me.'

'So do I, darling.' Maggie knelt on the floor to tie the pale blue ribbon round Laura's dark curly hair.

'Is he ever coming back to us?'

She had such a sad look on her face that Maggie just had to sweep her into her arms. 'I hope so,' she whispered.

'Well, I reckon it's rotten of him not to come home,' said Jamie.

'I'm sure he has a good reason,' said Maggie, standing up and regaining her composure. 'Now come on, we mustn't be late.'

The dancing around the maypole went well and the children who had had more rehearsals than at the Jubilee didn't get into such a tangle as the last time. Maggie decided to sit at the back of the playground. She didn't want to talk to Laura's teacher in case she asked about Tony. Her eyes misted over. Tony would have loved to have been here. He was very proud of everything Laura and Jamie did. Maggie was convinced he wouldn't stay away from them for long, not of his own free will.

That evening she was glad of Eve and Dan's company, and after a lot of persuading decided to go with them to the Dog and Duck. She felt very uneasy at the looks she received when they walked in.

'Still no news then, Maggs?' asked Gus.

'No.'

'Can't say I like the coppers hanging round here all the time.'

'Why's that then, Gus?' asked Eve. 'You got something to hide?'

'No I ain't.' He leant across the bar. 'I'll tell yer something else, old Ding Dong ain't none too pleased about it either.'

Maggie wanted to scream. How did they think *she* felt?

Gus's wife, Beatie, gave them a wave and came over. She was a short well-groomed woman, whose hair had been allowed to go grey naturally. Her pale face had just a hint of make-up, not like most of the landladies round here, who looked like they had just come off the stage. 'Have this one on the house, love.' She smiled at Maggie, then glared at her husband. 'Take no notice of him. Just remember if there's anythink I can do to help, let me know.'

'Thanks, Beatie. Do they think,' Maggie nodded towards the group of men at the bar who were deep in conversation, 'that I enjoy having the police keep coming round asking me questions?'

'Course they don't, love, but, well, you know most of 'em are into some dodgy dealings one way or another. Go and sit down and I'll bring the drinks over.' She returned with a flash of the lovely rings she always wore, with large stones that glinted when they caught the light.

'Thanks, Beatie.'

At the end of the week Maggie added up the takings from the stall. Now she had Tony's books to go by she noticed they were down considerably.

'OK, Maggs?' asked Bill, when he brought Saturday's takings up to her.

'You ain't took a lot this week,' she said, after counting out the day's money.

'Ain't got any new stock, 'ave I?'

'Sit down, Bill,' she said quietly. 'Nobody's been to ask about Tony?'

'Only that copper.'

Maggie bit the end of her pencil. 'I know some of the auction rooms Tony used to go to. I might nip along there, and I'll see Benny next week – he might have a few bits.'

'D'yer want me to come with you?'

'No, I don't think so. But if anybody's got something to sell, get word up here to me quick.'

'You gonner take over the stall then, Maggs?'

'Looks like I ain't got any choice.'

'Well, I reckon you're very brave.'

Tears filled Maggie's eyes. 'I've already got two mouths to feed, and in a few months there'll be another.'

Bill looked embarrassed. 'So you don't think Tony's coming back then?'

Maggie didn't know how to answer him.

Chapter 6

On Monday morning, after taking Laura to school, Winnie said she would keep her eye on Jamie. Maggie took the bus to one of the auction rooms she knew.

She'd forgotten the dank musty smell of this place. After studying the catalogue she wandered around, browsing through some of the junk on display. Chipped china, dented saucepans, rusting lawn mowers and garden tools – who would want garden tools and a lawn mower in Rotherhithe?

'It's Maggie, ain't it? Maggie Ross? I ain't seen you here for years.' The short tubby white-haired man came hurrying over towards her. He held her close and kissed her cheek. 'This is a nice surprise.' Wally looked around. 'Where's that old man of yours then?'

'Hallo, Wally,' said Maggie, ignoring the question.

'So how you keeping then? And what you doing round this way?'

Wally was an auctioneer. Could he be the W in Tony's book? Maggie hadn't thought about him as Tony had told her he'd retired. 'Thought you was at home putting your feet up.'

'Na. Couldn't stand it, and the missis couldn't stand me

under her feet all the time, so I thought I'd come back. I only do a couple of days. Still, it keeps me out of mischief and in the know.' He put his arm round her shoulders and laughed. 'See he's still getting his wicked way then.' Wally pointed to Maggie's stomach. 'How many's that make now?'

'Only three.'

'So where is the old bugger?'

'He's busy, so he asked me to have a look round,' lied Maggie. There was no way she was going to tell him the truth – well, not yet anyway.

'So he's sent you out buying?'

'Sort of.'

'What's he got his eye on then? Could always let you know if someone else is interested in it.'

'Don't really know. It has to be cheap. Perhaps a couple of vases, or cutlery. Just anything we could sell quick and make a profit.'

Wally looked uneasy. 'I'm surprised Tony sent you along. He always reckoned the little woman's place was in the home.'

Maggie smiled. 'I told him I needed a day out, so he said I'd have to work for it.'

Wally laughed. 'Yer, that sounds like Tony. 'Ere, come this way.' Wally took her arm and led her to a corner. 'So how much yer got to play with?'

'Not a lot.'

'Did he say if he's ready to shift some of the big stuff again?'

'Don't know. Why?'

Wally looked about him suspiciously. He lowered his

voice. 'See that sideboard over there.' He nodded towards a large ornate oak sideboard. 'Well, the drawer's locked and key's missing.' He looked around again and moved closer to Maggie. 'I happen to know there's a lot of silver cutlery in that drawer, it's the real McCoy, and if I could get a mate to buy the sideboard, then whatever's inside comes with it, and we could split the difference. Just so long as he keeps his mouth shut.'

'How do you know what's in that . . .'

Wally took her arm. 'Trust me,' he whispered.

'Don't anybody else know?'

'Only the bloke what cleared the house. Course, he wants a cut.'

'Why don't he get a key and sell it?'

'It's to do with an old girl's estate. That way the money would have to go to the next of kin.'

'Tony's done this sort of thing before then?'

'Yer. A few times. Didn't you know?' Wally looked concerned.

She laughed, she wanted this conversation to sound light-hearted. 'You should know Tony by now: he don't tell me everythink.'

'So why's he sent you down here now?' His tone had an edge of suspicion about it.

'He had to go away, and Bill said the stall was getting a bit low.' Maggie bit her lip anxiously.

'Sounds fishy to me. He bin away long?' Wally rubbed his chin.

'No,' said Maggie quickly. 'Just a few days.'

''Ere,' he looked round again before speaking, 'he ain't . . . you know, inside?'

Fear took hold of Maggie. Prison had crossed her mind, but surely the local police would know if he had been arrested elsewhere. She laughed again. 'No, course not, somethink to do with a auction in the country, and he fancied a few days away.' Although she had to carry on this easy-going banter, she felt she was getting in deeper and deeper with her explanations.

'That sounds like him.' Wally took her arm and held it tight. 'But you would tell me the truth now, wouldn't you?'

Maggie nodded smiling, but she could feel the undercurrent in his words.

'That's all right then. So, yer lookin' fer cheap stuff to sell on. D'you wanner wait for the auction?'

'No, I've got to get back.'

'Right then, gel, follow me.'

'Wally, do you want me to tell Tony what you said about that,' she moved her head towards the sideboard, 'when I get home?'

'Na, this lot'll go today. Some lucky sod's gonner make a few bob. But, Maggs, tell him ter come and see me real soon.'

'Anythink I should tell him about?'

'Na, just tell him I wanner see him, that's all.'

They wandered around and Maggie picked out to buy a hand mirror that had the silver peeling off the back, two small vases, a pair of miniature brass dogs, and a set of cut-glass bowls.

'You sure you can manage to get these bits home? If you fancy leaving them with me I could get the van round to you tonight.'

'No, thanks all the same, I'll be able to manage.' She

didn't want Wally anywhere near the market.

'Please yerself. Give that dirty old man of yours me best.'

'I will.'

'Say, why don't you and Tony come round home one of these evenings?'

'I'd like that.'

'Tell Tony to pop in and make the arrangements, and we could see about getting another game of cards going.'

'I will.' Maggie dutifully kissed his cheek and left.

As she sat on the bus all that Wally had told her about their scam went over and over in her mind. How often had they done that sort of thing? Her thoughts turned to that exercise book. Some of those initials were W. Could that have been dealings with Wally? Had something gone wrong? Could Tony be in prison somewhere? If so, would Inspector Matthews know? There were so many unanswered questions. She didn't really like Wally – he'd always seemed devious. She had seen this morning what sort of deals Wally was prepared to do, so maybe Tony had been keeping this kind of thing from her. She sighed. Perhaps she was trying to find some excuse for Tony leaving her.

As soon as she arrived home Maggie went straight to the cupboard and got out the exercise book. There were dates next to the initial W, but the entries still didn't make sense. She looked through the other book, the one that had all the money written down. If only this one had dates then she could see if they matched.

She went back to her purchases and carefully emptied her bag on to the table. She was pleased, she had picked out some nice bits, and with a cleanup they should bring in a few bob. Tomorrow she would go and see Benny the rag-and-bone man. She began to sing, then, remembering, suddenly stopped. Why was she happy? Nothing had changed. She sat down. She didn't want to be the one in charge, running the business, making the decisions. Please Tony, she begged silently, come back.

The following day Maggie went to Benny's yard. Though it had been a few years since she'd seen him, she knew Benny still lived here, as Tony often mentioned him, and laughed about his carrying a torch for his mum, Bella.

Maggie pushed open a small door set in the large corrugated door that fronted the yard and stepped through. Inside were piles of rusting junk: old mangles whose wooden rollers were almost worn away, tin baths with holes in, and a heap of broken furniture. Who would ever buy this rubbish? The smell of horse dung took her breath away – Benny lived over the building that housed his horse. Maggie carefully picked her way across the yard to the iron staircase that ran up the outside of the building.

She was only halfway up when the door at the top opened.

''Ere, what d'yer want?' Benny stood in the doorway looking down on her. He suddenly recognised her and a great smile lifted his thin but stern weather-beaten face. 'Well, if it ain't little Maggie Ross. What you doing round these parts, gel?'

'Hallo, Benny,' panted Maggie as she got to the top of the steep stairs.

'Come on in, gel. I've got the kettle on, just making meself a cuppa. Want one?'

Maggie wasn't all that sure she wanted anything to drink.

What state would his cups be in?

'Well, I'll be . . .' He pushed his greasy trilby back, scratching his forehead as he did so. You couldn't tell what colour his hat had once been – it was always a standing joke that Benny must have slept in it, since nobody ever saw him without it.

Benny was a thin wiry man who gave everybody the impression he was lazy and slow like his horse, but his pale blue eyes were always darting about, never missing a thing.

'Sit yerself down, gel. This is a nice surprise. What brings you round these parts?'

Maggie sat on the edge of the chair. Benny had one large room with the kitchen at one end and his bed at the other; it looked neat and tidy. He had lived alone all the years Maggie had known him; apparently his wife had died soon after they were married.

Maggie had made up her mind to tell Benny about Tony. He might know something, and had always been kinder than Wally.

As if reading her thoughts he suddenly sat next to her and asked, ''Ere, ain't nothing happened to yer old man, is there?' He sounded genuinely concerned.

Maggie looked at him. 'Benny,' she whispered, 'Tony's missing.'

'Sorry, gel, I don't get yer. What d'yer mean, missing? I only saw him, what, a week or so ago.'

The whistling kettle broke through the quiet. 'Just a tick, I'll make the tea.' He took a brown china teapot from the cupboard and after warming the pot he put two carefully measured spoonfuls of tea in and filled it with boiling water. He then took a bottle of milk from a galvanised bucket that stood on the floor, sniffed it and looking up, smiled. 'It's all right, it ain't gorn orf yet.' He brought the tray of tea things over to the table Maggie was sitting at. 'Ain't got any biscuits to give you. Nellie, that bloody horse of mine, eats 'em as fast as I buy 'em. Right, gel, now tell me what this is all about.'

Maggie went through the story. Benny didn't speak, but he listened very intently, his only movement to pour out the tea.

'So,' he said, when Maggie had finished, 'what d'yer think could have happened to him?'

'I don't know. Eve asked me if there was anybody else.' Maggie sniffed and fumbled in her handbag for a handkerchief.

'Did he take any of his clothes?'

Maggie shook her head.

Benny patted her hand. 'Well then, I don't think you've got any worries on that score. He was a bit of a ladies' man in his day, and he always liked to look good, but he did love yer, Maggs, you knows that, don't yer?'

She nodded. 'But I wish he'd kept me a bit more . . . I don't know.' She threw her arms up in the air. 'Told me more about what was going on.'

'Why's that, gel? Do you think he's mixed up in some funny business?' He coughed. 'We all like to dabble a bit, but what I mean is, real dodgy stuff, with right villains?'

'I don't know. I went to the auction room yesterday and Wally wanted Tony to buy a sideboard that he said had a lot of silver in.'

'That does happen now and again,' said Benny, leaning back in his chair and lighting his pipe. 'But you have to be

74

in the know, and trust the person you're dealing with.' He was lost in a cloud of smoke. 'Mind you, I've never got on with Wally. A bit of a double-dyed villain, if yer asks me. Sell his missis fer a shilling.' He laughed. 'Still I s'pose most blokes I know would sell their missis fer a shilling.'

'Benny,' said Maggie quietly, 'I've been to the police.'

He sat forward and waved his hand to clear the smoke. 'You 'ave? And what did they 'ave ter say?'

'Not a lot. I had to look at a body they took from the river. But I didn't know who it was.'

'That wasn't very nice for yer.'

'What do I do, Benny?'

'Now then, gel, dry yer eyes. You go on home and look after them two little 'ens of yours. I'll ask around when I'm out and about on me rounds. You'd be surprised what bits of information you can pick up when you're supposed to be busy. What about his muvver? What's Bella got to say about all this?'

'I don't know, I haven't told her yet.'

'Oh I see.' Benny sat back again and smiled. A dreamy look came over him. 'Always had a soft spot for Bella. I reckoned I would 'ave married her if she hadn't already been hitched to old Jim.'

Maggie smiled; she knew all about this one-sided romance. Tony often laughed to his mother about the fact that he could end up having Benny for a dad. That remark would bring Bella's mighty hand landing round Tony's ear, almost knocking him off balance.

'That was a good thing her getting that nice little house at Downham – mind you, I missed all that lot when they moved away.' He grinned. 'Made quite a few bob out of those places. Couldn't believe what some of 'em left in 'em.'

Maggie could see Benny was in a reminiscent mood. 'Benny, I've got to be the buyer now for the stall.' She tried to bring him back to business.

'Yer, I suppose you have till Tony gets back. Is that what you was doing at the auction room?'

'Yes, and I was wondering if you've got any bits I could buy, just to keep things ticking over, you understand. After all, I've still got to find the rent for the stall and the flat, pay Bill and feed the kids.'

'Course you have, gel. Come downstairs and we'll have a butchers through me stuff. There's a few bits you might be interested in. But promise me you'll look after yerself now.'

Maggie smiled. 'I promise.'

Once again Maggie made her way home, her bag full of various items that came from Benny's storeroom that was part of Nellie's stable. Maggie knew that, with a good cleanup, she could sell them at a nice fat profit. Everything she bought and sold would have the price on and would then be entered in a book. That way, when Tony came back he would be able to see what an asset she was to the business.

She picked up a china shaving mug and smiled. She was sure it had a silver rim. Benny must have known that. She turned it round, it was very nice. 'This will do for Alan's birthday on Saturday,' she said out loud. If she could find the right box it would look very expensive.

Chapter 7

It was six o'clock on Friday evening when Eve walked in. Maggie was doing her books.

'Just thought I'd pop in to see how you are. What're you doing there?' asked Eve.

'I'm writing down everything I buy and sell, so when Tony comes back he can see how well I've managed.'

'So you think he'll be back then?'

'I've got to hope, and keep the stall going.'

'Well, my girl, have you made a fortune yet?' asked Eve flippantly.

'No, but I'm not doing too bad.'

'Bill looked right miserable packing away when I came past. He was having a moan to that bloke Cooper.'

'What about? I've got his wages.'

'I don't think he likes the idea of working for a woman.'

'It is only temporary.'

'That Tom Cooper's a bit of a mean-looking sod.'

'He's all right. Him and Tony always seem to hit it off.'

'He was having a right go about the coppers hanging round asking questions.'

Maggie sat back. 'Eve, do you think Tony will ever come home?'

Eve took a packet of cigarettes from her handbag and lit one. 'I don't honestly know.'

'He's been gone two weeks now.' Maggie stood up. 'You would have thought I'd have heard something by now.'

'I would have thought so. Has that Inspector said any more?'

'No. Eve,' there was a catch in her voice, 'if Tony was alive surely he would let me know?' Tears began slowly to trickle down Maggie's cheeks.

'Yes, course.' She nervously tapped the end of the cigarette into the ashtray. 'Maggie, you mustn't give up hope.'

Maggie wiped her eyes. 'What am I supposed to think?'

'I honestly don't know. So,' said Eve, quickly changing the subject, 'have you made up your mind yet? Are you going to Alan's birthday party tomorrow?'

'Yes.'

'Will you tell them?'

'Think I'll have to. They're sure to ask where he is, and Laura or Jamie will tell them quick enough.'

'How are they taking it?'

'Well, Jamie has started wetting the bed, and that's something I can well do without. When the new baby arrives I'll have more than enough washing.'

'What about Laura?'

'She doesn't say a lot. She seems to have gone into a shell. A couple of times at night I've heard her crying and when I've gone in she stops and pretends to be asleep. When they break up for the summer holidays I'm gonner take 'em to Ramsgate for a few days. Here, you don't fancy coming with me, do you?'

'Dunno. Let's wait and see what happens by then, shall we? Have you told the kids?'

Maggie nodded. 'I thought they should have something to look forward to.'

'Yer, I suppose you're right. Maggs, what about Tony's mum?'

'I'll have to tell her soon, she'll be wondering what's happened to him.'

'He didn't go and see her that often since she was moved out Downham way, did he?'

'About every couple of weeks, so he would be more or less due to go there this Sunday morning. Just as long as Benny don't go over and tell her first.'

'What, old Benny the rag-and-bone man? He's not still struck on Bella, is he?'

'I think so.'

'He don't go over there, does he?'

'Dunno. Bella ain't said.'

'You don't think she would know anythink about Tony, do you?'

'Shouldn't think so. 'Sides, if he was there she'd soon send him packing.'

Eve smiled. 'I guess so. Bella Ross is a very formidable lady.'

When Eve left Maggie thought about Tony's mother. How would she take the news? And what would Alan have to say about it? She cleared the table. Well she'd know the answer to that one tomorrow.

Saturday, 1 June was warm and sunny all day. It was late afternoon when Maggie and her children, who were looking very smart, caught the bus to Alan and Helen's house at Hither Green.

As they walked down the road Maggie couldn't help but admire the lovely houses. Was she wrong not wanting a place with a garden for the children? It would be nice to hang out the washing on a proper line, and not in a tiny yard with the sheets flapping against the fence. And a bathroom indoors – that must be heaven in the winter. She sighed. Perhaps the time had come to talk to Tony about it, see if they could afford even to rent anything like this.

The door was opened by Helen, who was, as usual, looking very chic. The long powder-blue frock that clung to her slim figure made Maggie feel in her present condition fat, dumpy and inferior. Helen's make-up was perfect, and with her fair hair elegantly cut, she looked like she was worth a million dollars.

'Maggie dear,' she said, bending her head towards Maggie and planting a kiss on her cheek. 'How are you?' She lightly touched Maggie's stomach. 'Getting nice and plump, I see. Still, it don't last for ever. Only about three months to go, isn't it? Mind you, I'm so glad we only had one child. I don't know where you get the energy from to deal with two, let alone when you've got three to contend with.'

Maggie smiled a false smile.

'Come on in. Go and join Doreen and the other kids in the garden,' Helen said to the children, standing to one side to let them into the house. Turning to Maggie she added, 'Doreen takes up all of my time, what with dancing and piano lessons, and the hundred and one other things she gets involved in. By the way, where's that good-looking husband of yours? Is he coming over later?'

'Daddy's gone away,' said Jamie over his shoulder.

'Oh,' said Helen, raising her perfectly shaped eyebrows. 'And where's he gone to?'

'Dunno,' said Jamie.

Helen smiled. 'Shoo, out in the garden, children. So where is Tony then?' she asked Maggie as she ushered the children along the passage.

'I'd rather talk to Alan first, if you don't mind, Helen.'

Helen looked put out. 'Why, has he done a runner?' She laughed. 'Is it some dark secret you'd rather not tell me about?'

'No, but I would still rather like to talk to Alan first.'

'Please yourself. I'll tell him you're here. I must say you're making it sound very interesting, but don't keep him from our guests for too long, will you?'

Maggie waited for Alan in the kitchen. She looked round at the green and white cupboards, everything smart and crisp, just like Helen. She stood admiring the food neatly laid out on the small table for their friends – and felt very tempted to stick her finger in the red jelly. Helen had told her they didn't eat in the kitchen, they always ate in the dining room. Maggie smiled. They were bloody lucky to have a dining room.

'Maggs, Maggie. Helen said you were here.'

Her brother took her in his arms and kissed her cheek. He was taller than her and his fair hair that time had darkened was now slightly greying at the temples. But his blue eyes still twinkled. Today he looked relaxed and very handsome in his white open-neck shirt and grey flannels.

Maggie had always loved her brother, but over the years things had soured slightly; his wife, Helen, had come between them. She had too many airs and graces for Maggie's taste – for instance, she didn't like her friends knowing they had a stall in the market. She always told them that Tony had a shop. But Helen wasn't above fawning over Tony whenever she had the chance.

'So, Helen said something about Tony. He's not here then?'

'No. Alan, I know this is your birthday, and I don't want to spoil it, but I'm very worried. Is there somewhere we could talk?'

Alan frowned and looked concerned. He took Maggie's arm. 'We can go in the front room.'

'By the way, happy birthday.' She handed him a box that contained the shaving mug as they went along.

'Thanks.' Alan beckoned for her to sit on the fancy green brocade sofa, while he sat in the matching armchair facing her. 'Now what's the problem?'

'Tony's been missing for two weeks.'

Alan looked shocked. 'What do you mean, missing?'

'He hasn't been home.'

'Sorry, Maggs, but what are you saying? He's left you?'

Maggie was getting agitated. 'I mean he's gone missing, disappeared.'

'Disappeared?' repeated Alan. 'Have you been to the police?'

Maggie nodded and went into great detail about all that had happened.

'What can I say? Is there anything I can do to help?'

'No, not really.'

82

'How are you managing, moneywise, I mean?'

'The stall's not doing too bad.'

'But what about stock?'

'I've managed to get a few bits.'

'But what about when the new baby arrives?'

Maggie rolled her eyes. 'Christ, I hope Tony's back by then.'

Alan sat for a while in thought. He stood up and walked to the window. 'Maggs, I don't want to sound a Jonah, but has Tony got any kind of insurance?'

'Only the penny policy his mum took out when he was born, I think. Why?'

'Well, that's better than nothing, I suppose.'

'Alan, you don't think he could be . . .' She couldn't bring herself to say the word.

'We have to look at all possibilities, but of course until we've got a body you can't do that much.'

Maggie was stunned. He was talking as if Tony was dead, and it was all so matter-of-fact.

He came and sat next to her. 'Look, don't worry about it. I'm sure Tony will turn up soon with a very plausible excuse. You should know him by now.'

'But Tony wouldn't go off without telling—'

The door was suddenly pushed open. 'Come on, you two. You shouldn't monopolise him, you know, Maggie.' Helen looked from one to the other.

'Well, I don't see him very often,' said Maggie tersely.

'We are rather busy with this and that. Now come on, Alan, some people out here are dying of thirst.'

Alan stood up. 'We'll talk about this later.'

Helen smiled. 'This sounds most interesting. I hope your

dear Tony hasn't gone off and left you?'

The silence pounded in Maggie's ears.

'Helen,' said Alan, 'don't jump to conclusions.'

'Oh dear. Have I hit a raw nerve or something?'

'Alan will tell you later.'

Helen smiled. 'I can't wait. Now come on, the pair of you.'

Maggie and Alan made their way into the garden. The children were busy playing in Doreen's little playhouse at the end of it and their laughter and yells told everybody they were enjoying themselves. Alan put a drink in Maggie's hand. It was comforting to stand here with the warm early evening sun playing on her back. Yes, Tony was right, a garden would be nice for the children.

Different people, whom Maggie had met briefly before at Alan and Helen's dos came up and talked, but most of it was idle chitchat about what they had, and what they'd done. A few times when Maggie glanced across at Helen she seemed to be looking at her rather quizzically. When Helen realised Maggie was staring at her she quickly joined a group, throwing her head back and laughing very loudly. Maggie wondered if she really enjoyed this life, or if it was all a sham.

As the evening wore on Maggie caught sight of Jamie yawning. 'I think it's about time we went,' she said to Alan.

'Sorry we've not had time to have a proper chat. Look, I'll pop over next week, say Saturday, then you can tell me more about your troubles.'

'OK,' said Maggie. She was a bit put out that he would wait a whole week before coming to see her, even though he had a car.

'Tony might be back by then,' he said, cheerily, 'and I'm sure he'll have quite a tale to tell.'

'I hope so,' she said as she went to find the children.

Things were still the same when Alan called on Maggie the following Saturday.

'Alan, I don't know who to turn to next,' said Maggie. 'I wish Mum and Dad were alive.'

'You've got me and Helen,' he said softly.

Maggie looked at him. She wanted to say, 'Yes, but how often do I see you?' but she knew that wouldn't really be fair. 'Have you told Helen?'

'Course. She reckons he's just gone off on some wild-goose chase.'

She would, thought Maggie. 'Would you like a cup of tea?'

'Thought you'd never ask.'

Maggie went into the kitchen and made the tea. 'I forgot the biscuits,' she said, putting the tray on the table.

'Maggs,' called Alan after her. 'I know I shouldn't ask, but d'you think Tony . . .'

She quickly returned to the living room, her eyes blazing. 'No I don't think there was – is – another woman. Everybody asks me that. Did Helen say she thought there was?'

'Well, Tony was a bit of a lad.'

'He loves me, he always has. He wouldn't just go off and leave me. And he loves the children.' She sat on the sofa next to her brother. 'And what about the new baby? I know something's happened to Tony, I just know it.' Her tears fell, and Alan put his arm round her heaving shoulders.

'Try not to worry, Maggs. I'm sure someone will come up with the answer soon.'

'I hope so,' she sniffed.

'Have you been over to see his mother yet?'

'No.'

'I think you should, you know how she dotes on him.'

'Yes.'

'Look, I've not got anything on next Saturday, I'll come over and pick you up and we can go and see her together. Can you get someone to have the kids?'

'I'd take them with me, they like to see Granny Ross.'

'Well, please yourself.'

'Alan, do you have a bank account?'

'That's a funny thing to ask. No, why?'

'I just wondered how you would go about finding out about one, that's all.'

'Why?' he answered quickly. 'Have you found some money?'

'No.'

'Maggs, did Tony have much money?'

'No, we've got a few bob in the Post Office, but I wondered if he might have put some in a bank.'

'If he did there would be a bank book to tell him what he had. Have you looked for anything like that?'

She nodded.

'And did you find one?'

'No.'

'Then I think you can safely say that Tony hasn't got a bank account.' He stood up. 'Look, I'd better be going. Helen might start moaning if I'm late for dinner.' He kissed her cheek. 'Take care, see you next week.'

Maggie stared at the door, thinking Alan didn't really seem all that worried about her, but what did she expect him to do? And what about when the new baby arrived? How would she manage? She put her head in her hands and wept.

Chapter 8

The following morning Maggie decided she wouldn't wait till the next Saturday for Alan to go with her to Tony's mother, she'd go today. Who knew, Bella might even have some idea where to try next.

'After dinner,' she said to Laura and Jamie while they were finishing their breakfast, 'I think we should go and see Granny Ross.'

'Goody,' shouted Jamie. 'She's always got lots of sweets in her house.'

'I like Granny Ross. She told me that when we get a garden she was going to buy me a puppy.' Laura got down from the table and helped Maggie to take the dirty dishes into the kitchen.

Maggie shuddered. That was the trouble with Bella Ross – she was a very generous woman but sometimes her generosity could get out of hand. 'Well, we haven't got a garden, so we can't have a puppy,' said Maggie crossly.

'Will Daddy be there?' asked Jamie.

'I don't think so.'

'Mummy, has Daddy gone away for ever and ever?' asked Laura.

'Course not.' Maggie was busy at the sink washing up.

'Some of the kids at school said he's gone to prison.'

Maggie spun round, still holding the wet washing-up mop aloft. The water ran down her arm. 'Who said that?'

'Some of the bigger kids.'

'Well, you tell them it ain't true. And I'll be up that school giving them a bit of my mind if they keep spreading stories like that.' She continued washing up aggressively. That afternoon, dressed in their best clothes, they took the train to Downham.

For the second time in just over a week Maggie was walking down a tree-lined road though this time there were neat council houses' either side. Laura and Jamie went skipping on ahead to Granny Ross's house. The thought kept invading Maggie's mind that it would be a lot better for them if they did have a garden and somewhere to play other than the market. Just because she and Tony had been brought up in Rotherhithe didn't mean their children shouldn't have the right to play on green fields. She wondered if she had been selfish over this. When Tony came back they would definitely start to make plans.

Bella Ross was standing at her front door when Maggie walked up the path.

'Maggie, Maggie love. What a lovely surprise! It's lovely to see you.' She threw her arms round Maggie and clutched her to her ample bosom. 'The kids went straight through to the garden. Anyway, how are you all?'

'We're all right. What about you? How's the leg?'

'See, I'm managing fine without me stick, but only for short distances.' She looked up the road. 'Tony not with you?'

Maggie was pleased the children had gone ahead, she didn't want them blurting it out. 'No, not today. Shall we go in?'

'Course. Let's go in the kitchen.'

Maggie followed her down the passage and into a bright modern kitchen.

'I'll put the kettle on. Look at those two out there,' said Bella, gazing out of the kitchen window and smiling. 'You'll have to let them come over for a week in the summer holidays; you'll need a break as you get nearer your time. Sit yourself down.' She pulled out a chair from under the table. 'How are you keeping then, love? And where's that son of mine got to?' Bella Ross spoke with such warmth Maggie was made speechless.

'I don't know quite how to tell you this . . . but . . .'

'What is it? You look worried.' Bella sat down, her face ashen. 'It's Tony, ain't it? It's me boy. What's he bin up to? He ain't in the nick, is he?'

Maggie shook her head. 'No.'

Bella put her hand to her mouth. 'Oh my God, it's worse? It's worse?' she repeated. Tears filled her eyes and ran down her cheeks. 'What's happened to him?' She clasped Maggie's hand. 'He's in hospital?' When Maggie didn't answer she whispered, 'He ain't dead, is he? Tell me he ain't dead.'

Maggie too had tears in her eyes. 'I don't know,' she whispered. 'I really don't know.'

Bella dabbed at her eyes. She sat up. 'What d'you mean, you don't know?'

Maggie swallowed hard. She gently patted Bella's rough work-worn hand. 'He's been missing for over three weeks, and nobody seems to know where he's gone.'

91

Bella pulled her hand away and jumped to her feet. 'Three weeks, and you've only just come over here to tell me!'

'But—'

Bella wasn't listening to Maggie. 'Three weeks, and what have you done to find him?'

Maggie wanted to shout at her to sit down and listen. To tell her her son wasn't a baby, that he should've let her know what was happening, that she was worried sick too – but instead she said quietly, 'I've been to the police . . .'

'The police!' screamed Bella. 'The police! Why?'

'I thought they could help me.'

'And what did they have to say?'

'Not a lot. I even had to go and look at a body they'd taken out of the docks.'

'Oh my God.' Bella quickly sat down again. 'Who was it?'

'I don't know.'

'That must have been awful for you.'

'Yes it was. Mum, do you know if Tony . . . well, has he been in trouble before?'

'Trouble? What d'yer mean, trouble?'

'I don't know. I went to see Wally at the auction rooms and he was telling me that him and Tony used to do deals, and I was wondering—'

'Don't talk daft, girl. All traders do deals.'

'I know. But what if he'd upset someone?'

'Christ, they wouldn't take him away just for doing a deal. Why, my old man was one of the biggest rogues under the sun, but he never put himself or me in any danger. Na, I think you're barking up the wrong tree there, love.'

'But where do I go from here?'

Bella poured out the tea. 'You wanner go and see Benny. He'll tell you if there's any funny business going on.'

'I went to see him last week.'

Bella slammed the teapot on the table. 'What? You went and saw him before coming to tell me?'

'I didn't know who to turn to. Besides, I wanted some stuff for the stall.'

'So, who else knows?'

'Well, all the market, and Eve and Dan.'

'Never trusted that Eve. She was always flaunting herself. Bit of a tart if you ask me. You know I thought that there was something going on between her and my Tony at one time.'

Maggie tossed her head in the air. 'That was a long while ago, before we got married.'

'You know about it?'

'Course, Tony told me. But I've never said anythink to anybody, didn't see the point.'

'Yer, s'pose you're right. I wonder what your brother will say?'

Maggie thought before she answered that. She didn't want Bella to know that she was the last to hear about Tony, so she said nonchalantly, 'I'm going to see him next Saturday.'

'Oh. I bet that stuck-up snotty-nosed wife of his will have a thing or two to say about it.'

'I expect she will,' said Maggie wistfully.

'Now about Tony. I can't believe he's just gone off and left you and the kids.'

'Neither can I. I was hoping he might have got in touch with you.'

'I would have clipped him round the ear and sent him packing if he had.'

'That's what I mean. I really do think something must have happened to him.'

Bella wiped her eyes. 'Course not. Look, we'll have to put our thinking caps on. Now what can we do next to find him?'

'I wish I knew.'

'So, who was the last to see him?'

'Mr Goldman. He saw him at the station, said he was catching a train.'

'Catching a train?' repeated Bella. 'Did he ask him where he was going?'

'You know Mr Goldman, he don't ask things like that.'

'Pity he ain't nosy like the rest of us and asked him where he was off to.'

Maggie played with the spoon. 'Mr Goldman thought he had gone to look at a cottage.'

'A cottage? Where?'

'You know, the one he's always on about in his mind.'

Bella laughed. 'Always had fancy ideas, that boy of mine. D'you think he went there, wherever it is?'

'It wouldn't take him three weeks.'

'No, love, you're right.'

'I'm worried that he might be lying in some hospital, you know, lost his memory or somethink.'

'I suppose that is a possibility, but surely he would have had some kind of identification on him.'

'That's what Eve and the Inspector said.'

Bella sat back. 'Three weeks you say? So how you managing?'

'Bill's been running the stall, and I'll have to do the buying till he comes back.'

'Yes, I suppose you will.' Bella looked thoughtful. 'Don't worry, Benny will help you on that score, he'll come up with some bits.' She gave a little smile. 'D'you know, he asked me to marry him after Jim died?'

'We always knew he was fond of you. So why didn't you?'

'He's nice bloke but he's been on his own for too long. 'Sides, I couldn't put up with his horse shitting in the garden.'

They both gave a little half-hearted laugh.

The back door was pushed open. 'Granny, can we have a drink?'

'Course you can, my boy. Tell Laura to come and get it.'

'OK,' and with that Jamie ran away.

Bella stood watching them. 'They're a couple of nice kids. You must be very proud of them.'

'Yes I am,' said Maggie. 'We both are, and that's why I don't think Tony has gone away of his own free will.'

'You could be right, love. I'm sorry to say it, but you could be right. But who would take him? 'Sides, what was he doing catching a train?'

'I only wish I knew.'

'He can't just disappear. Ain't you any idea who he could have gone to see?'

Maggie shook her head. 'I don't know where to turn without him. If he don't come back soon I'll have to find the rent and everythink else.'

Bella looked sad. 'You shouldn't be worrying like this, not in your condition. You shouldn't have to be the breadwinner. But you have got to think of what to do now. Taking care of yourself and the kids is a big responsibility for your young shoulders.'

For a while they were both silent with their own thoughts.

When it was time for them to leave Bella pushed two pounds into Maggie's hand.

'I can't take this,' she protested.

'Yes you can. I don't want you to worry about money as well, I've got a few bob tucked away.'

'Bella, have you ever had a bank account?'

She laughed. 'What the bloody hell would I want with a bank account? No, love, you always want ter get the cash in yer hand, then when you've spent it no one can take it away.' She kissed Maggie and the children. 'Now I don't expect you to come traipsing over here every couple of days, so drop me a line, and when that son of mine walks his arse in, you send him over to me to sort out, and I'll tell yer, he'll get more than a clip round the ear for making you, and me, worry like this.'

Maggie kissed her mother-in-law's cheek. 'Thanks. Take care.'

They waved back for as long as they could.

Well, thought Maggie, that was another hurdle over. In some ways she felt sorry for Tony, for when he did come back everybody would be having a go at him. She smiled. But he'd grin and with his winning ways he'd talk himself out of it. And in the meantime, financially, she'd have to manage, just like Bella said.

On Monday morning Maggie was surprised to see Inspector

Matthews walking round the market. She hadn't spoken to him for over a week and thought the police had lost interest in Tony by now.

'Is there any news?' she asked casually.

'I'm afraid not.'

Maggie could see some of the stallholders going into a huddle and looking at her suspiciously.

'Do any of Mr Ross's relations live round here?'

Maggie began walking back to her flat. 'No, his mother lives at Downham, but she don't know where he is.'

'You've told her then?' said the Inspector as he slowly walked along with her.

'Yes.' They reached her front door. 'Would you like to come up for a cup of tea?'

'That would be very nice. Thank you.'

They went up, Maggie pushed open the door and Inspector Matthews took off his grey trilby and placing it on the chair, smoothed down his dark straight hair with both hands.

Maggie went into the kitchen to put the kettle on. 'It's warm today,' she shouted out.

'Yes, it is,' he replied.

He pointed at the photo of the children when she walked in.

'They're a fine pair.'

'Thank you. Are you married?'

'No, not now. I lost my wife a few years ago.'

'I'm sorry,' said Maggie quickly.

'She caught TB.' For a fleeting moment he looked sad. 'We didn't have any children.'

'Would you have liked some?'

'Yes. They make a home, don't you think?'

Maggie laughed nervously. 'I don't know about make it, they're very good at wrecking it.'

'I'm sure that's not true. You have some nice pieces up here.'

Maggie felt like kicking herself. Had he only come up so that he could have another look round, just to make sure nothing had been pinched? 'My husband has a good eye for a bargain.'

'I can see that.'

As they sat drinking tea, Maggie was on her guard, very careful what she said to him.

He looked at his watch. 'I must be going.'

'Inspector Matthews, have you any idea what could have happened to Tony?'

'I'm afraid not.' He stood up and picked up his trilby, twirling it round in his hands.

'But he couldn't have just disappeared off the face of the earth. Someone must know where he is.' Tears welled up in her eyes. 'Have you tried the other police stations? Could he be in prison somewhere?'

'No, you'd have been told. His description has been circulated, and until someone comes up with something, I'm afraid there's not a lot we can do. Thank you for the tea.'

Maggie opened the door for him. 'Goodbye.'

When she heard the front door shut she waited a couple of minutes, then hurried down the stairs.

''Ere, Maggs, what's going on?' asked Fred, as soon as she stepped outside.

'Nothing, why?'

'What's he got to say about all this?' Fred inclined his

head the way she guessed the Inspector had taken.

'Not a lot. Nobody seems to have any idea what's happened to Tony.'

'Can't say I'm that pleased to have a copper nosing round here, keep asking questions.'

'Well, I ain't that pleased at having to be nice to one, but what else can I do?' Maggie tossed her head and walked on.

'All right, gel?' shouted Mrs Russell.

'Yes thanks.'

'I hope you're looking after yerself,' she said when Maggie got closer.

'Yes I am. I went over and saw Tony's mum yesterday.'

'Did you now. How's old Bella getting on? Heard she broke her leg.'

'Yes she did, but it's on the mend now.'

'That's good. She could always do a good knees-up, hate to think of her having to sit back and watch. She was a gel in her time. Always liked old Bella,' said Mrs Russell reflectively.

''Ere, Maggs,' Mr Cooper called out. Maggie walked over to his stall. 'Young Bill was telling me you've bin ter see Benny, the rag-and-bone man.'

'Yes, I had to get some more stock, why?'

'No reason. He couldn't shed any light on what's happened to Tony then?'

'No. You don't know if anybody . . . well, I don't know . . . had it in for him, I suppose?'

'No. It's a funny business, and I can't say I like the idea of these coppers keep popping up all the time.'

'Nobody does.' Maggie wanted to cry, to run away from all this.

''Ere, you all right, gel? You've gone a funny colour.'

'Yes, I'm all right. It's just that I don't know how this is all going to end.'

'Well one thing's certain, you've got to look after yerself and think about those kids of yours.'

'Yes I know.'

Maggie was very near to tears. But how could she look after the children and keep out of debt? She began to walk away. I suppose I could always borrow money from Alan if I was really desperate, but what would Helen have to say about that? she thought. Then there was Tony's mum – she'd said she had a few bob she could let them have. But how long would that last? She was so upset she had forgotten what she'd gone down for. She wanted to be left alone, and as she climbed back up her stairs she knew she must face the fact that she was in charge of her life until Tony came back – whenever that would be.

Chapter 9

On Saturday, when Alan arrived at Maggie's, he was very cross to learn that she hadn't waited for him to take her to Tony's mother.

'Why should I have waited? What good would it have done?' Maggie protested.

'Well, Helen thinks—'

'Alan, I don't care what Helen thinks.'

'Oh pardon me. We are only trying to give you some advice, you know.' Alan walked to the window.

'I'm sorry, it's just that I don't know which way to turn.'

'Well, what did Bella have to say about it?'

'Concerned, worried, like everyone else, but didn't have any answers.'

The babble from the market drifted up.

'And what do that lot down there think of all this?' He waved his hand at the market.

'Not a lot. They didn't like the coppers coming round asking questions, but that's dropped off a bit; we don't see them much now.'

The door was suddenly flung open and Eve came breezing

101

in. 'Hallo, Alan. Maggs said you might be over. Is Helen with you?'

'No, Doreen has a touch of the snuffles, and Helen didn't take her to her dancing classes.' He sat on the sofa.

Maggie felt guilty at not asking about his family. 'Is Doreen all right?' she enquired.

'Yes, but you know what a fusspot Helen is.'

Maggie smiled. 'Well, all mothers are a bit like that,' she said. But not as fussy as your wife, she thought.

'So, Alan, what's your opinion about this thing with Tony?' asked Eve, sitting next to him.

'Don't know what to think. But let's face it, he always liked to dabble in all sorts of things, didn't he?'

'So you think he might be in some sort of trouble then?' Eve crossed her long legs and blew the smoke from her cigarette high into the air.

Alan shrugged. 'Could be.' He looked at Maggie.

'D'you fancy a cup of tea?' she said quickly.

'Yes please,' said Alan and Eve together.

In the kitchen Maggie's knuckles turned white as she clenched her hands in temper. Why did everybody think Tony was up to no good? They didn't seem to care that he could have had an accident and lost his memory.

Soon after Alan finished his tea he said he had to go. As he kissed her cheek he said, 'Now don't forget, Maggs, if there's anything we can do to help, just let me know.'

'Thanks, Alan.'

'Bye, Eve.'

'Bye.'

When Alan shut the door, Eve stood up. 'Is that it? He didn't mention money.'

'I can't expect him to give me anythink. After all, he does have a lot of expenses.'

'Yer, I suppose he does.'

'Anyway, so far, thanks to Benny, I'm just about managing. Look, I must go down to Bill.'

'Course. Do you fancy coming out tonight?'

'Don't know.' She didn't feel happy at sitting in the pub without Tony and relying on everybody else to buy her drinks. Although Tony and Dan spent most of the time standing at the bar chatting and arguing with Gus over the Blackshirts and trying to put the world to rights, he always used to be there, and even after all these years when he gave her a wink and one of his smiles, her heart leapt.

'Well, think about it. Me and Dan will be over about eight.'

They walked down the stairs and out into the sunshine together.

'See you tonight,' said Eve as she went in the opposite direction to Maggie.

Maggie stood at the stall while Bill went for a pint. She watched the people coming and going, kids licking ice-cream cornets, and the mothers giving them a clout when they dropped it and started yelling. The young women who didn't have screaming kids hanging on to them were wearing pretty floral frocks. There was something about the summer that put a smile on most people's faces. She was miles away when Tom Cooper came over and stood beside her.

'Why don't you get yerself a chair? You shouldn't be standing around, not in your condition.'

She smiled. 'Thanks, Tom, but I'm all right.'

'Still no news then?'

'No.'

Tom was a real rough diamond: his thick dark bushy eyebrows that almost covered his eyes made him appear menacing. Tony always liked him, but a lot of the other stallholders didn't take to his ways, especially the fact that apart from selling material he did a few deals on the side, often undercutting them.

'Didn't like it when that copper was 'anging round.'

Maggie was getting very tired of hearing this. 'Nobody did,' she said quietly.

'I presume you've been ter see Bella?'

'Yes.'

'What's she got ter say about it?'

'Same as everybody else, but I think the novelty's wearing off round here a bit now.'

'Well, those bleeding Blackshirts shouting and yelling on the corner helps. Can't say I like what they're saying. Superrace indeed. Trouble is they keeps the punters up that end listening to 'em. If I had my way I'd run the lot of 'em out o' town.'

Maggie laughed. 'I shouldn't try if I was you. They're a lot younger and a lot fitter than you.'

'Yer, s'pose they are. But I'm a lot bigger. 'Ere, missis, keep that bloody kid of yours off me barra. Don't want bloody ice cream all over me stuff.'

A mouthful of abuse came from the mother and the child.

'And to you, ducky, as well.' He turned to Maggie. 'Don't know what the world's coming to. You wouldn't have caught me talking to an old man like that.'

Maggie laughed. 'Well, you wouldn't be hanging round a material stall for one thing.'

'Na, I'd be too busy tormenting that bloody monkey.' He pointed to the organ-grinder who was busy turning the handle on his machine, filling the market with tinny music. He was surrounded by scruffy children. 'It bites, you know?'

'Well, you shouldn't torment it. I've told Jamie and Laura to stay well away from it.'

Tom grinned. 'And I'd be pinching the apples, and making sure I didn't get another good hiding from me ma. 'Allo, Wally, what you doing round this way?'

Maggie quickly turned and was surprised to see Wally from the auction room walking towards them.

''Allo, Tom, Maggs. Just thought I'd 'ave a stroll round this way ter see how things were getting on. Tony about?'

'No,' said Tom. 'Ain't—'

Maggie quickly pulled Wally's arm. 'Look, when Bill gets back we'll go up and have a cuppa.'

'I'd rather have a pint. It's a bit warm today.'

'OK.'

'Tony in the pub?'

Maggie saw Tom open his mouth, about to speak, so she asked, 'Tom, will you keep your eye on the stall and the kids while me and Wally go up the Dog?' She wanted to tell Wally about Tony in private.

'Yer, course, Maggs.' He looked very puzzled.

They walked into the Dog and Duck, and Maggie went straight over to Bill, who was propping up the bar, making a pint last as long as possible.

'What yer having, gel?' called Wally after her as he moved towards the bar.

'Just a shandy. Bill, when you've finished could you get back to the stall? I want to have a quiet word with Wally here.'

'Was just going anyway,' said Bill quietly to Maggie. 'I've seen that bloke before. He's one of the blokes Tony's done deals with.'

'Yes I know.'

'One shandy, and a pint of the best,' said Wally, putting the drinks on the table. 'Oh, you going, son?'

'Yer, gotter get back. See yer later, Maggs.' Bill left the pub.

Maggie would rather have talked to Wally in her home but she didn't want to make a fuss.

'So,' said Wally, sitting next to her and taking the top off his beer, 'where's that old bugger got to now?'

'Wally.' Maggie looked around. Thankfully most of the other customers were deep in conversation. The sound of the Blackshirts shouting, and the traders' voices trying to sell their wares came drifting through the open door. 'Wally,' repeated Maggie, 'Tony's gone missing.'

'What?'

Wally's voice was loud, and a couple of the other customers looked over in their direction.

'What d'yer mean, missing?'

'Four weeks ago, he went out, and hasn't been seen since.'

Wally's face turned bright red. Maggie thought he was going to explode.

'But it was only, what – a couple of weeks ago – you come to the auction rooms and said—'

'Yes, I told you he was just away.'

Wally leant back in his chair. 'I thought he was in the nick.' He sat forward and his eyes narrowed menacingly. 'You sure he ain't in the nick?'

'I'm sure, all right.' Maggie wiped her brow with her handkerchief. 'It's very warm in here.'

Wally grabbed her hand. 'Now you listen to me, gel,' he hissed. 'I want the truth, d'yer hear?'

'Wally, you're hurting me.'

'And your Tony could hurt me.'

'Why? What d'yer mean?'

He sat forward and looked around. Maggie could see Gus was looking in their direction. Although she felt a little afraid, she knew she only had to shout and he would come running, but she had to find out more from Wally.

Wally lowered his voice. 'Me and him had quite a little deal going.'

'What, like you told me about?'

'Na, more than that.'

Maggie rubbed her wrist. 'What sort of deal?'

He laughed. 'I ain't saying, but did he keep any notes or books?'

'No,' she said a little too quickly.

'You sure?'

'Well, if he did I don't know where they are.'

'What about money?'

'What about it?'

'Where did he hide it?'

Maggie laughed; she didn't want him to see how worried she was. 'If he had hidden any away, I'd have soon found it.'

'You wouldn't keep anythink from me now, would you?'

'Why should I?'

'Look, why don't we go back to your flat and have a look?'

'What for? And why should I?' repeated Maggie.

''Cos I don't want anybody to find anythink that might incriminate me, savvy?'

'Why should it? Wally, have you any idea what might have happened to Tony?'

'Na. But I tell yer this: if he's tried to double-cross some of them big boys, well, it's curtains for him, that's for sure – they play very rough.'

Maggie stared at him. What had he and Tony been up to?

'And I don't wanner be mixed up in this.'

Maggie picked up her glass. 'Could somethink have happened to Tony?'

'How the bloody hell should I know? All I'm saying is, if he ain't in the nick, then where is he?'

'I wish I knew.'

'Have yer finished?'

Maggie nodded.

'Right, then let's get back to your place.'

'What for?'

'To satisfy my curiosity.'

'What about?'

'Don't argue, just do as I say.'

Maggie looked pleadingly over at Gus, but he was busy with a crowd of thirsty customers. She had no choice but to go.

Walking through the market she tried to attract some of the traders' eyes, but they were all too busy trying to outshout their rivals for punters.

Where were the children? Even they would help to dispel this situation.

As she mounted the stairs to her flat, a great feeling of doom began to settle over her. So Tony had been mixed up with some shady people. She closed the living-room door. How could she have been so blind, and where was this money?

'Right, where did he keep his papers?'

'I don't know.'

'Now come on, gel, don't play games with me.' He knelt on the floor, pulled open the door in the sideboard and rummaged through it, scattering newspapers and knitting over the floor. He stood up. 'What's this?' He held up an exercise book.

'It's the book I've been keeping. An account of what I've bought and sold, so when Tony gets back he can see what I've . . .' Her voice trailed off as he searched through the pages. She snatched it from his hand. 'Give it back, that's mine.'

'Now come on, Maggs, I don't want any trouble. Just give me Tony's books.'

Suddenly she was very afraid. They were alone together and this man was very angry. What would he do to her? 'I can't give you somethink I ain't got.'

'You better be telling me the truth.'

Should she tell him that she'd hidden them in Tony's lockup, just in case the police came looking for them? Tony, why have you put me through this hell? she asked silently.

Wally moved closer and Maggie backed away, afraid he

would hurt her. 'What's so important about them anyway?' she blurted out.

'I don't want 'em to fall in the wrong hands, so if—'

'Yoo-hoo. Maggs, it's me.' The door was pushed open and Winnie stood there, filling the doorway. 'Fred said you was back and I was wondering—'

'Hallo, Win,' Maggie said eagerly. 'This is a friend, acquaintance,' she quickly corrected herself, 'of Tony's. Wally.'

''Allo there, I've seen yer around,' Winnie said. 'You got any news of that little sod?'

'No,' Maggie answered for him.

'What's been going on? What yer been looking for?' Winnie bent down and began picking up the newspapers. 'This 'ere knitting ain't gonner stay white fer long if yer keeps chucking it on the floor.' She looked at the pattern. 'This is a pretty little jacket.'

'Yes, I've made it before, for Laura and Jamie when they were babies, remember?' said Maggie. She wanted to cry and throw her arms round Winnie's neck, she was so relieved to see a friendly face.

'I'd better be going,' said Wally. 'Now remember what I told yer?'

Maggie nodded.

When he kissed her cheek she wanted to slap his face.

'Bye, Maggs. Bye, missis. I'll let meself out.'

When they heard the front door close Maggie fell into the chair and cried.

'So,' said Winnie, 'what was all that about?'

'Oh Win, what would I do . . . I don't know . . .'

'Look, I'll put the kettle on and stay with yer fer a bit.'

'But it's Saturday – what about your stall?'

'Don't worry, they're all keeping an eye on it for me.'

Maggie blew her nose. 'But how did you know . . .?'

'First of all old Cooper said you'd gone for a drink with Wally. He said he was worried about you as Wally's a shifty sod. Then Gus come up and said he thought you'd looked uneasy in the pub. Then Fred said you'd come up here and you looked a bit peaky. So here I am large as life and twice as handsome.' She laughed.

Maggie's tears fell. The kettle began whistling and Winnie hurried into the kitchen. When she returned with the tray she sat at the table.

'Maggs, I know it ain't none of my business, but what did he want?'

Maggie too sat at the table. 'Win, he reckons Tony's mixed up with some villains.'

'So, what's it to do with him?'

'Don't really know. He wanted Tony's books in case he was in them.'

Winnie began pouring out the tea. 'And is he?'

Maggie hesitated. She wanted to confide in someone, but didn't want to put anyone else in danger. But Winnie was like a mother to her, and she could look after herself. Maggie decided to tell her everything that she knew. 'I don't know, they're in some kind of code, they don't make any sense.'

'Did you show them to him?'

'No, I've hid them in case the police want them.'

Winnie patted her hand. 'Clever gel.'

That kind gesture brought forth more floods of tears from Maggie. 'Win, I'm so frightened,' she sobbed. 'What am I gonner do?'

'First of all you're gonner drink this tea, and wipe yer eyes. Crying never solved anythink. Then you're gonner face up to this thing.'

Maggie looked up. 'What d'yer mean?'

'Well, I don't think Tony's coming back. Thought so for a bit now. Let's face it, he'd never go off and leave you and the kids, not of his own free will, now would he?'

Maggie shook her head.

'So,' continued Winnie, 'you've gotter be mother and father to your two, three when that one comes along. And you've gotter provide a roof and food. It's a pretty tall order, me gel, but you ain't the first, and you won't be the last. And if anybody offers you help, don't stand on yer high horse, you take it.'

Maggie remembered Bella had tried to tell her this, though she'd wanted to avoid facing up to it. 'Do you think he's dead?'

'Dunno what to think, but I do know if he could get in touch, he would. But remember, life's fer living, and you've gotter look after yerself.'

Maggie gave her a weak smile. She was so lucky to have someone like Winnie to lean on.

'Right, I'd better be going, and remember, gel, all that lot down there,' she waved her hand at the window, 'well most of 'em anyway, will always be around if yer want 'em.' She stood up and walked to the door. 'Oh, and by the way, if that cowson Wally ever comes round 'ere again worrying you, you send him down ter me.' She shut the door after her.

Maggie sat for a while thinking about Tony. He owed it to her and the children to come back, but till then she had to do what Winnie had said. She was right. She had to get on with her life, for her children's sake as well as her own. Their future was up to her, and who knew, perhaps she could make a go of it. She could even try new things on the stall. A slight smile lifted her sad mouth. She would show Wally and the rest of them. She had to.

Chapter 10

Maggie waited until the children had finished their tea before she sat at the table. 'Now I want you both to listen very carefully. I've got something to tell you.'

'I bet I know what it is,' said Laura, her mouth turning down.

'Bet yer don't,' said Jamie.

'I bet I do. How much then?'

'Shh, the pair of you,' said Maggie.

'You're gonner tell us we ain't going to Ramsgate, ain't yer, Mum?' Laura was looking defiant.

Maggie was taken aback. With all her other problems she'd forgotten about her promise. 'No,' she smiled. 'Course we're still going. It's just that Daddy won't be coming with us.'

Jamie looked up at her, his pale blue eyes beginning to fill with tears. 'Is it 'cos Daddy's gone to prison?'

Maggie was shocked at that remark. 'No, course not. Who told you that? Was it those kids at Laura's school?'

'No, them down there.' He pointed to the window.

Maggie knew she had to try and brazen this out. 'You shouldn't be listening to the grown-ups' conversations, young man.'

'Well, where is he then?'

'I don't know.' Maggie was thinking that in some ways she wished Tony was in prison. At least then she would know his whereabouts, and that he was still alive. 'I don't know where Daddy is, he's gone away,' she said softly, holding back a sob.

'Why's he gone away then?' asked Laura.

'I don't know, but I'm sure he'll come back to us one day.'

'Don't he love us any more?'

'Of course he does.'

'Then why did he go away?' asked Jamie.

'I told you, I don't know,' Maggie's voice began to rise – she couldn't answer their questions.

'We ain't been that naughty,' said Jamie, wide-eyed.

'Well I reckon he's rotten,' said Laura. 'He didn't even bother to come and see me dance round the maypole.'

'I'm sure he would have done if he could.'

'Na,' said Jamie. 'It's too sissy fer Dad. I ain't doing it when I go ter school.'

Maggie tousled his hair.

'Don't, Mummy.'

'Come on, you can go out for a short while. Then after Bill's put the stall away and brought the money in, it's bed. I'm going up the pub with Eve and Dan for an hour or so.'

'What about us, can we come?' asked Laura.

'No you can't. I'll ask Mr Goldman to keep an ear out for you, so no running about, d'you hear?'

They both nodded vigorously.

'And then, if you're really good, perhaps tomorrow we can go and see Granny Ross.'

116

'Yippee!' yelled Jamie. 'I'll be good.'

'So will I,' said Laura, 'and, Mummy, can we still go to Ramsgate?'

'Course.'

Laura came and put her arms round Maggie's neck. 'You won't ever leave us, will you?'

'No, of course I wouldn't, but I will have to go away for a week or two to get this new baby, but don't worry, I'll be back.'

'Can we have a baby girl?'

'We'll have to take what they've got.'

'Can we have two?' asked Jamie, scrambling on to Maggie's lap. 'A boy and a girl? Then we've both got someone to play with.'

'I don't think they'll let me have two. Besides, it'll be very small for a long while.'

'Was we very small?' asked Jamie.

'Yes, and you were both very beautiful.'

They giggled.

'What happened to Jamie? He ain't very beautiful now.'

'Nor are you,' he said.

Maggie laughed. 'You are still very lovely, and I love you both very much.'

'How much?' asked Jamie. 'This much?' He held his arms out wide.

'Much more than that. Now, do you want to go out and play for a while before Auntie Eve gets here?'

They both scooted down the stairs. 'And don't get into any mischief,' Maggie called after them, adding to herself, 'All the love they have for us, Tony – how could you leave them?' She began clearing the tea things away before Bill brought in the takings.

★ ★ ★

Beatie gave them a wave as soon as Maggie, Eve and Don walked in the pub. It was very crowded, but Eve managed to find a seat as Dan pushed his way to the bar.

'You all right, gel?' Beatie asked, coming over to Maggie. 'Gus was dead worried about you when you came in lunchtime. He said you looked ever so upset.'

Eve glanced up. 'You was in here lunchtime?'

'I'll tell you about it in a minute,' said Maggie. 'It was good of him to tell Win.'

'Was it trouble then?' asked Beatie, worried.

'No, not really, just someone looking for Tony.'

'Did he say what he wanted?'

'No.'

'Didn't have any news then?'

'No.'

Beatie twisted a large diamond ring on her finger round and round. 'Remember, gel, we're all here to help if need be.'

'Thanks, Beatie.'

'Well, what was all that about?' asked Eve, as soon as Beatie had gone back to the bar.

Maggie told Eve everything about Wally.

'He sounds a right arsehole to me. Wait till Dan finds out about—'

'Don't say anythink to Dan,' said Maggie quickly. 'Well, not tonight anyway.'

'Why?'

'Ain't really nothing to tell.'

'OK. So where's these books then?'

'I've hid 'em.'

118

'Ain't yer gonner tell me where?' asked Eve petulantly.

'No.'

'Thanks. So after all these years—'

'Look, Eve, if you don't know, then no one can make you tell 'em.'

Eve laughed. 'Christ, Maggs, you're beginning to make it sound like somethink out of a cloak-and-dagger film.'

Maggie laughed. 'Well, you always was a nosy cow.'

'Thanks. I can just see me swearing not to tell the villains your secret.'

'Trust you to be swearing.'

They both burst out giggling.

Dan put their drinks on the table. 'What's tickling you two?'

'Not a lot,' said Eve. 'A bloke called Wally came over and brought Maggie in here lunchtime.'

'Eve, I told you—'

'Yer, so Gus was saying. He said he was worried about you.'

'Christ,' said Maggie, 'everybody's keeping their eye on me. I can see if I want to carry on with someone it'll have to be far away from me own doorstep.'

'You could try Ramsgate,' laughed Eve.

'Yer, but I'd wait till you've got rid of that lump first,' laughed Dan. 'It's a bit off-putting.'

A cheer went up when Ivy, who lived in the tenement buildings round the corner, walked in. Pints of beer were quickly put in front of her as she sat at the piano. Her large bottom hung over the piano stool, and when she played her thick arms wobbled. Her fingers, like fat sausages, pounded the keys and conversation almost ceased as everybody joined in the sing-song.

A smoky blue haze clung to the already yellowed ceiling. It hung round the dropped pendant lampshades that stuck out from the red plush walls. They hadn't been cleaned in years, so nobody knew if they were supposed to be plain or coloured glass.

Maggie felt relaxed for the first time that day. She glanced around the pub. Although it was old and in need of a coat of paint it had a warm atmosphere, and very happy memories. The large mirror behind the bar was one of Tony's finds, a typical pub mirror, very ornate with gold scrolls along the top and down the sides. Large bunches of coloured grapes were etched in every corner. She half smiled, remembering the trouble they'd had trying to fix it to the wall.

This was all such a contrast to Beatie and Gus's flat upstairs, which was well furnished and immaculate. Maggie had only been up there once, and that was when Gus used to have a poker school after hours. It had been she and Eve who, while walking home from the pictures, had overheard two policemen saying they were going to raid it. They'd run on ahead and banged on the back door. Why had she suddenly thought about that? That was years ago, long before Laura was born.

Maggie looked at her watch, it was almost ten o'clock. 'I'd better be going home,' she said to Eve.

'I'll come with you,' said Eve.

'You don't have to,' replied Maggie.

'I fancy a cuppa.'

'OK.'

'Be along in a while,' said Dan.

Maggie and Eve said their good nights to Gus and Beatie and wandered down Kelvin Market. The moon was full and the air warm.

'It's so peaceful down this end,' said Eve, as they strolled along arm in arm.

'So far. Just so long as those Blackshirts don't start any trouble.'

'Dan's been reading about all what's going on in Europe. He says things ain't that good over there. 'Ere, you don't reckon your Tony's run off and joined the army, do you?'

Maggie laughed. 'What? Can you honestly see him taking orders from anyone?'

'No,' said Eve, dismissing the idea.

'You can't believe this is the same place with all the racket that goes on in the day. It's so quiet now,' said Maggie.

'That is till chucking-out time.'

'And then with the trains up there, dogs barking and the cats fighting, and drunks singing . . .' Maggie laughed.

'Yer, well, it ain't exactly a peaceful street.'

Maggie pushed open the door to her flat and was taken aback to see Laura and Jamie sitting at the top of the stairs. 'Why ain't you in bed?'

They rushed down the stairs and, crying, flung themselves at their mother.

'What is it, what's wrong?' asked Eve, fussing round them.

'A man come and got us out of bed,' sobbed Laura.

'What?' screamed Maggie. 'Who was it? I'll kill 'im. My babies. What did he do to you? Why didn't you call Mr Goldman?'

'Mummy, Mummy,' Laura was trying to make her mother listen.

'Laura,' Eve took her to one side and sat on the stair next to her. 'Tell me what happened.'

'This man—'

'What did he look like?' yelled Maggie.

'Maggs, give her time. Let's go upstairs.'

Slowly they made their way up.

'Now sit on the sofa, both of you, and tell me and Mummy all what happened.'

'I'm gonner get the police.'

'Maggie, sit down. Let's hear what they've got to say first.'

Maggie, with tears streaming down her face, did as she was told.

The man they described must have been Wally.

'I'll kill him if he's hurt them,' said Maggie, jumping up.

'Maggie,' Eve's voice had a sharp edge to it, 'sit down and let them finish.'

'He didn't hurt us, Mummy. He said you told him he could come here, he said he was looking for Daddy's book.' Laura wiped her eyes on the bottom of her nightie.

'So why are you both crying?' asked Eve softly.

''Cos he told us our daddy was dead.' Jamie's face was ashen. With one hand he was clutching his teddy and the other was holding the front of his pyjama bottoms trying to hide the wet patch.

'The wicked bugger. The bloody wicked sod.' Maggie jumped up again.

'It ain't true, is it?' asked Laura.

'We don't know,' said Eve. 'I only wish we did.'

'We told him our daddy didn't have any books, he only reads the newspapers.'

Maggie knelt down and threw her arms round her daughter's neck. She wanted to laugh at the innocent words.

Jamie pushed his way into Maggie's arms.

'I'll make a cup of tea,' said Eve, going into the kitchen. While she stood waiting for the kettle to boil, she cried softly to herself. 'Please come back to them, Tony,' she wept, 'they desperately need you.'

When Dan came to collect Eve, the children were tucked up in bed. When she told him all that had happened he was outraged.

'You say he works at the auction rooms?' He began pacing the floor and balling his fist. 'I'll go over there Monday and have a word with him.'

'But, Dan,' said Maggie, 'we've got no proof it was him.'

'Why didn't Mr Goldman come up?' asked Dan, still pacing up and down.

'The children are told not to make any noise,' said Maggie.

'And it was that bloody bloke telling them Tony was dead that upset 'em,' said Eve.

'Look, I'm taking 'em to see Bella tomorrow and I'll tell her what happened. She'll know how to deal with him,' said Maggie.

'Hmm,' said Dan, 'I still reckon I ought to go and see him and knock his block off.'

'Well, he didn't take anything,' said Maggie. 'But I wish he hadn't said that to the kids.'

'You look tired,' said Eve. 'If you want me to stay the night, I will.'

'I'll be all right.'

'I'll pop over tomorrow night then,' said Eve.

'OK.' Maggie kissed Eve's cheek.

When they left Maggie sat on the sofa and let her mind drift to Tony. Could there have been some little thing in the past she had forgotten about? If only she had taken more interest in some of his dealings. But in many ways Tony played his cards close to his chest, said he didn't want to bother her with his business deals. Why was Wally so worried about those books? Tony had always been a wheeler-dealer like his father before him – it went with the job – but were some of these transactions so big as to warrant this behaviour from Wally? On Monday she would go and see Benny again. There had to be more to all this than anybody was letting on.

She looked in at the children. Jamie was tossing and turning. This had upset him. 'Please don't wet the bed again,' she whispered.

'Mummy.' Laura sat up.

Maggie went to sit on the end of her bed. 'Now come on, settle down.'

'If Daddy's dead why ain't we been to his funeral?'

Maggie gazed down at her daughter. She had been busy working this out for herself. 'We don't know if he is,' said Maggie, holding back her tears.

'But that man said—'

'Shh, you don't want to wake Jamie.'

'But, Mummy—'

'I know that's what that man said, but we don't know if it's true.' Slowly a tear trickled down Maggie's cheek. 'Now come on, you've got to be bright to see Granny Ross tomorrow.'

'I like Granny Ross. Mummy, what was our other Granny like?'

'Very kind. My mum and dad would have loved you two.'

'Her name was Laura, wasn't it?'

Maggie nodded. This conversation was so painful.

'Do I look like her?'

'No, you look like your dad. Now sleep. I'm going to bed, so don't disturb me till the morning.' Maggie kissed Laura's forehead. At the doorway she turned to blow her a kiss.

'Mummy, what if that man comes back again tonight?'

'He won't.'

Maggie closed the bedroom door. She went downstairs and wound the front door key, which hung on a piece of string behind the letter box, round and round the lock. Nobody was coming in without her knowing. As Winnie had said, Maggie had to be both father and mother to her children now, and nobody was going to harm them.

Chapter 11

Bella's dark eyes were blazing with anger. 'That Wally's a rotten sod, telling the kids Tony's dead. I'd like ter get my hands on him. I'd make him squirm, walking into your place, nosing about. My poor little darlings, fancy upsetting 'em like that.' Bella sniffed as she put a plate of biscuits and two glasses of lemonade on to a tray, then fished in her overall pocket for her handkerchief to blow her nose. 'And you say he wanted to see that book?'

'It seems like it.'

''Ere, take these out to the kids. Tell 'em they're having a picnic, that'll please 'em.'

'Thanks, Bella,' Maggie smiled, and quickly returned from the garden with the empty tray.

'Benny ain't come up with any ideas then?' asked Bella, who was sitting at the table looking very pensive.

'Not yet. I'm gonner go and see him in the morning,' Maggie sighed, and a tear ran down her face. 'What am I gonner do? I'm so miserable.'

Bella moved her chair closer. 'Well, I'm glad you brought this lot over to me.' She tapped her son's book and notes that were lying on the table. 'Nobody will get their hands on 'em over 'ere, only over my dead body.'

'Please, don't say that.'

'Sorry, Maggs, but I think we've gotter face up to it. I reckon Wally's right: Tony must 'ave been mixed up in some real dodgy business, and he's either laying very low till it all blows over, or,' she hesitated for a moment, 'he's dead.'

Maggie sniffed. 'Let's look through these together. Perhaps between us we can make some sense of 'em.'

They read through everything, trying to tie up figures, dates and names, and although some made sense, with most of them they just drew a blank.

Maggie sat back and threw the pencil on to the table. 'If only I could find a bank book, or something like that, then I would know how much money we're talking about.'

Bella rubbed her eyes. 'What sort of place has Wally got now?'

'Very nice, so Tony always reckoned when he went over there to play cards.'

'Did he go very often?'

'A couple of times a month, I s'pose – never took that much notice.'

'Could he have got a posh place on his wages?'

'Dunno. Unless his wife has money.'

'Never liked him, or her, stuck-up cow, always had plenty to say, tried to make out she was better than us market traders.'

Maggie laughed. 'Sounds a bit like Helen, my sister-in-law.'

'Yer, but your brother ain't bent! Wally's sort are for ever looking for a deal. Mind you it's always been like that on that market.' Bella sat back. 'My old man could be a right sod at times, but I always made sure I knew all what went on.'

'Did he ever get into trouble?'

'Always made sure he kept one step in front of the law.'

'Has the market changed much since his days?'

'Na, only the people. Had some right characters through that market, and a lot of poor buggers as well. Don't forget there's been a war and a depression. It was bloody hard in the twenties to make a living, not like today – you lot 'ave got it easy. I only wish I could get out and about more. I'd go and sort that Wally out. Bloody leg.'

'Well, wait till it's better. Then you can go and sort him and his missis out. I tell you what, in August, after Laura's broken up for the holidays, I'm taking 'em to Ramsgate for a few days. Why don't you come with us?'

'I'd like that, Maggs. That'll be real nice. I'll pay me way.'

'I hope so,' Maggie grinned and stood up. 'We best be going, it's school for madam tomorrow.'

'How you managing, gel?'

'Not too bad at all, thanks to Benny. He managed to let me have some stuff at a good price.'

Bella smiled. 'I'll always have a soft spot for him.'

'So why don't you marry him?'

Bella screwed up her nose. 'Could you honestly see me living over that stable?'

Maggie shook her head and laughed. 'No, definitely not.'

'That bloody horse of his should have been in the knacker's yard years ago.' Bella moved to her dresser drawer. 'Here, treat the kids.' She put a ten-shilling note in Maggie's hand.

Maggie gasped. 'I can't take this.'

'Course you can.'

'You gave me some money last week. I don't want you to think I only come over here—'

'Give it a rest. Christ, if I can't do something for you lot, well then Gawd help me.' Bella stopped. 'Remember, you're all I've got now.'

'But—'

Bella sniffed. 'Save it towards the kids' holiday.'

Maggie gathered the children from the garden and made her way to the front door. 'Thanks. I'll let you know if anythink happens.'

'Bye, kids. Bye, Maggs, take care.'

As Maggie walked to the station she felt a great love for Bella. She was right, Tony would never leave her or his mother, not of his own free will. So where was he?

When they turned the corner into Kelvin Market, Laura and Jamie ran on ahead laughing. But Maggie was filled with alarm when, after reaching their front door they came running back, their faces full of fear.

'The front door's open,' shouted Laura. 'I hope that man ain't inside again.'

Maggie hurried to her door and with the children hiding behind her, carefully pushed it open. She gasped. 'Mr Goldman, what are you doing here? What's happened?'

The children poked their heads round Maggie's skirt and cried out in fright.

The old man was sitting on the bottom of the stairs, blood running down the side of his face. 'I fell over,' he croaked. 'I was hoping to get back inside before you came home.' He began to struggle to his feet.

'What are you doing in here?' asked Maggie.

'I didn't know you was out, and when I heard a noise coming from your place . . .' He swayed and held on to the wall.

'Someone's been here?'

He nodded.

'Was it Eve?'

'No, it was a short stocky grey-haired man.'

'What?' screamed Maggie. 'That bloody bloke, I'll kill him.'

'You know him?' asked Mr Goldman, looking confused.

Maggie nodded. 'Did he say what he wanted?'

'I didn't get a chance to ask.'

'Mummy! Mummy!' screamed Laura. 'That's the man what come into us last night, ain't it? Mummy, I'm frightened,' she cried, clinging to Maggie.

'He's been here before?' asked Mr Goldman, clutching his handkerchief to his forehead.

'Yes, he came here last night.'

Jamie was squeezing Maggie's hand. 'I'm gonner go and find a copper, I'll have him put away for hitting you.'

'He didn't really hit me, he just pushed me, but it shook me up a little.'

'Well, if you're sure.' Maggie looked down at this poor fragile man sitting holding his head. She wanted to scream. How could anyone do this? What the hell had Tony been up to to bring this grief to so many? 'Do you mind if I just pop up to make sure everything's all right?' she suddenly asked. 'You kids stay down here and look after Mr Goldman.'

Maggie was breathless and uncomfortable as she mounted the stairs. She was also beginning to get very angry. How dare this man walk into her home? She should have removed the key, but nobody carried their door key with them in Kelvin. Should she tell the police?

She pushed open the living-room door. It was as she expected. Everything had been pulled out of the sideboard and scattered over the floor. She quickly pushed it all back. 'If I get my hands on him I'll wring his bloody neck,' she said, storming into the children's room. The contents of the drawers were scattered over the bed. She hurriedly put them back, too. There was no point in the children seeing this; it would only upset them. She closed her bedroom door on the mess in there that she would have to sort out later.

She put on a forced smile as she made her way down the stairs.

'Everything all right?' enquired Mr Goldman.

'Yes, there's nothing to worry about. Now let me get you back into your shop and see to that cut,' said Maggie, taking his arm.

'Thank you, that's very kind of you.'

Slowly they made their way into the tailor's.

'Laura, take that stuff off that chair,' said Maggie.

'Where shall I put it?'

'On the counter.' Maggie guided Mr Goldman to the chair. 'I'll get some hot water and a towel and bathe your head.'

'That's very kind of you. Everything is in the kitchen,' he smiled weakly. 'But really, I'm fine.'

Maggie very gently wiped the blood away; the cut didn't appear to be very deep. 'That's better. It don't look too bad. Now, are you sure you're all right?' she asked, straightening up.

'Yes thank you. Would you like a cup of tea?'

'I'll see to it in a minute. First of all just tell me what happened.'

'Well, I heard this noise, and when I saw your front door was ajar, I pushed it open wider and called out. You understand, I was just enquiring to make sure you were all right. I know you don't let the children bang about like that, and I was wondering if perhaps you might have been taken ill or something, and were trying to attract my attention.'

Maggie smiled. He was such a kind old man.

'When I looked up the stairs I saw this man, short and stocky, like I said. And he had bushy hair.'

Laura cried out, 'It is him, Mummy, it is him.' Her eyes were full of fear. 'Is he still upstairs?'

Jamie was at his mother's side, holding on to her hand.

'Course not,' said Maggie light-heartedly. 'Just been up there, ain't I?'

'He ran down the stairs when I called out. He pushed me to one side, and that's how I hurt my head. I'm sorry, I shouldn't have been so nosy.'

'You weren't nosy. I'm glad you was here.'

'He woke us up last night,' said Jamie, gripping Maggie's hand very tight.

'He did?' asked Mr Goldman.

'I was out and he came in the flat,' said Maggie.

'Did he steal anything?'

'No, he's looking for something of Tony's.'

'Is it very valuable?'

'No.'

'Just an old book, so he said,' piped up Laura.

'How did he know I was out today?'

133

Jamie gave a little sob. 'It was me. I told him we was going to see Granny Ross. I'm ever so sorry.'

Maggie put her arm round him and held him close. 'You mustn't be sorry, it wasn't your fault.'

'You'd better take your key off the string,' said Mr Goldman, 'just in case he comes back again.'

Maggie felt Jamie's body tighten. 'Yes, I suppose I should, but it's such a job getting up and down those stairs every time somebody calls.'

'I could have your key, and you can tell your friends to get it off of me.'

'Would you mind?'

He tapped her hand. 'Course not. Anything to help.'

'Thank you, I'll do that right away. I'll put your kettle on first, then we can have that cup of tea.'

'There's still no news of Tony then?' Mr Goldman called to Maggie, who'd gone to the kitchen.

'No,' she said walking back.

'I wish I'd have asked him where he was going that day.'

'You weren't to know you might have been the last to . . .'

'There, there, love, you mustn't think the worst. Now, what about this tea?'

Over tea Maggie told Mr Goldman that this afternoon she had been to see Bella.

'Ah Bella,' said Mr Goldman. 'A lovely woman. Everybody on this market loved Bella.' He leant forward. 'Do you know, when she was young she had wonderful long black hair. And those eyes. They would flash with temper, or sparkle with happiness.' He sighed. 'All of us young bloods were in love with her.'

Laura giggled. 'What, my granny?'

'Yes, my dear. We were all young once,' said Mr Goldman pensively. 'And your granny was a very beautiful woman. D'you know you could almost span her tiny waist with two hands.'

Maggie smiled. 'I know, I've seen photographs of her.'

'And are you keeping well, my dear?' he asked Maggie.

'Not too bad. This business with Wally has shaken me up a bit, and this warm weather don't help. I'll be glad when September's here.'

'Mummy's taking us to Ramsgate in the holidays,' said Laura.

'That'll be nice for you. Would you like me to come up and sit with you this evening?'

Maggie smiled. 'No, thanks all the same, but I'll be all right. Eve's coming round very soon. Come on, kids, bed. I'm very sorry, Mr Goldman, that this happened.'

'You ain't going out again and leaving us, are you?' asked Jamie in alarm.

'No, love, course not. Bye, Mr Goldman, and thank you for the tea.'

'You look after yourself, young lady, and remember, I'm always here.'

'Thanks,' she said as she ushered the children through the shop door, and she meant it.

'Yoo-hoo, Maggs. Come on, open the door.' Eve was rattling the letter box.

'Just coming,' said Maggie, as she plodded down the stairs.

'What's the game?' asked Eve, looking behind the door. 'Where's the key?'

'I'll tell you upstairs.'

'Well, if you ask me it's a bit daft you traipsing up and down these stairs every time somebody comes to your door.'

'I'll tell you why when I get me breath back.'

Eve threw her handbag on the table. 'Now what's all this about?'

'I'll put the kettle on.'

'You sit down, you look all in. You all right?'

Maggie sunk into a chair and, shaking her head, let a tear slowly trickle down her cheek.

'Maggs, Maggie, what is it?' Eve was on her knees in front of her friend.

Maggie went into detail of all what had happened that afternoon.

Eve jumped up. 'That sod again. I'm sorry, Maggs, but I reckon Dan'll be round there in the morning giving him what for.'

'I'd rather he didn't get mixed up in all this. I'm gonner see Benny first thing, then I'm going to the police.'

'D'you think that's wise?'

Maggie looked surprised. 'Why?'

'Dunno. It's such a mess. Did he find those books?'

'No, I took them over to Bella this afternoon.'

'So that's why you've taken the key away now? It's a bit late, though, ain't it?'

Maggie nodded. 'I didn't expect him back. Till I get another one cut, if at any time I ain't in, Mr Goldman's got a key.'

'Poor old devil, I bet that shook him up.'

'Yes it did, and it didn't do me a lot of good, I can tell yer.'

Eve took a deep breath and looked directly into her friend's eyes. 'Maggie, I think you've got to come to the conclusion Tony ain't coming back, and you've got to start looking after yourself, and those two.' She inclined her head towards the children's bedroom. 'And that new one as well.'

'At the moment I don't feel as if I've got the strength to go on.'

'You'd better find it then, me gel.' Eve threw her arms round Maggie's neck. 'Remember, I'm always here for you.'

Maggie couldn't answer.

Eve held her tight as deep heart-breaking sobs racked Maggie's body.

Chapter 12

As the police station was en route to Benny's rag-and-bone yard, Maggie decided to go there first.

'Could I speak to Inspector Matthews, please?' she asked the fresh-faced policeman standing behind the desk reading through some papers.

He looked up. 'What's it in connection with?'

'My husband. Tony Ross.'

'Oh yer. Just a moment.' He disappeared through a door behind his counter.

Almost immediately another door was opened and Inspector Matthews came striding towards her. He held out his hand and shook hers warmly. 'Mrs Ross. How nice to see you. Any news?'

'No. Could we go somewhere and talk?'

'Course. Follow me.'

Once again Maggie was in his office.

'Please, take a seat.' He pushed a chair towards her. 'What's brought you here to see me? And where's your little chap?'

'Winnie's looking after him.'

'I see. Now, how can I help you?'

As Maggie started to tell him about Wally walking into her flat, she began to wish she hadn't been so hasty in coming here. She didn't mention his name as she was suddenly frightened of telling the Inspector too much.

He sat back in his chair, turning his pencil over and over in his hands.

Maggie noted his hands looked soft, so different from Tony's and most of his mates'.

'So what you're saying is that this man, who you say you don't know, came to your flat looking for something of your husband's, and accidentally pushed Mr Goldman to one side, causing him to cut his head?'

Maggie nodded. When he repeated her story it sounded very trite.

'How do you know he was only looking for something of your husband's?'

'That's what he told Mr Goldman.'

'So what was it that was so important?'

'I don't know. He didn't tell him.' Maggie began fiddling with her handbag. She could feel a flush creeping up her throat.

'Did he take anything?'

She shook her head.

'And what does Mr Goldman want to do about this assault?'

'Oh nothing, he doesn't know I'm here.'

'And you are quite sure this man didn't take any of your belongings?'

Maggie lowered her head, suddenly feeling very silly. 'No.'

'I'm sorry, Mrs Ross, but I don't understand why you're telling me this if nobody wants to do anything about it.' He leant forward. 'And you are certain you don't know who he was?'

Maggie shook her head. 'I'm sorry, I'm only wasting your time.' She wasn't going to tell him about Wally scaring the children the night before. She went to stand up.

He threw his pencil on his desk. 'Just a moment. So you think this could have some bearing on your husband's disappearance?'

'I don't know.'

'And you don't have any idea who broke into your flat? How long has your husband been gone now?'

'Over a month.'

'And you've heard nothing?'

Maggie shook her head. 'I'd better be going.' This time she rose to her feet quickly.

Inspector Matthews was also on his feet. 'I'll call in later and have a quick look round.'

'I'll be out for a while.'

He smiled. 'Anywhere interesting?'

'No, only to see Benny, the totter, to see if he has anything I can sell on the stall.'

'You wanner watch him, he's a bit of an old reprobate.'

'Benny's a kind man.'

'Yes I know, but I still wouldn't trust him. How are you managing?'

'Not too bad. Not used to being the breadwinner. I must go,' she said quickly. 'Bye.'

'Bye, Mrs Ross. I'll be round this afternoon, if that's all right with you?'

Maggie nodded, and closed the door. She wished she hadn't come to see him. It hadn't solved anything.

★ ★ ★

As the door closed David Matthews sat back down in his chair and lit a Park Drive cigarette. Maggie Ross was a lovely young woman. What had that husband of hers been up to? And where was he? Was there another woman? If not, why would he just go off and leave her and those smashing kids? And with another on the way. He tapped the end of his cigarette into the ashtray, his thoughts wandering. Maybe Tony Ross had been involved in something really dodgy. Perhaps he had welshed on a deal. There were plenty of villains in this area who would think nothing of doing away with anyone that upset them. Could he be lying in some warehouse with his skull bashed in, or in a sack at the bottom of the river? Was there anywhere else he could go to try and find out about what had happened to the man? Why, after bothering to come here, didn't Mrs Ross tell him who had come looking for something in her flat? He was certain she knew exactly who it was, but it couldn't have been one of the usual band of thugs – they would have taken everything.

He sat back and drew heavily on his cigarette. He had to admit he hadn't been too worried about this case. Foolishly he'd let his enquiries go cold as he had always assumed Tony Ross would turn up. But now, after all this time there had to be something more to all this, and he had to try to get a few answers. He stubbed out his cigarette aggressively and, taking his grey trilby from the hat stand, left his office. Maybe Benny the totter would provide a clue.

'You look done in,' said Benny, as Maggie slumped into a chair.

'I was a bit worried you might be out,' she said, pushing the damp strands of hair from her forehead.

'Would have been if Nellie had behaved herself. Don't think she wanted to go out today. Played about somethink rotten when I tried to put her harness on, so I thought: bugger it, let's have a day orf.'

Maggie smiled. 'I'm glad you did.'

'Now love, I expect you want a cuppa, don't you?'

Maggie nodded.

'Well, after that we'll go down and take a look at my stock. I've got a few nice little pieces I think you might be interested in.' Benny warmed the teapot and, after putting the carefully measured amount of tea in, added the boiling water.

'You ain't heard nothink more about Tony, I suppose?' asked Maggie.

'No, can't say I 'ave. I've asked around, but no joy so far.'

'Benny, Wally from the auction rooms paid me a visit on Saturday and again Sunday.'

Benny sat at the table next to Maggie. 'He did? What'd he want?'

'I didn't see him. I was out when he came. He woke the kids up and told 'em Tony was dead.'

Benny sat back and looked at her. 'He did what?' he said slowly, and his voice was full of anger. 'The wicked sod. What'd he do that for?'

'He said he was looking for Tony's books.'

'Did he find them?'

Maggie shook her head. 'He came back again on Sunday when I was over Bella's. He pushed poor old Mr Goldman over and cut his head.'

Benny tutted loudly and began pouring out the tea. 'Always said that Wally Marsh was a bad one. Is the old boy all right?'

'A bit shook up, but he's fine. I went to the police station before I came here.'

'And what did they have to say?'

'I felt a bit of a fool, really. I didn't tell the Inspector who it was, because, well, I was frightened to. I think I was wasting Inspector Matthews's time. But I was so angry with Wally, walking into my place like that.'

'He ain't got no right ter do that. I wish I was younger – I'd teach him a thing or two. You'll have to take yer key away from behind the door, love.'

'I've done that. Benny, what did Wally and Tony get up to? And why does he want those books?'

'Where are they now?'

'At Bella's.'

Benny smiled. 'D'yer know, I'd like to go over and see her sometime.'

'Why don't you? She'd be pleased to see you.'

'I might just do that one Sunday. Could always give her a hand with her garden.'

'Benny, about these books? They must be important. Did Tony ever tell you . . .?' Maggie began to toy with her spoon. 'Tony always liked you, you know.'

Benny pushed his greasy trilby back and scratched his forehead. 'Yer, I know. He loved a chat.' He stopped and looked up. 'Someone's coming up the stairs.' He rushed to the door and threw it open. 'Yer, what d'yer want?'

'Just a chat, Benny, just a chat.' Without being invited, David Matthews walked in.

'Mrs Ross,' he said politely, and removed his hat.

'Benny, you know Inspector Matthews?' said Maggie.

'Yer,' growled Benny. 'Well, what d'yer want this time?'

'As I said, just a chat.'

'Do you want me to go?' Maggie stood up.

'No, course not,' said David Matthews. 'Any tea left in that pot?' he asked Benny.

'You've got a bloody cheek. I'll just put a drop o' water on these leaves.'

'Thanks.'

'Well, what did yer want to chat about?' said Benny, banging the teapot on the table.

'About Tony Ross really.'

Benny sat down. 'Don't yer think if I knew anythink I'd tell this here little lass? Known her fer years, I have, and I wouldn't keep anythink from her.'

'I believe that. But what I would really like to know is who he did deals with.'

'How would I know?'

'Oh come on, Benny, everybody knows what you get up to. You must have heard something.'

Benny began to pour out the tea. 'All I know is that Tony, and Wally at the auction room, was mixed up in somethink. Don't think it was anythink big, mind, and that's *all* I know.'

David Matthews sat back. 'Was that who came poking his nose round your place?' he asked Maggie.

She nodded.

'Now listen,' said Benny. 'Don't you go telling him it was Maggie what put you up to this. You leave her out, d'yer hear?'

The Inspector lit up a cigarette. 'We've known all about

the rackets they get up to, but until somebody complains we can't lay a finger on them. I wouldn't have thought that it was bad enough for Tony Ross to scarper though.' He looked at Maggie. 'Would you?'

She shook her head. 'Look, I must go. I can't expect Win to look after Jamie for too long. Thanks for the tea, Benny.'

'I'll come down and help you pick out a few bits.'

David Matthews quickly drank his tea. 'I'll come with you.'

'Why's that?' asked Benny. 'Yer wanner have a quick poke round so you can see if all me stuff's kosher or not?'

'No, I'm not interested in your bits, unless you've got the crown jewels down there.'

'Why's that? Good Gawd, they ain't gorn missing as well, have they? Can't trust anybody these days,' Benny laughed. Although he didn't like coppers this one seemed fair, and unusually, he did have a sense of humour.

'No, it's just that I've got the car outside and if Mrs Ross wants any help with her purchases I can take her.'

'That's kind of you,' said Maggie. 'But I can manage.'

'Don't be daft, Maggs. If he's gonner give yer a lift make the most of it. 'Sides, that means you'll be able to take a bit more than usual.'

Maggie smiled. 'OK. I'll say that, Benny, you've always got an eye open for more business.'

'That's what it's all about, gel. Stick with me and you won't go far wrong.'

Maggie struggled into the passenger seat of David Matthews's car, her bulk beginning to make her movements difficult.

'Thank you for giving me a lift.'

'It's my pleasure, Mrs Ross. Looks like you've got a good eye for trinkets.'

'Yes, I seem to be buying different things to what my husband did.'

'But are they selling? That's the most important thing.'

'Yes. I'm keeping account of everything so that when he does come back he can see what an asset I am to the business.'

He stopped the car at the top of Kelvin Market. 'I'll give you a hand to get them up to your flat.'

'You don't have to. You can leave them with Bill and I'll collect them later.'

'It's no trouble. In fact, it's a good excuse to get out of the office for a few hours.' He helped Maggie from the car and collected her goods from the back seat.

'All right, Maggs?' shouted Tom Cooper.

'Yes thanks, Tom.'

Winnie gave her a wave.

'Jamie been all right?' asked Maggie.

'Yer, no trouble.' Winnie looked the Inspector up and down. 'Everythink all right with you?'

'Not bad.'

'Give us a shout if yer needs anythink?'

'Will do.'

'Seems the entire market's keeping their eye on you,' said the Inspector, noting everybody watching him walking with Maggie.

'Yes, they're a good bunch.'

'Do they know Wally Marsh came to your flat yesterday?'

'I don't know. Mr Goldman might have told them.'

'Why didn't you tell me you knew who it was when you came in this morning?'

Maggie blushed. 'I didn't want to.'

'Why?'

'I'll just open the door and then I'll take those.' Maggie went to take the box from him but he held on to it.

'It's heavy, I'll take it up for you.'

Upstairs she threw her handbag on to the table. 'You can put it down now,' she said anxiously. She wanted to get rid of him as soon as possible.

He put the box on the table and quickly took off his trilby. 'Mrs Ross, may I sit down?'

'Yes. What do you want?'

He twirled his hat round and round in his hands. 'I'm going to make a few more enquiries about your husband. You see, now I know he was an associate of Wally Marsh, I'm going to look into it a bit deeper.'

Maggie sat down. 'Do you think you will find out any more from Wally?'

'I don't know, but I'll be calling in again if I get any news. Will that be all right?'

Maggie nodded. 'Yes, of course.'

The Inspector stood up. 'I'll see myself out.' He closed the door quietly behind him.

Maggie sat at the table. She had to find out more about why Wally wanted those books. Tomorrow she would go and see him and perhaps do a deal with him: the books for information about their associates. It was the one way she could see she might be able to track Tony down.

Chapter 13

For a long while after Maggie and the copper had left, Benny sat and stared at the newspaper, his thoughts on what had been said earlier. He put the newspaper on the table. 'If only I could find out more about what's happened to Tony then I'd be in Bella's good books. In any case, I'll go and see her on Sunday,' he said out loud. 'Better make sure I've got a clean shirt on if I want to impress her.' He smiled. 'Might even have a bath. Wish I could persuade her to marry me. I could make her happy, and I need a good woman to look after me in me twilight years.'

He laughed and carefully folded the newspaper. His thoughts went back to the last time Tony came to see him, just a week before he disappeared. Benny hadn't told Maggie that he'd been, or how worried he'd seemed. Tony had casually mentioned he was in a bit of trouble, though that was nothing new for him, but he'd never said what about or that he was afraid of someone. Benny stood up. 'Silly sod,' he mumbled. 'If only he'd told me the full story I could have some idea where to start looking for him.'

He went down to the stable and put a nosebag on Nellie. He lovingly patted her head. 'We should 'ave gone out today, old girl. I don't want any of your nonsense tomorrow, d'yer hear? Did you see the way that copper was nosing round and casting his beady eyes all over the place? They don't miss a bloody trick. He knew Maggie was coming over here buying so it gave him a good excuse to look round. Must think I was born yesterday.' He stopped. 'I wonder if that copper knows more than he's letting on? I think I'll go and have a word with that Wally Marsh tomorrow, old girl, so I don't want any more of your tricks.' He smiled and gave Nellie another loving pat as she nuzzled close to him. As he closed the door his thoughts went to Maggie. He just hoped she didn't get too chatty with that copper.

Bella Ross was up and about very early for her on a Monday morning. She struggled on to the train, cursing her leg that was still giving her a little pain. The pent-up anger she was feeling towards Wally Marsh had given her the strength she needed to go out. She looked out of the window as they got nearer to her part of London. Downham was all right, but she came from the Smoke, and that would always be where her heart was.

She thought about Maggie. How dare Wally upset her and those lovely kids! She loved Maggie and Tony, but even he'd been a sod in his time. As a kid he was always in trouble, but always just managing to keep the right side of the law. It was different with the stallholders – if he'd been caught pinching he'd come home with a bright red ear where someone had given him a clout. Bella had often wished her and Jim had had more kids like all good Italian families did, but they hadn't been so lucky.

She smiled. Maggie could be a bit of an ostrich at times, preferring to bury her head about Tony's wheeling and dealing. Bella sighed. Maggie knew what had gone on between her friend Eve and Tony, but as she said, that was before they got married. Well, thought Bella, let's hope that was the end of it.

When Bella got off the train she caught the bus to the auction rooms.

She stood outside just looking at the windows. The whole place had been tarted up since she was last here, but that had been many, many years ago. Memories of her dear Jim came flooding back. Despite his faults, gambling and womanising, she had loved him with all the fiery passion that flowed in her Italian blood. She was never quite sure if her son had inherited any of his father's weaknesses, but if he had he never let on.

She pushed open the door and just managed to catch sight of the look of disbelief on Wally's face before his expression changed and he rose to greet an old friend.

The auction rooms' new young bloods looked on curiously as Bella was hailed as a long-lost soul. For years Jim had bought from this place, not all of it straight and above board, and they had made a good living.

Bella smiled at her welcome. 'Nice to see you again too, Wally. Me daughter-in-law – you know our Maggie – she said you was still here. Thought you would have retired years ago.'

'I did. How you keeping, then?'

'Not too bad.'

He took her arm and led her well away from the other men, to the far end of the showroom. 'Have a seat.' He pointed to a large, very old tapestry sofa.

Bella looked at it. 'Just as long as it ain't running alive.'

Wally laughed. 'Still the same old suspicious Bella. No, it came from a very respectable house.'

Bella sniffed. 'They can be some of the worse. Dirty cows, some of those toffs are. And not so much of the old. Anyway, mate, how are you?'

'Not too bad either. I did retire, but I got under me old girl's feet too much, so I come back again. Don't do a lot – not now – only a few days a week. So, what're you doing round this way? You live out Downham now, don't you?'

'Yer. I came back to see you. Heard you and my Tony had a good scam going.'

Wally's face fell. 'Shhh, keep yer voice down.'

Bella looked round, still smiling. She bent her head closer. 'Well, did yer?'

'Only the odd bit that come in, nothing big, mind.'

'So, where's my Tony now?'

'Don't ask me.' Wally too looked round in case his raised voice had attracted attention. 'Found himself a little floozie I shouldn't wonder. Always liked a bit a skirt did—' He took a sharp intake of breath as Bella's sharp elbow found his ribs.

'What d'yer do that for?'

'I'll give you take my Tony's name in vain. Now come on, tell me what this is all about.'

Wally's face flushed and he looked angry. 'How the bloody hell should I know?'

'Don't give me any of that. I know you went to Maggie's place looking for his books, and what was you doing frightening my dear little grandchildren? I tell yer,

Wally, you'll have to answer to me over that.' Bella
moved closer. 'That was a bad move. Those kids mean
the world to me.'

'How d'yer know that? Anyway, I didn't frighten 'em, I
was just—'

Bella was smiling as she took hold of a large lump of
flesh under his arm. She squeezed, then twisted it.

Wally screwed up his face in pain, but he didn't cry out.

'Cut the crap. So come on, what was you looking for?
What gives?'

Wally turned grey.

Bella put her face close to his. 'And don't give me any
old flannel. You ain't talking to young Maggie now, you
know. And what about poor old Mr Goldman?'

Wally took his handkerchief from his pocket and patted
his damp forehead. 'What about him?'

'You're lucky he ain't pressing charges.'

'It was an accident. I didn't mean to hurt him.'

Bella sat back and fiddled with her handbag. 'Try telling
that to the beak.'

Wally was sweating.

'Now what was you after in Maggie's place?'

'Nothing.'

'Rubbish! I know all about you. Remember I was wheeling and dealing here years ago, so I know all the ropes.'

Wally's face was full of misery as he sat back.

Bella felt good. At last she knew she was about to get
some answers to her questions, and they could lead to her
finding her Tony.

David Matthews sat in his car outside Maggie Ross's flat,

his thoughts with her. Why would her husband go off and leave her and her kids? She was a fine-looking young woman with that pretty blonde hair and such blue eyes, so very different to Jean, his late wife.

He turned on the engine. What made him think like that? He had loved Jean and had been heartbroken when she and their new-born baby died.

He quickly lit a cigarette and slammed the car into gear. It was time to have a word with Mr Wally Marsh.

When he walked into the auction room it looked as if the place was empty. Then he spotted a group of people at the far end.

'Give him some air,' called out someone.

David Matthews moved closer. 'What seems to be the problem?'

'He's passed out,' said the woman, sitting next to Wally, slapping the back of his hand.

'How bad is he?'

'Dunno. Anyway, who are you?' asked Bella.

'Inspector Matthews. I've got my car outside if you think he should go to hospital. He don't look too good to me.'

Bella straightened up. 'You're the copper what's looking for my Tony, ain't yer?'

David Matthews looked surprised. 'Are you Mrs Ross?'

'Yes.'

'What are you doing here? I thought Maggie – Mrs Ross, your daughter-in-law said you lived at Downham.'

'That's right. But I had to come and see Wally here. Now the silly sod's gone an' passed out on me.'

David Matthews wanted to smile. Bella Ross was a woman he could get along with; she was like Maggie's friend Winnie, the salt of the earth who called a spade a spade.

Wally groaned.

'He don't look too good,' said one of his fellow workers. 'I reckon he ought ter go to the doctor's.'

'He'll be all right,' said Bella. 'Tough as old boots, is Wally.'

'He's gone blue round the mouth,' said the Inspector. 'I'll run him to the hospital. Would you like to come with me, Mrs Ross?'

'Yer, why not? I fancy a car ride. Then you can take me on to see Maggie.'

'Yes, ma'am,' David Matthews smiled. Bella Ross must have been quite a girl in her time.

Maggie sat down and kicked her shoes off. Her window was wide open but there was no fresh air. Her feet were swollen, making her shoes tight. She thought about what Winnie had said. She knew she was in charge of her life now. Tomorrow she would go and see Wally as she'd promised herself she would, and make him tell her what had been going on. If there were other blokes involved perhaps she could go and see them too, and find out the truth. And she'd have a go at Wally about him coming into her flat and frightening the kids. If she shouted loud enough he'd be sure to tell her what he knew just to shut her up.

Maggie looked at the clock. It was late afternoon and Laura would be coming out of school soon, so she made her way down the stairs.

Before she reached the hall, there was a loud banging on the front door and a hand poked through her letter box, fishing around for her key. Maggie stood on the stairs mesmerised.

A pair of eyes peered through the slit. 'Maggs. Maggie, you there?'

Maggie laughed and quickly pulled open the door. 'Bella, what a surprise!'

Bella was standing with Inspector Matthews right behind her. Maggie froze. The look on Bella's face told her something was wrong. 'What're you doing over here? What is it? What's happened? It's Tony,' the words rushed out.

Bella looked around. 'No, gel, it ain't Tony. Can we come in fer a bit?'

Maggie stood to one side. 'Course. I must ask Win to keep an eye out for Laura.' She left them slowly climbing the stairs.

'Was that Bella?' asked Winnie, when Maggs appeared at her stall.

Maggie nodded.

'She don't alter much, does she? Mind you, she don't look too happy. What's she doing with that copper?' Winnie suddenly stopped and put her hand to her mouth. 'Oh my Gawd, you ain't . . .?'

'I don't know what they want. Could you keep an eye out for Laura?'

'Course, love.' She took Maggie's hand. 'Don't worry about the kids.'

Maggie half smiled and turned. What were they going to tell her? Her legs felt heavy and trembled as she climbed the stairs. When would this nightmare end?

'Hope you don't mind, love, but I've put the kettle on.

Me and the copper here's parched.'

'What you doing over this way?'

'Been up the hospital.'

Maggie slumped into the armchair. 'The hospital?' she croaked. 'Why? What?'

The kettle's loud whistle sent Bella scurrying as fast as her leg would let her from the room.

Maggie looked at the Inspector. 'Is it Tony?'

He appeared surprised. 'No. We had to take Wally Marsh to the hospital.'

'Wally Marsh?' repeated Maggie. 'Why, what's happened? And what's Bella doing with you?'

Bella walked in carrying the tray of tea things. 'Here, Maggs, you ain't never gonner believe this but Wally Marsh – you know from the auction rooms – well, he's gone and had a heart attack.'

'No,' said Maggie. 'When?'

'This morning. We was just sitting talking when all of a sudden he went this funny colour.' She straightened herself in the chair. 'Mind you, after seeing my Jim, I knew what was wrong with him. Reckon he did it on purpose, crafty sod.'

'Who?' asked the Inspector, grinning. 'Your husband?'

Bella tutted loudly. 'No, silly sod. Wally.'

'What was you doing there?' asked Maggie.

'Went ter see Wally. I wanted a few answers as to why he keeps coming here.'

Maggie opened her mouth but no sound came out.

'That's why I happened to be there. I too wanted a few answers,' said David Matthews.

Maggie sat back.

'Here, love, get this down yer, you look all in.' Bella handed her a cup of tea.

'Is he . . .?'

'Not when we left the hospital,' said Bella, spooning sugar into her cup.

'Did Wally tell you what you wanted to know?'

'No, he was past talking by the time I walked in,' said the Inspector.

'What about you, Bella? Did he tell you?'

'Na. Didn't get a chance. We'd no sooner sat down when he said he had a pain. I thought he was buggering about at first. Even dug him in the ribs.'

David Matthews quickly looked up.

'It's all right,' grinned Bella. 'It wasn't the side of his heart.'

'What about his wife?' asked Maggie. 'Does she know?'

'One of the lads from the auction room went and told her. She arrived at the hospital just as we left. She's a stuck-up cow. Never did like her.'

Maggie looked at Inspector Matthews. 'So you haven't got any more answers?'

He shook his head. 'No, but I'll be making some more enquiries. By the way, Mrs Ross, you said "keeps coming here"? So Sunday wasn't the first time he'd been here?'

Maggie looked at Bella. 'No. I didn't tell you, but he came here Saturday night.'

'And d'you know, he told those lovely kids of hers that Tony was dead. That's why I went over – to sort him out. Bloody disgraceful . . .'

David Matthews smiled. 'Well, you certainly did that.'

'I didn't expect him to finish up in hospital. Serves him right.'

'Did he threaten you?' he asked Maggie.

'No, I was out.'

'Oh, I see.' The Inspector looked grave. He finished his tea and stood up. 'I must go. Thank you for the tea, Mrs Ross.'

'That's all right,' said Bella and Maggie together, which made them laugh.

'I'll see myself out.'

When he left Bella said, 'He seems a nice bloke for a copper.'

Maggie smiled but didn't answer. That too was exactly what she had been thinking.

Chapter 14

Six weeks had passed since Maggie had actually spoken to her brother Alan, the week after his birthday when he had come to take her to see Bella. They wrote now and again, and the last letter said he would be over Saturday, today.

Maggie was pleased to see he was alone, and as she made him a cup of tea, she told him what had happened over the past weeks.

Alan was very angry when he heard about Wally frightening the children, and pushing Mr Goldman over.

'He wants locking up. What's that policeman doing about all this?'

'Not a lot really.'

'Bloody incompetent, if you ask me. Where is he now?'

'Who?'

'This Wally bloke.'

'In hospital, he's had a heart attack.'

'Serves him right.' Alan was pacing the room.

'Alan, sit down, you're making me dizzy.'

He gave her a worried glance and sat at the table. 'Still no news then, Maggs?'

'No. I don't know what to think, and now this business with Wally.'

Alan fidgeted with his fingers nervously.

'Is there something on your mind?' asked Maggie.

'I didn't like to mention it before, especially now. But, Maggs, about that money I lent Tony – is there any chance—'

Maggie went pale. 'What money?'

He looked very uncomfortable. 'I wouldn't normally ask, well, certainly not under these circumstances, but Helen wants to go on holiday and—'

'Alan, I asked you what money.'

He looked up. 'Don't you know?'

'No I don't,' she replied angrily.

'Didn't Tony tell . . .?'

'No he didn't. How much was it?'

'Twenty quid,' he mumbled.

'What? Twenty pounds? What did he want twenty pounds for?'

'To get some stock, so he said.'

'Stock. He could buy a whole bloody warehouse full with that sorta money. Did he say what kind of stock?'

'No, and I didn't ask.'

'When was this?'

'About three months ago.'

'And you never told me.'

'Why should I? I thought you knew. 'Sides, after all this I didn't want to worry you.'

'So why you asking for it now?'

'As I said, Helen wants to go away, and she said you should—'

Maggie banged the table. 'I might have guessed it was bloody Helen.'

'Come on now, Maggs, it ain't the first time this has happened.'

Maggie looked up. 'What d'you mean?'

'He often borrowed money from me.'

'I didn't know that. Did he ever say what it was for?'

'Stock.'

'But we only sell rubbish.'

'He liked a game of cards, and the dogs, didn't he?'

Maggie nodded.

'Well, that's what I reckon it was for, but to be fair he always paid up, some times quicker than others.'

Maggie sat stunned. She knew Tony liked a flutter, but twenty pounds was a lot of money.

Alan was still talking. 'Me and Helen think he's got himself mixed up in something big and he's laying low till it all blows over.'

Maggie looked at her brother. 'I ain't got twenty pounds, Alan. We're just about keeping our heads above water. We did have thirty bob in the Post Office but I had to take that out.' Tears began to trickle down her cheeks. 'Where's this all going to end?'

'I'm sorry, Maggie.' He put an arm round her shoulder. 'Say, could you get it off of Bella?'

'No I couldn't,' she yelled, brushing him away. 'I'll just have to try and find it, won't I?'

'I'm really sorry about this. But I did promise Helen a holiday, and we've had quite a bit of expense, what with one thing and another, you understand.' Alan was clearly embarrassed at this conversation.

Maggie stood up and went over to the sideboard. 'I've got two pounds here that I was saving to take the kids to Ramsgate in the holidays. You'd better take that.'

Much to Maggie's surprise he took it eagerly.

After he left Maggie sat at the table and tried to work out her money. There were still nearly two weeks until August, so perhaps she could just about scrape enough together to go away. She mustn't break her promise to the children.

That evening Maggie told Eve about Alan's visit.

For a few moments Eve sat silent. She lit a cigarette, then said with venom, 'The bastard. He come over here just for his money? He ain't been near since that time he was going to take you over to see Bella.'

'But he has written a couple of times,' said Maggie defensively.

'And he took that two quid you was gonner take the kids away with?'

Maggie nodded. 'Eve, it was money Tony had borrowed.'

'Yes, so you said, but to ask you for it now . . . I can't understand Tony borrowing off him.'

'Why did Tony have to borrow off of anybody? Alan said it was for stock – if that's the case, where is this twenty pounds worth of stock?'

'Don't ask me. I still reckon your brother's got a bloody cheek. D'you know, I reckon that cow Helen's at the back of all this.'

'Doesn't matter who's at the back of it, Eve, where am I gonner get Alan's eighteen pounds from? I ain't got nothing to sell.'

'Dunno. Let him sweat for it.'

'I can't. After all, it is his money, and Tony shouldn't have borrowed it.'

'Suppose you're right. How are you managing? The truth now, Maggs.'

'Not too bad. But I don't know for how long when this baby comes. I'll have a job to get over to Benny's, for a start, and he don't always have anything worth buying. I wish I'd taken more interest in what Tony was doing, then perhaps I too could find other dealers.'

'And you might have known what else he got up to.'

'I suppose I have been a bit daft.'

Eve looked at her friend. 'I can let you have a few shillings to help out.'

'Thanks all the same, Eve, but I can't get into any more debt.'

'Call it a gift towards the holiday.'

'No, I couldn't.'

Eve didn't argue.

They sat for a while, both deep in their thoughts.

'Maggs, why don't you come up the Dog tonight? You could do with a bit of cheering up.'

'I don't like leaving the kids, not after what happened with Wally.'

'But he's in hospital now.'

'As far as we know.'

'Well, I think you ought to try and have a quiet word with Ding Dong Bell.'

'What, the bookie's runner? What good will that do? He ain't gonner give me any tips on what's gonner win the two thirty, now is he?'

'I know that, silly. But he might be able to tell you how

much Tony spent on betting, and who he associated with. Those blokes seem to know everything.'

'That's true. I could go in the morning.'

'Would Ding Dong be there then?'

'Dunno, but Gus will be able to tell me.'

'Sounds like a good idea. I must go, I'll call in later.'

'Thanks, Eve. But you don't have to.'

Eve smiled. 'Just like to make sure you're all right.'

Maggie tried all week to see Ding Dong but he wasn't around. Gus told her he reckoned the cops were after him and was lying low.

'As soon as he shows up I'll let you know,' said Gus. 'I could send him along to you if yer like?'

'That might be better. Then I could have a quiet word with him at home.'

It was Friday and the end of term. Laura and all her friends came out of school, laughing and giggling, loaded down with their end-of-year work.

'We going to Ramsgate tomorrow, Mum?' Laura asked eagerly.

'No, next week.' Maggie had just about managed to make enough for their trip. She took some of the many papers Laura was trying to balance.

'I'm ever so glad Granny Ross is coming with us.'

Maggie smiled. 'So am I.'

As his mother and sister were with him, Jamie got a little cheeky when they passed the stalls and tried to act grown up. He picked up an apple.

'Oi, put that back,' yelled Fred.

'How much?' he asked Fred.

'To you, my boy, ten bob,' laughed Fred.

He quickly replaced it in its neat paper nest. 'Mummy, did you hear that? He wants ten bob for that mouldy apple.'

'It ain't mouldy,' said Fred indignantly. 'I bet if I said you could have it for nothink yer'd soon take it, wouldn't yer?'

Jamie nodded.

'Well, go on, take it yer cheeky devil.'

Jamie ran away laughing.

'You shouldn't encourage him,' said Maggie. 'But thanks anyway.'

'I see Bill's keeping everything in order down there.' Fred nodded his head towards Tony's stall.

'Yes, but I don't know for how much longer I'll be able to get over to Benny's for stock.'

'I reckon Benny'll bring over a few bits if you asked him.'

'I expect he would, but I've got to try and be independent. I'd like to find other places to buy from, but till I have this baby I can't get about that much, and carry the goods home with me.'

'I can always pick up any bits with me van, you know.'

'Thanks, Fred. I don't know how I'd manage if it wasn't for all you lot to keep an eye on the kids when I have to go out.' Maggie opened her door and made her way slowly up the stairs.

That evening, when the children were in bed, Maggie got down to the list of clothes she was going to take to Ramsgate next week. Some needed buttons, and others wanted the odd stitch. She sat back and put her hands on her large stomach. Despite her problems with Alan, and her backache, she was feeling pretty good with herself. The market traders had had a whip round for some pocket money for the kids to take away with them. Of course, Bella was always willing to help. Maggie would often find a ten-bob note in her handbag when she got home from visiting her. She hadn't seen Bella for over a week. What would she have to say about Alan? She would be angry with Tony, especially as it looked as if the money had been used for gambling, and she would want to help, but eighteen pounds was a lot of money.

Maggie smiled. The romance between Benny and Bella hadn't progressed, and they'd had a good laugh after Bella had told her how he'd been over to see her wearing a brand-new shirt with the cardboard stiffener still wedged under the back of the collar. Maggie said he must have meant business.

Bella reckoned he'd even had a bath, and his sparse bit of grey hair had been plastered down with some sort of grease.

It would be nice for both of them if they could get together, thought Maggie, but she could never see Benny giving up his horse and stable to live with Bella, and Bella certainly wouldn't live with Benny, so it was stalemate.

Someone banging on the knocker roused Maggie from her thoughts. Thinking perhaps it was Ding Dong at last, she slowly made her way down the stairs. 'All right, all right, I'm coming. Keep it down, will you?' Maggie opened the door and two large men pushed her roughly to one side, walked in and quickly closed the door behind them. Maggie stood motionless.

'Well, where is he then?'

Maggie had never seen these men before and quickly took in their appearances. The older man was clean shaven with piercing blue eyes. He was wearing an expensive-looking grey suit and matching trilby, with his white hair just showing.

'Who?' croaked Maggie.

'You bloody well know who we mean: that old man of yours.'

'I don't know. What d'you want him for?'

'Our money,' said the younger, slightly slimmer man. He too was well dressed, in navy blue. He was dark and had a slight five-o'clock shadow. His dark eyes, almost hidden beneath bushy eyebrows, narrowed menacingly.

Maggie began to shake. 'Oh no, not somebody else,' she said softly, sinking down on to the stairs.

'Shall we go up? Then you can tell us where he keeps it hidden,' said the older man.

'There ain't any money here.'

'Don't give us that, darling.' The younger one roughly grabbed her arm and pulled her to her feet. 'We know all about Mr Tony Ross and the deals he does. So the boss here,' he jerked his thumb over his shoulder in the direction of the older man, 'wants his money.'

Maggie pulled her arm away and rubbed the red mark that was forming on her bare skin.

Slowly Maggie climbed the stairs, her heart beating furiously and her thoughts racing. What if they woke the children? She sat nervously on the edge of the sofa. 'Who are you?'

'Friends of your husband, so where is he?'

Maggie was taken aback. They didn't know Tony was missing. 'He's not here.'

The younger one, who was about twenty, began walking

round the room. 'We know he ain't in the pub, been there.' He went to open the children's bedroom door.

Maggie jumped up. 'Don't go in there. My children are in there asleep.'

'Sit down, Reg. We don't want to upset the little woman. You can see what a state she's in, and we don't want her dropping that lot while we're here, now do we?'

Reg sat in the armchair.

'Now, young lady. Are you going to tell us where your old man is?' The older man took a cigarette from a fancy engraved gold case and lit it with a posh lighter.

'I don't know.' Maggie was shaking with fear, and very slowly tears began to trickle down her cheek.

'For Christ's sake, gel, don't start crying. Mr Windsor here can't stand women crying.'

Maggie felt sick. What did these men want?

Mr Windsor picked up the heavy brass ashtray. He fondled it. 'Nice place you've got here. Mind you, I'm a bit surprised. Thought you would have lived somewhere a bit smarter.'

'What do you want?' sniffed Maggie.

'I told you – me money.' He smashed the ashtray down on to the table, making Maggie jump.

'I don't know nothing about my husband's affairs.'

'Well, in that case, missis, we'll just have to start looking for ourselves.'

Reg grinned and stood up. One by one he cracked his knuckles loudly.

Maggie's head swam, she thought she was going to pass out. 'There ain't no money here,' she said, trying to keep her voice down. 'You ain't the first to come looking. Wally

Marsh was here a few weeks ago and he . . .' She suddenly realised what she'd said: she'd told them Tony wasn't around.

'Well, well, well. So it's true then? Someone has done away with our dear Tony?' Mr Windsor waved at Reg to sit down. He put his face close to Maggie's. 'Or else he's done a runner.' He sat back. 'You say Wally Marsh was here? And pray what was he looking for? It couldn't have been money?'

Maggie was trying to think fast. 'I don't know. When I went to ask him he'd gone into hospital.'

'Yes, that was very unfortunate, poor Mr Marsh. I didn't know you were a friend of the family's, not having seen you at his funeral.'

'Wally's dead?' gasped Maggie.

'Yes, didn't you know? We began to get worried about our money when we didn't see Tony at the church yard. We all knew how fond of Wally he was.'

Maggie began to feel sick. 'Please, Mr Windsor, won't you tell me what this is all about?'

He slowly got to his feet and stood in front of Maggie. He took hold of her shoulders and gripped them hard. He was very close, and as he towered over her she could feel his hot breath on her face.

'It's about that bastard husband of yours. He owes us a great deal of money, and if he don't get it to us quick, we'll have to take it in kind.'

Maggie's head was pounding. She wanted to ask them so many questions, but was afraid. What had Tony been doing all these years? How much did he owe? And what had it been for? These men didn't know where he was, and Wally hadn't known – or had he? In any case, that was too late now.

Mr Windsor pushed her back in the chair and moved towards the door. 'We'll be back. Perhaps you'll have some answers or money for us next time.'

Reg came over and dragged Maggie to her feet. He put his face close to hers, and the smell from his bad breath made her feel sick. 'Now just you remember, Mr Windsor don't like to be messed about with. So when that husband of yours does turn up, tell him we're coming back to collect what he owes.' Grabbing both her arms he shoved her hard backwards, hitting her head against the wall.

He grinned, pulled at his shirt cuffs, then opened the door for his master.

As they went down the stairs, Maggie silently slumped to the floor.

Chapter 15

Eve was pleased Maggie had given her a front door key after that do with Wally. At least she didn't have to drag her down those stairs every time she came to see her. Over these past months she had felt increasingly sad as she walked down Kelvin Market. Eve worried about Maggie and this new baby. How would Maggie manage to pay the rent and run the stall when the weather turned?

It was late evening. All the stalls had long been put away, the rubbish had gone, and somehow after the hustle and bustle of the day there was an air of quiet loneliness about the place. The fact that Tony Ross wasn't around with his jokes and laughter didn't help. Eve smiled to herself; he was a bloke all the women could so easily fall for. A train rattling above broke the silence and her thoughts went back to the talk in the pub earlier.

Tony wasn't the most popular bloke in there at the moment. They had all been talking about poor old Ding Dong being picked up by the coppers. Most of them blamed Tony for buggering off like that and bringing the coppers snooping around. Dan had been up at the bar, while Eve had kept quiet and listened. Gradually people began to talk about Tony. Gus reckoned he owed money to just about everybody. Was this the reason he'd done a runner?

Eve felt sorry for Maggie, she had always trusted Tony, and now it looked as though he had let her down. Eve knew that if she had played her cards right it might have been her having babies and sitting at home waiting for Tony, but that was something she had never wanted. Life was for living, and she would never be like her mother, who had had seven kids and countless miscarriages, and who had spent her life struggling from one pregnancy to another. The day Eve met Dan was the best day of her life. They both had the same attitude: to live for today. He was fun, and she loved him.

Eve looked up at Maggie's window. The light wasn't on, but perhaps she was having a quiet doze. Maggie was beginning to look very tired. Trying to run the stall, this business with that Wally bloke, and then on top of all that Alan asking for money, it was causing her a lot of extra grief.

'Where the bloody hell are you, Tony Ross?' Eve said to herself.

She didn't call out as she mounted the stairs, not wanting to startle Maggie or wake the children. She slowly pushed the door to the living room open and peered in. It took her a few moments for her eyes to adjust to the gloom, but then what she saw had her rushing to her friend's side.

Eve fell to her knees and cradled Maggie's head in her hands. 'Maggie, Maggie. What happened? Oh my God.' She sat back on her legs. 'Maggie, Maggie, can you hear me?'

Maggie groaned.

'Don't move.' Eve rushed into the kitchen and grabbed the towel that hung behind the door. She pushed it between her friend's legs. Maggie was lying in a pool of water.

Eve was bewildered. What if the kids came in and saw their mother in this state while she was getting help? But she had to do something. She gently pushed open the children's bedroom door. They were both sleeping peacefully. There was nothing for it, she would have to get help, and the nearest place had to be the Dog and Duck.

Eve ran all the way. She pushed the door open and breathlessly yelled out for Dan. Everybody looked round.

'My God, gel, whatever's the matter? You look like you've seen a ghost.' Gus was leaning on the bar.

'Where's Dan?'

'In the bog, I think.'

'Eve, you all right?' asked Beatie, frowning. ''Ere, you ain't just witnessed a murder, have you?'

The others near the bar laughed.

'No, I ain't. It's Maggie. She's lying on the floor in her flat. I think she's having the baby.'

'Oh my Gawd,' said Beatie. 'Gus, phone for an ambulance. I'll come back with you, Eve. What about the kids?'

'They're still asleep, or they was when I left 'em.'

'They on their own?'

'Yes.'

'You should have knocked up Mr Goldman.'

'Didn't think of that. Please hurry.'

'I didn't think the baby was due for a few weeks yet,' said Beatie.

'It ain't.' Eve was about to push open the door marked Gents when Dan came out.

'Hallo, love. You decided to come back for a quick one then?' said Dan, walking leisurely up to the bar.

'Dan, you've got to come back to Maggie's with me.'

'I'll just finish me beer first.'

'No you won't.' Eve grabbed his arm and pushed him out of the door.

As the three of them ran back Eve told Dan what had happened.

Eve fell to her knees beside Maggie once again as she lay groaning. She took her hand and gently squeezed it. 'I'm here, Maggs. You're gonner be all right.'

'It's OK, Maggs,' said Beatie. 'Gus has called an ambulance. Dan, go and wake the kids, dress 'em and take them up the pub.'

Dan nodded, his face went pale when he saw Maggie, and eagerly he did as he was told.

'Will she be all right?' asked Eve, looking anxiously at Beatie.

'Course. She ain't the first to have their baby on the floor, and I don't suppose she'll be the last.' Beatie gave a little laugh. 'And I reckon that's where a lot of the dirty deeds start out, don't you, on the kitchen floor?'

'The men, Reg . . .' whispered Maggie.

'Don't worry, there ain't no men here, love,' said Beatie.

Maggie drew her legs up and screamed out in pain.

They heard Laura cry out. 'Mummy, Mummy! What's wrong with my mummy?'

'Dan, hurry up and get those kids out,' shouted Eve.

'Auntie Eve, what you doing to my mummy?' said Jamie, coming into the room with his teddy under his arm, his hair tousled, and rubbing his eyes.

Eve stood up and with her arm round Jamie's shoulder gently ushered him away and out of sight of his mother. 'It's all right. Mummy's just going to the hospital to get the new baby.'

'Why is she laying on the floor?'

'She's having a little lay down, she's very tired.'

'Oh.'

Eve was pleased he didn't want to pursue it any further.

'Will we take the new baby to Ramsgate?' asked Laura, coming into the room and trying to see what was happening.

'You'll have to wait and see,' said Dan, easing her towards the door. 'Come on, I'm taking you up the pub.'

Jamie's face lit up. 'Can we have an arrowroot biscuit? Daddy used to buy us those.'

'I think I could manage one of those,' said Dan. 'And what about some lemonade?'

'I want some as well. It's all dark out here . . .' Laura's little voice faded away as they disappeared down the stairs.

Tears slowly slipped down Eve's face. 'Those poor kids,' she said.

'They'll be fine,' said Beatie. 'I wonder what brought this on?'

'Could be all the worry about Tony. She's been under a lot of pressure lately.'

'H'mm,' mused Beatie. 'And if he don't turn up soon then it ain't gonner get any better for her.'

A few minutes later two well-built ambulance men walked in.

'Eve, you go with Maggie. I'll clear up here, then I'll see to the kids,' said Beatie.

'Thanks, Beatie.' Eve watched as the men carefully carried Maggie down the stairs. 'You'll have to tell—'

'Don't worry,' said Beatie. 'I'll let everybody know what's happened.'

Eve sat in the ambulance holding her friend's hand. She wanted to cry. Maggie was very distressed and she looked a terrible colour. A little prayer raced round Eve's mind: Please, Maggs, don't die.

'Benny Jones. What the bloody hell you doing here at this time of morning? And on a Saturday as well? You should be out earning a few bob.' Bella Ross was cross. She was in her old dressing gown and hadn't done her hair. 'You'd better come in. Don't want all the neighbours to see me like this.'

Benny removed his trilby, which wasn't the usual grotty old one he wore for work, and followed Bella down the passage. Suddenly Bella realised he looked both clean and very worried.

'What's up then, mate, that horse of yours died?'

Benny sat at the kitchen table. 'Dan New came to see me very early this morning.'

Bella glanced over her shoulder as she filled the kettle. 'What, Eve's Dan?'

Benny nodded.

'Didn't know he knew where you lived. What did he want?' Suddenly it hit Bella. She slammed the kettle on the gas stove. 'It's my Tony, ain't it? They've found his body. He's dead, ain't he?' Tears welled up in her big brown eyes.

Benny quickly hurried over to put his arms round Bella and hold her close. 'No, girl, it ain't Tony, it's Maggie.'

'Maggie!' she screamed, pushing herself away from him. 'Maggie? What's happened to her?'

'Calm down, love. Maggie's all right, but I'm afraid the baby was born dead.'

Bella stared at him for a moment. 'The baby . . . But it ain't due till . . . Poor Maggs.' She began to cry.

Benny held Bella round her wide shoulders. In all this sadness he wanted to smile. They must have looked a strange pair, a bit like Laurel and Hardy. He was thin and wiry, while Bella was round and cuddly.

Gradually her tears and sobs subsided and she drew away from him. 'Sorry about that,' she mumbled, fishing in her dressing-gown pocket for her handkerchief. She dabbed at her eyes. 'How do you know all this?'

'It seems Eve was with her at the hospital and when Beatie from the pub phoned to see how she was, they told her not too good. Eve didn't leave till the baby, another little girl by all accounts, was born. She phoned the pub, Dan was still there, and told him to come over and see me and ask me to tell you. He looked terrible – been up all night, so he said.'

'Why?'

'He promised Eve he'd look after the kids.'

'The kids.' Bella quickly put her hand to her mouth. 'Where are they?'

'They're in the pub. Beatie and Gus is looking after them till Eve can pick 'em up.'

'I've got to go and see Maggie, and I'll have to look after the kids. That bloody son of mine should be here. It's his fault she's lost that baby. I'll kill him when he walks his arse in here. I mean it, I'll bloody well kill him.'

'Do you want to go to the hospital first, or see the kids?'

'The hospital.' Bella half smiled. 'D'you know, we was going to Ramsgate next week. That would have been nice.'

'Perhaps you can still go when Maggie comes out. It might do her good.'

'Yes, you could be right – and, Benny, thanks.'

'What for?'

'For being a real mate and coming over and letting me know.'

He looked embarrassed. 'You know how I feel about you, Bella, and I'd like to be part of your family.'

'Now don't start on all that nonsense again. I'm going upstairs to get dressed otherwise I'll have me neighbours talk about me entertaining a man in me dressing gown. You can make another cup of tea if you like.'

Benny sighed as Bella left the room. Perhaps one day he might make her see that being together would be nice for both of them. For who knew how long they had left?

Maggie opened her eyes and tried to focus on a man who was walking down the ward carrying a bunch of flowers. 'Tony?' She desperately wanted it to be Tony.

He smiled. 'Maggie, sorry, Mrs Ross, I hope you don't mind me coming to see you. I was round the market this morning and I heard what had happened.'

David Matthews sat on the chair next to the bed and placed the flowers below her feet.

Maggie, who looked pale and drawn, gently eased herself up in the bed and pulled her bed jacket round her shoulders. She looked up the ward apprehensively. 'I thought only relatives were allowed in the maternity ward.'

'That's the one good thing about being a policeman – I

only have to say I want to ask you a few questions and that opens all kinds of doors.'

Maggie was suddenly wide awake. She shuddered at the memory of what had happened last night. Did he know about those men coming to her flat? 'Questions? What sort of questions?' she asked.

He smiled. 'That was just a ploy.'

She sunk back on the pillows. Tears filled her eyes. 'You know I lost my baby?'

He shuffled in the chair. 'Yes, yes, I do know. I'm very sorry about that. Everybody on the market's talking about it. They are all very upset.'

Maggie looked away.

He stood up. 'I'm sorry. I shouldn't have come.'

Maggie turned. She half smiled. 'It was very nice of you, and thank you for the flowers, they're lovely. I hope you got them off Mrs Russell?'

He didn't reply. At the door he turned and waved.

Maggie closed her eyes.

David Matthews stood outside the hospital and lit a cigarette. It was such a shame that Maggie Ross had lost her baby. She was a wonderful mother. If only he had some news, any news, about Tony Ross. He got into his car. The word was that the affable Mr Ross was in a lot of debt. Well, he certainly didn't spend much on his wife and kids. They weren't hard up, but they didn't live in the sort of luxury that the volume of his gambling money seemed to suggest.

His thoughts were rambling. How would she manage when winter came and the weather turned bad? She wouldn't be able to get the stall out every day then.

Matthews noticed the Blackshirts on the corner. The Nazis were a despicable bunch, and the papers were full of what was happening in Europe. What if there was another war? Who would look after Maggie Ross then? She was a lovely young woman who needed love and affection.

David Matthews sat for a long while wondering what his next move could be to try to find Tony Ross. The dog track knew all about him. They called him the big spender, and added that he'd been a big loser too. The bookie's runner, a Mr Bell, who was arrested a few days ago, said Tony owed him a lot of money. In fact, it appeared he owed money all round. The Inspector ground the end of his cigarette into the ashtray and started the car engine. He only hoped Ross hadn't been involved with Reg Todd and Mr Windsor. That could really be trouble for him now they were out.

Another thought struck him: it could also mean danger for Maggie. David Matthews banged the steering wheel in anger. 'Sod you, Tony Ross,' he said aloud. 'You don't deserve Maggie and those lovely kids.'

Chapter 16

Everybody waved as Maggie, with David Matthews at her side carrying her bag, turned into Kelvin Market.

'Good ter see you back,' said Winnie, wobbling up as soon as she caught sight of her. 'We're all really sorry about the baby.' She kissed her cheek and, smiling, gently patted Maggie's arm. They were old friends and didn't need to say comforting words.

'Everything all right?' Maggie asked Bill as she came up to the stall.

'Not too bad, Maggs. Could do with a bit more stuff. Benny brought a few bits over. I ain't paid him, though.'

'Don't worry, I'll get it sorted out. Bella been seeing to your wages?'

'Yer, ta.'

As Maggie moved on, her thoughts stayed with the stall and the pathetic display. How could they exist on what that must be taking?

'See yer still got that bloody copper in tow,' shouted Tom Cooper good-naturedly.

'Take no notice of him, love. You've been good for me business,' yelled Mrs Russell.

'Lovely ter see yer back, gel,' said Fred warmly.

Maggie couldn't believe her eyes when she pushed open the living-room door. The flat seemed to be full of flowers and fruit.

'Sit yerself down, Maggs. Kettle's on. You are gonner stay for a cuppa, Inspector?' Bella was beaming.

'If it's not too much trouble.'

The racket coming up the stairs told Maggie who was about to burst in.

'Mummy, Mummy!' The door was flung back and banged hard against the wall as Laura and Jamie came bounding into the room.

'We ain't half missed you,' said Jamie, burying his head in her lap.

'Hope you've been good while I've been away.'

Laura sat beside her. 'Granny Ross said they didn't have any babies left. Is that true?'

Maggie put her arm round her daughter's shoulder. 'I'm afraid Granny Ross is right.'

'Well, I reckon it was rotten of the hospital to tell us we was gonner have one, then take it away.'

'You can always ask again for another one,' said Jamie.

Maggie smiled. 'I don't know about that. You see, I have to ask Daddy first.'

'I don't see why. Daddy ain't here now.' Laura was pouting. 'Perhaps you could ask Uncle Dan. He might be able to help.'

David Matthews laughed. 'I don't think that would be such a good idea.'

'Auntie Eve might not like it,' said Maggie.

'Why? Don't she like babies, then?'

'Only mine.'

'Can we still go to Ramsgate?' asked Laura.

'I don't know.'

'Oh Mummy, you promised.'

'Give yer mum a chance to get her coat off,' said Bella.

'She's ain't got a coat on,' said Jamie.

'Well, can we go out and play then?' asked Laura.

'Yes, off you go, and don't get into any mischief.'

Laura smiled. 'Mummy's back,' she said, skipping out of arm's reach and adding defiantly, 'And don't you be like that hospital and break a promise.'

'Well, my being away didn't seem to bother them very much,' said Maggie to her mother-in-law.

'Don't you believe it. We had quite a few tears, and Jamie's been wetting the bed again, and Laura's been shouting in her sleep.'

'Oh Bella, I'm sorry. Have they been a lot of trouble?'

Bella smiled. 'No, it's been a real pleasure. It's taken years off me. Mind you, I don't know how you managed up and down those stairs all the time, and that bloody washing got caught on the fence more times than I care to remember. And as for dragging that tin bath up the stairs on Fridays... I dunno how you've been managing.'

'I'm sorry I've been a nuisance.'

Bella laughed. 'You ain't been a nuisance, love. I've enjoyed it. Fred brought the bath up for me, and put it away after. I wouldn't like having an outside bog again, though. Didn't like creeping out there in the dark.'

'You're getting soft,' said Maggie.

'Reckon I am. You wait till you get a nice house with it

185

inside, then you'll wonder how you managed.'

Maggie tried to hide her feelings, knowing that was what Tony wanted – a nice house.

'Sounds like you'll be glad to get back home,' she said.

'Na. In fact I reckon my house will seem like a morgue after I've been here for a couple of weeks.'

'I know how you feel,' said David. 'It must be nice to come home to a warm friendly house.'

'Where d'you live then, son?' asked Bella, pouring out the tea.

'Greenwich.'

'Oh very nice. Got a house, have you?'

'Yes, but it feels a bit empty at times.'

Maggie stirred her tea. She suddenly felt embarrassed. 'Thank you for bringing me home,' she said softly.

'It was no trouble.'

Bella took the cups into the kitchen.

'Maggie – do you mind if I call you Maggie?'

She laughed. 'Course not, everybody else does.' For some unknown reason she wanted to keep the conversation light-hearted.

'Maggie, could I come round and—'

'You don't normally ask. Have you any more news?'

'No, but I would like to come and have a chat with you one evening, that's if you don't mind.'

'No, course not. Is it about Tony?'

'In a way, yes.' He stood up. 'Well, I think I'd better be off. Got to do some work sometimes.'

'I hope I haven't kept you.'

'No, course not. Bye, Mrs Ross,' he shouted.

Bella poked her head round the door. 'Bye.'

When they'd heard the front door shut Bella asked, 'What was that all about?'

'I don't know. He said he wanted to see me.'

'About Tony?'

'I don't know.'

Bella sat next to Maggie. 'You know what I reckon?'

Maggie shook her head.

Bella straightened herself up. 'I reckon he's setting his cap at you.'

'What?' Maggie laughed. 'Don't talk daft. I'm married to your son, remember. 'Sides, he's a policeman.'

'He is rather nice, though, and very considerate – that is, for a copper. You could do worse. And he's got a house.'

'And he might live with his mother. 'Sides, I ain't looking for anyone else. I'm married.'

'I think we've got to accept that Tony's . . . Well, you know . . .'

'No, I don't know,' said Maggie angrily. 'I'm surprised at what I'm hearing, and surprised at you accepting that Tony could be dead. And now you're trying to get me married off.' Her voice rose and her tears began to flow. 'What did I do to make him run off like this?'

'I dunno, love, and I ain't trying to get you married off. I'm sorry, Maggs, I wouldn't upset you for the world, especially after what you've been through lately. I just want to see you and the kids happy again, but I think we should face up to—'

Maggie jumped up. 'I ain't staying here to listen to you. I won't be happy till Tony comes back. I love him – d'you hear? – and I know he'll be back, I just know he will. You wait and see.' She rushed into her bedroom and slammed the door.

Bella sat back, acknowledging her thoughtlessness, knowing Maggie was down after losing the baby. She walked to the window and looked down on the market. Somehow she had to tell Maggie what Benny had told her, that he thought Tony had been involved with a Mr Windsor and a gambling syndicate. If he owed that man money that could mean trouble for all of them if he came here. Benny said Windsor was a nasty bit of work. They would have to look at those books again. Did the W stand for Windsor, and not Wally as they had first thought? And what kind of trouble had Tony got himself – and Maggie and the kids – into? In some ways it would be safer for her to have that copper hanging around.

Maggie's arm was being gently shaken. 'Mummy, Granny Ross said are you getting up for tea?'

She sat up. 'Sorry, darling. I must have dropped off.'

Laura climbed on the bed and sat beside her. 'Have you been very ill?'

'No, not very.'

'Then why was you in hospital for such a long time?'

'I was a bit ill and very tired.'

'We missed you. I wanted to come to see you in hospital but Granny Ross said the nurses wouldn't let me. I think that's ever so rotten of 'em, and them not having any babies as well. We've got haddock for tea. Are you going to get up?'

'Yes, my darling.' Maggie sat up and hugged her daughter.

'Feeling a bit better?' asked Bella when Maggie walked into the living room.

Maggie nodded. 'I'm sorry for going off like that.'

'Don't worry about it. It was my fault.'

As they sat at the table both Bella and Maggie couldn't find the right words to say. But they both knew Tony was filling their thoughts.

At six o'clock Eve came racing up the stairs. She threw her arms round Maggie's neck.

'It's good to have you back home, I've really missed you, and I'm so sorry about the baby. What d'you think brought it on?'

Maggie shrugged, smiled and said, 'I wish I knew.' She wasn't going to tell anyone about Mr Windsor, or his sidekick Reg Todd. 'Thanks for coming back and taking care of everythink. I dread to think what effect it would have had on the kids to see me like that.'

Eve shrugged. 'That's what friends is for. That was good of that copper to take Bella to the hospital every day, wasn't it?'

'Yes, it was.'

'What's he like then?' asked Eve, peering into the mirror and running her little finger over her bright red lips.

'He ain't a bad bloke for a copper,' said Bella. 'Think he's got a soft spot for our Maggs here.'

'Don't start on that again,' said Maggie, giving Bella a dirty look.

'Oh dear, have I asked the wrong thing? Is he good-looking though?'

'Trust you to ask that,' said Maggie.

'Well, is he?'

'He's not bad at all,' said Bella. 'And he's a widower.'

'Is he now?' said Eve. 'And he's taken a shine to our Maggs then?'

189

'No he ain't, and she talks a lot of rot sometimes.'

'Sounds like I'll have to meet this bloke.'

Bella tutted and laughed. 'Can't keep yer hands off 'em, can yer? Remember you're a married woman.'

'Did your brother come and see you?' asked Eve, changing the subject.

'No, but he sent a letter.'

'Well, I reckon all this worry about his money could have brought this on,' said Eve.

'What money?' asked Bella quickly.

'Ain't she told you?'

'No she ain't.'

'Eve, it ain't nothink to do with Bella. This is between me and my brother.'

'If it concerns that son of mine, then it's to do with me as well.'

'Tony borrowed some money off him, that's all.'

'How much?'

'A few pounds.'

'How much?' asked Bella forcefully.

'Twenty pounds,' said Maggie.

'What?'

Maggie didn't answer.

'And do you know, that brother of hers had the cheek to take the two pounds Maggs was saving to take the kids to Ramsgate with.' Eve sat back.

'Eve, I told you, it's none of your business.'

'That's settled it. We're going to Ramsgate as soon as you feel up to it,' said Bella. She waved her finger at Maggie. 'And I don't want any arguments about it, it'll be my treat.'

'I can't let you pay for—'

Bella held up her hand. 'Shut it.'

Eve giggled. 'So, do as you're told. When you thinking of going then?'

'It's up to Maggs.'

'I don't know. What about the stall and the stock? I noticed there wasn't that much when we came past.'

'Benny's been keeping his eye on things for you, and I've been keeping yer book up to date. By the way, I didn't tell yer before but old Wally Marsh died.'

Maggie almost said, 'I know,' but quickly recovered. 'He did? When?'

'A week or so before you went in hospital.'

'Was that the sod that come here?' asked Eve.

'Yer,' said Bella. 'I went to see him at the auction room, you know. In fact it was me and the Inspector what took him to the hospital.'

'Well, you ain't got any more worries about him turning up on your doorstep then, have you?' said Eve.

'No,' said Maggie thoughtfully, and she wasn't going to tell them that it wasn't him she was worried about. 'We could go to Ramsgate the week after next if you like.'

'Only if you feel up to it.'

Maggie smiled. 'I'll be all right. Besides, the kids need a break.'

'So do I,' said Bella laughing, 'after all this washing and ironing. I don't know how those two get into such a state.'

Chapter 17

Laura and Jamie looked tanned and happy as they skipped along Kelvin Market holding the sticks of rock they were going to give the stallholders.

'I reckon they'll be a right sticky mess when they get 'em,' said Bella.

Bella had laughed when Laura told them what they wanted to buy everybody. 'I can just see old Mrs Russell, and Mr Goldman trying to get their teeth round that.'

But Maggie was pleased they wanted to share some of the money the traders had given them.

Where was Winnie? She was always the first to greet them. Her stall was there, and she knew they would be home today. 'Where's Winnie?' she called to Ada.

'She didn't come back from the pub. Fink she met a couple of old cronies she used to know.'

'Did she say if she'll be back later?'

'I would fink so,' came the reply. 'Only hope she ain't legless.'

Maggie was concerned. Winnie never left Ada in charge all day, especially on a Saturday, their busiest day. Perhaps she was in the flat with a cup of tea waiting. That would be the sort of thing Winnie would do.

'All right then, Fred?' asked Maggie smiling.

'Yer, gel. You look as if you've all had a good time.'

'Yes, we have. I see Winnie's gone off.'

'Yer.' Fred carried on serving his customers.

'You gonner stay over the weekend then, Bella?' asked Maggie, when they reached her front door.

'If you want me to, love.' Bella put her bag on the floor while Maggie opened up. 'But I don't want to get in the way, and I'll have to go home soon to pay me rent. Don't want 'em chucking me out.'

Maggie sensed this light banter was to hide the anxiety she too was feeling. Although she guessed Winnie would be upstairs and even though Wally was no longer on the scene, she was still very apprehensive at what they could find if Mr Windsor had paid her a visit while they'd been away.

Their few days' holiday had been a huge success, thanks to Bella and the wonderful weather. They could never have had so good a holiday without Bella's money. Maggie had felt relaxed and happy sitting in the warm sunshine watching the children play on the sands, but now, as she returned home, all the old worries and uncertainties began to crowd in on her.

Had Mr Windsor been back? How was Bill managing? The stall was looking half empty. The week after next Jamie would be starting school, which would give her more time to try to find stock.

'You could always move in with Benny if they did chuck you out,' Maggie laughed half-heartedly as they mounted the stairs.

'Don't start on that bloody nonsense again. This weather

and these stairs kills me feet. Won't be sorry to get these shoes off.'

Maggie pushed open the living-room door and stood in the doorway for a moment just looking round. She let out a sigh of relief. It was just as she had left it. 'Yoo-hoo, Win, we're home. Are you there?'

Bella was right behind her. 'I tell yer, gel, I was a bit worried at what you might find in here.'

Maggie turned on her. 'Why? Wally's dead.'

'Oh yer, so he is.' Bella knew she would have to tell Maggie soon that Mr Windsor was out of prison and would come looking for Tony. But would that be worrying her unnecessarily? Did he know where Tony lived?

'Win, are you here? We're home,' called Maggie, walking into the kitchen.

She came back out. 'That's funny, she ain't here.'

'P'raps it's like Ada said, she's had a skinful with some old mates.'

Maggie frowned. 'But that's not like Winnie.'

'Well, don't worry about her now, just put the kettle on. I'm parched.'

That evening when the children were in bed, and after Bill had brought in the day's takings, Bella and Maggie sat waiting for Eve to arrive.

'The stall ain't doing so well, is it, Maggs?'

'No, I'm worried. You don't think Bill's . . .?'

Bella shook her head. 'No, he's an honest enough lad. D'you know what I think the trouble is: lack of the right kinda stock.'

'It's the lack of any kind of stock. Some of that rubbish

has been hanging about for years. I'll have to go to see what Benny's got on Monday.'

'People have changed. They seem to have a few bob these days for silly knick-knacks. Look at what was on sale down at Ramsgate. You'll have to find other places to buy from, try to go a bit up-market.'

'I know, but what? And where will I get the money from to buy that sort of stuff? And will it sell?'

'You could give it a try. I'll have a talk to Benny next week. I'm surprised Winnie didn't come back to see you,' said Bella, changing the subject.

Maggie moved over to the open window, the noise of the market packing away drifting up. 'So am I. I see Fred and Tom are putting her stall away. You don't reckon she's been taken ill, do you?'

'Wouldn't like to say. Na, that lot down there would know soon enough. She got her stall out this morning, didn't she?'

'So Ada said. She didn't come back after going to the pub.'

'And she was all right then?'

'I expect so.'

'D'you think she got Brahms?'

'Dunno. Still, if she did Gus would tell someone, surely?'

'Unless she managed to stagger out on her own.'

Maggie sat down. 'I could pop up to the Dog later, then if they don't know, tomorrow I'll go round her place, that's if she ain't here by then.'

Bella gave a little grin. 'I know I shouldn't say this, but then you know my warped sense of humour, gel. This market'll get a bad name if all the traders keep disappearing.'

'Bella, what a rotten thing to say. Mind you, if it got in the papers with pictures, somebody might recognise Tony.'

Bella didn't answer.

Eve threw her arms round Maggie when she came breezing in. 'I ain't half missed you.'

'Christ, we've only been gorn a week,' said Bella.

Eve looked lovely. She was wearing a small beige straw hat with an upturned brim. Her light floral frock fitted snug over the hips, then flared out.

'You look very nice,' said Maggie.

'Treated meself. D'you like it?' She did a twirl.

'Lovely,' said Bella. 'Only wish I was a few stone lighter.'

'Well, you two look as if you had a nice time. It's been bloody hot up here, I can tell you. Look at your tanned faces. I really envy you. Did you have a paddle? Did the kids enjoy it?'

'Yes they did, and they brought you back a stick of rock.'

'Did they? Can I go and thank 'em?' asked Eve, going to their bedroom door.

'If you like.'

Eve was back almost at once. 'They're fast asleep.'

'I expect they're worn out. It's been a long day for 'em.'

'They look ever so well, and young Jamie's hair has gone really fair. I left Dan in the pub – d'you fancy a drink?'

'I was going to call in to see Gus, but I can't leave the kids for too long.'

'Course you can,' said Bella. 'I'll look after 'em. Go on, go out and enjoy yourself for a half-hour.'

'I wouldn't mind.'

'Right, grab your bag and we'll be off,' said Eve, poised at the door ready.

'You got enough for a drink, Maggs?' asked Bella.

'Yes thanks.' She was glad Bill had taken a few shillings today.

'Well,' said Eve, when they were outside, 'did you really have a good time?'

'Yes we did.'

'I'm glad.' Eve put her arm through Maggie's. 'Now, Mrs Ross, what's the future got lined up for you?'

'I wish I knew, Eve. But one thing's for sure, I've got to try and earn enough money to keep our heads above water, and to pay off Alan.' Maggie wanted to add, 'And Mr Windsor as well,' but she knew that wouldn't be wise – not just yet anyway.

Maggie was greeted like a long-lost soul when she entered the pub. It was the first time she had been in there since she'd lost the baby. Drinks were put in front of her at an alarming rate, but with Eve's help she made sure she didn't offend anyone. She was pleased that neither Tony nor Inspector Matthews was mentioned.

'You're looking really well,' said Beatie, sitting at their table. 'That holiday's done you the world of good.'

'I couldn't have done it without Bella's help.'

'She's a good 'en. The way she looked after those kids of yours while you was in hospital – well, she's a diamond.'

'I know, and I'm gonner miss her when she goes back home.'

Dan put another drink on the table.

'Thanks, Dan,' grinned Maggie. 'But I think I've . . .'

He leant closer. 'It ain't from me, it's from Ding Dong. He's just walked in.'

Maggie looked up and waved to him. The last she'd heard he'd been in the clink. She wanted to run over to him right away, but knew she couldn't. 'Thank him, oh and, Dan, could you ask him if he'll be around on Monday morning?'

'Why's that, gel? You want to put a bet on?' asked Beatie.

'No, I'd like to have a chat with him, that's all.'

'If it's about Tony, well, gel, if you want my advice I'd call it a day. After all, you ain't seen hide or hair of the old bugger for months now, have you? I think Bella's given up about ever seeing him again. It's a shame.'

Gus began yelling for Beatie.

'All right, all right, I'm coming. Can't sit down for a minute before he starts shouting for me.' Beatie stood up.

'Beatie, was Winnie in here lunchtime?'

'Dunno, I was upstairs.' Beatie moved over to the bar.

'What was that about?' asked Eve.

'Winnie didn't put her stall away and I wondered if she'd been in here.'

'So why do you want to see Ding Dong? Is it about Tony?' asked Eve.

Maggie nodded. She giggled – the drinks were going to her head – and when Ivy began playing she sang her heart out, and all thoughts of Winnie went completely.

When Ivy got to a sentimental song Maggie wanted to cry. She missed Tony so much and longed for his arms round her, and to be made love to.

When Ivy changed her tune so Maggie's thoughts changed. How was she going to manage to pay off Tony's debts? And exactly how much did he owe? How was she going to live and keep the children fed, and clothed? The drink was making her feel very sorry for herself. Tears began to trickle down her cheeks. Ivy began belting out 'Pack Up Your Troubles in Your Old Kit Bag'. Maggie wished she had an old kit bag she could just pack all her troubles into and then throw it into the Thames.

She woke with a thumping headache. Gently she lifted her head off the pillow. She could hear the children laughing, and Bella singing. She lay back down again. They didn't need her.

A racket in the living room brought Maggie back to her senses. It was Winnie's voice. What was she doing here on a Sunday? She moved as quickly as her head would allow, grabbed her dressing gown and went into the living room.

'Good morning, miss,' said Bella breezily. She turned to Winnie, who had a swollen, bruised cheek. 'D'you know, me and Eve had to almost put her to bed last night, she was in a right old state when she got home.'

'What happened to you?' asked Maggie, her voice thick with sleep. 'Where was you yesterday?'

'Could I have a quiet word?'

'Course. Come in the bedroom.'

'Don't mind me,' said Bella curtly.

Maggie closed the door and sat on the bed.

'You look bloody awful,' said Winnie.

Maggie smiled. 'I know, and me mouth feels like a sewer. But say, have you seen yourself? How did you get that? I know, you walked into a door.'

Winnie looked in the dressing-table mirror. 'As a matter

of fact I did walk into a door, or to put it another way, the door came and hit me.'

Maggie laughed. 'Oh me head. Don't give me that, Win.'

Winnie sat on the chair. 'I got this because of your old man.'

'What?' Maggie felt the colour drain from her face. 'You've seen Tony?' she whispered.

'No, but I seen those two blokes that was with him that time in the pub and I asked 'em about Tony.'

'You did? What did they look like?' asked Maggie, almost dreading the answer.

'The older one was well dressed in grey, and the other one was bigger and . . . You all right?'

Maggie felt sick. 'Yes, thanks, got a bit of a hangover.'

'Serves yer right, silly cow. As I was saying. I went up the Dog for a quick one yesterday lunchtime as it was so bloody hot, and there as bold as brass was these two blokes sitting there. I said to Gus I thought they were the blokes that was in there with Tony.'

'Gus didn't say anythink last night.'

'Probably didn't think any more about it. Anyway, when I turned round, they'd gone, so I downed me stout and went out to try and see 'em. They was just getting into a car so I banged on the window. Anyway, to cut a long story short, they told me if I didn't know where your old man was, to piss off and mind me own business. Well, I told them in no uncertain words what I thought about them.'

'Tea up,' yelled Bella. 'D'you want it in there?'

Maggie opened the door. 'If you don't mind.' Maggie took the two cups from Bella.

'What's she got to say for herself that's so private?' asked

Bella in a hushed voice, nodding her head towards the bedroom.

'I'll tell you all about it later.'

But Bella didn't look too happy as she closed the door.

'So why didn't you go back to your stall?' asked Maggie.

'I was going to, but I wanted to find out what they knew so I banged on the car window again. Well, the young one – he didn't half look wild – shoved open the door and caught me face. I fell over, and as you can see I ain't no lightweight. The old man rushed round, picked me off the ground and shoved me in the car. I tell yer, gel, I was frightened ter death. I thought they was gonner kidnap me. Anyway, they took me to the hospital, then scarpered. In the car the old one was giving this Reg a right telling off, said he was worried somebody might have seen what happened. So anyway, be the time I got out of the hospital I knew it was too late to put the stall away. I wasn't worried as I guessed Fred and Tom would do that for me, and I had to get back to Mum.' She took a gulp of her tea. 'This morning I thought I'd have a stroll round to the lockup just to see what Ada had been up to, then I thought I'd better pop in to see you and let you know what happened, and to find out if you had a nice holiday.'

Maggie sat listening. 'I'm glad you did. Yes, we had a good time. Win, I was getting worried about you.' So Tony has caused someone else pain, she thought.

'Don't worry about me. I'm all right.'

Maggie stood up. 'It ain't all right,' she shouted angrily. 'There's you, Mr Goldman, how many more? Did they tell you why they wanted Tony?'

'No.'

'It's about money. It's all about money.' She threw her arms into the air. 'He owes my brother eighteen pounds. Wally came here for his books, so God only knows what that was all about. Mr Windsor, that's the old boy's name, came here for money, and I've no idea what he owes him.' She sat down again. 'I don't know what I'm gonner do. I'm at my wits' end.' She put her head in her hands and wept.

Winnie put her arm round Maggie's shoulders. 'Go on, love, you have a good cry. Does Bella know about this?'

Maggie shook her head.

The bedroom door flew open. 'What's going on in here? What have you been saying to upset her like this?' yelled Bella.

'Bella, I think you'd best send the kids out, then we'd all better sit down and have a chat.' Winnie was still holding Maggie close.

Bella glanced from one to the other – they looked so sad and dejected. 'They've gone out to play already.'

Winnie helped Maggie to her feet and into the living room. After settling her on the sofa she said to Bella, 'You sit here with her and I'll put the kettle back on.'

They sat drinking tea while Winnie told Bella all what had happened, and then Maggie told her about Mr Windsor coming to the house, but not about Reg pushing her.

When they finished Bella walked to the window. She peered down on the market. It always looked so empty on Sundays. Apart from the trains the only sound that came drifting up was from the Salvation Army band. 'I've got something to tell you now.'

Two heads shot up.

'You know somethink?' asked Winnie.

'Just that Benny told me about this Mr Windsor. Maggs, I didn't say anythink before as I didn't want to worry you. I didn't know he'd been here.'

'Who is he?' asked Maggie.

'He's part of a big betting syndicate, and it seems Tony's mixed up with him, and, according to Benny, if anyone owes him money, he can be a very nasty piece of work. You'll have to go and see that copper of yours,' said Bella. 'You can't go on being threatened like this.'

'Look, you don't 'ave to mention to him about what happened to me, do you?' asked Winnie.

'Why's that?' asked Maggie.

'Well, as I said, it was an accident really.'

Maggie turned to Bella. 'Anyway, what can the Inspector do?'

'I'm sure he'll be able to tell you all about Mr Windsor,' said Bella.

'What if it's somethink I don't want to hear?'

'I think we've got to face up to it, gel, there's a lot we don't want to know about, but . . .' Bella sighed. 'At least we know Mr bloody Windsor ain't done nothink to Tony otherwise he wouldn't be looking for him.'

Maggie hadn't thought of that.

Chapter 18

On Monday morning, although Maggie knew she should be going to see Benny to buy stock, she thought that going to the police station was more important, even though she had promised Winnie not to mention her dealings with infamous Mr Windsor.

'Maggie,' said Inspector Matthews, when he saw her sitting in the waiting area. 'I must say you look very well after your holiday. Did you have a nice time?'

'Yes thank you.'

The young policeman standing behind the counter looked up, full of curiosity.

'Well, Mrs Ross,' said the Inspector, glancing across at him, 'what can I do for you?'

Maggie looked around.

'Come through to my office.'

Sitting in the chair he offered, she was cross with herself. Why did she always feel embarrassed in this man's company?

'I think there is something I should tell you. In fact both me and Bella – Mrs Ross – think you should know.'

David Matthews sat back and played with a pencil.

Maggie fiddled with her handbag. 'You see, there is this Mr Windsor, he keeps asking about Tony, and Saturday—'

The pencil snapping in two made Maggie jump. David Matthews threw the pieces on to his desk. He leant forward. 'Have you seen Mr Windsor?'

Maggie nodded. 'He came to the flat.'

'When?' The question came like a gun shot.

'That evening before I went in the hospital.'

David Matthews jumped up and walked round the desk. 'Why didn't you tell me before? What did he want?'

'Money that Tony owes him.'

'Which you haven't got? Maggie, now tell me the truth, did he . . . did he knock you about?'

'No.'

'Are you sure? He has a reputation, you know. And you're sure he wasn't the cause of you losing the baby?'

'Course.'

He sat on his desk facing her, his face full of concern.

She was aware of his eyes searching her face, but couldn't meet his gaze. She could feel his warmth close to her. 'I think it was just one of those things,' she said softly.

Suddenly he bent down and, taking hold of her shoulders, pulled her to her feet. 'Please, Maggie, you must be careful.'

'Inspector Matthews.' She quickly stood up, and although she wanted to melt into his arms, she pushed him away. She needed someone to hold her and take care of her, but she was married to Tony.

'Please call me David.'

Tony flooded her thoughts, and she moved away. 'That ain't very professional.'

He moved back to his seat behind the desk. 'I'm afraid I don't feel very professional when you're around.' He quickly took a cigarette from the packet that had been thrown amongst the papers that were strewn over his desk and lit it, angry with himself for almost losing his self-control.

Maggie sat down. She didn't know what to say. She had wanted him to make a pass at her, but now . . . 'Inspector Matthews,' she said slowly and very deliberately, 'I don't think Mr Windsor could have hurt Tony, otherwise he wouldn't be looking for him.'

David blew the smoke high into the air. 'That's very true, Mrs Ross.'

Maggie felt a barrier had been placed between them, and it had been her doing.

'You do know that Mr Windsor has been in prison?'

'No.' Maggie was taken aback.

'And that he runs a very large betting syndicate.'

'Bella did mention something about that.'

'Well, I believe that your husband has gone to ground because he owes a lot of people a great deal of money.'

Maggie felt her face pale.

'First there was Wally Marsh, and then—'

'Inspector, I know Tony owed money, but I do feel he would have contacted me in some way if he could. You see we love each other very much, and he would never do anything to hurt me and—'

'Maggie,' he ground his cigarette stub into the overfull ashtray, 'how can you sit there and say that when he wasn't around when you lost the baby? And he's supposed to be fond of his mother, but he hasn't got in touch with her either. And what about your lovely kids?' David Matthews lit another cigarette. 'No, I'm sorry, but I think he's gone, left the country. He knew he would be—'

Maggie jumped to her feet. 'No. You're wrong,' she cried. 'He loved me and the children, and he wouldn't go away without me. Not for good,' she added in a whisper.

'Well, what other explanation can you give for his disappearance?'

'I don't know.' She sat down.

'Would you like a cup of tea?'

She shook her head.

'Would you like me to run you home?'

She could only nod. 'I should really be going to see Benny.'

'I could take you there first if you like.'

'I'd better.'

But when they got to Benny's he was out.

The journey back to the market was silent. Maggie sat staring in front of her. She wondered what was going through David Matthews's mind, but couldn't look at him.

She would have been shocked to know that he was thinking of ways to find out the truth about Tony Ross, and with some hope, a body. That at least would settle Maggie's status – widow rather than abandoned wife.

'Did you have a special reason for coming to see me this morning?' he asked.

'Yes. I was worried about Winnie.'

'Winnie on the market?'

'Yes.'

He stopped the car. 'What's happened to her?'

'It seems Mr Windsor was in the Dog on Saturday and, Winnie reckons he was one of the last to see Tony, so she went to have a word with him, and his minder . . .'

'Reg Todd.'

Maggie nodded. 'He accidentally hit Winnie with the car door. They took her to hospital. She's all right, though,' added Maggie quickly.

He started the car again. 'It seems as if I should be having a word with our friend.'

'Who, Winnie?'

'No. Windsor.'

'I don't think that would be such a good idea.'

'Why?'

'I wouldn't want them to come back to me or Winnie.'

'Don't worry, I'll find some way of pulling him in.'

'Thank you for the lift.' Maggie didn't attempt to hang around, she didn't want him to come upstairs.

'I'll be in touch,' he called through the car window.

As she walked up the stairs she queried her own feelings. Why didn't she invite him in? The children and Bella were there. What was she afraid of?

'I'm home,' she called out, pushing the living-room door open.

''Allo, love.'

Maggie was surprised to see Benny sitting in the chair, and in his work clothes.

'Hallo, Benny. I've just been to your place. I didn't see your horse, where is she?'

'Shoved a nosebag on her and left her round the corner. Young Fred down there gets right narked when she starts rummaging among his fruit.'

'I'm not surprised,' said Maggie, glancing in the mirror as she removed her navy straw hat. 'How's business?'

'Not bad. I've brought a few bits over for you.'

'Thanks.'

'You're back quick,' said Bella,. smiling. 'Did he bring you home?'

Maggie nodded.

'I was telling Benny here that you're thinking of expanding the business.'

Maggie sat down. 'I don't know how. I've got to find the money first.'

Bella tutted and tossed her head. 'I keep telling her we should be in this thing together.'

'She's right, you know, gel. Seems these days that people have got a few more bob to spend on fripperies, and you're just the gel to sell it.' Benny leant forward. 'D'you know, I reckon with the right sort o' gear you could do very nicely down there.'

Maggie was getting tired of all this advice. 'So what gold mine do you suggest I start looking for to buy all this stuff that's gonner make me a millionaire?'

'You don't have to be so flippant about it, gel. Benny's only trying to help.'

Suddenly it all seemed too much for her. She could feel her patience snap like a broken string. 'Everyone's only trying to help, but what good is it doing? I've got two kids and a shitty business that's just about paying the rent. What am I gonner do?' she cried.

'Pull yourself together for one thing,' said Bella drily.

'I don't want to pull myself together, I want to be left alone, and I don't want to keep having handouts.'

'We're only trying to help,' said Bella haughtily.

'I shouldn't need help. If your son had been a bit more truthful and told me what he'd got himself into I wouldn't be in this state now.'

'I suppose he didn't want to worry you.'

'Worry me? Worry me? So what the bloody hell do you think he's doing to me now?'

'He must have a reason.'

'Like what? Go on, tell me. Am I suddenly gonner get a bundle of pound notes pushed through me letter box with a letter saying, "Sorry, love, but I had a few gambling debts. Here's some money to keep 'em sweet as I don't want you and your friends to worry about being beaten up"?'

'You don't have to talk to Bella like that, love,' said Benny. 'Not after she's paid for you all to have a nice holiday.'

'That's it, ain't it? She pays for this and that, she ain't got a bottomless purse. And I don't like taking money off her.'

'I did my bit towards the holiday 'cos I wanted to.'

'I know, and I'm really grateful. But I still think Tony should show himself. I hate him, d'you hear? I hate him for what he's doing to me and the kids.' Maggie sat in the chair and wept.

Bella went to put her arms round her.

'Go away. Leave me be. I don't want to keep relying on you.'

'I don't mind. After all, we are family.'

'I don't want to be family. I want to be left alone.'

'Oh very nice, I must say.' Bella began collecting the tea

things. 'I ain't staying where I ain't wanted.'

'Well, go then. And if that son of yours turns up, tell him to drop dead. That way at least you'll get his insurance.'

Bella stood riveted to the spot.

'Maggie, that's a dreadful thing to say,' said Benny, pushing his trilby back and scratching his forehead.

'That's it. I ain't staying here to listen to this sorta talk.'

'Well, go on then, shove off. Leave me alone.'

Benny looked from one to the other. 'Maggie, I don't think you should say things like—'

'And you can go, an' all. I don't want any more of your condescending handouts.' Maggie walked into her bedroom and slammed the door.

When she heard the front door shut she began to cry. At first it was a gentle cry, then as she got angrier it became a wail and she pummelled the pillow with hate, anger, and frustration.

'Maggs, Maggie? You all right, gel?' Winnie's voice broke into her distress.

She sat up and wiped her eyes.

'What the bloody hell's been going on up here?'

'Why? What d'you mean?'

'There's you looking like you've been crying for hours, and there's Bella storming off down the road, swinging her bag and pushing everybody out of the way, and poor old Benny in tow, trying to keep up. Bella's face looked like thunder. When I asked if everything was all right I just got a mouthful of abuse and told ter mind me own business.' Winnie sat on the bed.

'I told Bella to clear off,' said Maggie.

'Oh, that's very bright, I must say. Why?'

'I don't know really.' She gave a loud sob. 'I just feel I want to be left alone, I suppose.'

'Well, love, you shouldn't upset Bella, of all people. After all, she's been good to—'

Maggie jumped off the bed. 'That's the bloody trouble. She's been good to me, and all I seem to do is take from her.'

'But it's family, gel, and if we can't look after family then where would we be?'

'And I don't need you to tell me that.'

'Oh very nice, I must say. What's got into you?'

Tears filled Maggie's eyes. 'I thought it would have been obvious.'

'Course it is, love. You've probably got a bit down after losing the baby, but you've got to be positive about all this.'

'So what's your suggestion?'

'I'll put the kettle on. By the way, did you go and see your policeman?' she called from the kitchen.

'Yes,' replied Maggie.

'Well, what'd he say?'

'Not a lot really. He might pull that Mr Windsor in.'

'I ain't gonner make a complaint,' said Winnie quickly, coming back. 'Don't want the likes of him coming sniffing around.'

'He said he'd find some excuse.'

They were sitting drinking tea when Winnie said, 'You know, you'll have to make your peace with Bella.'

Maggie held her cup with both hands. 'I know. But I've got to try and find a way of managing on my own.'

'Now how yer gonner do that?'

'I don't know, Win. I really don't know.'

'What about that brother of yours? Can't he help?'

Maggie tossed her head. 'Can't see him being of any use, not with the money I owe him.'

'You mean Tony owes him as well?'

'Me, Tony, what's the odds? Helen will still want it all back.'

Winnie poured her tea in the saucer and began slurping. 'Have you heard from him lately?'

'He wrote to me when I was in hospital, but he ain't been over. Probably didn't think it was worth it till I'd got some money for him.'

'Is it much?'

'Eighteen pounds.'

'Phew, that's a tall order.'

'I know.'

'How many more does Tony owe to?'

'I dunno. And I don't know how I'm gonner pay 'em back.'

'I always liked Tony, but now after all this – well, I reckon he's turned out to be a right cowson. And if you ask me—'

'I don't want any more advice, thank you.'

'And let's hope we don't have a bad winter, 'cos it gets bloody hard down there then.'

Winter was the last thing on Maggie's mind; she was too worried about the present. 'Winnie, what am I gonner do?'

'You've just got to go on. Think of the kids.'

They sat quietly for a while, then Winnie said, 'Look, I'd better go. You all right now, love?'

Maggie nodded. 'For the time being.'

Maggie sat going over and over in her mind ways to salvage the situation, but they all came back to money, and the lack of it to make a start. She looked round the room. If the worst came to the worst, she could always pawn something, but what? This was her home and everything meant so much to her. Besides, did she really want everybody to know how bad things were?

It was Bill knocking on the living-room door that brought Maggie out of her thoughts. She had been thinking about all she'd said to Bella and Winnie. She knew she was wrong, but how could she tell them that part of the reason things were getting on top of her was the fact she needed someone to love her and look after her.

''Allo, Maggs,' said Bill, putting his leather money apron on the table and snatching his cap from off his head.

'Sit down, Bill.'

He sat on the edge of the chair. 'You all right?' he asked.

She gave him a slight smile. 'Just a bit low, that's all.'

He nervously twisted his cap in his hands. 'Maggs, I know things ain't very good down there.' He nodded towards the window. 'We've gotter start doing something soon. What chance is there of you getting more—'

'Benny did bring a few bits in. I haven't sorted them out yet. But I'm gonner see about it tomorrow. I know I should have gone out today, but, well, somethink come up.'

'I saw Bella and Benny rushing down the road. I thought they might have got some news.'

'Bella had to go home.'

'Thought it looked like she had a bee in her bonnet. Everythink all right?'

215

'Yes, she had to pay her rent in case they threw her out.'

'Oh.'

Maggie stood up. 'What sort of things do you get asked for now?'

'Don't get asked for much at all really.'

'Oh come on, Bill, people must say somethink.'

'Well, a lot of punters are doing up their places and some ask for fancy plates and pictures to put on the walls.'

'That's interesting,' said Maggie thoughtfully.

'You ain't thinking of getting that sort o' stuff, are you?'

'Don't know. Why?'

'Don't want too many breakables.'

Maggie laughed. 'And if I decide what to sell, while you're working for me, you'll do as I say.'

He flushed and looked down at his cap. 'Don't yer think Tony's coming back then?'

'I don't know.' She wanted to add that at this moment she didn't care. 'But in the meantime I've got to look after my kids, and with the winter coming, I've got to think of better ways of making a living.'

Bill stood up. 'I best be going.'

Maggie emptied the contents of the apron on to the table.

Bill moved towards the door. 'Maggs, *will* you be running the stall?'

'Some of the time. Why?'

'Nuffink. Bye.'

When she heard the front door shut Maggie began counting out the money.

'This is ridiculous. This won't keep a sparrow alive,' she said out loud, and began piling up the few coppers and silver. Two and six. Bill hadn't even earned the rent and his

216

wages today. She got her notebook from the sideboard and started a new page. She licked the lead of her pencil. 'Well, girl, this has been quite a day for you. So far you've upset Bella and Benny, and Winnie didn't look that pleased, and now poor Bill's worried about his job.'

Chapter 19

The following morning Maggie went to the auction room where Wally had worked. After studying the catalogue she waited for the auction to begin as she thought it would give her some idea what the dealers were buying.

She sat on the edge of her seat fascinated, carefully watching as item after item was sold, afraid to move in case they thought she was bidding. Bill appeared to be right. Wall plates and pictures were selling very fast, but right out of her price range.

At the end of the auction she wandered around turning over some of the goods that were left. If only she could go upmarket and not have to bother with all this rubbish. She managed to buy a few items, among which was a chipped china butter dish, a small milk jug and sugar bowl, and a glass cake stand. She was very taken with some odd bits of jewellery, and bought a couple of cheap rings, various coloured-bone bangles and round pearl button earrings that ranged in sizes. Twice she picked up a diamanté brooch and some matching earrings and twice she put them down. They were a bit more than she was prepared to spend, but would they sell?

She knew she should save some money for the rent and it was Jamie's fifth birthday next Monday. What could she get him? He would be starting school that day as well. Thank goodness she didn't have to buy him any new clothes, as Bella had already taken care of that before she left. Bella. Guilt filled Maggie. Should she go and make her peace with her? She stepped back.

'Careful, love.' An elderly, portly grey-haired man held her arm to steady her.

'Sorry.' She knew she had trodden on his foot. 'Did I hurt you?'

'No, you're only a light little thing. I see you like pretty things.' He too picked up the jewellery.

'Yes, but will it sell?'

'Depends on your clients. D'you have a shop?'

'No, a stall at the market.' Maggie began to wander to the far end of the room.

'Don't know about that trade. What sort of mark-up do you have?' he asked, trailing behind her.

'I could only put a few pence on them.'

'Do you do the buying?'

'Most of the time.'

'I don't think I've seen you here before.'

'No, I don't usually come to the auction.'

'So, what brings you here today?'

Maggie felt like telling him to mind his own business, but thought better of it. 'Do you work here?' she asked politely, ignoring his question.

He laughed. 'Good heavens no. I just pop in to buy a few bits of furniture, and to see what's selling.'

'So did I. Do you have a shop?'

He nodded. 'Inherited it from Father a few years ago. I wanted to get rid of it, but Mother won't hear of it. But I must admit it is very lucrative.'

Maggie wanted to laugh. He looked well into his fifties, so how old was Mother? Together they wandered back. 'So where's your shop then?' Maggie was drawn to the jewellery again.

'Peckham.'

'That's quite near to—' Maggie didn't know why, but she suddenly stopped. She wasn't going to tell him it wasn't that far from Rotherhithe. 'Is it just furniture you sell?'

'Yes. We like the old stuff that has real character.'

'Oh I see.'

'Could I take you for a coffee or something?'

'No I'm sorry, I have to get back.'

'You have a husband waiting for his dinner, I suppose?'

'Something like that.'

'There is another big auction at the beginning of October, perhaps I'll see you here then.'

'Perhaps.'

'Here, let me give you my card. Who knows, your husband might be interested in buying a nice antique chair or table. We have some really beautiful pieces.' He fished in his wallet and handed Maggie a card.

She laughed. 'I shouldn't think so but thanks all the same. Freeman's Fine Furniture. Sounds very grand.'

'You, my dear, will always be sure of a warm welcome at our shop.'

'Thanks, but I must go. Bye.' Maggie put his card in her handbag. Her thoughts were still on the jewellery. She would dearly love to buy it, but knew she had to be cautious. As she walked to the door she wondered what Tony would have done. 'You have to invest money to make money' was one of his favourite sayings. She suddenly stopped and turned on her heel. She had changed her mind.

There was a heart-fluttering moment as she handed over nearly all her cash for the jewellery. 'What's the odds? Nothing ventured, nothing gained,' she said bravely to herself, walking outside and patting her handbag. Although her purse was empty she was pleased with her purchases. After all, it was very pretty and bound to sell.

When Maggie turned into the market she saw Ding Dong ahead, walking towards the Dog. She quickly caught up with him.

''Allo, gel, everythink all right?' he enquired when she called his name.

'Not too bad.'

'I was just going in for a quick half. D'yer fancy one?'

She nodded. Although drinking at lunchtime was the last thing on Maggie's mind, she did want a word with him, and hopefully they might be alone, as apart from the traders not many people frequented the pub this early in the week.

Inside Maggie moved to a seat away from the bar and Rene, who was listening with rapt attention to a tale one of the breweries' reps was telling her.

''Ere y'are, gel, get that down yer.'

'Thanks, Ding Dong. I was very sorry to hear you've been pulled in again.'

'Yer, me case comes up next week. Bloody nuisance, but there you are. It goes with the job, I suppose.'

'What d'you think you'll get?'

222

'Just a fine, I reckon.' He bent his head closer. 'Yer see, if I get the right judge I'm all right as he likes a bet on the side.'

'Did Tony have many bets?'

Ding Dong laughed. 'I should say so. Must have lost a packet over the years. You still ain't 'eard nothink then?'

'No.'

'I must say I miss taking his money.'

It was Maggie's turn to look round and then move closer. 'Does he owe you much?'

Ding Dong looked uncomfortable. 'A bit.'

'How much?'

He took a swift noisy drink from his pint and wiped the froth from his lips with the back of his hand. 'Well, it ain't ser much me, yer understand, it's the big boys.'

'How much?' Maggie asked again.

'Dunno orf hand. Must be in the region of about, what, forty smackers all told.'

Maggie took a loud gasp. 'Forty pounds.' She felt sick.

'It's round about that, give or take a few quid.'

'And is some of that Mr Windsor's?'

It was Ding Dong's turn to take a loud breath. This time he moved his chair closer. 'What d'yer know about him?'

'Not a lot. He came to see me.'

Ding Dong went pale. 'He did? When?'

'A while back.'

'What'd he want?'

'Money, like everyone else.'

'Does he know Tony's done a runner?'

Maggie was playing with her glass, she looked up. 'Yes. What makes you so sure Tony's only run off?'

'Well, it stands ter reason. He owes a lot and he's gorn orf to make a few bob so that when he comes back he'll be in the clear.'

Maggie hadn't thought of that. 'But surely he would have told me where he's gone?'

'Dunno about that.' He sat back. 'Yer see, my theory is that what yer don't know, well then yer can't tell anybody, 'specially the likes of Mr Windsor.'

She certainly hadn't thought along those lines before.

'Fancy another?' He picked up his glass.

Maggie shook her head. 'No, thanks. And is some of that money Mr Windsor's?'

'Most of it.'

'What about you?'

'Nuffink really, just a couple of bob.'

'If you tell me how much I'll pay you back.'

'You don't have to do that, gel. I liked your old man. Always gave me a drink, even when he didn't win, so let's call it quits. I'll just get me pint.'

Maggie was thinking over what Ding Dong had said when Beatie came and sat next to her.

'He's had to go off.' She pointed to where Ding Dong had been standing. 'Gus wanted a bet on the two thirty. Well, how're you keeping? Bella got the kids?'

'No, they're out somewhere. They'll be yelling for their dinner soon.'

'Bella gone back home then?'

'Yes.' Maggie wasn't going to tell her why.

'So, what you been up to then?'

'I've been to the auction this morning. Thought I'd have a look round and see what's selling these days.'

224

'You finding it hard then, gel?'

'A bit.'

'So what is selling then?'

'Well I thought I'd try a few new things. Got a bit of jewellery here. Say, what d'you think?' Maggie took it from her bag and laid it on the table.

'Not bad.' Beatie picked up the brooch and turned it over. 'Give it a good clean and I reckon you should sell it OK, just as long as it didn't cost too much.'

'No, only a couple of bob for the lot.'

'Don't care for this cheap imitation stuff meself, I prefer the real thing. I must say.' She looked across at Gus. Satisfied he was busy talking she bent her head closer, 'That's something I do miss your Tony for. As you well know, now and again he'd come in with the odd trinket or two, and at a very reasonable price, and no questions asked.'

Maggie sat open-mouthed.

'Mind you, we never see you done up with yer rings and things. Me, I have ter wear me finery all the time, just in case Gus takes it into his head to sell 'em back to him, or pawn it.'

'Did you get all your rings from Tony?' Maggie asked in a hushed voice.

'Yer, most of 'em, but then you must know that. He said you didn't want 'em, said they was too flash for you.'

Maggie smiled. 'Oh yes, I forgot.' She didn't like to say that she had never seen them before they adorned Beatie's fingers. Were they real? If Tony had given them to her, at least she would have had something to pawn. But where did Tony get them from?

Beatie was still talking but her words weren't registering. 'I must go.' She stood up.

'Maggie, I said have you got your snaps yet?'

'Snaps?'

'Pictures of your holiday. Bella said she took some good ones.'

'Oh yes. No, Bella's still waiting for 'em.'

'Let me see them when you get 'em. Like to see pictures of the sea, as that's the nearest I'll ever get to it.' Beatie laughed. 'Look after yourself, gel.'

Maggie walked out into the sunshine. 'Well,' she said to herself, 'that was a very enlightening half-hour In fact it's been a very enlightening morning all round.'

Bill looked anxious when he saw what Maggie was displaying on a corner of the stall that afternoon. 'Don't know about selling all these fancy bits,' he said.

'Well, we can only give it a try.' Maggie stood back and admired her handiwork. She had carefully cleaned the bits she'd bought, and arranged the items of jewellery on a piece of black cloth she'd managed to get Tom Cooper to part with. 'I think it looks very nice.'

'Yer, 'sall right.'

Maggie smiled. She could see he wasn't impressed. 'Well it makes a change from broken lamps and rusty tools.'

'S'pose so.'

She hoped the punters would be more enthusiastic than Bill.

Chapter 20

Saturday morning Maggie was singing as she got herself ready to go down to the stall. 'Come on, you two, hurry up and finish your breakfast. I've got to go down and give Bill a hand.'

'Why?' asked Jamie.

'I like to chat to people and see what they'd like to buy.'

'Why?' asked Laura.

'I have to do the buying now, and I want to make sure it's right, otherwise we might starve.'

'We won't starve, will we, Mum?' asked Laura, worry puckering her suntanned brow.

Maggie laughed. 'Course not. Now come on.'

'Mummy, we gonner have a tea party on Monday for Jamie's birthday?' asked Laura.

'I think we could have a few children in after school.'

'I'll be all growed up then,' he said, beaming.

'Daft, you don't get grown up just 'cos you're going to school,' said Laura.

'Well, it's more growed up than being at home.'

'Stop it, you two. You'll have to tell me who's coming to this birthday tea.'

'Will Granny Ross come?' asked Jamie.

'I don't know.'

'I hope so. She gives us nice presents.'

'She didn't say goodbye,' said Laura.

'She had to leave in a hurry.'

Laura slid down from the table. 'Don't you like Granny Ross?'

'Of course I do.'

'Did you like Daddy?'

Maggie felt her heart lurch. 'I love your daddy very much.'

'So why does everybody leave us?'

Maggie was at a loss for words. What had she done turning Bella away like that? She had to go to her and make her peace, if only for the children's sake.

'Will Daddy be here for my birthday?' asked Jamie, licking the bowl that had had his porridge in.

'I'm afraid not.'

'Will he be here for my birthday on the twenty-fourth of November?' asked Laura.

'I can't promise.'

'I wish he would come back. I ain't got no one to play football with.'

Maggie stooped down and held him tight. 'I miss Daddy as well.' She blinked back a tear. It wouldn't do to let the children see her crying.

'Why don't you ask Uncle Dan to play with you? Or what about that policeman that comes to see Mum? He ain't got no kids.'

Maggie looked up at Laura. 'How do you know that?'

'I asked him.'

'Do you think he'd take me to the park?' asked Jamie eagerly.

'I don't know, he's a very busy man,' said Maggie, straightening up.

'Well, I'll ask him to come to my party, then I'll ask him to take me to the park.'

Laura gave Jamie a nudge. 'He might get you a new football.'

Jamie's eyes lit up. 'Would he? Mummy, could you ask him if he would?'

'No I won't. You can't go round asking people for presents.'

'Well then, he ain't gonner come to my party if he don't bring me a present.'

'Jamie, I can't tell him that.'

'Oh go on, Mummy. If he ain't got kids of his own he might like to take Jamie out.'

'I don't know.'

'Oh please, Mummy, please.'

Maggie smiled as she tousled Jamie's hair. 'You two have the cheek of the devil.'

'Will you, please?' pleaded Jamie, smoothing down his hair.

'I'll see, but I won't make any promises. Besides, he might be too busy. He has a lot of crimes to solve.'

Maggie was upset that this was going to be the first birthday that Tony wouldn't be around. If he was in hiding would he remember the date? If so, would Jamie get a card from him? Maggie suddenly felt hopeful. Monday could be the day she had been waiting for. 'Now come on, you two, shoo, I've got a lot to do.'

As she did the washing-up Maggie reflected further. What if Jamie did get a card from Tony? That would be the best birthday present ever, just to know he was still alive and thinking of them. Jamie needed a man around and she thought about what he'd said. Should she ask David Matthews to his tea party? Was it wrong? She smiled to herself. Well, it wasn't her idea, and he could only say no. She would go and ask him on Monday morning after the postman had called, and tomorrow she would have to go over to Bella and say sorry.

'Good ter see you down here, Maggs,' said Winnie.

Maggie nodded and grinned. Over these past few months she had enjoyed the few hours she had spent tending the stall. The noise, smell, chatter and bustle had a thrill of its own. She felt she belonged.

'I'm pleased ter see you've got a bit of new stuff,' said Winnie, picking up a ivory-coloured bone bracelet. 'I reckon that'll do all right round here. We ain't had this sorta stuff here before.'

'Well, not many have had money to spend on themselves,' said Maggie, fiddling with her display. 'I hope we take a few bob today. I've got to get something for Jamie's birthday.'

'When's that then?' asked Winnie.

'Monday.'

'Monday? I reckon this lot don't mind chipping in and getting him somethink. Here, Ada, keep yer eye out. I'm just gonner go round and squeeze a few bob out o' these tight-arsed sods. Won't be long.'

'But, Win . . .'

230

'It ain't no good you shouting after her, Maggs. She won't take no notice of yer,' said Bill. 'Once she gits a bee in her bonnet, she's off.'

Maggie laughed. Bill was right, there was no stopping Winnie when she started something.

Half an hour later Winnie returned. 'Here you are, gel. There's a few bob there.' She handed Maggie a paper bag. 'Watch the bottom don't fall out. I even managed to con a couple of bob out of Gus.'

Maggie was surprised at the weight of the bag and almost dropped it. 'Winnie, I can't take all this.'

'It's mostly pennies. 'Sides, ain't fer you, it's for young Jamie. Now go on, take it upstairs and count it out, then tell us what he wants. I reckon old George in the toy shop will knock a bit off of whatever it is.'

Maggie could feel the tears well up in her eyes. These people were so kind. 'I know he wants a football.'

'Reckon there's enough in there to get him half a dozen. No, get him somethink else. What about a scooter?'

Maggie had to wipe away a tear that had spilled over. 'He'd really love one of those. He was hoping that Tony would make him one.'

'Don't like those home-made things. He could end up getting splinters, and those bloody ball-bearing wheels make a bloody racket on these cobbles. No, get him a posh one.'

Maggie hugged Winnie, 'Thanks, I'll pop in later. Mind you, he won't want to go to school and leave it.'

'He's starting school? It don't seem five minutes ago he was born. A lot of water's flown under the bridge since then.'

Maggie could only nod and quickly turned to rearrange the items on display.

'I must say it suits you being down here.'

Maggie looked up to see Alan and Helen standing there. She pushed the paper bag out of sight. 'Hallo, you two. You look well. Where did you go for your holidays after all?'

Helen plumped up the back of her hair, and smiled. 'We went to Devon, to a lovely hotel, and we had lovely weather. You should see my tan.' Her voice was loud enough for Tom Cooper to catch.

'It ain't yer tan I'd be interested in, gel, it'll be yer white bits – that's if of course you ain't been sunning yerself in the nuddy.'

Everybody laughed and Helen went very red.

'So what you two doing round this way?' asked Maggie, dreading the answer. She quickly glanced at the bag of money; she wasn't going to part with any of that.

'We thought we'd pop Jamie's birthday present over, and the little gift we bought the children, just a small souvenir, you understand.' Helen sounded very patronising.

'That's very kind of you. Would you like to come upstairs?'

'A cup of tea would be very welcome,' said Alan. 'Are you sure you can leave the stall?'

'Course. Bill always looks after it. I'm just down here to get people's reactions to the new things I've got.'

Helen took an earring from off the display. 'I must say you seem to have got hold of some very interesting bits and pieces.'

'Do you like those?' asked Alan quickly.

'They're not bad, but not really my taste.'

Helen quickly put it back on the stall, but Maggie could sense by the way she analysed it that she liked it, so that surely was silent praise indeed.

'Won't be long,' said Maggie to Bill. 'Keep your eye on everythink.'

'Sure.' He winked.

As she made her way to her flat she hoped Alan wasn't going to ask for more money.

Helen settled herself on the sofa. 'So, where are the children, out with Mrs Ross?'

'No, she had to go home, they're around playing somewhere.'

'Don't you worry about them mixing with some of those scruffy kids down there?'

'No, they've known them all their lives.'

Helen visibly shuddered. 'Well, I'd be worried sick that they might come home with fleas or impetigo or something.'

Maggie chose to ignore that remark.

'Did you manage to get away, after all?' asked Alan.

'Yes. Bella paid for our holiday.'

'Alan said you were thinking of going to Ramsgate. Was it there you went in the end?'

'Yes, we had a lovely time,' said Maggie, smugly. 'I'll just put the kettle on.'

When she returned to the living room, Helen was busy rummaging through her bag. She brought out a small parcel. 'Here's a car for Jamie's birthday, and I bought them both a little joke cup.' She handed Maggie two tiny china cups that had 'A present from Devon' written on them, and they had holes all round the top; they also had a handle.

'You have to try and see if you can drink out of them without spilling any liquid,' she said with a smirk.

Maggie turned them round. She couldn't see Jamie and Laura getting very excited about these; they would have preferred a stick of rock.

'I'll show you how you do it,' said Helen, eagerly taking one from Maggie's hand. 'See, you drink through the hole in the handle. I thought they were very clever and I can just see your two taking them to school and fooling all the other children.'

'Thank you, they are very good.' The kettle's whistling took Maggie into the kitchen.

'How is Doreen?' Maggie asked when she returned with the tea tray.

'Very well. She's with a friend for the day. They have a very large house at Eltham,' said Helen.

It had to be a very large house, thought Maggie.

The conversation lapsed when a urgent banging on the front door sent them hurrying down the stairs.

'It's Jamie,' yelled Fred. 'He's up there, been in a fight, so Laura said.' Fred pointed in the direction of the pub end of the market.

'Oh no.' Maggie hurried up the road with Alan on her heels.

Jamie was sitting on the pavement with blood on his shirt.

'Who did this?' screamed Maggie.

'It was that boy,' said Laura, pointing at four scruffy-looking boys standing on the opposite side of the road. They began laughing and walking away.

'I'm all right, Mummy, honest.' Although Jamie had tears

in his eyes he grinned and wiped his nose with the back of his hand, spreading the blood across his face.

'Come on, I'll take you back home. And as for you lot,' shouted Maggie, 'you'd better keep your hands to yourselves otherwise you'll feel mine. He's a lot younger than you.'

'Yer, and what you gonner do, bring yer fancy copper ter give me a hiding? Look, I'm quaking in me boots,' shouted one of them.

The others started laughing.

'Saucy sods,' said Maggie. 'I've a good mind to go—'

'Leave it, Maggs,' interrupted Alan. 'It's not worth getting into a scrape over.'

She glared at Alan. 'What d'you mean? Look, he's hurt.'

'No I ain't.'

'What's going on up here?' said Winnie, puffing up to them with Helen at her side.

'Look at Jamie's nose. Those kids did it,' she pointed to the backs of the boys, 'and Alan here won't go after 'em.'

Alan looked sheepish.

'Well, Maggie, you can't expect Alan to look after your brood as well. That's Tony's job, and he should be here to—'

'Don't start, Helen,' said Alan.

'Well, didn't I say earlier that you shouldn't let your children run about in the street with all this riffraff?'

Winnie tutted and tossed her head at Helen.

Maggie felt it was best to ignore Helen and turned to Jamie. 'What was all this about?'

'They said you was a copper's nark.'

'Me?' Maggie was taken aback. 'Why did they say that?'

''Cos you go out with a copper. I told 'em you didn't go out with him, he only comes round 'cos me dad's gone away. Then they all laughed at that so I kicked the one with the cap in the shins, and he punched me on the nose.'

Winnie burst out laughing.

'I don't think it's any laughing matter,' said Maggie angrily.

'Well, he was defending your honour.'

'Come on, let me take you home and get you cleaned up.'

Maggie held Jamie's hand. In many ways she was very proud of him, certainly more than of her brother.

As soon as he was cleaned up Jamie was off out again.

'And don't get into any more arguments,' shouted Maggie behind him. She noticed Helen wince. She wouldn't shout out like that, it wasn't ladylike.

Soon after that the living-room door burst open and Eve came in, laughing.

'Jamie's pleased with himself, told me he's been in a fight, and guess what?' said Eve. 'I've just been invited to a birthday . . . Hello, Alan, and Helen. What are you doing over this way?' There was a hint of sarcasm in Eve's voice.

'We've brought young Jamie's present over.'

'That's nice of you. See you've been away as well.'

'Yes, Devon, a very expensive hotel.'

'Lucky old you. Here, Maggs, I love the new stuff you've got.'

'Do you? Do you think it will sell?'

'I should say so. Bill's sold that diamanté brooch and earrings already.'

'He has?' Maggie was overjoyed. 'I was a bit worried it might be too expensive. I'd spent over my budget, and what with Jamie's birthday coming . . . I wonder who bought them and if they'd like me to look out for more.'

'De-da!' Eve opened her bag with a flurry and produced the earrings and brooch.

'Oh Eve, you shouldn't have bought—'

'I wanted them.' She moved over to the mirror and put the earrings on. 'Well? What d'you think?'

'They look smashing,' said Maggie. 'But I can't let you pay full price. You can have 'em for what I paid for 'em.'

'I will not.'

'I can't take your money.'

'Don't talk daft, you're supposed to be making a living,' said Alan. 'And if Eve's happy paying that price, well then, that's business.'

'But she's also a friend,' said Maggie.

'Maggs, you wasn't exactly charging the earth for 'em,' said Eve, turning her head so when they caught the light they sparkled.

'There's no friendship when it comes to money,' said Helen. 'As your husband knew only too well.'

'Trust you to come out with something like that,' Maggie snapped. 'I ain't got any more money for you, Alan, if that's what you've really come for.'

'We didn't. Helen, I do wish you hadn't said that, especially in front of Eve.'

'Eve knows all about it,' said Maggie, glaring at Helen.

Helen ignored her and, taking a powder compact from her handbag, peered into its mirror and proceeded to powder her nose.

'We only came over to give Jamie his present,' said Alan, looking very uncomfortable. 'If you've finished your tea, dear, then I think we'd better go.'

Helen snapped her compact shut with a loud click. She tutted, stood up, brushed down her frock and silently left the room.

Alan kissed Maggie's cheek. 'Sorry about that.'

'That's all right. Bye, Helen,' Maggie called down the stairs.

There was no reply.

'Bye, Maggie,' said Alan. 'I'll be seeing you some time.'

When they heard the front door shut Maggie angrily banged the table. 'Why does she always have to make me so wild?'

'It's one of her charming ways,' said Eve.

'And why did she have to be here when Jamie got a punch on the nose?'

'Winnie told me what happened. He's very proud of it, you know.'

Maggie smiled. 'I know.'

'What are these?' She picked up one of the cups.

'Helen brought them for the kids. They're a joke – you have to drink out of 'em without spilling any.'

'You can't, that's impossible. It'll fall through all the holes.'

'That's the joke. You drink through the handle.'

'Oh,' said Eve, obviously not very impressed.

'Eve, did you really buy that stuff because you liked it? Or was it just to help me out?'

'I really like it, and I'll tell you something else, I reckon Helen did too.'

'I thought so, but she's probably too stuck-up to buy anything off of me.'

'That's her loss. I was watching her face through the mirror when I put them on, and she almost turned green with envy. If you can get hold of any more stuff like this I'd like to browse through it first before you put it on the stall.'

Maggie's face broke into a smile. 'I never know when to believe you.'

'Well I'll tell you this, there was two of us arguing over them.'

Maggie laughed. 'Oh yer? So how come you won?'

'I ain't telling. But I think you could be on a winner with this stuff.'

'There's only one trouble with all this.'

'What's that?'

'Where do I get the stock from?'

Eve shrugged. 'Where did you get this lot from?'

'The auction, but it's only stuff they get hold of now and again and it could be weeks before they get any more.'

'Well, don't ask me. You're supposed to be the buyer now.'

Maggie sat down. 'Eve, you know those lovely rings Beatie wears? Well, it seems Tony sold her most of 'em.'

'No.' She laughed. ''Ere, you ain't thinking of going in for the real stuff, are you?'

'No, don't talk daft. What I'm saying is that Beatie thought I knew all about it, but I didn't.'

'So, he done a few deals on the side. You always knew that.'

'Yes, but not very expensive stuff.'

'So how do you know they were expensive?'

'Beatie said she only liked the real thing.'

'But we don't know they're real, do we?'

'But Beatie would have. I expect she's had 'em valued.'

'Dunno about that. She couldn't very well take 'em into a proper jeweller's now, could she? They could have been knocked off.'

'But Tony would have known.'

'Exactly. Let's face it, gel, your Tony could spin a right old tale when he wanted to, and he was a bit of a rogue one way and another.'

'Yes I know.' Maggie stood up and went over to the window. She looked down to the market. 'But what did he do with the money?'

'He must have gambled it away,' said Eve softly.

'Eve, this bloke Mr Windsor – he runs a betting syndicate – Tony owes him forty pounds.'

'Bloody hell.'

Maggie turned. 'Eve, I'm so frightened.'

Eve went to her friend and held her close. 'I know.'

'What am I going to do?'

'I wish I knew, Maggs. I only wish I knew.'

Chapter 21

When Eve left, and the children had finished their dinner, Maggie was down on the market again. It was then she found out from Bill how Eve had managed to buy the bits of jewellery. She was telling the truth, there was another woman interested in it, but Eve had offered more money.

'Was that wrong, Maggs?' asked Bill, looking worried.

'No, course not. After all, business is business.' But Maggie wasn't really pleased about it. She felt Eve might have done it out of sympathy, and she didn't want people feeling sorry for her.

A number of the other small pieces of jewellery had gone and that cheered her up, and she hoped that once she found another source to buy from, it could be the turning point in her fortunes.

She stood with the warm comforting sun on her back, trying to work out the best way to display to its advantage any future stock. She enjoyed talking to the women that came and browsed, and managed to get a few ideas of what they would like to see. Some did ask after Tony, but she found their questions difficult to answer. One or two wanted to know if he'd been banged up inside. Prison was a part of

241

life round here. All she said was he had to go away, which got her a few funny looks.

Throughout the afternoon the noise and patter from her fellow traders was interrupted by the Blackshirts once more. Today they seemed louder and more intrusive than usual. Once or twice Maggie looked up, concerned that when the arguing and heckling got to the pushing and shouting stage it was beginning to get out of hand.

She told the children to keep well away from them. 'Stay down this end of the market.'

'You all want ter be bloody well locked up,' shouted Winnie to them. 'Go on, sod off.'

A young man wearing a black shirt came across to Winnie. He was tall and slim, and stood over her menacingly. 'When Hitler's race takes over this country, you, old woman, had better watch out.'

'Don't you talk ter me like that, you saucy sod. I remember what happened in the last lot, and what a bleeding bunch of savages the Germans was.'

'What's up, Win?' asked Tom Cooper, coming and standing next to her. He was as tall as the youth, but a lot broader.

'This young whippersnapper 'ere reckons we're all gonner be put down when the Germans get here.'

There was a catch in Winnie's voice, and Maggie could almost feel the sorrow and anger that was written over her face.

Tom Cooper went up close to the young man and with his finger poked him in the chest. 'Clear orf. Don't come round here causing trouble, 'cos we don't like the likes of you mouthing orf.'

The young man, who Maggie noted had gone white with

temper, clenched his fists. He looked around at all the hostile faces closing in on him, turned and walked away.

Fred moved up to Tom. 'Think they bloody well know it all. I tell ycr, mate, if there's another war I reckon we'd flatten 'em.'

'D'yer reckon there will be another set-to then, Fred?' asked Winnie.

'Wouldn't like ter say. Tell yer something, though, it'll be a bit different to the last lot.'

'What, the war to end all wars?' commented Tom Cooper cynically.

'Don't say that,' said Maggie. 'I couldn't bear it.'

'Well, I ain't got no one to lose this time,' said Winnie, walking away.

'My dad fought in the war,' said Bill. 'He got a bit of shrapnel in his leg. Me mum keeps it in a box on the mantelpiece.'

Maggie looked surprised. 'I didn't know that.'

'Never told anyone, only Tony.'

'Is he all right now?'

'No, he died a while back.'

Maggie stood and looked at Bill. Tony had never mentioned anything about him or his family in the years Bill had worked for him. Maggie felt sad that all Bill's mother had left of his father was a bit of shrapnel in a box.

Maggie turned away. Over these past months there had been a lot of things she was finding out about Tony, the main one being that he had never told her very much at all.

At the end of the day Maggie went upstairs and left Bill to put the stall away. The squeaking of the stalls and barrows' wheels as they rumbled over the cobblestones mixed with the chatter and noise drifting up through her open window.

Suddenly there was a lot of shouting and yelling and an almighty crash of glass. Maggie hurried to her window to see some of the Blackshirts running away laughing. She leant out and saw Tom, Fred and Bill hurrying from the lockup. They stopped in front of Mr Goldman's window. Glass was strewn over the pavement.

'You two stay here, I'm just going downstairs,' she said to the two anxious children's faces that looked up at her.

'Mummy, Mummy, please don't leave us,' cried Laura, her face full of fear as she threw herself at Maggie's legs.

'It's that man, he's come back again.' Jamie too rushed up to her with tears spilling from his eyes.

Maggie held them both. 'No it ain't that man. I told you, he's dead. It's just some silly young blokes throwing a brick through poor old Mr Goldman's window, and I've just got to make sure he's all right. I won't be long. You look out and see.' Maggie edged them towards the window. 'See, Tom, Fred and Bill's down there.'

'So why must you go?' asked Laura.

'Just in case Mr Goldman's been hurt.'

'Like when that nasty man pushed him?' said Laura.

'Yes, love.'

'Why don't people like Mr Goldman? He's nice,' said Jamie.

'I'm afraid there are some very stupid people out there. Now let me go, and I'll be back in a mo.'

A small crowd had gathered and Mr Goldman stood with his head bent, surveying the damage.

'Mr Goldman, Mr Goldman,' shouted Maggie as she pushed her way through.

He looked up.

'Are you all right?'

He came over to her. 'Yes thank you, dear. As it was Saturday I was out in my back room. Silly young things.'

'Has someone called the police?' she asked.

'Na. It's always the same, you never see a bleeding copper when you want one.' Tom looked very pointedly at Maggie.

'There's not a lot of point,' said Fred, coming over to them. 'We know who they was but we've got to prove it, and they're sure to stick together on their story.'

'I'll tell yer if I got me hands round their throats I'd give 'em Hitler.' Tom Cooper looked very angry.

'Why did they pick on Mr Goldman's window?' asked Maggie.

He took hold of her hand and gently patted it. 'I'm a Jew, my dear, and I'm afraid Hitler and some of his fellow men don't like us.'

'I think that's awful.'

'So does nearly everyone, but he has a very powerful charisma, and some people are beginning to think like he does.'

'Well, with a bit of luck they won't be round this way again,' said Tom Cooper. 'Otherwise they'll have us lot to answer to.'

Gradually the people began to disperse.

'We've got some tarpaulins in the lockup,' said Fred. 'So

Tom, young Bill here and me will nail 'em to your window for now, and we'll get all this glass cleared away.'

'Thank you, that's very kind of you.'

'Are you sure you're all right?' asked Maggie again.

Mr Goldman nodded. 'Yes thank you, my dear. You go on up to the children, they look very uneasy.'

Maggie looked up at the two small faces peering down on them. They did look very worried.

For a while the sound of banging filled the air as the tarpaulin was fixed over the window. Maggie sat thinking about what had been said about Hitler. Please don't let there be another war, she prayed silently. I've got enough to worry about as it is.

On Sunday afternoon Maggie and the children were on the train to Downham. She was very apprehensive. What sort of greeting would they get? But it was for Jamie's sake she had made the effort, and hoped Bella would also let bygones be bygones.

Her fears had been unfounded, for when the front door was opened they were as usual clutched to Bella's ample bosom like a long-lost tribe. She wasn't the kind of person to hold a grudge.

'What a lovely surprise,' she said, taking the children's faces and kissing them all over. 'And who's got a birthday then tomorrow?'

Maggie noted the expression on Jamie's face. He smiled weakly but didn't comment. Maggie guessed he was worried about a present.

As they marched down the passage Bella said over her shoulder, 'I was gonner get Benny to drop a little something off, but now you're here he don't have to bother.'

Jamie squeezed his mother's hand, and she looked down to see a very broad grin spread across his face.

Maggie was surprised to see Benny sitting at the kitchen table. He was very spruce and had even taken his trilby off, showing his sparse grey hair.

'Benny, I was coming over to see you this week.'

''Allo, love.' He stood up and kissed her cheek. 'I must say you're all looking well.'

'Benny come over and did a spot of gardening for me, so I give him a bit of dinner,' said Bella quickly, almost as if making an excuse for his presence.

'She's a grand cook,' said Benny proudly.

'I know,' replied Maggie. 'So, how's business then?'

'Not too bad. Managing to keep me head above water, as they say.'

'Where's your horse?' asked Laura.

'She's back home in her stable. Got her nose in her feed bag, I shouldn't wonder.'

'Why didn't you bring her to see Granny Ross?'

'I don't somehow think Granny Ross would like that.'

'I know bloody well I wouldn't. Christ, could you see me neighbours' faces if they had a horse and cart stuck outside all afternoon?'

'Still, they wouldn't have to go far for manure for their rhubarb,' laughed Benny.

'What do they want manure on their rhubarb for?' asked Jamie.

'To make it grow,' said Benny.

'Then they eat it?' Jamie's blue eyes were wide open with amazement.

'Lovely,' said Benny, grinning. 'I likes a nice bit of the old rhubarb pie.'

'Ehg!' said Laura. 'That's not very nice.'

'It smells,' said Jamie, holding his nose.

'Here y'are, kids, take this lemonade into the garden,' said Bella.

'Bella was telling me you're thinking of getting some new stuff. Any idea what line you're looking for?'

'Can I have a biscuit?' asked Jamie.

'Jamie,' said Maggie sternly, 'what have I told you? You wait to be asked.'

'Yer, I know, but when you grown-ups start talking you forgets all about us.'

'As if we could forget you,' said Bella, pulling him close and kissing him again.

This time Jamie did rub his cheek.

'Go on, off with you.' Maggie gave him a light pat on the bottom.

'So, he'll be five tomorrow?' said Bella.

'Yes, and they're back at school as well.'

'A big day for the boy then?' said Benny.

'Yes, I only wish his father was here to see it.' Maggie had a job to keep the sob from her voice.

'Still heard nothing then?'

'No, Benny, nothing. Bella, I'm giving Jamie a little tea party tomorrow after school, any chance of you getting over?' Maggie wanted to get away from the subject of Tony, which was still very painful to her.

'Don't think I can, love. See how I feel in the morning.'

'Ain't you well?' Maggie was suddenly filled with guilt as well as alarm.

'Just a few twinges. This leg still ain't right.'

'Keep telling her to go back to the quack, but you know what she's like.'

Maggie smiled, pleased Benny was concerned about Bella.

'Maggs, I've been thinking,' said Bella. 'D'you think if Tony's – you know – all right and hiding somewhere, he might send Jamie a birthday card.'

'I've been thinking that as well. I'll be down those stairs like a shot in the morning.' Maggie sat back and wiped her cheek with the back of her hand. 'It would be the best present ever,' she sniffed.

'Yer, well, don't hold out too many hopes, gel,' said Benny, clearing his throat.

'Talking of presents . . .' Bella hurriedly left the kitchen.

Maggie blew her nose. 'There was a set-to at the market last night. Those bloody Blackshirts broke Mr Goldman's window.'

'No! Did you hear that, gel?' said Benny to Bella when she returned holding a parcel. 'Did the police come?'

'No, he didn't want them to.'

'Poor old bugger,' said Bella. 'I dunno what this world's coming to. Is he all right?'

Maggie nodded.

'By the way, there's the photos of our holiday. They're very good, if I say so meself. You staying for a bit of tea?'

'If that's all right.'

'Wouldn't bloody well ask yer if it wasn't.'

'Can I take these and show Win?'

'Course.'

'We mustn't stay too long. Remember school tomorrow.'

Bella sat down. 'Little Jamie starting school. I bet you'll shed a few tomorrow.'

Maggie could only nod. Tears were very close today. She knew that tomorrow her baby would be, as he would say, 'all growed up', and there wasn't another one to fill his place.

Chapter 22

It was very early and Maggie lay in bed listening to the whoops of delight as Jamie rushed into the living room and began opening his presents. He was shouting for Laura and Maggie to come and see what he'd got.

Could this be the day she had been waiting nearly four months for? At last some sign that Tony was still alive? Would he send Jamie a card or present?

Maggie slipped on her dressing gown. It would be a while before the postman came.

Jamie, wearing the Red Indian outfit Bella had given him, was racing round the room on his scooter. Thank goodness it has rubber tyres and not those noisy ball-bearing wheels, thought Maggie as she quickly jumped out of his way. 'After school you must go round and thank all the traders. And you mind the paint work, young man.'

Jamie grinned. 'The truck Auntie Eve give me is just like the one Uncle Dan drives. He said he'd take me out in it one day. Can I go, Mummy?'

'I should think so.'

Between getting breakfast, helping to open presents and getting the children ready for school, Maggie watched and listened for the postman. She worried that Jamie might be sick with all the excitement.

Suddenly the plop of letters falling to the floor raised a yell from Jamie and he rushed from the room.

'Be careful,' she shouted after him. 'Don't fall down the stairs.'

He raced back into the living room, clutching an assortment of envelopes. 'I'll open 'em, then you can read 'em to me.'

'Let me help,' said Laura.

'No,' he said, hiding them behind his back.

'Oh, Mummy, tell him to let me.'

'Now sit at the table, both of you, and we will read them together.' Maggie's hands were trembling as one by one Jamie handed her each birthday card to read. Apart from the usual ones from all the market traders, Eve and Dan, Alan and Bella, there was one from David Matthews.

'You gonner ask him to my party this afternoon?' asked Jamie.

'I'll see.'

'Oh Mummy, you promised.'

'He may be too busy.'

Gradually the collection of envelopes was reduced to a heap of litter, and the cards carefully stacked on the sideboard.

'I'll put them all up properly later,' said Maggie, taking some of the dirty dishes into the kitchen. 'Now come on, get dressed, it's nearly time for school.'

In the kitchen, away from the children's eyes, she stood and let her tears fall. Had Tony forgotten Jamie's birthday?

'Mummy, would you tie my tie for me?'

Maggie turned and through her tears smiled at her son standing there looking very smart in his new white shirt and grey trousers, with his tie hanging round his neck.

'Mummy, what you crying for?'

Maggie bent down and hugged him. 'I'm crying 'cos my baby's all growed up and leaving me.'

'I ain't leaving. I'm only going to school round the corner.'

'If that hospital had let you have that baby it promised you, you wouldn't be left on your own.'

Maggie looked up to see Laura standing in the doorway. She had never mentioned the baby since Maggie had first come home from the hospital.

'Yes, darling, you're right. But we can't always have what we want.'

'I asked God to let Daddy come to my party,' said Jamie. 'D'you think he will?'

Maggie thought her heart would break. 'I don't know.' She wiped her eyes, gave a little laugh and tousled his hair. 'I'm being silly. Now stand still while I try to do a proper knot.' This should be your job, Tony, she thought. She was sure Tony wouldn't let his son's birthday pass without something. Perhaps the next post would bring the long-awaited answer.

Maggie helped Jamie on with his new blazer that Bella had bought, and tucked up the sleeves. 'You'll soon grow into this.'

When they got down into the market most of the traders were standing looking at Mr Goldman's window.

''Allo, love. Fancy those bleeders doing this,' said Winnie to Maggie. 'If I had my way I'd kick all their arses. Do the police know about this?'

'He didn't want any fuss,' said Fred.

'See you in a jiff,' Maggie said to them as she shepherded Laura and Jamie past. She didn't want them to start asking questions and getting upset about the incident again.

Winnie began to walk back to her stall with Maggie, but Jamie hung back. Winnie glanced over her shoulder and, giving him a wink asked, 'So, who's this young man you're walking out with then, Maggs?'

'Don't you go messing me hair up, 'cos Mum's put water on it to keep it down. And don't kiss me.'

Maggie laughed. 'Well, he was my baby till this morning, now he's all growed up.'

Jamie took hold of his mother's hand.

'I won't kiss you then, not today. Happy birthday, son,' Winnie laughed, but Maggie noted her eyes became watery.

Alone with her thoughts, Maggie walked back very slowly from the school.

'All right then, gel?' asked Winnie. 'It must be a great wrench when the last one goes.'

She nodded and said sadly, 'I was hoping there'd be a birthday card from Tony.'

Winnie didn't have an answer.

'I'll get Jamie to bring you down a bit of cake after his party.'

'Blimey, how big's this cake?'

'Not very big, but we've only got about four or five kids coming. I only hope they bring handkerchiefs this time. At Laura's they didn't stop sniffing, and a couple had the longest candles you ever saw.'

'That was in the winter,' said Winnie. 'We all get candles then, especially standing around out here.'

Maggie laughed. 'I'd better start getting ready for 'em.'

While Maggie was busy preparing for the tea party, someone banged on the front door. Maggie froze. Who would come calling at this time of morning? Her heart lifted. Could it be her Tony? There was no key behind the door now. She ran down the stairs and flung open the door.

'It's you.'

'Who were you expecting?' asked David Matthews.

'Well, certainly not you. You'd better come in,' she said before she had time to think about it. She looked up and down the market. Everybody was busy so perhaps she wouldn't get too many remarks.

David removed his trilby and followed her up the stairs. 'I had to come over to see Mr Goldman and his window.'

Maggie pushed open the living-room door. 'But I thought he didn't want the police involved. Have a seat.'

'He didn't.' David sat down. 'The officer on the beat saw the window had been smashed, so he called in and asked him what it was about. When I heard about it I thought I'd come over and have a word, just to make sure it was Blackshirts and not our friends back again.'

Maggie flinched at the thought of Mr Windsor. 'That was a good idea. Thank you for Jamie's birthday card.'

'It's my pleasure. Looks as if he's had plenty.'

'Yes.' She wanted to say, But not from the one person he really wanted one from. 'Would you like a cup of tea?' she said instead.

'If it's not too much trouble.'

'I was coming over to see you later.'

'You were?' He looked concerned.

'Yes. Jamie would like you to come to his birthday tea. I

told him you may be too busy.'

'I'd love to come. As a matter of fact I've got a present for him. Has he got a football?'

'No, but that was high up on his list.'

'I was going to bring it over after school anyway.'

'Well, you'll certainly be his favourite today.'

David's eyes met hers. 'What about you?'

Maggie felt embarrassed and quickly looked away. 'I don't know what you mean.'

'I'm sorry. How did he take going to school?'

'Couldn't wait to leave me. I just about managed to give him a kiss.'

'He's a fine lad.'

'He looked so grown up in his blazer and tie. I only hope I've tied it right.' Maggie's voice had a slight catch in it. 'I'll put the kettle on. There's the photos from our holiday on the sideboard,' she called from the kitchen.

David Matthews came into the kitchen holding the photographs. 'These are good. It looks as if you had a nice time.'

'Yes we did,' said Maggie filling the teapot. 'Would you like a biscuit?'

'No thanks.' He followed her back into the living room.

'I was hoping Tony might have sent him a card but . . .' Once again tears welled up in her eyes.

'Maggie, I honestly think you've got to accept that something has happened to Tony.'

'I'm beginning to feel that way as well. If he was alive I'm sure he would have sent him at least a card.' Maggie fished in her overall pocket for her handkerchief.

David took her hand. 'I don't like to see you so upset.'

His sympathy warmed her and the tears flowed.

'Please don't cry.' He put his arm round her shoulders and held her close.

'I'm sorry,' she sniffed, 'but the thought of Jamie starting school just . . .' She looked up at him and their lips met, gently at first, then with a passion that surprised her. She wanted to be loved.

'I'm sorry,' he said, breaking away. 'I shouldn't have done that.'

Maggie blushed and bent her head self-consciously. 'Well, I didn't exactly stop you, did I?'

'No, but I was in the wrong.'

Maggie moved away. 'I must get on.'

'Of course.'

'You will come back this afternoon?'

'If you're sure.'

'Yes, I'm sure,' she whispered.

Jamie came racing out of school and Maggie couldn't believe her eyes. His shirt was out of his trousers, his socks were down inside his shoes, and his tie skew-whiff. He had a grin from ear to ear on his cheeky face.

'Well, did you like it?'

'It was smashing. The bestest day of me life.'

'Good. What happened to that smart little lad I sent to school then?'

'You should have seen him in the playground, Mummy,' said Laura. 'He was tearing about like a mad thing. I told my friends he wasn't really my brother.'

'Oh Laura, how could you?'

Laura pouted. 'Well, he was mad.'

Maggie laughed. 'Come on, let's get back home and get

you tidied up, young man, before your friends arrive.'

'Did you go and see that policeman?' asked Jamie.

'He had to see Mr Goldman, so he popped in.'

'Is he coming?'

'Yes.'

'Great. Has he got me a present?'

'You'll have to wait and see.'

Jamie skipped and ran all the way home, not stopping to talk to anybody.

An hour later two other boys, and a girl to keep Laura happy, were sitting at the table eating fish-paste sandwiches followed by jelly and ice cream.

Only one little boy had a cold, and when he wasn't sniffing he made full use of his shirtsleeve.

'That policeman ain't come,' said Jamie grudgingly.

'Don't talk with your mouth full,' said Maggie. 'I expect he'll be here later. He is a very busy man.'

Maggie took some of the plates into the kitchen. She leant against the cooker and gently touched her lips. She didn't want to admit to herself how much she had enjoyed his kiss. She only knew it had to be wrong.

The knock on the front door sent Jamie flying down the stairs to answer it.

'Mummy, Mummy, look what the policeman give me.' Jamie thrust a football into her hands.

'It's very nice,' was all she could manage to say.

'I've got Saturday off, so could I take Jamie to the park?'

'Please, Mummy, please.'

'How can I refuse? But only if you're sure.'

David Matthews looked at her and his smile softened. 'Oh I'm sure all right.'

Maggie couldn't take her eyes away from his. She wanted him to kiss her and hold her again, and she knew he was thinking the same.

'What time?' asked Jamie, breaking the spell.

'Whenever it suits you, young man.'

'I'll be up early.'

'Can you stay long?' Maggie asked David.

'I'm off duty.'

'That's good. Now you can see me blow out me candles,' said Jamie.

'I'd better light them first,' said Maggie.

David followed her into the kitchen. 'I could stay all evening, if that's all right with you.'

She knew she should be saying no, but her heart was ruling her head. 'That would be nice.'

The cake with its five candles blazing was duly carried into the living room. The loud off-key rendering of 'Happy Birthday to You' brought a big smile to Jamie's cherubic face. He took a deep breath and quickly blew the candles out.

'Did you make a wish?' asked Maggie.

He nodded.

'Tell me,' said Laura.

'No, 'cos it won't come true if I tell.'

Maggie kissed his cheek. 'That's right. You let it be your secret.'

At last the children left. David was in the kitchen helping Maggie with the washing-up.

'I haven't been to a tea party for years,' he said, placing a plate in the cupboard. 'I'd almost forgotten how to play blind man's buff.'

'We always have a few children in for tea on their birthdays.'

'You are very lucky, they are smashing kids.'

'Thanks.'

'Tony's a lucky bloke.'

'David,' she put the washing-up mop down and faced him, 'if he was alive I'm sure he would have sent Jamie a card. I think I have to really believe he must be . . .' her voice had a sob in it and she couldn't bring herself to say the word, it sounded so final.

It was just as the children were going to bed that Eve and Dan came in, and after the good-night kisses the first question Eve asked was, 'Did he get a card from Tony?'

Maggie shook her head. 'By the way, Eve, Dan, this is Inspector Matthews.'

David stood up. 'Please, call me David.'

'Are you here on official business then, David?' asked Eve.

'No, I was this morning. Had to come over to see about Mr Goldman's window.'

'That was bloody awful,' said Dan. 'Want locking up, the lot of 'em. When's he getting the new glass in then?'

'Tomorrow.'

'That was a bit of luck for you,' said Eve, 'having to come over here for that.'

'Yes, it was, then it seems I'd been invited to Jamie's party.'

'Oh?' said Eve, raising one of her finely pencilled eyebrows quizzically.

'I think Jamie only invited him hoping to get another present,' Maggie said quickly.

'And did he?' asked Eve.

'Yes, David gave him a football.'

'I bet you was the most popular bloke,' said Dan.

'It did go down rather well,' said David.

'And the fact he's taking him to the park to play on Sat'day,' said Maggie.

'Not on duty then?' asked Eve.

'No, not unless somebody murders somebody.'

'Well, let's hope it's a quiet day for you.' Eve sat back on the sofa.

'I think I'd better be off. It's been very nice meeting you all.'

Maggie went down to the front door with David. 'Thank you for Jamie's football.'

'Don't mention it. And I'll see you on Saturday.'

'Yes,' said Maggie. 'That'll be nice.'

Maggie was a little disappointed that he made no attempt to kiss her good night and as she made her way upstairs said under her breath, 'And I really look forward to Saturday.'

'Well,' said Eve, echoing Maggie's thoughts, 'did he kiss you good night?'

Maggie could feel herself blushing and quickly turned away. 'Don't talk daft.'

'Let's face it, he is rather dishy.'

'He don't seem to be a bad bloke – for a copper, that is. That was nice of him to give Jamie a football,' said Dan.

'Is he married?' asked Eve.

'He was. His wife died; she had TB.'

'That was rotten for him. Where does he live?'

'Greenwich way, I think. Eve, you're so bloody nosy.'

'Just keeping a beady eye out for me best friend.'

'Yer, I bet.'

'Greenwich way, eh? Very smart too, and he is rather nice – and you could do worse than keep him hanging around.'

'I don't want him hanging around,' Maggie protested.

'Come on you two, give it a rest,' Dan chipped in. 'Eve, we'd better be off, got a busy day tomorrow.'

'OK.' Eve stood up. 'I'll tell you somethink for nothink: I reckon he fancies you. He's got that look in his eyes.'

Maggie laughed. 'Go on, scram.'

When Maggie closed the front door she stood leaning against it for a while. Eve was right. He was nice, and Maggie knew she could be very happy and relaxed in his company, and feel very safe, which was something she hadn't done for quite a long time.

Chapter 23

Maggie had taken the children to school, and as she returned the noise and hubbub from the glaziers repairing Mr Goldman's window brought back to her Saturday's scene. She hoped it wasn't going to be repeated. What if Mr Goldman had been near that window or, worse still, her children playing there? She shuddered at the thought, and carried on with the tidying up. All the while she was thinking about stock. Most of the rough bits and pieces Tony had bought in the past were still stuck on the stall. The china and odds and ends she'd bought had gone. She had to go and see Benny. Just lately he seemed to be coming up with some real bargains at very reasonable prices that enabled her to put on good mark-ups. She had asked him if he was charging her the right price, but he'd grinned and said he was in this business to make money, not do anybody favours. Maggie's thoughts went to Bella. Did Benny sell her, Maggie, the stuff cheap because he was sweet on Bella, or was Bella paying the difference?

Maggie was about to put their holiday photographs in the sideboard drawer when the card that the old gentleman she'd met at the auction room had given her caught her eye.

Freeman's Fine Furniture. Peckham High Street. She stood studying it for a moment or two. Maybe he would know where she could buy some more jewellery at a reasonable price.

That's what she wanted to sell, and she decided that instead of seeing Benny she would go along and ask this acquaintance. After all, she had to find another supplier soon.

It wasn't a very long bus ride to Peckham and not many shoppers were out and about on a Tuesday morning. She pushed open the door to Freeman's and the bell above rang loud and frantic. She peered into the drab interior. It took a moment or two for her eyes to adjust to the gloom. The musty smell of old furniture mixed with wax polish filled Maggie's nostrils. The showroom was full of large heavy-looking items. She wandered over to a beautiful table and carefully ran her fingers over the wood. It looked very expensive.

'Yes?' An abrupt deep voice made her spin round. An old woman emerged from the shadows at the far end of the room. She had draped round her bent shoulders a bright red silk shawl with a deep fringe that swayed as she moved. She leant heavily on a stick and shuffled towards Maggie.

'Oh, could I speak to . . .' Maggie stopped. She didn't know the man's name. She smiled the broadest smile she could muster. 'I think it must have been your son, Mr Freeman? I met him at the auction room. He told me about your shop.' Maggie felt very nervous and intimidated by this old woman, whose eyes appeared to be very dark brown, almost black, and penetrating. As she got nearer, Maggie could see the skin on her wrinkled and lined face was practically translucent, and her hands liver-spotted.

'My son? What do you want with my son?'

'I would like to ask him about buying stock.'

'Stock? What kind of stock? And pray, where is your shop? We don't want any competition round here, young lady.'

'I don't sell furniture. I have a stall on Kelvin Market. I sell jewellery.'

'Jewellery? We don't sell jewellery. What do you want with my son?'

'I met your son last week at the auction room. I wondered if he knew of anywhere else I could buy from.'

'Get out.'

'I beg your pardon.' Maggie drew herself up to her full five foot three.

'I said get out. We don't want the likes of you dirty old costermongers round here, common market trash, you lot are.'

Maggie was boiling with anger. 'How dare you speak to me like this? I ain't a costermonger. I only came to see your son, not to be insulted by the likes of you.'

'Get out.' The old woman flapped her hand as if shooing a fly away. 'I've met your sort before, coming round here on any pretext to get your hands on my Charles and his money. Little gold-digger.'

Maggie stood with her mouth wide open. 'I ain't after your son. I'm a married woman with a couple of kids.'

'That's what they all say. Now get out, d'you hear? Get out.' She raised her stick menacingly. Maggie flew for her life.

Maggie stood for a while outside the shop, trembling,

trying to gather herself together before she found the strength to move away. Her mind was in a turmoil. What sort of woman was this? And how could they do any business with a woman like that around? And what about that poor man – fancy having a mother like that.

Maggie caught sight of a café on the opposite side of the road. She quickly crossed over, went in and sank into a chair.

'You all right, love?' asked the large woman behind the counter. Her face below her white mobcap was flushed and jovial-looking.

'Yes thank you.'

'Look a bit peaky ter me. What d'yer fancy?'

'A cup of tea, please.' Maggie noted she was the only customer.

Strong tea in a thick cup was duly placed in front of her.

Maggie couldn't believe what had just happened, and felt she had to tell someone. 'I've just been into Freeman's.'

'Was you on your own?'

Maggie nodded.

The woman laughed and, wiping her hands on the front of her white overall, went behind her counter. 'I bet you've just seen old mother Freeman. She's a nutter. Every young pretty girl what walks into that shop she thinks is a potential threat to her.'

'Why?'

'She don't want anybody to take her dear Charlie away from her.'

'I only went in to ask him about stock. I couldn't believe it. I thought she was going to hit me with her stick.'

'Yer, she can be a bit frightening at times.'

'So where does she keep her precious Charlie then?'

'He was probably out delivering furniture. They have a very good business over there – well, ever since Charlie took it over.'

'I can't see how, not with a mother like that.' Maggie sipped her tea then sat back. 'I've certainly had a wasted journey then.'

The woman leant on the counter. 'So what sorta furniture was you looking for?'

'Not furniture. I sell bits and bobs on a stall, and I was thinking of selling jewellery.'

The door opened and another customer walked in, carrying a round wicker basket. Maggie couldn't see what was inside. Her long black tangled hair was twisted and pinned on top of her head. She was wearing a voluminous black frock that reached the ground and she looked very gypsy-like.

'Tea and a bit of dripping toast please, Doris. And I'll have some of that lovely thick jelly from the bottom on it if yer don't mind.' She took a sprig of heather from her basket and walked towards Maggie.

'Here, girl,' Doris shouted over. 'Lil here might be able to help.'

Maggie looked at the woman. She was unkempt and looked as if she hadn't two ha'pennies to rub together, so Maggie couldn't see how she could help her.

Lil came and sat at Maggie's table. 'Buy some lucky white heather, love. And what's she on about?' She inclined her head towards Doris.

'She's just had an encounter with old mother Freeman,' said Doris.

Lil threw her head back and laughed. 'I bet you gave her something to think about. Was you after her Charlie?'

'No I wasn't.' Maggie was getting fed up with this conversation.

'So, gel, what was yer after?'

Maggie was a bit apprehensive about telling this woman what she wanted. But she didn't have much choice in the circumstances, and who knew, she may be able to help her. 'I've got a stall,' she wasn't going to say where, 'and I'm looking for some stock. I'd like to buy jewellery. Only cheap stuff, you understand.'

Lil sat forward. 'Paste, glass, that sorta thing?'

'Yes,' said Maggie, leaning forward eagerly. 'Do you know where I—'

'Dunno. What's it worth ter me?'

'I'm sorry. I don't understand.'

Lil turned to Doris. 'See she ain't been in this business long. Look, love, you don't ever get something for nuffink, even information has ter be paid for.'

Maggie sat back. She suddenly thought about Tony. What would he say in this situation? 'How do I know what you're telling me is good information?'

Lil laughed again. 'Maybe she ain't ser green. Pay fer me cuppa and toast and I'll tell you fer nuffink.'

'Two cups please, Doris.'

When Doris put them and Lil's toast on the table she too sat down with them.

Lil poured the tea into her saucer and began to drink making loud slurping noises.

Maggie sat there staring.

'Couldn't take her anywhere, could you?' said Doris.

'Here, watch it, gel,' said Lil, wiping her mouth with the back of her hand. 'Otherwise I'll take me custom elsewhere. Now listen, young lady. If you go along to Percy's Emporium, and tell him Lil sent yer, he'll see yer all right.'

'What's an emporium?' asked Maggie.

'A posh name for a shop that sells a load of old rubbish,' said Doris.

Maggie looked at Lil. 'I don't want to buy a lot of rubbish.'

'Don't listen to her,' said Lil. 'He does a good line in costume jewellery, and if you buy a few bits he'll give you a good discount.'

Maggie was trying hard to suppress her delight. 'So where is this Aladdin's cave then?'

'Over the Elephant, I'll write his address down for yer.' She produced some paper from her basket and much to Maggie's surprise, wrote the address in a well-formed hand. 'And don't ferget to tell him Lil sent yer.'

'No, no I won't. Thank you very much. I'll go over there right away. Doris, give Lil another cuppa.' Maggie put the paper in her handbag and gave Doris money for the tea.

'Let's have a butchers at yer hand, love.'

Maggie looked surprised. 'Why?'

'She tells fortunes,' said Doris.

Maggie reluctantly put out her hand.

Lil took hold of it and after studying her palm, gently ran a long tapering finger along one of the lines. 'Just as I thought. You've had a lot of grief lately. Am I right?'

Maggie nodded.

'Well, gel, I'm afraid there's a few more tears ter come. I can see a lot more grief for you before it starts to get better.

But I can tell yer that in the end it will all turn out all right.'

Maggie looked at her hand. 'Can you tell me how long I've got to wait for it?'

'No, sorry.'

Maggie sat forward. 'What else can you see? Can you tell me about—'

Lil waved her hand at Maggie. 'Show's over.' Lil poured her tea into her saucer again.

'Well, I'll be off now,' said Maggie, sorry the reading had come to an end. There was so much she wanted to ask her. 'And thanks once again.'

'Good luck to yer, gel. 'Ere, take this to give yer luck.' She handed Maggie a sprig of heather. 'And take care. And let yer heart rule yer head.'

Maggie left the café in a state of bewilderment. What did the woman mean? And what else was going to happen to her? Was Lil really a gypsy? She put the heather in her bag, wondering whether it would bring her luck. She glanced across the road at Freeman's. What a good thing Charlie had been out.

Maggie couldn't believe Percy's Emporium. It *was* just like an Aladdin's cave. Her eyes grew wider and wider as she slowly wandered around. Beads glinted. Brooches sparkled. Fancy paste animals that had bright green and red eyes twinkled. There were tiny ornaments on stands, lovely shaped glass vases, and beautiful wall plaques. Maggie wanted to run round gathering up everything she saw. She crossed her fingers and prayed the price would be right. She waited till she found an assistant on her own, then asked, 'Excuse me. Where can I find Percy?'

'He's over there. Is there anythink I can get you?'

'No thanks.' Maggie knew the woman's eyes were following her as she went to the far end of the room. 'Excuse
me,' she said to a portly balding man bent over a box. 'Are
you Percy?'

He shot up and their eyes were level. 'Yes, who wants to
know?'

'I'm Maggie Ross, and I've just been talking to Lil.' She
gave a little laugh. 'I don't know her other name, and she
told me you might sell me some stock for my stall.'

He looked her up and down suspiciously. 'Did she now?
That wouldn't be Gypsy Lil, by any chance, would it?' he
replied gruffly.

Alarm filled Maggie. What had that old woman sent her
to? 'I don't know.'

'She's a bloody old witch.' Maggie turned round to see
the woman she had first spoken to standing behind her.

'Be fair, Mabel, she does have an uncanny knack of
predicting things,' said Percy, looking up at the woman.

'I don't trust her, and you shouldn't either.'

Maggie was looking from one to the other. All she
wanted was to buy some stock, and now it seemed she had
got herself involved in a family argument. 'I'm sorry, I must
have made a mistake.'

'No you ain't. What was it you wanted?' asked Percy.

'Well, you see I've got a stall and I was looking for
jewellery, only cheap paste.'

'Come with me.'

Maggie followed him to the end of a long counter.

'This the sort of stuff?'

She nodded. Earrings, necklaces, brooches and little hair

ornaments. She could have hugged him. 'How much?' she asked, carefully replacing the brooch she was fondling.

'How many?'

Maggie couldn't answer. 'It depends.'

'How much you got to spend?'

She was desperately trying to work out what she could sell them at. 'Couldn't you give me some idea what you will charge me for a few bits?'

'If we make you up a pound's worth, how would that do?' asked Mabel.

'Well yes, I suppose so.' That way Maggie could at least see what she would get for her money.

Percy laid out the objects on a tray. 'These do?'

Maggie was quickly trying to work out what she could sell them for. 'I could go to another ten shillings,' she said.

'You don't want to believe everything that Lil tells you, yer know,' said Mabel.

'Oh, why's that?'

'Reckons she can tell the future, she's just a fraud.'

Maggie gave a silly little laugh. 'I don't listen to all that nonsense.'

'She kept telling us we was gonner have this great disaster. Well, as you can see we're still here. But she put the bloody fear of death up poor old Percy here. I reckon it was just a ploy to get him out – her son's always took a great interest in this place.'

Maggie didn't comment, but she listened carefully while Percy bagged up her goods. Why was Mabel telling her all this? Percy was such a quiet man and Maggie could see who was in charge of the business.

'I hope we can do business again, young lady,' said Percy.

'So do I.' Maggie smiled. She felt happier than she'd felt for a long while.

She sat on the bus and, smiling, patted her handbag, pleased with its contents. She thought about what Lil had told her. Even if there was going to be more grief, at least there was light at the end of the tunnel. So perhaps Tony was going to come back after all. She desperately hoped so. Then her life would be complete.

Chapter 24

As the week progressed Maggie became more and more thrilled as her purchases appeared to bring a lot of interest from punters and stallholders alike, and she was selling well.

Saturday saw her smiling and brimming with confidence when people came and chatted, and bought.

'Reckon you wanner charge a bit more for this stuff,' said Winnie, sauntering over as the lunchtime lull approached. She picked up a brooch.

'Not yet. I'll wait till people get used to seeing it.' Maggie took hold of Winnie's arm and gently ushered her away from the stall. 'Look at Bill's miserable face. He ain't all that pleased about it.'

'That's his hard luck.'

'But what if he wants to leave, how would I manage without him?'

'Offer him more money.'

'I can't. I ain't exactly making a fortune.'

'Well, get more stuff and put a penny or two on the price. You'll soon cover his wages.'

'I can't afford to buy more, not just yet.'

'Look, Maggs, it ain't for me to tell you how to run your business, but see how today goes, then look what you've got left, and if you really think it's gonner work, why don't you take out a loan?'

Maggie looked shocked. 'What? Me borrow money? You of all people should know what happened to Tony over that.'

'Yes but that was for gambling, not stocking the stall.'

'I don't know.'

'Well, think it over. You don't want an opportunity like this to pass you by. It's you that's got to feed you and the kids now. Remember there's always eyes and ears round here looking for something new to flog, and if they see you doing well, well, before you know it everybody will be selling this stuff.'

'They wouldn't, would they?'

'Give 'em half a chance. Some of 'em would sell their grandmother for a bob or two if they thought they'd get away with it. By the way, a word of advice, gel. Don't let on to anyone who your supplier is.'

When Winnie walked back to her stall Maggie was stunned. She stood and thought about what she'd said. Would someone else get hold of stock like hers? What if they got it cheaper? Where did Percy get it from? All these questions were going through her mind. And what about a loan? She looked at the stall. It really did look rather pathetic. She needed more stock from Benny as well as Percy to make it look special, and borrowing money was something she would have to think really hard about if she wanted the stall both to look right and to pay. And, after all, Christmas was coming.

All morning business had been brisk, and Maggie knew

she would have to go and see Percy on Monday.

'Hallo, Maggie,' said her brother, coming up and giving her cheek a kiss as she stood behind the stall.

'Alan. Helen, what are you doing over here?' Maggie offered her cheek to Helen for the obligatory kiss. 'Two Saturdays in a row.'

'We'd thought we'd just pop over and see how you're doing. This looks nice,' Alan picked up a diamanté hair slide.

'You should have seen what we've sold,' said Bill. 'Can't say it's my line, but Maggie 'ere seems to think it's OK.'

'Been doing well then, have you?' Helen asked him.

'I should say so.'

Helen picked a pair of large pearl earrings off the black cloth. 'It's not the sort of thing I'd wear, but I expect they would sell well over this way. People round here like things that are cheap and cheerful.'

Maggie gave Helen a sarcastic smile. 'Would you like a cup of tea?' she asked.

'Why not?' said Alan.

'We can't stay too long. Remember we have to pick Doreen up.'

'Just a quick one,' said Alan.

Maggie felt like telling them not to bother, but she guessed they had another reason for this visit.

As soon as they were in the flat Maggie asked, 'Have you come over for some more of your money?'

Helen gave Alan a sneering look.

'No, course not,' said Alan quickly, looking very embarrassed.

Maggie could see by Helen's expression she was behind this.

'So things are going well down there? Who's looking after the children while you're on the stall?' asked Helen.

'Well, they're at school all week, and on Saturday they usually play round here.' She went into the kitchen.

'I didn't see them,' said Alan, following her.

'No, they're out.'

'Who with? Eve?'

'No. Inspector Matthews.'

'What, the policeman who's supposed to be looking for Tony?' enquired Helen, walking into the kitchen.

'Yes.' Maggie began filling the kettle.

'What they doing with him?' asked Alan.

'David bought Jamie a football for his birthday and as today is his day off he took them both over to the park.'

'David, eh. And you let him?' said Alan.

'Course, why shouldn't I?'

'Sounds to me like he's trying to get his feet under the table.'

'No, Helen, he isn't. He's a very nice man.'

'Is he married?' It was Alan's turn for the questioning.

'He's a widower.'

'That's convenient,' said Helen, looking at her nails.

'What d'you mean?'

'And what does Bella have to say about this cosy arrangement?'

'Helen, sometimes I . . .' Maggie wanted to give her a piece of her mind but decided against it. 'She likes him.'

'You wanner watch it, Maggs. If Tony comes back and finds this nice little setup – well, I dread to think what would happen,' said Alan.

Maggie slammed the kettle on the gas stove and turned

on him. 'If Tony does come back, first of all he's got a lot to answer for, and second, if he can't be bothered to send his only son a birthday card, then if you ask me he ain't worth worrying about.' Tears sprang to Maggie's eyes.

'My, my, we are touchy.'

'Helen,' said Alan, and looking sheepish put his arm round Maggie's shoulder. 'I don't want to upset you, Maggie, but I do worry about you.'

She shrugged him away. 'What did you really come over here for, money?'

'No, I told you, to see how you are.'

She dabbed at her eyes. 'As soon as I can I'll pay back a bit more of what Tony owes.'

'That's not what I'm after.'

'I must go down to Bill,' she said, breaking away from Alan and heading for the door.

'What about our cup of tea?' asked Helen.

'You'll have to have it next time.' Maggie didn't want to talk to them.

After that episode Maggie went over to Winnie. 'Who do I see about getting a loan?'

'They upset you?' Winnie inclined her head in the direction Alan and Helen had taken.

Maggie shuffled her feet.

'What'd he want? His money?'

'He didn't say as much, but that was the real reason. It's her, you know.'

'Is that what you want the loan for? Look, Maggs, you can tell me to shut up if you like, but to borrow money to pay Alan back – well, if you ask me it's a bit daft. Think of the interest.'

'Have you quite finished? I want the money to buy stock, lots of it, then if I make enough I can pay off Alan and everybody else.'

'It's gonner take you a bloody long time.'

'Then they'll just have to be patient, won't they?'

At two o'clock, just before closing time, Winnie took Maggie to the Dog and Duck to meet the loan club man, Mr Shore. She wanted to borrow five pounds. At first he was reluctant to lend so much, but after he'd explained the interest and charges and she was still keen to borrow, he agreed.

'Maggs, that's a lot of money,' said Winnie as they walked back to the stalls. 'You sure you're doing the right thing?'

'No, I'm not. But I've got to get some money from somewhere.'

'Yer, but you've got to pay a bloody lot back.'

'Well, it was your idea.'

'I know, but five pounds – what about the interest? Two bob in the pound, and the longer you have it the more you pay.'

'I know. I know. So I'll have to try and pay it back quick then, won't I?' Maggie tried to appear nonchalant about it, but deep down she felt sick. What was she thinking of?

Monday morning saw her over at Percy's again.

'Well, this is a surprise. Didn't think we'd see you so soon again,' said Mabel.

'Hopefully I'll be over every week.'

'So what yer buying this time?'

'About the same, but more of it.'

Mabel opened her watery blue eyes wide. 'How much yer got?'

Maggie held her breath. 'Four pounds.' She decided to keep a pound back in case she didn't make next week's rent. Then she needed money for Benny's bits. But last week's profit would take care of that.

'Four pounds?' repeated Mabel. 'Looks like you're on to a winner over your way.'

Maggie crossed her fingers. 'I hope so.'

The following two weeks saw Maggie becoming more and more self-assured, and once again she had been to see Percy. This time, as her profit was going up, she spent five pounds, but still kept a pound back for emergencies.

Another part of her life was happier too. 'Looks like he's becoming a regular visitor,' said Winnie as she and Maggie stood watching Jamie and Laura skipping down the road holding David Matthews's hand.

'It's only the second time this has happened, and it's nice of him to take them out, and they do like him.'

'What about you, gel?'

Maggie blushed. 'He is very nice.'

'But still a copper.'

Maggie turned to fiddle with her display. 'Don't start making something out of nothing.'

'How's Bella doing these days? Don't suppose we'll be seeing much of her once the weather turns.'

'I'm going to try and get over tomorrow. The stall and the buying seems to be taking a lot of my time.'

Winnie looked about her and moved closer. 'Paid off any of that loan yet?'

Maggie smiled. 'Hopefully I'll be able to pay off a pound this week.'

Winnie grinned. 'That's good. 'Ere, you ain't told anybody else, have you?'

'No, not even Eve, although she did want to know where I got the money from to buy this amount of stock. I told her Bella lent me a few bob.'

'Well, it certainly looks good.'

'Mummy, Mummy,' shouted Jamie as they ran towards her. 'Look, Uncle David bought us a great big ice cream.'

Maggie noted all eyes were on her. 'That was very kind of you, but you shouldn't have.'

'It was my treat.'

'Mummy,' said Laura, grinning and moving closer to her, 'Uncle David was telling us about his house. He's got a big garden and a tree he said he could put a rope over and make us a swing, but he said we'd have to ask you first if we could go.'

Maggie looked at David.

He shrugged his shoulders. 'I'm sorry, I should have said something before telling them. I can understand if you don't approve.'

Maggie was so embarrassed she wanted to die. She turned her back on the stallholders. 'We'll talk about it later. Bill, watch the stall while I see to the kids. Bye, David,' she said softly.

David came up close. 'Could I see you tomorrow?'

'No, I'm taking them to see Bella.'

'I could take you all in the car.'

'Oh please, Mummy, let's go in Uncle David's car.' Jamie's shrill voice stunned everybody into silence.

Maggie could feel eyes boring into her back.

'Oh go on, Mummy, please,' pleased Laura.

Maggie wished herself anywhere but there with everyone listening.

David moved very close to her. She could feel his breath on her cheek.

'Look, I'm sorry about this,' he whispered. 'I'll call round tomorrow, you can let me know then.' His words were for her ears only.

As David walked away Jamie said, 'You're mean. Why couldn't we go in his car?'

'Come on, Jamie, upstairs,' said Maggie crossly. Why did he have to say that in front of everybody? She didn't dare look at the traders. She knew all the remarks would come when it was time to put the stalls away. And she was right.

'I know it ain't none of me business, gel,' said Tom Cooper, 'but I don't think you should make an 'abit of letting that copper hang about.'

'I can't stop him,' said Maggie, making sure all the small pieces of jewellery were carefully boxed.

'Well, you could tell him you don't want him ter see the kids,' said Mrs Russell.

Maggie felt she had to stand up for herself. 'He ain't doing any harm. 'Sides, the kids like him and being taken to the park.'

A train rattled past, making conversation impossible.

'But when Tony does walk his arse back here he'll certainly have somethink to say about it.'

Maggie went and stood by Mrs Russell's flowers. 'Do you honestly think he's coming back?'

'We all like to think he is.'

'In the meantime I'm grateful for someone to take Jamie for a game in the park as his father don't seemed to be very bothered.'

'Maggie, stop that.' Mrs Russell smacked Maggie's hand. She was absent-mindedly pulling the petals off a daisy. 'That ain't gonner give yer the bleeding answer to yer prayers.'

Maggie smiled. 'Well, according to that daisy he don't love me anyway.'

'Who you talking about?' asked Mrs Russell.

'Tony, of course.'

Mrs Russell tutted and shook her head. 'I don't believe that fer one minute.'

'Just remember what I said,' said Tom Cooper. 'Send that copper packing.'

Maggie felt like telling him to shove off and mind his own business, but she knew she depended on these people to stand by her if she ever needed them. She smiled. 'I'll tell him,' adding silently under her breath, 'but will he listen?' And did she want him to?

Chapter 25

Maggie had just finished washing up the dinner things when Jamie rushed down the stairs to answer the knock. Maggie knew it was David.

She was wiping her hands on the bottom of her apron when he walked into the living room clutching his trilby. 'I'm sorry about yesterday. Did you get much stick from the others?'

'A bit.'

'I've got the car outside. Please, let me take you over to see Mrs Ross.'

She looked down at the two pair of eyes studying her and smiled. 'How can I refuse?'

'Goody, goody,' shouted Jamie. 'Can I take me football?'

'Jamie, behave.'

'Our gran's got ever such a big garden, but she ain't got no trees in it.'

David laughed.

'Right, into the kitchen you two and let me wipe your faces.'

'Oh Mummy, do we have to?' asked Laura.

'Yes.'

'Well, don't you be too rough,' said Jamie.

'We won't be long,' said Maggie, smiling at David.

It didn't take long for them to get ready and soon they were seated in David's car heading towards Downham, past green fields and tall trees.

'You have a bit of a journey to Greenwich every day.'

'It's not too bad. Going home in the winter to an empty house is the worse part of it. I would move nearer to Rother-hithe, but I like to do a bit of gardening, it helps relax me.'

'Is your garden bigger than our gran's?'

'I don't know, Jamie, I've never seen your gran's.'

'This a smashing car. What's it called?' asked Jamie.

'A Morris.'

'My daddy said he was gonner get a car, but he never did,' said Laura.

'Daddy said a lot of things,' said Jamie, 'But he never keeps promises. He didn't even send me a birthday card.'

'Well, I reckon he's dead like that man told us,' said Laura matter-of-factly.

Maggie looked at David.

'Why don't you have a game of I-spy?' said David.

'That's a good idea,' said Laura. 'I'll start.'

'Why is it always you? Mummy, let me start.'

'To save all arguments I'll start,' said Maggie, pleased David had moved the conversation away from Tony. The rest of the journey was full of laughter when Jamie and Laura weren't sure if the objects began with C or S.

''Allo, love,' said Bella, opening the door and kissing all three of them. 'It's good to see you.

''Ere, ain't that that copper's car?' she asked, coming out of the doorway.

'Yes.'

'Oh no, not more bloody trouble?'

'No, he just brought us over here.'

'Did he now? Go on into the garden, kids.'

'I've got my football what Uncle David gave me for me birthday.'

'Uncle David, eh?' Bella raised her eyebrows. 'Well, he coming in or not?' she asked.

'He wasn't sure.'

Bella walked down the path. 'Come on in,' she beckoned to him, then turned and walked back to her front door. 'Silly sod, what was he gonner do, sit there till yer come out?'

Maggie smiled. 'Probably. He's used to sitting in a car waiting for people. I half expected to see Benny here,' said Maggie when they went into the kitchen.

'He does come over most Sundays – been helping me with the garden.'

'Oh I see,' said Maggie.

'Don't say it like that. There ain't nothink wrong with him giving me a hand, and me giving him a bit of dinner in return, is there?'

'No, course not.'

When they were seated at the table Maggie opened her handbag. 'I've got a little present for you.'

'Me? Why? It ain't me birthday.'

'I know.' Maggie leant forward excitedly. 'You see, I've found this new place, Percy's Emporium, to buy from.'

'That's a bloody posh name. What's he sell, and what's his prices like?'

'Very good.' Maggie handed her a small brooch that had the word 'Mother' written in gold-coloured wire.

'This is lovely,' said Bella, admiring it. 'What'd it cost?'

'I ain't telling you, but don't worry, it ain't gold.'

'You must let me pay.'

'No, I told you it's a present. Besides, you spend enough on us, so let me treat you for a change.'

'So, has this Percy got some good gear?'

'I should say so, it's like a treasure trove.' Maggie went into great detail about how she met Doris, Mabel and Percy, and of course Mrs Freeman brought hoots of laughter. She also told them about Lil, and that she was a fortune-teller who had read her hand.

'Don't hold with that sorta thing,' said Bella. 'Could be very unhealthy. I hope you didn't take any notice of what she told yer?'

'She did tell me I was to expect more grief, but it will all turn out all right in the end.'

'Did she say how long?'

'No.'

'Well then, anybody could tell you that. Have you heard of this Lil?' she asked David.

'Can't say I have, so she hasn't got a record – well, not round our way anyway.'

Maggie laughed. 'Still it's given us something to talk about.' Deep down she was concerned with what Lil had told her, and she wasn't sure how she could cope with more grief.

All too soon it was time for them to leave.

As they moved up the passage Bella took hold of David's arm and held him back. 'I'm glad you brought Maggs over,' she said quietly. 'She could do with a bit of looking after.'

'Thank you for the tea. If she wants me to, I can nearly

always manage to alter my shifts and bring her over.'

Maggie noted the pain on Bella's face when Jamie took hold of David's hand.

Maggie held her close and whispered, 'Don't worry, we will always be around.'

The singsong they had all the way home was very off key, and conversation was impossible. But Maggie could see David was really enjoying himself.

'Would you like to come up for a cup of tea?' she asked when they arrived at her door.

'That would be very nice, but only if you're sure it's not too much trouble.'

'Let me get these two to bed first, then we can sit and have a chat. Thanks for taking us over there.'

'My pleasure.'

'And David, there's something I want to ask you,' she said, before turning to attend to the children.

He sat on tenterhooks waiting for Maggie to see to the children. Restlessly he lit a cigarette and wandered over to the window. What did she want to ask him? There were so many things he wanted to ask her. He had so much to offer her. He knew he was falling in love with her, but he also knew he had to be very careful not to show his feelings. He didn't want to frighten her away. If only there was some concrete news of Tony Ross.

'There, that's them down for the night.' Maggie closed the door. 'You can sit here while I put the kettle on.' She went to go into the kitchen.

David stubbed out his cigarette and was right behind her.

'It's all right, I can . . .' her voice trailed off as he came close to her.

'I'll give you a hand,' he croaked.

'You don't have . . .' Maggie felt silly, she knew she was sounding pathetic. 'David, please, don't.'

He knew it was wrong as he took her in his arms and kissed her warm inviting lips, softly at first, then full of passion. Maggie didn't resist.

He buried his head in her neck and whispered, 'I promised myself I wouldn't do this. But I can't help it. You are so lovely and look so vulnerable. I want to take you away and protect you and love you.'

Maggie gently pushed him away. 'This is so wrong.'

'Why?'

'I love Tony.'

'Do you? Deep down, do you after all that he's putting you through?'

'But what if he's dead?'

'But what if he's not?'

Maggie couldn't answer his question. 'I'll make the tea.'

They stood in silence watching the blue flame dance round the kettle. Neither knew what to say. Maggie made the tea and took the tray into the living room.

David sat on the sofa, while Maggie sat at the table.

'I'm sorry, Maggie.'

'It's all right.' She began stirring the tea in the pot vigorously.

'What was it you wanted to ask me?'

'It was about Mr Windsor. I've not heard anythink more from him.'

David came and sat at the table, touching her hand tenderly. 'No, he won't be bothering you any more.'

'Why?'

'I told him Tony was missing, presumed dead, so there was no use trying to collect his money as you didn't know anything about it, and if he did, he'd have me to answer to.'

Maggie pulled her hand away. 'Do you think Tony's dead?'

'What else can we think? It's what, almost five months – you would have heard something by now. He didn't send Jamie a birthday card, and from what you've told me about him I don't think he would have let that pass.'

Maggie looked down. 'You could be right, but how can I be sure?'

'If he changed his name when he left there won't be any records.'

Maggie's tears began to fall. 'What if he's wandering about not knowing who he is?'

'We've gone through that theory before. He must have had some form of identification on him – even his railway ticket would have told them where he came from.'

'I suppose you're right. Have I got to spend the rest of my life wondering if I am a widow or not?'

'I'm afraid that would be a possibility.'

Maggie looked up at him. Tears streaked her face. 'What am I gonner do?'

'Maggie, come and live with me.'

'What? I can't.'

'Why not?'

'I've still got to wait for Tony.'

'Maggie, I'm very fond of you.'

'Please, David, don't.'

'The children like me.'

'I know.'

'I'm off next Sunday, let me take you to my house. Please.'

'I don't know.'

'The children will love it.'

Maggie stood up. 'How could I just go off and live with you? What would the traders say, and what about Bella? She would be horrified. And what about the stall? Tony's dad, Jim, took years to get to that spot – I just can't throw it all away. And what about my brother? And what if Tony comes back?' she said softly.

'All these questions.'

Maggie bit her lip. 'But they have been my life.'

'But that part could end and you can start again.'

'I don't know.'

'Is that all that's stopping you from coming with me?'

'No. Yes. I don't know.'

'All I can say is that I mean it.'

'I wish this mystery could be cleared up.'

'So do I.' He stood up and took his hat from the chair. 'Maggie, don't let other people rule your life. You deserve to be happy.'

'You going? What about your tea?'

'I'm sorry. But I can't trust myself to stay here with you. I might say or do something I'll regret for ever. I'll collect you about eleven. Don't worry about dinner, I'll do something for us. I'll see myself out.'

He went. Maggie stared at the door. She didn't want him to go. But what *did* she want? She poured out her tea. Suddenly everything was going so well for her. She had found a good supplier and the stall was doing fine. She was even thinking of sending her brother two pounds next week, and she didn't have to worry about Mr Windsor, David had seen to him. She should be happy, but now he had given her another problem to solve. Part of her wanted to go with him, but she also knew she loved Tony, and had to be here for him, and that feeling would never go away.

Maggie hadn't seen Eve all week, and on Saturday night when she came round and the children were in bed Maggie said, 'David took us to Bella's last Sunday in his car.'

'Did he now? What did Bella have to say about that?'

Maggie laughed. 'I took her a brooch to soften her up.'

'You crafty cow.'

'No, it wasn't for that reason. She likes him. She reckons he's not a bad bloke for a copper.' Eve joined in with the last few words.

Maggie sat forward. 'Eve, he wants to take us to his house tomorrow.'

'What, over Greenwich?'

Maggie nodded.

'You going?'

'I don't know.'

'What do the kids say about it?'

'I haven't told them.'

'What you gonner do?'

'Half of me wants to, but . . .'

'Look, Maggs, I know it ain't none of my business.'

Maggie laughed.

'What's so funny?'

'Everybody says that, then they proceed to tell me what to do.'

'Oh well, please yourself, I was only gonner give you my opinion, but if you—'

'Sorry, Eve. Come on, don't get huffy. What was you gonner say?'

'I was gonner say that it wouldn't be a bad idea to go over. What you afraid of? Has he been coming on a bit strong?'

It was Maggie's turn to get rattled. 'No he ain't. And I ain't afraid of nothink.'

'Well, I think you are, and if you want my opinion I reckon you're falling for him.'

Maggie stood up. 'Don't talk daft.'

'So in that case why won't you go over there?'

'I didn't say I wasn't going, it's just that—'

'And the kids will be with you.' Eve laughed. 'That should stop any hanky-panky.'

Maggie laughed with her, but she knew her friend could see through her.

Chapter 26

The following Sunday evening after Maggie had put the children to bed, she plonked herself on the sofa next to David. 'I feel exhausted. Thank you for a really lovely day.'

David smiled. 'It should be me thanking you. Mind you, they certainly keep you on the go.'

'And you.' Maggie laughed. 'I'm surprised you could keep up with them, playing football, pushing them on the swing you made them, and doing our dinner.'

'I'm not that old. But honestly, I can't ever remember enjoying myself so much. They are a great pair.'

Maggie leant back. 'Yes they are.'

'I'm so glad you decided to come.'

'So am I.'

Maggie had been very impressed when David had arrived on the stroke of eleven. Jamie and Laura, who were all spruced up ready, were having a job to sit still and curb their excitement.

'Didn't have any choice, did I? I really would have been the wicked witch if I'd said no.'

He put his arm round her. 'You could never be wicked.'

Maggie moved away. 'Please, David, no.'

295

He held up his hands. 'Sorry.'

'You have a lovely house,' said Maggie. She knew she had to change the subject, even though she wanted David to hold her and kiss her, but if she allowed that where would it stop?

David lit a cigarette, fidgeting awkwardly. 'It felt good hearing all that laughter and noise today.'

'There was certainly plenty of noise.' Maggie tried to stifle a yawn. 'I'm sorry.'

'I think I should go. I have a busy day tomorrow.'

'So do I.'

'You over to see your Percy?'

She smiled and nodded. 'Don't you let Mabel hear you call him my Percy.'

'Everything still going well?'

'Yet it is.' She sat forward excitedly. 'I can't believe how well it's going.'

'They'll soon have to change the name down there to Maggie's Market.'

She laughed. 'D'you know, I've even managed to start . . .' She stopped. She had been going to say, 'paying Alan back, and the loan,' but she hadn't told David Tony owed money to her brother, or where she'd got the money from to buy the jewellery. 'Saving for Laura's birthday.'

'When's that?'

'Five weeks' time, November the twenty-fourth.'

'How old will she be?'

'Seven,' Maggie said wistfully. 'I don't know where the years have gone. It's on a Sunday so you must make sure you get that day off.'

'If you really want me to.'

'Laura certainly will, and so do I,' she said softly.

David resisted his desire to pull her into his arms and instead walked to the door. 'When can I see you again?'

Maggie shrugged.

'I'll pop in some time, and thank you again for a lovely day.' He lightly kissed her cheek.

Maggie closed the front door behind him.

Yes it had been a lovely day, she mused. David had a nice house, though not big like Alan's, and the children loved the garden. She softly sang to herself, letting her mind wander as she folded the children's clothes. She thought about the wedding picture of David and his wife that had stood on his sideboard. She looked a lovely woman, and he was so handsome smiling down at her, they must have been very happy. He said that now, because of her death, he threw himself into his work. When Maggie went upstairs to his bathroom she felt she wanted to go into his bedroom, not just to be nosy, but to see if he'd kept it as she imagined his wife would have done.

'So, what difference would it make to you?' she said out loud to herself.

The weeks sped past and Maggie couldn't believe how well the stall was doing. Although Benny was still providing her with some of the things Tony always sold it was the jewellery that was her first love. Every Monday she was over to see Percy, and every week she bought more and more with her profit as new customers came. Her business had really taken off.

'Your stuff's certainly bringing in new punters,' said Tom Cooper.

'It's good to see new faces,' said Winnie. 'Everybody seems to be benefiting. The word's definitely getting around.'

Maggie felt very proud and confident. She was even managing to pay back Mr Shore, the loan club man.

'I'm surprised you borrowed money off him,' said Gus one Monday when she went in the Dog to see Mr Shore.

'He's the only one I know who'll lend it to me.'

'Yer, at a price.'

'Well, I'm able to pay him back.'

'I hope so, love. I certainly hope so.'

Twice Maggie had been able to send Alan a two-pound postal order. She hoped this would keep him away. She didn't want him and Helen to keep coming over for they had the knack of upsetting her.

David was becoming a regular visitor most Sundays. That way, she told him, she wouldn't get so much hassle from the other stallholders as if he visited while they were around. Sometimes they went to Bella's, other times Maggie did the dinner and they went to the park, and on other Sundays they went to David's house. Although Maggie wanted him, and she knew he felt the same, they kept their distance. She didn't ask him to the pub when she went with Dan and Eve on a Saturday night as she didn't want Gus and the others to know she was seeing him socially.

'I dunno why,' said Eve one Monday evening when they were sorting over Maggie's latest buys. 'At least it keeps all them undesirables away from you.'

'I know, but I think they would resent me going out with him.'

298

'Why?'

''Cos I'm still married to Tony.'

'Yer, but Bella accepts him.'

'Only 'cos he's good to the kids.'

'Maggie, do you love him?' she asked.

'No, course not,' she answered abruptly.

'OK. Don't bite me head off. I only asked.'

'Sorry. Eve, I could get very fond of him, I s'pose, but only if . . .'

'It must be bloody hard, all this not knowing, and not having any of you know what. You don't, do you?'

'No I don't.' She couldn't tell Eve that she longed to be held and made love to. When would that happen again, if ever? 'It's Laura I'm worried about. I'm hoping Tony will send her a birthday card.'

'Do you still think he's alive?'

Maggie put the ring she was trying to display on some cardboard to one side. 'I don't know. I would like to think he is, but then again, if he was, and not telling me . . .' She blinked hard to stem a tear. 'We'll just have to wait and see if he remembers, won't we?'

'I hope he does. She's at a funny age.'

'I know.'

Maggie wasn't surprised to see Alan on the Saturday before Laura's birthday.

'Business seems to be brisk,' said Alan as he stood watching the customers come and go.

Maggie smiled. 'I'm doing very nicely, thank you.'

He took her to one side and, keeping his voice low, said, 'You know you didn't have to send me that money. You knew I'd be over some time and you could give it to me then.'

'I just wanted you and Helen to know that I intend paying you back every penny Tony borrowed.'

'But I don't want you to go short.'

'Thanks, Alan, but don't worry about me. I'm doing all right. Yes, love, a shilling a pair.'

'They're only a tanner in Woolworth's.'

'They may look like those, but I can assure you the backs won't fall off of these after one wear.'

The woman turned the earrings over, and put them on. She peered in the hand mirror Maggie kept on the stall. 'I must admit they do look better. All right, I'll have 'em.'

Maggie put the earrings in a small paper bag.

When the woman was out of earshot Bill said to Alan, 'She's got the gift of the gab, just like her old man.'

'What do you think of all this?' Alan asked Bill.

'Not a lot. Would rather be selling stuff like what Tony got – tools and the like. This lot's too sissy for me.'

Maggie laughed. 'As long as I'm paying your wages, you'll sell what I say.'

'She's getting bossy as well,' added Bill.

'I've got Laura's birthday present here.'

'Leave it here, I'll take it up later.'

'Her card's inside.'

'Thanks, Alan.'

'I suppose I'd better go.'

Maggie didn't offer him a cup of tea. She didn't want to leave the stall as she knew she made a better job of selling than Bill did. Also, she didn't want Alan hanging around any longer than necessary, then reporting to Helen on how well she was doing. She held her face close to her brother's for the obligatory peck on the cheek, then carried on serving.

That evening Maggie was busy making a jelly, cooking fairy cakes and generally preparing for Laura's birthday tea.

'I didn't get any cards today,' said Laura, coming into the kitchen.

'I expect you'll get them tomorrow. After all, your birthday isn't till tomorrow.'

'There ain't no post then.'

'I expect people will find a way.'

'What about them on the market? They ain't gonner leave it till Monday, are they?'

'Don't know. You'll just have to wait and see.' Maggie smiled. Laura's cards and presents were hidden away, but she wouldn't get the doll's pram they'd bought for her until Eve brought it round from her flat.

'Well, they better not forget me.'

'You don't even know if they've bought you anything,' said Maggie, pouring the cake mixture into the tin.

Laura's face was filled with alarm. 'I told 'em it was me birthday. They ain't forgot, have they?'

'Not telling.'

'But they always buy us somethink. Can I lick the bowl?'

'Shh, don't let Jamie hear, otherwise he'll want it.'

'Well, he can't, 'cos it's my birthday. Mummy, do you think Daddy will remember my birthday?'

Maggie was taken aback. The children rarely mentioned Tony these days – it was almost as if he had never existed – though sometimes Maggie would go to his wardrobe and hug his suits, just to remember his smell. 'I don't know, love.'

'I've said a prayer every night to tell God to remind him. Do you think he will?'

For a few moments Maggie couldn't answer, for she knew there would be a catch in her voice. She blinked quickly to stem the tears, then bending down she held her daughter close. 'I can't answer you. I only wish I could.'

Laura giggled. 'You've got all flour on your face.'

'Go on, cheeky, start getting ready for bed.' Maggie tried to sound cheerful, but she shared Laura's thoughts: would Tony remember? Or must she now accept that he was dead?

It was raining on Sunday but that didn't dampen Laura's spirits. And the afternoon had her jumping with joy when her school friends arrived. David had collected Bella and Benny, and Eve and Dan brought the pram round.

'Felt a right fool walking along pushing this,' said Dan.

'You didn't push, I did,' said Eve.

'I still felt a fool.'

Laughter and noise filled the flat. Even Mr Goldman came up to join in.

There was paper and cards everywhere.

When Bella and Maggie were alone in the kitchen Bella said, 'You've pushed the boat out on this one, ain't yer?'

'Well, now I'm earning a few bob what's the odds?'

'What about your brother?'

'I've been paying him back as well.'

Bella smiled. 'I'm pleased about that. That's a lovely doll,' she inclined her head towards the living room, 'that he bought Laura.'

'David's very good to them. What d'you think of the

clothes? I've been busy, ain't I?'

'They're very nice. Mind you, I dunno where you get the time to make 'em.'

'When the kids are in bed.'

'Do you see much of him?'

'Most Sundays, but you know that.'

'Yer, it's just that I wondered if he came here in the week.'

'No, he doesn't. That was good of Benny to give her that necklace.'

'He's not a bad bloke.'

'Well then, why don't you marry him?'

Bella didn't want to answer that question. 'I'm really pleased to see things are getting better for you. You've worked bloody hard.'

'I've got to thank that Lil for telling me about Percy. I couldn't do it without him.'

'You getting stuff at a good price from him?'

Maggie nodded. 'The more I buy the bigger the discount, and I think he likes me, as I always seem to get more for me money.'

'In some ways it's a good thing you lost that baby.'

Maggie stood and stared at Bella. 'How can you say that?'

'Well, you couldn't run the stall and look after a baby as well, now could you? Something would have had to go by the board.'

'I would have tried to manage somehow.'

'I know that, but all that traipsing round looking for stuff to sell before you found out about that Percy – that could have been hard.'

Maggie felt like telling her to shut up, she didn't want reminding of her lost baby, but she knew it was better to keep quiet.

'I'm pleased you managed to keep the stall going. Those licences are bloody hard to get hold of, 'specially up that end. Wouldn't like to see it lost, not after all the years we've had it. And a word of advice: remember you've got Christmas coming up, so you wanner get plenty of stock in for that.'

Maggie was pleased Bella was off on a different tack. 'Don't worry, I intend to.' And she wasn't going to tell anyone, not even Winnie, that she was going to take out a bigger loan to buy Christmas stock.

'I must tell you this. That Mrs Saunders – you know, who runs the haberdashery stall? – came up and give me the once-over. D'you know, she told me not to sell ribbons and the like otherwise she'd have my guts for garters.'

'What did you say?'

'Not a lot, just told her I only use ribbons to hang some of the bone bracelets on,' Maggie laughed. 'But guess what? Winnie told her that my guts wouldn't look very nice hanging on her stall and she couldn't see many girls wearing 'em. She didn't half get wild, and waddled off down the road muttering to herself.'

Bella also laughed. 'Winnie's a nice woman.'

'Yes she is.'

'I don't think her and that Mrs Saunders hit it off when Jim was there.'

'D'you know why?'

'I think one of her kids pinched a pair of shoes. Mind you, that's going back years.'

'But Winnie would never let that rest.'

As Maggie wiped the dishes her thoughts suddenly went to Lil. She must have got her prediction wrong, because in many ways this was a good time. She was happy and making money. But she also knew the grief would never really be over all the while Tony was away.

Chapter 27

Maggie sighed. It was dull and miserable outside, the kind of Monday morning when nobody wanted to leave their bed. Winter was well and truly on its way.

The postman dropping the letters through made her jump up, grab her dressing gown and rush downstairs. She was ever hopeful that there would be a birthday card for Laura from Tony.

Again she was disappointed, and hoped Laura wouldn't be upset before going to school. She would tell her the postman hadn't been yet.

She got dressed. This morning she was going to Percy's as usual, then at lunchtime she intended to see about getting a big loan. Maggie was pleased she'd managed to pay back four of the five pounds she'd first borrowed, and hoped Mr Shore would see his way to lending her the ten pounds she had in mind. 'Ten pounds,' she whispered. 'That's a lot of money, and a lot of interest to pay back.' But Percy had told her to get the stock in well before Christmas as he soon sold out of all the good gear. She smiled confidently to herself and, after putting the kettle on, set about preparing the children's breakfast.

Maggie shuddered when she opened the front door, she wasn't looking forward to being out and about in this weather.

'Did you have a nice birthday, young lady?' asked Winnie when she caught sight of Maggie trying to hurry the children along.

'Yes thank you, and thank you for my lovely doll's pram. Uncle David bought me a pretty doll with a real china head and brown eyes that open and close. When I get back from school I'll show you.'

'I'd like that.'

Maggie tightened Jamie's scarf. 'Laura can bring you all down a bit of cake after school. Now come on, kids, otherwise you'll be late. I'll have a word later on,' she said to Winnie over her shoulder.

On her way home from Percy, Maggie reflected as usual on her good luck at finding him. He too was talking about Christmas and the new lines he was getting next week. It was all going to be very exciting.

She took her purchases upstairs before going along to the Dog and Duck.

'Hallo, Rene. Thought Monday was your day off?'

''Allo, Maggs. Don't often see you in here at lunchtime,' said Rene. 'Gus has got the accountant in, so I've had to come in. Did you wanner see Gus?'

'No, I'm looking for Mr Shore. Has he been in yet?'

She leant over the bar, revealing more of her bosom, and bent her head closer. 'He's in the bog. Here, you ain't borrowing money off that shark, are yer?' So far Rene hadn't been in when Maggie had met Mr Shore to pay back any of the money.

Maggie couldn't deny it. 'Why do you say that?'

'Well, if yer don't pay up, it could be . . .' She stopped and looked up as the dapper Mr Shore came over to Maggie.

'Hallo, my dear. Come to give me some more of my money?' he grinned. 'Good customer, this one is,' he said to Rene.

He got out his book when he and Maggie were seated. 'Only a pound to go, plus interest. So, how much you paying me this time?'

Maggie looked round nervously. 'I would like to borrow some more.'

He licked his pencil. 'Don't normally let you have more till this lot's been paid up.'

Maggie sat back dejected. 'I can let you have it in a week or so.'

'How much more did you want?'

She cleared her throat. 'Ten pounds,' she said softly.

His head shot up. 'How much?'

She went to speak but he put up his hands to silence her. 'That's a lot of money, young lady, and a lot of interest.'

'What do I owe you now?'

He quickly added up the figures. 'As you've had it over a relatively short time I'll only charge you a pound interest.'

'But I thought you only charged two bob in the pound, and I only had five pounds.'

'Ah yes, I do, but then there's a charge for the loan, the loan book I gave you and administration charges, and if it went over three months there's another charge.'

Maggie sat back. What was she getting herself into? She was beginning to see how easy it must have been for Tony to get into deep water.

'So, do you still want ten pounds?'

She nodded. 'Will that be two pounds' interest?'

'Only if you pay it back within three months.'

There wasn't any way out; she needed more stock for Christmas. 'Yes, please.'

Mr Shore smiled and took out his wallet.

'Still paying off that money?' said Winnie when Maggie came back from the Dog and Duck.

'Getting there,' said Maggie breezily.

'It looks as though it was worth it.'

'Winnie, have you ever borrowed money off of him?'

'Na, never had cause to, but a lot I know have. I think he's as fair as any of 'em. Why?'

'Just wondered, that's all.'

'Laura was pleased with the pram then?'

'I should say so. It was really nice of 'em all.'

'So the tea party went all right?'

'Yes, Bella and Benny came over.'

'And did Uncle David then?'

'Yes, he did as a matter of fact.'

'Just remember to keep yer feet on the ground, gel. Don't get carried away. You never know what's round the corner.'

'Well, I don't think it will be Tony. He never even sent her a card.'

'The cowson.'

Maggie had been dreading Laura coming home from school. Would she ask about a card or had she forgotten?

'What you looking for?' asked Maggie that afternoon as Laura sifted through the papers on the sideboard.

'I thought there might be a card from Daddy,' she said quietly.

'There better not be,' said Jamie. ''Cos he didn't send me one. He don't love us any more.'

'I'm sure he does. It's just that he didn't have me to remind him,' said Maggie, fighting for the right words to say.

'Well I reckon that man was right,' said Jamie, 'and he's dead.'

That statement shook Maggie, it was so forthright. For the first time it occurred to her that Wally might have been telling the truth.

'I think we must accept that something has happened to Daddy.'

'See,' said Jamie. 'Told you so.'

'Now come on, sit up at the table. You can finish off the jelly and cake.'

'Great,' said Jamie, scrambling on the chair.

That night, when Maggie went to tuck them up, Laura was softly crying.

'Laura love, what's wrong?'

'Was Jamie right when he said Daddy don't love us any more?' she sobbed.

Maggie held her close. 'I can't answer your questions truthfully, Laura, because I really don't know.'

Laura's sobs racked her tiny body. 'Has he gone away 'cos we've been naughty?'

'No, my darling.' Laura seemed so small and vulnerable. At that moment Maggie hated Tony viciously. How dare he make his children so unhappy? She kissed her wet cheek. 'Now settle down. You don't want to go to school with red puffy eyes, do you?'

Laura shook her head. 'Mummy, I didn't wish for Daddy

to come back when I blew out my candles.'

'Oh,' said Maggie. She couldn't think of any comforting words.

'You see, Jamie did, and it didn't come true.'

Maggie thought her heart was going to break. She choked back a sob. 'Do you want to tell me what you wished for?'

'No, just in case telling won't make it come true.'

Maggie smiled and kissed her. 'Remember we've got Christmas to look forward to next,' she said, trying to make it sound lighthearted.

Laura gave her a weak smile. 'Good night, Mummy. You'll never leave us, will you?'

'Never.'

'Promise?'

'I promise.'

The rest of the week saw the traders battling with the rain and cold. On Friday when Maggie went down to see Bill he looked very miserable.

'What's wrong with you?' asked Maggie.

'I'm cold and fed up.'

'Why? You know what being on a stall's like, you've done it for years.' But Maggie too was worried about the weather.

'To tell the truth, Maggs, I miss Tony.'

Maggie began to feel angry. 'So do I, but walking around with a long face ain't gonner bring him back, and it don't encourage people to hang around and look over the goods.'

Bill shuffled to his feet. 'No, I know. It's just that I dunno what to say when these women put on the stuff, then peer in the mirror and ask me what I fink, as if it matters.'

'Course it matters. They like a bloke's opinion.' She smiled. 'Anyway, how's your mum?'

'She's not too bad. Her sister from Essex is coming on Sunday.' He brightened up. 'I like my uncle, he's a smashing bloke. He was in the air force during the war. Mum says him and me dad were the best of mates. Don't see him very often. I think they want me mum to go there for Christmas. I hope so – it'll be a nice change from just the two of us sitting looking at the fire.'

'Don't you go out with the lads?'

'Sometimes, but at Christmas they usually stay in with their families, 'Sides that, I wouldn't leave me mum, not on her own.'

Maggie smiled. 'Let's hope we have a good Christmas, then I might give you an extra Christmas box.'

At least the thought of that brought a smile to Bill's face.

The following Monday Maggie was full of excitement about going over to see Percy. She hadn't told anybody she had borrowed ten pounds. The children were having their breakfast when there was a banging on the front door.

'I'm coming, I'm coming,' Maggie said, hurrying down to open it. 'Winnie. What you doing here? What's wrong?'

'Just letting yer know, gel, that Bill ain't turned up. Your stall's still in the lockup.'

'What?' Squabbling from upstairs made Maggie look round. 'I'll get these two off first, then I'll be along to sort it out. I wonder if he's all right?'

'D'you want Fred and Tom to get it out for you?'

'No, no thanks. I've got to go and see Percy so the stall

will have to stay put for today. This afternoon I'll go round and see if Bill's all right.'

'Please yerself. See you later.'

Maggie closed the door. As she ran up the stairs to stem the argument, she said to herself, 'That's all I need at the moment – Bill being ill.' She admonished herself for being selfish. It could be that his mother had been unwell.

On the way home from Percy's Maggie sat on the bus and smiled to herself. Her bags were loaded, she had spent every penny she owned. 'Alan will have to wait till after Christmas for some more of his money. So will Mr Shore.' She felt so happy and confident that for now she ceased to worry about her debts.

Later that afternoon she went to Bill's mother's house for the first time. It was in the middle of a dirty and run-down row of terraces in a miserable area. The houses looked like Bella's had done before it was pulled down. Skinny scruffy kids with runny noses, who, even though it was cold and damp, didn't have any shoes on, were running about or pushing babies in prams that held two and three children. Maggie shuddered and knocked on the door.

No one answered. Perhaps Bill was at the hospital. She began to get agitated and banged again, this time much harder.

The next door opened. 'Ain't nobody in then, love?' asked a thin seemingly old woman.

'Don't look like it.'

'Fought young Billy might be there. His mum, Jenny's, gorn off.'

'She in hospital?'

'Na, love. She's gorn ter stay with her sister out Essex

314

way for a few days. They took her yesterday in the car. Nice car he's got. Mind you, it's a good fing too, if yer asks me. Wouldn't be surprised if she didn't stay there fer good. She ain't been all that well lately – it's her chest yer know – and this damp don't help none. Her sister and her old man – lovely couple they are, and good to her – they've been wanting her ter go up there fer years, but it was young Billy what kept her here.'

'So where's Billy now?'

'Dunno. He went with 'em, but I fought he was coming back. P'raps he changed his mind.'

Panic filled Maggie. What if he had gone to live in Essex? What would she do without him?

Maggie thanked the woman and left. As she walked home her mind was churning over and over, and she was full of fear at the prospect of managing the stall alone. She wasn't strong like Winnie and one or two of the other women who took their stalls out day after day. She couldn't rely on Tom and Fred for favours as after a week or two they'd get fed up. And what about the children? She would have to get them to school and still feed them, then there was the washing and . . . Perhaps I'm worrying unnecessarily, Maggie thought. I've got plenty of stock, thank goodness, and if I run out . . . well, I'll just have to wait and see.

Maggie told Winnie about what had happened.

'Don't worry about it, gel. We'll make sure you don't lose out if he's gorn off. But I can't see him letting you down like that, not at this time o' year.'

But the following morning there was no sign of Bill again. Fred helped Maggie to get set up, and between them

Winnie, Fred, Tom and Mrs Russell kept an eye on it till Maggie came back from taking the children to school.

At the end of the day they all helped her put it away.

All week it was the same, and Maggie was cross there hadn't been any news from Bill.

On Saturday morning when Eve came round and heard the story, she stayed to help out.

'I ain't half enjoying myself,' she said, after serving a customer. 'Mind you, I wish I'd put thicker drawers on. There's a bloody draft blowing up me knicker leg.'

Tom Cooper laughed. 'I've got some lovely red flannel on me stall, gel. Come over and I'll get yer measured up.'

'You wanner watch him, gel,' said Mrs Russell. 'He'll be asking yer to take yours off for a pattern.'

'Now that's what I call a good idea,' said Tom.

Despite the cold, all morning there was plenty of laughter and easy-going banter. Maggie too was enjoying herself, and she was selling well.

Towards the afternoon Eve said she had to go and get Dan's tea ready. 'I'll be round later.'

Trade had died down and the hurricane lamps that hung from the stalls had been lit. Despite the cold a warm glow hung over the market and the lovely smell of roasting chestnuts filled the air. Since the incident with Mr Goldman's window the Blackshirts had moved to another corner, a street away from the market and their shouts no longer disturbed the traders.

Maggie stamped her cold feet and banged her hands together to try to bring some life back into them. She joined in with the carols coming from the Salvation Army band. Three weeks to Christmas, and if trade stayed like this, and

Bill came back, it would be great. She felt warm and happy inside. She was showing everybody she could manage.

''Allo there, me old Maggs.'

Maggie turned and saw Bill staggering towards her. 'Not so much of the old. Bill, you all right?'

He giggled. 'I fink I'm a bit pissed.'

'Oh very nice,' said Winnie. 'And where yer been all week?'

He held on to the stall. 'Bin out with me mates. I have got mates, yer know.'

'I expect you have,' said Maggie. 'Win, can we borrow your chair? Now sit down here, Bill, and tell me why you've not been here.'

'Well, it's like this. I do miss Tony, yer know, Maggs?'

'Yes, Bill, we all do, but getting drunk's not gonner help him or me. I need you here, so where have you been?'

'Did I tell yer me auntie came ter see me mum?'

Maggie nodded. The state he was in there was no point in trying to hurry him.

'Well. Me auntie and me uncle Ron came ter see me mum and we all went to Romford – that's in Essex, yer know. Me uncle's got a car. I like me uncle, yer know. We had a smashing day, and when it was time ter go, me mum said she didn't want to go back home. Me auntie's always on to her to go and live with 'em.'

'What's he doing here?' said Tom, catching sight of Bill. 'You should be 'ere helping Maggie, not piss-arsing about. And what's he doing sitting down? He should be on his feet.'

'He's having a job to stand,' said Winnie. 'Been sniffing the barmaid's apron, if you ask me.'

'He's drunk?' asked Tom.

'Yer,' said Winnie.

'What's going on over here?' asked Fred. 'I see, so he's turned up then. Where's he bin?'

'That's what we're trying to find out,' said Winnie.

'Don't mind them,' said Maggie, beginning to get a little impatient. 'Where have you been all week, and why have you got drunk?'

Bill laughed. 'Stayed with me auntie for a few days, then I went up the West End wiv some of me mates. Met some lovely ladies.'

'Oh my Gawd,' said Winnie. 'I hope he ain't caught nothink.'

'I remember when I went up west and my—'

'OK, Fred,' said Winnie. 'We'll hear all about that another time. Carry on, son.'

Bill laughed. 'I've had a smashing time. Well, I had to find out what . . . well, you know, what it was like first, didn't I? D'yer know what some ladies—'

'They ain't ladies, son,' said Tom.

Bill had a huge grin on his face. 'Well, I fink they're ladies, and after that I went and joined the army.'

Everybody was stunned into silence.

'Ain't yer gonner congratulate me? There's gonner be another war, yer know, so I fought I'd get in first, and then I'll be a sergeant.'

'Bill,' said Maggie quietly, 'what does your mother have to say about this?'

'I ain't told her yet.'

'But after your father—'

'Yer, I reckon she'll be a bit upset.' He laughed again. 'If

I get a bit of shrapnel in me, she'll have a pair then to put on her mantelpiece, won't she?'

Maggie threw her arms round his shoulders. 'Bill. Oh Bill, you stupid young boy. Your mother is gonner be heartbroken when she knows.'

'Yer, but she's got Auntie Milly. 'Sides, she's better off up there. D'yer know, they've got a lav inside. 'Sides, it's better than round here with the fog.'

'I think you'd better come upstairs with me and have a lay down.'

'Yer, I do feel a bit tired.'

'Not surprised,' said Tom, grinning. 'He's probably worn himself out with all that unaccustomed exercise.'

'Keep an eye on me stall, Winnie, while I take him upstairs,' said Maggie.

Tom helped Maggie get Bill on his feet. 'Put your arm round me shoulder.' Bill was almost a head taller than her.

'Can you manage him?' asked Tom.

'Just as long as he puts one foot in front of the other.' Maggie thought they must have looked a funny pair, staggering along together.

'When you going in the army, son?' called Winnie after them.

'Monday,' came back the answer.

Maggie almost dropped him. 'Monday! But how am I gonner manage?'

Bill didn't answer, his eyes were closed and he still had a silly grin on his face.

'I bet you're dreaming about your lovely ladies,' she said to him.

He just nodded.

As they steadily mounted the stairs Maggie's worries crowded in. What if there was going to be another war? Would Tony come back to them then? And what about Bill's mother? She didn't need another casualty in her life.

Chapter 28

Jamie and Laura thought it very funny to see Bill sound asleep on the sofa. His loud snoring was sending them into fits of giggles.

'What's he doing here?' asked Eve when she arrived later that evening.

Maggie went through the whole story.

'So, how you gonner manage the stall on your own now he's going?'

'I don't know, especially as this should be our busiest time of the year.'

'Well, I'd throw him out, letting you down like this.'

'I wouldn't do that, Eve. He's not had it easy.'

'So what does he reckon the army will do for him then? That ain't no bed of roses.'

'He's young, so let's hope he makes a go of it.'

Eve's face softened. 'I enjoyed being down there today, so I'll give you a hand on Sat'days. How many till Christmas?'

'Thanks. Three. Christmas Day is on a Wednesday this year. I'll be glad of an extra pair of hands. I'll pay you.'

'I hope so, even if it's only a pair of earrings.'

'I think I'll be able to manage a bit more than that.' Maggie looked down at Bill. 'It's his mother I feel sorry for. I don't suppose he'll be here for Christmas.'

'I still reckon he's a silly sod. Fancy joining up.'

'What if he's right and there is another war?'

'Like Dan says, we'll worry about that if and when it happens. He said he can't see Baldwin leading us into another one.'

'God, I hope not.'

'Have you talked about Christmas with David yet?'

Maggie shook her head.

'Will you spend it with him?'

'Dunno. I'll have to see Bella sometime over the holiday.'

'How will you get stock and run the stall?'

'I must have known something as I've already bought a lot. It's only Benny I've got to see, but he always keeps a few good bits for me.'

'Is that it, all what's on the stall?'

'No, I've kept some back.'

'That's a bit daft.'

'Not really. If you don't let the punters see it all at once, they think there's only one or two left so they'll buy them, not knowing I've got another half-dozen up here.'

'You crafty cow. No, honestly though, I'm glad you're making a go of it. If Tony ever did come back you'd find it hard to take second place down there now, wouldn't you?'

'Yes I would. But perhaps I could have a bit of his stall and still sell jewellery.'

Eve smiled. 'One thing's for sure, he'd certainly see a different Maggie.'

'Have I changed that much?'

'Only for the better, and stronger. Now what's gonner happen with him?' Eve pointed to Bill, still sprawled out and snoring.

'He'll have to stay here for the night. Then perhaps David will take him home in the morning.'

When Maggie walked into the living room the following morning Bill was sitting holding his head.

She laughed. 'Believe me, I know exactly how you feel.'

'You do?' he croaked. 'Can't ever imagine you getting drunk.'

'I've had me moments. Fancy a cuppa?'

'Please. Me mouth feels like a bit o' sandpaper.'

Maggie handed him a cup of tea and sat beside him. 'Bill, do you remember why you got drunk?'

He slowly nodded. ''Cos I'd joined the army.'

'What made you do that?'

'Me uncle was telling me what a good time him and me dad had.'

'But your dad died because of the war.'

'I know. Me uncle was in the air force, but I still thought I'd go in the same regiment as me dad. I want to go, Maggs, I really do. I'm sorry if I've let you down.'

She patted his hand. 'Well, let's all hope there's not another war, and you'll soon be a sergeant.'

'I hope I ain't been a nuisance.'

'Course not. So, what you gonner do now?'

'Well, I've got to go home and get packed.' He laughed. 'That ain't gonner take long. Then I'll get a few of me mum's bits together and leave the rent next door, then Uncle Ron's coming over to sort everythink out.'

'Ain't you gonner say goodbye to your mum?'

He shook his head. 'I'm gonner write her a letter. Then when I've finished me training I'll be able to go and see her.'

'You've got this all worked out. She's gonner miss you though, and she'll be very upset.'

'I know, but I've been thinking about this for a long while, ever since those Blackshirts broke Mr Goldman's window. That really got to me and I felt I wanted to do somethink about it, but I didn't want to leave me mum on her own. But now I don't have to worry about her.'

Maggie kissed his cheek, causing him to blush. 'You're a smashing bloke, and I hope you come and see us in your uniform. Now, what about a bit of breakfast?'

'Thanks, Maggie, I'd like that. And Maggie, I only wish your story could have a happy ending.'

Maggie swallowed hard. 'So do I Bill. So do I.'

That afternoon, when David took her and the children to Downham, Maggie told Bella and Benny all about Bill.

'It made me look at him in a different light,' she said. 'I never knew he was such a warm sensitive lad.'

'I s'pose we all try to hide our lights under bushels, so the saying goes,' said Bella. 'But fancy him going and joining the army.'

'It's his poor mother I feel sorry for,' said Maggie.

'What d'you think, Dave, d'you reckon we'll have another war?' asked Benny.

'Wouldn't like to say. Things don't look good over in Europe, and now Mussolini's walked into Abyssinia that could spell trouble.'

'Now let's stop all this war talk,' said Bella. 'More to the point, how are you gonner manage without Bill?'

Maggie shrugged. 'I don't know.'

'Well, I reckon he could have waited till at least after Christmas.'

'So do I, but there you go, he didn't, so I'll just have to manage. Eve's gonner help out on Saturdays, so that's useful, and if I can afford someone else who I can trust, then I'll take them on.'

'That's the trouble – trying to find someone you can trust,' said Bella. 'What about stock?'

'Got most of me Christmas stuff in.'

Bella looked shocked. 'You 'ave? Where d'you get the money from?'

'Saved it,' lied Maggie, 'and if Benny could bring me over some of his little treasures, then everythink will be great.'

'Oh, that's all right then,' said Bella.

'Don't get a lot this time a year,' said Benny.

'I'd come and give you a hand, but I can't stand about, not in this cold, not now. Getting too old.'

'Bella, you'll never be too old. 'Sides, I wouldn't expect you to. And talking about Christmas, you coming over to me for the day?'

'Don't you think you'll have enough to do without feeding me? 'Sides, how would I get over there? Ain't no trains running Christmas day.'

Maggie gave David a glance. 'We'll talk about that nearer the time.'

'In fact me and Benny was discussing it just before you come in. He said he'd like to spend it with me, so p'raps you could all come over to me.'

'We'll see,' said Maggie. She didn't want to make plans that might not include David.

All the way home Maggie was deep in thought, wondering what would happen in the next three weeks. Would she hear from Tony?

'Penny for them,' said David.

'They ain't worth a penny.'

'You've been very quiet since we left Bella's.' He took a quick look over his shoulder at the two children nestling under the tartan blanket. 'I think they're asleep. Maggie, are you worried about another war starting?' he said in a very low voice.

'In some ways, but at the moment my biggest worry is getting the stall out and selling the stock. I don't know how I'm gonner manage on me own.' Worry was keeping her voice low.

He patted her hand. 'We could easily solve that one.'

'How?'

'You could come and live with me. Give up the stall. I could look after you.'

'David, don't start on that again. You know I would never do that.'

Giggling came from the back seat.

'I'd like to go and live at Uncle David's,' said Jamie.

'Please, Mummy please, let's go and live in his lovely house,' shouted Laura.

'Sorry,' said David, 'I thought they were asleep.'

'Oh go on, Mummy, please,' piped up Jamie. 'We could play in his garden and—'

'I said no. Now all shut up.'

The journey was finished in silence.

When they arrived at Maggie's door David asked, 'Do you still want me to come up?'

'Course. If you put the kettle on I'll get these two to bed.'

'Mummy, why can't we go and live in Uncle David's nice house?' whined Laura.

'Because I say so.'

'We could have a bedroom each and I wouldn't have to sleep in the same room as him.'

Jamie jumped up and down on his bed making the springs ping. 'Go on, Mummy, please. That'll be great. I could hang all me planes up and leave me toys all—'

'Jamie, shut up and stop that. We are not going so don't let me hear any more of it.'

'Well, I think you're mean,' said Laura.

'And we wouldn't have to go down to our rotten lavatory. I hate all those rotten spiders.'

'Jamie, get to bed.'

'Daddy always said he was gonner get us a nice house. Now we could have one you won't go.'

'Daddy said a lot of things but he's not here now.'

'I bet you told him to go away. It's your fault and I hate you.' Laura's face was red with anger.

Maggie stood dumbfounded. She loved her children so much and she knew they loved her, but how long had this been building up? She tried to cuddle Laura but she hid under the bedclothes. 'Come on now, Laura, you don't mean that.'

'Yes I do,' came the muffled reply. 'Go away.'

Jamie slid under his bedclothes. 'And I hate you as well, so don't kiss me good night.'

Tears ran down Maggie's face. Anger built up inside her

and she stormed out of their bedroom, slamming the door behind her.

David jumped to his feet and she entered the room. 'Maggie, is everything—'

Her face was like thunder. 'No it ain't.'

He went to hold her but she pushed him away.

'What's wrong?'

'You've just turned my kids against me.'

'I don't understand.'

'Get out!' she screamed.

'I beg your pardon.'

'I said get out. I don't ever want to see you again.'

'I'm sorry. What have I done?'

'You know I won't live with you. You know I won't leave this place. But no, you have to keep on. You and your fancy talk have turned my children against me.'

David gave a little nervous laugh. 'I'm sure they don't mean it.'

'You didn't see the hate in their eyes all because I won't walk away from everything Tony worked for. Now please leave.' She picked up his trilby and handed it to him.

'But, Maggie, I—'

'I don't want to hear. Now go.'

'Well, if you're sure.'

'Oh believe me, I'm sure.' She held open the door.

They hadn't noticed the living-room door being quietly opened. Jamie and Laura ran and held on to David's legs.

'Please, take us with you. We don't want to live here,' said Laura.

'We don't like going outside in the dark to the lav,' said Jamie.

David looked bewildered. 'I'm sorry,' was all he could think of to say.

'You two, get back to bed at once.' Although she was close to tears Maggie's voice was strong.

'You're rotten,' said Laura, turning away from her.

'Come on now, do as your mother tells you.'

'Will you come and take us to your house again?' asked Laura, releasing her grip on David's leg.

David looked at Maggie, who moved away from him.

'Not if Mummy doesn't want to. Now go on back to bed.'

'Will you come and tuck us in?' asked Jamie.

'I'd better not. I must go now.' He picked up his hat and left.

Laura and Jamie ran into their bedroom. Maggie could hear them crying. She too sat and cried. What had she done? Why didn't she want to go and live with David? She knew she was falling in love with him, and he could make them all happy. But she also knew she could never leave the flat in case Tony ever came back. Was this how she was going to spend the rest of her life, waiting?

When Maggie opened her swollen puffy eyes the following morning all that had happened yesterday filled her mind. How could her children hate her? Why did David have to say that in front of them? He knew they often pretended to be asleep if they thought they would hear something to their advantage.

It was quiet outside, the street sounds muffled. She got up and drew back the curtains. She couldn't see out for the thick fog. She sat back on the bed. 'Oh no,' she moaned aloud. 'This is all I need. Nobody will come out in this weather.' She wandered into the kitchen, still talking to herself: 'I must get the children up. I'll buy them a comic or some little treat, anything to show them I love them a lot.'

She pushed open the bedroom door and went to shake Laura. 'Come on, love, time to—' The bed was empty. She rushed over to Jamie's bed and threw back the clothes. His bed too, was empty.

Her screams were heard by Mr Goldman, who began banging on her front door with his fists. 'Maggie, what's happened? Open this door. Maggie!'

When the door was opened, Maggie stood there ashen-faced.

'My dear, whatever's happened?'

'It's Laura and Jamie . . .'

'Oh my God.' He tried to push past her, but she did not move. 'What happened to them?'

'They've gone, Mr Goldman. They've gone. They've run away.'

'Gone? What? What d'you mean, they've gone? Gone where? And who took them?'

'Nobody. They've just gone.' Suddenly the enormity of this hit Maggie and she began screaming again.

'Maggie, please, calm down.' He took hold of her shoulders. 'Please, Maggie, calm down. They can't have got far, not in this weather. Now go up and get your coat. You'll catch your death of cold standing here in your nightclothes. Have they taken anything with them?' Mr Goldman began coughing. 'This fog gets down your throat. They can't be that far away.' He took hold of Maggie's arm. 'Now do as I say.'

Maggie turned and dreamlike went upstairs. 'This is all

David Matthews's fault,' she yelled, suddenly coming out of her trance and rushing into the children's bedroom. They had taken their hats, coats, scarves and gloves, and their wellingtons.

She grabbed her coat and flew down the stairs.

'Where do you think they would have made for?' asked Mr Goldman.

'Greenwich.'

'What? That's miles away. Why would they go all the way to Greenwich?'

'That's where David Matthews lives, and they want to live in his house.'

'I see. Look, why don't you go into the Dog and wake the landlord. He'll help you.'

Maggie began crying. 'Why should all this happen to me? What have I done to deserve such misery?'

Mr Goldman had a job to put his arm round Maggie's heaving shoulders as he was shorter than her. 'There, there, my dear, they can't have got far.' He suddenly straightened up. 'Have you looked in the lavatory?'

She shook her head. 'They wouldn't go in there, not in the dark, they're too frightened. Besides, they've got a bucket under their bed.'

'Well, I think perhaps we'd better start there, just in case. Let's do that first.'

When they pulled open the rickety wooden door, from two deathly white faces two pairs of wide open eyes were staring at them. They were huddled together like babes in the wood. With their teeth chattering loudly they managed slight smiles. Maggie threw herself at them and held them tight.

Mr Goldman gently patted their heads. 'Now come, the pair of you. You've given your mother quite a nasty shock. I think we should all go back in the warm, don't you?'

Two heads nodded vigorously.

Maggie laughed and cried together. They were safe.

Chapter 29

Once upstairs Mr Goldman went into the kitchen to put the kettle on while Maggie lit the fire. She sat rubbing the children's cold hands and feet.

'Why on earth did you do a thing like that?' she asked.

Laura looked at Jamie. 'We didn't think you'd care if we ran away.'

Maggie held them close. 'You silly girl, of course I care. I love you both so very much.'

'We was going to see Uncle David, but it was too foggy, so we decided to stay in the lav. We couldn't get back indoors 'cos we'd shut the front door, but we knew you'd find us,' said Laura.

'It was ever so cold in there,' said Jamie, getting closer.

Maggie put her arm round them both. 'Now promise me you will never ever do anything like that again. I would die if I lost you two as well.'

'Do you want me to stay and make the tea?' asked Mr Goldman, coming back into the room.

'Only if you want to,' said Maggie.

'If it's all the same to you I'll get downstairs. I do have a lot of orders to finish before Christmas.'

Maggie stood up. 'Of course. Thank you for being here.'

He took her hand. 'That's what life is all about, my dear. Besides, there are times when you've been there to help me. Now go on back and give them plenty of love.'

'I will, and thank you.' Maggie kissed his cheek.

'Now you two, it's hot porridge and toast for you.'

'What about school? Will we be late?' asked Jamie.

'No, but after your little adventure I think it best that you stay home.'

'All right then,' said Laura. 'But only for today.'

Maggie was pleased they both liked school so much.

'Mummy, why won't you let us go and live with Uncle David?' asked Laura.

'You could marry him,' said Jamie. 'Then it would be like in our storybook and we could all live happy ever after.'

Maggie sat between them. 'Now I want you both to listen very carefully to what I've got to say. First of all I love you both very much, and the reason I won't go and live with David is because if your daddy came back and the flat was empty, he wouldn't know where to find us, would he?'

They both shook their heads.

Jamie looked puzzled. 'But we don't know where Daddy is, do we?'

'No, Jamie, we don't, but until I'm certain that he won't be back I shall live here for ever.'

Laura picked at her fingers. 'Mr Goldman would tell him if we moved away.'

'Yes, I know that, but I still want to wait and see.'

'Don't know why,' said Jamie. 'It'll be more fun with Uncle David.'

'D'you think Daddy will ever come back?' asked Laura.

'I don't know. Now how about that breakfast?'

As Maggie stood in the kitchen stirring the porridge she thought over what she'd told them. Did she really believe in her heart that Tony would return, or was she just looking for an excuse not to go and live with David?

The thick, yellow swirling fog persisted for two days. It was a real peasouper and clung to everything. Very few people ventured out and even the trains stopped running.

Maggie felt she was trapped inside her home. She looked at the shoe boxes filled with the jewellery. Ten pounds' worth. Panic filled her. If she couldn't sell it before Christmas, what would she do about the money she owed? She put the boxes away again. There were a few more selling days to go, so she could only hope the weather improved. She knew Benny would be over when he could and that she could pay him later. But that would mean more debt.

It was Thursday before the stall came out and Maggie was pleased that although she only took half a crown, it was just enough to pay the week's rent for the stall. After that, things just ticked over.

Saturday morning saw Eve muffled up to the eyebrows.

Winnie laughed at all the scarves she had wrapped round her neck.

'Well, I ain't standing here freezing me whatsits off.'

Tom Cooper gave Eve a wave. He liked her because she was always ready for a dirty joke and good laugh. 'You ain't got any whatsits,' he shouted over to her.

'No, I know. They got froze off last week. So, Maggs, how's things?'

'Not too bad.' Deep down Maggie was worried. Although

trade was steady there were only two more Saturdays after this one to Christmas. Would this lot be cleared by then?

'Seeing David tomorrow?' asked Eve.

'Don't think so.'

'He working?'

'Something like that.' He sometimes had to work on a Sunday so that didn't come as any surprise to Eve. But Maggie didn't know whether or not he would come round.

At the end of the day, when the stall was locked away and Eve had left, Maggie sat and counted out the takings. Thirty bob. By the time she had bought food, coal and paid the rent there would be nothing left to pay off the loan or Alan, and Christmas was getting closer. She chewed the end of her pencil. Had she been overzealous and bought too much stock? What if she couldn't sell it? Would Percy take it back? How would she pay Mr Shore, and if it went over three months what interest would she end up paying?

Maggie felt her stomach churn. So much for trying to be the big businesswoman. It was all going wrong.

All day Sunday, between her chores, Maggie kept looking out of the window hoping David would turn up, but by the evening she knew her hopes had been in vain. Had he gone for ever as well?

Monday was the start of another wet and windy week. Maggie could have cried with the cold that, despite the many layers of clothes, ate its way into her bones, and the lack of customers didn't help to lift her spirits. Those that did come up to her stall had their heads bent and gave her a quick cursory glance, all eager to get back home. Maggie felt her face was frozen into the smile she tried hard to maintain. She spent a lot of time jumping up and down in an effort to bring life back into her feet. She had never realised it could be so cold and soul-destroying just standing around waiting for people to spend a few pence.

Even Winnie, who always looked on the bright side, was getting downcast. By Wednesday Maggie wanted the comfort of David around and she tried to think of an excuse to go to the police station to see him.

Thankfully, on Saturday the weather improved a little. At least the rain had stopped, and Maggie felt more optimistic as she displayed her stock.

'I hate this time o' year,' said Winnie.

'Don't you like Christmas then?' asked Maggie.

'Na, not really. Me and Mum just sit and listen to the wireless. Where's Eve?'

'Dunno, she's late.' Maggie looked at the shops. The shopkeepers had begun to decorate their windows. 'You going to put up any bits to make the stall festive like?' she asked Winnie.

'Might put a bit of holly round the shoes,' she laughed. 'Got ter be careful none falls inside otherwise I could lose a customer.'

'I thought I'd drape a bit of greenery round and some sparkly paper, might help the sales.'

'Not doing so well then, girl?'

'Not bad, but we've got to get into the spirit.' All the while Maggie was keeping her eye out for Eve. But it was Dan who came up to her.

'Eve's got a filthy cold. I told her to stay in bed, but she was worried about you on your own so I said I'd come round and give you a hand.'

'Thanks, Dan. Poor Eve. Will she be all right?'

'Yer, I'll give her a good dose of whisky when I get back. Now d'you wanner go up and see to the kids?'

'If you don't mind. Win here will give you a hand if you get rushed off your feet.'

Winnie laughed. 'Chance would be a fine thing, love.'

Upstairs Maggie gave the children their dinner, banked up the fire and once again made her way down to the market.

'That bloke round the corner's selling the same sorta stuff as this, but a lot cheaper,' said a woman, picking up a bone bracelet.

'What?' yelled Maggie. 'There ain't any other stalls round there.'

'Na, he ain't got a stall, it's a suitcase.'

'Oh no,' cried Maggie. 'That's all I need. You stay here, Dan, while I go round and give him a piece of me mind.'

Maggie rushed round the corner in time to see the old man hurrying along the road carrying his suitcase.

'All right then, missis?' said the policeman who had been watching him.

'Why don't you arrest him?' yelled Maggie. She felt like jumping up and down with temper.

'We won't worry too much about the likes of them, only if they're causing an obstruction. We just tell 'em to move on.'

'But he's taking my trade.'

'Oh yes, you've got a stall round the corner.'

'Yes I have, so what you gonner do about it?'

'Nothing. Come on now, live and let live. After all, he was a soldier and was wounded, so he told me.'

'Didn't look very wounded to me.' She glared defiantly at him, hands on hips.

A few people had stopped to listen when they heard Maggie's raised voice.

'Now come on, missis.' The policeman took hold of her arm.

'Leave me be.' She tried to shrug him off but he was holding on to her very tightly.

'Yer, leave her alone,' shouted a man in the small crowd that was now gathering.

'What she done then?' asked another.

Maggie had tears of temper and frustration running down her face.

The policeman was getting embarrassed. 'Now come on, missis, move on otherwise I'll have to take you in.'

'Well, go on then, arrest me,' she said defiantly.

'She's got two kids at home. Leave her be,' yelled a woman. 'What's she done anyway?'

'I'm only trying to look after my rights.'

'Oh, she's one of them,' said a young man in the crowd.

'I have to pay rent. That bloke doesn't.'

'Maggie! Maggie! What the bloody hell's going on?' Winnie's voice could be heard above the din.

Maggie turned to see her waddling towards her.

'OK, officer, I'll take her.' She grabbed Maggie's arm. 'What the bloody hell d'yer think you're doing?'

'I wanted that copper to arrest that bloke that was selling without a licence.'

'Yer, and you very nearly got yourself arrested. Silly cow. Good job that Mrs Black came and told us, otherwise you might have been carted off.'

'Don't care if I was. It ain't fair,' said Maggie, slumping along like a spoilt child. 'I have to pay rent, he don't.'

Maggie turned and gave the policeman a filthy look and shouted, 'He should be locked up.'

'There's a lot of things not fair in this world, and you being locked up in prison ain't gonner feed your kids. Now get back to your stall,' said Winnie.

'What if he comes back again?'

'Who, the copper?'

'No, that bloke with the suitcase.'

'There's not a thing you can do about it.'

'We'll see about that.'

'Now you listen to me. Don't you dare do anythink daft like that again, d'you hear?'

Maggie nodded.

'Think of those kids.'

Maggie certainly gave the traders something to chew over for the rest of the day.

Dan found it very funny. 'That would have been a turn-up for the book, you in clink.'

'It ain't funny, Dan,' said Winnie. 'She was very stupid and I was worried.'

'Eve will be sorry she missed that. She would have given him a run for his money. I ain't half enjoyed meself today.'

Maggie smiled. Dan had been trying to be as helpful as Eve but he was clumsy. His large fat fingers broke the backs off two pairs of earrings when he rushed to serve a good-looking well-built young girl. They stood laughing and giggling like a couple of kids as he tried to put the earrings on her.

'Good job Eve ain't here,' said Winnie. 'She'd give him what for.'

'It's all good harmless fun,' said Maggie. But she wasn't

340

so pleased when he got a gold-coloured chain necklace so twisted in a girl's hair that Maggie had to break it and put it to one side.

The afternoon wore on. The lamps were lit, and the Salvation Army began playing carols, but as darkness fell so did Maggie's optimism, and she couldn't get into the festive mood. That man with the suitcase was bothering her. Would he be back next Saturday?

It was getting late and nobody was making any attempt to move away.

'Why ain't we packing up?' asked Dan, looking anxiously at his watch.

'Always try to hang on a bit later these last couple of Sat'days,' said Winnie. 'And you can't go till the others move off.'

Maggie looked at Dan. 'If you want to get back to Eve I understand.'

'I can't leave you.'

'Well, I can't move, not till they do. I thought being up this end was an asset, but it can also be a nuisance.'

When it got to nine o'clock Maggie was beginning to panic. 'I'll have to go up and see to the kids. They ain't had any tea yet. And I expect the fire's out as well.'

'Look, pack all your stuff up and we'll see about putting your stall away later on,' said Winnie.

'Thanks.'

'I best be off,' said Dan. 'You had a good day then?'

'Not too bad.'

'It's been bloody cold though, ain't it?'

Maggie nodded. 'Give me love to Eve. Hope she's better soon.'

'So do I. Bye.' He waved to them and made his way home.

'He's a nice bloke,' said Winnie. 'That Eve's lucky to finish up with someone reliable like him.'

'Yes, she is,' said Maggie, thinking about the small amount of money nestling in her stallholder's apron pocket.

She raced up the stairs to find the children huddled together on the sofa.

'We're ever so cold,' said Laura.

'And hungry,' added Jamie.

'I'm sorry.' She poked the fire, making flames dance. 'I'll get your tea right away.' She threw her money bag on the sideboard.

Later that evening she got out her notebook and counted out her money. It was disastrous, and with Christmas so near she wondered how she'd manage. What could she do to shift the stock?

On Sunday Maggie hoped that David would visit them, but once more she was disappointed. Was he as fond of her as he had said? She'd hoped he'd come back, for the children's sakes. Everything was beginning to make Maggie really miserable and she couldn't see any way out.

The following week, again the wind and rain dampened everybody's spirits, despite the cheerful holly and Christmas trees hanging round Fred's stall and fairy lights twinkling in the shop windows. Rows of chickens and turkeys were hanging outside the butcher's. Maggie looked in the toy shop. What could she buy Jamie and Laura for Christmas? Should she blow everything she earned on them, or should she try and pay back some of the money?

Overnight it became very cold, freezing the streets and pavements and making them very treacherous, so once again few people ventured out. Maggie's fortunes were looking bleaker by the day.

On Wednesday afternoon Maggie was very surprised to see Benny coming towards her.

''Allo, gel,' he said. 'Got a few bits for you.' His eyes had lost their sparkle and Maggie noted they were red and bloodshot, and he didn't have his work clothes on.

'Hallo, Benny. You look very smart. Don't often see you round this way in the week, or out in this weather. You should be at home in the warm with your feet up. Everything all right?'

He nodded.

''Allo, Benny,' said Winnie, coming over. ''Ere, where you off to all tarted up? You ain't gotter see a policeman, have you?' She laughed and turned to Maggie. 'That's the only time we see 'em dressed up is when they've got to appear in front of the beak.'

'No, I ain't gotter see a policeman. It's just that it's too cold to be out sitting on a cart. 'Sides—' He stopped to blow his nose.

Winnie's attention was drawn to her stall. 'Just coming, love.'

'I don't know how Bella managed to run her stall in this cold,' said Maggie, banging her hands together.

'You been ter see Bella lately?'

Alarm filled Maggie. 'No, not for a couple of weeks. Why?'

Benny shuffled his feet. He looked uncomfortable.

Maggie suddenly realised he looked very sad. 'Benny? What's happened?'

He swallowed hard. 'It's Nellie.'

'Nellie?' repeated Maggie. 'What, your horse?'

'Yer. Thought Bella might have told yer.'

'No. What's happened to Nellie?'

'Knacker's yard.'

Maggie felt upset. 'Knacker's yard. She ain't . . .?'

He nodded.

Maggie touched his arm. 'Benny, I'm really sorry. She was a lovely old thing. What happened?'

'She fell and broke her leg. So I had to have her put down.'

'That's awful. What you gonner do?'

'Dunno. She's had a good run, been part of me life fer years. Better than a wife – at least she never answered back.' He gave her a slight smile.

Maggie patted his hand. 'But she couldn't keep you warm in bed though, could she?'

'No, love, you're right there.'

'What are you gonner do?'

'Dunno. Ain't done nothink without Nellie.'

'Will you be over Bella's on Sunday?'

'Should think so. Don't know what to do now, though. Feel like a ship out o' water. Can't walk the streets on me own, can I?' He looked so sad.

'I'll try and get over this Sunday, but this weather hasn't been so good.'

'You selling well?'

'Mustn't grumble.' How could she tell him things weren't that good? 'I've got to see Bella to find out about what we're all doing for Christmas.'

'Will Dave bring you over?'

It was Maggie's turn to look uncomfortable. 'I don't know.'

'Everythink all right with you two?'

'Yes, of course.'

'Bella's a fine woman, you know.'

Maggie nodded. If only she was as strong in character as her.

When Benny left she felt really down.

'Poor old Benny,' said Winnie when Maggie told her. 'He's had the horse fer years.'

'I know.' Maggie began putting her stock into boxes. She couldn't help selfishly thinking how Benny's misfortune would affect her. When things did get better and she had some cash for more stock, Benny would no longer be able to supply her.

'Hello, Maggie.'

A familiar voice brought a smile and a blush to her face.

'David.' She quickly looked round.

'What the bloody hell does he want?' said Tom Cooper. 'Not more trouble.'

Winnie came over to Maggie and David. 'Ain't seen you round here for a while. I hope it ain't bad news.'

'No, not at all, just making sure everyone's all right.'

Winnie inclined her head towards Maggie. 'Have you told him you nearly got arrested on Sat'day?'

'No I ain't, and I didn't.'

'Arrested?' David was taken aback. 'What for?'

'I just had a few words with a policeman, that's all.'

Winnie laughed. 'Thought you might be here to run her in.'

David looked from one to the other. 'No, I was just passing, that's all. Are you sure everything's all right?'

Maggie knew everybody was taking an interest. 'It is now.' She would have loved to throw her arms round his neck and kiss him long and passionately.

He moved closer, and bent his head towards her. Maggie held her breath.

'I'm sorry I haven't been around but . . .' He looked up at the faces. 'Look, can we talk?'

'I've got to put my stall away, then we'll go upstairs.'

'Let me give you a hand.'

To Maggie suddenly it was Christmas. The fairy lights in the shop windows were burning brighter and even the trees and holly on Fred's stall seemed to be greener.

'First time I've seen a copper working,' said Tom Cooper when David began pushing the stall.

'Can see he ain't used to it,' said Winnie.

'Quick, get out his way otherwise yer might get run over. 'Ere, mate, is it an offensive to be run over by a market stall?' said Tom, jumping out of his way.

Everybody was in good humour and stood back laughing as David battled with the two wheels, trying to keep them straight over the cobbles.

Maggie laughed. She realised it had been a while since she had laughed, and it felt good.

When they reached her front door Maggie saw that David looked serious.

'Anythink wrong?' she asked.

'I wasn't sure what kind of welcome I'd get.'

She smiled. 'It's the good-will-towards-men time of year. Besides, I've got over my tantrums now.' She pushed open the door. 'I had a bit of trouble with another bloke selling, and I did have a problem with them two.' She nodded towards the stairs.

'Not through me, I hope.'

'Well, yes, it was in a way. You see they were coming to see you.'

'See me? When? How?'

'I'll tell you later.'

ct so dark and

Chapter 30

'Uncle David,' yelled the children when Maggie pushed open the door and he walked in.

Then Laura looked guilty and slumped into the chair, trying to make herself as small as possible.

'It's all right,' said Maggie, guessing she felt a little apprehensive about seeing David again. 'I'll make the tea.' Maggie stood in the kitchen, happier than she'd been for days. He had come back to them. The loud chatter from the living room told her the children were over their fear of never seeing David again, and their laughter was a joy to hear.

David was told about how they only got as far as the lav in their attempt to run away. He in turn told them never to do that again, otherwise Father Christmas wouldn't visit them if he didn't know where they lived. They hung on to his every word.

Jamie giggled. 'It was ever so cold, and ever so dark and creepy in there.'

'I was worried about the spiders,' said Laura.

'You told me there wasn't none,' said Jamie.

'I only told you that so you wouldn't cry.'

'I didn't cry. Well, not very much.'

Maggie kissed the top of his head. 'Anyway, you won't be doing that again in a hurry.'

Maggie went on to tell David about Nellie. 'Poor old Benny, he was so upset.'

'He's had that horse for as long as I can remember,' said David. 'I like Benny, he's a real character. A bit bent at times, but not a real villain. I wonder how he's going to get about now? Can't see him buying another horse, not at his time of life.'

'I'm going over to see Bella on Sunday and she'll tell me all the news.'

'You must let me take you.'

Maggie looked at the two faces grinning at her. How could she refuse? 'OK.'

Soon it was time for the children to go to bed. Maggie would have liked to have sent them off as soon as she walked in – she wanted David to herself.

'Well, that's them down,' she said, closing the door. 'Mind you, I don't know about sleeping. They're very pleased to see you, you know.'

'What about you?'

She smiled. 'Me too.'

'I'm sorry about my big mouth. I shouldn't have kept on to you, but I hate to see you unhappy and worried.'

'I'm all right.'

'Are you? Now what's this about you almost being arrested?'

Maggie laughed and told him all that had happened. 'I was very angry. He was taking my customers away, and I can well do without that.'

'And I can well do without you being run in. Seriously, though, how are things?'

'Not bad, I suppose.' She wasn't going to tell him the truth. 'David, why are you here? And in the week as well.'

He lit a cigarette. 'I couldn't get to see you last Sunday as I had to go up north. The weather's really bad up there.'

Maggie sat up. Something in the way he was speaking told her that this wasn't strictly a social call. 'David, have you had any news?' She was dreading the answer.

He tapped the end of his cigarette into the ashtray.

She wanted to scream at him to get on with it, but she could sense it was something he wanted to say very carefully, and she suspected it was something she didn't want to hear.

The door opened and Laura asked, 'Mummy, will Benny be at Granny's on Sunday?'

Maggie jumped up. She wanted to push her out of the room. 'I expect so, why?'

'Now Benny ain't got Nellie, me and Jamie's gonner do him a drawing of a horse.'

She smiled. 'That's very nice of you. Now, back to bed. Remember it's school tomorrow.'

The door closed, and Maggie sat down again. 'David, is it about Tony?'

'It was.'

'Was!' she cried out. 'What d'you mean, was?'

'I had to go up north. Yorkshire to be exact. You see they had a bloke in custody, and they wanted him to be identified. It was in association with a murder and nobody knew anything about him, just that he came from London.'

'Murder?' Maggie felt her head swimming.

'It was a nasty business. He'd killed his wife.'

'His wife?' repeated Maggie.

'He said she was his wife. He was a cockney, and said his name was Bill Bailey. Well, they knew that was a joke to start with, and wondered if he had a wife and another life somewhere else. They went through the files of missing men, dark-haired, early thirties, looking for anything that showed he had other connections and one of the names they came up with was Tony's. As it was my case, I had to go.'

Maggie felt the colour drain from her face. 'And was . . .?'

'No. After all we have his photo on file, remember, so I could tell them it definitely wasn't Tony.'

'Did you see the man?'

'Yes, I spoke to him.'

'Did you know him?'

'No. Are you all right?'

She nodded. 'Will this nightmare ever go away?'

'Not till he walks back into your life, or they find . . .'

'David, why did you come over here to tell me all this, getting my hopes up and then—'

'I had to see you again. I was looking for an excuse.'

'Did you need one?'

'I wasn't sure.'

Maggie stood up and looked out of the window. She wanted to kiss him and tell him he was more than welcome in her home, but she couldn't speak. At this moment she didn't know what she wanted most, Tony dead, or alive.

'Well, am I?'

She nodded.

'Do you still want me to take you to Bella's on Sunday?'

'If you don't mind.'

'It'll be my pleasure.'

She smiled. 'I was hoping you'd say that.'

When David left it was with just a kiss on the cheek. Maggie knew that he too felt under strain.

As David drove home he knew that Tony would always come between them, and it would take time to get back on the understanding they had before he'd put his foot in it. How he wished it had been Tony up there; then he would have been out of Maggie's life for good.

It was the last Saturday before Christmas. Eve was better and was as usual enjoying herself, laughing and joking with everyone but Maggie was on edge. Was that bloke round the corner? She wanted to go and see, but she was aware that everybody thought she'd been making a big thing about it, though they didn't know the financial trouble she was in.

Maggie wasn't that surprised to see Alan. She was pleased he was alone, and as usual she felt guilty about his money.

'Helen OK?' she asked.

'Yes, very busy getting ready for Christmas. We're having a few friends over on Boxing Day. Any chance of you getting over, Maggs?'

'I don't think so.'

'Got plenty of mistletoe?' asked Eve.

'I think Helen's getting it today, so I mustn't hang about. Got to give her a hand, you know.'

'Alan,' Maggie moved away from Eve, 'I ain't got any more money to give you just yet, what with Christmas and everything.' She kept her voice very low.

'I didn't come over for that. So how's things? You managing without Bill, then? Selling plenty?'

'Not too bad.' Maggie had written and told him about Bill going in the army.

'There's a little gift for you and the children.' He handed her a paper carrier bag.

'Thanks. Yours is upstairs. I'll just pop up and get it. I won't invite you up as I don't like leaving Eve on her own for too long.'

'I understand, I'll wait here for you.'

Maggie hurried away. She hated this bland conversation. Tony and the money he'd borrowed had caused this rift between them.

Alan left and the afternoon dragged on. Maggie was worried. It wasn't the sort of day she'd been hoping for. Twice she managed to go round the corner to see if the man with the suitcase was taking her trade, but she never saw him. She knew the takings would be down, and that night when she counted out the money fear gripped her. Only two more trading days to Christmas.

Maggie sat back and looked at the pile of silver and coppers. What should she do – send Alan another pound or pay back some to Mr Shore? 'No, bugger it,' she said out loud. 'After I've put the rents and coal money away I'll spend it. We're gonner have a good Christmas. Monday I'll get a tree, get the fairy lights and the decorations out, then I'll go to the toy shop. I'll even get me and Laura a new frock. Everybody will have a great Christmas. After all I don't owe any to Mr Windsor, and the rest will have to wait.'

On Sunday Maggie was very quiet as David drove her to

Bella's. She wanted Bella to come to them, but knew it would be a big chore, and at the moment half of her didn't want Christmas at all.

'So are you coming to me?' asked Maggie, trying hard not to make the invitation sound too half-hearted.

'No, love. Me and Benny 'ere reckon you should come over here. It'll give you a break. 'Sides, when have you got time to do the shopping?'

'I can always pop to the shops, they ain't that far away. But how would I get over? We'd have to come late on Christmas Eve.'

'We can't do that!' yelled Laura frantically. 'Father Christmas might not find us.'

Maggie smiled. 'I'm sure he will, he's very clever.'

David gave a slight cough. 'Look, I'm not doing anything that morning so I could bring you over.'

Bella laughed. 'Where you spending the day, then?'

'I shall be on—'

'Look, if you're not on duty why don't you spend it with us?' she interrupted.

Maggie couldn't believe it. This was all that she had wanted to happen.

'I'd like that. I am normally on duty over Christmas, as I don't have anyone to share it with, but I can always make other arrangements.'

'Right, that's settled then,' said Bella. 'I'll expect to see you about one. That'll give me a chance to get it all ready.'

'What are you doing, Benny?' asked Maggie.

'Well, as he ain't got Nellie to worry about he's coming over here the night before,' said Bella. 'And don't look like that. We're going up the pub, and he's staying in the spare room.'

Maggie felt like laughing out loud. 'Well, let's hope you don't get too drunk to do the dinner.'

'I'm so glad I'm going to see you over Christmas,' said Maggie, after they arrived home and the children were in bed.

'I'm pleased as well.' He walked to the door. 'I won't stay, got a lot of paperwork. I'll see you on Christmas morning.'

He was keeping his distance, thought Maggie as she closed the door behind him. She was in a turmoil. Although she'd kept him at arm's length that's not what she really wanted. Had he changed his mind about her living with him?

Maggie's thoughts turned to Christmas Eve. She should have asked him to come over as Eve and Dan were taking her to the pub. But what if she had a few too many drinks? She knew she would throw caution to the wind and beg him to stay. But what if Tony came back?

David's thoughts were also on Christmas Eve. If only things were different. If only Maggie would let go. But he knew she never would.

It was late on Christmas Eve when the stall was finally put away. All afternoon, despite the carols coming loud and joyful from the Salvation Army and the drunks singing bawdy songs, Maggie felt cold, tired and irritable. She had so much to do she wasn't sure she really wanted to go out tonight.

Everybody else had been full of the Christmas spirit. All

day people had been waiting at Fred's stall and he had been working flat out. Mrs Russell had sold almost all her flowers, but Winnie, Tom and Maggie had had very few customers.

'Food's what's on their minds today,' said Winnie, banging her hands round herself to keep her circulation going.

When the punters finally began to drift away Fred took Winnie's arm and Tom grabbed hold of Mrs Russell and they danced and sang as bottles were passed round. Fred said it was to keep out the cold. Maggie tried to join in, but her heart wasn't in it. She still had most of the stock left even though she had been selling it off cheap. There was no way she could pay Alan, or any of the loan. The little money she had left after paying the rent and coal went on presents. 'Sod it,' she said to herself as she climbed the stairs. 'I'll let 1936 look after itself.'

The lights on the tree sparkled and two eager little faces looked at her when she walked in, making her forget her own misery.

'After tea it's a bath.' The thought of dragging the tin bath up the stairs and filling it made Maggie feel more dismayed. Her thoughts went to David's bathroom. If she moved in with him she wouldn't have to do this.

'I've left me list on the table,' said Jamie, squeezing the flannel over Laura and making her squeal. 'Should we leave something for Father Christmas to eat?'

Maggie smiled. She had to be cheerful for their sakes. After all, Christmas was for children. 'I think we could leave him a biscuit and a drink.'

'What about his reindeer?' asked Laura with a worried expression.

'I hope he's going to leave them outside. Now come on, jump out.'

She rubbed them dry. Their faces were glowing with delight. Maggie held them close. They smelt so clean and fresh and she loved them dearly. 'Now bedtime.'

For once there were no arguments. Maggie finished emptying the tin bath and struggled down into the yard with it.

As she draped the damp towels around the fire guard she reflected on past Christmas Eves. They had been so different. Bathed and fed, the children were in bed and out of the way by the time Tony came home, usually a little worse for drink. They would then go to the Dog and by closing time Tony could just about walk home. Then, after playing Father Christmas, they would make love. Remembering, Maggie let a tear run down her cheek. She desperately wanted to be loved. To have someone to hold her, caress her, and to make her feel a whole woman again. She so desperately wanted to be looked after. Please, Tony, she begged silently, after all this time, let me know what's happened – let me get on with my life.

The scene at the Dog and Duck was a familiar one for Christmas Eve. Gus was wearing his red Father Christmas hat and Beatie had tinsel draped all over her, and everyone was happy and singing. It seemed to Maggie that she was the only one who was miserable and felt out of place, though she did her best not to show it.

After a few drinks she too relaxed and was soon up dancing with the rest of them.

'Want us to come up with you?' asked Eve, when they reached Maggie's front door.

'No thanks. I'm going straight to bed after I've done me Father Christmas bit.'

'Maggie.' Eve held her tight. 'We all know how hard it is for you and what you're going through, more so this time of year. I only wish there was something I could do.'

'So do I, Eve.' She choked back a tear. 'And thanks for all your help.'

'That's what mates are for,' said Dan, hugging Maggie in turn.

'We'll see you on Boxing night, that's if you fancy coming out for a drink.'

'Thanks. I'll see.'

'Then we've got New Year's Eve. Christ, we've had some great New Year's Eves in the past, ain't we, girl?'

'Trust you to open your big mouth,' said Eve, giving Dan a push.

'Why? What did I say?'

'Good night, Maggs,' said Eve, pulling Dan's arm. 'You've got as much tact as my arse,' she said, dragging him down the road.

Maggie laughed as she watched them go. She could hear Eve going on at Dan till they turned the corner. If Dan was in a loving mood he'd better play his cards right before he got home.

Before she closed the door Maggie looked up at the sky. It was black and full of stars. The air was cold and crisp – definitely a night made for love.

She sighed. 'Well come on, Mother Christmas, let's get this job over.' She stopped at the bottom of the stairs, thinking. Dan was right, they had had some good New Year's Eves, but that was all passed. Let's hope they could go into the next one with a bit more hope.

She tingled with the thought of what that could bring.

Chapter 31

'Thank you, Bella, that was delicious,' said David, pushing his chair back from the table. 'I don't ever remember having a Christmas dinner like that before.' He stopped. He looked sad. 'Well, not for many years anyway. And that pudding.'

'Thank you, son. Made it meself, always have done.'

Maggie wanted to hold him close. She would know how to look after him.

'And me and Jamie found a thru'penny bit in it as well,' said Laura.

Bella gave Maggie a wink; that had been arranged. Bella's face was glowing with drink as well as praise. She was wearing her bright green crêpe paper hat that came from a cracker, at a jaunty angle. She was still grinning at David. 'So, how about you doing the washing up then? Better than singing for yer supper.'

They all laughed.

'See, you don't catch me saying too much,' said Benny, pushing the red paper hat he was wearing back from his eyes.

'And you can give him an 'and,' said Bella.

'No, I'll do it.' Maggie began clearing the table.

'Me and Benny will just have a quiet sit-down with the kids,' said Bella, following the children who had rushed off into the front room to play with their new toys.

'It won't be very quiet in there,' said Maggie, filling the washing-up bowl with hot water and throwing in a handful of soda from the stone jar on the windowsill. 'I'm so glad you could stay. Tea towel's in that drawer.'

'So am I, it's been really great.'

Maggie was conscious of him standing close to her. She could feel his warmth. If only she could let her real feelings take over. She turned and her paper hat fell to the floor. They both bent together to retrieve it. Their eyes and hands met. Maggie thought she would die of anticipation.

'Mummy, Mummy,' said Laura, rushing into the kitchen, giggling. 'Granny and Benny's fast asleep and they ain't half snoring.'

'Well don't wake them.' She turned to the sink and carried on with the washing-up.

It was in the evening after the tea things had been put away and they were all sitting round the fire having a quiet drink that Bella suddenly announced, 'By the way, Maggs, I've got to tell yer, me and Benny's getting married at Easter.'

Maggie almost dropped her glass. Her mouth fell open but no sound came out. Suddenly tears were rolling down her cheeks.

'What you crying for, love?' said Benny, taking her hand. 'Don't you like me?'

'Oh Benny, I love you, and I'm so pleased for the pair of you.' She threw her arms round his neck, then jumped up to hug Bella.

'Congratulations,' said David.

Maggie was drying her eyes.

'What you crying for, Mummy?' said Laura.

'It's just that I like to see people happy.'

'Well, I think you're soppy,' said Jamie.

'Can I be your bridesmaid?' asked Laura.

'It won't be that kind of wedding,' said Bella.

Laura returned to the puzzle she was doing. 'I would have liked to be a bridesmaid.'

'Why are you waiting till Easter?' asked Maggie.

'The weather's a bit better then, that's all, and it'll give Benny time to clear out all his rubbish from over that stable.'

'It ain't all rubbish.'

'Well, you ain't bringing it here.'

Maggie smiled. Theirs was certainly going to be a very interesting marriage.

'If you want a hand, remember I've always got the car,' said David.

'That's real kind of you, son,' said Benny. 'I might well want a hand.'

'When did all these plans start?' asked Maggie.

'A couple of days ago. He's like a fish out o' water without that bloody horse, and he was round here most of the time, so I said we might just as well be married and stop the neighbours talking. That way I'll get a few bob out o' him as well for his bed and board.'

Benny laughed. 'Don't you believe her. She's got a very soft spot for me.'

'Yer,' said Bella. 'The only soft spot I've got's in me bleeding head.'

The laughter and toasts to Benny and Bella followed, but Maggie felt ill at ease. Nobody had mentioned Tony. It was just as though he didn't exist any more.

It was when they were leaving that Bella took Maggie to one side.

'I know who you're thinking about and I only wish he was here, love,' she said tenderly. 'And I wish you was happy as well. I can see it in your eyes you're not, and there ain't a thing I can do about it.'

Maggie held her close. 'I'm all right. Just as long as you're happy and certain you're doing the right thing.'

'I am, Maggs. Been fond of the old goat for years, but don't tell him that. It was that horse that stood in the way.'

Maggie kissed her. 'Thanks for a lovely Christmas.'

'You take care. Me and Benny will be over to make sure you're all right.'

As David drove them home Maggie sat back and reflected on the day. In her eyes it had been almost perfect.

'Would you like a cup of tea?' she asked, after David had carried a tired little Jamie up to bed.

'Yes, please. He's heavy when he's asleep.'

'It's been a long exciting day for them.'

'And as for Benny and Bella . . .' he said, settling himself on the sofa.

'Yes, that was a surprise. I wonder what Tony will make of it – a new dad.' Maggie hurried to the kitchen when the kettle boiled.

David was right behind her. 'Maggie, I'm not going to pull my punches. I love you and I want you to come and live with me.' She went to speak but he held up his hand to stop her. 'I'm not going to say any more. I don't think you'll ever be free from Tony, and a home waits for you if ever you want it. I want to make love to you now, right this minute, but I won't. Now I'll have my tea and go.' He went back into the living room.

Maggie's eyes were wide open. What could she say? Was this going to be the end of their friendship?

'David,' she said, following him with the tray of tea things. 'What if I was free?'

'That would put a different light on things, wouldn't it? But you're not.'

His attitude frightened her. It was almost an ultimatum.

'Give me time.'

'Of course.'

'You will still come and see us, won't you?'

He smiled. 'Of course.'

She wanted to throw her arms round him and take him to her bedroom. But this wasn't the way she'd been brought up. If I was Eve things would have certainly been different by now, she thought to herself.

That evening the pub was quiet till Maggie told everyone about Bella and Benny. They all decided it was the best thing that could have happened to them, and despite the absence of the newly engaged pair an impromptu party was held in their honour.

Maggie didn't take the stall out on Friday, the day after Boxing Day, and she shouldn't have bothered on Saturday as business was bad and she certainly didn't need the steady drizzle to dampen her spirits. The only light relief all day was telling everyone about Bella and Benny. Winnie decided to have a collection and get them a present.

'They'll be tickled pink,' said Maggie as she was handed the bag of money.

'What yer gonner get 'em, love?' asked Winnie.

'Don't know. I'll have a think about it. I'll let you know before I get it, though.'

The stalls were put away early and Maggie knew her takings were a disaster again. She counted out the money Winnie had given her. Two pounds. That would pay her rents and the coalman for the next two weeks. She put the money in the drawer, feeling both tempted and guilty. Would the traders find out if she kept it?

That night she tossed and turned. She lay in bed thinking about the money for the present. What had she got herself into? Why did she think she was cleverer than Tony? Was she just like him? He hadn't stolen, but he had run away from his responsibilities. To her, her children's welfare was the most important thing in her life, and if it meant stealing to keep them warm and fed she was prepared to do that. Besides, she thought, turning over, I don't think the traders would really mind if they knew the reason.

She desperately needed the money. She looked round the flat. That mirror would have to go. Monday, she'd go to the pawn shop.

After a fitful night Maggie woke to the sound of rain beating on the window. Thank goodness it was Sunday. She turned over and went back to sleep.

David sat in his dining room watching the rain drip from the bare trees. Everything in the garden looked dejected and lifeless. This is how he felt without Maggie. He wanted to go and see her but what excuse did he have? How could he make her see she was wasting her life? But what if Tony Ross came back? Would she still want Tony? David felt guilty at almost brushing him aside, but what else could he do? 'If I'd stayed I would have made love to you, and that could have been the end of our friendship. I love you, Maggie Ross,' he said to himself, 'and those lovely kids, and I know we could be happy.' Bella had made up her mind to get on with her life, but Maggie hadn't the same freedom. Where the hell was Tony Ross?

David decided to go to work. He couldn't stay here feeling sorry for himself. At the station there was always something to do, and someone to talk to.

'Anything interesting happened over the holiday?' he asked the young officer at the desk, when he arrived.

'No, sir. Not on our patch, only the usual drunks. There's been a big fire over the Elephant. A warehouse went up, suspected arson. Seems an old boy got killed.'

David stood still, then slowly walked back to the desk. 'Do you happen to know the victim's name?'

'A Mr Collins, Mr Percy Collins. Does it ring any bells, sir?'

'No, not for me, but I know someone it will affect.' He turned and left the station.

'David,' said Maggie. 'I didn't expect to see you here today.'

'I've just come from the station. Children, would you mind going to your bedroom? I've got to talk to Mummy.'

Maggie fell back on to the sofa. 'Oh no.'

Laura and Jamie for once did as they were told without any questions.

'No, Maggie, listen. It's not Tony, it's Percy.'

'Percy. What, the Percy I buy from?'

'Yes.'

'What's happened to him?'

'I'm afraid he's dead.'

Maggie felt the colour drain from her face. 'Oh no! He was such a nice old man. How did it happen?'

'His warehouse burnt down and he was trapped inside. They think it might have been deliberate.'

'Who would do a thing like that?'

'I don't know. I haven't been over there yet, but I will.'

'Poor Mabel, is she all right?'

'There wasn't any other name mentioned.'

Maggie suddenly put her hand to her mouth. 'Lil. Lil, she said they would have a tragedy, and she said I . . .' Maggie's tears fell. 'She told me I would have a lot more grief in my life,' she cried, burying her head in David's shoulder.

He put his arm round her and gently held her close. He wanted to kiss away her distress. Her sobs hurt him.

When she pulled back he handed her his large white handkerchief.

She blew her nose. 'Thank you. I'll wash it.'

'Don't worry about it.'

'Can you find out more about how it happened for me?'

'Yes, I'll go over tomorrow and ask around.'

'I'd like to go to Percy's funeral.'

'I could always take you.'

'Thank you. David, what more grief could I have?'

'I don't know, and I don't think you should take too much notice of what an old woman told you.'

She gave him a weak smile. 'Well, time will tell.'

'What will you do about stock?'

'I don't know. At the moment I've got more than enough to keep me going, it's the selling that's the problem.'

'Are you having money problems?'

'No, course not. Would you like a cup of tea?'

'Thought you'd never ask.'

When Maggie opened the door Laura and Jamie came in.

'What have you been up to?' asked David.

'Been doing drawing,' said Laura, looking round.

'What did you want Mummy for?' asked Jamie.

'I had to tell her something.'

'Why does my mummy always cry when you come here?' asked Laura.

'She doesn't always cry.'

'A lot of times she does,' said Jamie.

Laura sat next to him. 'D'you know, I think she loves you and don't want our daddy to come back.'

Jamie wriggled in beside David. 'And we think she wants to live at your house.'

David smiled. 'Whatever your mummy decides is OK by me.'

Chapter 32

The alarm broke into Maggie's troubled sleep early on Saturday morning. She buried her head in the pillow and groaned. She didn't have to get out of bed to know it was another dark dismal day with the rain beating down like stair rods. Nobody would venture out today unless they were mad or really had to, and then it would only be a quick shop for their essentials. It was to be yet another awful barren day. Nobody would come out in this weather to buy a pair of lousy earrings.

She turned over and gazed at the ceiling. Worry was making her feel ill. In the two weeks since the New Year she had only managed to take the stall out once. Already 1936 had started terribly and seemed to be going from bad to worse. Since Christmas Maggie hadn't even taken enough to pay the rent on the stall or the flat. Coal and food were her first priority.

She cast her eyes round the bedroom. She had taken so many of her trinkets to the pawn shop, careful not to remove anything that would be noticed by Bella or Eve. She had told them she'd got a good buyer for her large mirror, and they accepted that. She looked at her hand. There was always her engagement ring. But that would feel as if she had severed her finger. She studied the five-diamond ring. If it came to it, that too would have to go.

She worried about the mounting interest on the money she owed Mr Shore. Maggie wanted to cry, she felt so guilty about keeping the traders' money for Bella's present, but what could she do? The children had to be kept warm and fed. She wanted to tell someone about the mess she'd got herself into, but who?

She gave another moan and turned over. The fact that Percy's Emporium had burnt down and she wouldn't be able to buy more stock when she finally managed to shift the large amount she already had was another problem she could foresee. She got cross with herself. That was selfish and wicked. Percy was dead. Poor Mabel had to start a new life, knowing Percy's death was brought about by himself, getting drunk and knocking the paraffin stove over. 'Well at least Mabel *knows* he's dead,' she said out loud. Was Lil right? Was this the grief she had told Maggie to expect?

In some ways she could understand Tony running away. This was how he must have felt when everything was closing in on him.

To think she was so happy up until a few weeks before Christmas. She had been selling well, and even managed to pay Alan back a few more pounds. Only one to go, then she took out the big loan. How long would that take to pay back at this rate?

Maggie dragged herself from her bed, made a pot of tea and took it into the living room. She sat at the table absentmindedly stirring the leaves round and round in the pot, and as always when she was alone, thoughts of David filled her mind.

She was really very fond of him, and knew she could love him if she could let go of her hopes about Tony. But was it hope now or just the final confirmation that Tony was dead that was stopping her from loving David? She knew that at the back of her mind she still lived in the hope that Tony had lost his memory and would return one day. All those years of happiness just couldn't be swept away.

Maggie toyed with the spoon. David wanted to offer her so much. He had a lovely house and the children adored him, and he had a steady job, and could give her the security she longed for. And, as Eve would say, on top of all that he was good-looking. She sighed. How could she just go and live with him? What if Tony did come back? But somehow she knew he wouldn't, not now.

A letter plopped on the front doormat. She went down to retrieve it, feeling sorry for the postman trudging about in this rain.

The envelope felt damp and the ink on the postmark was smudged. She didn't recognise the handwriting and as she climbed the stairs, began to open it.

When she reached the top she pulled out the letter. It was just one page. A photograph and another envelope fell to the floor. Picking them up she glanced at the envelope. It bore Tony's handwriting and was addressed to Mrs M. Ross. Her heart began beating fast and tears filled her eyes. She looked at the photo. Tony was laughing and had his arm round a woman a lot younger than he. Tears of joy streamed down Maggie's face. She was laughing and crying at the same time. She felt dizzy and sick with excitement. He was alive. At long last he'd written to her. But who was this woman? She staggered into the living room and sat at the table. Her hands were trembling as she read the single sheet of paper.

The address was Cardiff, Wales, and dated 8 January 1936. What was he doing in Cardiff? They didn't even know anybody in Wales.

Dear Mrs Ross,

I'm afraid I don't know your Christian name as Peter never told us about you or any of your family. I assume you must be a relation of some sorts. I found this letter in his drawer and it had a note attached asking this to be posted in the event of anything happening to him.

Well, I'm sorry to say our dear Peter had a terrible accident. It was just before Christmas. The sea was running very high. Everybody said he was silly to take the boat out, but then if you knew Peter you would know what a headstrong devil he was.

His body was washed up two days later. My daughter is still devastated. You see, they were hoping to be married at Easter.

Maggie gave a little cry. 'Oh no.' She read and read that paragraph, trying to make the words sink in. He was going to get married. Putting the letter on the table she picked up the photograph. On the back was written 'Peter and Thelma, November 1935.' Through her tears Maggie looked at Tony with his arm round this pretty young woman. They were laughing and looked so happy. This was taken in November, the month of Laura's birthday. Maggie sat as if in a trance. She couldn't believe what she had just read. Her tears continued to fall.

'You did lose your memory. I was right all along, and now you're dead. My darling, my darling,' she whispered. 'And we never said goodbye. You were going to marry this girl at Easter not knowing you still had us.'

Suddenly it hit Maggie that he'd written her a letter. Even as she wanted to shout and scream, throw herself into the street, to cry and cry, it somehow struck her as bizarre that he might have been married at the same time as his mother. Maggie knew she had to control herself and try to remain quiet for the sake of the children, who thankfully were still in bed.

'How could you do this to us? Why did you leave us? Now you're dead. Or somebody calling himself Peter is dead,' she said softly, gently running her fingers over his smiling face. Although stunned, she knew she had to finish the letter before reading Tony's explanation.

If you know of any member of his family, perhaps you would be kind enough to pass on this sad news. I couldn't let you know about his funeral before as we hadn't been through his things till after he was buried, it was then we found this letter. Incidentally he is in our local cemetery and we are having a monument put on his grave. It the short time we have known Peter, we all loved him very much.

I thought you might like this photo of Peter and my daughter. They were so happy.

If you are ever down this way, please come and have a chat and a cup of tea.

Yours very sincerely,
Mrs Eileen Walker.

They didn't know he had a wife and family, so what did they think was his surname?

As much as she wanted to read Tony's letter, Maggie couldn't bring herself to open it. It had her name and address on the envelope, in his hand. She turned it over and over. If only David or Eve, or even Winnie was here, they could read it to her. But she wasn't sure she wanted everybody to know.

Slowly Maggie began to prise the envelope open. She was afraid of its contents.

The first few pages were written in pencil, and very scrawly and all over the place, which was unusual for Tony as he took great pride in his handwriting. There was no address, but the date was Friday, 17 May 1935. Maggie gasped and put her hand to her mouth. That date was etched in her mind, the day he disappeared.

My darling Maggie,

I must write all this down while it's still fresh in my mind. You see at this moment I fear for my life.

I expect by now you are wondering where I've gone. Well, it is a very long story, and I hope that in the end you understand and forgive me.

Forgive my handwriting as I am sitting on a train writing this. Fortunately I managed to win a few bob on the horses to pay my fare. This train is going to Cardiff, always fancied spending a holiday in Wales.

My darling, I haven't always been straight with you. But I have always loved you, and since we got married I've never fooled around with anybody else, you've got to believe that. You and the kids mean everything to me, and I hope that by the time the new baby's here all my problems will be just a bad dream and you'll never read this letter, well not till years later when in our old age we sit and have a good laugh over it.

Today I had the misfortune to bump into a bloke who'd just come out of prison. As you know I've always liked a little bet and unfortunately I owed Mr Windsor a few bob.

Maggie was in shock. He had known all about them and he hadn't cared.

Well, to cut a long story short, Mr Windsor is a real villain and he threatened to, would you believe it, kill me. It was then that I decided to make a run for it and got on the first train that come along.

I know he won't hurt you or the kids, that's not his style, besides, he don't know where I live.

As soon as I've made enough money to pay him off I'll be back, large as life and twice as handsome. Just remember I love you and the kids very much.

All my love, Tony. xxxx

'Don't you believe it,' sobbed Maggie. 'How could you, Tony? It was through him I lost our baby.'

There was another page that was written in ink. It didn't have a date on it.

My dear Maggie,

I have decided to write to you because by now you should have our new baby. One day I will post this and then you'll understand why I did what I did. You are always in my thoughts, and when I'm on my knees in church I pray you are all well and I only wish I was with you.

I still haven't made quite enough to pay back Mr Windsor, so it's best I stay low.

It might sound a bit morbid but I'm leaving a note to ask Eileen, that's my very kind landlady, to post this if anything happens to me. The reason being that I've changed my name and bought a small fishing boat, and the sea can be a very lively lady. You know me. I had to do something on my own, couldn't work for a boss. Imagine me fishing. It's a great life, and young Jamie would love it, away from all that smoke and fog.

I expect you're managing all right, they're a good bunch on the market, and Mum will always see you all right, she's got a few bob stashed away.

I hope in the near future we shall all be together again. If not in this world, then it will be in the next. I love you.

Tony. xxxx

Maggie was stunned. So many thoughts were milling about in her head: what will Bella say when she reads it? How dare he just walk away and leave all his responsibilities, and how dare he write this letter when he was with that girl? Would he have ever come back to us? 'Why, Tony, why?' she cried out, first in anger, then in self-pity. She picked up the photograph. 'I've been a good wife. We could have sorted out your problems if only you'd told me and not run away. I've got problems but I've got to stay here and face them.' She threw the photo to the floor. 'You bloody two-timing bastard. So how do you think we—' Maggie stopped when she saw the living-room door open.

'Why are you shouting, Mummy?' asked Laura.

'Hallo, love. I'm angry with the weather,' Maggie smiled, quickly gathering up the photo and letters and stuffing them into her overall pocket.

Laura came and sat at the table. 'Why are you crying?'

'Somebody I know has died.'

'Who?'

'You don't know them.'

'Who's the picture of?'

'Nobody you know. I'll get you some porridge. Is Jamie awake?'

'No.'

Maggie went into the kitchen. She looked at the photo again. She wasn't really telling Laura lies. The man in the photo wasn't anybody she knew. This was a man who called himself Peter something, not the daddy they had known and loved.

Maggie stood slowly stirring the porridge. When Bella reads this she'll swear he'd gone off his head, she thought.

Maggie could hear Jamie and Laura squabbling. Suddenly she had to get out. She needed to talk to someone. Eve was the closest.

'Sit up and behave yourselves,' she said, walking into the living room carrying two bowls of steaming porridge. 'Now listen to me very carefully.'

Laura's head shot up. Her face full of expectation. 'Is it Daddy that's dead?'

'Why did you ask that?' Maggie sat at the table, unable to stop the tears.

'Well,' said Laura, her eyes blinking quickly, 'I heard you shouting about a two-timing bastard.'

Jamie looked up and loudly took in his breath. 'You mustn't say that,' he said, shocked.

'That's what Mummy said, and that's what Tom Cooper says about Daddy, so I thought . . .' her voice trailed off.

'Yes, you are right, it is Daddy,' Maggie said softly.

'But you said it wasn't someone we knew.'

'Yes, I know I did. You see I didn't know what to say.'

Jamie's eyes grew wide. 'Where is Daddy?'

'He had to go away, and he's had an accident.'

Laura began to cry. 'Was he run over?'

'No, he drowned.'

'Daddy can't swim,' said Jamie, his voice breaking as he tried to control his tears.

'Will we be going to his funeral?' asked Laura, wiping her eyes.

'No, I'm afraid not.'

'Why not?' asked Jamie.

'Daddy has been buried already.'

'My friend went to her granny's funeral,' said Laura. 'She said everybody was crying, but she didn't 'cos she didn't like her granny, but she said the cakes they had after were ever so nice.'

Maggie wanted to smile. With Tony being away for so long he had become almost a stranger to them. 'I've got to go round to see Auntie Eve this morning, so for an extra special treat I'm going to take you to the Saturday morning pictures.'

'Wow.' Jamie jumped up in the air. 'Really, Mum?'

'Course. Now finish your breakfast.'

'We'll get ever so wet,' said Laura, sounding grown up and practical.

'We can dry out round Eve's.'

Jamie was stuffing porridge in his mouth. 'My mate goes every Sat'day, and he says the Lone Ranger's really brave.'

'Jamie, don't talk with your mouth full.' Maggie was thankful their tears had quickly disappeared.

Later, when they stepped outside the door, the wind and rain took their breath away.

''Allo, Maggs. Bloody awful day, ain't it? Only had a couple of punters so far. You was wise not to get your stall out. I'm 'aving a right job keeping everything tied down.' Fred stamped his feet to keep warm. Rivulets of rain dripped off his trilby when he moved his head.

'It might brighten up later,' said Maggie, fighting to get her umbrella up.

'Won't be a lot of point staying if it don't clear up,' he called after her, but his last words were lost in the wind and rain as Maggie quickly moved on.

'Christ, what you doing round here, and in this weather as well? You're soaked.'

'I had to talk to someone.'

'Well, it must be very important to drag you out on a morning like this. Where's the kids?' asked Eve.

'I took 'em to Saturday morning pictures. I've got their wet things here.'

'Leave 'em in the hall and come through. I'll make you a

381

cuppa, you look like you need one.'

'Is Dan around?'

'He's in bed, why?'

'I'd like him to be here.'

'Why?' Eve's face turned ashen. 'Christ, you've heard from Tony.'

Maggie nodded.

'Dan, Dan, quick get up.' Eve rushed from the room, shouting all way to their bedroom. 'Yes, it is important. Now get up.' She was back almost at once.

Maggie was sitting on the sofa. 'You'd better read this.' She handed her Mrs Walker's letter.

Eve sat next to her and began reading. She let out a gasp. 'I don't believe it,' she said softly.

'Hallo, Maggs,' said Dan, walking into the living room. His hair was tousled and he began tucking his shirt into his trousers, his braces dangling round his knees. 'So what's all this about?'

Eve handed him the letter and Maggie passed Tony's letter to her.

Once again Eve was stunned into silence.

'Who's this Peter then?' asked Dan.

Maggie gave him the photograph. 'Read the back.'

'The two-timing sod.' Dan stood up. 'When did you get this?'

'This morning. Why?'

'Well, I reckon we ought to go to this 'ere Mrs whatser-name and tell 'er we want his real name to be put on his gravestone.'

'Dan, sit down and read this.' Eve passed the first sheet of Tony's letter to him.

Dan flicked the corner of the page. 'Fancy the silly sod running off like that. If we'd known we could have all rallied round.'

'I don't think so,' said Maggie. 'Not with the amount he owed.'

'True,' said Dan. 'But not to let you know. Not to even . . .'

'Wait till you read this page, Dan,' said Eve, handing it to him. 'I reckon he's gone round the twist, all this church and praying stuff.'

'Christ, he couldn't pay his debts but he could buy a bloody boat,' shouted Dan.

'He probably borrowed it,' said Maggie. 'It's the bit from her mother saying her daughter was going to marry him what upset me the most. What did he reckon he was going to do with me, send Mr Windsor round to finish me off?' She began to cry.

Eve put her arm round her. 'Come on, Maggs. Don't let that sod get you down. You've done all right without him so far.'

'No I ain't. I ain't took enough this week to pay the rent.'

'I'm sure your landlord will understand,' said Dan, looking uncomfortable.

'I don't even know what name he's been buried under,' sniffed Maggie.

'Does it matter?' asked Eve.

'What if in years to come the kids want to know, what can I tell them?'

'You could always write to that woman,' said Dan.

'Yer, and tell her daughter her so-called boyfriend was about to commit bigamy,' said Eve caustically.

Maggie began to cry again. 'What's Bella gonner say?'

'I don't know. I expect she'll be as stunned as we are. Dan, put the kettle on again, there's a love.'

'Would you like something a bit stronger than tea, Maggs?'

She shook her head. 'I've got to pick the kids up from the pictures soon.'

'Dan'll do that for you. When you gonner see Bella?'

'I'll go in the morning. I don't think I can cope with going today.'

'If you like I'll go with you,' said Eve.

'No thanks, I'll be all right.'

Eve stood up and took a cigarette from the packet on the mantelpiece. She offered Maggie one. She shook her head. 'Maggie,' said Eve blowing the smoke in the air, 'will this make any difference between you and Dave?'

'I don't know. Why?'

'Well, you're a free woman now. When are you seeing him again?'

'Tonight. He's coming over for a bit of tea, and he's going to help Jamie with that plane they're making.'

'Would you move in with him?'

'No, course not.'

'There's nothing to stop you marrying him now.'

Maggie didn't answer.

Eve sat next to her. 'Do you love him?'

'I don't know. I think I could.'

'Look, give it time. He's a smashing bloke and thinks the world of you, and the kids, and they like him.'

'I know, but I don't want him to think that—'

'What, that you're just looking for a meal ticket and a

good home?' Eve stood up and pointed her finger at Maggie. 'Now just you listen to me. Tony was all right, but he left you in a bloody mess. If he really loved you he would have been here when you lost that baby, and besides that, he reckoned that Mr Windsor wouldn't hurt you, but he did, didn't he?'

Maggie's head shot up. 'How do you . . .? I never told—'

'I ain't that daft, and when you started calling out about men I guess somebody had been to see you, and then there was the bruises on your arm.'

'Does anybody else know?'

'No. Thought it best to keep it to meself. Then there was that bloke Wally scaring the living daylights out of the kids. I couldn't see Dave ever letting you down like that.'

'Shut up, shut up,' shouted Maggie, putting her hands over her ears. 'I don't want to hear any more.'

'What's going on in here?' asked Dan, walking in with a tray of cups and saucers.

'I was just telling her a few home truths.'

'Oh.' Dan walked over to the sideboard and took a bottle of whisky out. He poured some into each of the cups.

Maggie was crying. 'What am I going to do?'

'Drink this tea, for starters. Then me and Eve will take you and the kids home, then you can start thinking about yourself and your future for a change.'

Maggie gave them a watery smile. 'I suppose you're right.' But the thought that was going through her mind was that now she was free, would David Matthews still want her and her debts?

Chapter 33

On the way home, Eve and Dan stopped at the eel shop and bought pie and mash for dinner. While Maggie was putting it on the plates Jamie was racing round the flat with his coat inside out and buttoned at the neck.

'Jamie take that coat off and sit at the table.' Maggie was on edge and beginning to lose her temper.

'It's me cape. I'm the Lone Ranger.'

'I don't care. Now be quiet and sit still.'

'Come on, son, do as your mother tells you,' said Dan softly, taking his coat.

'Auntie Eve, did Mummy tell you our daddy's dead?' asked Laura as she poured the parsley liquor over her mash.

'Yes, she did.'

'Well, at least we know now why we didn't get any birthday or Christmas presents from him. Has he been dead a long while?' She sounded very grown up and confident.

Maggie looked at Eve. What could she tell them? It was Dan that gave her the answer.

'I think he must have been, but Mummy only found out today.'

Laura smiled. 'Oh, so that's why we went to the pictures, and not to his funeral.'

'Something like that,' said Eve.

Maggie was relieved she had quite happily accepted that explanation.

As the afternoon wore on Eve and Dan were reluctant to go.

'I don't like leaving you on your own,' said Eve.

'I'm not on my own, not with these two tearing about.'

'Look, we'll come round this evening. What time will Dave be here?'

'About seven, I expect. He's not on duty tonight.'

'I like Dave,' said Dan. 'Even if he is a copper.'

Maggie smiled. She wasn't going to answer that. 'I'd like to see David on my own for a while, so if you can make it about eight, that'll give him time to walk out if he wants to.'

'Why should he walk out?' asked Dan.

'I'm not unobtainable now, am I?'

'He won't do that.'

'How can we be sure?'

Dan smiled. 'I know he won't.'

Eve stood up. 'We'll see you later.'

They exchanged goodbye kisses, and Maggie was left with her thoughts.

Maggie looked anxiously at the clock. He was late. The rain was still beating down. Had he had to go out on a case? Was he all right? It was times like this when she worried about him that she knew she was very fond of him.

'I hope Uncle David hurries up. I want him to show me how to do this bit.' Jamie was looking at all the odd-shaped pieces of wood strewn over the table that somehow were miraculously going to be turned into an airplane.

At last there was a banging on the knocker.

'It's Uncle David,' shouted Jamie, racing from the room.

Maggie could hear him excitedly telling David about their going to the pictures.

'Hello, Maggie,' he said, walking in and putting his hat on the sideboard. 'I'm sorry I'm late. Had to see to some paperwork.'

'That's all right.'

'You didn't take the stall out today, not in this weather, did you?'

'No, didn't see the point.'

'Our Daddy's dead,' said Laura.

David's head shot up. 'What? How d'you know?'

Maggie handed him the letters. 'Read this one first.'

He took the letters, and sat on the sofa. As he began to read Maggie noted the change of expression on his face. He didn't make any comments. She handed him the photograph.

'Come into the kitchen while I put the kettle on.'

David followed her. He closed the door. 'How could he do this to you?' he exploded. His voice was full of anger but carefully modified. 'And to think he was going to get married while he still had you. He wants bloody horsewhipping.'

'Shh, please don't.'

He held her close and whispered, 'Oh Maggie, what can I say? All that you've been through, and now this.' He buried his head in her neck and kissed it.

Tears began to fill her eyes. 'I thought he loved me.'

'He probably did in his own way, but I think you've got to face up to it, Tony Ross did what Tony Ross wanted to.'

The door was pushed open and they quickly jumped apart.

Jamie was standing there with a piece of balsawood in his hand. 'Could you show me where this bit goes?'

Maggie turned to the sink. She didn't want Jamie to see she was on the verge of tears again.

'Course,' said David. 'Come on.'

Maggie and David didn't have time to talk alone again for almost as soon as the children had gone to bed Eve and Dan arrived.

They spent most of the evening discussing the situation.

'When you going to see Bella?' asked Eve.

'Tomorrow,' volunteered David. 'I'm taking them over in the car.'

'Wonder what she'll make of it?' said Dan.

'What about all this money he owes?' asked Eve.

Maggie felt her stomach churn. What about all the money *she* owed? If she couldn't get the stall out soon the interest would mount up on her loan. She still hadn't told anyone about it. 'I'm gonner try and pay off me brother, though it'll take a while, but I'm afraid Mr Windsor really will have to sing for his. There's no way I can pay all that back.' Maggie stopped. She knew there was also the money for Bella's present. Because of the bad weather and the stalls not being taken out, Winnie hadn't asked her what she was getting them.

'Don't worry about him. I suggested Windsor wrote off the debt when Tony disappeared and he came bothering you. He knows I'm on the scene now so he won't threaten you again.'

Maggie smiled at David.

It was nine o'clock when Dan suggested they went to the Dog.

'I'd rather not, not tonight,' said Maggie.

'I'll stay here as well,' said Eve.

'Come on, Dave old man, surely you could do with a drink?'

He looked at Maggie. 'Would you mind?'

'Course not.'

'You'd better take a key,' said Maggie.

Eve looked at her surreptitiously.

'Well, I don't want to keep rushing up and down the stairs,' she said defensively.

The front door was closed quietly.

'Well,' said Eve almost at once, 'you gonner marry him?'

'Give us a chance. Besides, he ain't asked me.'

'But would you?'

'I don't know.'

Eve lit a cigarette. 'If you ask me you'd be a bloody fool not to. Do you love him?'

'Not like I loved Tony.'

'Well, he was your first.'

'And the father of my children. I'll make us a cuppa.'

Eve sat back on the sofa when Maggie left the room. How could she make Maggie see that David would be the best thing that ever happened to her? What if she blackened Tony's name even more? But Eve knew that would be pushing their friendship to the limits and that was something Maggie could do without at the moment.

Eve nervously tapped her cigarette into the ashtray. She wandered over to the window. She could say they had an affair after they were married and that would be the last straw in Tony's character assassination. It would be a lie of course but with her reputation before she married Dan, Maggie would believe that. She loved Maggie and wanted her to be happy with David. Even though Eve had wanted Tony all those years ago, after he got married he did remain true to Maggie, until now. Her saying anything now would cost her their friendship. And what about Dan? She loved him very much. Tears filled Eve's eyes. And losing him and Maggie was something she wasn't prepared to do.

'You all right?' asked Maggie, sitting at the table.

Eve dabbed at her eyes, nodded and joined her. 'Maggie, I want you to be happy.'

'Give me time, Eve. Give me time.' She sighed. 'Eve. I've done something, and I've got to tell someone or I'll go mad.'

Eve looked up surprised. 'Look, if you're gonner tell me you and Dave have . . . well, it ain't nobody's business but yours.' She smiled. 'Not that—'

'No. It ain't that. And by the way we haven't. It's just that I've . . . I've got myself into a lot of debt.'

'What? How?'

'Before Christmas I borrowed ten pounds from a Mr Shore, he's a moneylender, and I can't pay it back and all the time the interest is building up and . . .' The words came bubbling out faster and faster.

Eve sat back. 'Oh Maggs. What can I say? Ten pounds. Christ, that's more than what Dan earns in a month. We all thought you was doing so well down there. What with the nice frocks you bought Laura and yourself for Christmas, and the money you spent on—'

'I know, I know, I was a bloody fool. But I needed stock and how was I to know the weather was going to be that bad?' She banged the table. 'Eve, what am I gonner do?'

'I don't know, Maggs, I really don't know. What about your brother, have you paid him back yet?'

Maggie shook her head and tears ran down her cheeks. 'Not all of it. There's something else.'

Eve face went white. 'What else?' she whispered.

'Winnie got up a collection for Bella and Benny and I spent it on the rents and coal and food . . .' The words were lost in sobs.

'Oh my God.' Eve stood up and took another cigarette from her handbag. 'I would have thought you of all people would have learnt your lesson from Tony and the money he owed. Just how did you think this would all end?'

'I don't know. I've been pawning as many things as I dare. Oh Eve, my life's in such a mess.'

'I must admit you have been a bit of a silly cow.'

Maggie burst into tears. She was glad of the relief of telling someone, but she also needed sympathy and wasn't getting it.

'Does Dave know?'

Maggie shook her head. 'No, only you.'

Eve began pacing the floor. 'I just don't know what to say.'

'Eve, what am I going to do?'

'I dunno.'

'I can't even think of marrying David, not with all these

debts. He might think I'm only marrying him for security.'

'Not if he loves you, he won't.'

'I can even understand Tony running away. That's what I want to do right this minute.'

'Oh yes, and where would you go? Wales?'

Maggie's tears flowed. 'Don't be funny.'

'Funny is the last thing I feel,' said Eve, sitting down again. She looked up at the clock. 'They'll be back soon. Do you want us to stay?'

Maggie nodded.

'Well, you'd better do something about your face. You look a mess.'

'Eve, what would you do?'

'Look, you've got to make up your mind if you're gonner tell Dave or not. I can't see any way out of it; this ain't gonner go away.'

'No, I know.'

'Well then, what's it to be? Do you want us to stay and be here with you, or . . .?'

'I think perhaps I'd better be on me own. Tomorrow I'll go and see Bella and tell her everythink.'

'You'll have to do that anyway. Let's hope she ain't gotta bad heart, otherwise you might—'

'Shut up, Eve.'

'Pardon me, sorry I spoke.'

'I'm sorry, it's just that I'm so on edge. I just don't know what to do for the best.'

'If you want my advice, for what it's worth, I'd come clean, tell 'em all. That way once the tittle-tattle dies down they'll have nothing to hang on to and you can bury Tony in your mind for ever.' Eve crushed her cigarette into the ashtray. 'Now, have you got anythink stronger than tea in this house?'

'There's a bottle of whisky in the sideboard.'

'That'll do.'

The whisky didn't give Maggie any Dutch courage, and when David and Dan came back she suddenly lost her nerve.

'Don't bother making yourself comfortable,' said Eve, putting on her hat. 'We're gonner go.'

'I wanted one of Maggs's cheese sandwiches.'

'I said we're going.'

'What's upset her?' said Dan. He grinned. 'See you've been at the whisky. S'pose you're all randy and can't wait ter get me home, then?'

'Shut up, you silly sod. Maggie wants to be left on her own.'

Dan patted David on the back. 'This could be your lucky night, mate.'

'Shut up,' shouted Maggie.

Dan sat back down and looked astonished.

'What's wrong?' asked David.

'Sit down, Eve.'

'But, Maggs—'

'I might as well get it over and done with.'

David looked worried. 'What is it?'

They all sat very quiet while Maggie told them the whole story.

When she'd finished she went into the kitchen, leaving them stunned. Eventually Eve followed her.

'I think you'd better make Dan his cheese sandwich,' said Maggie.

'Yer, yer. OK.'

All the while Maggie busied herself making tea she listened for the living-room door to shut. Then she'd know she had lost David for ever. But all she could hear was the clinking of glass, the whisky being poured out.

'Well,' said Dan, when they went back into the living room, 'we reckon we could have an answer to some of your problems.'

Maggie looked at David.

'I don't know much about market stalls.'

Maggie giggled, partly because of the whisky and partly in relief. 'I couldn't see you selling jewellery.'

'Not selling the goods, but selling the licence.'

Maggie sat up straight. 'I couldn't do that. It ain't mine to sell.'

'It ain't Tony's now, is it?' said Dan, munching on his sandwich.

'No, I know, but what would Bella say?'

'That's something we could find out tomorrow.'

'How much d'you reckon it's worth? I could ask at work,' asked Eve.

'Dunno, but some of the traders would know,' said Dan. 'And hopefully it could be enough to pay off that loan shark.'

'And as for the money for Bella's present, well, I'm sure she would rather have you spend it on the children, don't you?' said David.

Maggie very slowly nodded. 'I expect so, but it was still stealing.'

'And as for your brother, he'll have to wait. Besides, he shouldn't have been such a silly sod lending it to Tony in the first place,' said Dan.

'You two got this sorted quick,' said Eve.

'Yer, well, when you get a couple of intelligent blokes together it's surprising what you can come up with.'

'That's all very well,' said Maggie, 'but what if Bella won't sell the stall, and what am I going to live on after that?'

'You'll have to get yourself a job,' said Eve. 'That way you'll be sure of money coming in every week.'

'But what about the kids?'

'Look, Maggs, take one thing at a time. Dave here's taking you to see Bella tomorrow so you can get that sorted.'

Maggie sat quietly thinking it over. Was this a light at the end of a long dark tunnel? Eight months of uncertainty. Now Tony was dead she didn't feel anything. Maybe her love for him had died months ago.

'Look, Maggs, we'll be off.'

'All right, Eve.'

'I'm off as well. I'm giving them a lift,' said David.

'You don't have to go, do you?'

'I think it best. I'll be over tomorrow.'

They said their good nights and Maggie was alone. David had been very distant. Why didn't he want to stay? Was it all over between them? She loved him and wanted him, but she wasn't sure whether he wanted her now.

She would have to wait till tomorrow to find out that.

Poor Bella. Maggie was dreading telling her that, after all this time, the hope and wondering was finally over. Her son was dead. Bella was strong and she was going to start a new life with Benny, so Maggie hoped this wouldn't upset her too much. But then there was the business of selling the stall – how would Bella react to that?

Chapter 34

Maggie was silent on the way to Bella's. It was a journey she had been in fear of making ever since Tony went away.

The noise from the back of the car told her the children weren't interested in grown-ups' worries.

'Hallo, you lot,' said Bella on opening the door, then crushing them one by one to her ample bosom. 'Thought you might be over. Benny, go and light the fire in the front room, there's a love. It's all laid up ready.'

Benny kissed Maggie's cheek as he passed them. 'Good ter see you. Bring yer bits in here, kids. This fire don't take long to get going.'

Bella was beaming. 'Never thought the day would come when I'd be lighting two fires in one house. Christ, I remember when we could just about afford the coal for one. What's up? You two look like you've lorst a tanner and found an 'apenny.'

Maggie gave her a slight smile.

'Right, that's them sorted,' said Benny. 'I'll just wash me hands.'

'I'll go and stay with the children for the time being,' said David.

'Why? What's happened?' Bella's eyes were darting from one to the other as David left the room.

'Bella, I've had a letter.'

Bella sat at the table. 'From Tony?'

Maggie nodded. She put her hand on Bella's. 'I'm afraid he's dead.'

'But you said . . . a letter? But how?'

'You'd better read them,' said Maggie.

Tears filled Bella's eyes as one by one she read the letters and passed them to Benny.

'How dare he do this to you?' Bella's reaction wasn't what Maggie had expected. 'The bastard. Gitting married indeed. If I'd have known about this I'd have been down there and chopped off his bleeding cobblers.'

'What did he tell all these lies for?' asked Benny. 'And how could he say he was gonner marry this girl?' He was studying the photograph.

'I know he was me son, but to do that to you and those lovely kids. I'll never forgive him, you know. Never. Good job my Jim ain't here. He'd give him a right pasting.' Bella quickly left the room.

Maggie went to stand up.

'Leave her be, love,' said Benny. 'Let her have five minutes on her own.'

Maggie nodded. 'I might as well get every bit of bad news over at once.'

'What bad news?'

'I'll wait for Bella to come back, if you don't mind.'

'No, course not. I'll put the kettle on.' Benny looked worried.

A few minutes later Bella came back into the kitchen.

'Sorry about that.' She was still wiping her bloodshot eyes.

'Bella, I might as well upset you a bit more, and if you want to chuck me out – well, I understand.'

Bella opened her eyes wide. 'You gonner get married? Well, I can't say I blame yer, he's a nice bloke.'

Maggie looked embarrassed. 'No, I ain't getting married. It's . . . I'm finding this very hard.'

Benny and Bella were hanging on her every word.

'Bella, I've got myself into a lot of trouble.'

Bella jumped up. 'Christ. You're not having a baby?'

'No, no, I'm not. I ain't done nothink to . . . no. I'm in a lot of debt.'

'What d'you mean? I know you've been trying to pay off Tony's debts, but that don't mean to say you should have got yourself—'

'No. Bella, listen.' Maggie went into all the details of what she owed, and the money for the present.

'I see what yer mean,' said Bella finally.

'But you only did it for the kids,' said Benny.

'And my own ego as well. You see, I thought I was as clever as Tony.' She hung her head and nervously played with her fingers. 'But I wasn't. Dan and David have come up with a scheme to help me out, but it will need your approval.' Maggie hesitated. 'I could sell the pitch.'

Maggie waited for a reaction, but when Bella didn't reply, she stood up and gathered up her handbag.

'Where're you going?'

'Well, you don't want me around, so I'll be off. Don't worry, I'll never stop the children from seeing you any time you want. And one day I'll write to the women in

Wales and find out what name Tony used so if you or the children ever want to visit his grave, you'll know which it is . . .' Maggie's last few words were lost in her sobs. She turned to go.

'Sit down.' It was an order from Bella that startled even Benny.

'Right. How do you feel about him?' Bella inclined her head towards the front room.

'I like him, but I don't know about . . .' Maggie dabbed at her eyes. 'And I don't want him to think I'm only looking for somewhere to . . .'

'He don't think that. 'Sides, you don't have to be in a hurry to do anythink. Go and get him.'

Maggie did as she was told.

'Right, young man.'

Maggie was suddenly terrified. Oh no. Was Bella going to tell David to marry her?

'Maggie here's told us the whole story. And I reckon what you and Dan suggested is a damn good idea. She shouldn't be out in all weathers, and leaving those kids on their own anyway. As for the money she owes that loan shark, well I reckon the pitch is worth that much, and the money for the present, well we can forget that.'

'But what can I tell the other traders?'

'Tell 'em you bought us a pair of sheets. Then even if any of 'em do ever come over here, which I doubt, they'll never see them. But as for your brother, that was my son's debt so I'm gonner pay it off.'

Maggie went to speak but Bella put up her hand to silence her.

'So, that's all your immediate problems out of the way.'

'How you gonner manage?' asked Benny.

'I don't know. It's not as though Tony took out any insurance.'

'Well you couldn't get it anyway,' said David. 'Not without a death certificate.'

'That means I can't get his penny-a-week one out?' said Bella.

''Fraid not,' said David.

'The sod. All right, don't look at me like that. I know he was me son but I can't believe he would do a thing like this.' Tears filled Bella's big brown eyes again.

Benny put his arm round her. 'Come on, love. Remember we've got our wedding to look forward to.'

Bella's head shot up. 'How can you think of that at this time? I've lorst me son.'

Maggie and David looked at each other and shifted in their seats.

'Look,' said Maggie, 'we'll go, leave you on your own to get over the shock.'

'No, stop and have a bit of tea first.'

'Only if you're sure.'

Tea was a very strained affair. Maggie was pleased Bella managed to keep her feelings under control in front of the children, but she still looked very tearful.

'I shouldn't have jumped down Benny's throat like that, but I couldn't help meself.'

'He understands,' said Maggie, as they did the washing-up.

'Yer. I'll take him for a drink later, that'll cheer him up.'

'The wedding still on?'

'I should say so. Every time I think that Tony might have been getting married at the same time . . .' She sniffed and fished her handkerchief out from her apron pocket. 'I don't know what he was thinking of.'

'Unless they had money?'

'S'pose that could have been the reason. He was a bastard.'

Maggie put her arm round Bella's shoulders. 'We've all got to try and put it behind us. You've got a new life to be getting on with, and I know Benny will make you happy.'

'I know, but what about you? Have you got anythink to look forward to?'

'I don't know. But I do have the children.'

'That's the one good thing that came from Tony.' Bella smiled and dabbed at her eyes.

'Come on, let's go in the front room. It'll soon be time for us to go.'

'Do you want me to come in?' asked David when they arrived at Maggie's door.

She looked at him. She had to know how he felt about her. 'Only if you want to.'

He smiled and closed the door behind him. 'I'd like to very much,' he whispered.

Maggie felt her heart leap. This was what she wanted to hear. She ushered the children into their bedroom.

'Uncle David, will you read us a story?' asked Laura, poking her head round the door.

He looked at Maggie.

She shrugged her shoulders. 'That's up to you.'

404

He grinned and took her hand. 'Please, and I would like the job for life.'

'Back to bed, Laura.' When the door was closed Maggie turned to David. 'I don't want you to think—'

He pulled her close and kissed her. 'Maggie, I've loved you for such a long while and it would make me so happy, now that you're free, if you would marry me.'

She threw her arms round his neck and held him tight. 'I too have loved you, but been afraid of my feelings.'

'Hurry up,' shouted Jamie, from the bedroom.

'Well, have I got this job for life?'

'Only till they grow up, or we have one of our own.'

'I'd like that very much.' David walked into the children's bedroom with his arm round Maggie's slim waist. 'Me and Mummy have got something to tell you.'

They began giggling.

'How would you like it if me and David got married?'

Jamie jumped up. 'Great. Would we go and live at your house?'

Maggie nodded.

'Will you get married when Granny and Benny does?'

Maggie looked at David.

'I suppose if Benny and Bella wouldn't mind we could have a double wedding.'

Maggie giggled. 'That'll be different.'

'So, Mummy, could I be your bridesmaid?'

'I should think so.'

It was Laura's turn to giggle. 'See, I told you that if you didn't tell anyone your wish when you blew out your candles it would come true.'

Maggie looked puzzled. 'What did you wish for then?'

'That you and Uncle David would get married and that we would all live happily ever after.'

Tears filled Maggie's eyes. She suddenly thought of Lil. At last her grieving was over. The happy time was here, and with David she knew it would go on for ever.

Katie's Kitchen

Thank you, Emma and Samantha, for this title.
Love you lots.

Chapter 1

Katherine stared at the man sitting opposite her, her green eyes wide and blazing. 'What do you mean there's nothing for me?' she said, fighting back tears. She was angry with Gerald for humiliating her like this.

Mr Cannon, a tall middle-aged man, looked the perfect solicitor, but he appeared uncomfortable as with his finger he eased the stiff white shirt collar away from his flabby neck. His morning suit did nothing for his pale complexion.

'I'm sorry, Mrs Brown, but as the late Mr Edwin Brown didn't leave a will, and unless you can prove you were married to the late Mr Edwin Brown, produce a marriage certificate, there is nothing I can do to help you.'

Katherine's mind was racing. What was she going to do? She was thirty-eight, with a twelve-year-old son to bring up. 'Are you sure there was no will?'

Mr Cannon cleared his throat. He was sitting behind a very neat and tidy wide desk. 'As the late Mr Edwin Brown's solicitor I can assure you he never made one in my presence.'

'Could there be one in the house?'

'I shouldn't think so. He always conducted his business affairs through me.'

Katherine felt stifled. The windows were tightly shut and heavily draped even though it was a warm bright spring morning.

Mr Cannon looked over his rimless glasses. His mouth twitched and he appeared embarrassed. His black hair was sleek and flat against his head and when he glanced down at the papers in front of him the glow from the gaslight above his head made his hair shine.

Katherine sat bewildered. 'How long can I stay at the house?' she asked quietly.

A slight smile lifted Mr Cannon's thin mouth. 'Mr Gerald Brown, the deceased's younger brother, has kindly offered to let you stay in his employment. As you know he has taken over the business and the house. Unfortunately you will have to leave the house if you do not wish to work with him.'

Katherine didn't need to be told who Gerald was. She didn't want to work with him or for him. As soon as she received the solicitor's letter telling her she would have to leave her home she knew it was Gerald who had told Mr Cannon about her and Edwin's 'arrangement'. When she'd confronted Gerald about it he had told her to see Mr Cannon.

Much to Edwin's dismay she could never see eye to eye with his brother. Gerald couldn't wait to get his hands on Edwin's estate. He was a waster and a womaniser. What could she do? She had Joseph to think of.

Mr Cannon continued. 'I'm sorry, but I'm afraid I do have to ask rather . . .' he hesitated, 'shall we say rather difficult questions. You do understand I am only acting on Mr Gerald Brown's behalf. Were you married to the late Mr Edwin Brown?'

Katherine shook her head. 'No.'

'But your name is Brown?'

She crumpled the black lace gloves nestling in her lap, then painstakingly smoothed them out again. She looked up. 'No. I was only known as Mrs Brown when we opened the restaurant. We met on the ship when we both came back to England from Australia in 1900.'

'Twelve years ago. You've done extremely well in that time.'

'We both worked very hard. When we opened the restaurant it seemed easier at the time to answer anyone, staff and customers, who called me Mrs Brown. But I didn't expect him to die and not leave a will. He was only fifty-eight. I've worked hard helping him, now I've got nothing to . . .' Tears tumbled from her eyes and plopped down on to her hands. She took a spotless white handkerchief from her small black brocade drawstring bag and dabbed at her eyes. 'What's going to happen to me and my son?'

Mr Cannon sat back and put his fingertips together. 'I'm sorry, Mrs . . . er, er, Brown, but I must ask, is the boy Mr Brown's?'

Katherine shook her head. 'No, he's my husband's. You see as far as I know Mr Carter is still alive, and I'm still married to him.' Did he need to know all this? And did all solicitors ask such impertinent questions?

Mr Cannon was visibly shocked. 'Don't you know?'

Again she shook her head. 'He stayed in Australia.'

'I see. Does your son know about this?'

Katherine nodded. 'Yes.'

'Did he call the late Mr Brown Papa?'

'No. He always addressed him as Grandpa. Edwin was very good to Joseph, making sure he had a good education. They were very fond of each other, and Edwin was like a father to me.'

'Is your son's name Carter?'

'Yes.'

'Didn't that cause complications?'

'No. I never explained it to anyone, we didn't see that it was anyone else's business.'

'I see,' Mr Cannon repeated. He wrote something on a piece of paper in front of him.

Katherine's mind was in turmoil. What if there was a will, where would Edwin have hidden it? She must begin looking before Gerald moved in. Gerald – his name made her cringe. Edwin was always so good to him and told her many times that if she had been free he would have liked to see her wed to his

3

brother. Katherine knew Gerald was devious. She had to get home, get to Edwin's room before Gerald.

'Is that all?' she asked eventually.

'I'm afraid so.'

She stood up. She had to go, get out of here. She was filled with panic. What was she going to do for money? How would they survive? 'Excuse me, Mr Cannon. Will Gerald Brown pay for Edwin's funeral?'

'Of course, it will come out of the estate.'

'Thank you.'

'I will see you in church on Friday,' he sighed. 'It will be a very sad and painful occasion for you and your son. Mr Brown will be sadly missed.' He held open the door and she swept past him, her long expensive black mourning gown rustling as she moved.

Katherine stood at the front door of their house, which overlooked Green Park. She loved this part of London. This was the home she and Edwin had shared for ten of the twelve years she had known him. Their house, with furnishings she had chosen. It wasn't overlarge, but it had a garden and a stable. It had been a happy place with plenty of laughter. Now she was about to lose it. Edwin had been a good man and she had been very fond of him, but even he never thought he would go so soon or so quick. As she opened the front door, Joseph came out of the drawing room.

'Uncle Gerald's been here.' Joseph was a tall slim lad who looked older than his twelve years. He seemed upset, and Katherine's heart was full of love for him.

'Did he say what he wanted?'

'He went into Grandpa's study.'

Panic again surged in Katherine, but she knew she had to act calmly to hide her fear from her son. She moved across the hall and stood in front of the large ornate mirror, the dust dancing where it was caught in the beams of bright sunlight. She removed the hatpins that secured her large-brimmed black hat and, carefully taking it off, placed it on the small green brocade chair that stood next to the hall stand. She gently ran her fingers up the back of her chignon. Her deep red hair blowing in the wind while she was being seasick was what Edwin said he had first noticed about her.

'What did Gerald have to say?' she asked, looking at her son in the mirror. She smoothed down the folds of her gown over her small waist; she was still very shapely.

'Uncle Gerald wanted to know if we were going to stay here. What did he mean? Are we leaving here, Mama?' Joseph, fairer than his mother, looked at her, his pale blue-green eyes full of sadness and bewilderment.

Katherine turned to face him. 'I'm afraid so.' She hadn't wanted to upset her son, so when she received the letter she went to see Edwin's solicitor to make sure she hadn't been told a lie.

'But this is our house.' Joseph's voice was full of pain.

'It was.'

'But where will we go? This has always been our home.' Frustration began to fill his flushed face.

'Yes I know, but it belongs to Gerald now.'

'But why? He didn't live here with us.' His voice had a slight tremor.

'I know. It's a long story, I'll tell you all about it one day.'

Joseph looked upset. 'I don't understand. Why can't we stay here and live with Uncle Gerald?'

'I'm afraid that isn't possible.' Katherine bent down and hugged him to her.

'Where will we go?' he asked again, freeing himself from her.

'I don't know,' she said out loud. Then to herself added: 'I only wish I did.'

Katherine closed the door and looked round Edwin's study. It was warm and manly. The smell of his expensive cigar smoke hung in the air. She opened the drawers in the desk and sorted through the papers. There was nothing she didn't know about. She sat in his armchair and studied the room. Where would he hide a document like a will? And would he have any reason to hide anything from her or any member of the household?

Perhaps Gerald had got here first . . .

Katherine put her head in her hands and wept. She wept for Edwin, Joseph and herself. What would happen to them now? She brushed the tears from her cheek and let a smile lift her sad face as her thoughts drifted to when she first met Edwin.

She had been leaning over the side of the ship being very seasick. She felt terrible. Every wave sent her hanging over the rail, her red hair blowing wild in the wind, and her body rejecting everything. They had only left Darwin a day ago; there were six months of this ahead of her. She let out a long groan and slumped to the deck.

'Can I help you?'

Katherine looked up at the friendly face. 'Only if you can make the ship keep still.'

The man smiled and sat beside her. He was tall and well-built with a shock of uncontrollable light brown hair. White lines caused through screwing up his blue eyes against the Australian sun appeared whenever he looked serious. 'I'm sorry I can't do that. Would you like me to help you back to your cabin?'

She shook her head. 'No thank you, that only makes me feel worse.'

'Would you like me to get you a drink of water or something?'

'Please.'

'The name's Edwin, Edwin Brown,' he said when he returned and handed her a glass of water.

'Pleased to meet you. I'm Katherine Carter.' She held out her hand.

'You're English.'

She nodded. 'So are you.'

During the long months that followed Katherine learnt that it wasn't only the sea that was making her sick, she was also expecting a baby.

She and Edwin became close friends. He told her he was going back home to England to start a business. He had made a little money in Australia but felt a longing to return home.

'It's a young man's country, new and exciting,' he had said. 'Full of opportunities for the young.'

'But you're not old.'

'I'm forty-six.'

She didn't have an answer to that as in another twenty years, when she reached his age, she too would be considered old.

'Also,' continued Edwin, 'I recently heard my mother has passed away and I have a young brother that I feel needs looking after.'

'I'm sorry. How old is your brother?'

'Gerald's twenty-five,' Edwin laughed. 'I know that's not young, but Gerald has always been Mother's baby, and in her eyes he could do no wrong, and I'm afraid now, well, who knows . . .?'

He was a year younger than Katherine. She remembered thinking to herself that he sounded a bit of a weed.

'What line of business are you considering going into?' she had asked, changing the subject.

'I rather fancy opening a restaurant. In a classy place somewhere.'

'Did your family have a restaurant?'

'Good heavens no. My father worked on the railway. He died when I was on my way to Australia ten years ago. I would have liked to come back right away, but Mother insisted I stay. My wife, whom I met in Australia, died in childbirth two years ago. The baby died too.'

'I'm so very sorry,' said Katherine. 'Do you have any other children?'

'No.' He smiled as if trying to blot out a painful memory. 'So you see now, well, I feel I should go back. What about you? Are you going back to your family?'

'No.' Katherine was definite about that. If her parents did take her back, which she very much doubted, she would be the laughing stock of the village they lived in. Those women would never leave their husbands. That part of her life was a closed book.

Katherine sighed and, leaving Edwin's armchair, moved over to the window. 'You were my family, dear, dear Edwin. What will I do without you?'

All the while they stood at the graveside Katherine could feel Gerald's dark smouldering eyes on her, boring into her. She put a protective arm round her son's shoulders. Joseph had taken Edwin's death very hard, and now that they had to move, it was all proving too much for him.

Gerald thanked the vicar and the assembled guests began to slowly move away. They were going to the restaurant. The restaurant she and Edwin had built up. Katherine had told Gerald she didn't want to go, but he had insisted. He came towards her and took hold of her arm forcefully.

Bending his head towards her he said in a hushed tone, 'I've arranged for the carriage to be at your disposal until the end of the month.' He stopped and gave a fellow mourner a nod and a brief smile, then added, 'He will take you and the boy to wherever you wish.'

She looked at him. He was thirty-seven, tall and slim, always well-dressed and very good-looking. Edwin had found him a good position in one of their suppliers' offices. He had never married but there were plenty of young women who would gladly grant him any favours, and he wasn't above boasting about his latest conquest.

'You are being a very silly woman, you know. You could always come and work for me, and you and Joseph could stay on at the house. He doesn't want to move.'

She quickly looked up. 'What have you said to Joseph?'

'Nothing.' He bent his head closer. 'We could be partners in more ways than one.'

Katherine didn't answer. He was still holding her arm tightly; as they moved across the uneven ground, she stumbled and trod on his foot. 'I'm so sorry,' she said smiling and without sounding remorseful. Under his fixed smile she saw him grimace.

'You know we could be very good together.'

Brushing his arm away she stopped. She knew the time had come to make a stand. She turned and faced him, and said rather loudly, 'Gerald, I don't know what sort of woman you take me for. I was very fond of your brother. Although we lived in the same house we never married. We never shared the same bed or even the same room. He was like a father to me, we were never lovers.'

Gerald looked about him, clearly agitated. 'Katherine, for God's sake keep your voice down,' he hissed.

'So you see I would never work or live with you, as I haven't the same respect for you as I did for Edwin.'

The people within earshot had stopped to listen. There were many raised eyebrows as well as intrigue and amusement on some of the men's faces, but the women looked shocked and were shaking their heads in disgust.

'Come along, Joseph, we have to go.' She began to move away.

Joseph looked at Gerald with blind hate as his mother ushered him to the waiting carriage. In so many ways Katherine could see herself in him – she couldn't hide her feelings either.

When they arrived home Katherine was still angry. She told Joseph to go to his room to make a start collecting all he wanted to take with him. He was not happy about leaving.

'I always thought Uncle Gerald liked you.'

'He probably does in his own way, but he still wants the house.'

Joseph stomped up the stairs. Katherine was beginning to worry – was he going to be difficult?

She sat in the drawing room looking out over the garden. The daffodils were still tight buds waiting to burst open. Soon they would be producing their annual display, then everything would look fresh and green. The garden would be a blaze of colour but she wouldn't be here to see it.

Tears ran down her cheeks. She loved this house and the thought of leaving it filled her with dismay. How would she manage? Where would they go? Edwin had been a wonderful person and partner. If only he'd made a will. *Had* he made a will? Katherine knew he would have made sure she'd have been well provided for if he'd had the chance, but his death had been very sudden. Surely she was entitled to something after all she'd put into the business. But not if Gerald could see a way of getting his greedy hands on all they'd worked for. Her thoughts went to Edwin and when after all those months at sea they'd finally arrived back in England.

By the time the ship had docked at Tilbury, Edwin Brown knew a lot about Katherine. How she had come from a well-to-do family in the north and was engaged to a Mr Thomas Carter. She was very young when she married, and soon after, her husband had been offered a good post in Australia. He took the job but Katherine had hated the heat and the flies and she had never felt well. She never told Edwin till much later in their relationship that most of her illness was the result of many miscarriages brought about by her husband's violence. It was after one particularly bad time, when she feared for her life, that she knew she had to return to England. Mr Carter refused to let her take their son, Robert, with her. Katherine spent many months torn between her sanity, health and her beloved boy.

When Robert was eight years old Mr Carter sent him to a boarding school many miles away, and Katherine knew she wouldn't see much of him from then, so after a great deal of soul-searching, she left. Although she had two sisters she could never go back home, the family would never accept her. She had married well and no woman left her husband for something so trivial. After all, she had promised to love, honour and obey, and like all good women, that had to be until death parted them.

It was when they arrived in England that Edwin offered her a home. By this time she had become very fond of him. Two months later her second son, Joseph, was born.

Soon after Edwin opened a small teashop, Katherine found she had a gift for cooking. The business had grown, and they moved into larger premises near to Green Park and opened the restaurant. Afternoon tea was always accompanied by a small trio playing in the background, and the beautiful chandeliers and tall potted palms all added to the grandeur.

Katherine sighed. What was she going to do now? Gerald hadn't mentioned money. Where would she go? If the worst came to the worst at least she had fine clothes and jewellery to sell. She stood up. Once again she was in charge of her destiny, and if she could travel halfway across the world on her own, she would get

11

through this. But although Edwin had helped mould her into an astute businesswoman, she was twelve years older now, and with a son to bring up alone.

Chapter 2

Katherine walked into the large kitchen. 'Dolly,' she called out.

A short, grey-haired, plump and jolly-looking woman came bustling out of the larder. Katherine could see she'd been crying.

She sniffed. 'I'm sorry Miss Katherine.' She took a handkerchief from her white apron pocket and dabbed at her eyes.

'I understand how you feel. Losing Edwin has been very painful.'

'It ain't only that,' sniffed Dolly. 'It's the thought of you and the lad going.'

'I know. I feel very upset about it.'

Katherine and Edwin hadn't believed in their staff at home being formal, and had encouraged them to call them by their first names, much to the dismay of Gerald and some of their friends and acquaintances.

When they first came to the house Dolly Webb and her husband told Katherine they thought it odd. But after a short while they found that they had never been happier in all their years in service. Dolly was their cook and general cleaner, her husband, Tom, a quiet, tall, thin man, their gardener and handyman, who also looked after the horse and carriage. They didn't have any children and lived over the stable. They were almost part of the family, joining in at Christmas and birthday parties. Katherine had always looked on Dolly as a lovely elderly aunt who showed her many short cuts in the art of preparing food and cooking.

'Where're you gonner live?' asked Dolly.

'I don't know. I have a little money, but it won't last for ever.'

'What about the lad's school?'

Katherine shrugged her shoulders. 'I don't know. I can't afford to send him any more.' She pulled a chair out from under the large deal table which dominated the warm friendly kitchen and sat down.

Dolly began to get angry. 'Watched him grow up, I have, he's a lovely boy.'

'Yes, I'm very lucky.'

'I reckon it's a disgrace that young Mr Gerald turning you out like this.' Dolly pulled out another chair and sat opposite Katherine.

'He isn't exactly turning me out, it's my decision to go. Besides, Mr Edwin didn't leave him any option.'

Dolly shook her head. 'He went so quick. I'm sure he would have provided for you if he'd known. Treated you like a daughter, he did.'

'I know.' Katherine sighed.

'You won't consider staying on at the restaurant then?'

'No, Gerald and I could never see eye to eye.'

'I'm gonner miss our little chats and laughs. We've had a few in here when we've been trying out new dishes.'

Katherine smiled. 'And we've had a few disasters.'

Dolly laughed. 'Yer, but it's been good fun. It won't be the . . .' There was a sob in her voice. She quickly rose and walked out of the kitchen, dabbing her eyes on the bottom of her apron as she went.

Katherine followed her and put her arm round her shoulders. 'Come on now, Dolly, promise me no more tears.' Katherine hugged her close. She too felt tears stinging her eyes.

'I'm sorry,' said Dolly. 'But we've got on so well together, always felt like one big family.'

'Yes I know, but that's all over now. I'm going to have to

look for somewhere suitable to rent.'

'Any idea where to start?'

'No. It can't be too expensive. I might even have to go over the water.' She smiled. 'Mr Edwin and I lived south of the river for a short while when we came back from Australia.'

'My young sister lives over there by the docks. Rovverhithe. Do you know it?'

'No, I can't say I do, we lived at Kennington.'

Dolly pushed past Katherine's boxes lining the hall ready for her move. She suddenly took hold of her arm. 'I know I shouldn't say this, but if you ever get settled and wants someone to, you know, do for you, you know where to find me.'

'I would love that, but at the moment I couldn't afford you, even if I did manage to find somewhere large enough.'

'Would work for you for nothing.'

'Well, I wouldn't let you.'

'Well, just you wait and see. You've got a good head on your shoulders, I can't see you down for long.'

Joseph descended the stairs, his face set in anger.

'Joseph, what's bothering you?'

'This.' He waved his hands at the boxes. 'I don't want to move away from here.'

'You're not the only one, but we don't have a lot of choice, do we?'

'You could go and work for Uncle Gerald. He said we could stay here then.'

'He's been here to see you?' Alarm bells rang in Katherine's head. Was Gerald trying to get round him?

'Yes. D'you know he's thinking of getting one of these new motor cars. He's going to take me round the show rooms to see them.'

Dolly took a sharp breath.

Katherine quickly looked at her.

'He said I could sit in it. Mama, it's going to be such fun. Please let us stay.'

'Joseph, I don't want to work for Gerald, and I certainly don't want to live in this house with him.' Gerald had been getting at her son. He knew his weakness and was playing on it to get at her.

'Why not?' Joseph began to kick his toe against the bottom stair.

'Please stop that.' Katherine tried to keep her voice under control. She could see Joseph wasn't to be reasoned with. 'Come along, you'd better come with me.'

'I'll tell Tom to get the carriage ready,' said Dolly, quickly moving away.

Katherine called at a few houses she knew might be available, but at the moment the rents were way out of her price range. Was that because she was well-dressed and arriving in a carriage? People got a false idea of her wealth and quoted prices accordingly? She knew what little money she did have wouldn't last very long if she had to pay a high rent. Should she bury her pride and go and work for Gerald? That at least would keep Joseph and Dolly happy.

The carriage was halted when they turned into Whitehall, police everywhere. A column of women came down the road singing and waving banners. They were wearing green, purple and white sashes.

'Who are they, Mama?' asked Joseph.

'Suffragettes.'

'What are they doing?'

'They are women who are fighting for their rights.'

Joseph wasn't listening as he excitedly gathered leaflets that were thrown through the open window. Katherine picked one up. It told of future meetings. In many ways she would have liked to join them. She too had rights that were worth fighting for.

It was a lovely day, and after Tom had battled with the traffic and abuse from drivers of the motors and omnibuses, he suggested they take a turn along the river.

As they approached, Joseph eagerly rose to his feet and put his head out of the window. 'Tom, please stop,' he called.

He jumped out. 'This is a wonderful sight. I wish I'd brought my sketchbook with me.' Joseph loved drawing.

Katherine too left the carriage and watched the boats on the busy Thames that glistened in the afternoon sunlight. Large and small ships used the waterway to ply their trade. Long lines of barges tied together were strung out like a necklace, those very low in the water probably loaded with coal and pig iron. They all appeared to move effortlessly, up and down, back and forth. It was very calming and peaceful. The suffragettes were still on Katherine's mind. She shuddered. She admired these women: you had to be very dedicated to risk imprisonment and go on hunger strike.

'Look at those sails,' said Joseph, breaking into his mother's thoughts. 'Could we go over there?' He was pointing to the other side of the river at a ship with its tall majestic sails gently moving in the slight breeze.

'I don't know, I don't know my way around that part.'

'Oh please. They look so lovely.'

'No I'm sorry, Joseph, I have far more important things to do. Besides, Dolly will be waiting to get our tea.' Katherine smiled up at Tom. 'And Tom will be wanting to get back as well.'

Tom nodded and although he too had a general air of sadness, managed to smile back. 'Only when you're ready, Miss Katherine.'

As they made their way home Joseph said, 'When I sit in the kitchen Dolly often tells me about her sister who lives over by the docks.'

Katherine looked surprised. 'You never told me that.'

'Didn't see any point. I would love to see the docks. Her brother-in-law's name's Charlie and he's a docker. He loads and unloads the ships. It sounds very exciting, and I bet he's a nice man.'

Katherine grinned. From what she'd seen and heard of dockers she wasn't so sure 'nice' was quite the right word to use.

For days she searched for suitable rooms, having lowered her sights from a house, but all the while getting more and more frustrated and worried. Everything she found in her price range was either a dark and dismal basement, or rooms in a house with many other people that was noisy and didn't look very clean.

Gerald continually returned to the house enquiring how long would it be before she left.

'You have another week before I move in,' he told her on his most recent visit. 'I hope you have found somewhere by then – that's if you really wish to leave.'

After he went Katherine sat and stared out of the window. What was going to happen to them? Where could she go?

'Do you and young Joseph want tea in the drawing room for a change?' asked Dolly interrupting her thoughts.

Katherine nodded.

'Not had any luck then, with the rooms, that is?'

'No. I don't know what I'm going to do.'

'Tom said you've started looking a bit further afield.'

'Yes, I can't afford any of the fancy rents some of these people are asking.'

'Can't say we're looking forward to Mr Gerald moving in. He's already talking about changing things.'

Katherine didn't reply. She didn't want to know. It was all too painful.

Dolly plonked herself on the window seat next to Katherine.

'Look, I know it ain't none of my business, and you can tell me to shut it if you like.' She took Katherine's hand. 'I was telling me sister all about this 'ere carrying on with Mr Gerald when we went over to see her last Sunday – she rents out a room, you know. Her place ain't as posh as this but she's clean.' Dolly straightened her shoulders. 'Which is more than can be said for a lot of 'em round there. Well, to cut a long story short she said you could stay there till you got yourself sorted.'

'That's very kind of her, but I don't know.'

'Her last lodger's just left. Nice young man. Gorn to work abroad somewhere, so she said.'

'But what about her husband and children?'

'Charlie don't mind. It helps out with the rent when there ain't a ship in, 'cos he only gets paid when he works. He's a stevedore.'

'I thought Joseph said he was a docker.'

Dolly took a quick intake of breath. 'Don't let Charlie hear you say that. You see, stevedores are the skilled ones. They load and unload the boats, making sure it's right. Wouldn't do to have the boat lopsided now, would it?'

Katherine shook her head.

Dolly continued, 'Milly's only got the boy at home now, young Ted – he's apprenticed to the barrel-makers – named after our dad he was. Her girl, Olive's, married. Her and Ernie, that's her husband, don't live all that far away. She's just found out she's expecting,' whispered Dolly. 'Nice kids the pair of 'em. It'll seem funny our Milly being a granny.'

Katherine didn't want to offend Dolly, but she hadn't envisaged living near the docks. The other side of the water didn't hold any enthusiasm for her. 'Won't I look a bit overdressed round that way?'

Dolly looked her up and down. 'Yer I suppose you would. But once Milly's told everybody your hard-luck story they won't worry what you look like. 'Sides, you could even send young

Joseph to school over there. They only charge a penny a week.'

It seemed as if Katherine's plight had been well and truly discussed.

'Anyway give it some thought. If you like, Tom'll take you both over in the morning.' Dolly looked down at her hands. 'If Mr Gerald gets one of these newfangled motor things what's gonner happen to Tom?'

'Tom?' repeated Katherine.

'Yer. If he gets rid of the horse, what will Tom do? He can't drive one of those things.'

Katherine couldn't answer. She had been so worried about her plight she hadn't thought anyone else might be affected by these changes.

'Miss Katherine, I hope you don't mind, but I did tell our Milly you might be over.'

'But I—'

'Don't worry about it now. I'll bring in the tea.'

Dolly left Katherine bewildered. Should she go and stay with Dolly's sister? It would only be temporarily till she found something more suitable. But Rotherhithe . . . Perhaps tomorrow she would ask Tom to take her there, just to have a chat to Milly. After all, it wouldn't do any harm, and besides, she didn't have a lot of choice. She only had a week to come to a decision. Either she stayed here and lived with Gerald – she shuddered at the thought – or tried to make a new life for herself and Joseph. But what about Dolly and Tom? What was their future?

The next morning Katherine was toying with the idea about going to Rotherhithe when she heard Gerald downstairs.

'Katherine my dear,' he said as she walked down the wide staircase. 'I was just coming up to see you. Could we go into the drawing room? I have a proposition to put to you.'

'I'll ask Dolly to bring in some tea.'

'No, leave that till later. Wait till you've heard what I have to say first.'

Katherine followed him into the drawing room and sat in an armchair.

'I know you don't like me – you've always made that perfectly clear – though I can't think why.'

Katherine quickly glanced at him.

'Oh yes,' he smiled. 'There was that Christmas when I tried to, as you called it, seduce you. It was only a Christmas kiss.'

Katherine drew herself up with indignation. 'A Christmas kiss? You tried to get your hand down the bodice of my gown.'

'Well I'd had a few drinks. Besides, no one noticed.'

'*I* noticed.'

'I always thought you were wasted on Edwin. You could have a far more exciting life with me.'

'Don't you dare take dear Edwin's name in vain. He was a good man.'

'Good yes, but boring with it.'

'I'm not going to stay here and listen to you insult Edwin.' She stood up.

'Please, Katherine, sit down. You see I know how much you will hate leaving this house, so what I suggest is that you stay.'

'Why? What do you want in return?' she asked sharply.

'I need a hostess. I've found that now I am in charge of the restaurant I have many invitations, and a lovely woman at my side would be such an advantage.'

'I would have thought you could have any woman you want.'

'Yes, but I need an intelligent one, one who can hold a conversation.'

'I will not stay here just to be your, your . . .'

Gerald threw his head back and laughed very loudly. 'Good God, woman, I am not asking you to come to some of the places I frequent, just the odd Masonic do and parties I have to attend, and of course you will be here to entertain my guests. In return I will give you an allowance, buy you a new gown when you require one and you can stay and live in the custom you have become used to.'

'Sir, I will not be humiliated. I will not be treated like a child. Given an allowance indeed!'

Gerald stood up and walked to the window. He stared out and said in a low voice, 'Why not? I have felt humiliated ever since you and Edwin returned from Australia. I have always been given an allowance.'

'Yes, because you couldn't look after yourself.'

'That's all changed now. I'm in charge of a very good business.'

'Yes, but for how long will it be a good business?'

'You will see. I intend to turn over a new leaf, for my late brother's sake, and I would like you to be at my side to enjoy some of the fruits of his and your labour.' He came and knelt in front of Katherine and took hold of her hand. 'Joseph can stay on at school. Please, Katherine, stay, for young Joseph's sake as well as your own.'

'Please, Gerald, get up.' She sat for a while in silence. She had to think about Joseph. 'At this moment I don't know. Will you require me at the restaurant?'

He stood up. 'No, the chef seems to be managing without you, or me for that matter.'

'Where will you live?'

'I shall be moving into this house.'

Katherine flinched.

'Don't worry I'll be over the other side, well away from your room.'

Katherine's mind was churning over. What choice did she have? 'I don't know. I am still in mourning.'

'Yes, yes, I know all about that but it won't last for ever.'

'I will have to think about it.'

'Very well, you have till the end of the week.' He gently kissed her cheek. 'Remember, till the end of the week.'

As he closed the door behind him Katherine sat thinking. Had she misjudged him? He was younger than Edwin and Edwin had given him everything he wanted, he had also paid off a lot of Gerald's gambling and drinking debts. Katherine had never told Gerald she knew about that. That was another thing that had turned her against him. They worked hard while Gerald spent hard. Could he have changed? Perhaps he had, now he was in charge of the business.

As she climbed back upstairs, Joseph, who had had a change of heart, becoming very excited at the thought of going to see Ted and Charlie whom he had heard so much about, followed her into her bedroom.

'I'm taking my sketchbook. Dolly said to ask Charlie to take me to the docks.' He sat on his mother's bed.

'Don't expect him to take you right away, he has to go to work.' Katherine began searching her wardrobe for something suitable to wear. It had to be black, of course, but most of her clothes seemed much too grand for Rotherhithe. 'Besides we're only going over to see Milly and the room, and if I don't like it – well, we won't stay.' She wouldn't mention Gerald had asked her to remain there.

'Will I have to sleep in your room?'

'I don't know, we will just have to wait and see.' Katherine finally chose a simple black cotton gown and removed the fancy collar.

'Well, I can tell Milly about what I want to do when we get there.' It seemed Joseph had already made up his mind. She smiled to herself. He changed his allegiance almost daily. Wait till he sees what it's like in the dock area, she thought. He might change his mind again.

'Dolly, are you sure your sister won't mind us turning up unannounced?' Katherine asked as they made their way outside.

'Course not. 'Sides, I told her you might be over if you can't find anything.'

Katherine wondered what else this family had planned for her as Tom helped her into the carriage.

'Young Milly loves it when we goes over to see her. This outfit always causes a stir when we ride up Croft Street,' he said, then added sadly, 'Mind you, I don't know for how much longer I'll be in charge of it.'

'Don't worry Miss Katherine with our troubles. She's got enough problems of her own,' said Dolly, handing Katherine a small brown paper parcel. 'Tell Milly we'll see her the end of the month. That's just a bit of knitting I've done for Olive's baby,' she said, gently patting the parcel.

Katherine smiled and sat back. She felt strange. All these people relied on her decision. What should she do? She had had this feeling when she went to Australia, and again when she returned to England. Was this to be the beginning of another new journey?

She took hold of Joseph's hand as the carriage began to move away.

'Don't, Mama,' he said sheepishly, pulling away.

Katherine knew he was trying to grow up. But she needed his warmth and comfort. He had a huge grin on his face. To him this was the start of a great new adventure.

Chapter 3

Tom was right, their carriage did cause a stir when they crossed the Thames and approached Rotherhithe. Much to Joseph's amusement children ran beside them shouting.

'Scram,' shouted Tom as he cracked his whip high above their heads.

They didn't take any notice and continued laughing and running.

'Look, Mama,' said Joseph excitedly, twisting back and forth. 'They've forgotten to put their shoes on.'

'This is a very poor area. I don't suppose they have any. Shoes come after food.'

Joseph looked shocked. 'They look very dirty and scruffy.' In his sheltered life he'd never come across poverty. This was a lesson he hadn't learnt at school. He sat back with a worried look on his face. 'Mama, are we going to have to live here because we're poor?'

'Not really, it's just that I have to watch my pennies now.'

'If we get ever so poor, will I have to go without shoes?' Joseph sat back, his brow puckered.

'Goodness me, I hope not.' Katherine began to wonder if it had been such a good idea bringing him here.

Tom turned into Croft Street with its row of back-to-back terraced houses. As soon as he stopped Milly came racing out of her house and stood at the side of the carriage as Tom jumped down and opened the door for Katherine.

'Been looking out the window then, gel?' Tom said to his

sister-in-law. 'Milly, this is Miss Katherine what we told you about.'

Katherine wondered how Milly knew they were coming on this particular day.

Milly curtsied. 'Pleased to meet you I'm sure.' She held out a thin bony red hand. 'I was dusting the front room when I saw you. Don't get many posh carriages down this street.'

Katherine grinned. 'And I'm pleased to meet you. I'm sorry we couldn't let you know we were coming, but Dolly said it would be all right. I hope we're not putting you out.'

Milly blushed. 'No, course not. I've been hoping you'd come. And this must be young Master Joseph. How do you do?'

Milly, a thin, wiry woman, wore her naturally curly brown hair twisted into a bun at the nape of her neck, though many strands had escaped the pins. Her pale blue eyes darted nervously about. She was a lot younger than Dolly, but it was hard to guess her age. Katherine thought she could be about thirty-eight, the same as herself. Milly ran her hands down the front of her spotless white overall.

Tom burst out laughing. 'Good Gawd, Milly, they ain't royalty. They're just Miss Katherine and— Oh never mind. Got the kettle on?'

Milly gave him a filthy look. 'Yes, course. This way.'

Tom adjusted the nosebag he'd put on the horse and stepped aside to let Milly lead them into the house.

Katherine noted that in a few windows the lace curtains were quickly pulled into place.

Joseph was studying Milly's feet. He seemed almost relieved that she was wearing shoes.

They followed Milly down the passage with the faint smell of lavender polish filling their nostrils. Small hand-made scatter rugs at the foot of the stairs and at the door of what Katherine guessed was the front room, rested on the shiny brown lino.

When Milly pushed open the kitchen door the warm friendly aroma of baking filled the air.

'Please sit down.' Milly pulled a chair out from under the table.

'I hope we're not putting you out,' said Katherine.

'No, no, not at all.' Every word was carefully chosen, and said slowly. 'I'll see to the tea.' Milly took one of the kettles from off the hob and went off into the scullery.

Katherine sat and took in her surroundings. The kitchen was of modest size but very clean and tidy. The table where she sat dominated the centre of the room and was covered with a plum-coloured chenille cloth that almost reached the floor. An empty cut-glass bowl stood in the middle. Two wooden armchairs either side of the fireplace had comfortable cushions and headrests, neat and very colourful, which Katherine assumed must have been embroidered by Milly. Above the well-black-leaded cooking range was a large mirror, and the mantelpiece was full of china and brass knick knacks. The hearth had been whitened and the brass fender shone. One side of the fireplace was taken up with a huge dresser with plates and dishes tastefully arranged.

Milly returned with a tray. Pretty cups and saucers and a plate of biscuits were neatly laid out.

'This is all very nice,' said Katherine, trying to hide the surprise in her voice.

'Milly always likes to do things right, don't yer, love?' said Tom.

Milly beamed as a slight flush crept up her face. 'Oh go on with you, Tom. Mind you, I do try. That's till Charlie gets in.'

Katherine was smiling from one to the other till her face hurt. What was wrong with Charlie? she wanted to ask. Did he beat Milly? She knew all about that. Was he a drunk? Did she want to be here?

'Charlie's all right,' said Milly quickly. 'It's just that when he's working on lampblack he gets in a bit of a state, but he can't help it.' She turned to Katherine. 'He's a stevedore, and if a ship comes in that's carrying lampblack he gets filfy, and we don't have a barfroom, so if the public barfs is shut the tin barf has to come in and sometimes he makes a bit of a mess – but I only let 'im do it in the scullery.' The words tumbled out.

Katherine quickly glanced at Joseph. His eyes were like saucers. She could almost see his mind turning over. This conversation was like nothing he had ever heard before. There would be a hundred and one questions to answer later.

'If you've finished your tea perhaps you would like to see your room?'

Katherine was stunned. They all assumed she would be moving here. She was being rushed into things. Was this where she wanted to live? 'Well, yes, that's if it isn't any trouble,' she replied politely.

Milly's face was filled with a smile. 'It ain't no trouble, and I'll be that pleased to have you here. Ain't had a real lady living here before.'

'But I'm not . . .'

'Take a look upstairs 'fore you makes up yer mind,' said Tom.

Katherine and Joseph duly mounted the stairs behind Milly. At the top Milly flung open a door. 'This could be your room.'

Katherine stepped in and held her breath. The lace curtain at the long sash window was gently swaying in the slight breeze. The room was bright and airy. She moved to the window. Below was a tiny yard like all the others in the row. Every house had a scullery attached to the back looking like a large carbuncle, and a smaller building that was back-to-back with next door, and which Katherine guessed was the lavatory. She turned. There was a large mahogany wardrobe whose full-length mirror reflected the room. The matching dressing table with pretty lace doilies set out on top had long spindly legs and a green velvet stool pushed under. The bed had a spotlessly white folkweave bedcover thrown over.

'This is a lovely room,' said Katherine, genuinely impressed.

Milly beamed with pride. 'Don't get all me nice bits out when I've got blokes in. Never take in any riffraff, mind. Wouldn't let to dockers or the like, let Mrs Harris across the road 'ave them. Most of me good stuff was our mum's. Dolly only wanted a few small bits as her and Tom's always been in service, so I was lucky enough to get it. Lovely ain't it?' Milly gently ran her hand over the dressing table. 'Won't let any of the blokes smoke up 'ere just in case they leave burn holes on it.'

'It is very nice. Do you and Charlie have . . .?'

Milly laughed. 'Na. Wouldn't let him near anything good. He's a bit like our Ted, clumsy.'

Katherine was getting a little worried about Charlie; now there was Ted as well.

'The lad can sleep in with Ted,' said Milly, gaining confidence. 'This is his room.' She moved out and pushed open another door.

The difference was dramatic, and Katherine could feel Joseph reel back. It smelt of stale tobacco, clothes were strewn over a chair, and odd pieces of woodwork were on the table, but despite that, Katherine could see it was clean.

'My Ted might be clumsy with his feet but he's good with his hands and he enjoys making things, and drawing.'

Katherine noted Joseph suddenly take an interest.

'Takes after his granddad. Ted's apprenticed to a barrel-maker round in the Old Kent Road,' said Milly proudly.

'You only have the two children?'

Milly smiled. 'Yes. Me daughter,' she shuffled Joseph down the stairs and whispered over her shoulder, 'she's expecting.'

'When's the baby due?'

'End of September. It'll be lovely being a grandma.'

Katherine was beginning to warm to this family. In many

ways it would be good to live with a woman who, like Dolly, made her main pleasure in life looking after people.

'Shall we go down? That's me and Charlie's room,' said Milly, walking past the last door upstairs.

'Well, Miss Katherine,' said Tom when they returned to the kitchen. 'What d'yer think? I know it ain't like the place you live in, but our Milly's a good 'en. She's clean, and she'll look after you.'

Katherine didn't know what to say. The thought of no bathroom was one of the drawbacks. 'What kind of rent did you have in mind?' she asked tentatively.

Milly looked embarrassed. 'Well, I usually charge me other lodgers five bob a week, that's if that's all right with you. That'll be for the both of you,' she added quickly.

Katherine looked across at Joseph. He was unusually quiet. She tried to read his mind but his face was blank.

'That will of course include all your food,' said Milly. 'I do charge a bit more for washing, but if you're here you might want to do your own.'

Katherine was amazed. She could manage that for many weeks to come. 'Well, Joseph, what do you think?'

He looked downcast. 'Don't know.'

'We've got to live somewhere, and perhaps Charlie could take you to the docks.'

'Don't know if I want to sleep in Ted's room.'

'Well, you can't sleep in with your mother,' said Milly sounding more confident.

'What about schools?' asked Katherine.

'There's one not too far away,' came the quick reply. 'My Ted went there.'

'I don't want to go to school round here,' Joseph mumbled while playing with his fingers.

'Joseph, that's not nice,' said Katherine.

He looked from one to the other then lowered his gaze, his face full of pain.

'What about another cup of tea?' asked Tom, trying to ease the situation.

Milly jumped up. 'I'll put a drop of water on these leaves.'

'Milly, I'm afraid I will have to look for work,' Katherine said quickly.

Joseph's head shot up.

'We can't live for ever on what I've got,' she added before there were too many questions.

'Let's see. We've got the biscuit factory. My Charlie will know more about that.' She took the kettle, whose lid was bobbing up and down, from off the top of the range and filled the teapot.

There were many things Katherine wanted to know, but at the moment she didn't want to show too much enthusiasm just in case somewhere better to live came up. But would it in just a week? Then there was still Gerald's offer to consider.

'If I decided to move in, would it be convenient say, Friday?'

'Could come tomorrow if yer like,' said Milly.

'I do have rather a lot of boxes.'

'Not to worry, we can stack 'em in the front room for now.'

Milly appeared to have all the answers.

'I know you'll be happy here,' said Tom.

Katherine finished her tea and stood up. 'Well, we had better get going.' She held out her hand. 'Thank you, Milly.'

Milly smiled a broad smile that filled her face. 'Wait till the neighbours round here find out I've got a lady living in. Old Ma Harris will go green with envy.'

Katherine also smiled, but it was false. She didn't fancy being the subject of local gossip.

Although Katherine tried hard to make conversation with Joseph on the way home, he remained quiet.

'Well,' said Dolly, as they walked in, 'you gonner move in with our Milly?'

'I really don't have a lot of choice, do I?' Katherine stood and watched Joseph run up the stairs.

Dolly looked a little put out at that remark. 'I know it ain't like this place, but at least she'll look after you.'

'Sorry, Dolly. Yes, I know she will, but after having my own home, I'm not sure I want to share someone else's.'

Dolly straightened her shoulders. 'Well, as you said, you don't have a lot of choice at the moment.'

'No, I know.' Katherine removed her hat. 'I'd love a cup of tea.'

'I'll bring it into the drawing room,' Dolly said coldly.

Katherine sat staring out of the window. She should go and talk to Joseph, but at the moment she just wanted to be alone and wallow in self-pity. She wanted to cry, but knew that wouldn't help the situation. She had to be positive. Why is it when you think your life is all mapped out, something happens to turn it all about again?

There was a slight tap on the door and Dolly walked in carrying a tray. 'I'm sorry, Miss Katherine, if I got a bit . . . well, you know. It's just that I don't like to see you down, and I know our Milly will make you very welcome.'

'I know. If I do go I'll have to leave some boxes here. Perhaps when you come to see Milly you could bring them with you.'

'Course we will. That's if Mr Gerald will still let us have some time off, and lets us use the carriage. I always feel ever so grand when we go over in it.' Dolly fiddled with her fingers. 'I only hope he lets Tom stay on if he does get a motor thingy.'

'But he'll still have the garden and the odd jobs.'

'Can't do a lot in the winter though, can he?'

Katherine was suddenly made to realise it wasn't only to be her that was having a change of lifestyle. Her departure could affect Dolly and Tom as well.

'I'm sure Gerald will look after you.'

'I'm not so sure. If he can chuck you and the boy out, he ain't gonner have a lot of time for us.'

Dolly left the room leaving Katherine to her thoughts.

After a while she knew she had to talk to Joseph.

'I am not going to live over there,' said Joseph as Katherine opened his bedroom door.

'You will do as I say, young man.'

'If you make me go I'll run away.'

Katherine sat on his bed. 'Please, Joseph. We must give it a try. I thought you were looking forward to going there.'

'Did you see the state of that boy's room? How could you expect me to live in a pigsty like that?'

'I'm sure Ted's very nice.'

'Well, I don't intend to find out. I'm going to ask Uncle Gerald if I can live here even if you go.'

'Joseph, you will not. I forbid it.'

'I'll work for Uncle Gerald.'

'Don't talk ridiculous. Besides, Gerald isn't your uncle.'

'I know that. And Grandpa wasn't my real grandpa. Why haven't I got any real relations?'

'You know why.'

'What about your mother and father, my true grandparents? Have I got any real aunts and uncles? You told me you once lived here in England.'

'That was a long while ago and, over the years, we lost touch. I expect they have all passed away by now.'

'See, you never cared about them, you're only interested in yourself.'

'Joseph,' Katherine's voice was full of anger, 'don't you speak to me like that. When you are old enough to understand I shall tell you the full story.'

Joseph hung his head. 'So why can't you stay here and make

me happy?' His voice trembled. 'You're selfish and I hate you. You left my father and my brother in Australia, now you're going to leave me.'

Katherine was taken aback at that statement. This was the first time Joseph had mentioned Robert. She had told him about his brother and his father, she had never kept them a secret, but not about the violence she had suffered. To throw this in her face now and tell her he hated her was more than she could bear.

'I would never leave you, but we have to be—'

'If you make me go, as soon as I'm old enough I'll run away. I don't want to live there, I want to stay here in my own bedroom.'

Katherine couldn't speak. With tears welling deep inside her she quickly left the room.

That night as Katherine lay tossing in bed her thoughts flew round and round between Milly, Joseph, Gerald and Robert. What did her son look like now? Did his father ever talk about her? Would she ever see him again? What Joseph had said still had her reeling with guilt. True she hadn't thought about her family here but she had left many years ago and knew she wouldn't be welcome. That's if they were still alive. Her parents had thought Mr Carter was wonderful, so full of ambition, and they had been very pleased at getting the last of their three daughters off their hands. They always said Katherine was wayward because she preferred books to sewing. And what about her sisters? They never did see eye to eye; was that because she didn't conform and behave like them? Well, now it had all backfired on her and she was alone.

Katherine hadn't been looking forward to moving to Rotherhithe, and this outburst with Joseph had finally made up her mind. She had been selfish. She had lost one son and she wasn't prepared to lose Joseph.

'Well,' she said out loud, 'tomorrow Gerald will have my answer.'

Chapter 4

After telling Joseph they were not moving and getting Tom to take the boxes that had been lining the hall back to her room, Katherine sat waiting for Gerald. The atmosphere between Katherine and her son was very hostile. Even Dolly greeted the new arrangement with mixed feelings.

'Only hope you're doing the right thing in staying,' she said.

'Only time will tell.' Katherine hadn't told Dolly the real reason for her change of mind.

'Well, till Milly lets that room the offer will still be there, that's if you fancy it.'

'Thanks, and tell Milly I would have been very happy to move in with her.' Katherine turned away. She didn't want to go into detail of why she'd had a change of heart.

When Gerald arrived he appeared to be genuinely pleased Katherine had decided to stay.

'I'll get Tom to collect my belongings from the hovel I live in.' He strutted round the hall. 'I must say I am really looking forward to moving into this house. Always admired your taste, my dear. I'm so glad you saw the sense in staying. So, perhaps this could be the beginning of a very happy liaison.'

Katherine flashed him a look which she hoped said 'Keep away from me.' 'I'll get Dolly to bring tea into the drawing room.'

'Katherine, wait. I am very fond of you, and I know it was Edwin's dearest wish that we got on. He always said that if you had been free he would have liked us to marry.'

35

'But I'm not free.'

He laughed, moving away. 'I promise not to get under your feet too much.'

'I'll fetch the tea.'

She stood in the hall for a few moments. Was she being too hard on him? After all, he had lost his only brother.

For the next two weeks Gerald was as good as his word. They saw very little of each other. He seemed to be busy with the restaurant and only joined Katherine and Joseph on Sunday for dinner. Joseph was happy but said very little to his mother, for there was still a big gulf between them that Katherine was determined to heal.

Katherine was also beginning to get bored. Needlepoint was not one of her strong points, and now she wasn't needed in the kitchen she wandered aimlessly about. Even her beloved garden didn't hold her interest for long. She needed to be busy, but what at? So far Gerald had not required her to exercise her social skills on his behalf.

'Katherine,' called Gerald, as he walked into the drawing room late one Saturday evening. He was handsome and looked immaculate in his evening dress. His dark hair shone as it caught the light when he moved across the room. 'I have some exciting news. A few of my friends have persuaded me to hold an Easter party here. A good idea, don't you think?'

'I don't know. We should still be in mourning.'

'Oh, I'm sure old Edwin wouldn't mind us having a bit of fun. After all, we can't bring him back, can we?'

Katherine would have liked to smack his face at the remark. 'This is your house now, and it's up to you. Of course you will have to hire extra staff.'

'I will leave all that up to you. It will give you something to look forward to. I must say you have been looking a bit down lately. Now I must dash. Just came back for a change of clothes. I'm off to the theatre after we close tonight.'

In many ways Katherine too would have loved to have gone to the theatre. That was one of the many things she missed, but would never have dared to tell Gerald.

Dolly looked angry when Katherine told her the news about the forthcoming party.

'So how many's coming to this 'ere do, then?'

'I don't know.'

'Will they be stopping overnight?'

'I don't know that either. When I find out more I'll let you know.'

'Can't say I'll enjoy having someone else mucking about in my kitchen.'

'It's only for one night.'

Dolly straightened her shoulders. 'Well, I never thought I'd hear you approve of this sorta goings-on.'

'I didn't say I approved. It's just that this is Gerald's house now and we have to make the best of it.'

'Suppose so.'

'I'll try and see Gerald and ask him to give me more details.'

'That's a laugh.'

'Why? What do you mean?'

'Walks in at all hours of the night and morning and then 'as the cheek to wake me and ask for food. Mind you, nine times out of ten he's three sheets to the wind.'

Katherine smiled. 'I expect he has to meet a lot of people.'

'You and Mr Edwin met a lot of people, but you didn't carry on like he does.'

'I don't hear him.'

'Well, he's crafty. Creeps in after you're in bed, and he don't get up till about noon, then it's straight down to the kitchen and out the back way.'

Katherine wanted to laugh at the thought of Gerald creeping about. 'I don't know why he does that. After all, it is his house.'

'Don't want you disapproving, so he said.'

'Then I only hope he's looking after the business side of things. I would hate to think that all our hard work . . .' Katherine stopped. It wasn't her business now.

'Well, that's up to him,' said Dolly disapprovingly.

It was early Sunday evening. Gerald hadn't been home for dinner. Katherine was taking a leisurely stroll round the garden when she heard his voice.

'Katherine my dear. I must say this is a pleasant surprise. Dolly said you wanted to see me.' Walking towards her he took hold of her shoulders and kissed her mouth hard.

She pushed him away. 'How dare you!'

He laughed. A strand of his dark hair fell over his face. 'I couldn't help it, you look so lovely and I thought—'

'Well, sir, you thought wrong. All I want to do is go over the arrangements with you for this party.'

'I told you, I'll leave all the details up to you.' He waved his hand dismissively. 'By the way, buy yourself a new gown.' He threw a small purse of money on to the garden table. 'And get any colour but black.'

Katherine looked at the purse. She felt like a kept woman. 'I don't need a new gown.'

'I'm sure you do. I don't know of any woman that turns down the offer of a new gown.'

'But—'

'Oh for God's sake, woman, don't make such a fuss,' he said angrily.

He followed her when she went in the house. She wanted to tell him there wasn't time to have one made, but gave up, he wasn't interested, and besides there were many gowns upstairs that he had never seen, so he wouldn't be any the wiser at what she wore.

In Edwin's study she picked up a pencil and paper from the desk and sat very upright in the armchair. 'We must sit down and discuss the guest list, and what time you wish the event to commence.'

He went to the drinks table and poured himself a very large whisky. 'Can I pour you a drink? Sherry perhaps?'

'No thank you.'

'Oh dear, I've ruffled your feathers. We are Miss Efficient, aren't we? You, madam, are a cold fish. I'm surprised Edwin let you stay in this house if you didn't share his bed.'

Katherine was blazing inside but tried hard to keep her feelings under control. She wanted to kill him, but she needed a home. 'Gerald, you are being very rude and offensive, and if Edwin had left a will I wouldn't be in this situation. Now can we get on with this list?'

Gerald stood behind her and lightly touched her hair. 'This is a beautiful colour. Edwin always admired your hair.' He bent forward as if to kiss her neck.

'Please, don't touch me.' She could feel his breath on the back of her neck and quickly stood up.

'Can't you show any warmth towards me? After all, you could be out on the streets if it wasn't for my generosity.'

'I am aware of that.' She sat down again. 'Now can we continue with the guest list?'

Gradually the list was completed. There were so many names Katherine didn't know, and the few she did were people she would never have had in her house.

The date was settled and Katherine in many ways was looking forward to being busy.

Joseph came down the stairs.

'Off to school then?' asked Katherine as she stood back to

admire the vase of flowers she had placed on the hall table.

'Uncle Gerald said I can stay up for this party.'

'Did he now?'

'Well, will you let me?'

'I shouldn't think so for one minute.'

'That's what I told him.'

'He's not your father.'

'I know that, don't I?' He pushed past her and slammed the front door.

Katherine walked into the kitchen. She felt like stamping her feet in temper.

'You look annoyed. What's got your goat?' asked Dolly.

'Gerald. D'you know he's told Joseph he can attend the party.'

'Don't say I approve of that, not with all the wine and drink that's been delivered.'

'I didn't order that much.'

'You didn't, but he did.' Dolly inclined her head towards the door. 'Take a look in the outhouse.'

'No, I can't be bothered. Dolly, what am I going to do?'

'Don't ask me. I only work here.'

The friendly atmosphere that had always prevailed in this kitchen somehow seemed to have been lost. Katherine felt an outsider.

'Have there been any other changes?'

'Not as far as I know.'

As the weekend of the party got closer so the food and flowers arrived and preparations began in earnest. Dolly and Katherine were kept very busy.

At eight o'clock on Saturday evening Gerald banged on Katherine's bedroom door. 'Come along, Katherine, let's go and meet our guests.'

'I'll be down in a moment.'

The guests began arriving by horse and carriage as well as motor cars. Joseph was hanging out of his mother's window.

'Why can't I go down?'

'Because I say so.'

'You don't let me do anything I want. I want to go and see those motors. Uncle Gerald is going to buy one and he said he would take me with—'

'Joseph, be quiet!' shouted Katherine. 'I'm sick of hearing what Gerald says and promises. Now, you can stay here and look out of this window if you wish. When Dolly has a spare moment I'll get her to bring you up a tray. I must go.'

Katherine left the room. Her heart wasn't in this, but she knew she had to put on a show, it was part of their agreement. She smoothed down her dark navy gown, the darkest she had that wasn't actually black.

A trio began to play. Gerald smiled and took her hand ready to introduce her to various people – there were very few she already knew.

'You look lovely,' he whispered.

As the evening wore on and Katherine moved about, she caught snatches of conversation and was surprised to hear her name linked with Gerald's. What had he been saying?

'Katherine my dear.'

Katherine turned to see Mrs Emily Hawthorn walking towards her.

She came and kissed Katherine's cheek. 'I was so sorry we missed dear Edwin's funeral. And now what's this we hear about you and Gerald? You do make a very handsome couple, and this house is very nice for you both.' While she was talking to Katherine her sharp beady eyes were darting round the room. 'Never been invited here before, but then you and Edwin didn't entertain that much, did you? Oh look, there's the actress Pamela

Courtney Jones, must have a word with her.' With that she turned and hurried away.

What was Gerald telling them? She must try to get him on his own, ask him to quash these rumours.

All evening he was busy with his guests. The wine was flowing and conversations were getting louder. The room was hot and stuffy and thick with cigar smoke. Katherine felt tired and miserable, she didn't enjoy the company of these people, they were noisy and showy.

She decided to take a walk in the garden to clear her head before going to bed. Her thoughts were full of Edwin. Young men were behaving foolishly, picking the flowers and tramping on the borders. Edwin would never have allowed this. Was this how her life would be from now on?

She tried to talk to Gerald but she could see he was in no mood for a serious conversation.

Before she retired to her room she looked in at Joseph. He was fast asleep. She smiled. The tray on his table had just a few crumbs left. Please let us be friends. I need a friend, she thought.

As she lay in bed the laughing and shouting drifted up. Motor car doors were being slammed and engines bursting into life. Every now and again a horse would neigh – how much nicer these sounds were. But this was progress, and she must accept it. Her life was changing now whether she liked it or not.

Chapter 5

Katherine woke and for a while lay listening to the birds singing. What did the future hold for her? For the second time in her life she felt trapped and miserable. How she envied the birds their freedom, they could fly away. After dressing she went downstairs.

''Ave you seen the mess in there?' asked Dolly, as soon as Katherine opened the kitchen door. 'Broken glass and all sorts.'

'No, I came straight in here.'

'It's a bloody disgrace. I hope we ain't gonner have too many of these dos.'

Katherine sat at the table as a cup of tea was put in front of her. She couldn't tell Dolly that she'd overheard people eagerly talking about the next one. 'That will be up to Gerald,' was the only answer she could give.

Dolly was busy bustling about. 'Tom's in there now clearing up. There's some burn holes in Mr Edwin's favourite chair. And someone's squashed their cigar out in the carpet. You wait till you see it.'

Katherine wanted to cry. This had been her house, now it was being taken over. She should have been strong and stood her ground. She should have gone to Milly's. 'Is Gerald up yet?' she asked.

'Shouldn't think we'll see him till dinner time.' Dolly clearly wasn't in the mood for any kind of polite conversation.

'What about Joseph?'

'He's out in the garden.'

All day Katherine had to listen to Dolly complaining about

the mess and the behaviour of some of the guests, while Joseph moped about grumbling that he never got to look over the motor cars properly.

'I wanted the chance to draw one up close, that's all, but you wouldn't let me.'

Katherine didn't reply. There was no point.

Gerald wasn't seen until afternoon tea was over. Katherine was sitting in the garden surveying the damage. Tomorrow she would ask Tom to help her make a start to clear it, she wasn't in the mood today.

'Last night was a huge success,' said Gerald, sitting next to her. 'And I have you to thank, my dear, for that.' He condescendingly patted her hand.

'I can't take the credit, it was the staff who made it go as smoothly as possible. Dolly isn't very happy about it, or the mess.'

'She works for me now, so she'll have to get used to it, won't she? You don't approve of my friends, do you?'

'No, and I don't know what you told them about me, and us. What did they mean?'

'I just happened to mention to one or two of my very close friends that, in the very near future, we may well be married.'

'Gerald, how could you? You know that to be a lie. You know I am already married. Can't you see I don't like you, or your friends, and I only stay here because, as you so rightly say, I have nowhere else to go.'

He smiled. 'I'm glad you see things my way.'

Katherine walked away in temper. Why did this man always make her so angry? Tears of frustration stung her eyes. Was it because he never listened to her? Or because he thought he could own her?

That night Katherine was tossing and turning in bed. Sleep

wouldn't come. Her mind was going over and over what Gerald had said when she heard the creaking of her bedroom door being slowly opened.

'Joseph? Joseph, is that you?' Katherine sat up.

He didn't answer.

She pushed back the bedclothes and slid out of bed. 'What's wrong?'

The door was clicked shut. Katherine froze when in the gloom she recognised Gerald's shape. Quickly grabbing her dressing gown and regaining her composure, she asked, 'What do you think you are doing coming into my room?'

'I've come to talk to you.'

'I'm sure we have nothing to talk about that can't wait till morning.' She wanted to move round the bed to get near the door, but he was blocking the way.

'Katherine, I'm in love with you. I have been for years. Since the first time I saw you. You are the reason I have never married.'

'Please, Gerald, this is ridiculous. Have you been drinking?' Katherine was shaking with temper and fear.

'Ridiculous, is that what you think?' He slowly moved towards her. 'Let me tell you, madam, that at this moment ridiculous is the last thing I feel. And yes, I have been drinking. I've been sitting downstairs trying to think of a way to make you like me.'

'Well, this certainly isn't the way, now kindly leave my room.' Katherine stepped back and fell against the dressing stool, stumbling to the floor.

Gerald quickly came towards her. She tried to scramble to her feet but her nightclothes hampered her.

He was on his knees, and with his arms round her he pulled her close. The smell of whisky almost took her breath away. She tried to pull away but he held her face tightly in his hands and passionately kissed her lips, face, and hair. She rocked her head from side to side in an effort to break free. She pummelled his chest and tried to push him away but he was strong. She wanted to scream out, but who would hear her? Her room was the other side of the house from Joseph's. His hands tore at her nightgown revealing her bare breasts. Like a wild animal he bit into her soft white flesh; she cried out in pain.

'You like it, don't you? You want me. You have been without a man for years,' he hissed.

'Let me go.' Her long hair caught on the buttons of his waistcoat and pulled her head back.

She screamed out hysterically and dug her nails into his cheek.

He put his hand over her mouth and she bit his hand.

'You bitch.' He pulled at her nightgown and it came away in his hands. She was naked.

She tried to get to her feet but he was holding on to her, his fingers digging deep into her flesh. They rolled on the floor with their legs entangled. He put his forearm across her neck; she couldn't breathe. With his free hand he pushed her legs far apart. She thought he was trying to suffocate her and somehow she managed to bring her hand up and hit his face hard. He sat back on his haunches and laughed. Then with the back of his hand he struck her hard across her face. Her teeth rattled and warm sticky blood filled her mouth. Her head was swimming.

Between her sobs she heard him say, 'I've waited a long while for this, and I'm going to have you one way or another.'

For Katherine everything went black and she didn't feel anything any more.

Slowly Katherine opened her eyes. She was still lying on the floor. Through the open window she could hear the birds singing their hearts out. Outside dawn was just beginning to break. Red streaks painted the sky. It took her a moment or two to get everything in focus. Every part of her body hurt. Gradually, after a great deal of effort, she got to her feet and sat on the bed. She looked down at her naked body. It was covered with red weals and bite marks. Long scratches ran from her breasts down to her waist. The bruises on her legs took on many colours. Ashamed, she hastily pulled a sheet over her nakedness. Her head throbbed and her body ached. When she caught sight of her face in the mirror she cried out and put her hand to her cheek. A yellow and black bruise filled one side of her face. She lay back and let her tears flow. 'How could you do this to me, Gerald?' she groaned.

When Katherine opened her eyes again the sun was up. She carefully got to her feet when she heard Joseph slam the bathroom door and clatter down the stairs. 'I'll wait till he's gone before I make a move,' she said to herself. Every movement was an effort.

Gradually, after she knew Joseph had left for school, she bathed, and when she felt a little stronger made her way downstairs.

'You're late,' said Dolly with her back to her. 'Tom's taken young Joseph off to— Oh my God!' Dolly quickly put her hand to her mouth and rushed to Katherine's side. 'What happened to you?'

Katherine tried to give her a reassuring smile, but it hurt.

'Did he do that?'

Katherine nodded and tears slowly rolled down her cheeks.

'Bloody animal, wants locking up. I knew you should have gorn to Milly's. You can't stay here, not now.'

'When Tom comes back perhaps we could have a word.'

'You go on up to your room, I'll bring you something nourishing. 'Sides, you don't want to come face to face with that cowson.' Dolly took hold of Katherine's hand. 'I don't like to ask,' she gave her a knowing look, 'but did he – you know . . .?'

Again Katherine only nodded.

'Wants bloody castrating. You wait till my Tom hears about this, he'll go mad. Why didn't you scream out?'

'I couldn't.' Katherine stood up. 'I will go on up.'

'I'll bring up a cuppa.'

As Katherine climbed the stairs every bone in her body seemed as if it were complaining. She just wanted to lie down and weep.

Dolly followed her up. She sat on the bed. 'Here, lay back and let me take your shoes off.'

Katherine did as she was told and closed her eyes.

'Tea's on the side,' said Dolly.

'If Gerald asks about me, tell him I've gone out.'

Dolly quietly closed the door and left Katherine to her thoughts.

She would have to leave this house, she couldn't stay under the same roof as Gerald, not now. Despite what Joseph had said she would get Tom to take them to Milly's today. She had to get away. Slowly she sat up. Her mind began to get things in order. She had to pack. She would only take essentials. Money and jewellery, and as many clothes as she could. Then there were Joseph's things she would have to take. Suddenly she felt stronger as she began to put her plan into action.

Gradually and very painfully she managed to fill two boxes. That was all she could take at the moment. Perhaps later, when Dolly and Tom visited her sister, they could bring a few more.

'Miss Katherine, what you doing down here? I was just coming up with some broth.' Dolly was leaning over a large steaming pot.

'Has Gerald gone yet?'

'Yes. And he didn't ask about you. He's got some nasty scratches on his face. Felt like giving him a piece of me mind, I did, but then thought better of it.'

'I'm going to stay at Milly's.'

Dolly's face lit up. 'You are? Oh I'm ever so glad. She'll look after you. When you going?'

'This afternoon, when Tom picks Joseph up from school.'

'So soon?'

'I can't stay another night under this roof. Do you think Milly will mind me turning up like that?'

'Shouldn't think so. Mind you, that's if she ain't already let the room.'

Katherine was filled with fear. She hadn't thought about that. 'Well, I'll have to keep my fingers crossed. I've packed two boxes, so when Tom's ready perhaps he'll put them in the carriage.'

'What about the rest of your stuff?'

'Have a sort through and if there's anything you'd like please take it, then perhaps you could bring the rest over sometime.'

Tom made no comment when he saw Katherine's bruised face. She guessed Dolly had given him all the details.

Katherine didn't leave the comfort and the obscurity of the carriage and sat waiting for Joseph to come out of his expensive school. All the boys were wearing uniform and it was hard to pick him out, but when he caught sight of Tom he bounded up to him.

'Didn't expect to see you here,' he said eagerly. 'Can I ride on top with you?'

'No, son, get inside.'

He looked a little puzzled as he opened the door. 'Mama, what are you doing here?'

Katherine sat back in the shadow as they moved off.

'Where are we going?'

She took hold of his hand but he pulled it away.

'We are going to live with Milly.'

'What? I told you I wasn't going to live there. Tell Tom to take me home. I am not going to . . .' His voice trailed off when Katherine sat forward. 'Mama,' his voice softened. 'What's happened to your face?'

'This is why we have to leave Gerald. He attacked me last night, and I'm afraid I fear for my life.'

For a full minute Joseph sat and stared at his mother, then he threw his arms round her and, hugging her close, cried, 'Why Mama? Why did Uncle Gerald do that to you?'

'I told you, we had a disagreement. I can't live in that house any longer – we are going to Milly's.'

Joseph sat back. 'But I don't like it there.'

'Well, I'm sorry, but I have decided. It's time to go.'

Chapter 6

After Joseph got over the shock of seeing his mother he asked what had happened. Katherine explained that Gerald had drunk too much and wanted her to marry him.

'So why don't you?'

'Because I am still married to your father.'

'I forgot. Anyway he lives miles away, so who would know?'

'Even if I wanted to, which I don't, it's illegal, and I don't love Gerald.'

'Does that matter? If you did marry Uncle Gerald we could stay at the house.'

Katherine chose not to answer that. Is that all he was worrying about?

'Perhaps he didn't mean to hit you.'

'I'm sure he did. Men do silly things when they drink.'

Joseph sat back and looked sad. 'But I don't want to go to Milly's.'

'Well, I'm very sorry, but that is how it's going to be. Besides, you don't know, you may like it there.'

'Don't think I will,' mumbled Joseph.

'That's quite enough,' said Katherine sternly.

Joseph didn't pursue the conversation any further and the uneventful journey continued.

Katherine was cross and hurt that he didn't seem to be very concerned at what Gerald had done to her.

Once again Milly was on her doorstep as soon as the carriage came to halt outside number 12 Croft Street. Tom jumped down and helped Katherine to alight.

Milly gasped when she caught sight of Katherine's face. 'I'm so pleased you've made up your mind to come,' she said, not commenting on the bruising. Two bright pink spots of embarrassment and excitement coloured her pale cheeks. 'Put those boxes in the front room for now, Tom.' She turned to Katherine. 'You've certainly got a lot.'

'Can't stay long,' said Tom anxiously. 'His nibs might start yelling for me.'

'I'll give you a hand,' said Joseph sullenly.

'I'd like to move in today if it's convenient.'

'Course. Charlie and Ted will give you a hand to get this stuff upstairs if we can't manage it. Kettle's on. I expect you'd like a cuppa, Tom?'

'Only if it's quick,' came the reply as they moved into the kitchen. Tom looked nervous and drank his tea as soon as it was put in front of him, then left.

'Now,' said Milly to Katherine. 'When you've finished your tea I'll show you where everything is. I don't go out much, but if at anytime you fancy a cuppa it's best you know where to look.'

Katherine was shown the scullery and all the cooking implements. She was taken into the back yard for a look into the lavatory, then followed a lesson on how to raise and lower the washing line. Next the large wooden mangle was uncovered for her inspection.

'Charlie said that if you did come over here he'd take you and show you where the biscuit factory is, and where the boy can go to school.'

'Thank you, that will be very kind of him.' Katherine put a restraining hand out to stop Milly from entering the house. 'Milly, Gerald, Mr Edwin's brother, did this,' she pointed to her face, 'when I wouldn't let him share my bed.'

'Guessed as much, but don't worry about it, most of the wives round here get beaten regularly, 'specially poor Mrs Addams across the road. Not that my Charlie would ever lay a finger on a woman. Reckons those blokes are cowards, can't fight men, most of 'em.'

Although Katherine felt very apprehensive she was beginning to warm to Charlie. Suddenly everything in her life was going to be so different.

'Not got bad neighbours,' said Milly, not taking that conversation any further. She peered over the low wall and lowered her voice. 'Mr and Mrs Parsons lives next door. Got two boys – don't see a lot of 'em, they works away, that's when they're not in clink. Mr and Mrs Duke live there,' she pointed to the other side of the yard. 'Quiet couple. Kids married and moved away. She's a bit of a busybody, but not nasty. We're lucky we don't have hordes of kids banging and shouting. Feel sorry for that lot across the road, they've got the Addams family to put up with.'

Milly was in an excited chatty mood, and Katherine didn't ask questions.

Between them and with Joseph's help, they carried the boxes upstairs. They returned to the front room, which had a damp unused feel to it. A hard uncomfortable-looking brown Rexine three-piece had been carefully positioned around the fireplace. A shining brass firescreen hid the empty grate. In front of the lace-curtained bay window stood a long-legged rickety-looking table with a large pot on top. It held a huge aspidistra. The dark green shiny leaves overhung and looked like a giant spider ready to pounce.

Milly stood back and proudly pointed to the grandfather clock in the corner. 'That was me mother's. It don't work, but it's a nice piece of furniture. Lovely wood. Ted gets in first, about six, and now we have the lighter nights Charlie works on a bit – that's when there's a ship in, of course. It's timber mostly at the Surrey Docks.'

Katherine smiled. 'Dolly will be bringing some more of my clothes when they come over to see you, not that I'll have a lot of use for them now.'

'Don't chuck any away,' said Milly in alarm. 'What you can't pawn p'raps we can cut up.'

'Do you do alterations?' asked Katherine, noting the sewing machine in the corner.

Milly grinned. 'Can turn me hand at most things.'

'Do I have to sleep with your son?'

Katherine was suddenly aware they had almost ignored Joseph.

'Well it's that or down here in the front room on the floor. I ain't putting a bed up in here for you. It's gotter be the floor.'

'I'd rather sleep on the floor if you don't mind.'

'I don't mind, it's you that'll find it hard.'

Katherine wanted to sweep him up in her arms and hold him close, but she knew he would hate that.

'Will we live here for ever?' he asked his mother.

'I don't know. When I get a job perhaps we could look for a small house.'

'Jobs round here ain't that easy to get.'

Joseph was very quiet and at times Katherine caught him studying her face. He was obviously very shocked at what Gerald had done. Such violence was all quite alien to him. What a blessing no one would ever see her body.

Katherine sat in the kitchen while Milly busied herself with the dinner. She glanced at the clock on the mantelpiece. It was almost six, soon Charlie and Ted would be here. Joseph had sat all the while in her bedroom with his books. He had made it very clear he didn't like this situation. Katherine was worried. Would he ever accept living here?

The laughing and noise from the passage told her that Ted and Charlie had arrived home together.

''Allo there, love,' said Charlie, pushing open the kitchen door. He wasn't overtall, but stocky and well-built, with the healthy complexion of an outdoor worker.

Ted followed, a tall thin lad whose pale colouring was the same as his mother's, such a complete contrast to his father's weatherbeaten looks.

'All right then, gel?' Charlie asked Milly. 'Dinner smells good.' His thick brown hair sprung up when he removed his flat cap and threw it on to the armchair. That was followed by a well-patched jacket that had definitely seen better days. The thick heavy metal docker's hook that Katherine had seen men dig into large sacks and timber to give them a grip when they had arrived at various ports, had been hitched over his wide leather belt, but was now carefully placed on the dresser.

'And you must be Miss Katherine?' Charlie stopped when he caught sight of her face.

'That Gerald did that,' said Milly quickly.

'Did he now? Well anyway, pleased to meet you. Won't shake yer hand as I ain't all that clean.' He slipped his braces off his wide shoulders and, letting them dangle, took the large black kettle from off the hob and disappeared into the scullery.

Milly smiled as she hung his jacket and cap on a nail behind the door. 'You're having a good influence on him, he don't usually do that till he's had a cuppa.'

'Yer, but it won't last,' said Ted. 'By the way, I'm Ted.' He looked down shyly. 'Where's yer boy then, missis?'

'He's upstairs,' said Katherine, pleased they didn't ask any more questions about her bruises.

'I'll go on up and have a word with him.'

'Don't you sit on that bed in your work clothes. I'll just nip up and get Charlie a clean shirt,' said Milly, leaving Katherine on her own.

After a few minutes Ted came clattering back down the stairs and Milly passed through with a shirt and then returned to the kitchen with the kettle.

'He said he'd like to see my drawings,' said Ted beaming.

'Well, they are good,' said Milly.

'Joseph also likes to draw, perhaps you could help him.'

'That's what he said. He's ever so quiet.'

'I expect he's a bit shy,' said Milly, clearly enjoying having her family around her.

'That's better,' said Charlie, walking in and rolling up his sleeves. 'Right then lass, how's my Milly treating you?' He pulled up his braces and standing in front of the mirror ran both hands over his hair that had been slicked down with water.

'Very well, thank you.'

'Ted, you can go and have a wash as well,' said Milly, handing him another kettle.

'But, Mum, I ain't had a cuppa yet.'

'It'll be on the table by the time you're finished.'

'Do you want me to get Joseph?' asked Katherine.

'You could do.'

'Just yell up the stairs,' volunteered Charlie.

'Miss Katherine is a lady, remember, and she don't yell,' said Milly, giving her husband a filthy look.

Charlie laughed. 'Yer, I forgot.'

Katherine hastily left the room. She didn't want to keep being called a lady and Miss Katherine, she was living in their home now. She had to become one of them, but how?

She pushed open her bedroom door. 'Joseph, are you coming down to eat?'

'I'm not hungry.'

'Come on now, don't be silly.'

'Bet she can't cook as good as Dolly,' he mumbled.

'I expect Milly can. They both had the same mother to teach them, remember. Anyway, why don't you come down and find out.' She knew he must be hungry, and the smell of the dinner wafting up the stairs would soon change his mind.

He slid to the edge of the bed.

'What did Ted have to say to you?'

'He said he would show me how to draw properly.' For the first time that day he smiled. 'After tea he's going to show me his sketches, that's what he calls them.'

'Do you know what his favourite subject is?' she asked casually.

'No, but he said I mustn't tell his mum about his sketches.'

Katherine was taken aback. What if they weren't the kind of thing she wanted her son to see just yet? 'So, will you tell me?'

'I don't know,' he said, pushing open the kitchen door.

''Allo there, young 'en,' said Charlie. 'Glad to have you living here with us.'

'Thank you, sir.'

Charlie threw his head back and laughed. ''Ere, Mil, did you hear that, he called me sir.'

'Well I told you, they've got very good manners, and it wouldn't hurt you two to take a leaf out of young Joseph's book.'

The first meal was full of laughter and chatter, as Charlie told them about his day at the docks. He made everything sound as if he enjoyed the hard work. Katherine could see Joseph was intrigued.

'Bit worried about all these strikes though,' said Charlie, pushing his empty plate away. He sat back and began rolling a cigarette.

'D'you think it'll get to the docks?' asked Milly, jumping up to collect the plates.

'Don't rightly know, love. It don't take much to set 'em off.'

'Well, I hope it don't happen. Don't know how we'll manage with only Ted's bit coming in.'

'You've got Miss Katherine's money as well now,' said Charlie.

'Anyway, we'll worry about it if and when it happens.'

'That was delicious,' Katherine said to Milly as she handed her her empty plate. She noticed Joseph's plate was also empty.

'She ain't a bad cook, is she?' Charlie smacked his wife's bottom as she passed his chair.

She blushed and giggled. 'Oh, go on with you. There's seconds if you fancy any.'

'Not for me, thank you,' said Katherine.

'That's not what I fancy,' said Charlie, giving Katherine a wink.

'Charlie Stevens,' shouted Milly, 'I trust you to watch your mouth. We have a child as well as a lady present.'

'I'm not a child,' said Joseph.

'And I'm not a lady,' laughed Katherine.

'And I was talking about having a pint,' said Charlie.

Milly sat down and laughed with them.

'Come on, Joe. Can I call you Joe?' asked Ted.

Joe nodded.

'Right, let's show me what you can do.'

'Please, Mama, may I leave the table?'

'Of course.'

'Oh, he's got such lovely manners,' said Milly.

Katherine looked round at the happy faces. Even Joe, as she guessed he had now been christened, was grinning. At that moment she knew she had made the right decision in coming here. She only hoped the neighbours would prove as friendly. With the way she spoke and her clothes, she felt, and was, an outsider in Rotherhithe.

Katherine had decided to wait a few weeks before she looked for work. She wasn't in that much of a hurry, not all the while she had a few sovereigns left. She hadn't returned the money Gerald had given her for a new gown.

* * *

The following morning Milly took Katherine shopping. As Milly closed her front door Mrs Duke from next door came out.

'Good morning, Milly.'

Milly was beaming. 'Mrs Duke, this is Miss Katherine.'

Mrs Duke was a large woman with rosy cheeks and her grey hair piled up on top of her head. Her white wrapover overall was tied tightly round what should have been her waist, but she was the same size all the way down.

'Pleased to meet you,' said Katherine, giving her a slight nod.

'Christ. Miss Katherine, eh? That sounds a bit posh for round here.' Mrs Duke had a slight lisp.

'Miss Katherine is staying with me till she finds suitable accommodation.'

'Down on yer uppers then, girl? See yer old man's been knocking you about. Oh look out, here comes that poor cow Mrs Addams and her tribe.'

Katherine gasped when she saw the woman walking towards them. She wasn't old but looked very weary; she was heavily pregnant and holding on to two small boys, one in each hand. Their clothes were tatty and well patched, but they weren't wearing any boots. Another child, who was struggling to see over the top of a large battered bassinet, was desperately trying to keep it going in a straight line. Inside a child sat at each end; one was much too big to be sitting in a pram and both were sucking huge grubby gobstoppers made from rag. Katherine guessed they were full of sugar and they almost covered their faces.

Two older girls deep in conversation were trailing behind. They all had masses of dark hair like their mother, and as they got closer Katherine could see that apart from the styes and yellow matter in most of the children's eyes, they were all the same dark blue.

'Hello, Mrs Duke, Mrs Stevens,' said Mrs Addams politely, with a slight nod. Her lilting Irish brogue was a joy to hear. 'I trust this fine weather is helping to keep your rheumatics at bay, Mrs Duke?'

'Yes thanks. You all right?'

'Mustn't grumble. Won't be sorry when this one's here.' She patted her large stomach.

'You'll only get yourself up the duff again.'

She smiled, lightened up her blue eyes. 'I expect you're right, but 'tis the will of the Lord.'

The two in the bassinet began yelling and fighting when the older one pulled the other's dummy out. The child holding the handle started to rock it violently. Katherine looked on in horror, she thought they would fall out with the intense movement.

'The Lord, eh?' said Mrs Duke, smugly crossing her arms. 'That's all very well, but He don't have to feed 'em, does He?'

'That's true,' said Mrs Addams, putting out a calming hand to steady the bassinet and shoving the dummy back into the child's mouth. She smiled. 'I trust you and your family are keeping well, Mrs Stevens? When does your Olive have her baby?'

'Not for a while yet. September sometime.'

'Well, send her over if she wants some advice.'

'It ain't no good her coming to you to find out how to stop 'em coming though, is it?' laughed Mrs Duke.

'No, Billy, don't do that, it ain't nice.'

Billy had broken free from his mother's hand and was sitting on the kerb picking his nose, then running his only clean finger down his tatty coat.

'That's a nice frock, missis,' said one of the girls who had been hanging back. She began to run her dirty fingers over the fine material of Katherine's dress.

'Leave it be,' shouted Milly.

The girl put her tongue out.

'Briony, you mustn't be so rude,' said her mother. 'I'm sorry, but she ain't used to seeing such fine cloth.'

Briony looked thin and undernourished. Katherine guessed she must be about the same age as Joseph. She looked up at Katherine with adoration in her eyes.

'Miss Katherine is staying with us till she finds something more in keeping with her lifestyle,' said Milly in a very pompous way.

'Oh yer, and what sort of lifestyle's that then?' asked Mrs Duke.

'Miss Katherine once owned a lovely restaurant, and my sister – you know my Dolly – well, she used to do for her.'

Katherine stood dumbfounded. They were talking about her as if she wasn't there. Was all her history about to be discussed? She was used neither to gossiping in the street nor being treated as an object of curiosity.

'So what yer gonner do round here then, girl, open a posh restaurant?' Mrs Duke threw her head back and laughed very loud. Katherine was fascinated that her bright pink gums held one lone tooth, which accounted for her lisp. 'Christ, this lot round here don't know what it is to sit at a table, let alone sit in a restaurant and use a knife and fork. No, girl, I think you'll have to think of something else.'

Opening a restaurant, especially round here, was the last thing on Katherine's mind.

'Mum, what's a rest— What that lady said?' asked Briony.

'I'll try to explain later,' said her mother. 'Now come on, we must be off.'

'They live across the road,' said Milly, when the Addamses were well out of earshot.

'She's got another three boys, the eldest goes to work and the other two run errands for the blokes down the market. A bit like bookies' runners they are, do all the dirty work,' added Mrs Duke.

Katherine didn't like to ask what a bookie's runner did. 'Don't the boys go to school?' she enquired instead.

'Na, can't afford it, poor cow.'

'How many children has she got all together?' asked Katherine, staring after them.

'Let's see. It'll be eleven when she drops that one,' said Mrs Duke.

'Eleven,' repeated Katherine. 'She can't be that old. How does she manage?'

'Dunno. They ain't been here that long, just a couple of years or so. Her old man works on the new tunnel. They brought a lot of Irish over to dig out the tunnel. Stinks to high heaven, he does. Still, I s'pose you and her have got something in common,' said Mrs Duke to Katherine.

'Oh, and what's that?'

'After work her old man goes to the pub then gives her a bloody good hiding when he gets home.'

Katherine cringed.

'Then,' continued Mrs Duke, enjoying getting into her stride, 'when they gets into a lot of debt, like the rent, they moves on, or so I heard. Poor cow, what sorta life's that?'

It was obvious to Katherine Mrs Duke knew all about them, and one way and another it shouldn't take her long to find out everything about this newcomer to Croft Street.

Chapter 7

Following Milly's instructions Katherine soon found the school and Joseph started the next day. She was pleased to hear he was far ahead of all the other pupils of his age. She had been worried he might have been picked on because of his smart clothes, but with Milly's help she managed to dress him down.

All week Milly was also busy in the front room with her sewing machine altering the gowns Katherine had managed to bring with her. With much laughter they removed most of the trimmings and took out the many petticoats, trying to make them suitable for Rotherhithe. Any they decided were far too grand finished up in the pawn shop along with a few pairs of her dainty shoes.

'You sure you want to do this to all these frocks?' said Milly, wistfully. 'What if you find yourself a good job – you might need them?'

'I don't think that will ever happen, and if it did, I could start all over again,' said Katherine, lightheartedly. But she knew she would never be in a position to wear such fine clothes again.

'Milly, you've made a lovely job of this one,' she said, holding a gown against her.

'What shall I do with all this cloth that's over?'

'Can you or your daughter make use of it?'

'Miss Kath – sorry, Katherine –' Katherine had asked her to drop the 'Miss' as it sounded as Charlie would say, 'too hoity-toity for round here' – 'you've been so good to us already. I've got so many lovely pieces in my workbox,' continued Milly, gently fondling the fine silk. 'Olive's baby's gonner be wearing some lovely things, and so will she when she can get into them.'

'I've got an idea. Sort out any pieces you can't make use of and I'll take them over to Mrs Addams.'

'You are kind.'

Katherine felt embarrassed. 'You don't think she'll take offence, do you?'

'I should say not.' Milly straightened her shoulders. 'She should be grateful you're taking an interest in her.'

'I don't want her to be grateful, it's just that young Briony always gives me such a lovely smile when I see her, but she has such sad eyes. I wish I had a daughter.'

'She has a lot to put up with, poor mite.'

That afternoon Katherine picked her way across the road, carefully avoiding the piles of horse dung, and knocked on the Addamses' front door.

Briony opened the door. The smell of dried urine filled Katherine's nostrils and almost made her cough. Briony was wearing a dirty frock that was at least two sizes too big for her. She was balancing one of the babies on her hip. He only had on a short vest and Katherine blanched at the sight of his red bare bottom. It was scabby and looked very sore. Briony's dark hair hung matted and lank, and with her free hand she pushed some strands behind her ear.

''Allo, missis, what d'yer want?'

'I'm sorting out some of my clothes and I was wondering if you would like this material that's left over.' Katherine held out a bag.

Briony quickly looked over her shoulder. 'I'd ask you in, but it ain't conveni— It ain't very tidy.'

'That's all right. Here, take this, I'm sure your mother can find a use for it.' Katherine wasn't that keen to go into the house.

'Thanks.' Briony's smile lit up her very pretty face.

As she made her way back to Milly's, Katherine noted that in a few of the houses the lace curtains moved slightly.

Katherine was happy. She had found a friend in Milly and every morning they would go off shopping together. Joe appeared to have settled down at school and most evenings he and Ted would sit and discuss their drawing. At the weekend Ted took him to the docks and Joe excitedly told his mother about the ships, and proudly showed off his sketches. Katherine had been shown the biscuit factory, the docks and many other things. She didn't want to go to work, but knew her money wouldn't last for ever.

It was the slums that upset her the most, the dirt and the squalor. Women sat outside their front doors with babies and children squabbling round their feet or sucking at their breasts. Young girls dragged the younger ones round with them. Shoes seemed to be unheard of. Katherine always felt overdressed when she passed these people, and she could feel their eyes boring into her back. After a few days one or two gave her a slight nod.

'Why do these people have so many children?' she asked Milly.

'Most of 'em because the old man says so. They have a few drinks then take what they knows is their right. Then the wives have to put up with more babies. Some of 'em go to any old crone who'll help 'em out – that's those that ain't Cath'lics, of course. Mind you, some don't always come off all right, poor cows, then they finish up in a pauper's grave.'

Katherine was shocked. 'You mean they die?' she asked softly.

'Sometimes.'

'I'm surprised that some of these women don't become suffragettes.'

Milly laughed. 'They ain't interested in getting the vote. Their main worry is where the next meal's coming from. 'Sides, most of 'em can't read.'

Katherine was beginning to find out it was an even more unfair world than she had ever imagined. So many had everything while others had nothing.

'I like to keep me place neat and tidy,' said Milly, almost as if reading Katherine's mind. 'Me mum was always a stickler for keeping the place nice and clean, so I suppose it rubbed off on me and Dolly.'

On Sunday Olive and her husband came to tea. Olive looked so much like her father, with her dark hair, brown eyes and a big ready smile. Ernie, a slim man, was quiet and wore a very serious expression, but they were a happy couple, eagerly looking forward to the arrival of their baby.

One morning after shopping Milly and Katherine were walking back down Croft Street when they saw Briony coming towards them. Her hair was tied back with a piece of string, she looked clean and was wearing a frock made out of some of the material Katherine had given her. It wasn't particularly well made, and she looked very overdressed.

'You look very smart,' said Katherine kindly.

She beamed and her beautiful blue eyes twinkled. 'I've got to go and see Mr Wilks in the ironmongers. He said he might give me a job.'

'How old are you, Briony?' asked Katherine.

'Thirteen.'

'You're a little older than my son, Joseph.'

'I tried to talk to him once but he walked away. He's a right snob, ever so stuck-up.'

Katherine grinned. 'I'll have a word with him.'

Briony began to move away. 'Don't bother. I don't need him to talk to, got plenty enough of me family. By the way, d'yer like me frock?'

'It's very nice,' said Katherine. 'Did you make it?'

'Na, me mum did.'

As she walked away Milly laughed. 'Poor little cow. Did you see the size of those stitches?'

'It was all done by hand,' said Katherine. 'She's very young to be going to work.'

'It's a case of having to.'

'I suppose it's good of Mr Wilks to give her a job.'

'That's as may be. But I can't say I'd fancy her serving me. Did you see the colour of her neck?'

Katherine nodded. 'She does smell a bit, I'll grant you that.'

'Don't suppose she's ever had a bath. It's a good job it's an ironmongers and not the grocers. Wouldn't fancy her touching me bacon or butter.'

'It's such a shame. She seems to have a good head on her shoulders despite everything.'

'I only hope for her sake all what we hear about old Wilks ain't true.'

Katherine stopped. 'What do you mean?'

'Well,' Milly also stopped. She looked around and said quietly, 'Some kids don't stay long, and talk is that he, you know, interferes with 'em.'

'That's dreadful. Are you sure?'

'Well, he's always got new kids in there, and that's what the rumour is.'

'No,' said Katherine, deeply shocked.

'It's what they say.'

'Don't any of the parents report him?'

'Who to? 'Sides, with some parents they worry more about the kid losing the job and the extra few shillings coming in.'

'That's awful,' said Katherine.

'That's life,' said Milly casually.

Briony was on Katherine's mind all afternoon. She liked her and wanted to help her, but how? Briony didn't go to school and the family obviously needed her wages so perhaps starting work could be something positive in her life. At least she would be away from the children for a few hours a day, and she would be meeting people. But what if Mr Wilks interfered with her? What was it with men? Did Briony have anyone to confide in if he did? Would she tell anyone if her job depended on it? Perhaps it was all rumours and he'd teach her to read and add up?

Katherine was still thinking of Briony when Joe came home from school. 'Why won't you talk to her?' she asked him.

'She smells.'

'That isn't a very nice thing to say.'

'Well, she does. 'Sides, I don't want to go near that family, they all smell. A lot of people round here smell.'

Katherine wanted to smile, but she managed to keep a straight face. 'She's going to work in the ironmongers.'

'Well, paraffin will be better than dried pee.' He ran from the kitchen into the front room which he now called his room.

Milly walked in from the scullery laughing. 'I heard that. He's got his head screwed on 'as that one.'

On Saturday Milly was busy making cakes for Sunday's tea. 'Dolly and Tom should be over tomorrow,' she said to Katherine, who was helping her.

'It will be interesting to find out how things are going at the restaurant and what changes Gerald has made to the house.'

'Do you still miss that way of life?'

Katherine brushed the flour from her hands. 'In some ways, but certainly not Gerald.'

'Not thought any more about going back then?'

'No. That part of my life is over.' It was true: if she did not yet feel entirely part of Milly's world, she certainly was not part of Gerald's.

'Do you worry about Joe?'

Katherine looked puzzled. 'I suppose I do, why do you ask?'

'He's always telling Ted he's going back there to live one day.'

Katherine sat at the table. 'He does?'

Milly laughed nervously. 'You know what boys are like, always telling each other things to make it sound good.'

'I hope that is all he's doing. I don't need any more worries at the moment. Milly, I must find something to do soon, my money won't last for ever.'

Milly looked embarrassed. 'I honestly don't think I could take any less, especially if the docks do come out on strike.'

Katherine flushed. 'Oh Milly, I'm sorry. I didn't mean that. Please forgive me. I'm so happy here.' She suddenly threw her arms round the startled Milly. 'You've made me feel I'm part of your family. And I wouldn't dream of asking you to . . . I'm sorry.'

'’S all right,' said Milly, straightening up. 'It's nice having you here.' She ran her hands down the front of her overall. 'You ain't given the biscuit factory any more thought then?'

'I don't think I'd like that. I'm not used to taking orders. I'm sure I'll think of something,' she said breezily – but to herself silently added, But it will have to be soon, very soon.

Chapter 8

Sunday afternoon found Milly backwards and forwards looking out of the front-room window.

'I wonder what's happened to Dolly?' she asked, clearly agitated.

'Could be Gerald had visitors and couldn't let them come over,' said Katherine, trying to ease the situation, but deep down wondering if he'd taken it out on Dolly and Tom for helping her to move.

'But she always lets me know if that's gonner happen.'

'P'raps she didn't have a chance,' said Charlie, looking up from his newspaper. 'There's pictures in 'ere about the *Titanic*. That must'a been bloody awful, all them lives lost, and after they said it wouldn't sink, an' all.'

Katherine shuddered. All week the newspaper placards and the paper boys had been shouting the tragic news about the sinking of the *Titanic*.

'Terrible thing, ships going down. They're sorta like living things, seem to have souls somehow. I remember me dad telling me about the *Princess Alice* sinking in the Thames,' said Charlie reflectively.

'I didn't know about that,' said Milly. 'You ain't said about it before.'

'Never thought about it before. Not many bought a paper in them days, not many could read. Me dad knew all about it though as he worked at Woolwich creek – that's where it sank, run down be the *Bywell Castle*. Seven hundred lives lost, so he said.'

Ted let out a long low whistle. 'Seven hundred, that's a lot of people.'

'Yer. Poor buggers. They was coming back from a day trip to Sheerness.'

'But it ain't as many as the *Titanic*,' said Ted.

'Well, that was an ocean-going ship, son. You was on a big ship when you come back from Australia,' said Charlie to Katherine as he folded his paper.

'Yes, but it wasn't as big as the *Titanic*.'

'Must'a been exciting though,' said Ted.

'Not when you keep being seasick,' laughed Katherine. She knew Dolly had told them about her background and how she came to be living with Edwin.

'Mama said I've got a brother who lives in Australia. I might go and see him one day.'

'You have?' asked Ted.

Katherine was taken aback at Joe's statement. 'Yes, Ted, he has. Robert was twenty last month.'

'That must'a been awful for you, leaving your son,' said Milly sadly.

'Yes, yes it was.' This was the first time Milly had mentioned this.

'What was Australia like?' asked Ted eagerly.

'Hot, with a lot of flies.'

'I'd like to travel,' said Ted.

'That's a laugh. Who'd wash yer socks?' asked Charlie. 'Mind you, I admire you. That was quite a journey for you to tackle on your own.'

'Yes, it was.' Even after all these years it was still very painful for Katherine to talk about. 'I wish there was some way I could get in touch with Robert. To find out if he's well.'

'Did you ever write to him?' asked Milly.

'I did when I first arrived back in England, but I never received a reply.'

'Perhaps he didn't get it?'

'That's possible.' But Katherine suspected his father had probably destroyed it.

'Don't know what I'd do if I ever lost one of mine,' said Milly softly.

'We get some ships in from Australia, but most of 'em come from Canada or Norway. Wood's the main stuff we handle at the Surrey,' said Charlie, quickly changing the subject.

Katherine liked Charlie. He was always ready to talk, even to women, which some men still regarded as beneath them.

'Tell you what, I'll take young Joe over a ship one day,' said Charlie.

'Would you?' His eyes lit up. 'I'd really like that.'

Katherine was pleased that he was beginning to settle down, but that was due mainly to Ted, who somehow enjoyed taking him under his wing. Most evenings you could hear them laughing together.

At the end of the evening Milly was upset Dolly hadn't been to see them.

'You might get a letter tomorrow telling you why,' said Katherine. But she too was apprehensive. What if Gerald was making Dolly and Tom unhappy? She was very fond of them. Was this her fault? She could have avoided it if she had stayed. That night she slept with a heavy heart.

The following morning Milly and Katherine were wandering round the shops when Katherine noticed a sign in the window of a place called Trent's: 'Help Wanted.'

Katherine stood looking at it for a few moments. 'I'm going in to ask what kind of help they want.'

Milly looked aghast. 'You can't go and work in there.'

'Why not?'

'Well, it ain't nice. It ain't proper for a woman of your—'

'I've got to do something.'

'I know, but that? You get all sorts in those places, real rough 'ens. Mind you, I ain't got nothing against a nice bit a saveloys and pease pudding, but you working in a pie and mash shop.'

'I'm going in.' With that Katherine swept inside.

After a few moments she came out with a huge grin on her face. 'I've got a job.'

'I don't think you should be working in a place like this. When you supposed to be starting?'

'Tomorrow. Look, why don't we go in and have a cup of tea?'

'Dunno.' Milly looked about her. 'Is anybody inside?'

'A few people.'

'Well, all right then.'

Katherine pushed open the door and ushered Milly inside.

'Two teas, please,' she said to the large red-faced man behind the counter. He lifted the heavy brown enamel teapot, poured out the tea, then wiped his hands down the front of his dirty white apron. 'That'll be tuppence. Just 'cos you're gonner work here you've still gotter pay.'

Katherine smiled, putting her money on the counter. 'Of course.'

'Sugar's there.' He pushed a tin bowl towards her. The spoon was caked with sugar that had turned brown.

After putting two heaped teaspoons of sugar in each mug she replaced the wet spoon in the sugar bowl and carried the two thick mugs of steaming dark brown liquid to the table where Milly was sitting.

'Oh my Gawd, what does he call this?' asked Milly, peering into the mug.

Katherine smiled. 'Tea.'

'How long's it been stewing?'

'I dread to think.'

Milly took a sip. 'Well it's warm. I'll grant you that. You sure you want to work here?' she asked, looking round.

'Yes.' Katherine sounded confident.

'It don't look very clean.'

'Perhaps he needs a woman round the place.'

'Bet he don't pay much.'

'Well, not at first and after all he did only want a young lad.'

'So how come you got the job?'

Katherine smiled. 'It's my winning way.'

'You'll be nothing but a skivvy.'

'Watcher, Josh, me old mate,' said an old woman walking in and plonking her basket on the floor. 'I'll have a nice cup of rosy.'

Katherine was taking all this in. She leant forward and asked Milly in a whisper, 'What's rosy?'

'Rosy Lee, tea. You've certainly got a lot to learn,' laughed Milly.

Katherine laughed with her. Milly was right.

Later that day Katherine was excitedly telling Joseph about her new job.

'The pie and mash shop? I pass that place on my way to school. It doesn't look very nice.'

'Well, I'll just have to wait and see. Who knows, I may be running the place soon.'

'Why? Is the old man going to die?'

'I shouldn't think so.'

The following morning Katherine felt a little apprehensive as she made her way to start work in Trent's shop.

'Good morning,' she said breezily.

'Oh yer. Christ, you look a bit dressed up for round here.'

Katherine knew the gown she was wearing really didn't look right, but she didn't have much choice.

'Right, now get this apron on and cut up those eels.'

The apron he handed her was dirty and Katherine turned up

her nose. It smelt of fish. She squirmed when she saw the live shiny black eels wriggling about in a large tray.

He handed her a large thick knife. 'What's a matter, woman, ain't you got no stomach for it?'

She half smiled. 'Not really used to doing things like this.'

'Well, you'd better learn quick. I did tell yer I just wanted a lad, but you said you'd done a bit of cooking, and well, that persuaded me to give you a trial.'

'Yes, I know, and I'm grateful, Mr Trent.'

He threw back his head and laughed. ''Ere, you'd better call me Josh like everyone else does.'

'Thank you.'

He was a tall, big man with a beer gut. He had a large nose and a florid face. His grey hair was sparse, his small watery blue eyes looked Katherine up and down. 'So, how comes you're round this way looking for work?'

'I've had a bit of trouble.'

'Not with the law I hope?' he said quickly.

'No, family.'

'I see.'

Katherine was pleased most of the bruising on her face had faded. Milly had warned her not to tell him too much otherwise it would be all round Rotherhithe before she got home. In any case Katherine didn't have any intention of getting too friendly; she was there to work, and that was all.

All morning she was kept busy pouring out tea, dishing out faggots, saveloys, pease pudding, jellied eels, meat pies and grey lumpy mashed potatoes. She filled jugs with parsley liquor, and in between did the washing up. After the shock of seeing her behind the counter the customers were polite and quiet. Gradually they began to ignore her and she quite enjoyed listening to the banter that came from the in-depth discussions they had. The subjects ranged from the *Titanic* to the suffragettes, the latter bringing a lot of noise from the men. It was obvious to Katherine that they didn't want women to get the vote, and thought the Pankhursts were a bunch of troublemakers. But it was the talk about strikes that brought the most reaction. Nearly all the men were really worried.

Josh Trent was a gruff man, who made sure she didn't stand around. 'Go over and wipe that table down,' he growled.

She picked up a cloth, it stunk and the feel of it made her heave. It felt greasy and slimy and was full of holes.

'Cor, we don't normally see the likes of you round here,' said a man sitting in the corner next to the marble-top table she was busy trying to clean. ' 'Ere, Josh, she ain't a bad looker – what's yer missis gonner say when she claps eyes on her?'

'Nothing, she's here to work.'

Josh had told Katherine he lived above the shop, but he hadn't mentioned a wife, and why didn't he have her down here helping him out?

'Don't hang about, woman,' he yelled. 'I said wipe it, not polish the bloody pattern off it.'

A couple of the men laughed and she felt cross as she made her way back behind the counter. She couldn't see how she could polish the pattern off of a marble-top table. 'Shall I make a fresh pot of tea?' she asked Josh.

'Na, that one will do till after lunchtime. Just leave it on the stove, that'll soon get it stewing.'

Katherine shuddered as she poured out the thick dark liquid, but the customers didn't seem to mind and drank it without question.

After the lunchtime rush the customers began to drop off. Katherine picked up the cloth and started to wipe the tables again.

'I like that,' said Josh.

Katherine looked up surprised.

'You didn't wait to be told. I like that. Some of the silly cows

I've had here have to be told to do every single thing.'

Katherine only smiled. She wasn't going to tell him about the restaurant, and that she knew all about staff.

When the last customer left Katherine was wondering if she should go. 'How long shall I stay?' she asked.

'Till I say you can go.'

She felt uneasy. 'You and your wife live upstairs?' she asked casually.

'Yer. She ain't too good these days.'

'Oh I'm sorry.'

'Why should you be, you don't know her.'

Katherine didn't have an answer, so she busied herself wiping the rest of the tables.

'Look, I'm gonner go out back and start cooking the meat for tomorrow's pies. You can manage out here.'

Katherine went back behind the counter and looked round. 'I'd like to give this place a good clean,' she said to herself.

The door opened and a young girl wearing a large black hat with a pink feather draped across the brim came in. She kept her head bent and slouched up to the counter. 'Cuppa,' was all she said.

Katherine quickly pushed a mug of tea towards her. The girl's two bright pink rouged cheeks looked clownlike on her pale face. 'Are you feeling all right?' Katherine asked.

'What's it to you?'

'I just thought—'

'Well, don't think, and mind yer own bloody business.' She took her tea and sat at the far end, the smell of her cheap scent following her.

A few moments later a man walked in. He was reasonably dressed, which was very unusual for round this way. He looked around but didn't come to the counter, just went and sat with the girl.

Katherine couldn't hear what was being said, but the girl looked very unhappy as she stood up and walked outside with the man.

Well, this place certainly has some strange customers, thought Katherine. But it looks as if it could be far more interesting than the biscuit factory.

Chapter 9

Josh let Katherine go about six. She was happy as she made her way back to Milly's.

'Well,' asked Milly, pouncing on her as soon as she walked in. 'How did you get on?'

'Very well. You're certainly kept on the go during lunchtime, then when it dies down Josh goes outside to make the pies and leaves me in charge.' She laughed. 'Mind you, he takes the money with him.'

'Cheeky sod,' said Charlie. 'So it's Josh, eh?'

Katherine grinned. 'It seems he likes everybody to call him that.'

'Been worried about you all day,' said Milly, plonking a cup of tea in front of Katherine.

'You smell a bit,' said Joe.

'It's the eels. Can I take the kettle into the scullery before dinner?' she asked Milly.

'Course.'

Katherine felt better after she'd washed and changed, and all through dinner she told them about her customers.

Katherine was a little worried that Milly still hadn't heard from Dolly. 'Would you like me to write to her?' she asked as they washed up.

'No, thanks all the same, but I can drop her a line.'

Katherine enjoyed working in the pie shop, and as the week progressed she found Josh was a fair man. The customers, who on the first day regarded her with suspicion when they heard her speak, began to accept her. She also noticed that now and again Josh disappeared upstairs. She guessed it was to see to his invalid wife, but he never mentioned her. Katherine wondered if she had ever worked down here. After that very first comment none of the men spoke about her, and Katherine didn't ask.

On Friday she was curious about the young girl who often came in and sat facing the door. Today she was wearing a very tight skirt that made it difficult for her to walk, and that large black hat with the feather again. It was much too old for such a young face. She had rouge on her lips and cheeks.

'What yer staring at?' she asked when she looked up.

'Nothing,' said Katherine quickly.

The man wearing a suit came to the doorway and the girl walked out.

Katherine was full of it when she got home. 'Such a pretty girl, and her friend was a lot older than her, and better dressed than most round here. He didn't come in.'

'Don't reckon he was a friend,' said Charlie. 'Sounds like more of a customer.'

'And how would you know about that, Charlie Stevens?' asked Milly.

Charlie winked at Katherine. 'Only what I've been told, old girl.'

'That's all right then,' said Milly.

Katherine smiled at Charlie. She guessed he had seen many of her sort hanging around the docks. What drove those girls to that sort of life?

Josh was very surprised when she took in some material for cloths the next day, and on Saturday she asked to take her apron home to wash.

'You ain't getting any extra money for it.'

'I don't expect extra, I just like things to be clean.'

'Please yourself, but I don't want yer making the blokes feel uncomfortable.'

'Why should they?'

He grinned. 'Most of 'em here are used to more than a bit of dirt.'

On Saturday Katherine received her first wage of five shillings. That was just enough to pay Milly and, for the moment, she could still manage Joe's school money – but how long would that last? She would make sure she was useful and then in a few weeks' time, she would ask Josh for a rise. That evening Milly read out the letter she'd had that morning from Dolly.

'She said she couldn't get over 'cos Mr Gerald's got rid of the horse and bought one of these 'ere motor cars.'

'I was going to go with him to get that,' said Joe glumly.

'Don't worry about it,' said Ted. 'We can have a ride in it when Tom comes over.'

'They don't know when they're coming over as Gerald keeps 'em busy with a lot of wild parties, so Dolly says,' said Milly, still holding the letter.

'I bet that doesn't please Dolly. Does she mention what he said about me leaving?' asked Katherine.

'No, only that he was very cross. She wishes you all the best, by the way.'

Katherine gave Milly a weak smile. 'Give her my regards when you write.'

'I will. I shall miss 'em not coming over here,' said Milly, sniffing and stuffing the letter back in her overall pocket.

'Perhaps one day you could meet her halfway,' suggested Katherine.

Milly smiled. 'Perhaps we could.'

At the end of the second week at Trent's Katherine knew she had made the right decision. She was really enjoying her work even if it was hard on her feet all day. It was when she had a name change she knew she had been accepted and was very happy about it.

'I ain't gonner keep calling you Katherine or Mrs Carter, it's too much of a bloody mouthful. What about if I call yer Kate?'

'I don't mind.'

'You look more like a Kate.'

Kate was pleased about that.

Very soon all the men followed suit. Some of the older ones enjoyed a laugh when she had to ask them to explain cockney slang, and she wasn't sure they were always telling her the truth. After a while many told her to call them by their first names, so it was that she began to talk about Percy, Bert, Bill and many more. Sometimes during their heated conversations she was asked her opinion, but she was careful how she answered. She didn't want to upset anyone, least of all Josh. She still hadn't seen Mrs Trent and nobody ever mentioned her.

Milly came in one morning when she was out shopping.

Katherine gave her a beaming smile. 'Sit down, I'll bring you over a cuppa.'

Milly laughed as she looked round. 'I must say it looks a bit cleaner in here. What yer done to the place?'

'Nothing really,' she said, putting the mug on the table. 'Just washed the lace curtain and cleaned the window and underneath the tables.'

'Well, it certainly looks brighter and better without all those dead flies lining the windowsill.'

'And these cloths smell better. Yes, Josh, before you say anything I'll put the money in the box. He thinks you might be trying to get away without paying.'

Milly fumbled in her purse. 'I wouldn't dream of it.'

'This one's on me,' said Katherine.

'Just been in the ironmongers. Young Briony don't look very happy.'

Katherine looked at Josh, who was deep in conversation with a well-dressed man Katherine hadn't seen before. 'You don't think,' she came round the counter and wiped down a table next to Milly's so she could lower her voice, 'you know, that Mr Wilks . . . you don't think he's . . .?'

'Dunno.'

'I wish I could talk to her.'

'Her mother's baby's due any day now, p'raps you could pop over then.'

'I could do, I could take her a little gift.'

A small boy wearing such a large cap that it almost covered his eyes, came in. He was very short and could hardly reach the counter. Standing on tiptoes he put a bowl and money on the counter. 'Faggots and pease pudding, please, miss.'

Katherine filled the bowl. 'Thank you, young Walter. How's your granny today?' She looked at Josh, he wasn't facing her direction so she quickly spooned another dollop of pease pudding in the bowl.

'She ain't too bad. This warm weather's doing her feet in, though. Swelled up like big balloons, they have. They look really rotten. 'Bye.' He picked up his bowl and left.

Katherine smiled. 'He's a nice little lad, told me his granny looks after him.'

Milly laughed. 'Good job this place don't belong to you otherwise they'd all be round here for a handout.'

'Shh.'

'Well, I must go. See you later.'

Josh was still in conversation and Katherine carried on with her chores. When she went out to the back yard to get some more potatoes ready to peel for the next day she heard someone calling.

She hurried back into the shop. 'Josh, I'm sorry to interrupt but I think your wife's calling.'

He looked annoyed. 'You can see I'm busy. Go up and find out what she wants.'

Katherine smoothed down her apron and made her way up the stairs.

'Yoo-hoo,' she called out. 'Which room are you in?'

'I'm in the bloody bedroom. Who are you and what d'yer want?'

Katherine pushed open the door from behind which the voice had come. The smell almost took her breath away. The room was stuffy and stank of urine and an unwashed body. It took a moment or two for her eyes to get accustomed to the gloom as the curtains were drawn.

'Who the bloody hell are you? And what yer doing up here? Where's Josh?' The woman who was sitting up in bed was small and wizened. She became very agitated. Her thin mouth was turned down and from her pale lined face faded blue eyes set in deep dark sockets stared out. They looked Katherine up and down. Her grey frizzy hair stuck up like a witch's and it didn't look as if it had been brushed or washed in years. Her gnarled hands and bent fingers twitched and pulled at the bedclothes.

'I heard you call out and as Josh is—'

'Josh? What you calling him Josh for?'

'He ask me to.'

'Did he now? So are you his fancy bit?'

'No. I work for him,' said Katherine haughtily.

'Oh you do, do yer? And how long 'as this cosy little setup been going on?'

'I've been employed by Mr Trent for three weeks now.'

'Oh, so it's Mr Trent now, is it?'

'Can I get you anything?'

'No you can't Miss High-and-Mighty. And where did he find you?'

'I answered his notice.'

'I bet you did. I told him to get a boy, not another tart. Mind you, you're a bit old for him, he normally likes 'em young.'

Katherine was finding it hard to keep her temper. Who did this woman think she was talking to? She wasn't a child. But she knew she had to hold her tongue, her job could depend on it.

'Your husband is busy at the moment, so if I can't be of any help I'll leave you in peace.' Katherine turned to go.

'No, hang on a minute. You say you work for Josh? What's yer name?'

'Kather— Kate.'

'Well, Kate, you can bring me up a cuppa, and I don't want any of that stewed stuff he dishes up to the customers. Make me a nice fresh pot. And if there is any hanky-panky going on down there, I'll soon find out about it. Got lots of friends who comes and sees me and tells me all what goes on. So make sure you keep yer nose clean.'

Katherine closed the door and took a breath. How could he let his wife stay in a room like that? And how long had she been there? What was wrong with her? And who looked after her? And who came to see her? It wasn't in the day, unless they came in the back way. All these questions were going over and over in her mind as she slowly made her way down the bare wooden stairs.

'Oh, there you are. Go on out front. What did old Nellie want?'

'A cup of tea.'

'Pour her one out and I'll pop it up.'

'But she wanted a fresh one.'

'She'll have what she's given. Well, go on then, move yourself. By the way, that was the landlord, Mr Sharman, I was talking to.

Make sure he talks to me when he comes for the rent. Now get Nellie's tea.'

Katherine hurried to the shop and poured out a mug of dark liquid. As she passed it to Josh she felt sorry for his wife. Fancy just lying there. She would wait till the right moment, then ask him if she could do something.

That evening she was full of it when she got home as she now called it.

'I'm going to ask him if I go in an hour earlier perhaps I could try to make her comfortable.'

Milly waved at her the wooden spoon she was using to stir something on the range. 'First it's Briony, then the kid in the shop, now it's his wife. Nobody worried about you when you was down and finished up with a pasting.'

'That was different.'

'Why?'

'I don't know. Perhaps it's because I like to think I can look after myself, and others aren't so strong.'

Milly turned and continued her stirring.

'Besides, I had you and Dolly looking after me.'

Milly laughed.

Charlie looked very worried when he came in. 'Looks like we might be on strike,' he said, throwing his cap on the chair.

'Oh no,' said Milly, hanging his clothes up as usual.

'Been dreading this for weeks. You'll have to manage somehow, love, if the worst comes to the worst.'

Katherine sat quietly listening to the distress in Charlie's voice.

'Don't worry, we'll get by,' said Milly, dishing up the dinner. 'There's plenty worse off than us.'

'I was hoping to give Olive's new baby something nice,' said Charlie.

'Don't worry, Dad. We'll manage,' said Ted. 'With me at work and Joe's mum, we'll all get by.'

Katherine smiled at Ted. He was a shy, sensible lad who didn't quite know what to call Katherine.

'And Olive will understand,' added Milly. ''Sides, it might not be for long.'

'Dunno about that. The miners and dockers up north have been out for weeks – that was till they got the minimum wage bill passed for miners.'

'Now stop all this talk about strikes and get on with your dinner.'

The rest of the meal was finished in silence.

As the week went on Katherine was getting more and more concerned about Briony.

'Do you ever see her now?' she asked Joe.

'Sometimes.'

'Do you ever speak to her?'

'No.'

'Joseph, next time you see her could you ask her how she is?'

'No I won't. She thinks I'm posh and stuck-up.'

'Perhaps you could try?'

'She'll probably spit in me eye.'

'She wouldn't do a thing like that, and it's *my* eye.'

He giggled. 'No it ain't, it's mine.' He ran away laughing.

Katherine could see she didn't stand a chance trying to keep him speaking well now he went to school here, but did she really mind? She smiled, not as long as he was happy, and next Sunday, 12 May, was his thirteenth birthday. Despite the fear of the forthcoming strike Milly and Katherine planned a little tea on that day. Olive and her husband were also coming. Katherine was sorry Dolly and Ted wouldn't be there, but in the letters Milly had from her, Dolly said they were all right. Katherine would have liked to have asked Briony over, but knew Joseph wouldn't approve of that.

Chapter 10

On Sunday the birthday tea was a great success. Joseph was thrilled with his drawing book from Ted. Olive gave him a book about boats, and Milly and Charlie gave him some socks. Katherine bought him a model of a motor car.

'Perhaps you'll have a real one, one day,' she said laughing.

'I'm sure I will,' he said with a serious look on his face. 'You see, I intend to get a job that teaches me to drive.'

'You've got another year at school yet,' said Ted.

'I know. I wish I could leave now. That Briony goes to work and she's only thirteen.'

'Don't think she's ever been to school,' said Milly. 'So you see how lucky you are.'

Joseph didn't have an answer.

He was pleased to receive a birthday card from Dolly and Tom.

'I'd like to go and see them one day. P'raps Uncle Gerald would give me a ride in his new motor, and he might teach me to drive.'

'I don't think that would be such a good idea,' said Katherine.

'See, you always stop me from doing what I want.'

Katherine left that statement unanswered.

'I will, you know.'

That too was left unanswered.

It wasn't till the following week that Katherine had the opportunity to talk to Josh about Nellie. She was pouring out a mug of tea he said she wanted.

'If you like I could take this up. Perhaps she would like me to comb her hair and try to make her feel a bit comfortable.'

'I pay you to help me, not act as nursemaid to her,' was the answer she received as he took the mug from her.

But it worried Katherine that his wife could lie upstairs day after day without a visitor or nurse.

When Katherine told Milly how she felt, Milly reminded her that he was the boss.

'That's as may be, but I still think it's heartless to leave her alone like that.'

Katherine knew she had to mind her Ps and Qs as jobs were going to get harder to come by, as at that moment, for most people, their biggest worry was the looming dock strike.

All week the men had been in and out of the shop, going to meetings and reporting back to those who had managed to get work that day. They had stood on the docks waiting to be called for work, then, disheartened, had come to sit in groups with their heads bent deep in conversation and worried expressions on their faces. Many times raised voices sent Josh over to quieten them down. But he was more concerned that they wouldn't have enough money for a cuppa.

'Feel sorry for some of 'em,' said Charlie after he'd been to another meeting. 'Worried sick about their little 'ens. They was saying they'll have to get the Salvation Army to open up soup kitchens or something if the worst comes to the worst.'

'Well, that's not a bad idea,' said Milly. 'After all, most of 'em spend a lot of time in the pub when they've got a few bob, and when they've had a few they all end up buying the *War Cry*.'

Katherine listened to these conversations with great sadness. These people had nothing but were willing to stand by their fellow workers and their convictions.

* * *

She was walking home one evening when Briony caught up with her.

''Allo, missis,' she said cheerfully. 'Heard you was working in the pie shop.'

Katherine smiled. 'Yes I am. I'm so pleased to see you, Briony.'

'Why?'

'Well, it's been quite a while since we bumped into each other, and I'd like to get to know you.'

'Why're you so interested in me, missis?'

Katherine was a little taken aback at her directness. 'I think you're a nice intelligent young woman, and I'd like to talk to you, that's all.'

'Your son don't think I'm nice. He's a right stuck-up little sod just 'cos he goes to school and wears posh clothes.'

'You mustn't take any notice of Joseph. Would you like to go to school?'

'Yer. Mr Wilks is teaching me to add up, he says I'm a quick learner.'

'Does Mrs Wilks ever come in the shop?' asked Katherine tentatively.

'Oh yer. She's nice. D'yer know, I can read a bit. Me mum teached me. She went to a Catholic school in Ireland for a little while before she met me dad.'

'I could always help you with your reading,' said Katherine.

Briony's eyes shone. 'Would you? I'd like that. Mind you, I don't get a lot of time. P'raps one Sunday afternoon when Dad's sleeping it off I could come over.'

'Of course. Whenever you can.'

'You must really be down on yer luck to come and live round here and have to go to work.'

'Yes, I think you could say that. How's your mother?'

'Not too bad. I wish she'd chuck me old man out though, and not keep having babies.'

'But your father does work to feed you.'

Briony laughed. 'He only goes to work to get money for booze and the horses. If we're lucky we might get any that's left – that's if he's won a few bob on the gee-gees. I could kill him sometimes. Mind you, me mum's clever. She always goes down his pockets when he's sleeping it off. Where's your old man? Did he do a runner?'

'No, it was me that left him.'

Briony's big blue eyes opened wide in amazement 'No! You mean you walked off and left him?'

Katherine nodded. She wouldn't say from the other side of the world – well, not yet.

'Did he beat yer?'

'Once.' Katherine thought that would be enough of an answer.

'And you walked off and left him just for that?' Briony laughed again, lighting up her pretty face, making her blue eyes twinkle. 'Christ, me dad beats me mum nearly every week. He reckons it keeps her under control, 'specially when he finds she's taken his last few bob.'

Katherine stopped and took Briony's arm. 'But your mother's having a baby.'

'That don't matter. If she lost this one she'd soon be having another.'

Katherine was shocked. 'Does your father hit you and your brothers and sisters?'

'Course. And with his belt.'

Katherine was amazed that this child took this way of life for granted. 'What about Mr Wilks?'

Briony smiled. 'He don't hit me. He's not a bad old man. In fact he can be quite kind at times. Lets me bring a broken candle home sometimes for free.'

Katherine wanted to ask if he did anything to her, but thought better of it. She would wait till she'd gained her trust. If his wife was around perhaps all the talk was rumours. They turned into Croft Street.

'When's your mother's baby due?'

'Couple of weeks, I think. I ain't never gonner get married.'

'You're young yet, you may change your mind one day.'

'Na, don't think so.' Briony stopped. 'There's that bloody priest again and that old Mrs Duke nosing.'

Katherine had been avoiding Mrs Duke since she started work. She didn't want her asking too many questions.

Katherine stood with Briony a short distance away and watched the bent figure dressed in long black flowing robes come out of the Addamses' house. He stopped and, looking back, shook his head. He took a handkerchief from a pocket, dabbed at his forehead then, holding the handkerchief to his nose, hurried away.

'I bet me mum's given him her last couple of pence. He tells her she'll rot in hell if she don't pay her way to heaven.'

'That's terrible,' said Katherine. 'He can't be a true man of the Church.'

'Dunno about that. All I know is that he puts the fear of God up me mum. He gets her on her knees chanting and patting her head and waving his smelly incense about. Do you go to church?'

'No, I'm afraid I don't.'

'I bunk off when I should be there. Can't stand all that stuff. Better go and help me mum. 'Bye, it's bin nice talking to yer.' Briony crossed the road.

'See you're still here then?' Mrs Duke folded her arms as Katherine walked past. 'Thought you might have moved on before now.'

'I'm very happy staying with Milly.'

'I bet she is as well.'

Katherine felt through the letter box for the key and quickly opened the front door. 'Been nice talking to you,' she said, closing the door behind her.

Katherine told Milly about the conversation she'd just had with Briony. 'She said the priest took money from her mother. I think that's dreadful.'

'It's a way of life with some of 'em round here,' said Milly.

'How can they take from people like that?'

'Fear,' came the reply.

'Of what?' asked Katherine.

'Not finishing up in heaven.'

All evening Katherine couldn't get Briony off her mind. She was trying to think of an excuse for going over and talking to her mother, but Milly advised her not to interfere.

'They won't thank you, and more often than not she'll get a bigger hiding from her old man for telling you what goes on in there. 'Sides, she might be over for a reading lesson.'

'I'd like that,' said Katherine, beginning to feel at ease living here. She had no regrets. At first Joseph had been troublesome, but he appeared to be settling down now he'd found he and Ted had a lot in common, and their laughter was a joy to hear.

Weeks went past and Briony didn't take up Katherine's offer to teach her to read.

'P'raps she'll have more time in the summer,' Milly said.

One fine warm evening, as Katherine made her way home from work, she couldn't believe her eyes when she turned into Croft Street. It seemed all the women were out of their houses and huddled in small groups on their doorsteps, talking in low whispers. Some were sitting knitting or sewing while children played in the gutter; others were drinking tea. An ambulance was outside the Addamses' house.

She hurried across the road, hoping to see Briony.

'Katherine, psst! Katherine!' called Milly in a loud whisper, beckoning to her frantically.

Katherine picked her way back over the cobblestones. 'What's happened?' she asked.

'It's Mrs Addams, been taken bad be all accounts.'

'Who called the ambulance?'

'It seems old Ida Fairfield. She was delivering the baby when complications set in. She sent one of the boys round for the doctor and he sent for the ambulance. It's been there a long while,' said Mrs Duke, who was sitting on her windowsill.

'Is Mrs Fairfield a nurse?' asked Katherine.

'Dunno,' said Mrs Duke. 'She might have been. She does most things round here. Helps out with a few potions when somebody's ill. She births 'em, lays 'em out, and she—'

One of the Addams boys came out and ran up the road, stopping Mrs Duke as she was in full flow.

She stood up. 'Reckon he's gorn for the priest,' she said excitedly.

'Oh no,' said Katherine. 'You don't think . . .?'

'Not surprised at what goes on over there. Be happy release if you ask me for the poor little cow.'

'You mean it could be Mrs Addams?'

'They wouldn't make all this fuss if it was just the baby. Na, it's got to be her. They'd just wrap the baby up and take it away.'

'What about the children?' Katherine was shocked at the way she was writing Mrs Addams off.

'They'll be better off in a home if you ask me. Was surprised to see you in Trent's. Guessed you was working as I see you go out the same time every day, but I thought that place was a bit below you. I nearly came in and had a cuppa when I saw you, but thought better of it. Can't go lining Trent's pockets.'

Katherine gave her a wan smile. To have Mrs Duke come in while she was working was the last thing she wanted.

'Katherine's only doing him a favour, just helping him out,' said Milly defensively.

Mrs Duke gave Milly a funny look. Katherine knew she didn't believe her.

When the priest walked down Croft Street Mrs Duke's face took on a smug expression. 'See, I knew I was right.'

'Is her husband in there?' asked Katherine.

'Na, he ain't home from the pub yet.'

'What about Briony?'

'She ain't home from work yet.' Mrs Duke certainly knew all that was going on.

'Shouldn't someone go and get Briony?'

'Not till we're sure the poor cow's gorn,' said Mrs Duke.

Katherine felt guilty at standing around waiting. She wanted to go inside, but like the rest of them she felt she had to wait and see what was going to happen. This was a major event. Normally they would all be hiding behind their lace curtains but today they were outside filled with anticipation and curiosity.

After a while the ambulance went away empty. Then the doctor and priest came out and stood for a while deep in conversation.

'She's gorn,' whispered Mrs Duke.

'It might be just the baby,' said Katherine.

'Na. It's got to be her.'

The priest and doctor moved away.

'What should we do?' asked Katherine. 'Those children will be in the house alone with Mrs Addams, and if she's—'

'Don't worry about it. When Ida Fairfield comes out she'll give us all the details,' said Mrs Duke knowingly. 'Think I'll just pop inside and bring a chair out. This bloody windowsill's a bit cold on me bum, and all this standing about makes me feet ache and don't do me piles much good either.'

'Ida Fairfield's probably laying her out now,' said Milly.

'She makes a very nice job of it as well,' said Mrs Duke. 'But Gawd help yer if you hang on to the pennies she puts on their eyes, she nearly goes mad.' Mrs Duke came up close. She looked around before adding the next sentence in a low voice. 'And if yer ever gets in trouble – you know what I mean – well, Ida's yer girl.'

Katherine laughed. 'I don't think I'll need Ida for that,' but she was intrigued with this conversation.

Once more a young boy came out the house and ran down the road.

'She lends money as well, you know,' said Mrs Duke, straightening up.

Katherine smiled. Ida Fairfield sounded like a very enterprising woman.

Charlie walked up to them. 'What's going on?' he asked.

Milly went into great detail of what they thought had happened.

'Well I want me dinner, so you'd better come in.'

'You don't sound very happy, mate,' said Mrs Duke. 'Who's crawled up your arse?'

'Out on bleeding strike, ain't we? I tell yer, missis, this is gonner be a bloody long hard struggle.'

'Well, we'll just have to make the best of it, won't we,' said Milly.

'Mrs Duke, will you knock and let me know when Briony gets home? I'd like to have a word with her,' said Katherine.

'Course, girl.'

Charlie, Milly and Katherine went inside the house.

'What d'you want to see Briony about then?' asked Milly.

'If it is her mother she may not have a black frock for her funeral.'

'I don't suppose she has.'

'Perhaps we can alter one of mine. Poor Briony, what sort of life will she have now?'

'Dunno. Was it all that good before?'

'Who will look after the rest of them?'

'Dunno. We'll have to wait and find out after the funeral,' said Milly.

'Don't reckon it'll be much of one,' said Charlie.

'But surely the Church . . .'

'Dunno about that,' said Milly. 'Mind you, we ain't had an Irish funeral round here before.'

'I believe they have a wake,' said Katherine.

'What's a wake, Mama?' asked Joseph.

'Well, they celebrate, have singing and drinking.'

'Now that don't sound a bad idea to me,' said Charlie grinning.

'And who will pay for all this then?' asked Milly.

'Don't know,' replied Katherine.

They had almost finished their meal when Mrs Duke banged on the door.

Katherine hurried down the passage.

'She's just come in, but mind, the old man's over there now. Can I come in?'

Katherine looked over her shoulder. 'Well I don't . . .' But Mrs Duke had pushed past her.

'Got a cuppa, Milly? I'm fair parched.'

Katherine looked at Charlie and shrugged her shoulders as Mrs Duke plonked herself at the table.

When Milly put a cup of tea in front of her, Mrs Duke poured some in the saucer. Joseph sat looking on silently as she slurped this noisily.

'Look, if you and Ted's finished,' said Milly, noting Joseph's face, 'why don't you go upstairs?'

They scurried away from the table like a pair of startled rabbits, laughing all the way.

'Now, Mrs Duke, I didn't want the boys to hear. So is she dead?'

'Yer, and it seems, so Ida said, that her body was covered with bruises, a right mess, great weeping sores, and she was so thin

100

that her bones were almost sticking through her skin.'

Katherine was shocked, and relieved they'd finished their meal.

Mrs Duke continued to hold the conversation. 'Well, the old man wasn't very pleased when he found that Ida had laid her out.'

'That's so very sad. So what's going to happen now?' asked Katherine.

'Dunno. Ida said the old man fell to his knees and, grabbing her in his arms, began rocking back and forth and wailing, bloody hypocrite. When Briony came in she took one look at her father and walked away. She's a good kid. Mind you, Ida said it's like a madhouse over there. There's the old man crying, the kids shouting and poor Briony trying to get 'em a bit of tea.'

'What happened to the baby?' asked Milly.

'Dead,' said Mrs Duke, very matter-of-factly. 'Ida wrapped it up in a piece of dirty cloth and laid it beside her, another girl be all accounts. They're gonner be buried together, so Ida said.'

Katherine shuddered. 'That poor woman.'

'Well, in some ways it's a happy release for her and the kid.' Mrs Duke was certainly enjoying her moment of glory.

'What will happen to the children?' asked Katherine.

'Probably finish up in a home,' sniffed Mrs Duke.

'Will the neighbours get up a collection for a wreath?' Katherine wondered.

Charlie laughed. 'You'll be lucky. With most of 'em on strike they've got to think of their bellies before they think of flowers.'

'Yes, but not all of them work at the docks,' said Katherine.

'No, but a lot like the shops and the pub rely on the dockers for their money,' said Milly.

'Well, I'd go and knock on the doors,' said Mrs Duke, 'but me feet play me up something rotten in this weather.' She looked pointedly at Katherine. 'I reckon someone should try. At least it shows we care.'

'Do we?' asked Charlie.

'I care about the children,' said Katherine.

''Sides, what good's flowers? That won't help 'em,' said Charlie.

'It shows a sign of respect.'

'I reckon any money you did manage to get should be given to them and not buy flowers,' said Milly.

'Any money you give 'em he'll use to buy booze,' said Charlie.

'Not if I give it to Briony,' said Katherine, warming to the idea of helping.

So it was settled that on Friday night Katherine and Milly would start a collection for the late Mrs Addams's family.

'Good luck, and I only hope you know what you're doing,' said Charlie offhandedly.

Chapter 11

At seven thirty on Friday evening Katherine and Milly set out to start collecting along both sides of Croft Street for the Addams children. Although Katherine wasn't expecting to be showered with money, she didn't expect to meet with such aggression. Many times they had doors slammed in their faces.

When front doors were opened wide enough for her to see inside, it was a shock. The noise, shouting and cursing made her want to run. Men waved their fists at her, and the babies sitting on women's wide hips were dirty and unclothed. Passages were full of rubbish and dirt, and some of the smells indescribable. There were a few like Milly who kept their homes neat and clean but these were rare. There were women with fear in their eyes who hardly opened their front doors, and those that did talked in whispers, telling her they were sorry but they hadn't received any money from the breadwinner yet. Others told her in no uncertain words to push off. Family came first round here. Some were sympathetic and managed to give her the odd halfpenny and farthing. All in all they managed to collect one shilling and thrupence ha'penny.

'It's not a lot,' said Katherine, as they sat at the table counting out farthings, halfpennies and pennies.

'Didn't expect a lot,' said Milly. 'Still, it's a nice thought.'

'I'll find out when the funeral is and I'll get three penno'th of flowers from us and give this money to Briony,' said Katherine.

'You don't have to get flowers, you know,' said Milly.

'I know, but I want to, and I said I'll pay for them.'

Milly looked put out. 'Just 'cos Charlie's on strike—'

Katherine put her hand on Milly's. 'You've helped me out, now it's my turn.'

'I'd try and get her on her own if I was you.'

Katherine nodded. 'Yes, I don't fancy going over there when Mr Addams is around.'

The following day when Katherine finished work she made her way to the ironmongers, pleased to see Briony was still there. She was busy filling a customer's can with paraffin. Katherine noted her pale face and dark circles under her lovely eyes. Her face lit up when she caught sight of Katherine.

''Allo, missis. What d'you want?'

'What time do you finish?'

'Not long now.'

'I'll wait outside and we can walk home together.'

Katherine gave Mr Wilks a smile and went out.

'So, how are you managing?' asked Katherine as they began to walk home.

'Not too bad. Young Bridget helps a bit. The boys can be a bit of a handful, but we'll manage.'

'Mr Wilks treating you all right?'

'Yer, he said I can have an hour off for me mum's funeral.'

'That's kind of him. How's the rest of the family?'

'All right. They don't like seeing Mum and that baby in the front room, though. Young Billy keeps having nightmares and Dad's threatened to lock him in the coffin and bury him with Mum if he don't behave.'

Katherine gasped. 'I'm sure your father doesn't mean it.'

'You don't know me dad. D'you know, he picked up our Kenny – he's our youngest – shoved the dead baby out the way and put Kenny in with Mum. He didn't half scream when Dad made him cuddle the cold stiff baby.'

Katherine couldn't believe it. This man sounded wicked or mad or both. 'When's the funeral?'

'Friday.'

'Have you got a black frock?'

Briony shook her head.

'I'm sure I can find you one. Why don't you come over to Milly's later on and we will sort something out for you?'

'Dad won't be having me accept charity.'

'It's not charity. I've got far too many gowns and I'd like you to have one.'

'That's ever so kind of you. I'll try and get over later.'

Milly was very angry when Katherine told her what the father did to the children.

'If you ask me, he wants locking up,' was Charlie's comment. 'He'd better watch out when those boys get a bit older. The old man might be found lying face down in some dark alley with his throat cut.'

'Don't talk like that, Charlie,' said Milly. 'It ain't nice. And don't you go saying anything in front of that young girl when she comes over.'

He grinned. 'As if I would.'

When Briony called, Milly and Katherine took her up to Katherine's bedroom.

'Cor, what a smashing room,' she said, standing in the doorway.

'Yes, I'm very lucky, Milly really does look after me,' said Katherine. 'Now, let me see. I think we can do something with this.' She held out a plain black cotton dress.

'I can't take that.'

'I don't see why not,' said Katherine.

'Let me hold it against you. I'll be able to take it in and shorten it a bit,' said Milly, promptly taking charge. 'Mind you, it won't want a lot off the bottom. You're quite tall, young Briony.'

Briony giggled as she held the dress against her. 'It is ever so nice, and I would feel ever so grand. But I don't think I should. Dad might not like it.'

'Don't be silly, of course you must,' said Katherine.

'Well, could I have it a bit shorter? Seen some pictures in a book about the ladies wearing frocks that don't come down to the ground.'

Milly smiled. 'I'll take a lot of this fullness out as well.'

'Could you make our Bridget one out of the scraps? That's if you don't mind.'

'Which one is Bridget?' asked Katherine.

'The next one down to me. She's gonner go to work soon.'

'How old is she?' asked Milly.

'She's a year younger than me. She'll be thirteen next month, and I'll be fourteen then, so Mum said.'

Milly looked at Katherine. 'I'll just pop down and get me pins.' She left the room.

'Briony, Milly and I have got a little money from the neighbours.'

'What you telling me for?'

'We want you to have it to help out.'

'What? I can't take it.'

'Why?'

'Me dad'll go mad if he thought everybody was feeling sorry for us.'

'Does he have to know?'

'He'll find it. He can sniff out money.'

'Well, it's not a lot. One and thrupence ha'penny to be exact. But it might help.' Katherine went to her dressing table and put the money into Briony's hand.

'I don't know what to say. I shouldn't be taking—'

Katherine patted her hand. 'Don't say anything, just make sure your father doesn't get his hands on it.'

On Friday evening Milly told Katherine the funeral was a very noisy affair with Mr Addams hanging on to the coffin weeping and wailing. The children were crying and looking terrified as they followed the handcart and the priest, who was chanting loudly and waving the incense about as they went slowly down the road.

'Yours was the only flowers. Briony and Bridget looked nice in their frocks. D'you know, young Briony wasn't crying.'

'She was probably storing it up for later. Grief's a funny thing,' said Katherine.

'I expect she's a bit worried about what will happen to her and the kids,' said Milly.

'She might have to give up her little job, which would be a pity as she does like it there.'

'Can't see that. Her and the boy that goes to work are the only ones bringing in any money, that's not counting the two boys that run a few errands. Don't think the old man gives 'em much, not to feed 'em and pay the rent.'

'Who'll look after the little ones when Bridget goes to work?'

'Dunno. Like Mrs Duke said, I reckon they'll put 'em in a home. That kind don't have any hope, do they?' said Milly with a sigh.

'No, they don't,' said Katherine.

On Sunday morning Katherine sat up ready to get out of bed. She sat on the edge to gather her senses. She didn't feel right, and when she stood up she felt giddy and nauseous. She quickly sat down as hot flushes swept over her. Was this confirming her worst fears? Since she moved in with Milly she hadn't had the curse, but she put it down to all the upset she'd had, and her age, even though she thought she was a bit young to be starting the change. Now she was sure what was wrong with her. She was pregnant, and Gerald was the father. She burst into tears. This was the worst thing that could happen to her just as she was getting her life together.

After a while, when her tears subsided, she slowly dressed and made her way downstairs.

'Good morning, Milly.' She tried to sound cheerful.

Milly looked up from the frying pan. 'You all right?'

Katherine sat at the table. The smell of cooking was turning her stomach and her legs felt like jelly. She was barely able to stand. 'Yes, I feel a bit funny, think I might be getting a cold.'

Milly gave her curious look. 'At this time of year?'

Katherine smiled and nodded.

'I must admit you do look a bit off colour.'

'Well, we do get all sorts in the pie shop, coughing and sneezing all over the place.'

'Suppose you do, fancy a bit of bacon?'

She swallowed hard. 'No thanks. As it's a nice day I think I'll go for a walk.'

'Please yourself.'

Katherine took her coat from off the nail behind the door and hurried up the passage. Outside she stood taking in great gulps of fresh air. She prayed Mrs Duke wasn't looking out of her window waiting to pounce on anyone to talk to.

Katherine's mind was churning over and over as she walked along. Questions were coming thick and fast. What was she going to do? What would Joseph say? What would they do for money if she had to give up her job? Or be given the sack if the strike continued for very long and Josh's business went down? With Charlie not working Milly couldn't keep her for nothing. The disgrace. She hated Gerald so much she wanted to kill him. He had taken everything from her, and now this. She didn't want his baby, she wanted to die.

As Katherine slowly made her way towards the docks she was confronted by the scene she had witnessed every day since moving to this area. Screaming children playing, fighting and racing round the street. Women sitting outside their front doors knitting or with babies at their breasts, young ones clambering over them, while others were yelling and shouting at their offspring. Could she finish up living like this? With all the noise and confusion she couldn't think straight. The smell of dinners cooking wafted out of the open doors and made her vomit. She stopped and held on to the lamppost.

'Go on, move on, yer dirty cow,' said a woman tutting and tucking a baby into a pram.

'Looks like a right old tart ter me. Bet yer bin on the beer all night,' said a woman, coming up to her and pushing her along the road.

'Bin on somethink or someone,' yelled another. 'Go on, shove orf, you old tom.'

Katherine wiped her mouth and after taking a deep breath hurried past them, afraid they would harm her. She didn't know where she was going. Should she go and see Gerald? But what good would that do? She couldn't marry him. She didn't want to marry him. Tears ran down her face. She felt so miserable and alone as she wandered on. This was the dock area and she didn't know it at all. Katherine thought about the swirling water. Could that be the answer to her problem? No, only cowards took their own lives. Besides, what about Joseph? There must be another way out.

When she turned the corner some girls had one end of a rope tied to the lamppost. At the other end a young girl wearing a dirty torn overall over a brown frock was busy turning the rope. A girl in the middle was skipping, and they both were chanting: 'Touch collar never holler. Touch lip never catch dip, never catch the fever.'

Katherine stopped and brushed her tears from her cheeks with her hand.

'What yer staring at, missis?' asked the young girl who was turning the rope.

'Sorry, was I staring?'

'Yes you was. What yer crying for?'

'Nothing. I seem to be lost.'

She stopped turning the rope. 'Well, yer don't wanner go down there.' She pointed along the road.

'Why?'

'Oh come on, Rose, don't stop and talk to 'er,' said the girl who was standing with the rope at her feet.

'No, she's upset, and we can't let her go down there.'

'Well, if she don't know, well then that's up to her.'

'Excuse me,' said Katherine. 'But what is down there?'

The first girl pointed to the name plate on the red-brick wall. It said 'Redfiff Road'.

'Down there's the smallpox receiving station. And if you go down there you could finish up with the pox.'

Katherine shuddered. 'Smallpox? Thank you,' she said, turning away.

The girls began laughing and chanting again. Were they laughing at her? At this moment she didn't care, she had to get back to Milly, her only friend.

Soon Katherine was back on familiar ground. She had made up her mind. As much as she hated the thought, she would ask Milly about Ida Fairfield.

Chapter 12

Katherine sat at the table and picked at her dinner.

'You sure you're all right?' asked Milly.

'Yes, of course.'

'Well, you look a bit peaky to me,' said Charlie.

Katherine smiled. 'I'm all right, really.'

'If you don't want that potato can I have it?' asked Joseph.

'Of course.'

'Here, don't you go telling your mates at school I don't feed you,' said Milly.

'I ain't got any mates,' he said, stabbing at the potato and putting it on his plate.

'Don't give me that,' said Charlie.

'They all think I'm too posh. Can't wait to start work.'

'And what are you going to do?' asked Katherine.

'I told you before, learn to drive a motor car. That's why I need feeding. I'm a growing boy,' he said, grinning.

Ted laughed. 'He's always hanging round that new place looking at the motor cars. You should see his sketches of 'em.'

Katherine knew she should be taking more interest in this conversation and be pleased that Ted and Joseph were getting on so well, but she couldn't concentrate.

All afternoon and evening Katherine was hoping to get Milly on her own but the situation never arose.

The following morning when she left the house, the thought of working with food was just about as much as she could bear.

' 'Allo there, Kate,' said Josh when she walked in. 'Christ, you look bloody awful. You all right?'

'Yes, thanks.'

'You don't look it.'

She smiled. 'That's not very complimentary.'

'Ain't known for me compliments.'

'Well, don't worry about me.'

Katherine knew she had to keep her food down and herself busy.

As usual they had the dockers filling the shop. It had become a meeting place for the strikers. At times the arguments became very heated and everybody appeared to be shouting at once. Josh wasn't happy that only a few mugs of tea were being consumed. Ron, the bookies' runner, wasn't happy either: nobody was putting a bet on. Josh had pointed him out to Katherine weeks ago. He'd told her what he did was illegal.

'So, just remember to say nothing to the coppers if they ask. You don't know nothing. It pays to keep yer nose clean and yer mouth shut, and out of other people's affairs round here.'

After the dockers left Josh looked worried. 'I hope this strike ain't gonner go on for too long. Still got me overheads, and you, to pay. Had the landlord in, he's worried about his rent.'

Katherine didn't need reminding that ultimately she could lose her job because of the strike.

Josh went out the back. Katherine was busy wiping the tables down when the young girl who had come in on her very first day appeared. She had been in before and after a short while men came and sat with her – most times people Katherine had never seen before. Then the girl would leave with them. Some were scruffy and dirty. Katherine shuddered at the thought of what she did with these strangers.

Katherine poured out her tea, the girl took it and sat in the far corner like before.

'What yer staring at?' the girl suddenly shouted out.

'Sorry, I was miles away.'

'Yer you was. What's a posh cow like you doing in a place like this?'

'Earning my living,' said Katherine aggressively.

The girl laughed. 'Bet yer don't get much.'

Katherine decided not to answer.

'Kate,' yelled Josh from the back. 'Pour the missis out a cuppa.'

'Would you like me to take it up to her?' Katherine asked eagerly, smoothing down her apron. She had been waiting for an opportunity to go up and see Nellie Trent again.

'You could do while we're quiet. But don't stand around chatting, and don't go putting any fancy ideas in her head. And don't go telling her too much about the strike. I don't want her worrying.'

Katherine smiled as she poured out the tea. The bell over the door rang and she looked up to see a well-dressed man, possibly an office type, which was unusual round here. Katherine thought she'd seen him in here before. He stood in the doorway and beckoned to the young girl.

She stood up and walked across the room, giving Katherine a grin. 'I bet I'll make more in half an hour than you'll make in a week,' she said as she sauntered past.

Yes, thought Katherine, but what about in a few years' time? Will you have someone to love you? And what if you have a— She was suddenly plunged into despair when she remembered her own plight.

As she climbed the stairs Katherine's thoughts were still on her own problem. She must have a word with Milly tonight.

She gently tapped on the bedroom door.

'Who is it?' called Nellie Trent.

'It's me – Kate. I've got your tea.'

113

'Well, come in yer silly cow, don't stand out there. Me tea'll get cold.'

Katherine pushed open the door and stood for a moment to get her eyes accustomed to the gloom.

'Put it down here.' The old woman flapped her gnarled bent fingers towards the table by her bed.

'Mrs Trent.'

'Nellie. Call me Nellie. Where yer been? Ain't seen yer for weeks.'

'Josh keeps me busy in the shop.'

'Yer, well he would. He said what a good worker you was. Reckon he'll be sorry to lose yer if this dock strike carries on for long.'

Katherine was taken aback that Josh and his wife talked about what went on. He had told her not to mention the strike, but she seemed to know all about it.

'He likes you, yer know. But don't get any fancy ideas about moving in.'

Katherine wanted to laugh. She couldn't think of anything worse than moving in with these two, but she was pleased he'd said he liked her.

'Nellie,' said Katherine, looking nervously over her shoulder, 'I know Josh said I mustn't stay up here too long, but would you like me to come up and comb your hair one day?'

'Why? What's wrong with it?'

'Nothing, but I thought—'

'Well, you thought wrong. Josh looks after me now.' She grinned. 'And if he says it's all right then that's all I worry about.'

Katherine was surprised at that answer. 'I'd better go.'

Nellie, ignoring Katherine, took hold of the mug with both hands and took a mouthful of tea.

'I said I didn't want this dish water. Next time bring me a proper brew.'

Katherine left the room. Why was Josh so against Nellie having visitors and a nurse, Katherine wondered as she made her way downstairs.

As the day dragged Katherine was again deep in her thoughts. What if the strike continued for a long while? What would happen to her? Would she lose her job? Would Josh lose the shop?

At six o'clock Katherine began to make her way home. She had to talk to Milly soon but with Charlie being home it was getting very difficult. He didn't go out for a drink now as money was very tight.

After dinner Katherine asked Milly if she would come to her room to sort out something.

'You ain't gonner give Briony any more frocks, are you?'

'No.'

'Well, can you wait till we've done the washing up?'

'Of course.'

They were halfway through it when Olive and her husband walked in.

Olive kissed her mother's cheek. 'Mum, me and Ernie are going over the West End on Saturday.' She smiled at Katherine. 'It's our wedding anniversary and we're gonner go and see a show, only in the gods mind.'

'That's lovely,' said Katherine.

'We thought as we were over the water we might go and see Auntie Dolly first, so if you've got a letter, we can take it.'

Milly's face lit up. 'That'll be really nice. You must tell us all about how she's getting on. Look, why don't you and Ernie come to tea on Sunday?'

'We could do. But you sure you can manage – you know with Dad being out of work and all that?'

'Course we can. Don't worry about it.'

'Well, I'll bring a cake.'

All evening Olive and Ernie sat with them. Katherine was

desperate to get Milly on her own, but it wasn't to be.

It wasn't till Friday that Katherine finally managed to get Milly alone in her room.

Milly sat on the bed next to Katherine as she told her her story.

Milly's mouth fell open. 'How long you known?'

'I've been sure for a week.'

'And you ain't told no one?'

Katherine shook her head. 'Milly, what am I going to do? The disgrace. What will Joseph say?' Great tears fell from her eyes. All her pent-up emotions bubbled up and she put her head in her hands and cried bitter tears.

Milly put her arm round Katherine's heaving shoulders and held her close. 'That Gerald's a wicked sod. He wants castrating.'

'Milly, what am I going to do?' she sobbed.

'Do you want to have it?'

Katherine shook her head.

'Well, the only answer's got to be Ida Fairfield.'

Katherine dabbed at her eyes. 'I don't want anyone else to know, and if she tells Mrs Duke . . .'

'Ida ain't that bad, or daft. She charges, though.'

'I can always sell something.'

'You ain't got much left, have you? And I don't think what frocks you've got left will cover it. What about jewellery?'

'All that I brought with me has gone. I didn't get a lot for it.'

'Well, you don't when those blokes know you're down on your uppers.'

'In fact all I've got left is my wedding ring.' She twisted the ring round her finger.

'Is it that sentimental?'

'No. But as I'm known as Joseph's mother I like everybody to know I was married.'

116

'Well, you can always get a brass one. Most of the women round here have hocked their wedding rings, that's them that had one in the first place.'

'Do you think that would be enough?'

'Should think so.'

'Look, tomorrow morning I'll get some senna pods and make you some strong tea.'

'Will that help?'

'Dunno, but anything must be worth trying. Can't afford gin. The senna pods might give you the runs and if that don't work then I'll go round and see Ida.'

'You won't tell Charlie, will you?'

'Not if you don't want me to.'

'No, I only want you to know.'

'He's going off early anyway. There's going to be a big rally in Trafalgar Square on Sunday and him and a lot of the dockers are going, so he'll be out most of the day planning it.'

'How are they going to get there?'

'It seems the union's putting on buses. It'll be like a day out for 'em.'

On Saturday as Katherine walked home she felt a little happier. She had got two shillings for her wedding ring and bought a thrupenny brass one from the jeweller. But would one and ninepence be enough? Fear grabbed her. What if it wasn't? Would Ida let her borrow the rest? She hated this living from hand to mouth every week. If the dockers hadn't been on strike perhaps she could have asked Josh for a small rise, but now it seemed her job could also be at stake. Well, with luck by this time next week her biggest problem would be behind her.

'Did you manage to see Ida?' whispered Katherine as they washed up.

'No, I didn't, she was out, but I'll pop round in the morning.'

Milly looked at the closed kitchen door. 'Here, I've made you this senna tea.'

Katherine screwed up her nose. 'Can't say I fancy the look of that.'

'Go on, get it down yer, and if it don't work then tomorrow I'll go and see Ida. She should be in on a Sunday.'

Although Katherine was disappointed at Milly not seeing Ida, she braced herself and drank the tea.

Sunday morning Charlie went off with his sandwiches. He kissed Milly's cheek. 'Don't know how long we'll be up there. Some real big nobs coming – let's hope they listen and give us all a living wage.'

Milly waited for Katherine to come out of the lavatory before she put her coat on. 'Anything happened?'

Katherine shook her head.

'Well, I'll pop out now,' she said over her shoulder as she walked up the passage and opened the front door.

'Olive. What you doing here? Did you have a nice time yesterday? How's Dolly?'

'Can we come in, Mum?'

'Course, silly me,' said Milly, stepping to one side.

'Was you just going out, Mrs Stevens?' asked Ernie.

'It can wait.' Milly quickly took off her coat. She suddenly looked worried. 'You was coming round later for a bit of tea. So why you here now?'

'Mum, it's Auntie Dolly.'

Milly put her hand to her mouth. 'Oh my God. What's happened to her?'

'She ain't well, and that Mr Gerald's got someone else living in and doing her work. Auntie Dolly and Uncle Tom've finished up in the basement.' The words tumbled out.

'What's wrong with her?' asked Katherine.

'Don't know. She's ever so thin and she can hardly speak.'

'Thin?' shouted Milly. 'Our Dolly's always been plump. What's wrong with her?'

'I don't know.'

'What did Tom have to say?' asked Katherine.

'Not a lot. He's still doing the garden, that's why that Mr Gerald lets them stay in the basement. If not, he said they'd have to get out. Oh Mum, he looks ever so old and weary. They was just sitting there.' A tear ran down her face.

'Dolly hasn't said anything in her letters, has she?' Katherine was very concerned about them.

Milly shook her head.

Olive gave a sob. 'They look like they're waiting to die.'

'Olive, don't say such a wicked thing,' said Milly. 'I've got to go over and see her. They'll have to come and move in here.' Milly was getting agitated.

'But you ain't got the room,' said Olive. 'And me and Ernie's only got the two rooms, so we can't help out, not with the baby as well.'

'We'll manage somehow.'

Katherine suddenly felt like a stranger. These people were going to look after their own, and she felt in the way.

'Joe will have to move in with Ted, and Dolly and Tom can have the front room. It won't be so bad.'

Katherine knew Joseph wouldn't be happy about that, as much as he admired Ted.

'I must go and see Dolly,' said Milly, quickly tipping the contents of her purse out on to the table. 'What will it cost to get there and back?'

'About sixpence or even a bit more. You have to get a couple of buses,' said Ernie.

'I've only got fourpence ha'penny,' said Milly, sitting at the table.

'I can't help you,' said Olive. 'We spent a lot yesterday. What about Ted?'

'He give me all he could on Friday.' Tears filled her eyes. 'Why did the bloody docks have to be on strike now.' She ran the back of her hand under her nose.

Katherine looked from one to the other. 'Milly, I've got a few pence you can have. It's enough to get you over to see Dolly.'

'But you wanted that money for . . .' She sniffed. 'I can't take that.'

'Yes you can. I'll go up and get it.' Katherine left the room. Upstairs she took the money she got from the jeweller out of her purse and sat on the bed. Tears filled her eyes. She was crying for Dolly, Tom and herself. If she gave Milly this money she had nothing left to sell to pay Ida Fairfield, and if she lost her job she wouldn't have anything at all, and would still have to have Gerald's baby.

Chapter 13

After Milly left, Katherine wandered about unable to concentrate on anything. Even preparing the dinner, which she normally enjoyed doing, didn't hold her attention for long.

'Where's Mum?' asked Ted when he finally left his bed.

Joseph was sitting at the table. He listened very quietly while Katherine explained all that had happened.

'Thought I heard Olive's voice,' said Ted.

'So Dolly and Tom could be moving here?' Joseph's voice was full of alarm.

'It looks like it.'

'Well, as much as I like Ted I don't want to sleep in his room.'

'Can't say I'd fancy it, but it's family, ain't it, and we've gotter help out.' There was a touch of anger in Ted's voice which was unusual. He was normally a quiet lad not given to voicing his opinions, or expressing his feelings.

Katherine was very angry with Joseph. He was just thinking of himself. 'Well I'm sorry, but we don't have any choice. It's either that or . . .' She didn't finish. How could she tell him all her other troubles? 'We'll have to wait till Milly gets home before we make any rash decisions.'

Ted said softly, 'I hope Auntie Dolly's gonner be all right.'

'I'm sure she will be,' said Katherine, glaring at Joseph.

All afternoon she sat in the front room looking out of the window. This was a cold room but Joseph was happy in here. He had a mattress on the floor and a small cupboard for his books. The few other belongings he possessed were in Katherine's room.

She sat and mulled over what he had. Was anything worth selling? Not really. Besides, that would be the last straw, especially if he had to move in with Ted.

'You're quiet,' said Ted to Joe as they sat on a narrow bridge over part of the docks waterway.

'Well, you're always telling me to shut up when we're fishing.'

'I know but we don't ever catch nothing. But it ain't that, is it?'

'No.' Joe let the piece of wood he was holding that had string tied to it, go limp. The other end of the string was dangling in the water below them; it had a safety pin bent open and a piece of a worm they'd managed to find stuck through it.

'It's this business with Dolly and Tom,' said Joe, shifting his legs, which were sticking through the iron railings, to a more comfortable position.

'Thought as much.'

'I like you, Ted, but I don't want to share your bedroom.'

'Well, go on, tell me what else we can do?'

'Don't know.'

'They've got to live somewhere. Mind you, I dunno how Mum's gonner manage to feed 'em with Dad being on strike. She's only got me and your mum's money coming in.'

Joe wedged his back against a post. 'I wish I was going out to work.'

'Your mum won't hear of it, not till you're fourteen.'

'I don't know why. I can never do what I want.'

Ted looked at him. 'D'you know, you are a selfish bugger. I don't know why I put up with you hanging round me.'

Joe was horrified. 'But I thought you liked me. You're the only friend I've got.'

'So whose fault's that? You want to listen to your mother. You're bloody lucky with the kind of schooling you've had.'

Joe wiggled his fishing line. 'I don't know why she worries about me going to school. I'm better than all of 'em there.'

'See what I mean? You're also a puffed-up little sod at times.'

'I'm not, am I?'

'Sometimes, especially when you put on all yer airs and graces.'

'Like when?'

'Well you won't talk to that Briony, for one thing, and I think she's got a soft spot for you.' Ted laughed.

'Briony? I don't like her, she smells.'

'She's always looking at you, and giving you the eye.'

'How can you say that? Here, you don't . . . you know, not with her.'

'No,' said Ted quickly, and looked away. 'I feel sorry for her, that's all. She's good to her family. It's a pity you don't start thinking of other people and not just yourself for a change.'

Joe was taken aback at Ted's comments. He began to reflect on the people round him. Since Edwin's death his mother had had to lower her standards, but she didn't complain. The Addams family had had a great tragedy but they still carried on. Charlie was on strike but he didn't keep on about it. Now Dolly and Tom were in trouble.

'I'm going to try and get a job after school,' said Joe suddenly.

'What's brought this on?'

'You, you've just made me realise what a selfish bugger I am.'

'You've just grown up, so welcome to the real world, and don't let your mother hear you swear or I'll get the blame.'

Joe laughed. 'And if I've got to share your room, just you make sure you don't leave those sweaty socks about.'

Ted put his arm round Joe's shoulders. 'You ain't a bad kid.'

'So, do you want me to have a word with Briony about you?'

Joe ducked as Ted went to give him a clout.

* * *

As the evening approached Katherine went into the kitchen. It would have been a waste of gas to light the lamp in the front room now every penny had to be accounted for. The boys were still out, and this morning Olive had told her mother they wouldn't be coming round for tea.

Sitting in Charlie's armchair in front of the fire was comforting and gradually she began to drift off.

She sat up when somebody banging on the front door made her jump. Who would knock like that? All the family used the key that hung on a string behind the letter box.

She hurried along the passage and pulled open the front door.

'You Mrs Stevens?' asked the man standing there.

'No, no, she's out. What did you want her . . .?' Katherine's voice trailed off when she realised he looked agitated.

'It's Charlie. Charlie Stevens.'

'Oh my God,' said Katherine, her voice breaking with emotion. 'Not more trouble. What's happened to him?'

''Fraid he's been nicked.'

'What, arrested?'

The man nodded.

'You'd better come in.' She was sure Mrs Duke must have heard their knocker, and any minute she would be poking her nose round the door.

The man stepped just inside the door and snatching off his cloth cap, stood in the passage pushing the door to behind him.

'What's he done?' asked Katherine.

'There was quite a skirmish at Trafalgar Square this morning and the police was called in to try to contain it. I must admit it did get a bit out of hand. Well, to cut a long story short the last I saw of Charlie Stevens and some others was 'em being thrown in the back of a Black Maria. He yelled out for me to tell his missis, so here I am.'

'Thank you,' said Katherine. 'Do you happen to know which

police station they would have gone to?'

'Na, can't help yer there.'

'I'll tell his wife as soon as she gets home. Thank you, Mr . . .?'

'Davis. Frank Davis.'

'Mr Davis.' She opened the front door just as Ted and Joe came along.

'Who was that?' asked Ted, watching the back of Mr Davis as he walked up the road.

'I'll tell you when you're inside.'

'You're making it sound very interesting,' said Joe. 'You haven't got yourself a man friend have—'

Katherine turned on him, her green eyes blazing. 'No I haven't.' She pushed open the kitchen door with such force that it banged against the wall.

'I'm sorry, it was just a joke.'

'Well, I don't need those kind of jokes, and for your information it was a man from the docks telling me that Charlie has been arrested.'

Ted's face went ashen. 'Why? What's he done?'

'It seems a lot of men were arrested just for being in the wrong place at the wrong time.'

'My dad ain't a troublemaker.'

'I know, and I'm sure they won't keep him for long.'

'What's Mum gonner say?'

'I don't know. Your poor mother has got more than enough to worry about without this.'

Tea was a quiet affair with just a sandwich, and as the evening wore on they all became fidgety and apprehensive.

'I wish there was something we could do,' said Ted.

'I know. Let's hope they're only going to keep them in prison overnight to teach them a lesson,' said Katherine.

'Prison,' said Joe. 'Will they really put him in prison?'

'I don't know.'

'I don't reckon it'll be that bad,' said Joe.

'How would you know?' asked Ted.

'Well, I don't think those suffragettes would keep being arrested if it was that bad.'

'S'pose so,' said Ted soulfully. 'See they've been at it again.'

'Doing what?' asked Katherine.

'It said on the placards outside the newsagents this morning that they've been smashing windows again.'

'Silly women,' said Katherine. 'Look, why don't you both go to bed? I'll wait up for your mother.'

'She's very late,' said Ted, a worried expression filling his face. 'She's not used to being out on her own. I hope nothing's—'

'She's all right,' said Katherine, gently tapping his arm. 'She's probably helping them to pack.'

'Just as long as she's not been smashing windows,' said Joe with a grin.

'If that was meant as a joke, young man, then I for one don't think it was funny.' Katherine looked very stern.

'Sorry. Where shall I sleep tonight?' he asked quietly.

'In the front room, and we'll see what happens tomorrow.' Katherine was dreading the tantrums and sulks if he had to go in with Ted.

Once again Katherine was alone with her thoughts. What else could go wrong? If only Milly would come home. She shouldn't be as late as this. Had she got lost, or in some kind of trouble? She didn't know her way about. Please God, don't let anything happen to her, Katherine prayed.

Her thoughts went to the suffragettes. She could never do things like that. They appeared to be very well organised. They must have a lot of help. She was sitting in the armchair, quietly thinking, when Milly finally walked in.

'Milly, you're late. Where have you been all this time?' Katherine jumped to her feet. 'Thank goodness you're home. I've been so worried about you. Sit down and I'll make you a cup of tea. Didn't Dolly and Tom come with you?'

Milly shook her head and, after removing her hat and coat, sat at the table and began picking at the tablecloth. 'She looks ever so ill.'

'Do you know what's wrong with her?'

'No. She said it started with a cold. She's got a terrible cough, and she's so thin. Was she thin when you left?'

'No. She was losing a bit of weight, but we put it down to all the extra work she was doing. How's Tom?'

'He ain't much better.' Tears filled Milly's eyes. 'I wish they'd let me help 'em. They're living in that bloody cold basement.'

Katherine filled the teapot and sat at the table next to her. 'Why won't they come over here?'

'Tom's still working, he's doing a bit of gardening for that Gerald, and you know Dolly – she likes to keep her independence.'

Katherine nodded and smiled.

'I think Dolly's worried she's got something that might be catching, and that's why she's not said anything. Where's Charlie, he in the bog?'

Katherine took hold of Milly's hand. 'It seems there was a bit of trouble this morning and—'

Milly jumped to her feet. 'You've let me sit here and all the time my Charlie's in hospital?'

'No, Milly, he's not in hospital.'

'Oh my God, it's worse.' Her tears fell.

'No, it isn't. What I mean is, he's in prison.'

'What?'

'A Mr Davis came and told me Charlie and a lot of others were taken to prison, but he doesn't know which one.'

Milly sat down. 'Why? What's he done?'

'It was to do with the strike.'

'My Charlie in prison? He's never been in trouble in his life. What we gonner do?'

Katherine choked back her tears. 'We'll have to wait till morning. Then we'll go to the local police station and see if they can find out what we have to do.'

'Will it cost money to get him out?'

'I don't know.'

'We ain't got none now, have we?'

Katherine toyed with the spoon in her saucer. 'Only a few pence.'

'My poor Charlie. Will they feed him?'

'I don't know.'

'Does Ted know about this?'

'Yes.'

'What did he say?'

'What can any of us say?'

'I can't believe this is all happening.'

'Well, they say trouble comes in threes, so we've had our share.'

Milly looked down at her hands. 'We ain't.'

'Why? What do you mean? There's my problem, Dolly and now Charlie. What else can happen?'

'That's a terrible journey, took me ages.'

'Milly, what else has happened?'

'I'm sorry.'

'Sorry, what for? I didn't mind giving you that money. Perhaps when we see Mrs Fairfield we can explain . . .' Katherine's voice trailed off. She felt uneasy. Somehow she knew this wasn't what Milly was talking about.

'You see when I saw the place Dolly was living in I very nearly went mad. They're couped up in that dark damp basement. That Gerald's got a lot to answer for.'

Katherine quickly took a breath; she'd almost forgotten about Gerald and what part he had to play in Dolly's illness.

'Well, I went and gave him a piece of me mind. D'you know, he just told me to shut up and go away. Said he wasn't interested in my affairs, and I was making it harder for Dolly, said he could throw them out on the street if he felt like it, and I should be grateful he was still letting them stay there.'

'That sounds like Gerald.'

'Then I saw red, didn't I, and I told him in no uncertain words what I thought of him. I told him he was a selfish bugger that didn't deserve all he'd got from your hard work. I knew I wasn't making it any easier for Dolly, but then . . .' Milly blew her nose. 'I'm ever so sorry, Katherine.'

Katherine sat with her eyes wide open. 'Why?'

'I told him about you going to have his baby.'

Katherine gasped. 'What? Why did you tell him that?'

'I dunno. It just all came blurting out.'

'But I'm not going to have his baby, I'm going to see Mrs—'

'He wants to see you.'

'What? Well, I don't want to see him.' Katherine began to feel threatened.

'He was very interested, and seemed very pleased.'

'I bet he was.' She stood up. 'How could you do that, Milly? I trusted you.'

'I'm sorry, Katherine, really sorry. As soon as I said it I felt like biting me tongue off, but he was standing there smirking at me like Lord High-and-Mighty, thinking he knew everything, so I told him something he didn't know about.'

Katherine was in shock; she couldn't cry. 'I'll have to move, find somewhere else to live.'

'Why?'

'I don't want him to come here looking for me.'

'But he don't know where you live.'

'Dolly still lives there, remember, and Gerald has a funny way of finding out things, and the last thing I want is for him to come here making a scene and forcing me to go back.'

'D'you think that's what he'll do?'

'He'll try. He's had everything else of mine, so I suppose he thinks this baby will be his right.'

'Oh Katherine, what we gonner do?'

'I don't know. I don't want him here. I don't want Joseph to find out about this.' She gently touched her stomach. 'And if I know Gerald, he'll take great delight in telling Joseph.'

'Oh Katherine . . .' Milly's eyes were full of sorrow.

Katherine put her arm round Milly's shoulders. 'We can't do much tonight, and you look very tired.'

'It's been a long day, and so much has happened.'

'Well, I suggest we go to bed, then tomorrow we'll see about finding out what's become of Charlie.'

'What a bloody mess,' said Milly.

'Yes, life is a bloody mess,' said Katherine sadly.

Katherine knew as soon as she closed her bedroom door that sleep wouldn't come. She lay on the bed staring up at the ceiling. What was going to happen to them? If she lost her job because of the strike where would they live? What could they afford? She could understand the suffragettes. She almost felt like joining them, anything to get back at men. When she closed her eyes she could see Gerald laughing at her. Should she bury her pride and go back to him? It would make a lot of people happy. She would insist Tom and Dolly were employed again. Joseph could have his old room, that would make him very happy. Tears ran down her face.

'Looks like you've got everything on your side again, Gerald,' she said out loud.

Chapter 14

Everybody was up and about very early on Monday morning.

'I couldn't sleep,' said Milly as Katherine wandered into the kitchen.

'I know how you feel,' replied Katherine.

'Mum, I'm coming to the nick with you,' said Ted.

'No, you go to work, son, we need the money.' Milly knew if he didn't go into work, like anybody else, he would not be paid.

'I'll go with you,' said Katherine. 'As it's on the way I'll go in to Josh and explain.'

'What if he sacks you?' said Milly in alarm.

'Well, we'll have to cross that bridge if and when it happens.'

'What about Olive?' asked Ted. 'She's gotter know before some busybody tells her.'

'Would you like me to do that?' asked Joe. 'I could go before I go to school.'

Katherine looked at him. This was the first time she'd heard him volunteer to do anything to help anyone.

'Thanks. I'd really appreciate that,' said Milly, going out of the door.

Milly and Katherine were very quiet as they walked to the shop.

When they turned the corner they were taken aback at the amount of men crowding round Trent's doorway and spilling into the road.

'Oh my God,' said Katherine. 'What's happened now?' She started to push her way through.

' 'Allo, Kate. I bet old Josh'll be glad to see you,' said a white-haired man.

'Why? What's happened?'

'It's so bloody crowded in there, we can't get in.' He leant against the wall and proceeded to push more tobacco into his pipe. When he was satisfied he put it in his mouth and puffed hard. Katherine was not going to get any more information out of him.

She got to the door and after elbowing a lot of men out of the way, managed to get through. She hurried behind the counter. 'Josh, what's happened?' she asked, straightening her hat. 'What's everybody doing here?'

'Thank Christ you're here. I'm running out of mugs. Ain't you heard?' He had to shout above the din. 'A lot of 'em finished up in the nick yesterday and all these are in here trying to sort something out. Hurry up and get your hat and coat off and start pouring out some tea. And make sure they pay.'

'But . . .' She was going to tell him where she was going but it was too late, he was round the other side of the counter and lost in the throng as he tried to collect the dirty mugs that were strewn about.

Milly pushed her way through the crowd and was being squashed against the counter. 'Looks like I'd better go on me own.'

'No, hang on a minute,' shouted Katherine as she ran the full teapot over the mugs, filling them to overflowing. 'Look, come round here and give me a hand.'

It went deathly quiet after a lot of spoon banging and shouting for order. A man stood on a table.

'Now we all know what happened yesterday, and if our mates is gonner get bail I think we should see the union blokes about it.'

A great chorus of 'Hear, hear!' went up.

'Right, I need to know who was carted off.'

'Milly, hang around,' said Katherine. 'We can find out where Charlie is from this lot.'

Names were being called out and written down, including Charlie's. Gradually the men drifted outside and along to the docks for a meeting with the union.

Frank Davis came up to Katherine and Milly and told them all the men had been taken to a police station near Trafalgar Square. 'They're going in front of the beak this morning. He'll probably let 'em off with a fine and a caution. Can't do a lot else, otherwise it could cause riots.'

'A fine?' asked Milly in alarm. 'Any idea how much?'

'Na, but don't worry about that, the union will have ter pay.'

'Are you sure?'

'They'd better, that's what we pay our dues for, for them to look after us.'

Both Milly and Katherine looked relieved.

'Right, Kate,' said Josh as the place began to empty. 'Better get some clearing up done ready for the lunchtime rush.' He laughed. 'I only wish.'

Katherine knew they hadn't been very busy since the strike started, but was afraid to ask too much in case he said he didn't want her any more.

'I best be off,' said Milly.

'Oh yes,' said Katherine. 'Thanks for your help.'

'Well, at least we should soon have one of our problems over,' she said smiling.

'You think you've got problems, missis,' said Josh. 'You don't know the half of it.' He went out the back.

'He don't know what we've got to worry about,' Milly whispered.

'And he's not going to find out,' said Katherine as she began clearing the tables and wiping them down.

* * *

As she walked home Katherine was almost afraid to turn into Croft Street. What if Gerald had found out where she lived? She sighed. Thankfully there was no motor car in the road.

The atmosphere was a lot happier when Katherine went in and found Charlie sitting in his chair.

He jumped up and gave her a big hug. 'Thanks, gel.'

'For what?' she asked, taking off her hat, which he had knocked sideways.

'Standing by Milly and helping her out with the fare to get over to Dolly.'

'It was nothing. How was prison?'

'Don't ask. Bloody awful. Don't think I'm gonner make a habit of it. What with one thing and another it's been a bloody awful weekend all round.'

'I agree with you there,' said Katherine, giving Milly a quick glance.

'Anyway,' continued Charlie. 'Thanks for giving Milly that money. I'm really grateful. She told me you sold your wedding ring. I'm sorry about that, she shouldn't have let you do it.'

'I didn't mind.'

'I know, but yer wedding ring . . . I wouldn't like it if Milly—'

'Charlie, I said it doesn't matter,' said Katherine forcefully.

'But it must'a meant something.'

Joseph was sitting at the table, drawing. He looked up.

Katherine felt her face flush with anger. 'Milly, I told you not to say—'

'I couldn't help it. I had to tell Charlie where I got the money from.'

'You're as bad as Mrs Duke. Your mouth will get you and me in a lot of trouble very soon.' She stormed out of the kitchen.

'Why is Mama so angry?' asked Joe.

'You and your big mouth,' said Milly, turning on Charlie. 'I shouldn't have told you.'

'Why? What did I say that was wrong?'

'Milly, why is Mama so angry?' asked Joe again.

'It doesn't matter,' said Milly dismissively.

But it mattered to Joe. What difference did a wedding ring make? Why was his mother so angry? He moved away from the table and went upstairs.

The gentle tapping on Katherine's door made her quickly wipe her eyes. 'Who is it?' she called.

'It's me,' said Joe. 'Can I come in?'

Katherine knew she couldn't refuse and opened the door.

'Why are you crying? Was your wedding ring so important?'

She shook her head. 'No, not really.'

'But you're still wearing it.'

She half smiled. 'No, this is brass.'

'Does it matter then?'

'Only if my finger goes green and drops off.'

Joe looked horrified. 'It won't, will it?'

'No.'

'Are we ever so hard up now?'

'Yes, I'm afraid we are.'

'So why did you give that money to Milly?'

'I had to. Come and sit down.' She patted the bed on which she was sitting. 'You see, I feel that in many ways it was my fault that Dolly is ill and Tom has lost his job.'

'Why?'

She put her arm round her son's shoulders; he didn't pull away. 'When I left Gerald I think he used Dolly and Tom as a kind of revenge.'

'But, Mama, what he did to you was wrong.'

'I know.' Katherine was pleased he now thought that way.

'Will Dolly and Tom come here to live?'

135

'I don't know. Things will be very hard if they do.'

'Is that why you sold your ring?'

'Yes.'

'What're we going to do?'

'Let's hope this strike doesn't last for too long.'

'I know you don't want me to leave school so I'm going to try and get a job after school, that'll help out.'

Katherine pulled him close and kissed his cheek. 'I'm pleased about that.'

'Don't you mind?'

'No, but you are a bit young. Where are you going to start looking?'

'I thought of going to that place that sells motor cars.'

'It's a long way away.'

'Don't matter. It's what I want to do more than anything else.'

'And why not?' she smiled.

He jumped up and threw his arms round her neck. 'I don't like to see you unhappy, and I promise I'll try to help and I don't mind if I have to sleep in Ted's room.' He laughed. 'He said he'd keep his smelly socks outside.'

Katherine wanted to hold him and kiss him. He had changed. He had had to grow up, and she loved him dearly. He knew jobs were hard to get but he was willing to try.

Milly knocked on her door, telling her the meal was on the table.

'Just coming. Go on down,' said Katherine to Joe. 'I just want to tidy myself up.'

When Joseph left she sat back down on the bed. How could she tell him her real problem? And would it be solved? And what would he say if Gerald came here looking for her?

'I'm sorry, girl,' said Charlie when Katherine walked into the kitchen. 'Didn't mean to upset you.'

'That's all right. What with one thing and another, I was just being a bit silly, that's all.'

Later that evening when Milly and Katherine were in the kitchen, Milly closed the door.

'I'm gonner go and see Ida tomorrow. I'm gonner tell her we'll pay as soon as everything gets back to normal.'

'Thanks.' But what was normal? thought Katherine.

Trent's wasn't very busy at all the following day, and Katherine grew more concerned for her job. She cleaned and swept and tried to make herself as useful as she could, and she kept out of Josh's way. She would have liked to go up to Nellie, but dare not ask.

As she left the shop she knew this couldn't last. He would have to sack her soon. What if she was ill after seeing Ida? That would be the last straw. More and more the option to go and live with Gerald seemed to be crowding in on her.

Milly gave Katherine a knowing look when she walked in, and Katherine followed her into the kitchen and closed the door behind her.

'She's busy tonight,' said Milly. 'But she said she'll see you tomorrow.'

'Did she say how much?'

'Three and six and no questions asked.'

'Three and six,' repeated Katherine in alarm. 'But that's over half my week's wages.'

Milly shrugged her shoulders. 'Don't look like you've got a lot of choice.'

'No. But it will take me for ever to save that.'

Milly smiled. 'When Charlie gets back to work we'll think of something.'

'But how long will this strike go on for?'

'Dunno.'

'And how long is Ida willing to wait for her money?'

'Dunno,' repeated Milly. 'But you can go over that with her.'

'Milly, do you think she would wait till Saturday to do . . . you know? Then I'll have Sunday to get over it.'

'Look, I'll take you round tomorrow night, then you can sort it all out with her.'

Katherine kissed Milly's cheek. 'Thanks. I don't know what I should have done without you.'

'Don't thank me till it's all over.'

'You sound as if you don't approve.'

Milly turned away. 'In some ways I don't, but then again it wasn't your fault you got in this mess.'

Katherine was taken aback. 'No, it wasn't. Do you think I should go back to Gerald?'

'No. But you leaving him has caused a lot of grief all round.'

Katherine was beginning to get angry. Everybody seemed to be blaming her for everything. 'I'm sorry for what happened to Dolly.'

'Well, when I can afford it I'll go over and see her again.'

Katherine didn't volunteer to go with her.

'Now come on, take these plates in the other room and sit down and have your dinner.'

Katherine did as she was told but she was upset at what Milly had said.

After dinner the following evening Milly and Katherine told the family they were going round to see Olive.

'What if Olive tells them we didn't go there?' said Katherine when they left the house.

'Charlie won't bother to ask questions when I tell him it was woman's talk.'

As Milly knocked on Ida's door Katherine felt her stomach churn and her knees go weak. The memory of all the miscarriages she had had in Australia came flooding back to her. All those lovely babies lost, and now she was deliberately going to get rid of one. She felt sick and wanted to run away. But what future would the child have? No, deep down she knew this was for the best.

'Come in,' said Ida, opening the door. Her face glowed with good health, her grey hair was in a neat bun and she was wearing a spotless white overall. There was nothing dirty or shoddy about Ida Fairfield.

They followed her down the passage and into the kitchen.

'Sit yourself down.' Ida pointed to chairs at the table.

Milly and Katherine quickly did as they were told. 'Right. How many months?'

'Two.'

'You sure?'

'Yes.' Katherine could have told her the exact day and time if she'd asked. It was stamped on her mind. So much had happened since Edwin's death. Ida's voice broke into her thoughts.

'Only had some silly cows in here three and four months, that can lead to all sorts of complications.'

Katherine played with her gloves. 'Mrs Fair—'

'Call me Ida, everybody else does.'

'Ida. I think Milly has explained our financial situation to you.'

'Yes, she did.'

'You see, all the while this strike's on we have to be very careful with our money.'

'I understand that. I hear you come from somewhere very posh, so did a bloke from the gentry get you up the spout?'

Katherine nodded.

'Married, is he?'

Katherine didn't answer.

'Want bloody shooting, they do. Mind you, it takes two, you know?'

Katherine wasn't prepared to go into details of what had happened.

'Ain't he prepared to pay then?'

'I haven't asked him.'

'More fool you. I shouldn't think he wants his wife to know all about it.'

Katherine wasn't going to pursue this conversation any further. 'So, Ida, are you prepared to wait for your money?'

'Yer, but I'm gonner get you to sign an IOU. Can't have you trying to get away with it when things get better.'

Katherine almost wanted to laugh. How many women sign bits of paper in order to pay later for an abortion? 'Would it be too inconvenient if I came straight from work on Saturday, then that will give me Sunday to get over it?'

'No, that should be all right. Ain't got no husband round watching what I'm doing, so me life's me own. Mind you, it was sad when I had to lay him out. Been gone over ten years now, but I still miss the old bugger.'

'Did you have any children?' asked Katherine.

'No, more's the pity. But then again I might have felt different about helping the likes of you if I had. Might even have tried to talk you into keeping it.'

Katherine shuddered. The last thing she wanted was a baby.

When they got outside Katherine sighed. 'Well, that's the first hurdle over.'

'Yes,' said Milly. 'Let's hope everything will be all right.'

'Why? What do you mean?'

'Well, it ain't natural, is it?'

'No. But do I have any choice?'

'No, don't suppose you do, and the last thing you want is a little 'en.'

'I'm very worried about it,' said Katherine as they walked along.

'If you like I'll meet you at Ida's on Sat'day.'

'Would you? I'd like that.'

'Well, that's settled. Now come on,' said Milly, tucking her arm through Katherine's. 'We've still got time to go and see Olive.'

In a few days' time another problem will be out of the way, thought Katherine. But how many more were waiting to crop up?

Chapter 15

On Saturday morning Katherine woke with fear in her heart. This evening she would be going to see Ida. She was dreading it. Was she doing the right thing?

The day seemed to drag and at last it was time for her to leave.

Josh handed her her wages. 'Look, Kate, I don't know how long I can keep you on. You've seen what business is like.'

She nodded.

'Come in on Monday and we'll talk it over.'

Katherine was upset as she left. Would this be her last week? She didn't want to have to leave. What other job was around? With the strike they needed the money. She was happy here, but other things were crowding in on her mind as she made her way to Ida's house.

'Oi, you!' A man was shouting after her.

She stopped and turned. 'Mr Addams,' she said, surprised that he would want to talk to her.

He reeled towards her. 'You're the tart what's been putting ideas into my Briony's head, ain't yer? Seen yer walking up Croft Street with all yer airs and graces.'

'I'm sorry?'

'You will be when I've finished with you.'

Katherine stood back; the smell of beer and his unwashed body made her catch her breath.

'I said,' he poked his fat dirty finger into her shoulder, 'you're the one what keeps giving my Briony ideas.' He belched loudly in Katherine's face.

She screwed up her nose in disgust and turned her head. She looked up the road, desperately hoping someone would come along. Milly said she would be waiting for her at Ida's, but that was streets away. Katherine silently prayed that she would come round the corner. Although she was frightened – drunks were so unpredictable – she knew she had to remain calm. 'If giving your daughter a few clothes gives her thoughts of her own, then yes, I'm guilty,' she said haughtily.

'Don't start giving me all yer fancy talk.' He rocked back on his heels, putting his hand on the wall to steady himself. 'I don't want yer charity. I can look after me family well enough, so keep yer snotty nose out o' our business.'

'I like Briony, I think she's a very nice girl, and I don't think you should stop me from giving her a treat now again.'

'Saucy cow. Don't you answer me back. Ain't ever had a woman answer me back.'

'It's a pity somebody didn't. You wife might still be alive if she had.' She went to move on.

He grabbed the top of her arms. 'What did you say?'

She tried to shake him off but he was gripping her very tight. 'Let go of me.'

'Now you just listen to me.' He shook Katherine and put his face close to hers. 'I loved my wife very dearly.'

'I said, let me go.' Although she was beginning to get very nervous, Katherine tossed her head and said defiantly, 'You can't frighten me.'

'We'll see about that.' He raised his clenched fist to hit her. As he let go, she stepped back and he overbalanced. She wasn't quick enough to get out of his way and fell to the ground with him. He fell heavily, hitting his head against the wall with a sickening thud as he went down.

For a moment they lay very still. Then shaking with fear Katherine got to her feet. She stared down at Mr Addams in panic. Why didn't he get up? What if he had injured himself? She couldn't just walk away and leave him.

As she stood over him, brushing the dust from her coat she noticed blood very slowly beginning to seep from beneath his head. She put her hand to her mouth and let out an almost silent scream. Carefully she bent over him. To her great relief he was still breathing. He was a drunk, and drunks often fell and were left to sleep it off. Should she walk away?

She stood up and looked around. It was very quiet in this street. There weren't any houses, just warehouses, windowless buildings which were closed for the weekend. Dirt and rubbish filled the gutter; in the light breeze paper blew about Katherine's ankles. She knew there was a pub at the end of the street – she had just passed it. Should she run back and get help? What if they blamed her? Gradually Katherine began to inch away from him. Milly would be waiting for her at Ida's.

''Allo there, missis.'

Katherine groaned when she recognised the voice of the person who was shouting after her, and quickly spun round as Briony came hurrying towards her.

'Thought it was you. 'Ere, ain't that me dad?' Briony ran the last few yards. 'What's he doing on the floor? And what you done to him?' She was on her knees cradling his head in her lap. She looked at her hand. 'He's bleeding,' she screamed. 'What you done to him?'

'I haven't done anything.'

'So why's he on the floor and bleeding?'

'We were talking and he fell and hit his head on the wall.'

'What was he talking to you for?'

'He told me not to give you any more things.'

'Did he now.' Briony calmed down and looked at her father with contempt. 'I've got to get him back home.'

Katherine thought she knew Briony, and was amazed that she

now sounded far older than her years. 'Look, I'm sorry, but I must go.'

'You can't leave me here with him. Can't you help me get him home?'

'No I'm sorry. Perhaps someone in the pub will help you.'

Briony sat back on her heels. 'Shouldn't think so. They're probably all in the same state as him.'

Katherine began to walk away. 'Look, I really must go.'

'What's your hurry? And what you doing round this way? It ain't on your way home.' Briony stood up. ''Ere, you wasn't meeting me dad, was you?'

'No I wasn't.' The idea was absurd.

'So, you meeting a friend? A man friend?'

'Briony, what I do is my business, so I trust you to keep out of it.' Katherine was beginning to get cross with this young girl. How dare she pry into her affairs?

'Well, my business is getting me dad home. And if I go to the pub and tell 'em the lady what hit him has scarpered they might come looking for you.'

'I didn't hit him.'

'Only you and me dad know that, and he ain't talking, is he?'

'Briony, are you trying to blackmail me into helping you with your father?'

She looked at Katherine with defiance in her face. 'Yer, think you could say that.'

'I thought you hated him.'

'I do.'

'So why don't you leave him here to sleep it off?'

''Cos if the coppers come along and put him in the nick we'll have to find money to get him out. And we ain't got any to spare, and they might put the kids away.'

'What made you come this way home?'

'I was looking for him. Thought I'd get him before he boozed all his wages away, but it looks like I was too late.'

Mr Addams began to moan.

'It's all right, Dad. I'm here, Briony. Me and the missis here's gonner take you home. Can you stand?'

He groaned again and tried to get up. Briony bent down to help him.

'Come on, give us a hand.'

Katherine did as she was asked and helped him stagger to his feet.

He leant heavily on them as they pushed, weaved and struggled with him along the road. At first he tried to hit out at Briony, but she told him in no uncertain words to behave. Then he began singing at the top of his voice.

Katherine felt so embarrassed. A few people smiled as they passed them, others looked at this sorry trio with contempt. They probably thought Katherine was part of the family.

As they slowly made their way back to Croft Street Katherine could have screamed. Why was this happening tonight of all nights? How dare this man confront her and get her involved. Why did he use that pub? She wanted to run away, she felt trapped. She couldn't tell anyone where she was going. Milly would be wondering where she had got to. What if Ida were going out later? It had to be done tonight.

As soon as they got to the Addamses' front door Katherine left them. She could almost feel the eyes following her from behind the lace curtains as she hurried back along the street. Was Mrs Duke watching her? When she didn't go into Milly's she knew there would be some questions asked.

Breathlessly she ran. She hoped she wouldn't be too late.

She banged on Ida's knocker and almost collapsed with relief when Ida opened her door.

'You're late.'

'There was a bit of a problem,' she panted.

'Problem,' said Milly, who was right behind Ida. 'What sorta problem?'

'It's nothing to worry about. I'll tell you about it later.'

'I was getting a bit worried about you,' said Milly, frowning.

'And I thought you'd got cold feet,' said Ida over her shoulder as they trooped down the passage.

'No, I'm all right.'

When Ida opened the kitchen door the strong smell of disinfectant almost took Katherine's breath away. The table was covered with newspapers. She stood in the doorway for a moment or two, fear filling her mind.

'Well, get yer drawers off then. Pull your skirts up and get up on the table and open your legs.'

Reluctantly, Katherine did as she was told.

Chapter 16

Katherine lay in bed watching the sunbeams filter through the curtains, her head full of what had happened last night. She brought her knees up to help ease the stomach cramps. Although she knew what she had done was for the best, it still troubled her conscience. This was something she would keep to herself for ever, another burden she would have to carry. Well, if Gerald did find her, he wouldn't have anything to call his now. Her thoughts drifted to Dolly and Tom. Milly hadn't heard from them and was worried. As soon as money allowed they would go and see them. A tap on her bedroom door brought her back.

'You awake?' asked Milly.

'Yes, come in,' said Katherine sleepily.

'Brought you a nice cuppa. How you feeling?' Milly put the cup on the small table.

Katherine sat up. 'Other than guilty, not too bad.'

'You'll be all right. It's a good job you had Ida do it. At least she knows what she's doing, not like some of 'em who go to any old dear. But then again if you ain't got two ha'pennies to rub together you'll go anywhere if it helps.'

Katherine smiled at those words of wisdom. 'Did any of them ask why I went straight to bed when we got back?'

'I told them it was women's troubles, and that seemed to satisfy 'em.'

'Thanks. What would I do without you?'

Milly dismissed that statement with a smile. 'Now, d'you fancy a bit of breakfast? What about a bit of toast?'

'Thanks,' said Katherine again. 'I'll be down in a minute.'

'You don't have to get up till later. Just you take it easy this morning.'

'Milly, you shouldn't have given Ida that sixpence, you know.'

'I had to give her something, just to show we ain't gonner welsh on the deal.'

'But you'll be those few pennies short this week. And what if I get sacked? We might need that. Ted doesn't bring in that much.'

Milly shrugged. 'We'll let next week take care of itself.'

'Do you think she'll charge us interest?'

'Dunno. Why d'you ask?'

'Well, she is the money lender.'

'Yer I know, but for all that, I wouldn't like to say. Now come on, drink this tea 'fore it gets cold.'

This question had been at the back of Katherine's mind, but she wouldn't know the answer till all the money had been paid. 'I wouldn't be surprised if Mrs Duke doesn't come banging on the door soon,' said Katherine, grinning and sipping her tea.

'I bet she's bursting to find out what happened and why you brought old Addams home. And you, my girl, was very lucky he didn't clock you one.'

Katherine had told Milly the story as they made their way home.

'I must admit I was a bit worried. But he was so drunk he probably doesn't remember anything about it.'

'Let's hope so. Right then, I'll go down and see to the dinner.'

Katherine lay back when Milly left. She felt a bit sore, but quite well considering. The money she owed Ida worried her and kept returning to her thoughts. She had never been in debt before. This strike must end soon so that they could all get on with their lives.

Joe tapped on her door. 'Can I come in?' he called.

'Of course.' She sat up and twisted her long hair into a knot. 'Come and sit on the bed.' She patted the covers.

'Are you all right?'

'Yes I'm fine.'

Joe looked at her suspiciously. 'I wanted to tell you about me job. Mr Lacy let me stay there all day yesterday, and d'you know he showed me all sorts of things. He loves those motors, and he gave me a shilling. He said I was a help.'

'A shilling? You are a lucky boy.'

'I ain't a boy. And you can have this.' He held out a sixpence.

'I can't take this.'

'Why not?' He looked downcast. 'D'you want it all?'

'No, of course not. It's yours. You earned it.'

'All the money you earn you give to Milly, so.'

'I know, but that's because she feeds us.'

'Well, I want to help. It ain't easy for Milly and you know Charlie's out of work, and I'd like to help, so please take it.'

Katherine wanted to cry. 'Oh Joseph,' she said, hugging him, 'you are a good boy.'

He wriggled free and sat up. 'Now why are you in bed? You look all right to me.'

'I'm getting up soon, so don't worry about it.'

He moved towards the door. 'Mama. We seem to be happy here, don't we?'

'Are we?'

'Think so.' He grinned and left.

Katherine looked at the silver coin in her hand. She did feel happy. She would give this to Milly, so she wouldn't be short. As she carefully got out of bed she felt as if her inside was going to drop out. 'Please God, don't let this last for too long,' she prayed.

Katherine had sat around all day Sunday but on Monday she

knew she had to go to the shop, so she slowly made her way to work.

When she walked in Josh said, 'Christ, girl, you look awful.'

'Thanks,' she said, removing her hat and sitting at a table.

'D'you feel all right?'

'Yes, thanks. Josh, shall we talk about my job?'

'If yer want. I'll pour us out a cuppa.'

'Have I got a job?'

'Let's put it this way: I don't wanner lose you, but as you know things ain't that good.' He put two heaped spoonfuls of sugar into both mugs and slowly stirred them.

'I see.'

He took the tea and sat at her table. 'What if . . .' he paused. 'What if you work for less money?'

'I can't do that.'

'Well, it's that or nothing.'

'How long would it be for?'

'Just till the strike ends and things get back to normal, then I can pay you like before.'

'What sort of wage would it be now?' She held her breath while waiting for the answer.

'What about four shillings, and see how it goes after next week? I might have ter put it down every week.'

'I'll have to see if Milly can manage on less.' Katherine played with the spoon, her mind quickly turning over. Was there any other place round here she could find work? 'Do you own this shop?'

'Well yes, in a way. I rent it from the landlord. Why?'

'Nothing. I just wondered, that's all.'

''Ere, you ain't got a fortune stashed away, have you, and you wanner buy me out?'

She laughed. 'If only. But it must be a little gold mine when things go well.'

He looked at her quizzically. 'It ain't bad.'

She sat up. 'All right. I'll work for less money, but only until the end of the strike, then I want six shillings a week.'

'Six bob,' he grinned. 'You're a good one, Kate. You ain't afraid of hard work, or speaking your mind. Don't hear you moan like some of 'em I've had. And the blokes like you. You've got a good head on your shoulders. OK, it's a deal.'

For the first time in months Katherine felt in charge of her life, and she had plans for her future.

'Well,' said Milly, when Katherine arrived home and opened the kitchen door. 'Have you still got a job?'

'Yes. But I have to take less money.'

'How much less?'

'I'm only going to get four shillings a week. Will you be able to manage on that?'

'I'll have to.'

'That's not all the bad news. He's going to review the situation again. I might only finish up with three.'

'Christ, that will be bad news. Ted'll be earning more than you, and he's only an apprentice.'

Katherine shrugged. 'That's the way it is, but it's only until the strike ends, then I told Josh I want six.'

Milly laughed. 'Well, I've got to hand it to you, you know how to drive a bargain.'

'Let's hope the dockers have the same luck.'

Milly took her hand. 'I'm glad to see you're looking a lot better. Everything all right?' Milly gave her a knowing look.

'Yes, it is now.'

For two weeks they just about managed, but at times the atmosphere got a little fraught. Charlie was getting more and more upset at not being the provider. When Olive came round with a pot of stew, that really upset him.

'We can't take this.'

'Course you can, Dad. I made much too much. 'Sides, Ernie will get fed up with it if he has to have it day in and day out.' She gave a little giggle. 'It ain't that bad.'

Milly put her arm round her daughter's shoulders and glared at her husband. 'I'm sure it's very nice. Take no notice of yer dad, love. I'll get a few extra bits of veg and that'll do us all.'

'I wish we could help more,' said Olive.

'Never thought I'd have to rely on me kids feeding me,' said Charlie, slamming the door as he left the room. Katherine had noted the hurt look in his eyes.

'I'm sorry, Mum. Have I said the wrong thing?'

'No, not really. He's just fed up, that's all. I won't be sorry when this is all over. I'm as fed up as he is with him under me feet all day.'

Olive turned to Katherine. 'How's Joe getting on? He was telling Ernie all about these 'ere new motor cars.'

'He seems to be very happy. He spends all day Saturday there.'

'Who buys 'em? They seem ever so expensive.'

'I don't really know.'

'Wouldn't have thought anybody round this way had that sorta money,' said Milly.

'I think it's because the garage is a lot cheaper this side of the water.' Katherine was proud he was bringing in a shilling a week – half of which he gave to Milly – even though she wasn't that happy at the state he got into.

'Just about manage to get his things clean,' Milly said, folding her arms. 'Gawd only knows what he gets up to in that place.'

'Well, at least he's doing something he likes,' said Katherine.

'Bloody lucky, ain't he?' said Charlie, coming back in. 'I can't even afford a pint.'

'Do you think it will end soon?' asked Katherine.

'Wouldn't like to say.'

'I feel really sorry for some of 'em round here,' said Milly. 'You see the rent man, then the tally man banging on the doors. They know they're home but no one opens the door.'

'Can't really blame 'em if they ain't got it to give him,' said Charlie. 'I bet they're sorry they bought stuff on the never never.'

'Seen some of it took away. It's really sad to see a woman standing at her door after the means test man's been and she has to watch her home being taken away just so she can get some money from the relief office.'

'If this goes on much longer we might be in the same boat.'

'Don't say that! I don't want to go on relief, and I couldn't bear to see me home go.'

'If the worst comes to the worst I'll try and find another job,' said Katherine.

Milly smiled at her. 'You're a good 'en, Katherine.'

She grinned. 'That's only because I don't want my bed to be sold.'

'It's the kids I feel sorry for,' said Milly sadly. 'Look half starved, some of 'em do.'

'That's what'll end it,' said Charlie. 'Most blokes can't bear the thought of the kids having to go without.'

As there was no sign of the strike breaking, Katherine knew it wouldn't be long before her money went down to three shillings. Then they would really be in trouble. Even though she was thinking of looking elsewhere for a job, she knew deep down that would never come about. She liked it at Trent's. Over these past weeks she was even managing to see Nellie now and again, and hoped that in time she could get her to talk about herself.

It was the middle of June when the strike finally ended. At last the docks were full of ships and the men had plenty of overtime.

Katherine was pleased Trent's was busy once more. Gradually things were getting back to normal. Debts were being cleared, people were beginning to smile again. So far she'd paid off two shillings of Ida's loan since her rise.

Milly was worried about Dolly. Charlie had promised to take her to see her as soon as he got a Saturday afternoon off.

'Can't turn down the overtime.'

Three weeks later, on a Monday evening, there was a lot of laughter as they sat round the table discussing the day out Milly and Charlie were planning to have on August Bank Holiday Monday.

Katherine looked round the table at the happy faces.

'Fancy Southend?' asked Charlie.

'Cor, I'd like some of that,' said Ted. 'Reckon there's plenty of girls down there. Reckon you could come with us, Joe.'

Charlie gave him a friendly clip round the ear. 'You ain't going nowhere, me old son. Well, not with us, anyway.'

'I hope you two ain't going out with girls,' said Milly. 'I never knows what you get up to when you're out.'

Ted grinned at Joe. 'Wouldn't tell you if we was.'

Katherine and Joe laughed together. She thought her heart would burst with the love she had for this family, and to see Joe happy again was more than she could have ever hoped for.

'We ain't had a day out on our own since Ted was born.' Milly's cheeks were flushed with excitement. 'But I must get over to see Dolly first.'

'Course, love. Think I might be able to manage next Sat'day afternoon, how would that suit you?'

Milly smiled at Charlie, and Katherine could see the great affection these two had for each other.

'That'll be lovely. You lot'll be all right, won't you?'

'No,' said Katherine gravely. 'I'm sure we'll starve and won't know—' She stopped when a tea towel flew through the air.

'You,' said Milly, walking round the table and picking the tea towel off the floor. 'Now, I'll leave something simmering so you won't have to worry.' She was interrupted by someone banging on the front door. 'Who can that be at this time o' night?'

'I'll go,' said Ted.

They all sat listening to the voices that floated back down the passage.

'That's Tom,' shouted Milly, jumping up. 'It's Tom and Dolly.' She ran out of the room.

Katherine's heart missed a beat. Were they alone, or was Gerald with them?

The voices stopped and it became very quiet.

Chapter 17

Katherine sat perched on the edge of the chair, shaking. All the fear and anger towards Gerald was closing in on her again. It seemed like a lifetime before Milly walked into the kitchen. Her face was ashen. Tom followed her, then Ted, who shut the kitchen door behind him. Tom was alone.

''Allo, mate. This is a nice surprise. How are you, then?' Charlie jumped up and shook Tom's hand vigorously. 'Where's Dolly?' he asked, noting Tom's concerned look.

'Sit down, Tom,' croaked Milly as tears streamed from her eyes. 'Charlie, our Dolly's dead.'

Katherine heard herself shout out loud, 'No, not Dolly. She can't be.'

Tom, who appeared to have aged a great deal, stood beside the table with his cap in his hand and his head bowed.

'Not our Dolly? Tom, what can I say?' Charlie clasped Tom to him and patted his back. 'I'm so very sorry. How did it happen?'

Katherine glanced at Joseph. The colour was visibly draining from his face.

'I'll make some tea,' said Katherine.

'Leave it a minute,' sniffed Milly. 'Let's hear what Tom's got to say first.'

Katherine sat down again. She didn't want to hear that her beloved Dolly had gone. She knew she would blame herself. If only she'd . . .

Tom was speaking very low. 'It was last night. Doctor said it was her heart. Mind you, she ain't been that well for a while

159

now.' He gave a weak smile. 'It's the way she always wanted to go.'

Milly sat at the table and dabbed at her eyes. 'I can't believe it,' she said softly. 'I ain't seen her for weeks. Sodding strike. I should have tried somehow to have got over there. I should have brought her back here.' With her anger Milly's voice rose with every sentence, and tears fell from her eyes. 'Never even said goodbye.'

'You can't blame yourself,' said Tom. 'It was meant to be. She was a stubborn old thing, and you wouldn't have got her here, not to live, anyway.'

Charlie put his arm round Milly's heaving shoulders.

Dolly, their round laughing Dolly, was no more. Katherine felt like an intruder. She wanted to share their grief, but felt it was wrong. She picked up the kettle that was always singing on the fire and took it into the scullery to make the tea.

Joseph was right behind her.

'Poor Dolly,' he whispered. 'I loved Dolly, Mama. She was like a lovely aunt and grandma all rolled into one.' A tear ran down his cheek and Katherine cradled him in her arms and, for a few moments, cried with him.

When he was in control he pulled away. 'I would have given up my room for her, you know.'

'I know you would.' Katherine wiped her eyes on the striped towel that hung on a nail behind the back door.

'What's Tom going to do now?' asked Joseph.

'I don't know. He may have to come here.'

'He can sleep on my mattress.'

'We will have to wait and see what he wants to do.'

Joseph went out the back door. Katherine let him be alone with his thoughts and grief. In his young life he had lost two people he had loved dearly, and who had helped shape his childhood.

As if in a dream, Katherine made the tea. The happy years she had spent with Dolly flooded back. The laughs and long conversations. But Katherine never really knew her. She didn't know her likes or dislikes, other than what was to do with running the house. She didn't know if she had ever wanted children. And Tom was always a quiet man who had kept his own counsel.

Katherine put the tea things on a tray and carried it back into the kitchen.

'Miss Katherine, you will come to her funeral, won't you?'

'Yes of course, Tom. When is it?'

'Thursday morning. That's what I've been doing all day – racing round trying to get things sorted out.'

She went and patted his hand. 'Don't worry, we will all be there. Now I expect you'll like a cup of tea?'

He nodded.

'What you gonner do now then, Tom?' asked Charlie.

'Dunno. Mr Gerald said I could stay on if I like, but I'm not sure.'

'Why don't you come over here when it's all over, just to give yourself breathing space?' said Milly softly.

'I might just do that. I need time to think. It'll be strange not having her around. Been together for over thirty-five years.'

'That's a bloody long time,' said Charlie. 'But as Milly said, there's always a bed here if you fancy it.'

'Thanks.'

'What did Gerald have to say about all this?' asked Katherine.

'Not a lot. Just that he was sorry, that's all.'

'Will he be at the funeral?'

'No, he said he's busy on that day and he'd rather leave it to the family.'

Katherine wanted to shout out, we don't want him sharing our grief, but was pleased she wouldn't be bumping into him.

'There won't be many there then, Tom?' asked Charlie.

'Na, just the family. Mind you, it's just as well if we've gotter fit in our couple of rooms after.'

Katherine thought about Edwin's funeral, and the large congregation that had filled the church, but there wasn't genuine love from that crowd, not like the love that would radiate from Dolly's true friends and relations.

'I'm sure Olive and Ernie will come, and what about you, Ted? Can you get the morning off?'

He nodded. Till now he had sat very quiet, just looking from one speaker to another.

'Someone had better go and tell Olive,' said Milly.

'Me and Joe will go,' said Ted. He seemed almost relieved to get away. 'I'll go an' get him.'

Ted found Joe sitting in the lavatory on the closed lid of the closet with the door wide open. 'What you doing in there?'

'Nothing. Just sitting thinking about the good times we had at that house. Dolly would always let me scrape the bowl when she made cakes. I loved Dolly, you know.'

Ted, his hands in his trouser pockets, gently kicked his foot against the door. 'We all did. But I wasn't lucky enough to know her really well.'

'She was a lovely lady.'

'Joe, wanner come round Olive's with me? Mum wants her to know.'

'Course.'

'You ain't gotter go home tonight, have you?' Milly asked Tom after the boys had left.

'No. Didn't get a lot of sleep last night. I don't have to go and sit with Dolly. The undertaker took her.' He blew his nose hard. 'Is it all right if I kip here just for tonight?'

'Course. Joe and Ted can go in together.'

'I don't want to put anybody out.'

Milly gave him a weak smile. 'This is the least I can do. I only wish I'd got the chance to see her 'fore she went.'

'I'm sure the undertaker will let you,' said Tom.

'Tom, what about money? Can you afford—'

'Don't worry about it. Me and Dolly have always put a bit by for a rainy day. Funny thing, Milly, she was on about sending you some as she guessed things was getting a bit rough for you.' He stopped. 'Never thought she'd be the first to go. I loved her, yer know, really loved her.' He buried his head in his hands and sobbed.

Katherine took the teatray into the scullery. He needed the family at this moment.

It wasn't long before Olive and Ernie came and joined this sad little gathering, and they sat and talked well into the night.

Katherine was nervous about going to the house again. If Gerald came back, how would she react? She knew nothing would stop her going to Dolly's funeral, but Katherine still hesitated as she made her way up the path to the house. She was pleased that everything looked the same. The roses were in full bloom, their scent wafted on the air. This had once been her house and she had loved it dearly.

'All right?' asked Charlie, coming out of the house and taking Katherine's arm.

She smiled. 'Yes, thanks. You go and look after Milly.'

'She wants to say her goodbye alone.'

'I can understand that.'

When Milly and the rest of the family had finished paying their respects, they came out of the tiny basement room where Dolly was lying, then Katherine and Joseph went in.

Dolly looked so peaceful.

Joseph gently kissed her brow, letting his tears fall on her face.

Katherine thought her heart would break for him and Dolly.

To see her lying there so still was very sad. Her face was thinner but a hint of a smile played round her lips. Katherine kissed her wrinkled forehead. She wanted to scoop her up and hold her, to breathe life into her. It was wrong, so wrong that a lovely lady like Dolly should go. She had been like a mother to her.

'You all right, Mama?' asked Joseph, wiping his eyes.

'Yes. Are you ready to go?'

He nodded.

Hand in hand they left the darkened room and walked out into the bright sunlight together.

The church was within walking distance and a vicar whom Katherine had not met before greeted them. She was grateful she didn't have to answer any questions. After Dolly was reverently and quietly laid to rest, the small party made their way back to Tom's.

They were sitting drinking tea when Gerald came in.

He stood in the doorway like the lord of the manor and gave them all a slight bow. He had a catlike smirk on his face. 'Hello, Katherine, Joseph.' He walked over and kissed her hand.

She wanted to pull it away but he was holding it very tight. 'Gerald, this is Dolly's sister and her husband, and their daughter and son-in-law.'

'We have met,' he said to Milly. 'And I am pleased to meet all of you, but I wish it were under better circumstances.'

The family only nodded in return.

'So, Joseph, you certainly have grown. Why don't you come and look at my motor car?'

Joseph looked at his mother. He didn't want to upset her.

'You may go if you want to.' Deep inside Katherine was seething. How dare he intrude on these kind people's grief? He hadn't even said a word about Dolly. And had Joseph forgotten why they had moved away from here? She wanted to tell Gerald to go and leave them alone, but she didn't want to make a fuss.

As they went through the door Gerald put his arm round Joseph's shoulders. 'So, my boy, how's life treating you?'

'Not too bad, sir.'

'If you don't mind me saying so, you don't look that prosperous, or well-dressed. Grown right out of your clothes, I see. Is that mother of yours looking after you?'

'Yes, sir. She works very hard.' Joseph tried hard to pull the sleeves of his jacket down.

Gerald stopped. 'She works?'

'Yes, sir. And so do I.'

Gerald looked shocked. 'You're working? What about school? Or can't your mother even afford that?'

'I only work on Saturdays, and that's at a garage. Mr Lacy, that's the owner, tells me all about the motors and shows me how they work.'

'Does he now? So what do you think of this one?'

As they rounded the corner Joseph stood and stared at the shiny black Humber. 'That is really beautiful,' he said wistfully.

'Have you ever been for a ride in one?'

'No, I've only sat in those we have, we don't have Humbers.'

'Well, come on, get in, we'll go for a little drive.'

Joseph desperately wanted to, but he knew his mother wouldn't approve and it would only cause friction. He looked at the house. 'I don't think . . .'

'Come on, don't worry about your mother. I'll explain to her that it was me who persuaded you. Now hop in.'

As they drove along Joseph thought he was in heaven. The smell of the leather as he sunk back into the seat was intoxicating. To own a motor car one day was what he wanted to do more than anything else in the world. To see the trees rushing past was, to him, pure magic. He wanted this moment to last for ever.

'So what do you think?' asked Gerald, as they turned back into the drive. 'She's lovely, isn't she?'

Joseph nodded and ran his hand along the walnut dashboard. 'She is wonderful.'

Gerald stopped. 'Is your Mr Lacy going to teach you to drive?'

'I hope so.'

'You know, Joseph, if you lived here I could teach you to drive this. Would you like that?'

'Yes, sir.' Joseph's eyes were sparkling.

'We'll have to have a word with your mother, won't we? And when you and your mother move back here, we could be a family. I'm looking forward to being a father.'

Joseph smiled. 'I don't think Mama would like that. I never called Edwin Father.'

Gerald laughed. 'I'm not talking about you, I'm talking about my child. Your mother will be back here for the birth of my child. I can't have it born in the slums.'

Joseph felt as if he had been kicked in the stomach. 'Child? What child?' he said softly.

'Didn't your mother tell you? She's having my baby. Well, she won't be able to keep her secret for long, not once she—'

Anger filled Joseph's face. 'You're lying,' he yelled. He raised his clenched fist to strike Gerald.

Gerald took hold of the boy's arm and held it tight. 'Don' t be so foolish,' he laughed. 'So, I assume by this little scene she hasn't told you?'

Tears welled up in Joseph's eyes. 'You're lying. My mother isn't having your baby.'

'Oh yes she is. Why don't you go and ask her?'

'She wouldn't, not with you. You attacked her. I saw her bruises.'

Gerald threw back his head and laughed. 'Is that what she told you? I guess you're old enough to know that sometimes, when two people are enjoying themselves, things can get out of hand. We were just having a little fun and games.'

Joseph felt physically sick. He ran from the car and threw himself against the door of Tom's flat.

'Good God,' said Milly, opening the door. 'Whatever's wrong with you?'

'Where's Mama?' he shouted.

Katherine came out of the kitchen and ushered him inside. 'Joseph,' she said angrily, 'please lower your voice.'

He threw himself at her and held her tight. 'Please say it isn't true,' he cried.

Katherine looked about her, embarrassed. 'What's not true?' Suddenly she realised what he was saying. 'Gerald,' she hissed. 'What has Gerald been telling you?'

Joseph stepped back. 'He said you were having his baby.'

There was a stunned silence from the room. Katherine felt all eyes on her. 'Milly, tell him it isn't true.'

Milly sobbed, 'I'm sorry, Katherine. It's all my fault.'

'It doesn't matter whose fault it was, just tell Joseph it isn't true.' Katherine's voice was loud and high-pitched.

'It ain't true now,' said Milly, dabbing at her eyes.

'Now?' said Joseph. 'What do you mean, "now"? So was it once?'

'Come on now, son. For a young boy you certainly ask a lot of questions.' Charlie looked uneasy.

'I ain't your son and I ain't a boy.'

'Joseph,' said Katherine, shocked at his outburst.

He was hurt and angry and, ignoring his mother, continued, 'And if you must know, since I've been living with you lot I've had to grow up, and that school I go to is a good place to learn about life.'

Mouths fell open.

It took all Katherine's strength for her to regain her dignity. 'You will apologise for talking to Charlie like that, young man.'

Joseph left the room in silence.

'I'll go and talk to him,' said Ted, hurrying behind him, eager to quell the situation.

'So,' said Charlie, 'what's this all about?'

'I'll tell you later,' said Milly. 'Wait till we get home.'

'You mean to say you was going to have a baby?' Olive's face was filled with disbelief.

'She's not now,' said Milly.

'And you knew all about it?' asked Charlie.

Milly's voice rose. 'For Christ's sake, Charlie, shut it. I told you I'll tell you later. I'm sorry, Tom. I shouldn't be shouting, not today . . .'

'This is all my fault. Tom, I'm so sorry about this. Please forgive me,' said Katherine.

'Don't worry about it.' He gave a little grin. 'At least it gave everybody something else to think about.'

Katherine put on her hat.

'Where you going?' asked Milly.

'I am going to find Gerald.'

'No, Katherine. No!' shouted Milly. 'You can't.'

Katherine swept past her, closing the door behind her.

Chapter 18

'Katherine, my dear, I always knew you would come looking for me.' Gerald came striding towards her where she stood on the doorstep. 'I'm so pleased to see that you are looking so very well and, I might add, as beautiful as ever, but if you don't mind me saying, not quite so smart.'

When he was close enough, she struck him hard round the face.

Putting his hand to his cheek he tried to laugh it off, but Katherine could see the anger in his eyes.

'So, to what do I owe this little outburst of temper? It can't be because I don't approve of your gown.'

Katherine could smell the drink on his breath and her thoughts quickly went to Mr Addams. What was it about drink? Did men need it to give them courage? Gerald angered her so much that she knew she couldn't talk rationally to him, so she turned and began to walk away. 'No. It wasn't just for your bad manners,' she said over her shoulder.

Gerald fell in step beside her. 'I'm sorry, that wasn't very gentlemanly of me. Please forgive me.'

'You know very well why I came to see you.'

'I know.' He jokingly put his hands up in a gesture of surrender. 'It's because I took Joseph out in my motor car. I didn't think you would disapprove so . . .'

Katherine suddenly stopped. 'You know full well I am not here to talk about that. How dare you say the things you did to Joseph?'

He took hold of her elbow, forcibly moving her along the path. 'Like what?'

She tried to shrug his arm away. 'Don't you think he has had enough to put up with without you upsetting him?'

'Oh, I know, you must be talking about our child. And he wouldn't "have to put up with" it, as you so charmingly put it – my, we are going downhill with our phrases, aren't we? – if you hadn't been foolish enough to move out.'

'There is no child.'

'Now you don't think for one moment I am going to believe that?'

'I can look you in the eye and tell you there is no child.'

'So why would Dolly's sister tell me otherwise?'

'You had better ask her.' Katherine tried to pull her arm away from his tight grip.

'I don't believe you.'

'You can think what you like. And if there had been a child I would never have told you.'

He pulled her round to face him, his eyes narrowed. 'I said I don't believe you. Now you just listen to me. When this child is born I will take it from you and have it brought up respectably in this house under my guidance. I can find out where you live and if need be, I'll bring you back here and keep you till after the birth, then you can go wherever you like. But you will go alone.'

She laughed in his face. 'You, sir, are unbalanced.'

'I've been trying to find out where you went, but Dolly and that tight-lipped husband of hers kept it very quiet. I even thought of telling them I'd found Edwin's will.'

Katherine looked up.

'I knew that would get your attention.'

'Did you?'

'No,' smirked Gerald, 'sadly for you, he really didn't leave one. No, I've been giving our situation a lot of thought. It was a bit of luck, Dolly dying. I knew you would be here for the funeral.'

'How dare you think Dolly's death was a "bit of luck"? I'm not going to listen to this.'

'You will listen.' He clasped the tops of her arms with both hands. Despite the protection of her coat she could feel his fingers digging into her flesh. 'You see, I want my name to carry on. I know I could have any woman I choose but I like your bloodstock.'

Katherine laughed again and broke free from his grip. 'My bloodstock. You know nothing about me.'

'I knew from Edwin that you were a determined woman who would face up to any challenge. And to come from Australia alone meant you were a fighter. But it was your beauty that made all the other women pale into insignificance. Men would envy me when they saw you on my arm. You know what they say about redheads – full of fire and passion.' He stood back and looked her up and down. 'I must admit I am a little disappointed by the way you have finished up, but we can change all that.'

'I'm not going to stand here and listen to your mad ravings!'

'Edwin wasn't man enough for you, but when that woman told me you were having my baby, I was overjoyed. You are certainly a woman I approve of to be the mother of my child.'

Katherine went to move away but he blocked her path.

'I've worked it out. So when I think you are almost due I'll come and get you. I don't intend keeping you till it's necessary.'

Katherine thought she was hearing things and laughed. It was a loud nervous laugh. 'Gerald. There is no child now. I lost it.'

He looked as if he'd been struck. His cheeks began to twitch and his face turned scarlet with temper. He clenched his fists. Katherine began to slowly back away, suddenly fearing for her life.

'How did that happen?'

'Mother nature.'

'I'll hang for you. Taking my child away.'

'You can't prove it.'

He raised his hand.

'Mama!'

'Joseph,' cried Katherine.

'I've overheard all you've said. Gerald, Mama is right, you are mad.'

Katherine picked up her skirts and ran to her son's side. He was right, he wasn't a boy any longer. He had grown up.

From the expression on Gerald's face, Katherine thought he would explode he was so angry.

'Get out. Get out. Don't you ever come to this house again. And take that . . . that gardener with you, do you hear?' He wagged a finger at them. 'Tell him you have just lost him his home and his job.'

Katherine took hold of her son's hand and hurried away.

'Don't worry about it, Miss Katherine. I ain't sorry to go.'

When Katherine and Joseph walked into Tom's she decided to tell them all what had happened. She told them she had lost the baby, but she could see in Olive's face that she knew, and that she disapproved, but then she was young and had a husband.

'I'm so sorry, Tom,' said Katherine.

'He is bloody mad, if you ask me,' said Charlie.

'Look, we had better start getting Tom's things together,' said Ernie, looking towards the door. He was very agitated. 'We don't want him here causing trouble.'

'It'll be over my dead body,' said Charlie.

'Don't underestimate him,' said Katherine.

'Right,' said Milly. 'All grab a bag and start filling 'em. Charlie, take the sheets off the bed and fill 'em with the bedding, then tie 'em up.'

'We ain't got that much,' said Tom.

'I know, but we ain't leaving nothing.' Milly was in her element, organising.

They were loaded with bags and bundles as they all made their way down the drive.

Katherine turned and looked back at the house. Tears filled her eyes at the happy memories of long ago. She knew she would never return.

'It's all over now,' said Milly, putting her bundles on the ground and putting her arm round Katherine's shoulders.

'Yes, yes it is.' Katherine turned away.

It was too late for her to go to Trent's, and although she would be a day's pay short she didn't care.

As they sat on the bus Katherine thought about Dolly. In many ways she would have enjoyed today. She always loved a bit of scandal, but she would never have approved of what Katherine had done.

'Thought you might have made a bit of effort to get back yesterday afternoon,' said Josh when Katherine walked in on the Friday morning.

'There was a bit of trouble so I had to stay and help them sort it out.'

'Look, Kate, I know I let you down when the strike was on, but I didn't have a lot of choice now, did I?'

'What's brought this on?'

'Nothing.'

Ron, the bookies' runner, who was sitting at a table reading his paper, peered at her from under his large cloth cap. He was a small thin man whose eyes quickly darted about. He was always on the lookout for the law. He was friendly and enjoyed a laugh. 'He's only just found out what an asset you are to this place.'

Katherine laughed. 'I'm always telling him that.'

'Rushing round yesterday dinnertime like a blue-arse fly, he was.' Ron stood up and threw the butt end of his hand-rolled cigarette on to the floor and ground it out. 'Gotter go. Got a few bets to put on. See yer tomorrow, Josh, Katie.'

Katherine began singing as she worked.

'What you so bloody happy about?'

'Lot of things.'

'Well, pour out a cuppa for Nellie.'

'Shall I take it up?'

'If yer like.'

Katherine smiled. 'My, we are an old grumpy head this morning.' She ducked when she saw the dishcloth come flying through the air. She knew she made him happy, and he didn't want to lose her, so that could strengthen her position in the future.

'Hello, Nellie,' said Katherine, confidently walking into the bedroom.

'You're bloody cheerful today. Who's died and left you a fortune?'

'Nobody. It's just that suddenly I feel in control of my life. How about you, don't you wish you were in control?'

'No I don't.'

Katherine laughed. 'I could make you a lot more comfortable, you know.'

Nellie's eyes twitched. 'Why should you bother with me?'

Katherine sat on the bed. 'Because I think it's such a waste, you stuck up here on a lovely day like today. Don't you miss seeing the blue sky?'

'Can see it from me bed if I move round a bit.'

'Please yourself. But I'm sure with a bit of pampering life could be a lot better for you. Shall I close the door?'

'No, leave it open.'

Katherine smiled as she went down the stairs. She knew she was gaining Nellie's confidence.

Katherine piled pies, mash, saveloys and pease pudding on to plates, and jellied eels into bowls to be devoured here or taken home. She wiped her brow, it was warm work. After the lunchtime rush Josh went to the wash house out at the back of the shop to peel the potatoes for tomorrow. Katherine began cleaning the counter when the girl who arranged to meet men here walked in.

'Tea?' asked Katherine.

'Yer.'

'If you sit down I'll bring it over.'

'Why?'

'No reason.'

The girl eyed Katherine with suspicion. 'How long you been working here?'

'Must be, what, nearly three months.' Katherine put the tea on the table. All this time she had been intrigued with this girl but never had the chance to speak to her at length.

The girl lit a cigarette. 'You got any kids?'

'I have a son.'

'He at work?'

'No, still at school.'

'How old is he?'

'Thirteen.'

'Thirteen, and still at school? Blimey! I was out earning me living at ten.'

Katherine sat at the table. 'And how long ago was that?'

'Mind yer own business.' The girl pushed strands of her dark fuzzy hair under her large black hat.

'Don't you have any family?'

The girl blew smoke into the air. 'Why?'

'Are they dead?' asked Katherine softly.

The girl threw her head back and laughed. 'Na, the bloke me mum lives with has just come out of prison.'

When the girl's customer walked in, Katherine left the table.

They went out, leaving the smell of cheap scent behind. Katherine wondered where the girl took the men, and why she didn't finish up in the family way.

Tom was finding it difficult to settle down without Dolly. He couldn't get used to the idea of not working, and felt ill at ease hanging around the house all day, despite Milly trying to keep him busy with the odd job or two.

Even when Charlie told him he was pleased to have a drinking partner that didn't bring a smile to his sad face.

'P'raps Alf could find you a job in the pub,' said Charlie.

'That might not be a bad idea. I'll sound him out. I'll have to find work soon. Me money ain't gonner last for ever, and I don't expect you two to keep me in shirt buttons.'

Milly had told him to take his time in whatever he wanted to do.

Katherine knew he had quite a bit of money, and Milly didn't take a lot from him, but he was an independent man, and would always want to pay his way. He would go off for hours, not telling anyone where he'd been. Milly said she thought he went to the cemetery.

The other members of the Stevens household appeared to be contented.

Joseph was happy at the garage and eagerly waiting for his mother to let him leave school so he could work there full time. Everyone was pleased that he didn't cause any fuss about giving up the front room to Tom.

Ted's sixteenth birthday had come and gone. He was a young man now, but he still seemed to enjoy Joe's company.

On August Bank Holiday Monday Charlie and Milly took Tom to Southend-on-Sea for the day, and they enjoyed every minute of it. For days afterwards Milly talked about it.

At the shop Katherine was gradually winning Nellie's

confidence and now they often had a little chat. She still hadn't found out what was wrong with her, and why she stayed in bed. Katherine was pleased that at last she was managing to save a little from her wages, so things were definitely looking up.

The one person who seemed to be avoiding her was Briony. Even if Katherine went along to the ironmongers Briony made an excuse to hurry home and not to talk to Katherine. Did she really think that she, Katherine, was meeting her father?

It was Saturday evening, and Ted stood in front of the mirror, putting grease on his hair.

'Out again then, son?' asked Charlie.

Ted had been going out looking smart for a few weeks now, so everyone guessed he was meeting a young lady. He always said he was meeting Joe, but when Katherine consulted her son, he said he didn't know what she was talking about. They were keeping close together on this issue.

'What you tarting yourself up for, son? Got yourself a girl then?'

'No I ain't. I'm just going out, that's all.'

'I can see that,' Charlie laughed. 'Just as long as you remember to polish yer courting tackle.'

'Charlie Stevens, don't be so rude. Just leave him be. Have you got yourself a young lady then, Ted?' Milly had been dying to know.

Ted's cheeks turned bright red. 'No I ain't. I'm gonner meet Joe from work.'

'Joe didn't say he was going out,' said Katherine, grinning.

'He might not want to come tonight.' Ted was beginning to get flustered.

'I see.' Katherine gave Milly a knowing look.

'So where you going then, Ted?'

'I dunno, Mum. Don't keep on.'

'Move over, son,' said Charlie, pushing Ted away from the mirror. 'Let the dog see the rabbit. Me and Tom are just going out for a quick one, we won't be long.'

Milly tutted. 'I've heard all that before. Go on, be off with you. Good job I've got Katherine to keep me company.'

Charlie kissed Milly's cheek. 'See yer later, love.'

When they'd gone, Milly sat back in the armchair. 'I'm worried about Tom. He can't settle down at all.'

'It's hard for him to lose his job as well as Dolly. I still feel I'm to blame for that.'

'I dunno. I reckon that Gerald would have made his life a misery if he'd stayed there.'

'I think I'm inclined to agree with you,' said Katherine.

Ted poked his head round the door. 'I'm off, see you later.'

'Don't make too much noise when you come in,' Milly grinned. 'They can be a pair of noisy buggers when they get together. I wonder what they're up to.'

'They have been very secretive lately.'

'They're always that. It's all this going out tidy that worries me.'

'I haven't noticed Joseph going out tidy.'

'No, that's what worries me. I reckon my Ted's paying him to keep quiet.'

'Now that I can understand.' Katherine laughed. 'It's good to see Joseph happy. Moving here was the best thing that happened to both of us,' she said.

All evening they sat and talked. Milly was busy knitting and getting excited about the new baby. 'I'm very lucky. I've got so much.'

Katherine glanced at the clock. 'Ten o' clock. Joseph must have gone out with Ted. I hope he had something to eat at work.'

'Just like a mother. More worried about her son's stomach than who he's with.'

'He's with Ted.'

'Yes I know, but is there two young ladies?'

They laughed.

'I shouldn't think so,' said Katherine. 'Not if he went out in those dirty overalls.'

'That's true. I wonder where they've gone.'

'I'm sure they'll tell us if they want to.'

Their peace was shattered by someone banging hard on the front door.

Milly's face turned deathly white. 'Who can that be at this time of night?'

'I don't know. Perhaps it's Ernie, perhaps Olive's started.'

Milly jumped up. 'Of course. It must be him, silly bugger. He wouldn't use the key.' She flew down the passage and opened the door.

'Oh my God!' screamed Milly, her raised voice full of alarm.

For a second or two Katherine sat riveted, then she also raced up the passage.

Chapter 19

Katherine stood next to Milly, whose eyes were wide open at the sight of Briony standing there. 'Briony,' she whispered. 'What's happened?'

The young girl had blood on her face, hands and down the front of her frock. 'Ted, Ted,' she cried.

'Ted. My Ted?' screamed Milly.

Briony nodded, her thin body racked with sobs.

Milly sprang at her like a caged animal. 'What you done with my Ted?'

Mrs Duke suddenly appeared on the doorstep. 'What's all this racket? What the bleeding hell's going—' She didn't finish the sentence as she helped Katherine to prise Milly away from Briony.

Tears mingled with the blood on Briony's cheeks, turning the bright red smears to a soft watery pink. 'I ain't done nothing to Ted. I was supposed to meet him. I need him to help . . .' She couldn't finish the sentence.

Milly lunged at Briony again and, grabbing her shoulders, shook her violently. 'My Ted! What was you doing with my Ted? I'll kill you if you've hurt him.'

'It ain't Ted,' said Briony, sobbing and shaking her head.

'What's she bin doing with young Ted?' asked Mrs Duke.

'I don't know,' said Katherine. 'You'd better come in.' Katherine was pulling Milly away. 'We don't want all the neighbours to hear.'

'I can't leave the kids. I've got to go back. Please help me. It ain't Ted, missis, it's me dad.' She ran the back of her hand under her wet nose.

Milly jumped back as if she'd been scalded. 'Your dad? What's he done to my Ted?'

'Briony, what's happened?' Katherine was trying to take control.

'He's dead. Me dad's dead.'

Katherine also took a step back.

Mrs Duke put her hand to her mouth and let out a long gasp. 'Oh my God. How?'

All three women were dreading the answer.

'I've killed him.'

The silence that followed seemed to go on for ever.

Suddenly Milly broke the silence. 'What did you say?'

Briony didn't speak.

'How? Dead?' blustered Mrs Duke.

'Are you sure he's dead?' asked Katherine softly.

Briony nodded.

'We'd better go over and see,' said Katherine.

'Where's my Ted?' screamed Milly.

'I don't know, I ain't seen him,' sobbed Briony. 'I was s'posed to, but I . . .' Tears drowned the rest of the sentence.

'You was meeting my Ted?'

'Milly, let's talk about this later. Look, why don't you make her a cup of tea? Mrs Duke, you'd better come with me.'

'I can't leave the kids in there, not with . . .' sniffed Briony, 'Oh missis, please help me.'

Katherine threw her arms round Briony and held her close, as sobs racked her thin frail body. Katherine could have cried for this poor child who suddenly appeared small and vulnerable. She had lost all her bravado and courage.

'We'd better all come back with you,' said Milly.

They hurried across the road. Mrs Duke was shuffling and panting behind them, having a job to keep up.

Briony pushed open the front door. 'It's all right, kids, it's me.'

The three women stood in the dark smelly passage. The kitchen door flew open and a tight bunch of youngsters raced up to Briony and flung themselves at her, all trying to get as close as possible. Slowly they moved into the kitchen.

'Have you told 'em?' Bridget was standing in the corner, her voice harsh. Even in the dim gaslight they could see the tears glistening on her ashen face. She too had blood on her frock, and a baby on her hip.

Briony shook her head. 'Only that Dad is dead.'

'What's been happening over here?' asked Mrs Duke.

'Did she tell yer she done it 'cos she was jealous of me?'

'Jealous of you?' asked Katherine.

Bridget came towards them. She poked Briony in the shoulder with a skinny finger. 'Yer, she didn't like Dad being nice to me.'

'Nice? You call that being nice?' yelled Briony, taking the baby from her.

'Well, I liked it,' said Bridget. 'She didn't like it 'cos he showed her he loved me the best.' Bridget stood with her arms folded defiantly.

'It ain't love, it's dirty. And it's wrong,' said Briony.

'What's she talking about?' asked Mrs Duke.

Briony lowered her head. 'Me dad said he loved us, and he used to . . . He used to do things to us.'

'You don't mean . . . ?' Katherine hesitated. 'You don't mean touch your private parts?' she whispered.

Briony nodded.

'Bloody hell,' said Mrs Duke. 'The dirty sod. You mean ter say he . . . you know, to both of you?'

Briony looked up. 'He done it to me for a long while, even when Mum was here, but I didn't tell anyone. I didn't like it and he said if I told anyone he'd beat me and say it wasn't true.'

'How long has this been going on?' asked Katherine.

'With me, years,' said Briony. The baby began crying and she tried to comfort it with soothing noises and kisses.

'She didn't like it, but I did,' Bridget told them. 'When Dad took hold of me and kissed me and put his hands all over me it was lovely.'

Milly took the fretful baby from Briony and gently rocked it back and forth.

'Don't say that. Stop it, stop it!' Briony put her hands over her ears. 'It wasn't lovely, it was rotten. He hurt me.' She buried her head in Katherine's bosom.

'Well, I liked it,' said Bridget.

'Where were your brothers when all this was going on?' asked Katherine.

'They left home. They went after Mum died,' said one of the younger boys.

'Thought I ain't seen 'em around,' said Mrs Duke.

'How old are you, Bridget?' asked Milly.

'Thirteen.'

'Thirteen,' repeated Milly. 'Still a baby.'

'I ain't a baby, missis.'

'No, you're not, not now.'

'Briony,' said Katherine, gently pushing her away, 'where's your dad?'

'He's dead,' shouted another little Addams. 'Our dad's dead. Briony done it. She said she done it.'

'Where is he?' asked Katherine.

'Upstairs. I'll show you.'

'I'll go and look, you lot stay down here. Bridget, make sure they don't come up.'

Bridget pouted. 'Why? They've seen him.'

'I said, stay down here.' Katherine's voice was forceful.

'I'll stay here with them,' said Milly, still rocking the baby.

Slowly Katherine and Briony mounted the bare wooden stairs, with Mrs Duke close behind.

'Be careful. We ain't got any banisters 'cos me dad broke them up for firewood last winter. And watch your step in the bedroom as some of the floorboards is missing as well.'

She stood in the doorway. There was no door – that too must have been used for firewood. Katherine gently moved Briony to one side.

Mrs Duke, who was breathing heavily down Katherine's neck, peered into the room. The curtains, which looked like bits of rag, were stretched across the window. They could see Mr Addams lying on the bed. An old coat had been thrown over him, but a bare leg was sticking out.

Mrs Duke spoke first. 'Oh my God. What have you done?' She moved carefully into the room.

Katherine put her arm round Briony's shoulders and eased her away. 'What happened?'

'I didn't mean to kill him.'

'I'm sure you didn't.'

'Will they hang me?'

'Briony,' Katherine tried to keep the tone of her voice level, 'how did it happen?'

The frightened girl leant against the wall, fear in her eyes. 'I caught him with Bridget. He shouldn't have done it, not to her,' she sobbed.

Mrs Duke came and stood with them. 'He's dead, all right. Stabbed in the back. The knife's still in him, and he's starkers, naked as a new-born babe. We'd better get a copper.'

Briony began to shake uncontrollably. Her teeth chattered and her whole body was convulsing.

Katherine held her tight. 'No, wait,' she said, over her shoulder.

'What? Why? They've got to come and bring a doctor.'

'Just a minute. Wait till she calms down and can tell us how it happened.'

'We can see how it happened, she's stabbed him.'

Milly met them at the bottom of the stairs. 'Is he dead?'

'Yes,' said Katherine. 'Look, why don't you take all of them over to your house and give Briony a cup of hot sweet tea? She needs something to help her get over the shock.'

Mrs Duke straightened up. 'Well, I wouldn't have her in my house. She's a murderer. She might do for you if you take her to your place.'

'Don't talk such a load of rot. She thought she was protecting her sister.' Katherine was angry. Angry with Mrs Duke. Angry with Mr Addams. Angry with Briony, and angry with Bridget for allowing this to happen.

'Load of rot, is it? Always said there was something funny with this family and now they've proved it. Bad seed, the lot of 'em. You wait till my Stanley and the rest of the fellas hears about this. They'll run 'em out of the street, they will – all of 'em, kids an' all.'

'If you've quite finished, Mrs Duke, we'll be off,' said Milly. 'Perhaps you would like to go to the police then?'

'You bet I will!' She stomped down the stairs.

'Will she run the kids out of the house?' asked Briony. She looked at Katherine, her beautiful blue eyes red and swollen.

'No, she's all talk,' said Milly. 'Now come on, come and have a cup of tea.' Milly ushered Briony and the little band out of the door and across the road.

Bridget stood at the bottom of the stairs. 'I ain't going over there. I'm gonner stay here with me dad.'

Katherine looked at her. She wasn't going to argue, as she realised that the girl could still be in shock. 'Please yourself. You know where to find us when you feel like it.'

'Will they put Briony away?'

'I would think so.'

'What about the kids?'

'They will probably have to go in a home.'

'What about me?'

'I expect you will have to go with them as well.'

'I ain't going to no home.'

'Well, we will have to wait and see what happens. Now if you're staying here, when the police arrive you can tell them where Briony is.'

Katherine didn't want to leave her, but she knew if she tried to force her it would end up with a screaming match.

As Katherine made her way across the road her mind was in turmoil. She tried to imagine what must have been happening in that house. Poor Briony. They had been worried about Mr Wilks from the ironmonger's interfering with her. They never dreamt her father was doing things like that. Tears filled Katherine's eyes. And how was Ted involved? Were they lovers? Poor Briony, she could be hanged for murder.

They were sitting drinking tea when the front door slammed and they heard Ted and Joe laughing and talking all the way down the passage. Their laughter stopped when they opened the kitchen door and saw so many sad faces.

Briony ran up to Ted and threw her arms around his neck. 'I'm sorry I didn't meet you. I was . . .' She broke into more tears.

Ted's face flushed. He looked from one to the other, confused and embarrassed. He untwined Briony's arms from around his neck and, pushing her away, stepped back. 'What's going on?'

'Sit down, son,' said Milly. 'Something terrible's happened.'

'Our Briony's killed our dad,' said one of the children.

'What?' said Ted.

'I'm afraid it's true,' said Milly.

Joseph quickly took a breath. He looked bewildered as he glanced round the room at all the faces staring at them.

'How? Why?' asked Ted.

Briony sat down. 'I didn't tell you what me dad did to me, and when I saw him doing it with Bridget – well, I just lost me temper and got a knife . . .' Once again the tears fell.

Ted also sat down. 'You mean you killed your dad?'

She nodded.

'Why? What did he do that made—'

'Ted! Don't be so innocent, you know?'

He looked at his mother. His face became angry. 'He did that to you? And to Bridget? Then he bloody well got what he deserved!'

'Yes, but what about Briony?' asked Katherine.

'We'll just tell everybody what happened. They'll all say good job.'

'Not in the eyes of the law they won't.'

'You don't think . . . She won't go to prison, will she?'

'We will just have to wait for the police,' said his mother.

'Billy, leave that alone. I'm sorry, missis. Now you listen, kids. Don't you dare touch anything.'

Always the little mother, thought Katherine as Briony sat screwing the handkerchief she had given her into a tight knot.

It wasn't long after that the rumpus in the passage told them that Charlie and Tom were home. They must have arrived at the front door at the same time as the police and the doctor.

'What the bleeding hell's going on? There's a couple of coppers here and a Black Maria outside. What's this lot doing here?' demanded Charlie as he pushed open the kitchen door and saw the room full.

'For Gawd's sake sit down and I'll tell you all about it,' said Milly.

Katherine took the doctor across the road. When the police had been told all that had happened, and they had seen the body, they took Briony into Milly's front room.

'Will she go to prison?' asked Ted again.

'I'm afraid so,' said Katherine.

'What you been doing with young Briony then?' asked Charlie.

'I ain't done nothing. We just went out a couple of times, that's all. She's a nice girl.'

'So, Joseph, what were you doing while Ted was out with Briony?' asked Katherine.

'I stayed on at work.'

'Why didn't you tell us you was meeting Briony?' asked Milly.

'I didn't say 'cos I knew you wouldn't approve.'

'Too bloody right we wouldn't!' said Charlie. 'Bloody lot of scum bags, they are.'

'No we ain't!' protested Billy.

'See? Briony's not!' shouted Ted. 'She's nice, and what her dad did to her was rotten, really rotten. She's tried to look after all of them, but her dad never give her much money, she had to pinch it out of his pockets when he came home drunk, and he used to beat her.' Ted was almost in tears. 'I liked her, she was nice.'

The silence that followed was almost unbearable.

'I'll make another cup of tea,' said Katherine.

The kitchen door opened and one of the policemen came in.

'The doctor's getting in touch with the Salvation Army to take the kids away. Can they stay here till then?'

'How long for?' asked Charlie.

'Shouldn't be too long.'

'What about Bridget?' asked Katherine.

'She'll have to go as well. The doctor will be making the arrangements about the body. Trouble is it's late, and it may be a while before he can get things moving.'

'What about Briony?' asked Milly.

'She's coming with us to the police station.'

'What will happen to her?'

'She'll be charged with murder.'

'But she's only a child,' said Katherine.

'That's as maybe, but it's still murder.'

'Will they hang her?' asked Charlie.

'That's up to the judge. We've got to be off now.'

The shout that came from the front door sent them all racing out of the kitchen. They became wedged in the passage but were in time to see Briony run out of the house with a burly policeman behind her.

The kids started shouting. 'Go on, Bri! Run for it!'

'You've let her get away!' yelled the senior policeman, pushing past them.

'Couldn't help it, Sarge,' the other one said when they reached the street. 'She slipped away before I got a chance to put her in the van.'

'She won't get far.'

Ted grinned as the sergeant straightened his jacket.

'Where will she go?' asked Milly.

'Dunno,' said Ted.

'She went that way,' said Mrs Duke, who was standing at her door and pointing up the street.

'Could see that, missis, couldn't I?' said the policeman.

'Well, come on then,' said the sergeant. 'Let's get moving. We'll soon catch her up.'

As they drove away Milly turned to Mrs Duke. 'Trust you to have your two penn'orth! You didn't have to be so bloody helpful, did you?'

'She can't get away with it. After all, murder's murder, ain't it?' she said pompously.

'That's as maybe,' said Katherine, 'but at least it's not on our conscience that we didn't try to help her.'

Mrs Duke tossed her head, tutted, and went indoors.

Chapter 20

For the few short hours that were left of the night, nobody got a lot of sleep. As soon as dawn broke everybody began milling about. Milly began to worry that the Salvation Army had forgotten they had to collect the children. The house was at bursting point with kids screaming and yelling everywhere, and a steady stream filing out to the lav.

'It seems as if they've multiplied overnight,' said Katherine.

'You two!' shouted Milly, pointing a spoon at a pair of them. 'Stop that fighting!'

'She started it,' said the boy, picking his nose.

'I don't care who started it, I said stop it.' Milly sighed and carried on dishing out plates of porridge. 'I dread to think what it looks like out there,' she said, nodding in the direction of the back door as another child slipped down from the table and made his way through the scullery and outside.

'It wasn't too bad when I went out,' said Katherine, taking the youngest from the battered old bassinet.

'Do you think the police told them where they are?'

'Of course. Maybe it's because it's Sunday and they're busy,' said Katherine, as she changed the rag that was the baby's nappy.

'Even so, they should be looking after this lot.' Milly dished up more porridge to fill eager mouths.

'I'm sure we can manage for a bit longer. Just look at the state of this poor little mite's bottom.'

Milly straightened up. 'It's a bloody shame all round. I don't know what Ted and Joe think they were doing, dashing off like

191

that first thing. How do they reckon they're gonner find Briony? I told 'em I reckon she's in clink, but they wouldn't listen.'

'Well, it gives them something to do.'

'S'pose so.'

Katherine admired Milly. She had been so good, and was making these children as comfortable as possible. For a few hours they had slept huddled together on the kitchen floor, and now she was busy giving them breakfast.

'When will Briony come back?' asked one little girl as she stuffed spoonfuls of porridge into her mouth.

'I don't know,' said Katherine, who was busy buttering bread as fast as she could.

'Will Bridget come here?'

'I don't think so,' said Milly. She had been over the road earlier to collect what few clothes the Addams children had, and asked Bridget to come and have some breakfast, but she said she wouldn't leave her dad whose body was still in the house.

Two of the children giggled. 'She don't know what she's missing.'

'We don't get stuff like this at home.'

'Will we get nice food when we're in that home?' The little voices excitedly filled the kitchen.

'I expect so,' said Katherine. To them this was almost an outing.

It wasn't until after her father's body had been taken away that Bridget asked to come in.

'Would you like something to eat?' Milly asked her.

She nodded.

'Missis here said we'll get good food in the home.'

Bridget looked at the child who had spoken. 'We might all be separated.'

'Na, they wouldn't do that, would they, missis?'

Milly shrugged. 'I don't know.'

Charlie came into the kitchen. 'It's a good job I ain't still on strike. Couldn't afford to feed this lot if I was.'

'Well you ain't,' said Milly crossly. 'And a bit of bread and porridge don't cost the earth.'

He pulled a funny face. 'Pardon me. Sorry I spoke.'

One of the kids laughed. 'You ain't half funny, mister. Our dad wasn't funny.'

Charlie looked at his hands. 'Yes, well, enjoy your breakfast.' He went out to the lav.

Later that morning the Salvation Army came and took the children away. The youngest was bundled with what few bits they had into the large bassinet. There were no tears as they marched up the street. Katherine, Charlie, Tom and Milly stood at the door and watched them go. So, it appeared, did all of Croft Street.

'Bloody hell!' said Charlie. 'I reckon they'll be selling tickets soon.'

'Are those the kids of the murdered man?' asked a man whom they'd noticed asking questions of the women up the road. 'That woman said you've been looking after them, that right?' He was writing in a notebook.

Katherine noted Mrs Duke was among the gossips.

'Who wants to know?' asked Charlie.

'I'm Fred, a reporter.'

'Are you now? Well, I'm Charlie, a stevedore.'

Milly laughed nervously.

'No, come on. What's this all about? My boss told me to find out if it's true that his daughter killed him. Then it seems she was full of remorse and last night threw herself under a train. Poor little cow.'

Katherine felt her legs go from under her. 'Oh no!' she cried out. 'Not Briony.' She held on to Charlie's arm to steady herself.

Milly's face drained of colour. 'Ted.'

'You'd better come inside,' said Charlie.

Katherine and Milly sat at the kitchen table that was still full of breakfast things, in a state of shock.

'I'll make 'em a cuppa,' said Charlie.

'I'm sorry, ladies, I thought you knew. Everybody in Croft Street seems to.'

'Ted. Where's Ted?' asked Milly.

'Who's Ted, Mrs . . .?'

'My son.'

'What's he to do with all this?'

'Nothing,' said Charlie quickly. 'He's just popped out.'

'Poor Briony,' whispered Katherine. 'What happened?'

'As I said, she threw herself under a train late last night. Right old mess, be all accounts. The poor train driver's in a bit of a state. She was what, only thirteen?'

'Fourteen,' corrected Katherine, trying to keep her voice under control. She didn't want this man to see how much this news had upset her.

'Still, it's a good thing in a way. Saves her all that trouble of a trial and being hanged in the end.'

'Get out!' shouted Katherine. 'Get out!'

'Why? What have I done?'

'You'd better go,' said Charlie.

'Sorry I spoke,' said the young man.

Milly stood up. 'She was a lovely girl who looked after those kids when her mother died. So don't you dare say anything bad about her.'

'Go on, clear off,' said Charlie, holding the kitchen door open.

The reporter closed his notebook. 'Not to worry. Got all the details I need from your neighbours. Just wanted to make sure I got all the dirt. All right if I send a photographer round?'

'No it ain't! Now scram before I start to lose me temper,' said Charlie.

The young man stood up. 'OK. Keep yer hair on. Well, so long, all. Nice meeting yer.' He sauntered to the door just as Katherine threw a plate at him. It crashed against the jamb.

'Who crawled up her?'

'Get out!' shouted Katherine.

Charlie, who was taller and bigger built than the hack, grabbed his coat. 'You heard the lady.'

The young man left the room in a hurry and slammed the front door after him.

'Sorry about that,' said Katherine, fighting back the tears as she swept up the mess. 'I'll get a new one tomorrow.'

'Don't worry about it. I only wished I'd done it, and it had hit him.'

'Look, I'm going out to find Ted,' said Charlie.

'I'll come with you,' said Tom, who had been very quiet all through. 'Poor little mite. Bad business, this.' He shook his head. 'Bad business.'

After they left, Katherine and Milly sat for a while with their thoughts.

'I'll have to ask the police where they'll be burying her,' said Katherine as she let the tears trickle down her cheeks.

'I can't believe all this has happened.' Milly began absent-mindedly to pile up the dirty plates that were strewn over the table.

'I can't believe she would commit suicide. Not with the family to worry about. She was such a bright girl, she should have had everything to live for.'

'You always liked her, didn't you?'

'Yes.'

'I wonder what would have happened if Ted had got really serious?'

'I think he would have had a lot of trouble from Charlie.'

'For a while. But I could have got him to see sense if Ted had been really fond of her.'

'I think he was. But he won't say, not now.'

'That's something we'll never know.'

'She'll have to be buried in a pauper's grave,' said Katherine. 'What about her father? We never did find out where her mother and that baby were buried, unfortunately, otherwise they could have all been together.'

Tears quickly fell from Katherine's eyes. She was angry. 'What a wicked waste of lives. What a wicked waste.'

'You never know what goes on behind closed doors,' said Milly.

'More's the pity,' said Katherine.

Katherine was in her bedroom when Joseph, along with Ted, Charlie and Tom, returned.

'Can I come in?' asked Joseph at her door.

' 'Course. Have you heard what happened to Briony?'

Joseph nodded.

'Sit down. How's Ted taking it?'

He sat on the bed. 'Very upset. He liked her, you know.'

'We didn't till last night.'

'We went to the police station when some old women said a girl had been hit by a train. Somehow we knew it was Briony. They told us it was her and showed Ted a bit of the frock she was wearing.'

'Oh my God! Poor Ted. Why did they do that?'

'They said they wanted some sort of identification, but wouldn't let him see her.'

Katherine felt faint.

'You all right, Mama? You've gone ever so white.'

She gave him a weak smile. 'I'm fine. What about Ted?'

'A policeman took him and . . .' He hesitated. 'This policeman told Ted that he didn't think she – you know. What the papers are saying. He thinks she was running along the track when she slipped.'

Katherine put her hand to her mouth to stifle a sob. 'I didn't think she would take her own life. Those poor children.'

'Who's gonner look after them now?'

'They'll have to go into a home.'

Joseph looked down at his fingers. 'I feel ever so bad about all this.'

'We all do.'

'But I wouldn't talk to her. Ted was right. She was nice, and she made us laugh. She used to tell us what some of the kids got up to. She was ever so good to those kids, you know.'

'I know.' Katherine gently tapped his hand. 'We all have some regrets in our lives. Unfortunately we can't turn back the clock and rectify them.'

Joseph suddenly threw his arms round his mother and held her close and wept. He was weeping for Edwin, Dolly, and now Briony, and the child he had once been.

On Monday when Katherine walked into the shop Josh was leaning on the counter busy reading the newspaper.

'Morning, Kate love. Seen these headlines? They say this family comes from Croft Street. Ain't that where you live?'

She nodded and continued to remove her hat.

'Who's this old dear?' He pointed at a picture.

'That's Mrs Duke.'

'Did you know the family? They sound a right old lot to me.'

'I was very fond of Briony.'

'That the girl who used to work for old Wilks?'

'Yes. She was a lovely girl.'

He folded the paper. 'Don't sound very nice to me. She murdered her old man, then threw herself under a train. Couldn't face the trial, I reckon.'

'Do they say why she murdered her father?'

'No.'

'She caught him molesting her younger sister.'

'No!' Josh's eyes opened wide. 'It don't say nothing about that.'

'Well it wouldn't, would it? As far as the papers are concerned she was a murderess. She was only fourteen,' added Katherine softly.

'No,' said Josh again. 'Well I never. This is gonner be all the talk round here for days.'

Katherine was very aware of that.

As the morning wore on, so more and more people came in. There were photographers and reporters all asking questions, and a lot of people whom Katherine had never set eyes on before sat and looked at her.

'They might be a lot of ghouls to you, Kate, me girl, but to me it's good business.' Josh was beaming.

The questions came from all corners.

'They say you took her in?'

'Wasn't your landlady's son involved?'

'No he wasn't.'

'Well, that's what it says here.'

Katherine chose to ignore most of the comments. She wanted to run out. She didn't want her name to be associated with all this fuss, and she didn't want her name or picture in the newspaper. If Gerald realised it was her, she could just see him having a good laugh.

'It'll only be a five-minute wonder,' said Ron when he got his tea.

'I hope so,' said Katherine. 'I only hope so.'

'Hark at that silly cow,' said Josh.

Nellie was shouting out and banging on the floor.

'For Christ's sake shut it, can't you?' He walked into the dark passage and shouted back up. 'We're run off our feet down here.' There was a pause. 'You'll get your tea when we've got a minute.'

He came back. 'Take her tea up, Kate. Anything for a quiet life.' He tutted and cast his eyes up to the ceiling.

'What the bleeding hell's going on down there?' asked Nellie as Kate pushed the door open. 'Bloody racket.'

'It's full up.'

'Why, what's he doing, giving it away?'

Katherine smiled. 'No. It's because of the murder.'

'Oh yes. I heard about that. Josh said you live in that street, that right?'

'Yes, and I knew young Briony.'

'She worked for Wilks, didn't she?'

Katherine was always surprised at how much Nellie knew. 'Yes. She was a nice girl.' She put the tea on the bedside table and left the room. She didn't want to get too deep in a conversation as Josh would soon be shouting for her. She would tell Nellie all about it another day.

As the week wore on it seemed everybody wanted to get into the newspapers. There were pictures of Mr Wilks standing in his shop doorway. He had his arms folded and a smug expression on his face. There was another one of Mrs Duke, this time sitting on her windowsill with one or two others who lived in Croft Street. As the week drew to a close Ron was proving to be right. And by Friday it was almost back to normal.

Chapter 21

All week the atmosphere in the Stevenses' house had been very subdued. On Sunday morning Ted came into the kitchen carrying something in a paper bag.

'What you got there?' asked Milly.

Ted looked uneasy and didn't answer his mother. He turned to Katherine. 'You still going to try to find Briony's grave?'

'Yes. Why?'

'Well, when you said you might go I decided to make this, just to show where she is.'

Milly sat in stunned silence when he took a small wooden cross from the bag and very briefly showed them.

'That's lovely,' said Katherine. 'Do you want me to take it?'

'No.' He hastily put it back into the bag. 'I'd like to come with you, if you don't mind.'

'No, I don't mind. We may have trouble finding it. The police couldn't help much.'

'We can always ask the man in charge.'

'We'll try.'

When Ted went outside Milly looked at Katherine. 'I didn't know he was making that. That accounts for all the bits of wood in his bedroom. Did you know, Joe?'

He just nodded.

Later that morning Joseph, Katherine and Ted walked into the cemetery. They found an old man in overalls slowly sweeping a path. Katherine asked him where the people who didn't have any money or relations were buried.

'Over there.' The man stopped sweeping, and with his broom resting against his shoulder took a tin of tobacco from his pocket and carefully and methodically began rolling a cigarette. 'All the paupers in this parish finish up over there.'

The sad little trio went to the far side, passing the tall ominous-looking monuments. There were large stone crosses to mark the passing of loved ones. Angels with serene faces and cherubs with heavenly expressions looked down on them as the visitors picked their way across the graves. Some statues were old and weather-beaten, arms and noses falling off. Lichen and grass covered the ancient tombstones whose names had been worn away with time, and one or two had great chunks of masonry missing.

'Which one d'you reckon it is?' Ted anxiously asked Katherine as he moved from one dirt-covered hillock to another.

'I don't know.'

'These two don't look very old,' said Joseph. 'There ain't any weeds on them.'

They stood in front of two fresh mounds.

'I wonder which one is Briony?' Ted crouched down. 'I hope it ain't her dad. Would he be here?'

Katherine couldn't answer. Could Mrs Addams and her baby be somewhere near? If only she had asked Briony.

Ted took the cross from the bag and tears stung Katherine's eyes as she read what he had painted on it: 'BRIONY ADDAMS. Age 14. A good friend'.

'I hope this is the right one and this is the top,' he said, pushing the cross into the soft ground. He stood up and took a step back.

Katherine took Joseph's arm and gently moved him away, leaving Ted alone.

When Ted was ready the three of them slowly and silently walked from the cemetery. Katherine knew that for Ted things would never be the same. Losing your first love must be a terrible blow when you are just sixteen.

Days passed and everything and everybody began to drift along as normal. Even Milly was back on nodding terms with Mrs Duke, although Katherine said she would never forgive her for trying to put Briony away. Ted appeared to be getting over losing Briony. Tom had managed to get a job as a part-time pot man in the local pub and, much to Milly's relief, seemed to be settling down. Katherine was happy at work and Joseph said he lived only for Saturdays and the school holidays so he could be with Mr Lacy.

It was a Wednesday morning and at Trent's they were waiting for the lunchtime crowd when Josh asked Katherine to take Nellie's tea up.

'You busy down there?' Nellie asked her.

'No, not really, just the usual. It's better now the strike's over and all the fuss about Briony has died down.'

'That was a nasty business. Sit yourself down.'

'But—' Katherine looked towards the door.

'Don't worry about him. How long you been here now?'

'Getting on for five months.'

'You seem to hit it off all right with my Josh, don't you?' She eased herself up.

'Yes, he's a fair man.'

'Well, I must admit you've been with him longer than most, and you don't flaunt yourself.' Nellie shifted her position. 'Don't hold with that.'

Katherine gave her a faint smile.

'He likes you, you know. Reckons you could have been in business yourself the way you get stuck into things and don't hang around waiting to be told what to do. I'm glad you don't try to take things over down there. Don't say much about yourself, do you?'

Katherine laughed, but was immediately on her guard. 'There's not a lot to tell.' She hadn't told Josh anything about her past. At times, when the shop was quiet and they were talking together, he would ask her about herself but somehow she always managed to evade the questions. Was this a ploy to find out all about her?

'Well, did you have a business 'fore you moved round this way?'

'Don't be silly. Would I be working for Josh if I had?'

Nellie eyed her suspiciously. 'Might be if you're down on your luck. You talk nice and always look clean, and those frocks don't come from any pawn shops round here. And what about a husband? Ain't ever heard you talk about one.'

'He passed away.' Katherine was thinking quickly.

'Oh, I see.'

'He did have a good job,' she added, to justify her appearance.

'But boozed it all away, I s'pose,' said Nellie.

Katherine didn't answer. 'I must go otherwise I'll have Josh shouting for me.' She left the bedroom and slowly made her way downstairs. So much for her trying to find out about Nellie; Nellie was now probing her past.

'Been having a quiet word with Nellie then?' asked Josh.

Katherine wondered if this was a put-up job. What did he want to know? 'Yes. Josh, why won't she get up?'

'She does, when she feels like it. Those cups want rinsing out.' He rolled down his sleeves. 'I'm just going along to the off-licence 'fore they close. Nellie likes a drink at night.'

All day Katherine wondered why Nellie had asked her those questions. She hadn't told her the truth about her past, but then that was her business.

Tom was in the scullery whistling when Katherine got home.

'You sound happy.'

He turned from the sink where he was busy washing up.

'Didn't hear you come in, Miss Katherine.' He still couldn't drop the 'Miss'.

'Where's Milly?' She pulled the pins from her hat.

''Round Olive's. She sent a note to say she'd started, so Milly threw her coat on and left.'

Katherine put her hand to her mouth to suppress her joy. She was full of emotion. 'When was that?'

'This morning.'

Katherine smiled. 'At last, something nice is going to happen.'

'Yer, it's about time,' said Tom, turning back to his chores.

It wasn't long after that Charlie and Ted came in. Tom had put the pie Milly had made in the oven.

'About what time did Milly go off then, Tom?' asked Charlie.

'About eleven.'

'I wonder how long she'll be,' said Ted.

'She's not going to leave till it's all over,' said Katherine.

Ted grinned. 'I'll be an uncle.'

'I bet the old midwife will wish Milly further,' said Charlie.

'Not if it's Ida. Besides, it's a mother's privilege to be with her daughter,' said Katherine.

'We'd better get on with this pie Milly made this morning,' said Tom, carefully dishing out the pie and veg.

'What time d'you start tonight, Tom?' asked Charlie.

'Not till eight. He only likes me in to clear up. Don't want me hanging about for too long, might have to pay me more.'

After they'd finished dinner and the washing up they sat and waited for Milly to return.

Charlie looked up at the clock. He was getting anxious. 'She's a bloody long while. I hope everything's all right.'

'Of course it is,' said Katherine, hoping to reassure herself as much as Charlie. 'You know Milly, she won't leave till it's all over.'

'I know but it's nearly eight o'clock. I can't sit here any

longer, I'm going round to Olive's. I don't like the idea of Milly walking home on her own at this time o' night.'

'She'll be all right, Dad. 'Sides, they won't want you round there.'

'Ernie might. I know how I felt when your mother was having you and Olive. It ain't easy being outside waiting. No, I'll go round and give him a bit of support.'

'Why don't you take that bottle of stout round with you, then you can wet the baby's head,' said Tom. 'I'll bring another one in tonight when I finish.'

'Now that's what I call a good idea.' Charlie took his coat from off the nail behind the door.

'It's time I went to work anyway,' said Tom. 'I'll walk along with you.'

After an hour or so Joseph said, 'I think I'll go up to bed.'

'Me too. Can't do much down here waiting for news,' said Ted.

Katherine smiled and wished them both good night. She sat in front of the fire and watched the kettle's lid gently and silently lifting. The new life coming to this family was the best thing that could happen for all of them.

Katherine was dozing, and jumped when the kitchen door clicked open. She sat up and opened her eyes.

'Ain't they back yet?' asked Tom, taking his cap off.

Katherine shook her head. 'No. I'm getting worried, it's been a long while.'

'Look, why don't you go on up to bed?'

'I'd rather wait a bit longer.'

'I'll make us both a nice cuppa.' Tom had just picked up the kettle when they heard the front door close.

Milly walked into the kitchen, her face glowing. 'I'm a granny,' she said excitedly. 'She's got a dear little girl.'

Katherine leapt up and held Milly close. 'I'm so thrilled for you. Is Olive all right?'

Milly nodded.

'She's a real little cracker,' said Charlie, who was right behind her.

Katherine thought the buttons would ping off his shirt he looked so proud. 'What are they going to call her?'

Milly looked at Tom. 'Dorothy, after Dolly.'

Katherine swallowed hard.

'That's nice,' said Tom softly.

'Thought she might be carrying a girl, could tell somehow,' said Milly, her eyes dancing with pride.

'Would you like a cup of tea?' asked Katherine. 'Tom was just about to make one.'

'No, thanks all the same. Been drinking tea all day,' said Milly.

'That was a good idea of yours, Tom, taking that bottle round. Ernie looked like he could do with a drink when I got there.'

'She's got a mass of dark hair, and long legs,' said Milly.

'Was Ida there?'

'Ida?' asked Milly.

'Did she deliver—'

'No. A right upstart of a woman. Wanted me to wait outside. Well, I gave her a bit of me mind. Afterwards she thanked me for my help.'

'Will it be all right if I pop round to see her tomorrow after I finish the lunchtime stint? I won't stay long and I won't get in the way,' said Tom.

''Course. I'll be there most of the day. Katherine, I'll leave you all a bit of dinner, and I'll be back after I've seen to Ernie.'

'We can go out before you start work,' said Charlie to Tom. 'We've got to wet the baby's head.'

'Just as long as you don't drown yourselves,' said Milly, laughing.

Katherine smiled. There would be some celebrations going on tomorrow evening.

Olive's baby was lovely. She had lots of dark hair, and her dark eyes constantly looked about her. When Olive asked Katherine to be Dorothy's godmother she was overwhelmed and very proud at being invited to be part of this family. But when Katherine held Dorothy she felt a twinge of conscience. She would never rid herself of her guilt.

After the christening the party was soon in full swing, everybody enjoying themselves.

'Drink up,' said Charlie to Katherine.

'If he drinks to this baby's health once more we'll have him on the floor,' said Milly.

'Good job I didn't have twins,' said Olive proudly.

Charlie put his arm round his daughter's shoulder. His twinkling eyes misted over. 'You've made me a very happy man, love.' He tenderly kissed her cheek.

'Couldn't have done it without Ernie.'

'Yer, but he had the best bit.'

'Charlie Stevens, you watch your tongue.'

Charlie did a low sweeping bow. 'Yes, marm.'

Everybody shrieked with laughter.

'Bit different to the dos you had at the big house when Mr Edwin was alive,' said Tom, bending his head towards Katherine.

'Yes. In many ways this is much better. This is all family,' she replied, choking back a tear.

'Just you wait till Christmas,' said Charlie, trying to hold his drink steady. 'We'll really push the boat out then.'

'Well, thank Gawd you're back at work,' said Milly. 'And with Tom's bit and Ted getting a rise it should be a good one.'

Joseph sat next to his mother. 'Ma, can I talk to you?' He had long since stopped calling her Mama.

'Of course. I've just got to go and make a few more sandwiches. You can talk to me in the kitchen.'

After looking across at Ted, Joseph followed his mother.

'You can put these on that plate,' said Katherine. 'And then take them in the front room. Tell them they're fish paste.'

'As I'll be fourteen next May do you think I could leave school at Christmas?' It was said with a rush.

Katherine turned to him. Somehow she knew this was coming, and he knew she wouldn't start a fuss with everybody here. 'I suppose you want to start work?'

His face lit up. 'Yes, yes, please. Mr Lacy said I could start after Christmas so if it's all right with you—'

'Hold on a minute, young man.'

Joseph stopped in his tracks.

'I know you're not happy at that school, but are you sure you want to leave?'

Joseph nodded. 'I'm far in advance of any of them there.'

'I know, and I feel partly to blame because I took you from your old school. Edwin wouldn't have been happy at me doing that. But I didn't have any choice.'

Joseph looked up from arranging the sandwiches on the plate. 'I didn't think I would be happy living here, but I am, honest, and I really would like to go to work.'

Katherine put down the knife she was using to butter the bread and hugged him. 'Thank you.'

He pulled away. 'What for?'

'For sticking it. It hasn't been easy for you.'

'Nor for you.'

She brushed a tear from the corner of her eye. 'We've certainly had a few ups and downs this year.'

'Well, let's hope things will only get better.'

'I'm sure they will. You sound so very grown up.'

'I have grown up. I think when Briony died that made me realise all that she'd done for her family. To kill your father because of what he was doing to your sister, you've got to be very fond of someone to do that.'

'She was a nice girl.'

'Yes, and Ted was very upset about it.'

'I'm sure as time goes on his grief will fade, though it will never go away, and one day he will meet another young lady who will steal his heart.'

'I ain't gonner get married.'

'That's what all the boys say, but just you wait and see.'

'What was Australia like?'

Katherine was suddenly snapped out of her thoughts. 'Why? Why did you ask that?'

'I just wondered, that's all. Wouldn't mind going there one day. So you see, I don't want any woman hanging round me.'

Katherine wanted to laugh, but the thought that he was talking about Australia stopped her.

'I'll take these into the front room.' Joseph picked up the plate of sandwiches and walked out, leaving Katherine feeling utterly bewildered. What was going through his mind?

Later that evening, over the washing-up, she asked Milly what she thought about it.

'You don't wanner worry too much at what kids say. P'raps he'd just thought about it. Might be something they've talked about at school.'

'Could be. You don't think he wants to leave home, do you?'

'Na, course not. Could be he was just dropping a hint to put the frighteners on you, in case you said no to him leaving school.'

'Yes, that sounds more like it,' said Katherine, feeling reassured by Milly's common sense reaction.

'Ted was on about leaving home a while back when he couldn't get his own way,' Milly went on, 'but when I pointed out to him that he'd have to do his own washing and ironing he soon changed his mind. Anyway, since your Joe's been around, he's gone off the idea.' She put the plate she'd been washing on the wooden draining board. 'Seems all boys like to get their mothers worried from time to time. 'Sides, with Christmas coming up, he'll have more on his mind, especially now you said he can start work.'

Katherine picked up the plate and began drying it. She hoped Milly was right. Had she made Australia sound too exciting to a young man full of hope and adventure?

Chapter 22

Katherine knew that Christmas was going to be far better than she could have ever hoped for when she first moved to Rotherhithe. At work, she was surprised and very touched when some of the customers gave her their odd penny or halfpenny change and wished her a Merry Christmas.

'Blimey, you must have made an impression,' said Josh, observing. 'I ain't ever had nothing off 'em.'

'Well, you ain't as pretty as Kate,' said Ron.

'You watch it or I'll tell yer missis what you've done.'

Ron laughed. 'It's 'cos I've had a couple of good days at the dog track and I like to spread a little bit of good will towards me fellow men. Wouldn't hurt you to show a bit more good will. A few paper chains wouldn't come amiss.'

Josh nearly choked on his tea. 'What? Waste me money on things like that?'

Katherine laughed. She too would have liked to see a few decorations up, but Josh wasn't like that. She loved her job and this good-humoured banter. She was also surprised that some of the more sensitive men took her into their confidence when they were worried about their children or wives.

''Sides, I've told Annie all about Katie,' said Ron.

'Well, that's all right then,' said Josh. 'But don't expect her to give you a free cuppa.'

'Mean old sod. Where's yer Christmas spirit?'

'It's in a bottle and locked away upstairs.'

213

Before she left on Christmas Eve, Katherine took Nellie up a bottle of lavender water.

'I ain't got nothing for you,' she said.

'It's a Christmas present. I don't expect one back.'

'Well, that's all right then.'

Katherine had noted that over the past months Nellie had combed her hair and the curtains were open. Was she having some effect on Josh's wife, enough to make her start to take an interest in herself? But every time Katherine had tried to broach the subject of why she was in bed, Nellie shut up like a clam.

'Just a minute,' called Nellie, as Katherine was leaving. 'I've told Josh to give you a bit extra this week.'

Katherine stood in the doorway. 'What? Thank you.'

'Well, I dare say you can do with the money.'

'Yes. Thank you very much.'

Katherine made her way down the stairs. Once again Nellie had surprised her. Did she have more to say about the running of this business than anyone knew?

Katherine was amazed when she found Josh was giving her another week's wages. It was only Tuesday.

'Well, don't want you telling all the blokes I don't look after you.'

She kissed his cheek. 'Thanks.'

He smiled and touched his cheek. 'Don't let Nellie see you do that, otherwise she'll have me guts for garters. And don't be late on Friday.'

Katherine laughed. 'Have a nice Christmas.'

'Won't be much of one with just me and Nellie. Much rather be down here working.'

Katherine felt sad at that remark. If she hadn't moved in with Milly there could have been just her and Joseph sitting alone in rooms somewhere.

Katherine wandered past the shops. Many people were doing

their last-minute shopping. The butcher had chickens hung all over the outside of his shop and he was busy selling them off with lots of laughter and cheeky comments as he took them down with his long pole.

''Ere, I ain't 'aving this one,' shouted one woman as she pushed her way through the crowd. 'It's only got one leg.'

Laughter erupted as the woman took the chicken from her shopping bag by its neck and shook it at the butcher.

'It had two when it left here. I reckon you sawed it off when you got it home.'

'I ain't been home. Been in the pub having a quick one, ain't I?'

'Well, it looks like someone's gonner have a nice juicy chicken leg fer dinner tomorrow. Go back and ask 'em who pinched it.'

'I want me money back.'

'You ain't having it so clear off, you crafty old mare, and don't try any of yer old tricks on me. I wasn't born yesterday.'

'I'll send me old man round to sort you out.'

'Look, I'm shaking in me shoes.' The butcher shook his knees. He was a big man and it would have to be a very brave adversary who took him on.

Katherine smiled as she walked on. She knew a lot of women would be busy plucking these chickens all evening, getting them ready for tomorrow's dinner while their menfolk were in the pub.

The smell of chestnuts from a brazier was warm and inviting. Despite the damp and cold the hissing from the stallholders' kerosene lamps, and the shouts from the men trying to sell their wares all brought a great feeling of joy to her, as did the sound of badly sung carols from the youngsters rattling their tins under everyone's noses.

Bill and Bert, the brothers who had the flower and fruit stall, gave her a quick wave. Katherine gave them a smile. They were nice men, always friendly. They were well muffled up against the cold.

She slid down deeper into her coat and pulled her collar up. This was so different from the Christmases she'd had in Australia. They had been hot, with flies buzzing around all the while. It was too hot to eat during the day, and Christmas dinner didn't taste the same over there. What suddenly made her think of Australia? What would Robert be doing? What did he look like now? Her heart felt a longing to know how he was.

Then there were those Christmases she had shared with dear Edwin. They had to work late into the night in the restaurant on Christmas Eve, but Christmas Day they relaxed and enjoyed the celebration with Dolly and Tom. Dolly . . . the thought of her brought a lump to Katherine's throat.

Somehow she felt that this Christmas was going to be the best of all. She was happy living with Milly and being part of this community. They had very little, but were content to share and make the best of what they did have, and most of the time it was with a ready smile. She pulled up her coat collar and moved on. If only Edwin, Dolly and Briony were here to share it with her, but she knew she shouldn't dwell on the past.

Christmas for Katherine was just as wonderful as she knew it would be. The meal was delicious and with Olive, Ernie and the new baby, the kitchen was full of laughter and chatter. Come the afternoon they moved into the front room to relax and roast chestnuts on the cheerful fire. In the evening they played cards and charades, and finally it was time for bed.

For a while Katherine sat in her room reflecting. Over these past months she had been able to save, and even after giving Milly another sixpence a week she had managed to put a little away. She'd long since paid her debt to Ida Fairfield. She tipped the money out of the purse and began counting it. She wanted to help Joseph if he needed tools, but she also knew deep down she wanted to do more with her life. She wanted her own business, but it would take a lot more than the few shillings she had.

The New Year, 1913, started cold and very wet. Dense fog made everywhere feel dirty and damp. Men who hadn't been lucky enough to get work that day came to Trent's mainly to get warm as they sat with their cold fingers wrapped around their one and only mug of tea. They complained about the weather stopping the ships from coming up the Thames, while Josh complained they only wanted somewhere warm to sit and talk.

'Well, it's better than going home to have yer ear bent be yer old woman,' shouted someone when Josh was having a moan.

'And told ter pick yer feet up while she swept round yer,' said another.

'My old girl only asked me to bring the coal in the other day. I ask yer. I soon put her in her place. I told her straight – I'm the breadwinner so I'll do my job and you do yours.'

Katherine half smiled to look as if she were agreeing with him, but guessed his wife had a brood of youngsters to look after. She could understand that attitude when he was working in the docks, as the work was long and hard, but to sit in here and not help his wife was something Katherine always resented. Her job depended on her keeping quiet, though.

The air quality in Trent's, with all the pipe and cigarette smoke, was almost as bad as it was outside.

Charlie was getting restless as day after day he'd come home wet and miserable when the ships didn't arrive. When the odd ship did dock, the wood and sugar sacks were frozen and slippery, and every man was terrified of having an accident as no work meant no pay.

Katherine offered Milly more money but she refused.

'Now Tom's working and Joe gives me a shilling out of his wages we can manage for a bit.'

Katherine smiled. Joseph was so happy. He was doing something he really enjoyed.

Milly's voice cut into her thoughts. 'Besides, when things go good I always puts a little by, just in case. Charlie's been in the docks too long for me not to know bad times always seem to follow good.'

At last the winter gave way to spring and everybody was happy to see the ships waiting to get into the docks. Charlie worked longer hours.

At work Nellie seemed content and when it was possible enjoyed a chat. Katherine still hadn't found out what made her take to her bed, but she did suspect she got out sometimes. The smile on Josh's face told everybody the takings were up. Katherine asked for another rise. Life was good and she was more determined than ever to save. She wanted her own business. She wasn't sure what she would do but often she would daydream about being in charge and was thrilled to see her savings grow.

In June the biggest event that filled the papers and was on everybody's lips was Emily Davison throwing herself under the King's horse at the Derby. The pictures of the suffragettes lining the streets as her coffin passed by brought many heated discussions in Trent's. Even Katherine, who admired these women, thought that was a bit extreme.

There followed a long, hot, sizzling summer, and by the time August Bank Holiday Monday was almost on them, all at number 12 Croft Street eagerly decided to have another outing. Along with Olive, baby Dolly and Ernie, they all went to Southend for the day.

'Was it hot like this in Australia, Ma?' asked Joseph as he sat on the pebbles finishing off his ice cream.

'Hotter than this, and dusty.'

'Not my cup of tea,' said Milly. 'Don't really like this warm weather that much.'

'It's 'cos you've got too many clothes on,' said Charlie, lying back with his coat off and his shirt neck open. He was wearing a knotted handkerchief on his head.

'Well, I certainly ain't showing me legs off like some of 'em. Look at those tarts over there, showing all their knees. They don't have to hold their skirts up that high just to have a paddle.'

'Well, they've got nice pairs to show off,' said Charlie, raising himself up on his elbow and shifting out of the way of Milly's sharp finger.

'The boys are enjoying themselves,' said Tom. 'Look, they've gone up to those girls paddling.'

'I'm glad Ted washed his feet last night,' said Milly. 'I would have been that ashamed if he'd taken his socks off and his feet was dirty.'

The day went quickly and soon they were home, tired and happy.

At work Katherine had been very discreetly asking Josh about the shop. And once or twice she had seen the landlord come and talk to him. She knew now that she wanted her own business, but what and where? And, more important, where would the money come from to start? She had learnt from Edwin that you needed capital, and that was something she didn't have. The business had to be in food – she didn't know anything else – and she didn't want to move away from this area, but Josh wouldn't want her opening up a café near here.

One warm sunny Friday, there was nobody in the shop. Josh was out in the back room getting food ready for Saturday, which was always their busiest day.

Katherine was dreamily putting the clean mugs on the shelf under the counter when the young girl with the big hat and rouged lips came in. Today the perfume from her cheap scent was overpowering, and almost blotted out the odour of unwashed bodies and tobacco that mixed with the cooking smells always filling the air in Trent's. Sometimes they didn't see her for a week. Then the next she would be in almost every day. She seemed so young and didn't flaunt herself like some of the prossies. She wasn't loud and brash, although she could hold her own when some of the younger men made comments. Normally she just sat quietly with a mug of tea. The older dockers didn't ever appear to be that interested. Most Fridays she came in for one customer. Today Katherine could see she'd been crying.

'Are you all right?' Katherine enquired.

'Just give me a cuppa.'

'I'll bring it over.'

The girl, hobbling because of her tight skirt, went over to a table as far from the door as she could, and which was unusual, sat with her back to the entrance.

Katherine wanted to talk to her, so she sat at a nearby table. 'Is anything wrong?'

'No.' She took a cigarette from her handbag and lit it.

'If there's—'

'Just go away and mind yer own business, will yer, yer nosy cow?'

Katherine quickly moved off. She was worried the girl's harsh raised voice would bring Josh in, and he was always telling Katherine to keep out of other people's affairs.

He had got cross with her when she'd put a box on the counter to help young Walter's mother pay for his gran's funeral. She missed that little chap with the large cap coming for his gran's dinner. He was a good boy. She had since heard he had been sent away to another relation. 'I only hope they treat him all right,' she had said to Milly at the time.

Katherine looked across at the girl when she took a

handkerchief from her handbag and began wiping her eyes. She blew her nose hard. Katherine casually walked over to her table.

'I can see you're in some sort of trouble . . .' Katherine didn't get the chance to finish the sentence because the girl burst into tears. She looked up at Katherine, her dark brown eyes full of worry.

Katherine quickly sat at her table. 'Can't I help?'

The girl shook her head.

She reminded Katherine of Briony. What was it about these young girls who were full of bravado on the outside yet small and vulnerable on the inside? 'Look, please let me try to help you.'

'You can't,' she sniffed.

'If you're having a baby—'

'It ain't that.' She quickly looked at the door behind the counter, took a long hard drag on her cigarette and ground the butt into the ashtray.

'Don't worry, Josh is busy,' said Katherine gently, easing herself into the chair next to her.

'I know you think I'm a trollop, but I only go with men to help me mum out.'

Katherine was shocked. 'You mean your mother sends you—'

'No, me mum ain't well, and me dad . . .' She stopped. Fear filled her face. 'I shouldn't be talking to you.'

Katherine was intrigued. 'Please, if you need someone to talk to, who knows, I may be able to help.'

'I don't think so.'

'Is it your father that sends you out?'

The girl laughed; it was a hollow sound. 'He ain't really me dad. He don't like me or me mum but she give him a roof over his head and since he come out . . . Well, he's always hitting her and don't give her any money.' She stirred the remaining tea in her mug round and round. 'I shouldn't be telling you this, but you're always kind and you and Josh don't chuck me out like

221

some shops do while I wait for me customers.'

Katherine wanted to throw her arms round this child and hold her tight, for suddenly she looked so alone and lost. 'What's wrong with your mother?'

'When the doctor told her she ain't got long to live I promised her she'd have a nice funeral, and the only way I can earn money, a lot of money quick, was to go on the game. You see, me dad didn't know – he thought I worked in a shop. That was till yesterday, and when he found out he knocked me and Mum about.' She stopped again as tears ran down her face. 'I tried to stop him. He took all the money I've saved.'

Katherine could have cried with her. 'What can I say? Why doesn't your mother throw him out?'

She sniffed. 'She won't. She says she loves him and you know what they say about love being blind.'

'Is your mother all right?'

The girl shook her head. 'I've just come from the hospital. She's in a bad way. He told 'em she'd fallen down the stairs.' She wiped her eyes again. 'What if she dies? I ain't got no money to pay . . .' Sobs shook her sad body. 'And I promised.'

'Don't you have any brothers or sisters?'

She shook her head.

Katherine felt so helpless. 'I don't like to ask, but are you, you know, expecting a customer?'

She nodded. 'But I can't let him see me like this. Me Friday one's a nice bloke. A real gent.'

'Look, let me help you tidy yourself up. I'll get a clean cloth, then you can wash your face.'

'Why you doing this, missis? I ain't bin exactly nice to you.'

'I too have been in trouble, and we all need someone to give us a lift up the ladder of life.'

A slight smile lifted the girl's tear-stained face. 'That's a really lovely thing to say. My mum would like you.'

'I'm sure your mother is very proud of you.'

'Dunno about that.'

Katherine hurriedly rinsed out a cloth and gave it to the girl.

'Does your mother know what you do for a living?'

She shook her head.

'Won't your father . . . that man tell her?'

'No, he's crafty. He'll just take me money so that way he'll keep his mouth shut.'

Katherine was at a loss for words. 'What's your name?' she asked as the girl rubbed at her face.

'Grace. What's yours?'

'Here, I'm called Kate.'

Grace gave a little laugh. 'So this could be called Kate's kitchen then?'

'Kate's kitchen,' repeated Katherine. 'Don't let Josh hear you say that. But it's a good name.'

Grace powdered her nose and painted her lips. 'Do I look better?'

'Yes. Now please come back and tell me how your mother gets on, won't you?'

'OK. I'd better go and sit down. Me Friday man wouldn't like it if he thought I talked to you.'

Just a few moments later, Mr Friday came in. Grace walked to the door, and in the doorway she turned and gave Katherine a big smile.

Katherine was watching her leave when Josh came in.

'That all you gotter do, stand about grinning?'

'I was just going to clear that ashtray.' The words 'Kate's kitchen' were buzzing round her brain. Was this what she was looking for?

Her thoughts went to Grace. She'd called Josh by his name. He had never spoken to her – well, not in front of Katherine – and they had never even exchanged glances. She grinned. Why didn't he throw her out? After all, she only ever had one mug of tea, and sometimes she'd be there all afternoon waiting for customers. Was there something going on? She admonished herself for her naughty thoughts.

Chapter 23

'You're at it again, ain't yer?' said Milly, running her hands over the crisp white tablecloth, smoothing out invisible creases.

Katherine had been telling her about Grace. 'What d'you mean?' she asked, as she put the knives and forks out ready for dinner.

'Always worried about other people.'

'I can't help it. I hate to see these youngsters taking on the world.'

'What is it about you that seems to attract all the waifs and strays?'

'Must be me sympathetic ear,' Katherine said, laughing and putting on a cockney accent.

'So what's gonner happen to this poor cow then?'

'I don't know. If her mother dies before she gets enough money together for her funeral she'll be devastated.'

'Fancy having to go on the game to pay for your mum's funeral. Does her mum know?'

'She said not.'

'It's sad.'

'Then to have someone steal it from you.'

'It's a shame.'

'What if I told her about Ida Fairfield?'

'Ida? What could she do?'

'Perhaps she could lend her the money, if need be.'

'Maybe. But she ain't got a regular job, has she?'

'No. But I think what she does pays well. I could tell her about Ida when she next comes in.'

Milly laughed. 'You're a good 'en, Katherine, and no mistake.'

'Well, I only hope I've got enough for Joseph to bury me when the time comes.'

'Don't talk like that.'

'But it comes to us all in the end.'

'I know, but I expect to be around for a few more years yet.' Katherine kissed her cheek. 'So do I.'

'What was that for?' asked Milly, rubbing her cheek.

'I just felt like it.'

Throughout the week Katherine eagerly waited for Grace to come in, but even on Friday she still hadn't turned up. When her usual man appeared, he looked around, then walked out without saying a word.

'I hope her mother hasn't died,' Katherine said to Milly that evening.

On Saturday morning Mrs Duke was standing at her door. Katherine gave her a polite nod.

'See you're still living here then? Thought you might have been long gorn be now.'

Katherine didn't reply.

'You know what I did was right, so don't go giving me any of your holier-than-thou looks. Thought you might be starting a posh café be now.'

'I hope to one day.' As soon as Katherine said that she regretted it.

'Must be a bit crowded in there with all you lot.' She inclined her head towards Milly's door. 'Still, Milly must be coining it in now old Tom's odd-jobbing in the pub. And I see you've got your boy out working as well now.'

'I must go.' Katherine hurried away and let her thoughts turn to the business she wanted to start. She hadn't said anything to Milly in case she thought she was trying to get above her station, but if that slip of the tongue got back to Milly, she'd be very upset if she thought she was the last to know Katherine's plans. Fortunately Mrs Duke hadn't taken her up on it.

Katherine had been taking an interest in what Josh bought, and made notes. She discreetly asked Josh where he got his meat and potatoes from.

He laughed. 'Why's that? You wanner start buying in bulk?'

'No. I was just wondering if it was cheaper for me to buy them off you instead of Milly going to the market.'

'Shouldn't think so, not when I add on me bit of profit.'

'You old skinflint,' said Katherine, laughing, pleased he didn't make too much fuss about it.

All week Milly was talking about baby Dolly's first birthday. 'Can't believe she's a year old. Charlie's that proud of her.'

'And of course you're not,' said Katherine, smiling.

Milly beamed. 'Well, she is a little darling, ain't she?'

Katherine nodded.

'Olive's giving her a little tea party. I'm gonner make a small cake. I'll bring you all a bit back.'

Friday came round, and once again Katherine waited for Grace. She was delighted when she saw her walk in. 'How's your mother?' she asked, pushing a mug of tea towards her.

'Not good. I dunno how I'm gonner pay for the hospital, let alone anything else.' She lowered her voice. 'And I ain't been able to work much with going to see Mum every night.'

Katherine closed the door behind the counter. 'Josh is busy so I've got a moment or two. Grace, I don't want you to think I'm – well, you know – speaking out of turn, but if you need money, I know of a money lender.'

Grace's face turned pale with anger. 'I ain't going to no shark!' she yelled.

Katherine looked anxiously at the door. 'Shh! Keep your voice down. She's not a shark.'

'They're all sharks. 'Sides, what's in it for you? How much d'you get out of it?'

Katherine was taken aback. 'Nothing. I was just trying to—'

'Well, mind your own bloody business! I should have kept me mouth shut. I knew I couldn't trust you.' She snatched up her tea, spilling some in the process.

'But Grace,' Katherine called after her as she made her way to the far side of the café. 'You can trust me. I'm sorry.'

'What's going on?' asked Josh, pushing the door open. 'Who shut this door?'

'I did.'

'What for?'

'There was a draught round my legs.'

'Well, hard luck. Nellie wants a cuppa. You can take it up.'

Reluctantly Katherine poured out the tea. She wanted to talk to Grace. She wanted to help her, but Grace sat with her back to Katherine.

Nellie was sitting up in bed and looked happy. Over the months, the change in her was noticeable; even the windows had been open during the summer, making the place smell a little sweeter.

'Hallo, Kate. Guess what? It's me birthday.'

'Why didn't you tell me? I would have brought you a little gift or even got Milly to make you a small cake.'

A huge grin filled Nellie's pale face. 'Would yer? Would yer really?'

'Yes.'

'That's real kind of you. Ain't never had a cake – well, not for years.'

Katherine could see Nellie was in a good mood. 'Would you like me to help you get out of bed as it's your birthday?'

'Na. Might later on. Josh said he'd bring me a drop of whisky.' She lay back. 'He used to be a good husband.'

'He seems as though he takes care of you.'

'Yer, now.' The scowl returned and she slid down into the bed.

Katherine felt uncomfortable. This woman's moods changed so quickly. She stood for a moment in silence. 'Is there anything else I can get you?'

'No. And leave the door open.'

When Katherine went back into the shop Grace had gone. Had her Mr Friday come to collect her?

'Josh, why didn't you tell me it was Nellie's birthday?'

'Didn't see the point.'

'Have you bought her anything?'

'No. What does she need, lying up there day after day?'

Katherine felt like saying 'A little love and affection,' but he would have thought she was mad. 'Not a lot really, but a cake would have been nice.'

Josh laughed. 'A cake? And who the bloody hell would help her eat it?'

'Just a small one.'

'Na, she'll have a drop of whisky tonight, that'll keep her happy.'

'Why won't she get up?'

'Personal,' he said gruffly.

'Can she walk?'

''Course she can.' He turned away.

Katherine knew that the conversation was now closed.

Autumn turned to winter. Grace continued to come in to meet her clients but after getting her tea she kept well away from Katherine.

It was a cold dark November morning, and Milly was standing in front of the kitchen window as Katherine got ready for work. 'Just look at that rain,' she said. 'You're gonner get soaked.'

Katherine looked at the heavy rain falling straight from the sky like stair rods. It bounced noisily off Mrs Duke's roof, and the gutter overflowed. 'I'll take another pair of shoes with me. I don't like standing about all day in wet shoes. I'm glad Joseph keeps an old pair at work to change into.'

'What about your skirt? It'll get soaked.'

'I suppose I could take my other one, just in case.'

'Why don't you hang on a bit, just till it dies down? You can't go out in this!' said Milly in alarm.

'I must. I can't let Josh down.'

'Well, I shouldn't think there'll be many venture out in this.'

Katherine looked at the clock, then out of the window. 'I really must go. Saturday's our busiest day.'

Outside it was worse. She got to the end of Croft Street and her umbrella blew inside out. 'That's all I need,' she said angrily, throwing it to the ground. The rain stung her face. She trod in puddles, and rain from broken pipes splashed down on her. She was wet through in no time. The water squelched in her shoes, and her skirt, heavy with water, flapped and stuck to her legs. She felt cold and miserable.

'Good God, woman!' said Josh, when she pushed open the door. 'Fancy coming out in this.'

She stood and let the water drop from her. The brim on her black velour hat dipped and drooped.

'Look, get out back and use the towel. I didn't expect you to come out in this. You'd better get those wet things off.' He took her coat. 'Put your hat over the stove.'

'I hope it doesn't shrink, it's the only winter one I've got.' Katherine slipped her feet out of her shoes.

Josh laughed. 'Here, you're quite a little thing without shoes.'

'I've brought another pair with me, and a skirt to change into. Where can I go?'

'Well you can't go out to the lav, not in this weather. Stay here, I'll go out front. I'd better light the gas under the urn just in case we get some customers.'

Katherine shut the door that led to the shop and began to remove her skirt. It was heavy with water and she tried to wring it out. Her petticoats and blouse had stuck to her and she decided to take them off and wear just her overall. It wrapped around her generously, and with its long sleeves she knew she would be well covered, and not attract too many ribald remarks if she stayed behind the counter. She ran her hands over her white lawn chemise. It was wet but it would have to dry on her, as would her pretty lace-decorated cotton drawers. Before she put the overall on she took the towel from behind the back door and began drying her hair.

A terrific clap of thunder made her jump. She screamed out when the back door flew open and the chimney came crashing down into the yard, bringing many of the roof slates with it.

Katherine could hear Nellie screaming.

'Bloody hell, what was that?' Josh almost fell into the back room.

Katherine threw herself at Josh. 'It's the chimney.'

The wind and rain came in through the open door, blowing and saturating everything. Above the din they could hear Nellie screaming for Josh.

'Nellie! Nellie! It's all right, girl!' Josh pushed Katherine aside and raced up the stairs.

Katherine was fighting against the wind, trying to shut the door, when Nellie came in.

'What's going on down here?'

Katherine stood open-mouthed at Nellie standing there in her nightgown. She was a short woman who shuffled in leaning on a walking stick.

'See, I told you it was all right, love,' said Josh with his arm around her. 'The chimney's come off the roof.'

'I know that, don't I? I thought me bloody time was up. Frightened the life out of me it did.'

'Kate, get Nellie a chair from out front.'

Katherine went to move.

'What's she doing standing there in just her drawers and chemise?' screamed Nellie. 'Josh – you bin up to your old tricks again?'

Katherine could feel the flush of embarrassment creeping over her. She made a move towards her clothes that were scattered on the floor and, scrabbling them up, held them against her.

'No, Nellie. She got soaked coming here and she was changing her—'

Nellie's stick landed heavily on his shoulder.

'No, Nellie! It ain't what you think!'

'Don't give me that old fanny! I know what you get up to! Thought you'd know better be now!' Every word was said with force and a blow to Josh's body with her stick.

'Nellie, Nellie, stop it!' cried Katherine.

'And you can shut it an' all! I thought I could trust you, but no, you're like all the other trollops we've had here!'

Katherine thrust her wet clothes at Nellie. 'Look! See, I got wet through and I was just changing.'

'A likely story! You ain't the first, but if I have my way you'll be the last.' She turned to Josh. 'I told you to get a lad in, but no, it had to be another tart!'

'Nellie, it's not what you think.'

'You!' She turned to Katherine, who shrank back out of reach. 'Get out! Do you hear me? Get out!' She brandished her stick as Katherine tried to put on her wet clothes.

'Please, Nellie, you've got to believe me. Kate's a good worker.'

'I bet she is!'

'I don't pay her a lot, only what you said.'

'Might not be a lot for working here, but what about her other favours?'

Katherine gazed in amazement as Josh grovelled in front of this woman who appeared to be in control.

'How dare you!' Katherine couldn't stand by and let her name be ruined by this woman.

'Kate's a good woman,' said Josh, moving towards her.

'A good woman, is she?' The walking stick came down with a loud crack to the side of his head. He fell heavily to the floor. 'Good at what?'

Katherine looked at Josh lying on the floor.

'Come on, get up, you stupid sod!' Nellie prodded him with her stick.

He didn't move.

Katherine fell to her knees. 'What have you done?'

'Dunno, but I should have done it years ago.'

'I'll have to get a doctor. You could have killed him, you, you—'

'You'd better put some clothes on first,' laughed Nellie.

Katherine hurriedly pulled on her wet things and ran out, oblivious to the rain. She knew the doctor's was a few shops away. She banged hard on his door.

It was opened by a tall thin woman whose black hair was pulled back into a tight bun, giving her face a taut, pinched look. 'The doctor is busy. Call back on Monday.'

'I can't! Please, he must come to Josh.'

'Who is Josh?'

'Josh Trent who owns the pie and mash shop.'

'Oh yes, I know,' she said, looking down her long hooked nose. 'Why?'

Katherine brushed the rain that was running down her face away from her eyes with both hands. 'He's had an accident.'

'Wait there.' The woman closed the door.

Katherine began to shiver. What had Nellie done? And why did she think Josh and she had . . . ? That was unthinkable. The rain had seeped through everything she had on. She shivered. She was cold and uncomfortable. She stamped her feet to bring back life to them. She could have cried when she looked down. Now both pairs of shoes, which were all she had, were wet and probably ruined. She waited for what seemed to be for ever. Should she go back and try to help Josh?

Eventually the door opened. 'So you say Mr Trent has had an accident?' The doctor was a small dapper man. He pulled his trilby down over his eyes and put up his black umbrella. 'Well, come on, woman! Don't let's stand about in this weather or I'll catch my death!'

He was shorter than Katherine and took small running steps. She hurried beside him, dodging the spokes of his umbrella.

'The shop door's open,' shouted Katherine. 'He's in the back.' She pushed open the door. Josh was still on the floor where she had left him. Nellie was nowhere to be seen.

'How did this happen?' The doctor was on his knees. He took a stethoscope from his black bag. 'Help me to turn him over.'

Josh had a strange twisted expression on his face. A bruise was beginning to show on his forehead.

'Has he been attacked?'

Katherine didn't answer.

'I said did someone attack him?'

'What's going on down here?' Nellie's voice was feeble and faint. She staggered in, leaning heavily on a stick.

Katherine stared at her disbelievingly.

Nellie was wearing a tatty dressing gown and her hair was a mess. 'Doctor Ballard! What you doing . . . ?' She gasped and put her hand to her mouth. 'Josh! Josh! What's happened to my Josh?' She slowly and painfully made her way across the room.

'I'm sorry, Mrs Trent, but it looks as if your husband has

been attacked, and it's brought on a stroke.'

'A stroke!' She started to sway.

'Quick, get Mrs Trent a chair.'

Katherine continued to stare at Nellie in disbelief.

'Woman! Don't just stand there! I said get Mrs Trent a chair.'

Katherine felt this was a bad dream, a nightmare. Would she wake up soon? She put the chair in front of Nellie.

'I thought I heard a noise a bit earlier on. Then the chimney fell off and I called for Josh and he told me not to worry. He came down to get me a cup of tea. Who would attack him?' She looked across at Katherine.

'It wasn't me, it was you!' yelled Katherine.

Doctor Ballard looked up. 'My dear woman, that is a very stupid thing to say. You can see Mrs Trent can hardly walk. Now stop this silly nonsense and I'll go and see about getting him into hospital.'

'I'm going,' said Katherine.

'No. I want you to stay here and look after Mrs Trent.' He turned to Nellie. 'Is there anyone you can contact to look after you?' he asked in his best bedside manner.

Nellie wiped her eyes and slowly shook her head. 'No, I'm all alone.'

Chapter 24

As soon as the doctor had left, Katherine turned on Nellie. 'Why? Why did you say that to the doctor?'

Nellie laughed.

'You're mad!' screamed Katherine.

'Maybe. You see, I've had a lot to put up with from Josh these past years and I won't be sorry to see the back of him.'

'What? After all he does for you?'

Nellie didn't reply.

'I'm getting a pillow and a blanket for him,' said Katherine. She left Nellie sitting looking at her husband, but there wasn't any sorrow in her eyes.

Katherine quickly returned. She knelt down beside the sorry figure lying on the floor and put the pillow under his head and covered him with a blanket. 'How could you? He's your husband!'

'I know.'

'He's looked after you for years and this is all the thanks he gets.'

'You shouldn't judge people till you know what it's all about. I'm going back to bed.'

'Well, don't expect me to be around to answer your every beck and call. I'm going home as soon as I've made sure Josh is safe.'

'Why? You worried I might do him in?'

Katherine couldn't answer. That hadn't entered her mind.

'I wouldn't kill him if that's what you think.'

'I'm not so sure about that, and I don't want to be accused of anything.'

Nellie left the room.

Katherine went into the shop, turned off the urn and locked the shop door. The last thing she wanted was the place full of people.

She sat looking out of the window at the rain still beating down. What was going to happen now? With Josh ill, who would run the shop? She suddenly sat up. She wouldn't have a job. She had to talk to Nellie.

'Nellie?' She carefully pushed open the bedroom door.

Nellie was sitting in front of the window. 'Well, what d'yer want?'

'I want to talk to you.'

'Filthy day, ain't it?'

'Nellie, what's going to happen to you?'

'Dunno.' She didn't take her eyes away from the window.

'Why did you hit Josh?'

' 'Cos he's bin carrying on behind me back. He shouldn't have done that. He knows it makes me mad.'

Katherine sat on the bed. 'He wasn't, you know. I just worked for him.'

'Might not be with you, but he was having it away with someone.'

'Well, it wasn't me.'

Nellie turned to face her. 'Didn't think it was.'

'You must tell the doctor that I didn't hit him.'

'He won't believe me. He thinks I can't hardly get out of bed.'

'But you can.'

'Yer. I only took to me bed when he first started with this carrying on lark.' Nellie moved closer to Katherine. 'You see, Kate . . . Well, I might as well tell you all the story. But I tell yer what, why don't you make us a nice cuppa? I expect you could do with one.'

Katherine nodded. This could be a long morning, and she had

to know what this was all about, and where her future lay, and if she had one at Trent's.

As she waited for the kettle to boil Katherine was brought out of her daydream by banging on the front door. She glanced up; it was the doctor.

'I've got to get Mr Trent into hospital. Can't leave him here with no one to look after him. I've managed to get someone to take him. Now about Mrs Trent. Can you look after her?'

'Well, I don't know.'

He was bending over Josh, who hadn't moved. 'Remember it was your doing that probably brought his stroke on, so I think the least you can do is look after her.'

Katherine wanted to shout at him, make him listen, but she knew it was no use.

'Good.' He mistook her silence as yes.

Another banging on the door sent her hurrying into the shop. The butcher was standing there. 'The doc wants me to take Josh to the hospital. Me delivery cart's outside. Hope me and the doc can lift 'im. Bloody shame, him having a stroke like that.' The butcher looked down at Josh. 'Don't look too good, does he?' The butcher was a large man, and the doctor small, but between them they lifted Josh and put him inside the cart. Katherine stood in the doorway and watched them move away. The rain had wetted Josh's pale face. His eyes were still closed and he looked a very sad, sorry man.

Katherine took the tea up to Nellie.

'He's gorn then?'

'Yes.'

Nellie took the mug of tea and held it to her lips. 'This looks a bloody sight better than the stuff he gives to them poor sods downstairs.'

'Nellie, are you going to tell me what brought all this about?'

'Might as well.' She wiped her mouth with the back of her

hand. 'Mind you, there ain't that much to tell really. You see, this used to be me dad's place.' She stopped and looked round the bedroom. She patted the bed. 'This was me mum and dad's. When Josh married me he knew he was on to a good thing – walked right into a good business. Well, first Mum went, then Dad died, and that's when Josh started straying. I put up with it for a bit, then one day I'd had enough. I was working in the shop doing all the cooking and serving while he was out enjoying himself, so I went to bed and stayed there. That way he had to wait on me and run the shop, so that kept him busy and he didn't have time to go astray – that was till we had young girls working here. Caught him at it a couple of times, I did. After that I insisted we had young lads. That was till you come along. I somehow knew I could trust you, Kate. You've got breeding.'

'So why did you make all that fuss downstairs?'

'Dunno really. But it was a good excuse to give him a walloping.'

Katherine sat with her eyes wide open in amazement. She couldn't believe this woman would go to such lengths to make him suffer.

'Who will look after him when he comes out of hospital?' asked Katherine.

'I can't.'

'Who will look after you?'

'Dunno. I might write to me sister.'

'You've got a sister? But you told the doctor—'

'Yer, I know. She lives in Kent. She don't come up here, don't like London. I wouldn't mind going to stay with her for a bit.'

Katherine wanted to ask whether her sister would want her, but decided against that. 'Will you be able to manage financially?'

'I've got a few bob of me own. Dad made sure I wouldn't go short. 'Sides, the shop's in my name.'

Katherine was dumbfounded at all these revelations. She sat drinking her tea. How things could change in such a short space of time. Where would she go now? 'Nellie, when do you think you'll be going to Kent?'

'Dunno. I've got to think about that, and I shall need time to sort out things.'

'Josh? Kate? You there?' Someone was shouting at the bottom of the stairs.

'That's Ron, the bookies' runner,' said Katherine.

'He still comes here?'

'Yes. I'd better go down and tell him we're not open.'

'You can open up. You can run the place today, then we'll sort out some help for you later.'

'But . . . I . . .'

'You work here, so just get down there and open up!' Nellie's voice was loud and authoritative.

The last thing Katherine wanted was to work for Nellie.

'What the bleeding hell's going on?' asked Ron as Katherine came down the stairs. He banged his wet cap against his knee. 'She giving Josh a hard time?' He inclined his head towards the top of the stairs.

'Come on, Ron.' She took his arm and led him through to the shop.

'What's going on, Kate?'

She closed the door at the back of the counter. 'What do you know about Nellie?'

'Not a lot really. Where's Josh?'

'Sit down and I'll get you a cup of tea.'

With a puzzled expression on his face Ron moved over to a table, sat down, took his tobacco tin from his pocket and began rolling a cigarette.

Katherine knew she had to talk to someone. Soon everybody would be asking about Josh. The butcher would probably take great delight in giving his version, so she thought it best they heard it from her, and not any rumours that might grow. After all, she wouldn't stay after today – there was no way she was going to work for Nellie, and wait on her hand and foot.

'Josh is in hospital,' said Katherine, putting a cup of tea in front of Ron.

'What?' He took some coins from his pocket and put them on the table but Katherine waved them away. 'What's wrong with him?'

'He's had a stroke.'

'Bloody hell! When did this happen?'

'Early this morning.'

'What's gonner happen to this lot?' He waved his arm round.

'Nellie is taking it over and she expects me to work for her.'

'What?'

Katherine then went into great detail of what Nellie had told her, although she didn't tell him about her hitting Josh with her stick. 'Did you know Nellie was the owner?'

'Guessed as much. You see, me dad remembers her old man. Always wondered why she took to her bed, though. Did she ever say what was wrong with her?'

Katherine shook her head. She hadn't gone into Josh's indiscretions.

'So what happens now?'

'I'm not going to work for Nellie.'

'Can't say I blame yer. Mind you, we'll all be sorry to see you go, Kate.'

'And I shall be very sorry to go.'

'She won't be able to do much, stuck up there in bed, and if she does get someone in to run the place they'll soon see her off.'

'Don't know about that. Nellie Trent is a very shrewd woman. She was talking about writing to her sister.'

'Didn't know she had one.'

'She lives in Kent.'

'She can't run this shop from Kent.'

Katherine looked thoughtful. 'No, she can't.'

'Are you going to open up?' asked Ron.

'I think I will.'

'D'you want a hand?'

'I shouldn't be very busy, not on a day like this. Not many will venture out.'

'I'll hang about till lunchtime if you like.'

'Thanks, Ron.'

Katherine was right, she wasn't very busy. Ron left about one o'clock and an hour later she took a cup of tea up to Nellie.

'I'm going to close up now and go,' said Katherine.

'You can't go yet.' Nellie was still sitting in the chair. 'Who's gonner get me my tea?'

'You'll have to do it yourself.'

'I can't.'

'I'm going now the weather has improved. I don't want to finish up with a cold. My things are still wet from this morning. I'll get the takings.'

When Katherine returned Nellie counted out the money.

'Ain't much here,' she said.

'I haven't been very busy.'

Nellie snorted. 'I hope you ain't bin giving it away.'

'I'm off,' said Katherine, refusing to be drawn into another argument.

'You can't go yet.' Nellie was beginning to sound panicky. 'Will you be in on Monday?'

'Do you want me in?'

''Course. I ain't going down there. I ain't standing about all day serving that riffraff.'

'In that case I want a rise, if I'm going to be in charge.'

'A rise. Well, yes, I 'spect you would, but you're jumping the gun a bit. What if I get someone else in?'

'Well, that's up to you.' Katherine knew not many would work for her.

'We'll talk about it on Monday, and it'll only be till Josh comes back.'

'Do you think he will?' asked Katherine.

'Dunno.'

All the way home Katherine's head was spinning with everything that had happened. She almost ran into the kitchen, as she couldn't wait to tell Milly.

'You're early,' said Milly when she walked in.

'I've got so much to tell you.'

'Have a cuppa first,' said Charlie.

'And look at those shoes! Are your things wet?' asked Milly.

'Not now.'

'Well, get them off anyway.'

Katherine began laughing.

'What's so funny?' asked Charlie.

'It was me taking my clothes off that started it all.'

'Taking your clothes off?' repeated Milly. 'You've been taking your clothes off? You'd better tell us what this is all about.'

Milly, Charlie and Tom sat open-mouthed as Katherine went into all that had happened.

'Poor old Josh,' said Charlie. 'A stroke.'

'The old dear must be bloody wicked to do a thing like that,' said Milly.

'Well, she thought she had every right to.'

''Ere, Kate, she didn't really think you – you know, with Josh, did she?' asked Charlie.

Milly leapt up. 'Charlie Stevens! What a terrible thing to ask!'

Charlie was grinning like a Cheshire cat. 'Well, I only asked.'

Katherine too was grinning. 'No, she just felt she needed a good excuse to give Josh a hiding, only it turned out to be far worse than she thought it would.'

'And she can walk, an' all?' asked Milly.

'Yes. She's a bit wobbly, mind, but she can walk all right.'

'Fancy that place belonging to her,' said Charlie.

'You gonner work for her?' asked Milly.

'I don't want to. I reckon she'll have me up and down those stairs all day, but I haven't got a lot of choice.'

'You'll have to have help if you do decide to stay,' said Tom.

'I can't see her staying upstairs. She'll be down making sure I don't steal anything, or at the very least give someone a cup of tea and don't take the money.'

'What a turn-up for the book,' said Charlie.

'Well, let's hope by Monday she'll realise what an asset I am. I've already asked for a rise.'

Charlie laughed. 'Good on yer, girl. Don't you let her push you about.'

Katherine slowly stirred her tea. 'I wonder if she'll change her mind about keeping the shop?'

'Does she own it or rent it?' asked Tom.

'I don't know. Wait a minute. They rent it. I've seen Josh talking to the landlord. Why?'

'If she can't keep it open she's still got her rent to pay on the flat upstairs.'

'Yes, but what about Josh? She'll have to look after him when he comes home or pay someone to do it.'

'Well, you'll just have to wait till Monday,' said Milly.

'Yes,' said Katherine slowly. Her mind was already moving forward. 'Any idea what the rent on that place would be?' she asked.

'Dunno,' said Charlie.

'Why?' asked Milly. 'Here, you're not thinking of—'

Katherine laughed. 'Where have I got the money to start a bus—' Her voice trailed off. 'Ida!'

'Ida?' said Charlie and Milly together.

'Why not? I could borrow it from Ida and pay it back, it's a very good—'

'Just a minute. Hold on a tick, Miss Katherine,' said Tom, interrupting her. 'I don't like to put a damper on things, but what about Mrs Trent? Would she let you have it, and would you like her living upstairs?'

'He's right, you know,' said Milly.

Katherine felt deflated. She knew it wouldn't come to her that easily.

Chapter 25

All day Sunday Katherine felt low and moped about, her thoughts continually going to Josh. What was going to happen to him? What was going to happen to Nellie? And more important, what was going to happen to her and her job? She didn't want to work for Nellie.

'I think you'd better take some liver salts,' suggested Milly. 'I think you might be coming down with something.'

On Monday morning Katherine could hardly open her eyes. She tried to lift her head from the pillow. Her throat felt as if it had closed overnight, she was hot, then cold, and every bone in her body ached. 'Oh no!' she moaned out loud. 'I've got a chill.'

For days she was vaguely aware of Milly bringing her tea, propping her up and spoon feeding her hot broth, and slipping a stone hot-water bottle beneath her feet. Days drifted into nights. Time meant nothing.

'You know this is because you got soaking wet on Sat'day, don't you?' she heard Milly say, as cold flannels were placed on her hot, fevered brow.

Katherine tried to give her a hint of a smile; the last thing she wanted was to be lectured to.

She tossed and turned. She could hear herself shouting and calling from far away. She thought she saw Joseph sitting on the bed, but it was misty and she couldn't get him into focus. Then he smiled and held her hand. When she opened her eyes again he had gone. 'Joseph,' she croaked.

The door creaked open. But it wasn't Joseph standing there. It was Robert. He had grown so tall and handsome, but he looked very angry. 'Why did you desert me?' he shouted.

'Robert!' she cried out. 'You've come to see me!'

Her first-born came towards her.

'Robert, I didn't want to leave you. Please forgive me.'

'But you did leave me, and Father. We will never forgive you, never, never!' He turned and walked away.

'Robert!' she screamed. 'Wait!' She struggled to get out of bed. Hands were holding her down. 'Please let me go! I've got to catch him. I've got to tell him how handsome he is, and how much I still love him.' She tried to get away from the hands, but they wouldn't give way. She cried out and salty tears ran down her cheeks. Strands of hair brushed across her face. Someone was wiping her forehead. She couldn't move. Finally she gave up and lay back, worn out and exhausted. Her Robert had gone, and the blackness returned.

Katherine opened her eyes. Milly was standing over her.

'Welcome back.'

Katherine struggled to sit up. 'What time is it?'

'Ten.'

'What? I've got to get up! I'm late for work and I promised Nellie . . .'

Milly gently pushed her back against the pillows. 'You ain't going nowhere, not today.'

Katherine felt bewildered. 'Why? Milly, what day is it?'

'Saturday.'

'What? Where . . . ?'

'You, my girl, have been very ill. You have been delirious.'

Katherine frowned. She tried to remember. 'Have I been here almost a week?'

'Yes.'

'Was I that bad?'

'You had us very worried.'

248

Gradually things started to become clear. 'I thought Robert came to see me.'

'Only in your mind. It took all me and Charlie's strength to hold you down. You tried to run after him.'

'I'm sorry.'

Milly silently patted her hand.

'Have I been a lot of trouble?'

'No, course not.'

'I'd like to get up.'

'Well, wait till after dinner, then if you feel like it I'll help you into the chair. But only for a little while.'

'Yes, nurse.'

Later that afternoon Milly left her sitting in the chair. Katherine gazed out of the window, but not seeing the houses in her view. She let her thoughts go to Robert. What did he look like now? Would he be an older version of Joseph? Why in her mind was it him she most wanted to see?

She heard Joseph bounding up the stairs. He flung open the door and, falling to his knees, held her close. 'Oh, Ma! I've been so worried about you.'

She gently patted his head.

'I didn't like seeing you so ill. Are you feeling better now?'

'Yes thank you.'

He sat on the bed. 'You know you were shouting about Robert?'

'So Milly told me.'

'Do you miss him?'

'In a way. I shall always feel guilty at leaving him.'

'You never know, one of these days he might come to England.'

'He wouldn't know where to find me if he did.' She knew she had to steer the conversation away from Robert. 'Now, could you get me a cup of tea?'

He kissed her cheek. 'Course.'

Katherine sat back. Would she ever see her first-born son again?

Every day, thanks to Milly's care, Katherine got stronger. They sat and talked at length just like they did when Katherine first moved in, but now they were true friends. They talked about Dolly and Briony, and when Olive, now pregnant again, brought baby Dolly round, all work stopped.

'She's a little charmer,' said Milly, lifting her high in the air.

'Well, I hope you're gonner be as pleased with the next one,' said Olive.

'Reckon I'll have me work cut out then.'

'How you feeling, Olive?'

'Not too bad at all. Mind you, I won't be sorry when May's over.'

'At least you won't be carrying all through the summer.'

'That's true.'

'Your mother's going to let me go out at the end of the week.' Olive laughed. 'She's a good nurse, but a strict one.'

'Yes, I have found that out.'

'The pie and mash shop's closed,' said Milly, as they walked along. 'Charlie said someone told him the old girl's gone away.'

'What, for good?'

'Dunno.'

'What about Josh?'

'He didn't know what happened to him.'

Katherine felt sorry for the man she had looked on as a friend. 'Has she left her home and everything?'

'Dunno about that. Charlie didn't learn much about it. The butcher might know.'

Katherine hesitated when they reached Trent's. It looked sad and forlorn with its closed sign hanging lopsided on the door.

She thought about the laughter and the bawdy remarks, the arguing over politics, the sad time during the strike when the shop overflowed with angry men, and now about poor Josh. She gave up a silent prayer: please make him well again.

Milly took her arm. 'Come on.'

The butcher smiled and looked genuinely pleased to see her. 'Hallo there, Kate. Heard you was poorly. You feeling better now?'

'Yes, thank you. How did you know I've been ill?'

'Word gets around. Mind you, you don't look all that good, very pasty-faced.'

She smiled. She knew she wouldn't get too many compliments. 'Do you know how Josh is?'

'Na. When you didn't turn up on the Monday we all thought you'd jacked it in, but then one of the blokes from the docks said you was ill. Ron said he went in to see how Josh was and his missis was going mad that you hadn't turned up.'

'Had she got up?'

'She must have. She's bloody barmy. D'you know, she was gonner set about Ron with her stick.'

Katherine laughed.

'It wasn't funny. Poor bloke looked scared out of his wits. Think it must'a bin then that she decided to go away. Nobody will work for her.'

'Do you know where she went?'

'Na.'

'She said she had a sister in Kent. But what about Josh, is he still in hospital?'

'Dunno.'

'What hospital did you take him to?'

'The cottage hospital up the road.'

Katherine turned to Milly. 'Could we go there?'

'Not today. You've done enough for one day.'

'That's right, Kate. You mustn't overdo it.'

Milly fussed with her shopping bag. 'It's her first day out,' she said to the butcher. 'I'll have a pound of scrag end while I'm here.'

Katherine grinned. She felt like a naughty girl who'd just been allowed out.

The following day they went to the hospital, only to be told that Mr Trent had been sent to a home by the seaside to help him recover.

'Will he ever be well again?' Katherine asked the nurse.

'That's hard to say. Some people recover from a stroke while others remain like a cabbage for the rest of their lives.'

It upset Katherine to think of Josh as a cabbage.

As they walked home Katherine said to Milly, 'I'm going to take over the pie shop.'

'I ain't surprised. So, how do you go about that?'

'First, I've got to find out who the landlord is and what sort of rent he's asking. Then I'll have to buy stock.'

'And what yer gonner do for money, may I ask?'

'I'll go and see Ida.'

'Will you be able to pay her back?'

'It's a good business.'

'You've got it all worked out, ain't yer?'

'I must admit it's something I've been thinking about.'

'Have you now? Will you live over the shop?'

Katherine stopped. 'Oh Milly, I hadn't thought about that.'

'I can't stop you moving on.'

Katherine felt guilty. 'I shall really miss living with you and Charlie.'

Milly tucked her bag under her arm. 'Well, you ain't got it yet, and I for one don't believe in counting me chickens 'fore they're hatched.'

Katherine could see Milly wasn't going to be happy with the arrangements.

The following day Katherine went alone to the butcher's to

find out who the landlord was. He smiled when he heard what she had in mind.

'Mr Sharman. He comes every month for his rent. He ain't due till next week.'

'What day?'

'Mostly on a Monday.'

'What's he like?'

'Don't have a lot to do with him. I just pays me rent and he goes off. I think him and Josh got on.'

'Was he a tall smart man, with a paunch?'

'Sounds like him.'

'They used to chat. Do you mind if I ask how much rent you pay?'

'I pay twelve and six a week. That's for the flat an' all, mind. I don't reckon Josh paid as much as that as they've been there years, and her old man before that.'

'I know. If I happen to miss him could you get his address for me?'

'Sure. No, missis, I ain't got any liver left.' The butcher continued serving his customers.

'You look done in,' said Milly, when Katherine walked into the kitchen. 'Sit down, I'll pour you out a cuppa. Well, did you see him?' she asked sharply.

'No. The butcher said he comes on Monday. I have seen him talking to Josh at times.'

'What about, rent?'

'The butcher pays twelve and six a week, but I reckon I'll have to pay more.'

'Why's that?'

'It'll be a new tenancy agreement and all landlords look for a good excuse to charge more.'

'Well, you know all about that, don't yer?' Milly was definitely put out. 'But he may already have let it.'

'Yes, there is that possibility.' Katherine didn't want to think about that. She had made up her mind: this was what she wanted to do.

On Monday she went to the butcher's about the time she knew the landlord called. 'Has he been yet?' she asked.

'Not yet,' came the reply.

She took a slow walk down the road. She passed the stalls and shops, and looking into the ironmonger's, thoughts of Briony came flooding back. They never did find out if all the rumours about Mr Wilks were true. Now Briony had gone and the Addamses had moved away.

She felt sorry for Josh and hoped he'd be better one day. What would happen to Nellie? So many things had changed in the short time Katherine had lived in Rotherhithe. As she began to wander back she caught sight of the man she knew to be the landlord hurrying along, and quickened her step.

'Excuse me, sir! Excuse me.'

He stopped and, turning round, asked abruptly, 'Yes, what do you want?'

'Could I have a word?'

'What about?'

'It's rather private.'

'What's it about?'

Katherine looked anxiously around, feeling very uncomfortable. 'I would like to rent the shop.'

'You used to work for Josh Trent, didn't you?'

'Yes.'

'Yes, I remember now, used to see you in there.' He laughed. 'It was the hat that put me off.'

Katherine touched her hat.

'Josh used to speak very highly of you. Did you say you wanted to rent a shop?'

'Yes.'

'Now where would you get the money from to start a business?'

Katherine felt ill at ease and awkward at having to stand in the street to discuss her future. 'I have been in business before.'

'And you finished up working in Trent's? It wasn't that successful then, was it?'

Katherine didn't reply.

'Can't say I approve of women in business. But then again if your money's good . . . Now, which one did you have in mind?'

'The pie shop.'

'Sorry, that's gone.'

Katherine gasped. He had dismissed her plans in a flash.

He took her arm and bent his head closer. 'I do have another not too far from here, that's if you are interested.'

'Where is that?'

'Look, take my card and come and see me tomorrow. Perhaps we can talk about it in my office over a cup of tea.'

She looked at his card. 'Thank you, Mr Sharman. When will it be convenient?'

'About ten. I shall look forward to it.' He raised his trilby slightly and walked away.

Katherine stood and watched him go. There was something about the man she didn't like. But she had to go and find out about the other shop. Where was it? And who had taken the pie shop? If it was near, would there be trouble for her opening another so close? She would have her own shop and show him that this woman could run a business, she resolved. Besides, she had to do something soon as her money wouldn't last for ever, and Milly still had to be paid.

Chapter 26

Sharp at ten o'clock Katherine knocked on Mr Sharman's office door.

'Come in, my dear.' Without his trilby, his balding head emphasised his round florid face. 'Take a seat.' He sat back. 'Now, you said you would like to rent one of my shops?'

'Yes.'

'You said you were in business before?'

'Yes.' Katherine didn't want to reveal too much.

'That does sound rather unlikely seeing as where you finished up.'

'It was a while ago.'

'I see. Where was that? If I'm going to let you rent one of my shops I need to have references, you know.' He took up a pen and began writing.

She knew he didn't need references, so was this just a ploy to put her off? Women round this way didn't start their own businesses, only market stalls and the like. 'It was over the water.'

'I see. You're not one of these silly suffragette women who believe in women's rights, and all that, are you?'

Katherine had to hold her tongue. She wanted to be independent and tell him that she did believe in women's rights but didn't have the courage to be truthful about her feelings. 'No. I lost the business when my husband died.'

'So it wasn't really yours?' He sat back. 'What sort of collateral have you?' He bent his head forward. 'You do know what I mean by collateral, don't you?'

How dare he think she was an idiot? Katherine wanted to storm out. No man would have to answer these mundane questions. 'Mr Sharman, if you would be so kind as to tell me where this shop is I can let you know if it will be suitable for my requirements.'

He laughed. 'That's what I like to see, a woman with a bit of spirit.'

She felt herself flush with anger.

'The one I have in mind is in Perry Street.'

'Perry Street? What, under the arches?'

'Yes. Nice little shops.'

'They are horrible, and well away from everything.' She stood up. 'No thank you, Mr Sharman.'

'What sort of business did you have in mind, Kate? I may call you Kate?'

'No, you may not. My name is Mrs Carter, and I won't bother telling you what I need a shop for, as it won't be any of your concern. Good day, Mr Sharman.' She went to move towards the door.

'Please, Mrs Carter, sit down.'

'Why?'

He came round the desk. 'Please.' He pointed to the chair.

Reluctantly Katherine sat down.

'Why did you want Trent's?'

She toyed with her gloves. 'I know I could run it well. Who will be taking it over?'

He coughed. 'Well, at the moment we are still in the negotiating stage.'

'So, in other words, you haven't let it?' Katherine was feeling stronger. She knew she had this man cornered.

'I have been waiting for years for that property to become vacant.'

'Why? Just so that you could charge a lot more for the rent?

I'll give you the same as the butcher, twelve and six a week.'

'I can't—'

Katherine stood up. 'That's my offer, take it or leave it.' She turned and walked to the door. 'Good day, Mr Sharman.' She was shaking. Had she gone too far?

His laughter caused her to turn round.

'I like you. Come back and we will draw up an agreement. The rent is paid one month in advance, you know.'

She smiled.

'Mind you, if you don't make a go of it and miss a month's rent, you'll be out on your ear.'

'Don't worry. I intend to make a go of it and I won't miss paying the rent.' She sat, trying to look full of confidence, but deep down she was worried. What if Ida wouldn't lend her the money for her first month's rent?

'Will you be using the flat?'

'Yes. My son will be living with me.'

'You have a son? I don't know what state the place is in, but then that's not my problem. I sent builders round to repair the chimney Mrs Trent was complaining had fallen down.'

'What about the Trents' furniture?'

'She didn't leave any instructions.'

'But you said you've heard from Mrs Trent.'

'Not really. She just sent a note round about the chimney, said she was going away and she didn't know when she would be back.'

Katherine froze. 'So she could come back and take it all away from me?'

'No. Once you've signed the agreement the shop will be yours.'

'So what shall I do with the furniture?'

'Sell it.'

'I can't do that!'

'As I said, that, my dear woman, is your problem. Now do you want to sign this?'

She nodded and he pushed the agreement in front of her.

He walked to the door and held it open for her. 'It has been a pleasure doing business with you, Mrs Carter, and as soon as I get the rent you can have the keys.'

'Thank you.'

Katherine almost ran home. She couldn't wait to tell all of them her good news. But would they think it *was* good news?

'I don't think I fancy living above the pie shop. Will it stink of fish from those rotten eels?' Joseph was the first to air his views.

'I hope to be doing more than jellied eels.'

'What's the place like?'

'When I've paid the first month's rent I get the key.'

'Where're you getting that sort of money from?' asked Charlie.

'She reckons she's gonner borrow it from Ida,' said Milly sharply.

'D'you think that's wise?' asked Tom.

'Of course it is. If I want to start on my own.'

'Well, I don't reckon a woman should run that sorta business,' said Charlie.

'Why not?' Katherine was trying hard to keep her temper.

''Cos of the sorta blokes you get in there – I reckon they'll lead you a right merry dance.'

'Why should they? I've known them for quite a while now.'

'Yer, but that was when Josh was in charge.' Charlie began rolling a cigarette.

'You men are all the same. You don't like seeing women get on.'

'There's no need to get on your high horse. It's just that I reckon they'll try it on with a woman.'

'Doing what?' asked Milly.

'Not paying. Making out they ain't got any money and a woman's gotter be a soft touch.'

'Not this woman,' said Katherine with dignity.

'Have you thought about a nice little haberdashery?' asked Tom.

'No.'

'Well, I wish you luck then,' said Charlie.

Katherine wanted to scream. This is what she had wanted and all they could do was try to pour cold water on it. 'I may ask your help to get the place cleaned up, especially upstairs,' she said calmly to Milly. She wanted to involve her.

'So, when you seeing Ida?' asked Milly.

'Tomorrow.'

'I see.'

'For your sake let's hope she's in a good mood,' said Charlie.

'This is a business deal.'

'Yer, I know.'

At first Ida was a bit hesitant about lending her the money, but Katherine's enthusiasm quickly won her over. All in all, she borrowed five pounds, which she had to pay back at the princely rate of ten shillings a week, plus one pound interest.

As soon as she got the key Katherine hurried to the shop. Her shop. Mr Sharman had wanted to come with her but she preferred to be on her own.

She pushed open the shop door and took a deep breath. The smell of rotten meat nearly knocked her over. She hurried through the door to the back of the shop and rats quickly scurried away. She would have to get herself a cat.

Very carefully she made her way to the back door. The whole place seemed quiet and eerie. She almost expected Nellie to jump out on her or yell from upstairs.

She studied the yard with a fresh look. This was going to need a good cleanup. She couldn't bear a lot of unnecessary mess.

The place felt cold and damp. She made her way upstairs, not knowing what she'd find. Nellie's room was as she had left it. Even the chamber pot was still full and it stank. The bedclothes were in a heap on the floor. She opened the window and moved into the other bedroom that must have been Josh's. It wasn't very clean, but it was tidy. She sat on his bed. What could she do with all his and Nellie's clothes, and what about all this furniture? Should she use it till Nellie got in touch? At the moment she and Joseph had nothing but their clothes.

She shivered, and moved into the last room upstairs, the parlour. Ashes were still in the grate. She knew she could make this room warm and cosy. The thought of being in her own home after all this time brought a tear to her eyes. 'I am the mistress of all this,' she said out loud and, with her arms outstretched, turned a full circle. 'And nobody is going to take it away from me.'

Before she made her way back to Milly's she called in to the butcher. 'Tell everybody the pie shop will be open for business as usual on Monday.'

He grinned. 'That's great news, Kate. I wish you the best of luck.'

'Thanks. I'll be in for meat on Saturday, and I expect a good price.'

'For you, my dear, I'll do a good deal.'

As she walked home there was a spring in her step. She felt so happy. Christmas was only four weeks away – would all the Stevenses like to spend it with her and Joseph? She had to get the place into some kind of order first. Tomorrow she would start on the cleaning, and as far as she was concerned it would be a labour of love. Rotherhithe would be her home for ever.

At first Katherine worried Milly wouldn't go with her to clean up. She began putting many obstacles in her way, but eventually her curiosity must have got the better of her and she reluctantly decided to help. On Wednesday morning, armed with cloths and various other cleaning implements, they set off.

'What's that stink?' asked Milly when Katherine pushed the door open. 'Thought you said you'd emptied Nellie's po.'

'I did. Josh left the meat out. I did throw it all away but the smell still lingers.' Katherine hadn't told anyone about the rats.

'This kitchen could do with a good cleanup. What's it like outside?'

'Not that good.'

'Blimey! It is a bit of a mess,' said Milly, wandering out to see. 'Look at the state of this bog,' she added, gingerly pushing the door open.

'I know. I tried to keep it clean but Josh wouldn't buy any carbolic. I'll pop along to the ironmonger's later.'

All day they swept and scrubbed. They stripped the beds and bundled up Nellie's and Josh's clothes in the sheets.

'What you gonner do with 'em?' asked Milly, pointing to the bundles on the bed.

'I'll clean out a cupboard and put them in there for the time being.'

'At least the furniture ain't bad. That three-piece in the parlour could do with a bit of a clean, though. And those curtains look as if one wash and they'll fall to pieces. What you gonner do about sheets and stuff for you and Joe?'

'I don't know. I was thinking of going along to the draper's to see how much I can have on tick.'

Milly laughed.

'What's so funny?'

'You talking about having things on tick. When you first came over this way you didn't even know the meaning of the word.'

'A lot has changed.' She sat on the bed. 'Milly, I'm very fond of you and you've been very good to me and Joseph and I hope we remain friends for ever.'

'Course we will.' She sat next to Katherine. 'Sorry if I've bin a bit . . . well, you know. But it's just that I don't want you to go. It's been nice having a woman round the house. I can let you have some bedding. Don't forget I've got all Dolly's.'

'Will Tom mind?'

'No.' She began scratching her arm. 'I reckon you've got a few lodgers here. When you go along to the ironmonger's get a flit gun and I'll give these rooms up here a good going-over. When you reckon on moving in?'

'I'd like it to be Saturday.'

'So soon?'

'Well, I've got to get the shop open as soon as I can.'

'Yer, I s'pose you have. If you like I'll come and give you a hand till you're on your feet.'

'You are a real friend.'

'So when you opening?'

'Monday.'

'Christ! We'd better get a move on. You've only got a few days.'

'Yes, and I've got to do the cooking and clean up downstairs.'

'Well, let's get cracking then. But first I think we deserve a cuppa, don't you?'

'Be my guest.'

'Here, I hope we ain't gonner have to put the money in the box?'

Katherine laughed. 'No, no yet, we're not open.'

On Saturday when Joseph finished work he came to his new home.

'Joseph!' said Katherine, opening the shop door. She had been looking out of the window, waiting for him, and greeted him with a hug. 'Welcome to your new home.'

Silently he looked around.

'Go through that door.' She ushered him through the door behind the counter. A lovely smell of pies cooking filled the air. 'We will use this room down here as the kitchen. It stays nice and warm with the oven. I'll show you upstairs, and your very own room. You've waited a long while for this,' she said eagerly over her shoulder.

Upstairs he stood in the doorway. 'Is this mine?'

She nodded and put her arm round his shoulders. 'Yes, it's all yours. Come and see the parlour.'

It was warm and inviting, with a fire blazing in the grate. 'Well, what do you think? Do you like this room?'

'Where did the furniture come from?' he asked, looking around.

'It belongs to Josh and his wife.'

'What if they come back and want it?'

'I'll have to cross that bridge when I come to it.'

'But he isn't dead, and you've taken over his home, his belongings and his business. It's as if you've waited for him to go.'

'I didn't. If I didn't have this place the landlord would have let it to someone else and they might have thrown everything out. This way I can take care of it for them.'

'What if they don't come back?'

Katherine was surprised at his attitude. 'When I know for sure I'll send them the money for it.'

'But what if they want the shop back?'

'This is our home now.' She was getting a little tired of his questions. 'You used to be on about having your own room, but now it seems you've changed your tune.'

'I'll miss Ted,' he said.

'And I shall miss Milly, but we have to move on. We couldn't stay there for ever, and an opportunity like this only comes now and again. You always did hate changes.'

He smiled. 'It does look nice and cosy here. But we won't have to live on pies and saveloys, will we?'

'No, I think we can go to a roast on Sundays.'

Katherine was happy. This was what she wanted. She and Joseph were together in their own home, and nobody was going to take it away from her.

Chapter 27

On Monday Katherine was surprised at the number of people who popped their heads round the door to wish her good luck. At lunchtime she was rushed off her feet. She desperately needed help. Would Milly be prepared to come and give her a hand every day?

After lunch, when trade began to settle down, Ron, wearing a huge grin, came in. 'Hallo there, Katie love. It's good to see you back. We all thought you'd gone for good.' He rubbed his hands together. 'It's nice and warm in here. I tell yer, it's bloody cold out there.'

She looked at the steamed-up windows running with water, and brushed a stray damp strand of hair back from her forehead. 'This is hard work on your own.'

'Well, you could get a lad in like Josh used to.'

'That might not be a bad idea.' She pushed a mug of tea towards him. He reached into his pocket for the money. 'Have this one on me.'

'You're not gonner make a packet like that.'

'You've been a good friend, so the least I can do is give you a cuppa. Mind you, this is the first and the last.'

He laughed. 'D'you know, I reckon you'll make a go of this place. Good mind to open a book on it.'

'What's the odds?'

'You've certainly changed since working here.'

'I know, and it's for the better. Mind you, I'll miss Josh. He wasn't a bad old thing.'

'Yer, that was a bloody shame. He had a lot to put up with from her. I reckon she was a bit . . .' He put his finger to his forehead and twisted it. 'D'you think she'll ever come back?'

'I hope not. But you can never tell with someone like Nellie. She's just as likely to come swanning in here as if nothing has happened and expect to take over.'

He looked alarmed. 'You don't really think that, do you?'

'I don't know. After all, she just upped and left everything including her overflowing chamber pot.'

Ron was taking a mouthful of tea when Katherine said that. He laughed and the tea went everywhere. 'I've heard it all now!'

That evening, after she'd closed the shop, Katherine made her way upstairs to Joseph, who had come in earlier. He had quickly passed through, only stopping long enough to say hallo and glance around.

'You look tired,' he said, looking up when she entered the parlour. He was sitting warming himself in front of the fire.

'It's been a long day, but a very enjoyable one.' She plonked herself down on the sofa.

'But has it been profitable?'

'Yes. I've taken enough to pay the butcher and the ten shillings I owe Ida. Things are going to get better. The fruit pies I made went down a treat, but I will have to have help.'

'What about Milly?'

'She might do it for a little while. I was thinking of getting a young lad in.'

'Don't look at me. I'm not skivvying for anyone.'

Any idea she'd had of their running the business together was quickly quashed.

All week Katherine worked hard. She was disappointed Milly hadn't been in to see her, but knowing Milly, she guessed her absence was because she didn't want to get in the way.

Every evening, after she closed, she prepared the food for the next day and then early in the morning, long before she opened, she would be busy making pies.

Joseph sniffed the air when he came down for his breakfast. 'Those pies certainly smell good.'

'And it's nice and warm in here. Don't you get cold in the garage?'

'No, not really.'

She knew he wouldn't complain if he did.

The following Monday morning Mrs Duke appeared in the doorway.

'Heard you'd took this place over.' She waddled up to the counter. 'Had to come and black me nose, didn't I? Doing all right then?'

'Would you like tea?' asked Katherine, ignoring her last remark.

'How much yer gonner charge me?'

'You can have this one on me.'

'Yer, why not? Ta very much. Mind you, you ain't gonner make that much if you keep giving it away.'

'Don't worry, Mrs Duke. That's the first and last.'

Mrs Duke put her shopping bag on the floor and, taking her tea, went to sit at the table near the counter. 'Well, how you doing then?' She rested her elbows on the marble-topped table and clutched the thick china mug with both hands.

'Very well, thank you.'

'Must say I was a bit surprised when Milly told me. Thought you was gonner get something better. A bit more snobby.' Her eyes scanned every corner of the room.

Katherine smiled. 'This is just a start.' She turned and wiped down the counter.

'Well, it looks a bit cleaner in here. But you don't wanner make it too posh otherwise you'll send all the riff-raff away. They're used to spitting on the floor.'

'Not in my place they don't.'

Mrs Duke was looking round. 'What yer gonner call it then?'

'Call it?'

'Yer, it ain't Trent's now, is it?'

'Well, no.'

'It'll have to have a new name.'

'Yes, I suppose it will. But I can't afford a sign writer just yet, so that will give me time to think about a name.'

'I reckon Kate's Place.'

'Kate's Place,' repeated Katherine. 'That's got a nice ring to it. I could well call it that. Or what about Kate's Kitchen?'

'Yer.' Mrs Duke put her head on one side. 'That don't sound bad at all.'

'Right. Welcome to Kate's Kitchen.'

'In that case I'll have another free cuppa for a toast and me advice.'

Katherine laughed. 'I suppose I'll have to be Kate from now on.'

'Please yerself about that. Two sugars in it this time then, Kate. By the way, did you know Ron the bookies' runner's been caught?'

Kate sat down. 'No. I didn't.'

'Yer, he got run in last week.'

'I thought I hadn't seen him.'

'Goes up before the beak on Monday. Some of the blokes reckons he could end up getting a year.'

'No! Poor Ron. A year in prison.'

'Shouldn't worry too much about him, he's had a good run for his money. Well, I best be off.'

Kate watched her walk out of the door. Her thoughts were still on Ron. She would miss him. He had been a good friend.

* * *

Kate was a bit disappointed that it wasn't until Friday lunchtime that Milly called in, and she was very busy.

'Milly. Please come round here and pour out some tea.'

'Mrs Duke said you was rushed off yer feet.'

Kate smiled. She hadn't been busy when Mrs Duke was here, so had the older woman just been trying to make Milly feel jealous that she'd been here and Milly hadn't?

'You'll find the plates over there and there's plenty more mash out back,' said Kate quickly, as she put a pie and some mash in a dish a woman had brought in. 'Yes, these are apple.'

'Stick it on top. I can scrape the tater off when I gets home. Me old man won't know the difference.'

The pie was plonked on top and taken away.

After a short while Milly seemed at ease collecting dirty plates and mugs and emptying the overflowing ashtrays. In between Kate told her about Mrs Duke and the name they'd come to.

'So it's Kate from now on, is it?'

'Well, it's less of a mouthful than Katherine.'

'Our Kate's certainly made a difference to this place, ain't she?' said an old man who slapped Milly's bottom as she passed him.

'She works hard.'

'Yer, but it's the cooking what counts. Her pies are . . .' He kissed his fingers in a gesture of satisfaction.

Milly laughed. Kate could see she was enjoying herself.

Later, in a quiet moment, they were sitting having a mug of tea and Kate said, 'How would you like to work here with me?'

'Dunno. Charlie wouldn't like it if his tea wasn't on the table when he got home.'

'What if it was only during lunchtime?'

'Dunno. I'll have a word with Charlie. He can be a bit funny about wives working. Likes to think he's the breadwinner.'

'Please, I need someone. Besides, it will give you some money of your own.'

'Don't know about that.'

'Please, Milly.'

'I'll see. Now I must go.'

'Would you like to take some pies for Charlie and Ted and Tom's dinners?'

'Na, ta all the same, but I've got a rabbit pie ready to go in the oven.'

'Perhaps another day then. Would you all like to come here to tea on Sunday?'

'No, sorry. Olive and Ernie's coming round. You and Joe can come if you like.'

'Thanks all the same, but I expect I'll be busy.'

'Well, please yourself.' She kissed Kate's cheek and left.

Kate touched her cheek. Milly's kiss seemed to lack the warmth they had known. She almost felt as if Milly were trying to keep her distance. Was she trying to tell her something? Had Charlie put his foot down? He was normally so easy-going. Perhaps he was frightened of women getting too strong. Or was this awkwardness because Milly didn't want to work for her?

It was a quiet spell, and Kate was thinking things over while washing up, when the door opened and Grace walked in.

'See you've opened up again then?'

'Yes. Grace, it's so good to see you,' said Kate, wiping her wet hands on a cloth and pouring her out a mug of tea. 'Is everything all right?'

'Yes, ta.'

'And your mother?' asked Kate tentatively.

Grace sat down and took a cigarette from her handbag. 'She died.'

'I'm so sorry.' She put the tea in front of Grace and sat at her table.

Grace looked nervously about her.

Kate was at a loss for words. 'Are you expecting your Mr Friday?'

Grace nodded quickly. 'D'you mind me coming in here?'

'No, of course not. Did you manage to get enough for your mother's funeral?' Kate asked softly.

Grace shook her pretty head.

'I'm sorry.' Kate looked up when the door opened and a cold draught blew in. Mr Friday stood in the doorway and Grace quickly stood up and left, leaving her tea untouched.

'My God, it's cold out there!' The door opened again and an old man of about fifty, wearing a raincoat tied round the waist with string, staggered in. He moved close to the counter and Kate stood back. While he looked around he stroked his pepper-and-salt-coloured beard. His white hair was sticking out from under his dirty trilby. He swayed and held on to the counter.

'The name's Seamus.' He held out his hand to shake Kate's.

Fear gripped her. He was Irish and they had a reputation for being volatile around here. Why did he have to come in here? She wanted to throw him out. 'What do you want?' There was no warmth in her voice.

'Seamus O'Brien, and I'm pleased to make your acquaintance, my dear lady. Just heard the other feller's gone. Couldn't get on with him.'

Kate stood and stared. 'You're drunk!'

'Well, I do like a little tipple now and again. Just the odd one or two, you understand. It helps to keep out the cold.'

Thoughts filled her mind of the problem she'd had with Mr Addams. She was alone and had to remain calm. All the while she was behind the counter she was safe. 'A tipple?' She laughed half-heartedly and waved her hand in front of her face. 'You're knocking me over with the fumes.'

He laughed. It was a soft lilting laugh, causing his bright blue eyes to twinkle. 'I like you, like a woman with a sense of humour. Don't see many these days. Most of 'em are tight-lipped and tight-arsed.' He put his hand to his mouth. 'Begging your pardon, me dear! I'm sorry. That just slipped out. No offence meant.'

Although nervous, Kate wanted to smile, but knew she shouldn't encourage him. On the other hand he appeared to be a pleasant man. 'Did you want a mug of tea?'

'Now that's real civil of you. I don't mind if I do.'

'That will be tuppence.'

He held up his hands. 'Now there was me thinking you was giving it to me out of the goodness of your heart.'

'Tuppence,' said Kate, holding out her hand and desperately trying to suppress the smile that wanted to break through.

'My, you're a hard woman.' Seamus paid his money and sat at the table near the counter. 'What happened to the other feller?'

'He had a stroke.'

'Did he now? Is his missis still upstairs?'

Kate shook her head. 'No. How do you know about Nellie?'

He touched the side of his nose. 'Don't give to tell all me knowledge at once. That way you'll be pleased to see me again to find out what more I know about Nellie.'

Kate had to burst out laughing. 'You've certainly got a touch of the blarney.'

'Have you ever been to my fair isle?'

'No.'

'It's very beautiful.'

Kate thought about Briony and her mother. Would they both still be alive if the Addamses had never left? 'So what brings you over here, then?'

'Work. Not a lot doing over there.'

The brothers Bill and Bert from the market came in.

'Give us a mug of hot strong tea, Kate,' said Bill. 'It's bloody freezing out there. I'm glad I'm not a brass monkey.' He turned to sit down. 'Blimey! It's old Seamus. What you doing round this way again?'

Bert grinned and asked, 'When d'they let you out?'

'Yesterday.'

Bill laughed. 'You wanner watch him, Kate. Right old charmer, he is.'

'I've gathered that already.'

'She's lovely,' said Seamus. 'Listen to that pretty voice. Reminds me of back home. It sounds like a gentle stream trickling over stones.'

'Hark at him,' said Bill. 'His dad brought him over when he was a baby, and he's been in the nick most of his life.'

'What for?' asked Kate in alarm.

'I was just unlucky,' said Seamus.

'Unlucky be buggered,' said Bert. 'You was caught nicking, and more than once.'

'As I said, I was just unlucky. I kept getting caught.'

They all laughed.

'You know old Ron's finished up inside?' said Bill to Kate.

'Yes, I did hear.'

'He got six months.'

'My God, six months! What terrible deed did he do?' asked Seamus.

'Bookies' runner,' said Bert.

'Well, if you ask me he didn't run fast enough.'

'Bit like you then, Seamus,' said Bill.

'Yes, I think you could say that.' He grinned at Kate.

She could see he was another larger-than-life character that she hoped was harmless, and would add to the interesting people who had become part of her life.

Kate was more than pleased when Milly walked in the following day.

'I can only stay an hour,' she said, taking her coat off.

Kate threw her arms round her. 'Thank you.'

Tea, pies, mash, saveloys and pease pudding were all quickly distributed to the many waiting customers, and again with plenty of compliments for Kate's cooking. Kate could see Milly was enjoying herself, and the hour flew by.

'Sorry I can't stay any longer.'

'Thank you so much. It's been wonderful having your help. Will I see you tomorrow?'

Milly nodded. 'But not on Sat'day.'

'That's all right,' said Kate smiling, but she was worried. Saturday was Josh's busiest day, and now news was getting around about Kate's cooking, she was getting more and more new customers, and she knew they didn't like to be kept waiting.

'Give Charlie, Ted and Tom my love.'

'Right. I'll see you tomorrow.'

Kate looked at the pile of washing up. She had to have regular help, and soon.

Chapter 28

All week Kate was happy working with Milly, and although it was tiring, she knew Milly was enjoying herself. But the problem of how to manage on Saturday grew on Kate's mind.

'Do you know of anyone who could come in for a few hours?' she asked the butcher on Friday.

He shook his head.

'What about your wife?'

'Na, she's got more than enough to do looking after all the kids and giving me a hand.'

'That's the trouble. The women I can trust and know would be fine all have families, and Saturday's the day husbands want them around. And most young lads don't want to work for a woman.'

'Don't worry, something will turn up.'

But she was worried.

That afternoon Kate thought her prayers could be answered when Grace walked in. She quickly poured her a mug of tea. 'Grace, I'm so pleased to see you.'

Grace looked startled. 'Why?'

The two mugs of tea were put on the table and Kate sat beside her. 'I've got a proposition to make to you.'

Grace opened her brown eyes wide. 'What sorta proposition?'

'Do you work on Saturdays?'

'I don't need any more clients.'

Kate laughed. 'Not clients. How would you like to work for me on Saturdays?'

Grace looked thoughtful. 'Dunno. What would I have to do?'

'Serve, help me wash up, that sort of thing.'

'Dunno. How much?'

'Well it wouldn't be as much as you probably get, but if you don't work during the day, well, it's got to be better than nothing.'

'How much?'

Kate held her breath. She knew whatever she offered it wouldn't be anything like what Grace was getting. 'I'll give you two shillings.'

'Two shillings!' she exploded. 'For how long?'

'From about eleven to, say, three.'

'Four hours! Four hours for a lousy two bob?'

When Grace said it, it did sound very paltry, but Kate herself had only got six shillings working for Josh all week. 'That's all I can afford at the moment.'

The door opened and Mr Friday stood in the doorway and looked at Grace. She gave Kate a smile and walked out. Kate knew then that her ray of hope had gone.

'Joseph, I'm so worried. What am I going to do?' That evening she sat next to him on the sofa and poked at the fire with the poker.

He looked up from the book he was reading. 'I suppose you could always get Mrs Duke in to help you out. She'd like that.'

'Don't be so silly! Why haven't you got a nice girlfriend I could rely on?'

'You started this business.'

'I know, but I thought you might have shown some interest.'

'You knew where my interest lay.'

'Yes.' She twirled the poker round and round in her hands. 'I only wish Briony were still alive.'

Joseph put the book down. 'So does Ted.'

'Is he still grieving?'

'Think so. He's changed.'

'Death has that effect on those that are left,' she said sadly.

He put his arm round his mother's shoulder. 'I'll tell you what. Tomorrow I'll ask Mrs Lacy if she knows of anyone that will give you a hand till you get yourself sorted out.'

She patted his shoulder and smiled. 'Thanks.' She was pleased. At last he was beginning to show a little interest in her life.

Joseph had never raised the subject of going to Australia again, so perhaps Milly had been right, and he'd just been trying it on with his mother, though these days he was very quiet and self-possessed, and it was hard for her to know what he was thinking.

Saturday, Kate was feeling very harassed. First the urn wouldn't light, then while she was busy with that the potatoes burned dry. Then the saveloys burst. She screamed out in temper.

'What's that rotten smell?' asked Grace, when she walked through the door at the back of the counter and began to take her coat off. She wasn't wearing rouge on her cheeks.

'Grace!' Kate threw her arms round her, almost knocking off her large hat. She was so pleased to see her she thought she would cry. 'You've come to work here?'

Grace pushed her away and took off the hat. She tucked up the few loose strands of hair that had slipped from the bun that sat on top of her head. 'Only for today, just to see if I like it.'

Kate regained her composure. 'First you had better peel some more potatoes. What you can smell are those which I burnt. Make sure you take all the eyes out. Don't like to see black bits.'

'Fussy, ain't yer?'

'Yes, I am. I'll go out front and get the tea ready.'

All morning as they worked together, Grace was almost as interested in the different people that came in as they were in her. Her presence was a great source of amazement, and brought forth a few comments, for which she had a good-humoured, quick and ready answer.

The most frequent question was, 'Here! Ain't that the tart that comes in here looking for customers?'

Kate's answer was abrupt. 'What she does in her spare time is her affair.'

Grace was a good worker, and when the rush finally eased off she sat at a table with a cigarette and a mug of tea. A lot more of the fuzzy hair had escaped the confines of the pins and hung in attractive tendrils round her face. Her lipstick had disappeared and her nose was shiny.

'Look at the size of me ankles.' Grace began rubbing them.

'Well, those shoes don't help,' said Kate, joining her.

Grace laughed. 'I ain't used ter working upright on me feet.'

'I can't thank you enough. Will you be able to come next Saturday?'

'Yer, why not? Bloody hard work, though, but d'you know, I really enjoyed meself.'

'I'm so pleased.'

Christmas was almost on them, and the Sunday before, Joseph had helped his mother make paper chains, which they hung round the shop.

Kate had asked Grace if she would come in every lunchtime till Thursday, Christmas Day, as Milly was too busy. Much to Kate's relief, Grace had agreed.

On Monday morning when Grace walked in, she stopped in the doorway. 'I ain't ever been in a place with paper chains up before. It looks ever so pretty.'

'Thank you. My son Joseph helped me.'

She took off the hat. 'He sounds ever such a nice boy.'

'He is,' said Kate proudly. 'You'll have to meet him sometime.'

'I'd like that.'

Later that evening, when everybody was closing down for the night, Kate had been to the greengrocer's and was on her way back, dragging a heavy sack of potatoes.

'What are you doing there?'

Kate straightened up and put her hand on her chest. 'Seamus! You gave me the fright of my life. I was miles away then.'

'Sorry about that. Here, let me give you a hand.' He quickly and effortlessly hoisted the sack on to his shoulder. 'I would have thought the greengrocer would have delivered them, especially to a pretty lady like you.'

'Now then, don't let's have any of your old blarney. What are you doing round this way?'

'I'm off to the Salvation Army for a bed. I'm a bit early, and I ain't got the money to go in the pub so I just thought I'd walk around and soak up the Christmas atmosphere. I love Christmas.'

'Do you?' she asked as they strolled along. 'So do I.'

'Do you have a family?' he asked.

'Yes, I have a son, Joseph, although he likes to be called Joe, but I can't get used to that.' They reached the shop door. 'Would you like to come in for a mug of tea?' She couldn't believe her own ears. She was inviting a man, a drunken Irishman, into her home. What was wrong with her? Was she so desperate for company? She knew she shouldn't be inviting him in, but he had a certain charm, and he knew now she had a son, and although he wasn't upstairs, there was no harm Seamus thinking that he could be.

'Only if you're sure it's no trouble.'

'It's no trouble, the urn's still on. Besides, you saved me a lot of hard work. Mr Finch or his boy normally bring them down but they are both very busy and I want to get them peeled tonight.' She closed the door behind him. 'If you could take them through and put them on the table I'd be most obliged.' She pushed open the door behind the counter. 'I'll get the tea.'

'My, this is a warm cosy room. Is this where all the work goes on?'

'Yes.' She put two mugs on the table. 'Please take a seat.'

He quickly removed his trilby. 'This is most kind of you, my dear.'

She smiled. There was something about him she liked.

'Begging your pardon, but would you like me to stop and help you peel some of those?' He looked at the sack.

'I have got to get them all done tonight.'

'Well, that's all right then. So we'd better get started.'

She could have kissed him. It was late and the thought of sitting here until well past midnight filled her with dread. 'Only if you don't mind.'

He took his coat off. 'It'll be me pleasure, my dear. 'Sides, I ain't in no hurry to bed down with that lot of toe rags.'

'I suppose I shouldn't let you in here, not with your reputation.'

His eyes twinkled as his face crinkled into a smile. 'I'm hoping to give up me wicked ways, so you have no fear. I wouldn't want to upset you.'

Joseph looked startled when he walked in. 'Who's this?' he asked, looking pointedly at Seamus.

Kate smiled. With his shock of white hair standing up he did look a bit of a sight. 'Joseph, this is Mr O'Brien. He has offered to help me peel the potatoes.'

'Oh, I see.' A puzzled look flitted across his face. 'Why?'

'He's a customer and on his way to—' Kate stopped. She didn't want to tell him where, not at this moment.

'Pleased to meet you. I won't shake your hand, me boy, as mine're a bit dirty. I'm sorry I ain't Father Christmas, son.'

'It's not Christmas yet. I'm off up. Will you be all right?'

Kate smiled. 'Yes. I'll be up later.'

'Good night, son,' said Seamus. When Joseph closed the door he said, 'A nice-looking lad – he should go far.'

'I hope so. Did you have a wife?' asked Kate.

'No, was never out of prison long enough to get one. Lost your husband, did you?'

'Yes.' Kate thought that was better than a lot of explaining to this man who was almost a stranger.

'Thought so. You're a brave woman taking on a business on your own.'

'I worked for Josh and saw it was good. Could never understand Nellie, though. Did you know her?'

'Quite a while back. She was a pretty thing in those days.'

'What happened?'

'Well, she met Josh and married him.' He cut the conversation off quickly. Kate could see he didn't want to talk about it.

The sack of dirty potatoes gradually became bowls full of gleaming white potatoes.

Seamus sat back. 'Those should last you the rest of the week.'

She laughed. 'No, only a day. I shall be doing the same tomorrow night.'

'Would you like me to give you a hand?'

'Are you sure?'

'I ain't got nothing else to do.'

'Well, you must let me pay you.'

'I'll tell you what. How about tomorrow I come in and have one of your pies and a nice plate of mash for me trouble?'

'It's a deal.'

'Now I'd better be off. Don't want them locking me out.'

They wandered through the shop together. 'Thank you, Seamus. It's been very nice having you to help me.'

'It's been my pleasure, my pretty lady Kate.' He kissed her hand and went out.

As she closed the door she touched her hand and smiled. The potatoes were done and she'd enjoyed his company. He wasn't like other criminals who'd come into the shop; somehow he was different. What a pity he was Irish and a thief.

* * *

'Who was he?' asked Joseph aggressively, as soon as she opened the parlour door.

'A customer who offered to carry the sack from Mr Finch's, and he stayed and helped me.'

'Do you know him?'

'Not really.'

'Did Josh know him?'

'I think so. He didn't come in when Josh was here.'

'Why was that?'

'Joseph, what's with all these questions?'

'I don't trust him.'

'You've hardly met the man.'

'I know, but he's scruffy and Irish.'

'So, he's down on his luck.'

'I bet he is. P'raps he thinks he's found a nice rich widow and before you know it he'll be sitting at our table.'

'Joseph! How can you be so cruel? The man only offered to peel some potatoes.'

'Yes, I know. I'm sorry. It's just that you seem to be so happy now and I don't want anyone to spoil it for you.'

She held him close. 'Nobody is going to spoil anything for me, or you. But I can't refuse free labour.'

Joseph pulled away. 'I know that, but what did he want in return?'

'A free dinner.'

He sat on the sofa. 'Where does he live?'

Kate was quickly on her guard. 'He didn't say. But it must be round here somewhere.'

'Is he married?'

'Joseph!'

'Well, I only asked.'

'I *didn't* ask.' Katherine kept her fingers tightly crossed. She didn't like telling lies but if Joseph knew Seamus's background he wouldn't have him anywhere near the shop. 'Besides, it really isn't any of my business, or yours.'

On Christmas Eve the customers in Kate's were full of laughter and good humour. Some of the women, laden down with heavy shopping bags, moaned about all the extra work Christmas brought, but with Seamus around – he had taken on the job of washer-up as well as the potato peeler – he soon put a smile on their faces with his blarney.

'You're a right old charmer and no mistake,' said Grace, who was busy rushing back and forth, clearing plates and emptying ashtrays of those that bothered to use them.

All day some of the young men had been bringing in sprigs of mistletoe, and taking great delight in trying to catch hold of Grace, but she was slim and wiry and was only caught if she wanted to be.

'D'you know, Kate, I can't believe you've been here for – what? – must be well over a year by now,' said Bill, leaning on the counter and watching all the activity.

'Last year Josh gave me double wages.'

'No! And I always thought he was an old skinflint.'

'Well, it was Nellie really. I often wonder how they are getting on.'

'He might be dead for all we know.'

Kate looked wistful. 'Yes, he could be. I'll always be grateful to him for giving me this job.'

'Yer. Never thought you'd be in charge one day. You've certainly made a go of it. You and the boy staying here for Christmas?'

She nodded. 'This will be the first Christmas we've ever had on our own. I rather fancied doing the dinner myself.'

'What does the boy say about it?'

'Not a lot. He wanted to go and spend it with Milly.' Kate

leant forward. 'To be truthful, Bill, I haven't seen her all week, and she didn't really make any arrangements with me so I presume we will be on our own.'

'That's a bit daft, if you ask me. Milly thinks the world of you. I reckon she'll be expecting you.'

'Don't say that. We just can't turn up now, can we?'

'S'pose not. What you doing for Christmas, Grace?'

Grace stopped wiping a table down and straightened up. 'Nothink.'

'What about your family?' Bill had said it before Kate could stop him.

'Ain't got any.'

'Well, that makes two of us,' said Seamus. 'Say, how about you and me spending it together?'

'If you think I'm going to the Salvation Army hostel and sitting down to dinner with a lot of dirty old men then you've got another think coming.'

Seamus had told them earlier where he was going.

'Well, please yourself, me darling. But I'll be having a grand meal.'

Kate looked at Grace's sad face.

'Well, I'd better be going,' said Bill, 'otherwise I'll have Bert screaming at me. Got a busy day.'

Kate remained deep in thought. Joseph was going round to see Ted straight from work. Would Milly tell him what time she wanted them round for dinner tomorrow? Although she wanted to be on her own she would miss their company.

'What time you closing up?' asked Grace.

'A bit later, but you can go off if you like.'

'I'll only be going to the pub.'

'Will you be looking for customers then, girl?' asked Seamus.

'Yer. 'Specially one with a warm bed and a full larder.'

'Where are you spending Christmas then, Grace?' asked Kate.

'Dunno yet.'

Kate didn't like prying too much into Grace's affairs. After all, what she did out of the shop was her business. 'What about you, Seamus?'

'I'm not in any great hurry. Besides, it looks very dark and cold out there. Is it all right if I stay a while?'

'Of course.' Kate enjoyed his company. 'When I close up perhaps we can all go out to the back room and have a drink.'

Seamus gave her a beaming smile. 'Knew from the moment I stepped through that door that you was a civilised woman.'

'Is that all right with you, Grace?'

She nodded and turned away.

It was getting late when Kate finally closed the shop. The late-night shoppers came in for tea to keep out the cold, and the market men came in for the warm.

'Now what will you have to drink? I've got port and gin,' said Kate, as she walked into the back room.

'I'll have a nice drop of gin,' said Seamus.

'Port for me.'

Kate noticed Grace was very quiet, not her usual bubbly self.

After wishing each other a Merry Christmas they finished their drinks and Seamus took a small packet from his pocket and handed it to Kate.

'For you, my dear, and you mustn't open it till tomorrow.'

'Seamus, this is very kind of you, but you shouldn't have. You've only known me a short while.'

'I know, but you have shown me more kindness in these few short days than anybody has in the whole of my life.'

Kate could feel the tears sting the backs of her eyes.

'I ain't got you a present,' said Grace.

'I didn't expect one,' said Kate. 'But I do have a little something for you. I hope you like it.'

Grace's eyes lit up. 'Can I open it now?'

'If you like.'

Grace held the necklace Kate had chosen for her in the flat of her hand. 'It's lovely! I ain't ever had anything so lovely bought for me before.'

'It's only a cheap imitation,' said Kate quickly.

Grace quickly kissed Kate's cheek. 'Seamus is right, you are a kind lady. Now I must be orf, might miss a good punter.' She plonked her hat on her head and ran out.

'Grace!' called Kate, going after her. The door slammed. She was too late. 'I haven't given her her wages,' she said, walking back into the room.

'She'll be back on Saturday. She might need them be then. Well, I must be off.' Seamus picked up his trilby. 'I hope you have a nice Christmas, Kate. You deserve it.'

'Merry Christmas, Seamus.' She kissed his cheek and his whiskers tickled her lips. 'Will I see you on Saturday?'

'I would think so.'

'Here, take the rest of the gin. I'm sure you can find a use for it.' She handed him the almost full bottle. 'But don't get into any trouble.'

'Thank you. I'll finish off before I go to the Sally Army. They're funny about this demon drink.' He held up the bottle. 'Good night, Kate love.' He closed the door behind him and Kate was alone.

They were nice people who were down on their luck, and it made her feel happy to help them. She felt the small packet in her pocket. She looked at it and turned it over. She was very tempted to open it, but she had made a promise and she didn't want to spoil it. After all, Seamus was Irish and, who knew, it might have a magic spell on it.

Joseph came in just as she was filling her stone hot-water bottle.

'Milly said be round about one. I said we would. Is that all right with you?'

'Of course.' She couldn't disappoint him or Milly, but deep down, she would have liked to have spent the day at home – her home – and had Grace and Seamus share it with them, but then Joseph wouldn't have approved of that.

Chapter 29

Although Kate liked being waited on on Christmas Day, and being with Milly and the family, Grace and Seamus kept filling her thoughts. She wondered where they were, if they were alone and what they were doing. Kate hadn't told the family too much about them as Milly would tell her off for worrying about the waifs and strays she seemed to collect, and Charlie certainly wouldn't approve of a thief and a prostitute working for her. Their occupations were something she had kept from Joseph as well. She had just told all of them that she had a girl in to work on Saturdays – she didn't tell them her name – and that Seamus was more of an odd-job-man down on his luck, and that seemed to satisfy them.

Kate smiled at the present Seamus had given her – a pressed flower. He had written a little poem. He had told her he learnt to read and write in prison: 'Didn't want to waste me time.'

> Shamrock I have none, but nevertheless
> this small flower for a pretty lady must
> be second best.

She had put it away; she wasn't going to share this with anyone. No one else would see that, although he was a rogue, underneath, she was sure, he was a good man. He had told her he had been very fond of Nellie in his young days but that Nellie had preferred Josh.

'Could be because I was sent down a couple of times. Anyway, she wouldn't wait for me. Once when I came back I found out she'd married Josh and he wouldn't let me in this place.'

'I'm not surprised.'

'Never did find out why she took to her bed, though. I don't think he made her very happy.'

Kate smiled. She would never tell him the reason.

'Ma.' Joseph was tugging at her arm. 'It's your turn.' They were playing cards.

Everyone at Milly's was having such a good time. Olive looked happy and content at the thought of another baby on the way. Dolly was so good. When Kate held her goddaughter the burden of guilt about the baby she'd got rid of still hurt her. Had it been a girl or another boy? Kate sat and looked around her. Tom was beginning to look old and tired, while Ted was growing into a very handsome young man. Perhaps one day he would find love again. Charlie sat back with a contented look on his weather-beaten face. He was proud of his family, and he and Milly loved having them round.

All too soon Christmas was over and it was time for Kate and Joseph to leave.

'It'll be lovely to go straight to bed and not have to prepare pies.'

'Is the novelty wearing off then?' asked Charlie.

'No, of course not,' she replied quickly. 'Look at that moon,' she added, when he opened the front door. 'We shouldn't be having any snow tonight. See how bright the stars are.'

'It's very cold,' said Joseph, pulling his muffler up round his ears. 'Thanks for the mitts, Milly. They'll be good for work.'

'Just as long as you don't get 'em too greasy. 'Bye, love.' She held his face in her hands and kissed his cheek.

Kate felt a pang of jealousy. Milly's gift had been much better received than the shirt she had given him.

After all the goodbye hugs and kisses they made their way home.

'Did you enjoy yourself today?' Joseph asked as they moved along at a fast pace to keep warm.

'Yes I did. Milly is so good to us.'

'I know. Funny, isn't it? At first I didn't want to live with them. Now I like being with them.' He stopped. He couldn't tell his mother it was better than being stuck up in the flat above the shop most nights with no one to talk to while she was busy working.

'Would you like to move back then?' In many ways Kate knew her son wasn't happy.

'No, of course not, not now I've got my own bedroom. I miss Ted and Charlie though.'

'I expect you do.'

'By the way, Ted's invited me to a New Year's Eve party. D'you mind if I go?'

'No, but remember, no drinking. You are still only a child.'

'I'm not a child!' He sounded angry. 'I've been out to work a year now.'

'Yes, I know and I'm very proud of you.' She tucked his arm under hers. 'Now come on, let's get home.'

He wasn't sure if he would ever be able to call a flat above a shop home.

On New Year's Eve Kate thought she would ask Seamus and Grace to join her and see the new year in together.

'I'm sorry, Kate,' said Grace, 'but I'm meeting a customer. Would have been nice though.'

Kate was pleased she'd asked Grace first, as now she wouldn't ask Seamus. She didn't want to spend the evening with just him. But where was he? She hadn't seen him since the weekend and now it was Wednesday. She hoped he wasn't in any trouble.

'Now you're sure you'll be all right?' asked Joseph.

She had been deep in thought. 'Yes, yes, of course. I can always find something to do.'

'You could go to Milly's.'

'Yes I know, but I really must prepare this food.'

'Well, I'll be off.'

'Now you go and have a good time, and remember what I told you.' She waved the spoon at him.

Laughing he kissed her cheek and left.

How she envied him when he went out. Tonight she would be on her own, seeing 1914 in alone. She couldn't remember being alone on New Year's Eve before. She suddenly felt lonely. She missed Edwin and Dolly, even Briony. She could go and see Milly. They would probably go to the pub where Tom worked. It would be very lively, but was that what she wanted? She picked up the bottle of port. 'It looks like snow out there so I'll stay here and wish myself a happy new year.' She poured herself a generous glass of port. 'Good health, everybody,' she said out loud. 'I wonder what 1914 will bring.'

It was a cold start to the year. Milly now came in every lunchtime for an hour, and Kate was more than pleased to see her, and Grace continued to work every Saturday. Seamus came and went as the mood took him, or whenever he was sober enough to find his way to the shop. She was always pleased to see him and to listen to his tales, but was always careful not to pry. He would help with the washing-up as well as peeling the potatoes. Sometimes when Kate was in her back room that doubled as the kitchen, she thought of Dolly. How she would have enjoyed this life and the customers she had in.

At the beginning of March the weather improved slightly. Kate was waiting for Mr Sharman to collect the rent, quietly singing as she put the mugs on the counter ready for lunchtime.

'You sound happy, my dear,' said Mr Sharman, politely touching his hat.

'Mr Sharman, I have your rent ready.' She went to go into the back room.

He followed her. 'Mrs Carter, I'm afraid I have some bad news.'

Kate stood frozen to the spot. 'Nellie wants to move back,' she whispered.

'Not as far as I know. She told me Josh has died.'

'I'm so very sorry to hear that. She keeps in touch then?'

'Not really.'

'Do you have Nellie's address? I would like to send her a letter with my condolences.'

'Yes I do. But there was something else.'

Kate held her breath.

'She's coming here to see you.'

'Why? What does she want?'

'I don't know.'

'She can't take this away from me, can she? I've been building this business up and I don't . . .' Tears of anger were ready to spring from her eyes.

'Not really. You pay the rent. I don't think she will want to take over. It could be that she just wants her things.'

Kate sat down. 'I hope so. Did she say when?'

'Next week sometime.'

'Thank you, Mr Sharman.' She felt a little calmer when she gave him the rent book and money.

'You have done very well, Mrs Carter.' He looked round. 'It's all very nice.'

'Thank you. Have you got time for a cup of tea?'

'No, thanks all the same, but I must get on.'

She held open the door. He touched his hat and left.

Kate was worried. What if Nellie did want to come back? But

it wasn't hers now; Kate paid the rent. What did she want to come all this way to see Kate about? Perhaps it was just about her furniture, but why wait four months before getting in touch, and why didn't she write direct to her?

A week later Kate's eyes opened wide when Nellie came in. She looked so different. She had on a lovely black hat and her coat looked warm and expensive. She was still leaning on her stick but not as bent over as she had been.

'See you've tarted the place up a bit.' Her eyes darted round the room. She sat down and ran a gloved finger over the table.

'I've just given the place a good—' Kate decided to hold her tongue. 'I'll make you a special cup of tea. I was very sorry to hear about Josh.' She didn't want to say too much as all the memories of that dreadful morning came back.

'Yer. It was sad.'

Kate cringed. There wasn't any emotion in Nellie's voice. No sign of regret that she might have contributed to her husband's death.

'Did you want anything to eat?' Kate asked quietly.

'No, ta. I'm up here with me sister. Her daughter's getting wed, silly cow, and our Flossy's looking for something to wear.'

'Nellie! Well, if it ain't Nellie Trent.' Seamus came out of the back room wiping his hands on the bottom of his apron. 'I thought to myself, I know that voice. I may not have heard it for years but I would recognise those lilting tones anywhere.'

Kate smiled.

'Seamus O'Brien!' Nellie's face was a picture of disbelief.

He took her hand and kissed it.

She quickly pulled her hand back. 'What the bloody hell are you doing here? And you're still talking a load of crap.'

'Working for young Kate here.'

Kate grinned; she was far from young. 'Sit down, Seamus. I expect you two have plenty to talk about.'

'Sorry to hear about Josh.'

'It was for the best in the long run. He wasn't himself towards the end, you know. How long you been out?'

'A short while.'

'Hope you've got everything tied down out there,' she said to Kate. 'Can't trust him with nothing.'

'Now that's not a nice thing to say, Nellie love.'

'Well it's true, and I ain't your love.'

Kate carried on serving, but all the time she was watching Nellie and Seamus.

'Who's that talking to old Seamus?' asked Milly walking in, and, taking her hat off, she nodded towards Nellie.

Kate bobbed down and whispered, 'That's Nellie. Nellie Trent.' She had told Milly Josh was dead and that Nellie was coming to see her.

'How'd she get here?'

'Her sister brought her.'

'Where is she?'

'Who?'

'The sister.'

'Gone shopping.'

'What's Seamus doing talking to her, and getting on very well by the looks of it?'

'They knew each other years ago.'

Suddenly Seamus and Nellie's loud laughter burst forth.

'What does she want?' asked Milly with a worried look on her face.

'I don't know. We didn't get a chance to talk.'

A scruffy-looking woman banged hard on the counter with her money. 'You two! We gonner git any service round here terday? Standing there bloody yakking. I ain't got all day.'

'Coming up.' Kate moved away to fill a plate for the customer.

Kate watched the two old friends talking and laughing almost the whole of the dinnertime. She was getting agitated. What did Nellie want? And was she about to lose Seamus?

Finally Seamus stood up. 'Better get on,' he said to Nellie. 'Might not get any dinner if I don't get back to me chores.'

'Never thought I'd see you in a apron.'

'Well, Nellie me love, needs must when the devil drives.'

After he'd gone into the kitchen, Nellie beckoned Kate over. 'I expect you're wondering what I've come for?'

Kate sat down. 'Yes, I am.'

'When I told Mr Sharman I was coming up, he told me you'd taken the place over. Said you'd turned it into a little goldmine.'

'But I don't make—'

Nellie put up her hand to silence her. 'Anyway, seeing as how you've been hiring me furniture all this time, I thought I'd come and collect what's due.'

Kate sat with her mouth open. 'I've not been hiring your furniture! I didn't know what to do with it. Mr Sharman told me to throw it out.'

'Ah, but you didn't, did yer? And what about all this?' She waved her hand at all the tables and chairs. 'My dad bought these, so now I wants me money.'

'How much?'

'Let's see now. How long you been here?'

'Four months.'

'Well, I reckon a pound a month for all the lot's fair, so give me four pounds.'

'What if I throw it all out?'

'Now you wouldn't be that daft. Got some good pieces upstairs, I have, and you'd have to buy more. Tell yer what though, you could buy all the lot off of me.'

'How much?' Kate sat dreading the answer. Although she was now saving some money, would it be enough?

'Ten quid would be a fair price.'

'Ten pounds!'

'Yer. You can keep me and Josh's clothes and the bedding. I don't want that.'

'I don't think I've got ten pounds.'

'It'll be fourteen in all.'

'Fourteen!'

'Yer. Don't forget the back rent on 'em.'

Kate sat back. 'I haven't got that amount.'

'Well give me what you've got.'

'I can give you five pounds.'

'That all? Then that'll have to do for a start.'

Kate hurriedly left the shop and ran upstairs to get the money.

She sat on her bed and counted out five pounds. Should she give Nellie the two she had left? She pondered on that for a short while but decided against it. Should she have tried to beat her price down? No, Nellie was a shrewd woman and Kate knew she was getting a good deal. Besides, Nellie could be cruel, and who knew what she might have done? The last thing Kate wanted was a shop full of broken crocks and furniture.

'Ta,' said Nellie, looking at the money in her hand. 'You can send me a postal order for the rest, nine pounds in all. I don't think you'll welsh on the deal, you ain't like that. Always told Josh you was a good 'un. He should have made you a partner, then I would still be getting a bit. Ta-ta.' She stopped at the door. 'By the way, tell Seamus he ain't ever gonner share me bed. Might sound daft now, but I really loved my Josh for all his carrying on. And you take my word, girl, you can't trust that one' – she waved her stick at the door behind the counter – 'further than you can throw him. 'Bye, Seamus,' she called out.

He came hurrying out. He hugged Nellie close. Kate could see she didn't like it.

'Don't let us part again, Nellie love. It would break my heart if I lost you again.'

She laughed. 'Well, hard luck, mate. I'm going back to Kent. I've got a good sister, she looks after me, and I don't want for nothink.' She walked out.

'Well,' said Kate, 'that was certainly something.'

'What did she want? Begging your pardon, I didn't mean to pry.'

'No, that's all right. She wanted money for her furniture. I expected that. At least now I can say everything is mine, or it will be when I've paid for it. By the way, Seamus, there's some clothes of Josh's upstairs. I'll bring them down and if there's anything you'd like please take it.'

'You are kindness himself.'

'Oh, go on with you! I'm afraid Nellie told me to tell you that she doesn't care for you any more.'

'And I don't care for her. She's changed. She's a hard woman now, and she ain't pretty like she used to be.'

'We all change, Seamus.'

He laughed. 'Ah yes, but some of us do change for the better.'

'While we are quiet I'll go up and start sorting out those clothes. You can manage down here for a while?'

'Sure.'

As she mounted the stairs her thoughts were full of Nellie and Josh. Nellie had said she had loved him, but all those years she'd wasted, making him wait on her, not running the business together – she could have been a good businesswoman but now he had gone.

She pushed open the bedroom door. The room was full of light now and it smelt clean and fresh, so different from when Nellie had lived here. When everything was paid for it would be all

300

hers. At last she would be able to save a little and give Joseph some kind of inheritance.

Chapter 30

Kate didn't say a lot to Grace when she came in on Friday to wait for her man. So it was Saturday when she told her about Nellie coming in and Josh dying.

She looked very sad. 'I liked him,' she said.

'I didn't think you knew him. Well, I know you saw him but . . .'

Grace gave Kate a slight smile. 'In fact you could say I knew him very well.'

'How?'

'Well, he didn't let me come in here and sit about waiting for me customers without something in return, so now and again, when he give me the nod and after he'd shut up shop, I'd pop round and keep him happy.'

Kate looked at her in amazement.

'We used to, you know, in the shop. Quite exciting it was, knowing Nellie was upstairs.' She laughed. 'She'd bang on the ceiling shouting. Nearly caught us once and I finished up in that corner under the table. Funny old dear. She came hobbling in, waving her stick at him. Thought she was gonner bash him. It was comical to see him trying to do his flies up and run away at the same time. Poor old Josh.'

Kate grinned at that. 'Nellie knew he was up to something.'

Grace smiled. 'As I said, it was fun while it lasted. Mind you, I never thought I'd end up working here.'

'Do you like working here?' asked Kate.

'Yer, I do. It's warm and you make a good cuppa. It's bloody perishing some nights standing in a shop doorway with yer skirt round yer waist. That wind can blow a gale.'

'Grace, are you trying to shock me?'

'No, not really.'

Over the months Grace had been working with Kate they had developed a good relationship. Grace had changed. Her hair was more under control and her clothes and language weren't so outrageous.

'When Olive has her baby I can't see Milly wanting to come in. Would you like to come in every lunchtime?'

'Dunno. I'd have ter think about that. And I'd have to go early on Friday. Can't let that man down, he's very special.'

'Well, think it over.'

They both looked up when the door opened. A tall man shuffled to the counter. His bright blue eyes darted about and he had a worried expression. His blond hair was dirty and matted and his clothes scruffy.

He pulled up his coat collar. 'Please could I have tea?' He spoke with a thick accent.

'That's tuppence. Where yer from?' asked Grace as she cheerfully handed him a mug of tea.

Silently he held out a few pence in the palm of his hand.

Grace took tuppence. 'You don't come from round this way, do yer?'

He shook his head.

'So, where yer from then?'

'Germany.'

'Germany? We get a lot of sailors round this way. Your ship in the docks then?'

He nodded.

Kate didn't give him much of a glance. She was used to all kinds of people and different nationalities coming in off the ships. Grace was always happy chatting to the men, but Kate had told her, no picking up clients while she was working. Kate could never be sure that she didn't, and if Grace attracted the wrong kind of clientele, it could be very bad for Kate's reputation.

As the morning wore on they became very busy, but the German didn't move or buy any more tea. He just sat in the far corner, staring out of the window.

'Funny bugger,' said Grace, when he left about four.

'Perhaps he misses his home.'

'Yer, could be. He don't look very old, but you would have thought he'd have cleaned himself up a bit.'

'He may have been out all night.'

'Yer, and he might have jumped ship and sat here waiting till it sailed.'

'Suppose so, poor lad. It must be awful to be that unhappy.'

'He didn't look too pleased with life, did he? Right, time for me to be off. Got to get meself tarted up for tonight's customers.' She plonked her hat on her head and left.

Every day for the next week the German came at the same time, sat at the same table and left about the same time, after only having the one mug of tea.

'I'd chuck him out,' said Milly. 'Taking up all the table. He looks a bit funny to me.'

'He looks very sad.'

'You're at it again, ain't yer? Worrying about other people.'

Kate laughed. 'I can't help it.'

On Saturday Grace was behind the counter and Seamus was out the back, busy peeling potatoes, when the German walked in. Kate was stacking up the plates.

''Allo there, mate,' said Grace. 'See you're still around then.'

As usual he asked for tea and held out the money for Grace to take.

305

'This is a penny,' she said, holding up a penny, 'and this one makes two. Savvy?'

He gave her a slight smile and nodded. 'Twopence.'

'Yer, but we say tuppence.'

'Tuppence,' he repeated.

'That's right. What's yer name?'

The scowl returned and, picking up his tea, he quickly went to sit at his favourite table.

Kate shrugged her shoulders at Grace.

'He ain't very friendly, is he?' Grace commented.

'Doesn't seem to be.'

'He's very good-looking though. Blond hair and blue eyes. Very nice.'

'You don't miss much, do you?'

'Kate love, have you got a moment?' Seamus poked his head round the door. 'Will this be enough taters for Monday?'

'I'll come and look.'

Kate moved to the back room. 'I think so. I'll put them in the bucket outside.'

Suddenly Grace screamed out, 'Leave me be! Don't you bloody well touch me!'

Kate and Seamus both rushed into the shop together. The German ran from the shop with Seamus following close behind.

'What happened?' asked Kate, helping Grace to a chair. She was holding her wrist.

'He grabbed me. Look, I've come up all red.' She held her arm up.

'Why did he do that?'

'Dunno. Bloody pervert!'

'Did he touch you, you know, anywhere else?'

'Na, didn't give him a chance, did I? He might o' done, though.'

'What's going on?' asked Bill, hurrying in. 'Just seen Seamus rushing down the road after that German bloke. Bert's joined in the chase. He been pinching?'

'Only me,' said Grace. 'Look.' Once again the arm was put on display.

'What'd he do that for?' asked Bill.

'Dunno.'

'You wasn't giving him the come-on, was you?' asked Bill.

Grace quickly looked at Kate. 'Na, course not.'

The scuffle at the door caused them all to look up.

Seamus was pushing the German in front of him. 'Right, me lad. Now say you're sorry 'fore the missis here calls the rozzers.'

Bill and Grace's heads shot up.

'Here, steady on, Seamus! We don't want 'em poking about round here,' said Bill.

A small crowd had gathered in the doorway.

There was fear in the German's eyes as he looked from one to the other. 'Please, I only want to talk.'

'Well, you've got a bloody funny way of showing it. Look at me arm,' said Grace.

'I am very sorry.'

Grace rubbed her wrist. 'Well, that's all right then, but you do it again and you'll get me fist in yer face.'

He looked puzzled.

'I said,' said Grace very slowly and loudly, 'don't do it again.'

'He won't get the chance,' said Seamus. 'Reckon you ought to ban him, Kate.'

Kate tried to keep a straight face. 'I'm sure he meant no real harm. Give him a mug of tea, Grace, and go and sit over there where I can keep my eye on you and find out what he wanted.'

Grace went to the table carrying the tea. 'Come on, mate. Sit yerself down.'

The German looked at Seamus and Bill then, carefully avoiding them, did as he was told.

'Come on now,' said Seamus. 'It's all over.' He gently pushed people away from the door.

Every time Kate looked up, Grace, with her elbow on the table, was concentrating, trying to understand the German's broken English. Now and again she would look across at Kate and give her a wink.

After a while he stood up. He shook Grace's hand, causing her to giggle, and left.

'Well?' asked Kate. 'What did he want?'

'Poor bugger. I think he's jumped ship. Says he's staying with a friend, and he's looking for work.'

'Well, he won't find it sitting in here every day,' said Seamus.

'Where's he living?' asked Kate.

'He didn't say, but I reckon he's in a dosshouse.'

'Sad places, those,' said Seamus.

'He said if you don't mind he would like to come here again on Monday. It's warm, and it's better than walking the streets.'

'You tell him this ain't no dosshouse. He can't come here and sit all day with just one mug of tea.'

'Seamus, who owns this place?'

'Sorry, Kate, I was a bit hasty there, but I don't like to see you taken advantage of.'

'No one will do that and on Monday I'll have a word with him.'

Seamus looked upset. 'Kate love, you wouldn't be thinking of giving him me little job now, would you?'

'No – all the time you keep out of trouble, that is.'

He grinned. 'You're a fine woman and no mistake.'

'Christ! Look at the time,' said Grace. 'I'd better be off.' She rushed to the door, narrowly avoiding running into someone. 'Oops, sorry!'

Kate looked up. 'Hallo, Joseph. What are you doing home so early? Are you all right? You don't look very well.'

Joseph stood looking at the back of Grace as she hurried down the road. 'I don't feel too good. Who was that?'

Kate hurried round the counter with a worried look on her face. 'What's wrong? Go on upstairs. Seamus, keep an eye on things down here.'

'Who was that?' asked Joseph again.

'That was Grace, the young woman who works on Saturdays. Now go on up.'

Joseph was sitting on the sofa with his eyes closed when his mother came in with a cup of tea. 'What's wrong?' She held her hand against his forehead.

'Think my cold's got worse. That Grace is pretty, isn't she?'

'Grace is all right.' Kate was worried because Joseph was looking so pale. 'Now I think you should go to bed,' she fretted.

'What? I'm not going to bed. I'll be all right.'

'Didn't I say this morning that you should have stayed at home?'

'Ma, it's only a cold.'

'So why did Mr Lacy let you off early then?'

'My nose was dripping and I was sneezing. And we aren't very busy. That's all.'

'As long as you're sure. I'd better go down and see what Seamus is up to.'

When his mother left Joseph sat back. He wasn't going to tell her he had a pain under his ribs. She would be rushing him off to some doctor or another. His thoughts went to Grace. She really was very pretty. 'I'll have to try and get to know her. That'll make Ted jealous,' he said out loud.

On Sunday morning when Kate went in to Joseph, she found him in bed, bathed in sweat.

'Oh my God, what's wrong?'

'I can't move. I've got this pain here.' He touched his ribs.

Kate began to panic. 'I'll get a doctor.' She rushed out of the room.

Joseph tried to sit up, but fell back exhausted.

After the doctor had examined him he said he had a touch of pleurisy. He had to be kept warm and in bed.

'Ma, what about Mr Lacy?'

'Don't worry, I'll go round and drop a note through his door.'

All Sunday Kate was up and down the stairs, bringing Joseph hot drinks and cool flannels for his head.

'I'm really worried about him,' Kate said to Milly on Monday.

'He'll be all right in no time. I'll tell Ted to come round this evening to cheer him up.'

'Would you? That'll be lovely. He needs someone interesting to talk to.'

'Thanks for coming round, Ted. I'm getting fed up, stuck up here on my own.'

Ted sat on the bed. 'You've only been in bed a couple of days.'

'I know.'

'Brought you round some paper and a sharp pencil. Thought you'd like to do a bit of drawing.'

'Thanks.' Joseph struggled to sit up. 'Guess what? My ma's got a smashing girl working for her on Saturdays.'

'Oh yer?'

'She's got dark hair and goes in and out in all the right places.'

'Yer? How old is she?'

'Dunno. About eighteen, I reckon.'

'So she's too old for you?'

'Maybe.'

'I'll have to come in Sat'day and have a look.'

They sat idly chatting for a while, then Ted had to go.

'That was nice of Ted to come and see you,' said Kate, plumping up Joseph's pillows.

310

'He's coming again next Saturday.'

'That'll be nice.'

'I hope I'm better by then.'

'You'll have to be patient.'

The look on his face told Kate that was the last thing he was going to be.

When his mother left, he picked up the pencil and began idly drawing. It didn't matter how painful it was, he had to keep the picture of Grace in his mind's eye.

Chapter 31

During the day when Kate was busy, Seamus and Milly popped upstairs to make sure that all Joseph's needs were seen to. Towards the end of the week he said he was feeling a little better.

Although Joseph didn't approve of Seamus and only spoke to him when it was necessary, he had to find out more about Grace. 'Seamus, that Grace seems to be a bit of all right.'

Seamus gave him a long look. 'Yes she is, and your mother thinks a lot of her.'

'My mother thinks a lot of most people.'

'Your mother is a fine woman. Not many would take in the likes of Grace.'

'Why? What's wrong with her?'

Seamus quickly tried to cover his last sentence. 'I think she's been in a bit of trouble in the past.'

Joseph's eyes widened. 'With the police?'

'I don't rightly know. You see, it ain't any of me business. I best be going.'

That conversation put Joseph on his guard. He wouldn't ask his mother as she might laugh at him for taking an interest.

On Saturday Kate was surprised to see Ted walk in during the afternoon. 'Hallo, Ted. Everything all right?'

'Yes, thanks.'

'Thought you would have been round this evening.'

'Mum's going on a bit, so it's best I stay out the way. So I thought I'd come and see Joe.' As he was talking he kept glancing at Grace.

'That's kind of you. Go on up, he's in the parlour.'

Ted raced up the stairs, two at a time, and pushed open the door.

'I see what you mean, mate. She's certainly a good-looker. Have you found out much about her?'

'Oh hallo, Ted. Yes, I am feeling better, thank you. Her name's Grace and she's been in some sort of trouble. Is she down there, then?'

Ted sat next to Joseph. 'Yer, she's sitting talking to a bloke. Big, got fair hair.'

'I'll find out if it's her boyfriend.'

'So what did she do to get in trouble?'

'Dunno, nobody will tell me.'

'Has she been up here?'

'Na. Ma only sends up your mum or that Seamus.'

'Won't he tell you?'

'No. I think Ma's told him not to.'

'Oh, why's that?'

'Dunno, but it must be something really bad.'

'Can't be, your ma wouldn't have someone like that working for her, not if it was that bad.'

'You know my ma, always looking out for lost souls. Look how she tried to help Briony.'

Ted's expression changed. 'Yer. That was really awful what happened to her.'

'Yes, and I shall always feel rotten at not talking to her. D'you know, I reckon Grace has just come out of prison,' said Joseph, quickly changing the subject. 'Here, what do you think of my sketch of her?'

'That's really good. What does your ma think of it?'

'I wouldn't show her. And don't you go saying anything to her, or your mum.'

Ted grinned. 'As if I would. D'you fancy a cuppa?'

'Why not?'

'Good. I'll go down and get one.'

'Thought you might.'

When Ted walked into the shop Grace was behind the counter. He swallowed hard. His Adam's apple felt as if it had stuck in his throat and he could feel his face colour. 'Could I have a mug of tea for Joe and me?' He just about managed to finish the sentence.

'Thanks Ted, for coming round to cheer him up,' said Kate. 'He should be able to go out next week if the weather holds.' She was watching him look at Grace.

'Here yer are then, young feller me lad,' she said cheerfully.

Ted quickly looked down and picked up the tea when Grace smiled at him, and hurried up the stairs.

'Well,' said Joseph eagerly, when he walked in, 'did you see her?'

Ted put the tea on the table and, grinning, nodded. 'She really is beautiful. I've got to find out more about her.'

'Was she sitting with her boyfriend?'

'No, she was serving. But he was at the corner table watching her all the time.'

'I'll have to ask Ma all about her.'

'You've really captured a good likeness.' Ted was studying the picture Joseph had drawn of Grace. 'I think her eyes are a bit wider apart than that. You say she only works on Sat'days?'

'Yes.'

'I expect I'll be round to see you next week then,' said Ted, finishing his tea.

'Me or her?' asked Joseph.

Ted moved towards the door. 'You'll just have to wait and see.' He ducked when a pillow came through the air towards him. He laughed. 'I can see you're getting better.'

Ted's heart sank when he walked back into the shop: Grace

wasn't there, but the boyfriend was still sitting in the corner. *Was* he her boyfriend or just a customer whom she was casually talking to? She looked like the kind of person who would be friendly with anyone.

' 'Bye,' he called to Kate as he went out. 'See you next week.'

'Thanks Ted,' she replied. She smiled when she heard him whistling as he left the shop.

'What d'you wanner know about her for?' asked Milly sharply, looking from Ted to Charlie.

'Nothing. Just asking, that's all.'

'Charlie, say something,' said Milly.

'This paper's full of troubles. There's Ireland just waiting to flare up, then those silly suffragettes are still at it, and now Europe – it don't look too good over there.'

'Charlie! Speak to Ted about that – that Grace who works for Kate on Sat'days.'

'Is that the tart you was telling me about, the one what works for Kate?' asked Charlie, folding his newspaper.

Milly tutted. 'Yes. I've just said that.' Milly's mouth was set in a hard straight line. 'Always said Kate should be more careful who she takes on. There's that Seamus, he's a drunk and a thief, and then there's Grace. She ain't nothing but a—' Milly couldn't say the word.

Charlie laughed. 'And what about you? What dark secret have you got?'

'It ain't funny, Charlie Stevens. Kate will find herself in trouble one of these days, you mark my words.'

'You'll never stop Kate from taking in lost souls.'

'Why do you say Grace is a tart?' asked Ted.

' 'Cos she is,' said Milly. 'She comes in the shop to collect her customers.'

'Who told you?'

'I just know.' Kate hadn't exactly told her in so many words, but Milly had put two and two together.

Ted stood staring at his mother with wide open eyes.

'Ted, you know what your mother's talking about, don't you, son?'

Ted nodded. 'But she looks nice.'

'She does at work, I'll give you that, but you should see her when she's all dolled up and out on the game. All paint and powder.'

'I don't want you going out with that sort,' said Charlie, winking at his son.

'Don't you start encouraging him. You find yourself a nice girl,' said Milly, calming down. 'There's plenty of 'em about.'

Ted looked from one to the other. He didn't want a nice girl. He wanted someone beautiful like Grace. He left the room. As he walked upstairs he overheard his mother talking, so he stopped to listen.

'What is it with our Ted? First it was Briony, now this little madam. I'll have a word with Kate about it on Monday.'

'What can she do?' asked Charlie.

'Keep her eye on him.'

'Give him time, love. Let him sow a few wild oats first.'

'Is that what you did, then?'

'I ain't saying. But let him grow up and live a little.'

'Over my dead body.'

'He ain't a kid any more, you know. He's – what? – going on eighteen now.'

'He is still my baby.'

Ted closed his bedroom door.

'Grace.' Kate took Grace to one side when she arrived the following Saturday.

'What's wrong? I ain't been—'

Kate shook her head. 'It's nothing you've done. It's just that . . . Well, Milly's worried. It seems you have an admirer. Her son, Ted, will be in later and it appears he's – well – fallen for you.'

Grace threw her head back and laughed. 'What, that young lad what come to see Joe?'

'Yes, and I think my son is also smitten by your charms.'

'Oh, don't! I think I've heard it all now.'

'So please, have a word or something, but let him down lightly. Ted's been hurt once before and I would hate to see him hurt again.'

'So, what d'you want me to do, then?'

'Tell him you have a boyfriend, and you are going to get married.'

'Yer, I could say that.' She smiled. 'I feel rather flattered that I've got two nice young men fancying me.'

'Well, you are a pretty young lady.'

She giggled. 'Nobody's ever said that to me before.' She kissed Kate's cheek.

Kate was startled. 'What was that for?'

'Because you are a very nice lady.'

Later that day when Ted came in he went straight up to Joseph, looking very worried.

'Well, did you see her?' asked Joseph.

'Yes. Joe, me mum reckons she's, you know . . . one of those women that goes with men.'

'Oh.'

'You don't sound surprised.'

'Well no. You see Seamus said me mother wouldn't like it if I got too friendly with her as she said she was a bit of a loose woman.' He laughed. 'Ma said she was going to send her up to have a little talk to us.'

'Oh no! I'm going.' Ted began pacing the floor. 'I couldn't face her. What if she tries—'

Joseph threw his head back and laughed so hard he hurt his ribs. 'Don't say you'd be frightened of her?'

'No.'

When Grace went upstairs to talk to the boys, Kate could hear lots of laughter and she knew Grace was letting them down lightly.

'So?' asked Kate, when Grace came back. 'What did you tell them?'

'I told 'em I was getting married soon and that they were lovely boys and I hoped I had two sons just like 'em. I said I was ever so old.'

'And did they believe you?'

'I don't think so.'

'Thanks, Grace.'

But although Joseph had accepted that Grace wasn't for him, Milly didn't think Ted had, as she told Kate on Monday.

'He looks so miserable. I wouldn't be surprised if he didn't come in on Sat'day again just to see her.'

'I'll let you know,' said Kate.

For the next two weeks Ted came to see Joseph but most times he sat and gazed at Grace. Milly was beginning to get very concerned and voiced her worries to Kate again.

'Don't worry about it too much,' said Kate. 'It won't last. Joseph's going back to work next week and he doesn't finish till late afternoon on Saturdays, after Grace has left here, so Ted won't have an excuse to come round.'

Tuesday 12 May was Joseph's fifteenth birthday. He was preparing for work. Yesterday was his first day back and he had come home tired but happy. Now Kate looked round the shop, her shop. She was happy, she had almost everything she could wish for.

As Kate watched Joseph her thoughts went to his brother.

What did he look like? Was he tall, like Joseph? Was he married? She might even be a grandmother. A slight smile flitted across her face at that thought. But would she ever know?

Chapter 32

Every Saturday afternoon throughout May, Ted came and sat in the corner of the pie shop with just a mug of tea. Even Kate was beginning to get cross with his mooning about. Grace was making a big thing about sitting with the German, Kurt, whenever the opportunity arose, and their laughter would make Ted angry. Grace, making sure Ted was watching, would hold on to Kurt's hand and as she passed him would touch his hair.

'Ted, your mother isn't all that pleased, you know, about you hanging around here all afternoon,' said Kate, sitting next to him.

'I don't care. I'm going to go out with her one day, you'll see.' He nodded towards Grace. 'She don't go out with that Kraut, you know.'

'How do you know?'

'She told me she was getting married but I don't believe her.'

Kate didn't reply.

'I know she ain't going out with him 'cos I waited till he left here, then I followed him.'

'My God! If she found out she'd kill you!'

'I was very careful; he didn't see me.'

'Ted, you are being very silly.'

'I don't care. D'you know, if there is a war with Germany he'll have to go back or be interned.' He sat relaxed in his chair and put his hands behind his head. 'So you see, I have everything on my side.'

'Who told you that?'

'Some of the blokes at work. So it might be a good thing if there was a war.'

'Ted! You mustn't say things like that.'

'Well, it'll be that one out of the way.' He nodded towards Kurt.

Kate would have laughed if she didn't know he was serious.

'I know what she does, but I don't care.'

'Ted, I still think you're being a very silly young man.'

'Yer, that's what Dad says, and he said if I ain't careful I could end up with a dose of the clap, but that don't frighten me. I don't think she's as bad as everyone tries to make out.'

'But she's not interested in you.'

'She will be one day, you wait and see.'

Kate moved away. There was nothing she could do about this.

On Monday Milly didn't arrive as usual at lunchtime.

'Seamus, you'll have to come out here and give me a hand,' called Kate. She hated it when her customers tapped their money impatiently on the counter. She didn't like to keep them waiting as most of them had to get themselves or their husbands back to work.

Seamus came out from the back room, wiping his hands on his apron. 'What d'you think's happened to Milly?'

'I reckon it's Olive. The baby must be on its way.'

'Is it due, then?'

'Not just yet, but babies aren't known to obey the rules, and nothing will keep Milly away from Olive if she has started.'

Kate rushed about, clearing tables and dishing up food. Seamus was good at helping but he did like to stop and have a little chat now and again.

By late afternoon, Seamus had left and Kate was just finishing sweeping the floor. The door was wide open so she didn't hear Charlie walk in. He coughed, Kate looked up, and saw he looked very sad. 'Charlie, what are you doing here?' Fear gripped her as she kissed his cheek.

He took off his cap and rolled it nervously in his hands.

Kate felt the colour drain from her face. 'Sit down, Charlie. What's happened?'

'It's Olive's baby. It was born dead.'

Kate put her hand to her mouth. 'I'm so sorry. Poor Olive, how is she?'

'They've took her to the hospital as there's complications.'

'Oh my God! Is there anything I can do?'

He shook his head. 'Milly's taking it very bad. She went back to the hospital.'

'Who's got little Dolly?'

'We have.'

'What about Ernie?'

'He's at the hospital with Milly. Poor bloke, he's in a bad way.'

'I'll get my hat and coat and come back with you. Have you had any dinner?'

'No.'

'I'll bring some pies and mash and fruit pies. I've got enough for all of you.'

'Dunno if we feel like eating.' He began fiddling with the salt and pepper pots. 'Oh Kate, if anything happens to my Olive I don't know what I'll do.' He fished in his jacket pocket for his handkerchief and blew his nose hard.

She went to him and held him close. 'Nothing will happen to her. You mustn't think like that.' Her thoughts went to Mrs Addams. But this would be different. Olive was in hospital, she was a healthy girl and she had a lot of love around her.

'Sorry about that, Kate.'

'Don't worry.'

'I shouldn't show me feelings like that.'

'Why not? She's your daughter and you love her.'

'Yer I know, but it ain't very manly, is it?'

'Is that so important?'

'No, s'pose not. It's funny but I can share me troubles with you.'

'That's what friends are for.'

He sniffed. 'Thanks. Milly said she's sorry she didn't come in today. She couldn't let you know.'

Kate patted his back. 'That's the least of our problems. Now, let me get everything in my basket and we can be off.'

'What about Joe?'

'I'll leave a note, then perhaps Ted could come round and tell him what's happened.'

'Yer, it'll give him something to do.'

Kate was always flattered and pleased when they included her in their family.

Tom was sitting in the chair with Dolly on his lap when they walked in.

'She woke up so I took her out of her pram.'

Kate held out her hands and Dolly eagerly went to her. 'You're a lovely little girl and no mistake.' She gently kissed her forehead.

'Kate's brought some dinner,' said Charlie.

'That's kind of you, Miss Katherine.'

Ted looked very surprised to see Kate laying the table when he came in from work.

'Hallo, Ted.'

He quickly followed her into the scullery. 'What's wrong? Is it Grace?'

'No. It's your sister. She's in hospital.'

'Olive? Is she gonner be all right?'

'We hope so, but she has lost the baby.'

'Poor Olive! She was so looking forward to having another one.'

'Ted, when you've had your dinner could you go round and tell Joe? I'll be staying here for a while – well, at least till your mother gets back.'

'Yer, yer, of course.'

'Tell him to heat up a pie.'

'OK.' He began washing his hands in the scullery sink. 'D'you know, it seems that in this family every time you think things are going along all right something happens to upset the apple cart.'

'That's life, I'm afraid.'

'Yer, I suppose so.' He dried his hands on the striped towel that hung on a nail behind the back door. 'That pie smells good.'

After Ted left, Charlie, Tom and Kate sat gazing at the fire, waiting for Milly to come home.

It was a quiet entrance she made, so different from when Dolly was born.

'How is she?' asked Charlie, jumping up and taking her coat.

'Not too bad now. They've given her something to help her sleep. Mind you, she looks like death herself.'

'Where's Ernie?' asked Kate, taking the kettle from the hob.

'Gone home to bed. Poor lad looks done in. I said I'd keep Dolly here for a day or two. Where is she?'

'In the front room in her pram, sparko,' said Charlie.

'She's a good 'un.' A faint smile lifted Milly's troubled face.

Kate made the tea, and as she walked back into the kitchen, placing the tray on the table, she said, 'Look, I'll be off now. I'll send Ted home.'

'You don't have to go, you know,' said Charlie.

'I know that. I'll call in tomorrow.' One by one she kissed their cheeks, then left.

As she walked home she thought about Olive. She was still young enough to have another baby, but as Kate knew from experience, she would never forget this one.

* * *

When on Friday Kate told Grace what had happened, she was pleased that the girl volunteered to come in every day for a few hours.

Ted hadn't been in the shop for a couple of weeks and everybody was hoping he had got over his love for Grace.

Milly told Kate, when Kate went to see how Olive was, that Charlie was keeping him busy. Kurt was also making fewer visits.

'He's got a job,' said Grace one day when Kate commented on his absence.

'Where's that?'

'Round the docks somewhere, cleaning up, something like that. It's just casual labour.'

'Where's he living?' asked Kate.

'With me. He's a nice bloke and we have a few laughs together. I like him, Kate.'

Kate was taken aback at that statement. 'But what about your father?'

'He wasn't me dad,' she said quickly.

'I know, but he did live with your mother.'

'He buggered off when Mum died. D'you know, he didn't pay the rent or the coal man and left me a load of mess. I've only got a room but Kurt's been ever so good. He's been helping me get it looking nice.'

Kate was surprised to hear all this. 'What about, you know, your other job?'

'I don't take 'em back to my place, never have done. Him, me and Seamus go out together some nights for a drink when I ain't working. You know, Kate, I ain't ever had someone like him before. He's ever so kind, and I'm really happy.'

Kate smiled, but deep down she prayed no one would take this away from Grace.

'Old Seamus goes on a bit about Ireland. You'd think he'd lived there the way he talks.'

'I think he read a lot of books about it when he was in prison.'

'Yer. Right lot together, ain't we?'

Kate smiled. She knew they were but they all seemed to have found something.

At the end of June Olive came home, and although still weak, thanks to Milly's loving care she was improving daily.

'Don't know when she'll be strong enough to look after herself and Dolly,' said Milly one afternoon, when she popped into the shop. She had been out for a walk with her grandchild.

Kate went outside and peered into the pram. 'She looks so lovely, even when she's fast asleep.'

'Kate, I dunno when I'll be able to work for you again.'

'Don't worry about it. Now that Grace comes in I'm managing – that is, all the time I can keep Seamus away from the bottle. How long do you think you'll be looking after Olive?'

'Dunno. A few more weeks yet.'

A customer came up to Kate. 'Got a nice cuppa for an old friend?'

'Ron! Ron, how are you?'

'Not too bad.'

'You've lost a bit of weight.'

'Prison food ain't all that good.' He laughed. 'Reckon you could make a fortune selling your pies to 'em.'

'Don't think they'd let me.'

'I'll be on me way,' said Milly. 'It's good to see you back, Ron.'

'Ta.' He raised his cap to Milly and followed Kate into the shop.

'Well, what's all the news?'

'We thought you'd be away for at least six months,' said Kate, handing him a mug of tea. He went to pay but she waved his money away.

'Been a good boy, ain't I? Learnt it don't do to buck the system, so I got time off for good behaviour. It's good to be back, though. Missed me freedom. So, what's been happening?'

'Nellie came back.'

'No! What'd she want?'

'Josh is dead and she's living with her sister in Kent. She wanted money for her furniture.'

'Poor old Josh. I'm sorry to hear that. He was a decent bloke.'

'I've got Milly working in the week, or she was till her daughter lost her baby.'

'That's a shame.'

'I've got Grace – you know, the one that always sat waiting for her men friends – well, she works every day, and I've got Seamus O'Brien who washes up and does the potatoes.'

He laughed. 'Not old Seamus? He back on the scene?'

'Yes, do you know him?'

'I should say so.' He took Kate's arm and lowered his voice. 'You know he's been inside?'

Kate nodded. 'And so have you.'

'True.'

'But he seems to have mended his ways.'

'And so have I. What about Grace? She still on the game?' He gave Kate a knowing look.

'I think so, but as long as it doesn't interfere with her work here I'm not too worried at what she gets up to.'

'Sounds like a right motley crew to me.'

'Yes, I suppose it does, but they are nice people.'

'See you ain't changed the name outside yet.'

'No, had to pay off Nellie first before I could think about things like that.'

'I know a bloke what's a sign writer. I reckon he'd do it for you on the cheap.'

'That could be interesting.'

'It'll have to be out of hours, after he's finished.'

'Perhaps when you see him again you could ask him to pop in.'

'I'll do that, Katie love.'

It was the middle of July when Ted returned to Kate's.

When he walked in Grace looked startled. 'He's not gonner start coming back here again, is he?' she asked Kate.

'I hope not.' Kate hadn't mentioned to Milly that Kurt was living with Grace. 'Hallo, Ted. Everything all right at home?' Kate asked casually. 'Joe's not home yet.'

He stood at the counter and looked around, a grin spread across his face. 'See you've got rid of the Kraut.'

Kate began to clear away and didn't reply.

When he sat at a table Grace went over to him. Kate couldn't hear what she was saying but the look on his face told her it was something he didn't want to hear.

He stood up and stormed out.

'What did you say to him?' asked Kate.

'Told him I was marrying Kurt and asked him if he'd like to be a bridesmaid.'

Kate laughed. 'You didn't! Poor Ted. That's why he's gone off with a flea in his ear.'

'Yer, could be.'

Kate suddenly realised she could be telling the truth. 'Grace, you're not really thinking of marrying Kurt, are you?'

'Could be.'

'But he's not here legally. They will want to see his papers.'

'Yer, we know.'

'You've talked about this?'

'Yer. Seamus said he might know of someone who'll be able to help.'

Kate sat down. 'This is a bit of a shock.'

329

'Well, don't worry about it.'

After Grace had left Ted came in. He must have been waiting for her to go.

'Ted, what's wrong?'

'I forgot to tell you. Mum said they're all going to Southend again this Bank Holiday Monday and she said you've got to go with 'em.'

She smiled. 'D'you know, I think I will. Thanks.'

'Is it true? Is she really gonner marry that bloke?'

'She says she is.'

''Bye.' He walked out.

Kate felt sad as this time he wasn't whistling.

Chapter 33

Kate thought her life had settled down comfortably.

On the Saturday before the Bank Holiday, Grace and Seamus had both looked very nervous and guilty all day. They kept out of Kate's way and tried to avoid eye contact, so Kate knew something was wrong. It was almost the end of the day when they dropped their bombshell.

'What do you mean, you're leaving me?' screamed Kate, plonking herself at the table Grace and Kurt were sitting at.

'I'm sorry, Kate, but I love Kurt, and well, we've just got to go.'

'But why you as well, Seamus?'

He sat at the table opposite her and held her hand. 'It's like this, my dear Kate. We think a war is on the horizon, and Kurt here will be interned.'

'And I couldn't bear that,' said Grace.

Kurt held Grace's hand and smiled at her.

'So,' said Kate angrily, pulling her hand away from Seamus, 'what's that to do with you?'

'We're all going to Ireland,' said Seamus. 'Always wanted to see the land of me birth.'

'And if I want to marry Kurt, this is the only way out.'

'So how are you going to get there? Where will you get that kind of money from?'

'Kurt has got to know when the ships come in and he reckons there's one leaving for Ireland tomorrow night. He's seen the stoker who's said he can get us aboard.'

Kate was trying to take all this in. 'That means I'll be left on my own.'

'You've got Joe and Milly,' said Seamus.

'Can't you wait a few more weeks? There may not be a war.'

'We have to go tomorrow, as we may not get another chance,' said Grace. 'I feel awful at letting you down. You've been the nicest person I have ever met, except Kurt and Seamus. You've made me very happy.' Tears were brimming.

Kate swallowed hard. 'I can't believe this.'

'You are a very kind lady,' said Seamus. 'You have given me and Grace a chance and a reason for living. Who knows, perhaps one of these days when I've made me fortune I'll come back and take you out to a posh restaurant in London?'

That didn't hold any interest for Kate; she hadn't told them she ran one once.

They stood up and Grace threw her arms round Kate's neck and hugged her hard. 'I'm really gonner miss you.'

Seamus took Kate's hand and kissed it.

Kurt was smiling so hard Kate thought his face would crack. 'Goodbye and thank you.' His English was very hard to understand.

Seamus put a small parcel on the table. 'Just a little something to remind you of us.'

'I've got nothing for you. I can't even get you a wedding present, Grace. Oh please say you'll stay for at least another day?'

'I'm sorry, but we must get that ship.'

Kate hugged them. Tears were stinging her eyes. 'I've grown very fond of you two. Promise you'll write?'

'We will.'

'Grace, what about your Mr Friday?'

Grace laughed. 'You can have him.'

'Thanks.'

They left the door open and walked away.

Kate wanted to cry. She really did love these people. They had brought laughter into her life.

She opened her present. It was a small china jug with one of Seamus's poems attached.

> This jug is filled with kindness.
> The kind you gave to us.
> We hope the future gives you
> Love, hope, faith and trust.

She brushed the tears away and was still sitting at the table fondling the jug when Joseph walked in.

'You all right?'

She nodded and, standing up, put the jug in her overall pocket. 'I'll get your tea.'

'You don't look very happy.'

'I've just had some bad news.'

Joseph eased himself into a chair. 'What kind of bad news?'

'Seamus and Grace have left.'

'What do you mean, left?'

'They've gone to Ireland.'

Joseph laughed. 'What, gone off together?'

'Yes, in a way. Grace is going to marry Kurt.'

'That German bloke that Ted threatens to do in?'

'Yes.'

'What have they gone over there for, then?'

'It's all this talk about war.'

'What's he afraid of?'

'Well, he's a German.'

'Oh yes, that would make him run.'

'He wouldn't have a lot of choice.'

'No, s'pose not. Well, that's put paid to Ted's dream of marrying Grace. So, what's for tea?'

* * *

On Sunday Kate wished she knew what time their ship was sailing. She would have liked to have gone to the docks to see it off, though of course she wouldn't have seen them, not if they were stowing away. Please don't let them get caught, she silently prayed. Then she panicked. Would she even know if they got caught? Who would tell her?

All these thoughts were milling around as she prepared dinner. She was also trying to think of ways to get help. Perhaps Milly would come back again now that Olive was getting better. But who would do all those potatoes? The evenings she and Seamus would sit preparing the food for the following day were always a joy to her, and many times the chore would be accompanied with one of his many tales. She would miss him so much. 'I only hope you find what you're looking for,' she whispered.

'What did you say?' asked Joe, bringing her out of her daydream.

'Nothing. I was thinking out loud.'

'Are you still going with Milly and the family to Southend tomorrow?'

'I expect so. Look, don't say anything to Ted about Grace.'

'Why not?'

'Let him enjoy his day out first.'

'OK.'

Early on Bank Holiday Monday Kate arrived at Milly's with her basket overflowing with food. She put the basket on the kitchen table.

'Hallo, Olive. How nice to see you looking so well. Your mother has been keeping me informed about your progress.'

Without speaking, Olive stood up and walked out of the kitchen, leaving Kate standing with her mouth open.

'What have I said?'

'It's nothing,' said Milly quickly. 'Just her funny little way.'

Kate didn't think it was funny. In fact she was cross at being ignored. She wasn't that happy as it was, but was determined to enjoy herself today and would tell them all about Seamus and Grace later.

Tom said he didn't want to join them as he was feeling the heat. Milly was worried.

'We can't leave you on your own all day.'

'Of course you can,' he grinned. ''Sides, it'll be a nice change to be on my own for a while.'

'Well, I don't think we should go,' said Ernie.

'Why not?' shouted Charlie.

'It's all this talk about a war.'

'Christ, mate! If it does happen, they ain't gonner get over here, not while we've got the Channel. We'll soon chase 'em back. And I still reckon you ought to come, Tom.'

He shook his head. 'No, I'll be all right.'

'Leave him be, Charlie,' said Milly, folding nappies and filling the bottom of the pram with them.

Kate saw Tom looked tired and old.

Despite failing to persuade Tom to change his mind they finally left and happily made their way to the station. Ernie pushed Dolly in her bassinet, which would finish up in the guard's van. Kate was pleased to see that Ted and Joe were larking about in front. However, she was concerned at how Ted would take the news about Grace.

'Charlie, what's wrong with Olive?' asked Kate as they made their way to the ticket office.

He looked embarrassed. 'I don't know.'

'Yes you do. Why won't she talk to me?'

'She's not really been herself since she came out of hospital.'

Kate knew there was more to it than that.

The train was crowded, but everyone was in a bank holiday

mood and they arrived at Southend hot but happy, determined to enjoy themselves.

It wasn't till the end of the day, when they were walking back home from the station, that Kate had the opportunity to speak to Ted on his own. She told him what had happened. He didn't lift his eyes from the ground.

'I'm sorry, Ted, but she wasn't for you.'

'No, s'pose not.'

'You told him then?' asked Joe, bounding up to them.

'Joseph, behave!'

'Don't know why he's getting in such a state about her, she's only a—'

'I ain't getting in a state, so, Joe Carter, mind your own business.'

Joe shrugged his shoulders and they continued home in silence.

The following day, on 4 August, the news vendors and placards screamed that Britain was at war with Germany. The news spread like wildfire. Kate sat at a table looking out of the window. The door was wide open but the shop was empty. Young men were cheering and shouting as they made their euphoric way to one of the many recruiting stations that had sprung up like mushrooms. Some lads that Kate knew came and planted loud kisses on her cheek. She felt sad and alone, but pleased Joe wasn't old enough to join up. Her thoughts went to Grace and Seamus. She hoped they, along with Kurt, who wasn't a bad lad, would be happy in their new life.

'Don't worry, Kate,' someone shouted. 'It'll all be over by Christmas.'

She smiled and waved. 'I hope so. Good luck, boys.'

Business was very slow all day and just as she was closing Ted came rushing in and, throwing his arms round her, twirled her round and round.

'Ted!' she laughed. 'Put me down!'

'I've just popped in to say goodbye to you and Joe.'

Kate sat at the table. 'Why? What have you done?' She was dreading the answer.

He was beaming. 'Joined the army, ain't I? I'll show those bloody Krauts they can't mess with us.'

'Does your mother know what you've done?' asked Kate, getting her breath back.

'No, not yet.'

'She's going to be very upset.'

'I expect so. But I can't just sit here and wait for it to end, I've gotter do me bit.' He paused, and taking a cigarette from a packet in his pocket, lit it. ''Sides,' he said, blowing the smoke into the air, 'since you told me about Grace and the German it's a way of getting back at him. Who knows, I might meet him on a battlefield.' He laughed

'Ted, this isn't a game!' Kate felt a flush of anger. 'And you can't use that as an excuse to go out and get yourself killed.'

'I ain't gonner get killed.'

Kate stood up and paced the floor. 'My God! Your mother will never forgive me if she thought Grace was the reason you've enlisted. It's bad enough having Olive look at me as if I've committed a crime.'

'Yer, well. Olive's a bit emotional.'

'And you're not?'

'I must admit I was a bit upset when you told me Grace had gone off with that bloke.'

'Is that why you joined up?'

He stubbed the cigarette butt into an ashtray. 'Yer, s'pose it is in a way. But I would go anyway.'

'I only hope your mother believes you.'

'Ted! Ted, what are you doing here?' asked Joe, rushing into the shop. 'Have you heard the news?'

'I should say so. Guess what? I've joined the army!'

Joe stood open-mouthed. 'You lucky beggar!' He gave Ted a playful punch on the arm. 'I only wish I was old enough. I'd be off like a shot.'

Kate gave him a glance that almost said, over my dead body.

'So, when d'you go?' asked Joe.

'Soon. Got to have a medical first.'

'Well, let's hope you aren't half dead, otherwise you'll have to stay here.'

'Na. I think just as long as you can walk in you're fit.' He laughed, but it was a strange nervous laugh.

Please God, keep him safe, said Kate silently to herself.

The following day Milly came bustling in. She plonked herself and her basket on the chair. Kate could see she had been crying.

'What d'you think of that silly bugger joining up?' she sniffed, fumbling in her bag for her handkerchief.

'I'm so sorry, Milly. I've seen nearly all the young lads round here sign up. I suppose it's something they feel they've got to do.'

'Bloody daft, if you ask me. He's still a kid. You ought to hear Charlie going on about it.'

'I can guess,' said Kate, remembering his feelings about Olive. She walked round the counter, and after putting two mugs of tea on the table, sat beside Milly. 'What made him do it?'

'Dunno, said it was his duty. I ask you, his duty! A young lad like that. Charlie said it was the ones that got us into this mess who should be going off fighting.'

Kate was relieved she didn't say it was because of his love for Grace.

'Thank Gawd young Joe ain't old enough to go.'

Kate nodded in agreement. The thought of that upset her and she quickly changed the subject. 'You're not round Olive's then?'

'Na, thought I'd give it a bit of a rest today. 'Sides, she's got to learn to start standing on her own two feet soon.'

'Yes,' said Kate. She never thought she'd hear Milly say that. 'Milly, why was Olive so off with me on Monday?'

Milly toyed with her spoon. 'It was 'cos she lost the baby.'

'But why get upset with . . .' Suddenly the penny dropped. 'Was it because . . . ?'

Milly nodded. 'She thought that what you did was a terrible thing, but you don't want to take too much notice of our Olive.'

'That was a long while ago, and I wasn't very proud of it myself. But surely she knew the reason why I did it?'

'Course, but she needed to take her anger out on someone, and that person was you.'

Kate was upset. 'Well, thanks for explaining. How did she think I felt?'

Milly shrugged. She looked around and Kate could see she was embarrassed. 'You ain't very busy.'

'No. I only hope trade picks up. I've still got the rent to pay.'

'I was surprised when Ted told me about Grace and Seamus going. You didn't say nothing on Monday. Mind you, I ain't sorry to see 'em go.'

'Why? I'm left without any help.'

'No, I didn't mean that. It's just that Ted knows it ain't no use him hanging round here now she's gone.'

Milly didn't know Grace had gone off to marry Kurt.

'Kate, will it be all right if I come back for the hour or so a day?'

Kate could have kissed her. 'Of course. But are you sure about leaving Olive?'

Milly nodded. 'As I said, she's got to learn to cope. 'Sides, I'll be Ted's money short.'

Kate hadn't thought about the many women who would be a wage earner missing. It would strike some families very hard.

Although still sad about Ted, Kate felt happy at the thought of seeing Milly every day. 'Do you want to start today?'

'Why not?'

'There's some washing-up outside.'

Milly grinned. 'Thought there might be.'

Kate also realised that Milly needed something to take her mind off Ted leaving. After all, he was still her baby.

Chapter 34

That afternoon after Milly had left, Ron came in.

'Bloody awful news, ain't it?'

Kate sat at the table with him. 'What's going to happen, Ron?'

'Dunno. Think we'll just have to wait and see.'

'Do you think it will be all over by Christmas, as everyone seems to think?'

'Wouldn't like to say. By the way, tell Seamus his horse didn't come up.'

'Seamus, Grace and Kurt have left.'

'What, all of 'em?'

Kate nodded.

'What they pinched?'

'They haven't pinched anything.'

'So where they gone?'

'To Ireland.'

Ron burst out laughing. 'When did this happen?'

'Sunday. Kurt's been working in the docks and a ship was leaving on Sunday and they were smuggled out on it.'

'No! As stowaways?'

Again Kate nodded. 'Grace is going to marry Kurt, and as he's German, and without papers, it would have been a bit difficult, more so now.'

'I should say so. Mind you, they got out just in time.'

'Yes. I only hope they've done the right thing.'

'Don't look so worried. He couldn't stay here, could he?'

'No, but it's not really him I'm worried about.'

'She'll be OK, she's got Seamus with her.'

'I hope so. I thought everything was going along fine, then all this happens. Why does life suddenly come up and hit you when things are going well?'

'Sod's law.'

'It is as far as my life has been.' Kate stared out of the window and they settled down into an agreeable silence.

Ron put out his cigarette. 'Been busy?'

'No.'

'Seems quiet all round today somehow.'

'Yes, after yesterday. I think it's just started to hit people. Milly's boy's enlisted.'

'Glad mine ain't old enough.'

'So am I.'

'By the way, I ain't seen that bloke yet.'

'Who?'

'The sign writer.'

'Don't worry about that. That's the least of my troubles.'

Over the next two weeks business was slow.

'Can't see things getting much worse,' said Milly one lunchtime.

'I hope not. How's Olive these days?'

'Coping. Tom don't look that well, though.'

'I'll come round on Sunday to see him.

'Come to dinner. It'll be nice having young Joe at the table. Even Charlie's been off his food since Ted went. And we've only had the one card which didn't say much. Charlie's taking it hard.'

Charlie was poring over the newspaper when Kate and Joe arrived on Sunday.

'See most of the boys that signed up at the very beginning finished up in France,' he said, folding the paper and putting it under his chair. 'Don't know why we have to help them.'

'Is Ted out there?' asked Joe.

'Could be,' said Charlie.

'Lucky old Ted. Bet he's with all those French floosies.'

'Floosies?' repeated Kate in alarm. 'So much for a good education,' she said, looking at Joe.

'Ted can't speak French,' said Milly.

'You don't have to speak the language to be understood to get all you want.' Charlie winked at Kate. 'Signs is all you need; just as long as you can wave your arms about, you're in.'

Throughout dinner everyone was trying to be jovial, but Kate knew it was all a show. She was watching Tom. He had never been a great conversationalist, and today he was very quiet. 'How's work, Tom?' she asked.

'Not too bad, Miss Katherine. Don't do a lot.'

'Keeps him out of mischief, though,' said Milly.

He gave her a faint smile. Kate could see he wasn't well.

As the weeks progressed things gradually got back to normal. Kate's regular customers, those that were left, drifted back. The war wasn't going the way everybody thought it would, and at the end of the first month the terrible battle at Mons was on everybody's lips. As time went on Kate noticed many men and women wearing black armbands.

'D'you know, every time I see that telegraph boy come riding by on his bike me heart stands still.' Milly was drying the mugs. 'I dunno what I'd do if anything happened to my Ted.'

'You mustn't say things like that,' said Kate, but she too worried if Milly was a little late coming in, in case she'd had bad news.

'See they're asking women to go out to work.'

'My Olive gets very fed up. She'd like to get out more.'

'She can't go to work, not with Dolly to look after.' Kate was worried. What if Milly was thinking of having Dolly while Olive went to work?

'That's what I told her. We had a long talk about it. I suggested she comes in here for a few days a week. Would that be all right with you?'

Kate could have hugged Milly. 'I'd be more than pleased to have her, but—'

'I know she's been a bit of a cow towards you, but don't worry, she's a lot better now. I'll be having Dolly the days she works. If she likes it, she's even going to ask Ernie if she could do an hour or so on Sat'days.'

'That's wonderful news! Seems you've got all this sorted out.'

'D'you mind?'

'Mind? Of course not. I'm pleased all my problems are over.'

'Yer,' said Milly thoughtfully. 'Wish mine was.'

At the beginning Kate was apprehensive about herself and Olive working together. On Olive's first day she went about quietly doing what Kate asked of her. The next time she was in Kate suggested they had a cup of tea when the lunchtime rush finished.

They sat at the table.

'Olive, I know that you felt very strongly about what I did, but—'

'I'm sorry, Kate. I know I shouldn't have snubbed you like that after I lost my baby, but I couldn't help it. I was angry and wanted to hurt someone like I'd been hurt.' Her brown eyes misted over.

'I do understand, but I could never have been a good mother to Gerald's child.'

'I know.'

'It was bad enough leaving my son in Australia, and then to have to . . . I'm sorry.' Kate sniffed. 'I must be starting a cold.'

'It's all right. I understand.' She gently touched Kate's hand.

After that everything worked out just fine, and in a few weeks Olive and Kate were getting on very well. Olive was happy serving and talking to people, and didn't mind doing potatoes and any chores Kate asked her to.

'Dunno what you've done to our Olive, but she's brightened up a lot,' said Milly.

But one day when Olive came into work, Kate could see she had been crying.

'What's wrong?' she asked.

'It's that stupid husband of mine. He's joined up.' Olive wiped her eyes on the bottom of her overall. 'He's a married man with a child and he's exempt.'

'Why did he do that?'

'I dunno. Couldn't wait to get away from me, I s'pose.'

'I don't believe that for one moment.' But Milly had told Kate she thought her daughter and Ernie were going through a bad patch.

She had told her, 'When she ain't here she sits about moping all day, and that ain't no good. No man's gonner put up with that for too long.' Milly had been very worried about her daughter and Kate guessed it was she who had suggested Olive came to work here in the first place.

'He reckons he joined up now so he can get a cushy job before they called him up,' said Olive, interrupting Kate's thoughts. 'But I don't believe that. What am I gonner do without his money? What if he gets killed?'

'You mustn't think like that. Perhaps we can work something out with Milly. I'm sure she will have Dolly for you.'

'I've already talked to Mum, and I can do all day Sat'days if you'd like me to.'

Kate was overwhelmed. She could have cried out for joy. 'That's wonderful!'

When Olive had her first letter from Ernie and found out he

had a desk job in Wales it helped to cheer her up.

'Guess what? He's coming home for Christmas,' Olive told Kate eagerly some weeks later.

When Milly came in she said to Kate, 'Our Olive is a different girl these days. She's ever so happy.'

'I think it's the thought of Ernie coming home.'

Olive had changed in the past months. Gone was the dowdy way she dressed and did her hair. Somehow she appeared to have come alive.

'It's all your doing, Kate,' said Milly. 'Thanks. Ernie's gonner see a different wife when he gets home on leave next week. Might even find she's . . . you know' – Milly nudged Kate's elbow – 'when he goes back.'

Kate hoped not, as she selfishly thought that that could mean more staff worries.

Joe and Kate spent Christmas with Milly and the family. It was a very quiet affair.

Kate sat in the kitchen quietly talking to Tom while the others were in the front room playing with Dolly.

'Got to try and be cheerful for young Dolly's sake,' said Charlie, walking in. 'After all, Christmas is for kids. I only hope our Ted's getting a good dinner.' He went into the scullery. Kate didn't follow him – she knew he wanted to be alone with his thoughts.

'Bit different to the Christmases we had at the big house, Miss Katherine,' said Tom, pulling the shawl Kate had given him tighter round his hunched shoulders.

'That was a lifetime ago,' said Kate thoughtfully. 'And there wasn't a war on.'

'And my Dolly and Mr Edwin was here. I wonder how Mr Gerald's getting on?' He stopped when a fit of coughing racked his frail body.

'I expect he is managing,' said Kate, watching him anxiously.

Tom sat back exhausted and mopped his face with the edge of the shawl. When he recovered his breath he continued, 'I know I shouldn't speak out of turn but I'm glad you didn't stay with Mr Gerald.'

She smiled. 'I couldn't stay in that house after what happened.'

'I would think Mr Edwin would have turned in his grave if he knew what his brother did to you.'

'It's all in the past now.'

'Did you know Dolly looked for his will before Mr Gerald came to the house?'

Kate sat up. 'No, I didn't.'

'She didn't say anythink 'cos she didn't want you to think she was being nosy. She didn't find one.'

Kate slumped back in the chair. 'Well, that's one mystery that's always bothered me. I always thought Gerald had found it and destroyed it, though he said he hadn't.'

'No. Poor Mr Edwin. I expect as it all happened so quick, he didn't have time to make one.'

Kate patted Tom's hand. How different her life would probably have been if Edwin had. That had been the beginning of all her troubles.

As 1915 progressed everybody read the newspapers avidly. There was no end in sight to the war.

It seemed the whole world was being drawn into this conflict. Ships were being sunk and it was in May when the liner *Lusitania* was hit and that brought America into the trouble. Food was getting short, but most of the local traders kept Kate supplied at a price. Any shop that had a foreign name was a target for violence, even if the owners had been born in London. Kate was glad it was the name Trent above her shop; she would have been worried had it been something foreign. One of these days she would get it changed.

She often thought about Grace and Kurt, though she had never heard from them. Milly only had the odd card from Ted and she didn't know where he was.

In May too it was Joe's sixteenth birthday and Kate prayed the war would be over before he was old enough to join up.

'See they've got pictures of Lord Kitchener all over the place,' said Milly.

'Yes, I know. It worries me.'

'Mrs Duke was telling me that Mrs Bolton – don't think you know her – has lost two of her boys.'

'That's dreadful!' Kate looked at Milly. She knew she worried constantly about Ted and had aged considerably this past year. 'How is Mrs Duke?' she asked, to change the subject. 'Haven't seen her for I don't know how long.'

'She don't get out much these days. It's her feet.'

Kate smiled. 'Mrs Duke's feet have always been a topic of conversation for her.'

A week after Joe's birthday Milly didn't turn up for work. Kate was devastated and couldn't wait to shut the shop. As soon as the last customer left she closed the door.

After leaving a note for Joe she hurried round to Milly's and, pulling the key through the letter box, rushed in.

'Kate! I was just coming to see you,' said Charlie, looking up surprised.

'Why? What's happened?' She looked from one to the other. Milly looked a little distressed but not unduly worried. 'Is it—'

'It's Tom. He's had to go to hospital.'

Kate sank into a chair. 'What's wrong with him?'

'His chest, and he can't keep anything down,' said Milly, sitting next to her. 'Think he might have to go away to some sort of convalescent home for a special diet.'

'What, in wartime?'

'Yer. Daft, ain't it?' said Charlie.

Kate burst into tears. 'What's wrong?' asked Milly.

'I'm sorry. I thought it was Ted.'

'Oh Kate. I'm sorry I didn't let you know, but I went with him to the hospital and we had such a wait.'

She sniffed. 'It's all right.'

'Here, get this down yer,' said Charlie, handing her a glass.

'What is it?'

'Just a drop of whisky. Help steady your nerves.'

She smiled through her tears. 'To Tom and Ted, may they both come home safe and well soon.'

They both agreed with her.

A month later Tom died.

'The doctor said he was just worn out. Never got over losing Dolly, you know,' Milly said to Kate at the graveside.

'Well, he's with her now.' Kate put a small bunch of flowers on the mound of fresh brown earth.

A few days later Olive was helping Kate with the pies. 'Mum and Dad are looking old,' she suddenly said.

'I know.'

'That house is like a morgue now, with only the two of them rattling about in it.'

Kate smiled. 'It wasn't that long ago it was packed to overflowing. Have you thought about moving back in with them?'

'I did think about it, but Ernie don't think it's a good idea. I'm glad you got me and Mum to come and work for you. You've given us all a lift and a bit of spending money as well. I have to smarten meself up to come here.'

'No you don't,' said Kate quickly.

'I want to. 'Sides, you're a smart woman and I looked dowdy beside you.' She laughed. 'Then, when Mum has Dolly for a few hours that really pleases her, and on the other days she can come here and meet people. So she has the best of both worlds.'

'I'm more than pleased to have you both here with me. After all, you are my family.'

Olive smiled. She was a pretty girl, so much like her father.

It was a damp, dreary day on Monday 25 October 1915, a day that Kate would never forget. The gaslights in the shop hadn't been turned out all day and the windows were running with condensation. A few people came and went. Shoppers didn't stop very long – they were all eager to get home and into the dry. The men that came in at dinnertime sat at the tables waiting to be served.

'Who we got in helping today?' asked Bill, who came in from the market.

'Should be Olive.'

'Well, she's a bit late.'

'Yes, I know. I hope her baby's all right.'

'Reckon Milly would let you know if she was poorly.'

'I hope so.' Kate carried on dishing up the pies, mash and pease pudding.

'My missis wants to know where you gets your stuff from,' said Bill.

Kate smiled and wiped her damp forehead with the back of her hand. 'She shouldn't be going short, not with you and Bert in the know.'

He laughed. 'She thinks she misses out. Trouble is, there's so many things in short supply now.'

'I know. Tell her I've got some good connections, but it costs me, and sometimes I find I have to make do with something else.'

'Here, I hope we ain't gonner end up with horse meat in the pies.'

Kate laughed. 'Who knows what we'll finish up with.' She hurriedly put the dinners on the counter but kept looking at the door. She was beginning to get worried. Something must have happened to stop Olive coming in.

When Mrs Duke waddled in Kate felt the colour drain from her face.

'Kate love.' Her face looked full of grief. She came up and leant on the counter. 'I'm ever so sorry to tell you but—'

Kate dropped the plate she was filling and it fell with a crash to the floor.

'Bloody hell, Kate!' said Bill, looking up. 'Nearly choked meself. What yer trying to do, give us all a heart— Here, you all right?'

He hurried to the counter and helped Kate into a chair. 'Here, missis,' Bill said to Mrs Duke, 'what you bin saying to her?'

'I ain't said nothing yet. But you've guessed, ain't yer?'

Kate nodded. 'Is it Ted?'

Mrs Duke nodded. 'Can I have a sit-down, me bloody feet's killing me. I ain't walked this far fer years.'

Someone jumped up and gave Mrs Duke a chair.

'What's happened?' whispered Kate.

'He's bin killed.'

Kate could hear herself wailing but she couldn't stop. 'No, not Ted! Poor Milly! Poor Charlie! Who started this bloody war?' Tears were running down her face.

'Kate, Kate, calm down.' Bill was patting her hand. Someone was putting a mug of tea in her hands. 'Drink this,' said Bill. 'It's got a lot of sugar in.'

The usual babble that went on was suddenly silent. All eyes were on Kate. She took the mug with both hands.

'I'd like one of them,' said Mrs Duke.

'Coming up,' Kate heard someone say.

'When did Milly hear?'

'This morning.'

'Does Charlie know?'

'Don't think so, unless Olive's sorted that out.'

Kate sat back. 'I've got to go to her.' She looked about her. 'I must. Milly will need me.'

'Course she will,' said Mrs Duke. 'D'you want me to stay and finish giving all these men their dinners?'

A couple of them stood up. 'Don't worry about us, Kate. You go and see Milly,' said one of her regulars, who was wearing a black armband.

'This is a wicked world,' said Kate, staring into space. 'He was a young man with all his life in front of him.'

'There's a lot like that,' said Mrs Duke. 'There's a few now in Croft Street who've lost their boys.'

At this moment that was no consolation to Kate.

Gradually the shop emptied.

'You gonner be all right now, Kate?' Bill looked concerned.

'Yes, thank you. I'll walk back with Mrs Duke.'

'What about your boy?'

'Joseph? I'll leave him a note.'

'Will he guess?'

'I don't know. I hope not. Ted was Joseph's best friend.'

Kate locked the shop door and began the slow walk back with Mrs Duke. Although the old lady was talking, Kate wasn't listening; she was full of her own thoughts.

When they turned into Croft Street Kate felt her strength leave her. What could she say? Any words would sound inadequate. And no words would ever bring Ted back. She loved him like her own son.

'I won't come in, gel,' said Mrs Duke when they reached Milly's house. 'She don't want me in there fussing.'

Kate looked at Mrs Duke. Perhaps she wasn't such a bad old stick, and was more sensitive than she liked everybody to believe.

Chapter 35

Olive was in the kitchen holding Dolly on her hip when Kate walked in. 'Mum's upstairs,' she said in a hushed whisper.

Kate hugged them both. She swallowed hard. 'This is terrible news. Does your dad know yet?'

Olive shook her head. She put Dolly on the floor and wiped her tears away with the bottom of her pinny. 'It's always difficult to get someone out of the docks. Half the time the office don't know what ship they're working on. Mum thought it best we wait till he comes home.'

Kate went quietly up the stairs and pushed open Ted's bedroom door. Milly was sitting on her son's bed. She was chewing the corner of her handkerchief. Kate could see the screwed-up telegram in her lap. At her side were his drawings.

'Milly,' said Kate softly.

She looked up, her eyes red and swollen, her face tear-stained. She was suddenly an old woman.

'Milly. What can I say?' Tears ran freely down Kate's cheeks.

Milly stood up and holding each other close, they let their tears flow.

When they broke away they both sat on his bed. 'I was looking at these. That's Grace. It's a good likeness, ain't it?'

Kate nodded. 'It's very good. He was very talented.'

'She'll never know he's . . .' Milly couldn't say the word – it was too final. 'Wonder if she'd be upset?'

'I would think so. She was a sensitive young woman.'

'Oh Kate! What am I gonner do?' She gave a deep sob.

'I don't know.'

'I won't even have a grave to visit. It ain't fair. I want me boy back.' She gave a low moan.

Kate put her arm round Milly's shoulders. She didn't have an answer. 'Would you like me to go and meet Charlie and—'

Milly pulled away and shook her head, and after dabbing at her eyes, blew her nose. 'No, let him get home first. He wouldn't want to make a fool of himself in the street.'

'Would you like a cup of tea?'

'Yer, p'raps I would.'

'Do you want to come downstairs for it?'

'I'd better. Left poor Olive on her own all day.'

'She understands.'

They made their way downstairs.

'I've made some tea. I was just gonner bring it up,' said Olive.

'Where's Dolly?' asked Milly.

'In her pram in the front room. She's all right, she's dropped off.'

'She'll never remember her uncle.'

'Don't worry, Mum. I'll tell her all about him.' Olive sniffed as she poured out the tea.

Milly looked at the clock. 'You've finished early. How did you know?' she asked Kate. 'Who told you?'

'Mrs Duke came into the shop.'

'What, she walked all that way with her feet?'

Olive gave a faint smile. 'She couldn't walk without 'em. Sorry about that, Mum.'

Milly also let a slight smile lift her sad face. 'That's all right, love.'

They drank their tea in silence till Milly asked, 'Does Joe know?'

'No, not yet.'

For a while, the ticking of the clock on the mantelpiece was the only sound.

'I'm gonner stay the night,' said Olive, breaking into their thoughts.

'What about Dolly's things? Would you like me to go and get them?'

'No, thanks all the same. I'll pop round when Dad gets in.'

When they heard the key being pulled through the letter box they all tensed and sat up, waiting for Charlie to open the kitchen door.

''Allo, Kate, what you doing . . .?' His voice trailed off when he noted their faces.

Milly burst into tears and, rushing to him, hugged him tight.

He looked over her shoulder at Olive and Kate. Tears filled his eyes. 'Is it Ted?'

They both nodded.

'He's not . . .?'

They couldn't speak.

For a few moments the little group stood in silence as if in homage. The only sound was Milly's sobs.

It was Charlie who spoke. 'What did the telegram say?'

Milly fished in her overall pocket and gave him the screwed-up paper.

He straightened it out. 'Thought it might have been that he's been injured or taken prisoner. But this. This is so final.' He sat in the chair, and burying his head in his hands, he wept.

Kate picked up her hat, quietly said her goodbyes, and left. This was their grief, and it should be in private.

'I warmed up that pie,' said Joe when Kate walked in. 'Ma, what's wrong?'

Kate let the tears fall. 'Joseph, it's Ted.'

'Ted? Ted? What's happened to him?'

'He's been killed.'

Joe sat at the table. He stared at his mother, disbelief written all over his face. 'He can't be!'

'I'm afraid he has.'

Joe left the room and went upstairs. He didn't leave his bedroom all evening.

The following morning Kate gave him a black armband. 'Would you like this?'

'Yes. When did you make this?'

'Last night. I couldn't sleep and I had to have something to do. I've made one for Milly and Charlie as well.'

Joe kissed Kate's cheek. 'I'd better be off.' At the door he turned. 'I loved Ted like a brother.'

'I know.'

When she went to make his bed she was shocked at the pictures he must have spent the evening drawing. They were of faceless Germans lying in a field. Some had bayonets through their hearts, some were being hanged. They were violent pictures with barbed wire and guns. Perhaps it was good for him to get some of his anger down on paper.

Throughout the day many regulars came in and offered their condolences. It amazed Kate that so many people knew about Ted's death and cared.

'Thank you, Bill, for yesterday.'

''S all right. Bloody shame, though. Poor Milly and Olive. I bet they're taking it hard.'

'Yes they are. We all are.'

Kate felt she was in limbo, and throughout the day only did what was necessary.

Weeks later, things gradually returned to as normal as they would ever be. Both Milly and Olive came back to work. But it was Joe who was worrying Kate. He became morose and only spoke when spoken to. He spent hours in his room, drawing. The pictures were frightening, all about the war. Kate didn't show them to anyone although Joe knew she had seen them but made no comment. Somehow he had lost his sparkle.

At the end of November she found a note in his bedroom and her world crumbled. In it he said he had put up his age and had joined the army.

She sat silently in his bedroom. She couldn't cry, she was too much in shock.

There was someone banging on the door. They would go away soon. Someone was coming up the stairs. Perhaps it was Joe, he'd come back, they wouldn't take him. She eagerly pulled open the bedroom door.

'Milly! What are you doing here?'

'Kate! What's the matter? Why ain't the shop open?'

Kate handed her the note. 'How did you get in?'

'The back door was on the latch.' Milly read the note. 'Oh my God! What'd he do that for?'

'He loved Ted.'

'I know that, but this is— well, a bit extreme.'

'I think he felt he had to avenge Ted's death. Look at these pictures.' Kate showed Milly the drawings.

'They're frightening.'

'We don't realise what's going on in their minds.' Kate was shaking.

'Have you got any brandy in the house?'

'Why?'

'You're in shock, you need a drink.'

'No, I don't. I must get to work.' She stood up and threw the note to the ground.

Milly picked it up and, putting it in her pocket, followed her down the stairs.

'They might send him back when they find out his age,' said Bill.

'Dunno about that,' said someone else. 'Think they'll hang on to anyone daft enough to—'

'Shut it, mate!' said Bill.

'I was only saying.'

'Well, don't bother!'

All day Kate worked as if in a dream. All evening and half the night she kept herself busy preparing pounds of potatoes and making pies. When she looked at the many bowls of white potatoes, it struck her that Seamus would say, if he was here: 'You've got enough there to feed an army.'

She began to cry. Her baby had left her. All that they had been through together, and now she was alone. All she had was her shop. She felt so lonely and afraid. What if anything happened to him? Perhaps this was her retribution. 'Please, God, send him safely back to me,' she prayed.

She was overjoyed at her first postcard from Joe. It didn't say a lot, but at least she knew he was well and thinking of her.

Every day she read the papers, wondering where he was.

In December there was a lot of fighting in Turkey and a great many casualties.

Both Milly and Kate knew, like thousands of other women, that this was going to be a miserable Christmas.

There were no paper chains hanging from the shop's ceiling this year. There was no Christmas card from Joe.

'Come on, Kate, we've got to make the best of it for young Dolly's sake,' said Charlie as they sat down to dinner.

'Yes I know.'

With so many empty chairs at the table Christmas was a very half-hearted affair and everybody would be glad when it was all over and they could get back to work.

Would 1916 bring an end to this terrible conflict? Not many had any hope of that now. Kate's thoughts went to Joe. Where was he, and how was he spending Christmas? But what worried her most of all was whether she would ever see him again.

* * *

Joe sat in his trench clutching his rifle. He was cold and hungry. The order to fix bayonets had been given. The bombardment had been going on for days and he felt his head was going to burst. They had been told they were going over the top. It was Christmas and he knew he should be at home with his mother. He had never really thought of the shop as home till now. He remembered that warm place with the smell of her wonderful pies filling the air. Those memories brought a great longing to go home.

The only smells that permeated his nostrils here were mud, cordite and death.

A shell screamed over his head and he automatically ducked. The bloke next to him groaned.

'You all right, mate?' asked Joe, straightening up. He didn't answer. Joe asked again, but again the man was silent. Joe gently pushed him and watched him slowly slip face down in the mud. With his boot Joe turned him over, and in the half-light from the guns' flashes he saw half his head had been blown away.

Joe sat and stared. He shivered, then began to cry. He was scared. He didn't want to die. He wanted to be at home. Bile rose in his throat and he was sick over his mate, but he didn't know anything about it. He had gone to join Ted, like so many of them.

What am I doing here? Ted, why did you have to die? cried Joe silently.

At the beginning of March, Ron came in with a man Kate hadn't seen before. His overalls were covered with splashes of paint and he had a cloth cap pulled down over his eyes.

'This is the bloke I was telling you about, Katie love, and he said he can do your sign next week. That all right with you?'

'Yes, that's good. What do you want?' she asked the man.

He pulled on his homemade cigarette. 'Me money up front. Bin let down before.'

'Our Katie won't let you down. I can promise you that.'

'It'll have to be on Sunday. I work all week.'

'That's all right with me.'

'Don't let the Sally Army catch you working on Sundays,' said Ron.

'Some of us have ter work every day of the bloody week.'

Kate could see he wasn't a very happy man. 'How much?' she asked.

'A fiver.'

Kate swallowed. That seemed a lot, but she didn't argue and took the money from the box under the counter. 'I'll be out on Sunday, so will you be wanting anything?'

'Na, I'll provide everything. So, what'd you want it called?'

'Kate's Kitchen,' she said proudly.

'D'yer want a bit of fancy scroll work under the words?'

'That would be nice.'

'Right. I'll be 'ere about ten. Don't get up too early on Sundays, like to go to the pub Sat'day nights.'

'That's all right.'

On Sunday Kate could hear the man rubbing off Trent's name. She was quite excited – her name was going to be above the window and then it really would be her shop.

She gave him a mug of tea and left for Milly's.

'So, your name will be over the door?' said Charlie.

'Yes, I'm so thrilled about it. Only wish Joseph was here to see it.'

'Ain't heard any more then?' asked Charlie.

'No.'

'As I told Kate the other day,' said Milly, 'no news is good news. Right, dinner's ready.'

As far as Kate was concerned some news would have been welcome. 'I enjoy coming round here on Sundays, makes a change from eating alone all week.'

Much later, and before it got too dark, Kate hurried home. She wanted to see her name above the door. She walked up to the shop and looked up. Her face dropped. The words said 'Katie's Kitchen'.

'Oh, no!' she said out loud. 'That's not what I'm called! I'm a Kate, not a Katie. Only Ron sometimes calls me Katie. The man must have thought that was my name.' Well, she couldn't afford to have it changed so that's what it would have to be. She stood back to inspect it again. It did look rather nice though.

For days the new name was a talking point.

'I must say it does look rather grand,' said Milly as she stood back to admire it.

Some of the wags enjoyed singing, 'K-K-K-Katie, beautiful Katie . . .' But the novelty soon died down.

The letter that came at the end of April was completely out of the blue. It was Joe's handwriting and posted in England.

Kate frantically tore open the envelope and, after scanning the letter, sat and cried.

He was in hospital in Suffolk. He said he wasn't badly injured, and would be coming home shortly. He said he had so much to tell her.

'But he don't say when he'll be home then? Or how bad he's been injured?' asked Milly when Kate showed her the letter.

Kate shook her head. In many ways, she felt guilty that her son had been spared.

'And he don't say how long he's been there. I wonder what's wrong with him?'

'I wish I could go and see him.'

'He ain't given you his address. And what if he's on his way home? You might miss him.'

'You are right, but it's this waiting.'

'At least he's coming back,' said Milly sadly.

* * *

A week later Kate's prayers were answered when, just as she was closing, Joe walked into the shop. They both stopped and stared. For a few moments she stood looking at this young man whose army uniform hung on his lean frame. His face was pale and gaunt. He had lost his little-boy looks. In just these few months he had grown taller and older. There was even stubble on his chin.

She rushed to him and threw her arms round his neck. He flinched and she quickly stepped back.

'I like the name.' He nodded at the shop door and moved towards her.

'Sit down. Are you all right? Where were you injured?' She noticed he had a slight limp.

'I'm fine. Got a bit of shrapnel, that's all.'

'Shrapnel!' she cried out. 'Where?'

'In me leg, but it ain't that bad.' He began to cough.

'Joseph, that cough! Tell me, how bad are you?'

'Don't worry about that, that's left over from the pleurisy. But the leg – well, I was just bloody unlucky that's all. Only been out there a few days – we were in Turkey, and I got this, in me leg.' He fished in his trouser pocket and held out a small piece of metal.

Kate took it and turned it over. 'Where did it finish up?'

'Here.' He touched his thigh.

Kate quickly took a breath.

'It's all right.'

Kate didn't know whether or not to believe him. But she didn't care, she had her son back. 'So how long have you been in England?'

'Came back almost three months ago.'

'What? And you didn't bother to let me know!'

'Well, I know how you fuss so I thought I'd wait till I was on the mend.'

She turned away from him. 'All this worry I've had and you've been safe all the time. How could you?'

'I'm sorry, Ma. But I thought it was best this way. I didn't want you rushing all over the place. Besides, we never knew when we were going to be shifted.' He touched her hand. 'I could murder a cuppa. Been travelling nearly all day.'

'Let's go in the back room.' Kate couldn't resist giving him another cuddle when he stood up. Tears filled her eyes. 'I'm so lucky to get you back.'

'I've got a lot to tell you, and I've got to get some of the things I saw over there down on paper. Done some in hospital, but only outlines.'

'Those drawings you did before you went away were pretty horrific.'

'That's nothing to what I've seen.'

It was wrong that a young lad had been exposed to so much. 'Are you still in the army?' She held her breath waiting for an answer.

'No. They found out I was underage and now I've been injured I don't think I'll have to go back even when I'm old enough. Seems soldiers can't run fast with a gammy leg.' He sat at the table.

Kate let out a huge sigh. 'Thank God.'

'You'll never guess, but while I was in hospital I was with a lot of blokes from Australia.'

Kate almost dropped the cup she was holding. She sat down. 'The Australians are fighting?'

'There was a lot of 'em in the Dardanelles. Got quite friendly with one bloke, Pete. He lived near Darwin. Didn't you live there?'

She nodded. Fear gripped her again. Could her other son have been in this terrible conflict?

'I told him that. He couldn't believe you came back to England on your own. Reckons you must be quite a girl.'

She smiled half-heartedly, and put a mug of tea in front of her son.

'He's got my address and he reckons he's gonner look up your name when he gets back. It would be a right turnup for the books if he found out about my dad and Robert.'

Kate felt the blood draining from her face. She turned away from Joe and held on to the table. She felt her head swimming. She had so much to take in. First Joe was home and now she could one day have news of Robert, but did she want to know about her husband?

'This tastes good. Those Aussies all seem to be tall and good-looking. Must be all that fresh air. It sounds a great place to live. Would you like to go back there?'

Kate's heart froze. Surely he wasn't still thinking of going there? He hadn't said anything about that for years. 'It's got too many flies for me, and I couldn't stand the journey. Would you like something to eat?'

'I'm starving. The hospital food wasn't that good. The nurses were still going on about the Germans killing that nurse.'

'Edith Cavell.'

'That's right. Sad that.'

There was something different about him. He spoke with knowledge. He wasn't a young boy any more, he was a man.

'Milly and Charlie are going to be pleased to see you.'

'How they taking Ted's—'

'Pretty bad. Milly wants a memorial of some kind. Something to remind her.'

'Does she need something like that?'

'I think she's worried Olive's baby might not remember him and this way she'll have something to tell her children.'

Joe sat and played with the spoon in the sugar bowl. 'I'm gonner write about what I saw. I'm going to send my pictures to the papers. I'm going to make people see what I saw. Ma, it was awful!' Suddenly he began to cry.

Kate held him close. In so many ways he was now a man, but to her, he was still her baby.

Chapter 36

Everybody was pleased to see Joe back. There was laughter echoing round the shop again. Milly and Charlie were just as happy as Kate.

Kate heard Joe telling Charlie about some of the things he saw, and some nights his shouting would send her hurrying to his bedroom to comfort him.

His drawings were frightening, full of death and destruction: bodies lying in the mud; tortured faces on the dying; rats gnawing at bodies and flies buzzing all around them. There were bits of men strewn haphazardly over the pictures. Others showed men walking in lines with cloths over their eyes; they had been gassed. They were shuffling along holding the shoulder of the man in front, a pitiful sight.

Kate was deeply moved and upset at what she was seeing. It was beyond belief that men did this to their fellow men. And although he dismissed it, Kate knew Joe must have been near to the gas because of his cough.

One night Kate ran into his bedroom; he was shouting and flailing his arms about. 'You're not going to get me!'

'Joseph! Joseph.' Kate gently shook him. 'It's all right. You're home.'

He opened his eyes. He was bathed in sweat. He held her close for a while, burying his head in her shoulder. She could feel his tears through her nightgown.

'Let me get a cloth.' She gently eased him away and mopped his brow. She wanted to cry out. This was her son. She wanted to hold him and comfort him for ever. But he was a man now, and he had seen things that would have made older and stronger men crumple.

'Sorry about that,' he said, lying back exhausted.

'There's no need to be. Do you want to talk about it?'

He nodded and sat up. 'I don't think the smell of the dead will ever leave me.'

'Give it time.'

'You'd be talking to the bloke next to you only to find he was dead.'

Kate shuddered. Would he ever forget this?

She told Milly about his nightmares.

'It must be awful for these young lads. I wonder how my Ted went. Let's hope it was quick.'

Kate felt almost guilty at having Joe back and decided not to tell Milly too much after that. She had never shown her the pictures he'd drawn since coming home.

After a month, much to Kate's relief, the nightmares were getting less and Joe decided to go back to work. Mr Lacy was very pleased to see him. He had also started to send his pictures to the newspapers, but they were returned with letters saying they weren't what the public should see.

'One day they will get published, you wait and see,' said Kate, but deep down she had her doubts. People didn't want to see such carnage as it could be one of their own lying there.

August came round, and the war had been raging for two years. Two years since Seamus and Grace had left. Kate was still a little upset that they hadn't bothered to write to her. Ted had gone. Joe had been in the army and was considered a war veteran at the tender age of seventeen. Kate couldn't believe so much had happened in such a short time. She was intrigued as she picked up the letter addressed to Joe, with an Australian stamp, off the doormat.

'Who's it from?' she eagerly asked when he opened it.

'It's from Pete, Pete Higgs, the bloke I met in hospital,' he said excitedly. 'I told you about him, remember? Well, he's back home now. Fancy him bothering to write!' Joe read on. 'Guess what, Ma?' His voice was high with excitement. 'You are never going to believe this! His father said there was a man called Carter in the local government a while back – held quite a high office by all accounts. Pete says he's going to try and find out a bit more for me. That's great news! Wouldn't it be great if it was my father . . . ? Ma, you all right?'

'Yes.'

'And what about my big brother? I'd really like to know all about him. I wonder if he's been fighting in the war? You never know, I might even have been in the same trench as—' He stopped and folded the letter. 'Do we really want to know?'

'It would be nice to discover if Robert's married. I could even be a grandmother,' she said light-heartedly.

Joe laughed, which made him cough. 'You'd like that. Granny Carter sounds good.'

'It would be nice to hear from him.' But she wasn't so sure about her husband. Would he let Robert write to Joe? 'He was twenty-four last birthday,' she said reflectively.

'You still think about him?'

'Sometimes.' What if Joe wanted to go out there to find him?

That night Joe wrote to Pete. Kate was worried. He appeared to be very eager to keep in touch.

It was later that month that Kate received a letter from Grace. In it was a photograph of Grace, Kurt and Seamus. Grace was holding a baby.

To Kate
Sorry I aint wrote before but we was travelling about a bit.

Anyway me and Kurt got married and weve got Kate. Hope you like the picture. Shes really lovely. We called her after you as you're such a nice lady and I would never have met Kurt if I hadn't been working for you. Seamus is well and loves it over here, so does Kurt. They both send there love. We are all very happy here and when this terrible wars over perhaps we can meet up again. Give Milly my love as well as Ted and Joe. There two lovely boys.

Lots of love, Grace xxx

Kate had trouble reading Grace's writing. She stared at the photograph. They all looked so happy.

'So she married him then?' Milly had been reading the letter Kate passed to her.

'Yes. She looks a lovely baby.'

'Wouldn't show this to them out there,' said Milly, looking at the photo when they were in the back room.

'Why not? Most of the men knew Grace.'

'Yer, but seeing her with a German ain't gonner please 'em.'

It surprised Kate that Milly said that with such hatred in her voice.

'You gonner write to her?'

'I can't. She didn't put her address on the letter.'

'That was clever. Reckon she was worried, if you ask me.'

'Worried?' repeated Kate. 'About what?'

'In case you tell the authorities.'

Kate laughed. 'Why would I do that?'

'He's a German without papers.'

'Yes, I know that.'

'Well, if you didn't, someone else might.' Milly looked angry. 'Makes me wonder if my Ted didn't know what they were up to and that's what made him go.'

'I wouldn't have thought so.' Kate knew she was telling a white lie, but did it matter now?

'D'you know, if I thought that was the reason my Ted got killed I'd go over there and throttle 'em both with me bare hands.'

Kate was taken aback at Milly's hatred, but how would she have reacted if Joe had been killed?

She looked at the letter and photograph she was still holding and smiled faintly. It was a good thing there wasn't an address. Grace was a lot wiser than everybody thought she was.

The war and carnage continued in Europe. Every day the customers commented on the news of the heavy casualties at the front. It saddened Kate to see her friends and men she knew come in haggard and angry. So many had lost sons and brothers, and every day Kate thanked God that Joe was home with her again.

Food prices were soaring and Kate was worried about putting up her prices, but she didn't have a lot of choice.

'I hope you ain't gonner water this tea down too much,' said Ron one day as he looked in the mug Kate had just given him.

'I'll just have to let it stew a bit longer like Josh used to,' she said, trying to make light of it.

'It's the pies I'm worried about,' said another punter. 'Reckon we could be eating horse meat soon.'

Kate laughed. 'You'd soon know if you were. I'm told it's very tough.'

A new threat was beginning to worry everybody. Zeppelins were seen in the skies and they were dropping bombs.

'It's bloody terrible, innocent women and children being killed,' said Charlie one Sunday when Kate and Joe went to dinner.

'They must be a wicked bunch,' said Milly.

'Good job that Kraut buggered off to Ireland,' said Charlie.

371

'Reckon he would have been hanged, drawn and quartered be now.'

Kate could understand the hatred people had for the Germans.

'What we gonner do if those Zeppelin things come over here?' asked Milly.

'Keep out of their bleeding way, that's what,' came Charlie's reply.

They laughed, but it was a nervous, worried laugh.

Months later, a letter arrived from Australia addressed to Kate. She felt her legs go weak. It wasn't Pete's handwriting. She was alone. Should she wait for Joe to come home before opening it? Had Pete found Robert? After all, Darwin wasn't that overpopulated and if her husband had been in government it would have been quite easy to trace him.

She sat looking at the unopened envelope on the counter. Was it from Robert or his father? She didn't remember what his writing was like. She was trying hard to find the courage to open it. Was she about to find the one thing she had been missing for most of her life? What if it was from her husband and it was bad news about Robert?

It was beautifully written. Her hands were trembling as she picked up the envelope and opened it.

To Mrs Carter.

I was given your address by a young man who met your son while serving in the Australian army. His name was Pete Higgs. He said the young man's name was Carter, the same as mine. Could he have been my brother? The reason I ask is because he said this young man's mother once lived in Darwin.

Many years ago my mother left Australia to return to England. I was wondering if you are the same lady, my mother, as it is such a strange coincidence. Not many ladies have left Darwin and returned to England on their own.

Kate had to stop as tears were stinging her eyes. This was from Robert, her Robert. After all these years. She held the letter to her breast for a moment or two, then wiped her eyes and continued.

I remember my mother. She was a lovely tall lady with reddy golden hair.

Kate touched her hair that was now sprinkled with grey.

I was sent away to school when I was eight and didn't see you leave, and you never wrote. I never knew I had a brother. I know my father had given you a bad time and I didn't blame you.

My father died five years ago. He had a heart attack. He never talked about you. I am married but no children yet. Amy and I work hard on our sheep farm.

Darwin has changed since you were here. If you are my mother, please write to me. There is so much we want to know about you and my brother, and, who knows, one of these days we may meet up again. I do hope this letter hasn't offended you, and though you may have a life you do not wish us to share, I would like to know.

Yours hopefully, Robert Carter

Kate stared at the paper and let the tears fall. He wanted her to write.

'Kate, you all right?' asked Milly, coming into the shop.

She quickly brushed her tears away.

'What's wrong?'

Kate handed her the letter.

'Your son?' said Milly, when she'd finished reading it.

Kate nodded.

'Well, I'm buggered! After all these years. He sounds a really nice lad and keen for you to get in touch. This is a lovely letter. You gonner write?'

'Yes. I can't wait for Joseph to come home.'

'I bet he'll be pleased! Why didn't you write to him all those years ago?'

'I did, but his father must have destroyed my letters – that's if they ever got there.'

'Well, you can tell your son all that now.'

Kate grinned. 'D'you know, I've waited seventeen years for this day? If it hadn't been for Joseph . . . ' She suddenly stopped.

'Just think,' said Milly. 'If my Ted hadn't been killed, Joe wouldn't have joined up and you would never have . . .' Milly's voice had a sob in it. She went to the far side of the shop.

She had been echoing Kate's thoughts. 'I'm so sorry,' Kate said, going over to her and putting her arm round her shoulder.

Milly sniffed and fished in her pocket for her handkerchief. 'Well, I suppose some good's come out of it.'

'Yes, but it was a heavy price to pay.'

'Honest, Kate, I'm really pleased for you. You've certainly got a lot to tell him about.'

'Yes I have.'

'You've done a lot in your life.'

Kate also knew she was very lucky. Now she had everything she could wish for. She had two sons, even if one was the other side of the world, was mistress in her own home with a very profitable business. She let her thoughts drift to Edwin, the lovely restaurant they'd had, but she didn't miss it – she had her own pie and mash shop. Rotherhithe was her home now. She thought about all those who had helped to shape her life here. She looked across at Milly. She loved her and Charlie and Dolly and Olive.

Then there was Ted. He was with Briony now. Kate held back her tears. Why did he have to die for her to find happiness?

She looked through the window at all the hustle and bustle outside. Rotherhithe was a long way from Darwin, but not even the war and the Zeppelins would make her move now.

Hopes and Dreams

Dee Williams

Dolly Taylor and Penny Watts have been friends all their lives. Growing up in Rotherhithe, they left school at fourteen, and work in a factory making shell cases. Their childhood sweethearts, Tony and Reg, are away fighting and, as World War II rages on, Dolly dreams of escaping to far-off lands.

But, for now, American soldiers provide the excitement, breaking the monotony of factory life and nightly air-raids with music and dancing. Despite her loyalty to Tony, Dolly is attracted to Joe, a handsome GI, and when he proposes, she can't resist. But on reaching America, Dolly is shocked by the cold reception she receives. As she struggles to make friends and understand the man she married, Dolly wonders if she has made a terrible mistake. Will she have to return to Rotherhithe to find happiness?

Acclaim for Dee Williams' novels:

'An inspiring tale, full of surprises, intrigue and suspense' *Newcastle Evening Gazette*

'Flowers with the atmosphere of old Docklands London' *Manchester Evening News*

'A moving story full of intrigue and suspense, and peopled with a warm and appealing cast of characters . . . an excellent treat' *Bolton Evening News*

0 7553 0097 1

headline

madabout**books**.com

. . . the
Hodder Headline
site
for readers
and book lovers

madabout**books**.com

Now you can buy any of these other bestselling books by **Dee Williams** from your bookshop or *direct from her publisher*.

FREE P&P AND UK DELIVERY
(Overseas and Ireland £3.50 per book)

Hopes and Dreams	£6.99
A Rare Ruby	£5.99
Forgive and Forget	£6.99
Sorrows and Smiles	£6.99
Wishes and Tears	£6.99
Katie's Kitchen	£6.99
Maggie's Market	£5.99
Ellie of Elmleigh Square	£6.99
Sally of Sefton Grove	£6.99
Hannah of Hope Street	£5.99
Annie of Albert Mews	£6.99
Polly of Penns Place	£6.99
Carrie of Culver Road	£6.99

TO ORDER SIMPLY CALL THIS NUMBER

01235 400 414

or visit our website: www.madaboutbooks.com

Prices and availability subject to change without notice.

News & Natter is a newsletter full of everyone's favourite storytellers and their latest news and views as well as opportunities to win some fabulous prizes and write to your favourite authors. Just send a postcard with your name and address to: *News & Natter*, Kadocourt Ltd, The Gateway, Gatehouse Road, Aylesbury, Bucks HP19 8ED. Then sit back and look forward to your first issue.